INFILTRATION

ALSO AVAILABLE FROM STEERFORTH PRESS

Returning Lost Loves

The Way to the Cats

Musical Moment
And Other Stories

INFILTRATION

YEHOSHUA KENAZ

Translated from the Hebrew by Dalya Bilu

ZOLAND BOOKS
an imprint of
STEERFORTH PRESS
SOUTH ROYALTON, VERMONT

The author wishes to thank the Oxford Centre for Hebrew Studies
for its hospitality and assistance during the writing of this book.

For information about permission to reproduce
selections from this book, write to:
Steerforth Press L.C., P.O. Box 70,
South Royalton, Vermont 05068

Library of Congress Cataloging-in-Publication Data

Kenaz, Yehoshua.
  [Hitganvut yeòhidim. English]
  Infiltration / Yehoshua Kenaz ; translated from the Hebrew by Dalya
Bilu.— 1st ed.
      p. cm.
  ISBN 1-58195-205-8
  I. Bilu, Dalya. II. Title.
  PJ5054.K36H513 2003
  892.4'36—dc21

                              2003009891

FIRST EDITION

"No, it is impossible; it is impossible to convey the life-sensation of any given epoch of one's existence — that which makes its truth, its meaning — its subtle and penetrating essence. It is impossible. We live, as we dream — alone."

Joseph Conrad, *Heart of Darkness*

PART ONE

HEART MURMUR

At the last minute my life unfolded in front of my eyes. Like a movie or a bunch of slides flicking past with a quick, jerky rhythm. Images in black and white, the quality rather poor, as if they had been slightly eroded by the passage of time. Or like a dream, only without the literary, sometimes baroque, ambience that accompanies dream images, in my dreams at least. It had a kind of dry, laconic, businesslike severity, like the burst of shots after a summary court-martial. And there was a strong sense of urgency in the speed with which they changed places, something nervous and hurried, almost frantic, something final, decisive, never to be repeated, as if the strip of film in question would be automatically destroyed with this, its first and last use, by the very fact of its exposure. There was no sense of danger or longing, no fear, solemnity, pain, or surprise. Because everything had already happened before, somewhere on the frontiers of time.

The pictures suddenly stopped and a white light came down like a curtain on my closed eyes. The glaring white grew gray and in its center a circle of different, softer, external light gradually brightened, as on a still-closed stage curtain when the theater darkens a moment before going up on the first scene of the play. I felt my heartbeat and my breathing and I assumed that I wasn't dead. But until I opened my eyes my sense of time did not return in full and I wasn't sure exactly who I was.

The question suddenly became critical. I tried to clarify it with my eyes closed, without moving, for fear that if I changed my position, even slightly, something vital to my understanding would be irretrievably lost and I would never know the answer. I wondered what was happening. I couldn't remember anything except the images that had just stopped passing before my eyes. The thought that I wasn't dead, which ran through me in a flash, brought no glad tidings or excitement with it. I knew that soon I would open my eyes, but I didn't know what would appear before them. I sensed my consciousness returning, but some deprived, forgotten, nameless instinct urged me not to let myself be carried away on the returning stream of consciousness but to cling tenaciously to those images. More precisely: to the little that remained of them, pale shadows on transparent plates, gradually fading in the light pouring in from outside. Thanks to the exertion of my will, a few of the images remained quite coherently in my thoughts, like ideas, although by now it was already difficult to fit them back into the flow that had previously given them their narrative meaning. And in my determined attempts to conjure them up again, to repaint them according to the shadowy outlines remaining on the glass slides, like vapor on a windowpane, I succeeded in seeing them almost in their original form.

At last the plates became transparent and behind them dots came into view, scattered apparently at random, although I knew that they were arranged in some kind of pattern that escaped my comprehension. Gradually the dots turned into little black circles at the head of vertical lines, like quarter notes without the staves, each note in its place, waiting for a sign. A tremor ran through them, as at the pulsing of some distant beat, setting them in motion, upsetting the mysterious order in which they had been arranged, and slowly they began to move, thicken, and grow heavier. I saw the shadows of people I didn't recognize. I knew that I was one of them but which of them I did not know.

And while I was trying with all my might to revive the shapes and identities of those pictures dying and disintegrating inside me, I suddenly felt the bed of earth under my shoulders and the heaviness of my body sprawled on the humped, rough, and very steep, almost vertical ground. I must have been floating before; my body was so heavy now, so heavy that I wasn't even afraid of slipping down the slope, as if the weight of my shoulders were enough to counteract the downward pull. Afterward I felt my hips and my feet, and something inside me told me that I was bound to the ground and wouldn't be able to move a muscle. The sense of taste came back to my mouth with a stale, bitter smell, like the smell of a fish gone dry and sour, the smell of death. As if from a distance sounds began to reach me, at first like the low roar in a seashell, growing in volume until they were like stones tumbling down a mountain, like an avalanche. I wondered how much longer I could keep my eyes closed, protect myself from the light outside. Suddenly I felt the touch of a hand on my arm and my eyes opened of their own accord.

Two feet were planted at my head, and their owner, bare-chested in dark blue gym pants, was bending over me. At first his face was feature-less and his whole figure was a bright silhouette crouching against the background of a gray, dazzling metallic sky. The features came back to his face. I saw a high domed forehead, dull sandy hair, sunken little eyes, and the pimples spotting his face.

"Are you crazy? Why don't you get up? What's wrong with you?" His voice was harshly critical.

I couldn't say anything. Without moving my face, I let my eyes wander around and saw my friends lying on the ground like me in a circle, their faces pale as death, coming slowly back to life as the ones standing at their heads watched them wake.

"What did you want, to give me a fright? You think you could have scared me? You shit!"

Micky was mad. I must have really scared him. He pulled me violently by the arm until I was upright. "You did it on purpose didn't you? What kind of a trick is that to pull?" I teetered between the earth and the sky; I couldn't stand firm on my feet. I dropped to the ground. I sat up, resting my hands on the ground behind me. I felt giddy. The entire circle and the people standing behind them began spinning slowly around in front of me and Micky's face kept disappearing and then reappearing again. I wondered why I didn't want to wake up. There was something so elusive and appealing about those pictures, like signs from another world. I closed my eyes until the giddiness wore off. The pain of the grip came back to the corner between my neck and shoulder. I put my hand on the sore place and tried to stretch my neck. I heard the sound of voices behind my head. I recognized Avner's voice as he talked to Micky. Again I hated the clipped pronunciation, the emphatic Oriental accent, as if he were reading the Bible over the radio. I couldn't understand what they were talking about. All I heard was the sound of their voices and the bursts of laughter accompanying them. The voices receded, and I opened my eyes again. I looked around me. My waking friends gave back my reflection as in a mirror. How ugly this awakening was, how wretched the eye rolling, the limb jerking, the head shaking, the stupid, glassy looks from the frightened eyes, the gray faces, frozen in the terror of oblivion. After the beauty of the lost images, how degrading this sight was. The instructor went around the circle to see if everyone was okay, announced a break, and went away. I stood up and discovered that I had recovered my balance. I went over to Micky and Avner, who stood looking at Zero-Zero, who was lying on his side, his knees tucked up to his stomach in a fetal position, his head on his chest, covered with both hands. His shoulders shook as if he were crying or having a fit of the shivers.

Micky poked Zero-Zero's back with the toe of his shoe. "Stop making a fuss about nothing," he said.

Zero-Zero refused to remove his hands from his face. Rahamim stood next to him, short and tubby, his shoulders slumped and his hands spread out in a gesture of helplessness, although the smile on his face betrayed a certain surprised satisfaction. "I don't know what he wants of me," said Rahamim and burst out laughing.

"Is it really so terrible?" Avner asked me. He had been the first to volunteer when the instructor asked for someone to demonstrate the exercise on, before we did it to each other. A proud smile twinkled in his black, biblical eyes.

I opened my mouth to say something, but my voice failed me. A queer kind of croak came out of my throat, hoarse and unfamiliar, utterly unsuitable to the pronunciation of words. They looked at me in an amused way.

Zero-Zero took his hands off his face. His eyes were red, and it was impossible to tell if the redness came from the inflammation that made them permanently bloodshot, or from tears.

"I'll kill that bastard," said Zero-Zero and sniffed. "I'm telling you I'll kill him."

"What do you want?" said Micky. "All he did was obey an order. And now you'll do the same thing to him."

"And then I'll really kill him. I won't let go my hand. I'll squeeze and squeeze until he's got no breath left and he'll die. I'll strangle him like a Moroccan dog. You better believe it."

Zero-Zero was beside himself. He was always anxious about his health. Already on our first day on the base he had gone on sick call, claiming that he had heart palpitations. He was the only married man in the platoon, although he was the same age as the rest of us.

I cleared my throat and tried to get my voice back. My neck was still very sore. "I'm okay now," I whispered. "It's really weird. I still can't understand what happened to me."

"Maybe I went a bit too far," said Micky. "Whatever I do, I always do it too hard."

"It doesn't make any difference," pronounced Avner. "It only takes a second. The minute you get there, everything stops."

"It's death!" wailed Zero-Zero. He supported his head on his hands. His face was full of cuts from his morning shave. "I saw it right there in front of me, I swear on my mother's life I did."

We all laughed. I said: "Seriously, I saw pictures. I thought it was my life story, like you see before you die. And now I can't remember any of them. Just people. People's faces. Rows of people waiting for something. Maybe I saw you guys around me and I thought it was something else. But it seems to me my eyes were closed and it all came from inside me. I don't know. It's all gone now, wiped out. I can't stop thinking about it."

"Your eyes were open," said Micky. "I was looking at you the whole time. You only closed your eyes when you started to wake up. Before that they were rolling around like mad. I saw the whites of your eyes."

"Maybe that's why everything looked like a speeded-up movie and I didn't have time to see the pictures."

"You shouldn't think about it," said Micky. "It's morbid."

There was a look of revulsion on his face. I thought that maybe it was the memory of what I had looked like, lying on the ground rolling my eyes, that had caused his disgust. But it really was more his way of thinking. He saw the world as divided into sick people and healthy people. He was the first person I'd spoken to on the day we'd arrived on the base. We had been ordered to wait and we sat in our new uniforms with our gear, on a hill beneath a row of eucalyptus trees with white-washed trunks. We'd waited for a long time and nothing happened. Suddenly the fast-paced schedule had been interrupted and time dragged as if we had been forgotten. The people sitting around me looked like green animals. Micky, who was sitting next to me, looked around him with scorn and hatred.

"All the people you see here are sick," he suddenly said. "All of them, for your information, are cripples. Defective combat-worthiness! Medical Grade B!" He smashed his fist onto his knee and said: "Goddammit!" Then he added: "A-branch clerks, office workers. We're going to get basic training for girls!"

"That's what's worrying you?" one of the Jerusalemites asked him. Another Jerusalemite, whose friends called him Hedgehog, maybe on account of his bristling hair, said: "Don't worry. They'll make your life miserable here. Just the same as anywhere else. They won't treat you with kid gloves."

"Look," said Micky. "I happen to be a soccer player."

"I know," said Hedgehog. "You're Micky Spector from *Hapoel* Hadera."

Micky was not surprised to be so famous; at any rate his face showed no signs of surprise. "So you can imagine," he said, "that with my physical fitness I'll suffer less than the others. But that's not the problem."

"What is?"

"Heart," said Micky. "Until those lousy physicals I never knew I had a heart at all. And believe me I know what physical exertion means. And they have to go and shove me into Training Base Four with all the cripples."

"You feel it's a question of honor?" asked Hedgehog, innocent and ironic.

"You wouldn't understand," said Micky.

"What did they find in your heart?" asked Hedgehog.

"A murmur," said Micky.

"Me too!" said Hedgehog. "I don't even know what it is."

"You can ask me. I've studied the whole thing since the checkups began. I've become an expert. They say too much blood flows through the valves of the heart. The valves can't let all the blood through and then —"

"Do me a favor," said Hedgehog, "I don't want to hear it. Listening to it's enough to give a person a heart attack."

Micky Spector started laughing. His nose was flat, his lips thin, and in the sweat pouring down his face his pimples looked like coarse grains of sand. The August heat was heavy and humid. The new, dark uniforms stuck to our bodies, and the wool berets we had to wear at all times wet our foreheads and what little hair we had left after the military haircut. The air smelled of sweat. It was hard for me to see him as a soccer player. And it was even harder for me to see him as a famous person, his name a household word frequently mentioned on the sports programs on the radio. He was the first famous person I had ever met.

"This is going to be heartbreak platoon all right!" said Hedgehog.

The conversation took off, voices rose, but I didn't want to talk to any of them, not even the famous Micky Spector. I didn't want to be part of them. An inner voice told me that in rough times ahead I'd have to preserve all my strength, all my natural warmth, all my loyalty. I'd have to limit my contacts with the outside world, shrink into myself like the animals that adapt their color to that of their surroundings. Never make an unnecessary move, keep a low profile, and curl up like a ball to minimize the parts vulnerable to harm. Live on the borderline.

I didn't like their laughter, the jolly camaraderie, the equanimity with which they were suddenly facing the future. All this seemed to me to be aimed, not deliberately of course, at wrecking my strategy. I was horrified by the laughter rising from the Jerusalem gang whose leader was Hedgehog. There was one who was called Micha, whom they introduced to everyone as Micha the Fool. Everything he said made them laugh uproariously, and they never stopped slapping him on the back and encouraging him to say the things they considered so idiotic. And he himself enjoyed their ostentatious, vociferous affection. There was danger in the social seduction, in the appealing illusion that a sense of togetherness could provide protection or solace against the evil about to descend on us.

Suddenly there was a loud yell from the path opposite us. Immediately three recruits appeared carrying their guns, with their knapsacks on their backs. Their instructor was right behind them. The sound of his constant, savage yells were so at odds with the lightness of his step and the lazy apathy of his shoulder movements that he seemed to be putting on some sort of act. The three running men turned right onto the path between two rows of barracks and then veered left and disappeared from view. The instructor's shouts went on for a while, and then they too died away. Silence fell on the people sitting around me, who sat as if watching some riveting contest. Their faces were all turned to where the runners had disappeared. After a few minutes the shouts were heard again, this time to our left, and all heads turned in that direction. The three runners reappeared, the first, the second, and many seconds later the third, stumbling after his friends. His face was red and desperate, his breathing so heavy that we could hear his deep, rhythmic groans like a kind of accompaniment to the yells of the instructor immediately behind him. Again they passed us, continued to the end of the path, then turned left and disappeared. We immediately turned our heads to the left, waiting for them to reappear. And no one, not one of the dozens of men sitting there, opened his mouth or tried to crack a joke. But leaning against the eucalyptus trunk behind me, a tall fellow with a dark face and thick black eyebrows that met above his nose stood smoking a cigarette, whistling snatches of classical music to himself between one draw and the next, persisting in his irritating, provocative whistling as if none of this had anything to do with him.

The way we were sitting, we could have been watching a play. But the fear that had numbed me for the past few days, preventing me from taking anything at face value, now prompted me to believe that we ourselves were the actors and the play had already begun without our knowing it. There was no doubt in my mind that this long wait in the midday sun was not accidental, nor the result of forgetfulness or some technical snag. I knew that we were being tested. Someone had seated us here to check our reactions, to probe our weaknesses. Invisible eyes were probably surveying us from somewhere hidden in the dead space. Maybe they were taking notes, deciding our futures, speculating on which of us would break — who would survive. And thus, exposed to an invisible enemy, lacking imagination, lacking experience, we had only one advantage and we had to hang on to this advantage for all we were worth: our immunity as untouchables. This was a source of strength. The strange new laws held ancient echoes of danger. The terror of don't-come-near, of don't-touch. Already at the induction center the answers had stopped fitting the questions. Reality had started to disintegrate. The rite of changing clothes had been performed in frantic haste, leaving no gap for the unexpected in this no-man's-land between identities. Then I grew aware of this gift of the gods, bestowed like a blessed coat of mail onto those setting out on a journey against their fate. They had banished us from our homes, disguised our identities, and isolated us in quarantine, as if to hide the danger, localize it, and prevent it from spreading. I believed in the efficacy of this passive force, perhaps because the fear and the meaninglessness had made me feel sorrier for myself than I had ever felt before in my life, tempting me to take off for the borderland between reality and fantasy.

The runners reappeared again on our left. Now the distance between the two and the one had shortened, and the expression on the third one's face was terrible. The instructor kept up his rhythmic yelling, slowing down for a moment to let them get ahead. When the three soldiers had nearly reached the place where they were supposed to turn left, the third one fell to the ground and his knapsack rolled a few feet down the slope of the path. His friends heard the thud of his fall, turned their heads, and slowed their pace. One of them started to retrace his steps, apparently to go help the fallen soldier, but the instructor broke into a run toward them, and from his shouts it appeared that he was adding a few more rounds to their run. The two of them quickened their pace and disappeared around the left corner. The instructor approached the fallen recruit and kicked his leg to make him stand up. We could see the soldier's back rapidly expanding and contracting with his breathing. He tried to get up and fell onto the path again. The instructor yelled at him: "Get up immediately and begin again from the beginning or you're disobeying an order!"

The soldier stood up slowly and went to pick up his knapsack. On his way he glanced at us and for an instant I saw his face. His smile was full of mockery and hatred. He bent down, took hold of the knapsack, hoisted it onto his shoulder, and again turned toward us, an expression of loathing and contempt on his face. He set off, the instructor running behind him. At the corner the instructor stopped and stood watching him for a moment. Then he too disappeared.

"Imbecile," said Micky Spector. "Because of him they have to run the whole course again from the beginning."

He spoke as if he were an expert, but nobody agreed with him. After a tense silence everyone began to give their own opinion about what had happened. When the runners reappeared my companions barely glanced at them. Once again the barriers fell, conversation flowed freely, and the sound of laughter rose loudly in the air. The last vestiges of shyness and strangeness, which only a short while before had kept individuals and groups apart, were dispelled. Even the whistler of classical tunes stopped his irritating whistling and sat down with the rest of us. And then for the first time I heard Avner's biblical accent; its utter naturalness on his lips was precisely what made it sound so peculiar, artificial, and off-putting.

"You people don't understand the situation here," said Micky. "Over here anyone who's weak or falls down on the job gets everyone into trouble, not only himself. Over here being weak is like being a thief or a traitor."

"Nobody chooses to be weak," said one of the Jerusalemites, a boy with a long, austere face, whose tone made it easy to guess that he was speaking on his own behalf. He had brought his guitar to the training camp with him, and he held the blue canvas case between his knees all the time. "Being weak isn't something a person can change."

"That makes no difference," said Micky. "The fact remains that he's a burden to his friends — he burdens the strong with his weakness and himself."

Hedgehog stood up. There was an expression of anger and indignation on his face, whether because he found Micky's remarks illogical or out of loyalty to the Jerusalem fraternity. "Just a minute!" he cried. "Just a minute, I don't understand what you're getting at. What do you want a weak person to do? Turn himself into a strong one? It isn't up to him at all, that's the way he was born, and he suffers from it more than anyone else. So it isn't enough that he suffers for it every minute of the day, now you want him to feel guilty and immoral too? Maybe the only way for him to be okay as far as you're concerned is to kill himself and not be a nuisance to anybody?"

"I don't know," said Micky seriously, warming to his theme. He was obviously a keen debater who enjoyed shocking his audience with original and outrageous ideas. "I really don't know. I have no advice for him. I don't think he should be punished. He's his own punishment, after all, and ours as well! Suppose there's a plague and there's somebody who carries the germs and infects other people with the disease and they die of it. It's a fact that he caused their death, never mind if he chose it or not, or didn't even know it. But that doesn't make him less guilty or more guilty."

"So what in your opinion should the weak person do?" asked Hedgehog.

"I don't know. Why should I put myself in his place? I don't think I can solve his problem for him. It's not my problem and I don't know how to solve it either."

"Life isn't a soccer game," said Hedgehog.

"Are you telling me?" said Micky.

Again the runners came into view. This time there was hardly a gap between the first two and the third. They were running very slowly. They looked as if they were about to collapse under their loads. The sweat splashed off their faces as they ran; their rhythmic pants sounded like groaning sobs. Their commander, who seemed tired now too, passed without a glance in our direction. As if we weren't even there. He went into the barracks at the end of the row.

Micky looked at the recruits around him with a complacent smile, eager to see the impression his words had made. I wondered if he really meant what he'd said, or if he was just trying to shock them — out of the pure pleasure of polemics, or to keep himself occupied and not be left alone with his hated heart murmur. But something in what he had said bothered me. Could it be possible that being weak or strong was the result of a decision, a choice, like a sense of vocation? Perhaps everyone had something different to say to the world: What? I tried to remember my own moment of choice, but I couldn't. I could only imagine how alien I must have been to myself at that forgotten moment, and all the others like it.

"Are you speaking as one of the strong?" Hedgehog asked Micky.

Micky smiled sadly and said nothing. The Jerusalemites burst out laughing, happy at Hedgehog's victory, which they regarded as their own. "Which side are you on?" they cried. "The weak or the strong?"

"Look at them," Avner suddenly whispered into my ear. "I know them from Jerusalem. The spoiled darlings of Beth-Hakerem and Rehavia. Listen to them jabbering and cackling like hens: *tee-tee-tee-tee-tee*. When somebody needs help that demands real effort they'll always be somewhere else. They always know how to look out for themselves and let others to do their dirty work. That's the way they were brought up. My mother used to work in their houses. Domestic help, they call it. Every morning, when it was still dark, she would walk from our neighborhood to their houses. In the winter too, even in the snow. She didn't have the money for the bus fare. Sometimes she brought the little darlings' old clothes home. Believe me, it made me sick to wear them. Even then, when I was only a small child and I didn't understand anything."

I didn't know why he was telling me this or what it was that made him choose me for his confessor. But there was something so violent, so abhorrent in this intimacy that in my heart I immediately sided with the kids from the neighborhoods whose names rang melodiously and poetically in my ears, full of a pastoral charm.

"Maybe you really can't tell in advance," said Micky, "but that doesn't change my opinion, even if it's to my disadvantage personally."

But perhaps there was a sign nevertheless, something unconscious in our movements, a split second of absentmindedness, a moment of forgetfulness, that revealed a hint of the grand plan. In a world filling with new signs all the time this did not seem impossible.

At the end of the row of recruits sitting under the eucalyptus trees was a group of Iraqis and Moroccans. Peretz-Mental-Case was their leader. I remembered him from the induction center, chain-smoking and telling everyone he met about the poor state of his nerves. He was ready to support his claim with a letter (a short typewritten note, shabby and deeply creased, the paper sweaty and so worn with use that it was in imminent danger of separating into four equal sections), which he would whip out of his shirt pocket. He would scrutinize the reader's face, and as soon as the reading was finished, he would fold the letter up again carefully and return it to his shirt pocket, examining the other's face once more to see if he had taken his story to heart. Then he would smile bitterly and mysteriously under his narrow mustache and nod his head sadly as if to say: *Yes, yes, yes.* Now he was busy crushing a cigarette with the heel of his shoe. There was a pile of stubs at his feet. Next to him sat Sammy, a fairhaired fellow with small blue eyes, as expressionless as the eyes of a dead man, and a long, ugly scar that ran in a thin line down his face almost all the way to his jaw. He had been attached to us that morning at the training camp and announced with a certain pride that this was his third go at basic training He'd spent much of his previous training time in jail. Thanks to his experience he was an unrivaled expert on military life on both sides of the bars, and his Hebrew was better than that of his friends. His audience drank his words in thirstily, and also with not a little anxiety. Now Sammy pointed at the pile of cigarette butts at the feet of Peretz-Mental-Case and embarked on the tale of the ceremonial funeral that the regimental sergeant major of the base had given a cigarette stub left lying on the ground and ignored by the passing recruits. Peretz-Mental-Case whooped with loud laughter that was immediately choked in a fit of harsh coughing and ejected in a thick gob of phlegm. After that an embarrassing silence fell and Peretz poked at the scattered butts with the toe of his shoe, trying to push them into a pile. He looked to his right, at Rahamim who was sitting not far off, and called to him. "Ben-Hamo! Come here, do something!" And he pointed to the butts. They all burst out laughing and Rahamim laughed with them. He stood up and patted his uniform to shake off the earth and eucalyptus leaves that had stuck to it while he was sitting on the ground. The exaggerated movements of his hands and body increased the glee of his seated companions. Rahamin went down on his knees and began crawling at their feet, gathering up the butts that had collected there during the past hour, and when he had gathered them into one pile he didn't know what to do with them. "Dig them a grave!" said Sammy. But Peretz-Mental-Case picked up an empty cigarette pack that he had earlier crumpled up and thrown to the ground, pushed it back into some sort of shape, and held it out to Rahamim without moving from his place. Rahamim took the pack and began filling it with butts. When he had picked them all up and the pack was full he tried to give it back to Peretz, who told him to put it in his trouser pocket and find somewhere to get rid of it later. Rahamim, included in the joke, nodded and laughed gratefully, and the smile did not leave his face. He put the pack in his pocket, and when he saw that he was no longer needed he returned to his place not far from the group and went on listening to their conversation.

Two recruits in fatigue dress and hats came down the path carrying long tabletops with trestles on top of them. When they approached they stopped and surveyed us with amused expressions.

"Raw meat!" cried one of them. "Raw meat!"

For a moment silence descended on us as we sat there facing them. No one dared react to the cry, until Hedgehog jumped up.

"And you — what do you think you are? Not raw meat?" he yelled.

The two of them snickered and pulled faces of horrible disgust. "Raw meat!" they chorused, "raw meat!" And they went on carrying their load to the nearest building and disappeared inside. Hedgehog sat down again, and Peretz-Mental-Case muttered a long, complicated curse. For a long time after that there was no more laughing or talking, as if a cloud of insult and pain hung over us all.

There was something peculiar about the way they'd left us sitting there. The sun began to sink in the sky. There was none of the activity we had anticipated seeing in a training camp. And ever since the runners and their instructor and the two recruits who had yelled *Raw meat!* had disappeared, we were in the middle of a dead space. By now it was clear that there had been a hitch somewhere: Maybe they weren't ready to receive us yet — which added insult to injury. The strain and fatigue of the last few days rose to the surface. Voices were lowered. Not far from me the fellow everybody called Zero-Zero fell asleep sitting up. He was thin, stooped, and worn, with a long nose, his eyes and eyelids chronically inflamed, his face always wounded from shaving, and he never stopped complaining of queer pains in his heart, clinging to them as to his last salvation. When we were given our army serial numbers at the induction center he'd drawn a number ending in two zeros, and he'd told everybody of his good luck, saying that it would make it easier for him to remember. And these two zeros immediately became his nickname. Now his head hung on his chest, his upper lip with faint traces of down raised to expose large gums. One hand was clenched in a tight grip on his knapsack, as if he were afraid someone would steal it from him, while the other lay on his knee. A wedding ring glittered on his third finger like a medal from some other campaign, perhaps more glorious than the present one.

Next to him, reading a book in a foreign language, sat Miller, a German speaker who was a few years older than the rest of us. His face was as dark as old parchment and marked by suffering. His hair already had gray in it. He said nothing to anybody. His Hebrew was poor. In the induction center his bed was next to mine. I sometimes saw him sitting up in bed with a little suitcase on his knees, writing in a notebook. I imagined it was a diary. I knew that Germans often kept diaries preserving every detail of their lives. Now he was absorbed in his book, his face revealing nothing about its contents or his feelings as he read. Next to him sat Nahum, a religious boy who wore a black skullcap under his beret. He had a perpetual smile on his face, a shy, quiet, rather silly, very detached smile. He too kept to himself and only spoke when spoken to; his voice was weak and dull, and he smiled all the while. His eyes gazed at the space in front of him, opened a little wider than normal, apparently in concentration, but this wide-eyed look added an element of astonishment, perhaps even of terror, to the pure, calm, detached expression on his face.

At the end of the path we saw someone running toward us at last. A tall, broad-shouldered fellow, his knapsack on his shoulder, running with light, very springy steps. But for the badgeless beret on his head and the new, still-dark uniform, we would have taken him for one of the instructors. He came up and stood in front of us. His face was sunburned and slightly freckled, his hair was fair, his expression somewhat tense and arrogant. He dropped his knapsack to the ground, put his hands on his hips, and said in a hoarse, throttled, grating voice: "Hi fellows, my name's Alon. I've been attached to your platoon. I've just come from the company. They appointed me orderly-student for this platoon. Everybody get up and form up in threes. In a minute they'll bring your fatigues. Collect all the equipment over there at the side and re-form in threes. Move it. Stop fooling around. We'll all suffer for it. And tidy up your uniforms. You look like something the cat dragged in. The sergeant major gave me an order to get you ready. He'll be here pronto. And he wants you formed up. In threes." A faint smile appeared on his sunburned lips. "And I advise you not to fool around. And to shape up. Attention!"

CHAPTER 2

Did I see a flicker of fear in Micky's eyes, fear of the unknown moment to come? There was something suspect in his nonchalance, in his impatient gestures. Perhaps the truly strong are the ones without any imagination, the ones unable to picture some other possibility? And maybe what Micky called morbid was really the ability and the constant temptation to imagine that other possibility?

Micky said: "Don't go easy on me, you hear? Put all your strength into it, because I'm sure to resist. My life force is awfully strong, it can break out and rampage like a wild animal." He stretched his neck and fingered the artery that, when blocked, stopped the flow of blood to the brain. He smiled at me like an accomplice in crime, but there was definitely a worried expression in his eyes.

The rest break was over and we were summoned to line up in pairs in a circle around the PT instructor to practice silencing a sentry. The instructor went from pair to pair checking the grip and the clutch and the blocking of the artery to loss of consciousness. And once more we witnessed the spectacle of the fall and the ugly twitchings on the ground and the silence that came in their wake. The role changing made performance of the exercise difficult because the attackers had now experienced its effect on their own bodies, and they knew what their friends were about to feel. Their movements were more hesitant. And the attacked had now experienced its execution, and in advancing into the unknown their bodies reacted more forcefully with defensive and inhibiting impulses. The loss of innocence spoiled the pattern: Feelings and ambivalence interfered with a move that was intended to be purely and simply geometrical. When it was my turn to do it, Micky went limp and offered up his neck to make things easier for me, the weaker party. The instructor ordered him angrily to resist, so that the hold would be executed in conditions more approximate to reality. He leaned so far in my direction that I could hear him breathing. "*Go!*" he yelled in my ear. The sudden shout was so close and loud that it deafened me and for a moment I was stunned. When I recovered from the shock, the painful truth became clear to me: However much I wanted to do it, I would not be able to. This had nothing to do with any moral inhibitions or any feelings about Micky. It had nothing at all to do with my reason or understanding. My body refused to obey me, and its refusal was so stubborn that it seemed to have separated from me and taken up position opposite me like an enemy. I was to feel something similar on a number of occasions in the years to come, when I had to make a decision quickly without the possibility of real choice, when I was forced to take my fate into my hands and act. The whole thing lasted no more than a few seconds. A single instant revealed to me that I was nothing but one splinter of a shattered mirror each of whose fragments reflected the same picture but with different participants and on a different section of the continuum of time. In the arc of the circle in front of me three fallen men already lay, in various stages of death and resurrection, and behind me the other pairs awaited their turn. Before the echoes of the instructor's shouts died away completely in the empty space inside my head I saw Micky, with an anguished expression of anticipation on his face, swinging his hand backward and punching me hard on the shoulder. As he did so he said in a dry voice with a tone of would-be amusement: "It's good to die for our country!"

A sudden shameful, liberating glee descended on me, and I fell on Micky's hand and bent it until I forced him down. When I placed the crook of my arm on the place where his shoulder joined his neck to look for the artery, the instructor, having apparently lost all faith in me, crouched down beside me, tightened my grip on the exact spot, and squeezed my elbow to increase the pressure. Micky beat his feet twice on the ground, two dull blows that shook the earth under me, and his whole body writhed in the attempt to free his imprisoned head. "Don't let go," said the instructor, "don't let go!" perhaps because his hand sensed my grip loosening, and he increased his pressure on my elbow. Micky fell, swooning and extremely heavy, on my arm. His rampaging life force was silenced. I averted my eyes in order not to see his face, still held in the crook of my arm, and also perhaps because I didn't want to be in his pictures, if he too saw pictures like I had. "Don't let go!" said the instructor again. The next seconds were unbearably long. I turned my head and examined the instructor's eyes: Hadn't there been some terrible mistake? But he only repeated: "Don't let go!" I tried to resist the pressure of his hand on my elbow, and this time his fingers yielded and his grip loosened.

I knew that now I must not think about Micky but only about myself. My heart pounded and I tried to picture the rush of blood flooding the valves, churning its way from the veins to the heart and the heart to the arteries, and to hear the murmur accompanying the rhythmic heartbeats. But instead of a roaring tide of blood dashing against a blank wall, striving to break through, I heard a still small voice like warm, wet, red flowers slowly opening in the darkness of the deep heart's core. I turned around and saw Nahum standing opposite me with the perpetual smile of happiness and wonder illuminating his face. The black skullcap was fastened to his head with a woman's hair clip. He was standing next to Alon's body, having just forced him to the ground, and like me, apparently, he didn't know what to do next. Perhaps there was something he wanted to say to me, for he raised his hand slightly, as if to attract my attention, but he couldn't get the words out. He made a resigned kind of gesture with his hand and returned to himself.

In the end I dared to turn my face toward Micky. I saw him lying on his back, his face pale and gray, his eyes open, gazing at the sky. I leaned over him and he smiled, tired and contented.

"Did I rampage?" he asked, his voice quieter than usual.

"Yes, a little," I replied, to gratify him; I understood that it was important to him. I wanted to please him because of his fame.

"You don't see any pictures, you lose consciousness and everything stops. Until you wake up. Like in a deep sleep."

"The pictures that I saw were probably just the rest of you, standing over me," I tried to explain. "At first I couldn't remember anything, I didn't know who I was or where I was, and the pictures were my way of interpreting what I saw."

I immediately regretted having said this. I assumed that he didn't understand, or perhaps didn't want to understand, what I was trying to say. I didn't really understand it myself, only sensed something of its essence. Many years were to pass before I finally realized that I would never find anything that would give more meaning to my life than the stumbling, laborious, ever-renewed attempt to remember those elusive pictures, capture them and even perhaps, if only for a moment, bring them back to life.

Micky sat up, breathed deeply, stood and stretched his limbs. Then he started jumping up and down, shaking and swinging his arms and legs, as if he really had just woken from a deep sleep. Presumably this was the way he and his teammates warmed up on the soccer field before a game began.

The instructor was standing next to Hedgehog and Yossie Ressler, three paces away from us, when we suddenly heard him yell: "What the hell do you think you're doing, giggling like a couple of bitches in heat?" We drew closer. Hedgehog had evaded Yossie Ressler's attempts to grab him by the hand and was now prancing about behind him like a child at play. This was in complete contradiction to the principle of silencing-a-sentry, which required taking the target by surprise. But Hedgehog was unable to accept this basic assumption. After several repetitions of this childish romp, they both burst out laughing, bringing the instructor's wrath on their heads. He ordered Hedgehog to stand with his back to us and motioned Yossie to attack his friend. This time Yossie succeeded in seizing Hedgehog by the arm and forced him down without any trouble. The instructor sat on the ground with his legs crossed and watched them with an impatient, scornful expression on his face. Yossie tightened his arm around Hedgehog's neck, and Hedgehog immediately fell to the ground, where he twitched a moment and then fell still, as if deep in sleep.

The instructor rose, stepped softly over to the prone Hedgehog, and kicked him in the crotch. Hedgehog leapt up and opened his eyes in alarm. As soon as he opened them he realized his mistake. The instructor grabbed him by his bristling hair and pulled him to his feet. Hedgehog made a last, desperate attempt to extricate himself, muttering in a stupefied way: "Where am I . . . what happened?" The instructor landed a ringing slap on his cheek. Hedgehog recoiled and for a moment really was stunned. He put his hand to his head and sat down on the ground. "Get up!" yelled the instructor. Hegehog stood swaying on his feet. "Now do you know where you are and what happened?" asked the instructor. "No you don't. Not yet you don't. Because a recruit who tries to make a fool of his instructor gets special treatment on this base."

He called the whole squad to gather around him in a circle. The last of the fallen had already recovered and they too stood up. Everyone gathered to watch Yossie Ressler, under the active supervision of the instructor, put a half nelson on Hedgehog.

"I'm sorry," said Hedgehog, "I'm sorry." His voice trembled and broke. "I can't, I really can't."

There was a silence. Nobody laughed. And all around us lay the camp with its whitewashed paths and ugly eucalyptus trees and fences under the dusty summer sky, looking more and more like a vast desert without a single oasis that would welcome the wondering lost souls and quench their thirst for pity and forgiveness.

"Why can't you?" bawled the instructor.

"I don't know, sir," whispered Hedgehog. "I'm afraid."

The gym shorts were very wide on his slender body. His white skinny legs emerged shyly and timidly, full of agitation. His body writhed and twitched on the ground, as if thousands of insects were stinging him. And when repose finally descended on his body, there was still an expression of terrible anger and accusation against all of us on his face.

For the whole of the past hour we had been doing nothing else but this: Each of us had experienced both roles in this mysterious joke and also seen his friends doing it next to him, until it almost seemed that there was nothing left to get excited about. Like other unimaginable things. Like rites of humiliation, races in pursuit of illusory goals, dreamless sleep, and the unresolved riddles of an alien and capricious justice. Things that come to be taken for granted and lose their meaning in the end. Deep open wounds had healed with suspect speed; fear and desire and shame and disgust and pretense were growing ever duller with the sinking of the soul. Thus it was possible to believe that this too would sink and be borne away, becoming one more signpost marking the retreat to a new line in the battle for the fading memory of our lost honor. And the lesson was clear: There would be no resurrection. Ordered to watch Hedgehog lying motionless at our feet, like a pale, emaciated, anonymous corpse, we stood glum and silent in a circle around him, our heads bowed. A few paces in front of us stood the instructor, like the official representative of another world, his arms crossed on his chest, his face expressionless.

When Hedgehog regained consciousness and sat up to renew his acquaintance with the world around him, a smile of triumph spread gradually over his face, very different from the sly, inquisitive smile we were used to seeing there. He got up and stood next to the instructor. The smile of pride and triumph did not leave his face even as he stood waiting to hear his sentence. I did not know Hedgehog well, I did not know much about him or what kind of person he was, but I did know that somewhere between that last moment of fear, hope of rescue, begging for forgiveness, and this proud, triumphant smile, he, like the rest of us, had just lost something of what was best in him.

"At twenty-two-zero-zero hours both of you will fall in at the company office in turnout dress with clean weapons and beds and full equipment for special parade."

"Yes, sir," said Hedgehog, and his voice sounded almost happy.

"Yes, sir," said Yossie Ressler, his voice hardly audible.

"I didn't hear!" yelled the instructor.

"Yes, sir!" said Yossie loudly.

"Orderly-student will ensure carrying-out. Is there an orderly-student in this squad?"

"It's me, sir," said Hedgehog.

The instructor waved his hand in a gesture of scorn and despair. "You? You're the orderly-student? Alon!"

"Yes, sir!"

"You'll ensure carrying-out," said the instructor.

"Yes, sir."

A fifteen-minute break was announced again. We sat down next to the clump of eucalyptus trees on top of the hill overlooking the barracks. The afternoon hours had become twilight. Nobody seemed to want to talk. Some lay flat on their backs on the ground. Others sat leaning against the tree trunks. With the first cigarettes, hearts opened a little. Alon asked: "Why did you do it? Why couldn't you just go through with it like everyone else?"

"I don't know," said Hedgehog. "It was just stupidity."

"Not really," said Avner. "There are some people who always look for ways to shirk and evade their duty instead of doing the simple, obvious thing, like everybody else."

"I told him," said Yossie Ressler. "I told him it wouldn't work."

"Those PT instructors," said Sammy, "they weren't born yesterday."

"The army isn't a jail," said Alon. "It could be wonderful. But not here and not like this."

The tone of his words and the look he gave us were accusing, as if we were spoiling what should have been the best days of his life. He was from a kibbutz in Emek Beth Shean. The only kibbutznik in the squad and perhaps in the whole platoon. He was tall, broad-shouldered; his face, eyelashes, and hair looked burned by the sun, but this was apparently their natural color. His lips were cracked and sore, as if they were perpetually chapped. His voice came out in a strange, hoarse croak. In the beginning he tended to withdraw into himself, refusing to acknowledge us as his comrades-in-arms. He took no part in the group conversations, ragging, and arguments. He excelled in the training exercises and withstood the most exhausting conditions without any difficulty. All his social contacts were restricted to his role as orderly-student. Some people attributed this to snobbishness stemming from the fact that he was an arrogant kibbutznik. With hindsight, there is no doubt that this was not the case. His great height and physical fitness, his strong hands and sunburned, resolute face could not conceal the flicker of anxiety in his perpetually narrowed eyes, the delicate lines at the corners of his lips. There was something slack and weak, if not desperate in his posture as a whole, such as you might see in a person haunted by the wish to hear, if only once, the sound of absolute silence, although he knows that even if by some extraordinary chance the right conditions should suddenly present themselves, he would still be separated from his wish by the whisper of his breath and the pulsing of his blood. Afterward he softened a little and overcame his reservations. Did he compromise and yield to social pressures or did he perhaps decide that isolation would only remove him farther from his goal?

"What do they want of our lives?" sighed Zero-Zero, who had seen death face-to-face and had not yet recovered from the terrifying sight.

"Who're we supposed to strangle?" inquired Peretz-Mental-Case.

"The secretary in A branch? The regimental policeman at GHQ?" His friends burst out laughing.

"We're not all going to get office jobs," protested Alon.

"Right," said Zackie, whose parents according to him had been millionaires in Iraq. "Some of us'll be cooks and drivers and MPs."

"And some of us will be sent to combat units," said Alon, looking mysterious.

"Don't make me laugh," said Micky. "They don't send B-grade soldiers to combat units. I don't have to tell you that. They don't need invalids like us to fight, and for other jobs they prefer girls, to give the paratroopers a bit of fun."

"Ben-Hamo!" cried Zackie. "You're the only one of us who'll go to a combat unit. They'll take you to fold parachutes along with all the other girls!"

"You don't know what's happening in the army now," said Alon, with the obstinate expression of a baby refusing to return a toy to its rightful owner despite the pleas, threats, and coaxings of the grown-ups. "The period of soft jobs is over. There's no room for bull in the army now. Like they've stopped polishing badges and all that stuff. Since Dayan became chief of staff they've started building an army of men in this country. We're not playing games here. Practicing silencing-a-sentry isn't something they made up to torture recruits on Training Base Four. When the guys in a commando cross the border at night it's the only way they can eliminate some Legionnaire at his post without attracting attention. Or some sentry guarding a camp. Without anyone realizing what's happening. They slip through the Arabs like shadows. They know every tree and bush. Every wadi. And they slip back again without a sound. And when they go out on a raid everything depends on surprise. Until the tommy guns begin to shoot. And the grenades begin to explode. And the dynamite sends their HQ flying. And the Arabs don't even know what's hit them. And our guys are already getting ready to cross the border back into Israel again. It happens almost every night. But you don't know about it. You only hear about the big jobs. But sometimes just five, six paratroopers go out. Commandos. On a secret mission across the border. Suddenly they bump into someone. They have to bring him down with a half nelson. Quietly. Without a fuss. Before he shouts and gives them away. That's the real army. And gradually the whole army's going to be like that. Everyone'll be combat troops."

"In the meantime the Arabs are crossing the border and killing Jews all over the place," said the skeptical Zero-Zero. "By the time your army gets to be so full of fighters there won't be any Jews left here."

"Last week," said Peretz-Mental-Case, "some people from next door to my aunt in Kubeiba were going to bring their daughter home. She lives in a transit camp in Zarnuga. Her husband's a night watchman and she's scared of sleeping alone. And the next day they were going to have a celebration in their family. So that night they went to fetch her. And on the way some Arabs shot at them and killed the father, and a few more of the family are lying in the hospital now, and they wish they were dead too."

"They're in Rehovot and Rishon LeZion and Nes-Ziona, they go where they like, they even get into the kibbutzim, "said Zackie, "so what're you going to do about it? Silence the sentry?"

Peretz ground his cigarette out angrily and muttered a curse in Arabic. "You don't know them Arabs," he said to Alon, "I know them. All my life I lived with them. Those Arabs, they respect you only if you're strong."

"Exactly," said Alon. "And we have to be strong!"

"In Sparta," said Micky, "they used to throw the sick, weak, crippled babies out onto some mountain, so that they would die of hunger or so that the wild animals would eat them. Because they wouldn't grow up to be good soldiers and only be a burden to society and weaken it."

"In Sparta they were smarter," said Micha the Fool. And he explained: "That's a rhyme."

"In Israel," said Micky, "they've invented Training Base Four for the same purpose. That's where they chuck all the invalids and it's all much more humane. They even play soldiers with them, to give them the illusion that they're worth something. And I promise you that if a few of the gang that's roaming the country now came here to Sarafand, they wouldn't have any problem getting into the camp and doing whatever the hell they liked. Who'd stop them? The famous guards with their Czech rifles without striking pins who're afraid of the rats running past them in the dark?"

"That gang's a suicide squad," said Zackie. "They're not afraid of anything. Their captain's a guy called Abu Yussuf who swore to his mother to kill one Jew a day at least, and if a day passed without him killing a Jew then he wasn't a man. They went into an orange grove next to Nes-Ziona and killed the workers. They tied their legs together on top of their heads and chucked them into a hole in the ground. That's how they found them. Then they went somewhere else and killed some more Jews. No one'll catch them."

"Don't worry," said Alon. "We'll get them. We'll get the ones who send them here."

"And others'll come in their place," said Zero-Zero.

"That's why the whole nation has to be an army," said Alon. "Everybody has to be given arms and know how to use them. Girls too, and old men and children. Everybody. Every Jew in the country has to be trained. So they'll know how to fight. Everyone can contribute something. Everyone has to contribute his maximum. The maximum he's capable of. Not only in the army and the reserves. Every day. And it doesn't matter how fit he is or what his medical profile is. It's only a question of finding the right job for everyone to do. That way we'll be stronger than they are. If all the energy and talent and strength go just to that one goal. If people are prepared to give up other things that aren't important. And things that weaken them and harm the main goal. It's like the fingers on your hand" — Alon spread out his hand — "look, that's what the fingers are like separately. You can see the bigger ones and the smaller ones. The strong ones and the weak ones. And there's no strength in the hand. You can't do anything with it. Maybe just play the piano. Or neck with a girl. But like this" — now he clenched his fist — "all of them together, all of them equal. There's strength in that hand. That's how all the people in the country should be. That's what the people here were like before the state."

Micky stood up, stretched his limbs, and began jumping on the spot. Alon's vision of the clenched fist obviously left him cold. He smiled. "But some people don't have the least desire to live their lives in a country like one big kibbutz or army camp. Some people think their lives wouldn't be worth living without the chance to develop themselves according to their own private dreams, without striving for achievements and living their lives the way they see fit."

Alon seemed thunderstruck. "But those are private affairs, selfish ambitions!" he said. "That way people would only worry about themselves. Their own personal ambitions. They would leave it to the chosen few to defend them. To die for them. While they lived it up in the towns. And sat around in cafés all day long. And made money. And went to concerts and all that stuff. We wouldn't stand a chance. Never mind the infiltrators and the shooting on the borders. With that we can still cope. And I'm sure we'll succeed in the end. But what about when the second round comes? If the whole nation isn't prepared, we've had it.

"We need two things: personal example and discipline. Otherwise we don't stand a chance. And it has to begin from the top. The leaders have to be men. Not get in the way of the army doing what has to be done. And instead of playing politics all the time, they should see what's important and what's not. And from the top it'll seep down to the bottom. To the most miserable soldier. The most insignificant citizen. That's our only hope. And let me tell you," said Alon to Micky, "that the private individual is happier that way too. That's how he can reach his peak. His greatest achievements. Develop in the best way possible. Because whatever he does is connected to the general goal. To society as a whole. He feels that he's not living alone. That he's part of something much more important than his petty little problems, something bigger than himself. It gives him a lot of strength; a lot of faith in himself."

Micky spread out his hand, examined his fingers for a moment, as if wondering which of them to choose, and in the end raised the middle one and said: "This is my most important finger. I want to give it all the attention I can and I don't give a damn about the rest of them."

Micky's words elicited loud laughter and general agreement. Zackie too raised his middle finger and looked at it sadly: "It's sleeping, poor thing," he said, "from all the soda they give us to drink."

Micky leapt up and hung by both hands from one of the branches of the eucalyptus he had been leaning against earlier. He tensed his muscles and raised himself on his arms, lowered and raised himself, counting the number of lifts in an undertone, until his strength was exhausted and he hung there swinging backward and forward, breathing rhythmically, inhaling slowly through his nose and letting the air out quickly in a kind of brief whistle: *phew! phew! phew!* The whole exercise looked like an evasion of Alon's hurt, accusing silence. Micky's reaction to Alon's impassioned speech was uncharacteristic of him. The target was too easy. After all, anybody speaking seriously, with conviction or emotion, immediately exposes himself to derision, and any cynical remark, even the most pointless, will make him look like a pompous ass. The rules of fair play were usually instinctive in Micky's behavior. I assumed that it could only have been inner rebellion and personal enmity that had goaded him into departing from these rules now. And I assumed that Alon sensed this too. Perhaps he would take refuge in estrangement and arrogant isolation again, as he had at the beginning? Micky let go of the branch and dropped to the ground. He knew that Alon's words had been directed at him. Perhaps this was precisely what had given rise in him to hostility and aggression, as if these words had contained a threat to something deep and precious to him. And as always, aggression found strange ways of flanking to the exposed rear, the weak spots, far from the motivation that aroused it in the first place. The laughter and jokes about the effects of the soda had revived all spirits a moment before, but now they died down. The rest break was coming to an end. The brief summer dusk began to dim the light, and a kind of dull tiredness came down on us. There was a silence of the kind imposed by an inner command, a moment before the end of the rest break, perhaps in an attempt to draw out the time left and exploit it to the full.

Hedgehog, the orderly-student who had disgraced his role, stood up first, opened the leather shield of his watch, and looked at the time. There were a few minutes left. Suddenly Avner rose quickly to his feet, turned his back on the group, and walked a few steps away to the edge of the clump of trees hiding part of the paling horizon from us. The moon was already hanging over our heads, still unlit but ready to begin the night watch as soon as the time came. While we were still wondering what he was looking at we saw a red-spotted ball fall and bounce on the path at the foot of the hill, and immediately, in the flash of an eye, a dog; racing after it, its identical twin. The two dogs pounced furiously on the ball, fighting for their elusive prey. I had never seen dogs like them before. Their bodies were long and narrow, arched like bows, and their heads too were long and pointed. Their legs were tall and slender, their coats smooth, clipped, pale gray, shining with a silvery sheen on the soft protuberances of their spines and joints. The stripes of silver rounded and stretched rapidly but softly and harmoniously, rippling in waves such as a breeze might make on a calm, clear lake bathed in the light of the moon. This vision did not belong to the time and place in which we were imprisoned. The whole squad rose to its feet and went to join Avner, who was standing in front of us at a vantage point before which the whole horizon lay open. We saw him from the back, rooted to the spot against the background of the pale moon, still as a statue, in his dark gym pants and clumsy black boots and khaki socks, his head slightly lowered, and before we could reach his side, she entered our field of vision, running toward her dogs. At first she did not notice us standing next to the eucalyptus trees, and her run was free and light, her feet barely touching the ground and her head flung back. The smile illuminating her face, slightly flushed from her running, was apparently not meant for strange eyes to see. She hurried to the dogs and stopped next to them, her back to us, bent over them and began stroking them and patting their backs encouragingly. Then she laid her cheek on the ribs of one of them, rubbing up against its fur and belly, and with her other hand she encircled its back and stroked the ribs and belly on the other side. Then she bent over its sibling, but when she turned her face to lay her cheek against its body, her eyes were directed toward us and our presence was immediately revealed.

Even from where we stood we could see the sharp recoil passing like an electrical current through her body, and the practiced effort to inhibit the impulse, subdue it, and disperse it into a thousand tremors that merged imperceptibly into the overall movements of her body. The smile vanished instantly from her face, which flushed more deeply and took on a stern, proud expression. Slowly she rose from her crouch with her profile facing us. She was wearing a tight-fitting T-shirt with a whistle suspended from a cord lying on top of it, blue gym shorts with elastic hems hugging her thighs, white running shoes and short, thin white socks. Her fair hair was quite short, clipped back behind her ears, but curling abundantly over the front part of her head. Some of these curls fell onto her forehead, and their color was a shade between honey and gold, depending on the play of light and shadow cast by the rays of the sinking sun. The whistle, a slender, glittering chrome-plated tube, hung between her breasts like some rare, mysterious jewel. Her calves were rather muscular, but no more than allowed for by the strict harmony imposed by some marvelous musical law on all the proportions and lines and curves of her body. She wasn't tall, but the gym clothes emphasized the length of her legs, the gentle curve of her hips, the narrowness of her waist and the slope of her arms and the firm softness of her breasts and the majestic height of her neck. Her chin was cleft and her nose rather flat, and these two contrasted with her smooth cheeks and light brown eyes and delicate brows — as if they stamped her face with some alien harshness and underlined its expression of cold, haughty disdain. There was hardly anything in common between the noble wild animal that had galloped after the dogs with such natural, sensuous abandon and this reserved figure, measuring her movements and gazing at closed spaces like a stranger, the smell of danger tautening all the sinews of her body. She was a figure steeped in a kind of bright sadness. The swiftness of the transformation gave a special dimension of timelessness and ambivalence and mystery to this revelation of beauty from another world. As if we had just witnessed one of the metamorphoses described in ancient myths. And we stood on the low hill not far from her, like a little band of survivors from a shipwreck waiting to be rescued, half naked in our rags, utterly wretched and miserable opposite the marvelous girl who would not favor us with so much as a glance.

She knelt and picked up the ball. When she straightened up again she was rolling it between her hands, as if trying to make up her mind what to do next. And just for a second, as she knelt and stood, the smooth planes of her arms and legs were covered by shadowy golden sheen, as if they had grown a fine fuzz of yellow hair. She transferred the ball to her left hand and gripped it under her arm, while with her right she once more stoked the backs of the dogs crouching at her feet and sniffing her shoes. This was the sign. At the touch of her hand the two dogs rose. Slowly she started walking, the two dogs behind her. Haughty and reserved, with soft, measured steps, she passed us and receded down the path.

Avner turned and saw us standing behind him, transfixed as he was by the sight. His face was sullen, with a somber, worried look as if he just woken from a dream, and it asked as plainly as words: *Did you see what I saw?* No one said anything. As if keeping quiet could prolong the spell. Until Sammy broke the silence by saying, "That's Ofra the PT instructress," and he added a curse and spat.

"Is she from Training Base Twelve?" asked Avner.

"Yeah," said Sammy, "but she spends more time here than there. She's got troubles in Training Base Twelve."

"Oh man, if only we could have her to train us," said Zackie and sighed. "The first thing I'd do to her is put a half nelson on her —"

"I don't envy anyone who falls into her hands," said Sammy. "She's a snake, that one. Not a drop of pity in her. She sends you to jail for nothing. All she needs is to imagine someone said something. She's death, I'm telling you, death."

"Hasn't she got anyone on the base?" asked Avner. "Hasn't she got a boyfriend?"

Sammy laughed soundlessly. "Nope," he said. "She doesn't let anybody touch her."

"What, doesn't she like men?" asked Avner.

Sammy was silent, but there was a vicious smile in his dead blue eyes.

Again all eyes turned toward the girl receding down the path with her two dogs, as if to compare the sight we had seen with the new facts and test their effect. At the end of the path we saw our PT instructor coming back in our direction. We lined up in threes and looked at the path. He came up to her, stopped and smiled, and said something that we were unable to hear. She lifted her head and sailed past him without stopping or saying a word in reply. He turned around and looked at her for a minute in amusement, said something under his breath, laughed to himself, and came up to us.

Hedgehog bawled: "Atten*shun!*"

The instructor dismissed him with a disgusted wave of his hand: "The cowardly cheating girl can step back into the ranks. Alon!"

"Yes, sir!" cried Alon without enthusiasm. He stepped out of the ranks, stationed himself in front of us instead of Hedgehog, shouted "Attention!" and we stiffened and stood to attention again. The PT instructor was in a playful mood. "Back to the platoon at a run, and I want to see you lift your knees and hear you sing. Let Sergeant Ofra see what kind of men you are!"

We set out behind him at a run in time to the blasts of his whistle, but nobody felt like singing. The rhythmic swaying and mechanical movements induced a kind of stupor. "Sing!" yelled the PT instructor. Micha the Fool began to sing in a bleating voice: "She'll be coming round the mountain when she comes . . ." and a few others joined in rather dispiritedly. "I can't hear you!" shouted the PT instructor. More voices joined in. But he wasn't satisfied. He brought the squad to a halt. We waited for the yells and threats, but he looked at us in pretended perplexity instead: "What's the matter with you? Why don't you sing like men? One look at a pretty girl and the cat's got your tongue? Okay. Then don't sing. But run like men at least!" And we set off behind him again, with the thudding of our boots on the dirt track and rhythmic panting of our breath sounding like a blow and a groan, a blow and a groan, a centipede advancing blindly and stupidly along a never-ending path.

We saw her farther down the road in front of us with her two dogs and we almost caught up with her, but she turned off onto the path leading to the staff quarters. A beautiful, mysterious girl with a pair of dogs.

CHAPTER 3

"Maybe there's really something wrong with him?" I said.

"Rubbish," said Micky. "He's a malingerer. There's nothing wrong with him. He just hates washing. He's a dirty, stinking, lazy pig and he's getting his excuse ready in case he's caught."

"He's afraid to die," I said. "He's sick with fear."

"He's sorry for himself, that's all. Just look what he looks like," said Micky raising his voice so that Zero-Zero would hear, and pointing at him for good measure. "People like him would be better off dead. I hate people who feel sorry for themselves all the time, picking at their wounds and showing them off in public."

"Why are you talking so loudly?"

"Because I'm not a hypocrite and I don't hide what I think of people. I say what I think and I stand behind every word I say."

And as if to contradict what he had just said, he went up to Zero-Zero's bed, examined the figure lying there in a fetal position, and asked: "What's the matter with you?"

Zero-Zero said nothing.

Nahum, who was standing nearby with the usual surprised smile on his face, said: "Perhaps he should take something."

Zero-Zero moaned: "Just leave me alone. Don't do me any favors."

We left for the showers. "There's nothing wrong with him," said Micky. "He's a degenerate moron."

"Would you have left him out there on the mountain with the lost children of Sparta?" I asked.

"But we're all there already," said Micky. "Haven't you realized that yet? This is the place!"

In the shower room people from another squad were talking about what had happened to Miller. When they had lined up in threes in at the beginning of their PT session, he'd suddenly collapsed in the ranks and fallen to the ground like a lump of lead, jerked and twitched for a moment, and fallen asleep. They thought he had fainted. The PT instructor rushed up to him, forced his mouth open, and pushed a bit of wood between his teeth to prevent him from swallowing his tongue and choking. Miller was having an epileptic fit, the instructor explained to them, and added that he couldn't understand what someone like him was doing in the army in the first place. One of the recruits was sent to fetch help and the rest of them stood to one side with the instructor and waited. A few minutes later a medic arrived, and he too joined the spectators. Miller's sleep lasted about ten minutes. When he woke up and opened his eyes he wasn't surprised to see them all standing around and looking at him. The medic took him to the dispensary. Afterward, when the instructor demonstrated silencing-a-sentry on one of them, they were all horrified by its appalling similarity to the scene they had just witnessed. The instructor had to make them run and sing and knock them out with all kinds of exercises before they calmed down. But the sight went on haunting them, and the feeling that they had been reenacting Miller's fit still oppressed them now as they told the tale in the showers.

The instructor Muallem suddenly came into the shower room pushing Zero-Zero, with a terrified expression on his face and wearing only a pair of filthy underpants, in front of him. "The proper place for this piece of shit is the shithouse not the shower!" yelled Muallem and shoved him under the jet of water. The story of Miller's fit had left everyone feeling depressed, and consequently Zero-Zero's appearance in the shower did not elicit the response it deserved, or at any rate not the one expected by Muallem. He was the only one of the instructors who tried to ingratiate himself with the recruits and treated us with a degree of friendliness. Zero-Zero stood in his underpants under the shower without moving a muscle, full of mute protest and reproach.

We returned to the subject of Miller. The conversation aroused Zero-Zero's curiosity. He broke his vow and began to move his body under the water, even going so far as to wash his face and hair, and then he emerged from the shower, sat down dripping on a bench next to the wall, and pricked up his ears. Afterward he shook the water off his head and smiled. "As true as God, that did me good," he said. "I feel better now." He rubbed his bloodshot eyes with his wet hands.

When we returned to our barracks Miller had not yet come back from the dispensary. None of us knew who he was and what he was doing among us or what he was writing in his black notebooks. If we had discovered that he was a Christian, for example, or a Communist or a spy, we would not have been surprised.

It was only when we were standing in line for supper outside the mess that he reappeared and joined the platoon, his dark parchment face as inscrutable, foreign, silent, and old as ever. Nobody looked in his direction. Nobody ever talked to him. And now it was even more difficult and distasteful than before. He himself drew slightly apart, as if not to make the people around him uncomfortable by his proximity, evidently realizing how they felt. But the mere fact of his presence carried with it some fateful taint, a stigma that infected us all. The circle of untouchability and excommunication into which we had been cast from the beginning, and which had been suppressed from consciousness with the sinking of the soul, now tightened around us more implacably than ever. The foreign presence silenced everyone. Anything we said might be interpreted as in some way directed against him. But silence also, if it lasted too long, would only give rise to the same suspicion: that we were deliberately and demonstratively ignoring him.

"He keeps on staring at me in the showers," said Zackie and pointed at Ben-Hamo, who clapped his hands with hilarity, "staring and winking at me all the time. I don't know what he wants of me. What's the matter? What are you staring at?"

Ben-Hamo's movements became more and more exaggerated and grotesque. His voice choked with laughter as he repeatedly denied the accusation in order to increase the merriment. And Zackie went on complaining bitterly of the fate of his private parts, exposed to the lewdness of Ben-Hamo's looks. Rahamim kept on protesting and never stopped giggling for a minute. He knew that the role he had to play was more powerful and important than he was, more powerful and important than the truth. It was obvious that he too was enjoying the performance, that he was fanning the flames, that he would stoop to anything to increase the fun. Muallem, who was standing to one side and keeping order, came up to see what was happening. "Ben-Hamo!" he called. "Are you making trouble again? Cut it out right now, or I'll put you on report!"

"Sir," said Zero-Zero, "isn't there a law against it in the army?"

"Against what?" said Muallem. "Against dirty stinking pigs who try to get out of showering and want to infect their friends and the whole army with every disease under the sun?"

"But sir, I wasn't feeling well."

"You're a bloody malingerer. You know what we do to malingerers in the army? Bring me your mess kit!"

He examined Zero-Zero's mess kit and an expression of horrified disgust appeared on his face. "Go and clean it! Now! Get cracking!"

Zero-Zero went to the sinks to do what he was told and Muallem said: "God Almighty, the types we get here, one of you's worse than the next. Ben-Hamo, if you don't stop laughing I'll have you court-martialed!" At the sight of Rahamim's laughter and peculiar contortions, Muallem had a hard time not bursting out in laughter himself.

Zero-Zero returned with his mess kit and Muallem checked it again. "Disgusting," he said. "It's still dirty. Don't you even know how to wash a mess kit?"

"I did wash it, sir."

Muallem gave the mess kit back to Zero-Zero, who said: "Sir, I wasn't malingering, I swear I wasn't. I've got a heart condition. I couldn't breathe. I felt giddy, I thought I was going to die."

"I don't want to hear any more about it!" said Muallem. "If you're sick, go on sick call and let them send you to the doctor."

"I'll die before I go to that woman doctor . . . ," said Zero-Zero.

"Shut up!" said Muallem. "I don't want to hear any more."

The back door of the mess, the cooks' door, opened, and the cook's head peeped out. Sammy, who was standing at the end of the queue, looked sidelong at Muallem and, as soon as he thought the latter's eyes were averted, slipped out of line and crossed to the door, which shut quietly behind him. It seemed as if Muallem were looking away deliberately, in order not to catch Sammy out. Perhaps he didn't want to get involved with Sammy and his exploits, or perhaps all the instructors had decided to turn a blind eye and let him finish basic training without going to jail in order to be rid of him at last. Sammy himself avoided friction with the instructors and did what he was told, trying not to make himself conspicuous. Only sometimes he would whisper something in the thick voice that contrasted oddly with his boyish face, let out a curse that the instructors either didn't hear or pretended not to. Some people said that the cooks laid on big spreads for him in the kitchen with steaks and other delicacies, and sometimes he would bring his friends in the platoon freshly baked cookies or canned meat and fruit from the kitchen or the field rations, hidden in his trouser pockets. He was the only one of us who wasn't shaving yet. The ugly scar running down his cheek, a disfiguring birthmark or souvenir of some accident or knife fight, was the only sign of violence or any kind of emotion on his smooth, still, expressionless face.

As was his habit almost every evening, Miller placed his little suitcase, a shabby, well-traveled refugee suitcase, on his knees, opened his notebook on top of it, and began writing from left to right, line after line in a rapid, practiced hand. The dim bulb suspended from the ceiling cast a dreary light over everything. We had the evening off, with no training exercises or lectures scheduled. Everybody lay fully clothed on his bed, and only Hedgehog and Ressler, who had been given an extra night parade by the PT instructor, interrupted the silence with their childish bursts of laughter, which sounded more nervous than amused, like a cry for help. I lay with the back of my neck on the rectangle of folded blankets, their wool warming and tickling my skin. I half closed my eyes and saw in a blur, as if from a distance, the row of beds in front of me and the people lying on them, and I said to myself: *I don't know them. I don't know who they are, I've never seen them before in my life.* The more I repeated these words to myself, the more I felt the soft touch of sleep surrounding me and slowly bearing me elsewhere. I closed my eyes completely and the gentle gliding continued, in ever-widening circles. I wasn't asleep yet, for part of my consciousness described what I was feeling to me and advised me to get as much enjoyment as I could out of it. It was so different from the rough, panicky sleep that fell on me on other nights in this place, instantaneously, like a blow. Suddenly someone shouted: "Attention!" from the end of the barracks. And before I was aware of what I was doing I had jumped up and was standing in front of my bed, and like me all the others were standing in front of their beds, their bodies stiff, their faces listless and resigned. It was Muallem. He had come to inform Ressler and Hedgehog that their special parade had been pushed back. He was duty instructor that night and the one who had to review their parade, and it was hard to tell if he was motivated by concern for their, and our, sleep or if he just wanted to get the whole thing over. He gave them ten minutes to get ready. At eight o'clock on the dot they had to fall in before the company office with their beds made to regulation specifi-cations, with clean weapons, spick-and-span in turnout uniforms and full equipment, ready for parade. Muallem went away. The panic-stricken Hedgehog and Ressler didn't know where to begin. It was obvious that they had deliberately been given a ludicrously inadequate amount of time to prepare themselves, in order to make them run backward and forward for a couple of hours until they had been properly punished. We all went back to our beds and watched them rushing around in a frenzy, cleaning their weapons, polishing their boots, folding their blankets, and putting on their uniforms, looking frantically and repeatedly at their watches as they did so.

Alon got up and examined their weapons. "What difference does it make?" asked Yossie. "If he wants to he'll find something." But Alon took a couple of flannel rags out of his knapsack and went on cleaning the gun, holding it up to the light again and again to make sure no speck of dust was left in the barrel. By the time they began dragging their beds out it was already after eight. But it no longer mattered. They had to enter that interim state with which we were all familiar by now, in which actions were detached from their goals and means. They ran around like robots. Next to the door they got stuck with their beds, and like two blind animals they kept pushing them and pushing them without being able to get them through the narrow opening. Their faces looked like the faces of sleepwalkers. I knew that they were now covering themselves with the kind of protective skin that shields the feet of people who walk barefoot over smoldering coals. There was silence in the room, as if any word or touch might rouse them from their mystic trance, destroy their immunity, and bring disaster down on their heads. But Avner jumped off his bed and without a word hurried to the door, leapt over the two jammed beds, and from a position outside on the step helped them get out. Then he ran first with one and then the other, helping them carry their beds and get to the company office on time. Breathing heavily, he returned to the room and lay down immediately on his bed as if he had never risen from it at all; if he was caught helping them his punishment would be the same as theirs.

A little while later we heard their beds bumping against the door and Avner again jumped up and went out to help bring them in. They sat down, breathing hard, to clean their weapons. This time they did it without their previous panic-stricken haste, but at a deliberate, uniform pace, occasionally sticking a pinkie into the metal innards and contemplating the spot of black oil smeared on it before going back to work. And once more they set out, with Avner helping them carry their beds and running with them part of the way along the path leading to the company office, first the one, then the other, and then coming back and lying down on his bed, until the procession returned and the creaking of the beds was heard at the door.

Suddenly the sound of singing accompanied by an accordion rose from the opposite barracks. "On the road to the North — the frontier draws nigh, We'll wait for the foe, brother, when the time comes to go — On the road to the North . . ." At first the singing was quiet and orderly, but it got louder and louder and when the singers cried "When it's do or die, brother — On the road to the North there'll be a light in the sky!" they nearly brought the roof down on top of us. Alon, who was reading an old newspaper, put the paper down next to him on the bed, closed his eyes, and his croaking voice could be heard singing along softly with the rousing chorus. Someone else joined in and soon most of us were sitting on our beds singing at the top of our voices, in a burst of happiness as if we had reached a resting place on our hopeless wanderings. I knew that this moment too was only a mirage, one of those illusions that torment the souls of wanderers in the wilderness with the promise of quenching their thirst. I knew the heartbreak that invariably accompanies this, but I clung to it nevertheless, and when the first song was over the accordion in the opposite building began to play "The Little Goatherd in the Valley." Over in 3 Platoon they were always breaking into song, as if the pick of the company had been concentrated there, those whose spirits were unbroken, who knew how to get the best out of these days in basic training, which maybe weren't as terrible as I kept imagining them to be. In our barracks the singing died down somewhat, since most people didn't know the words by heart. But I did know them, and I sang them verse after verse, like someone singing a rebel song or underground hymn in the teeth of a tyrannical regime.

Hedgehog and Ressler, who seemed to be running around in circles, arrived at the doorway again, and again Avner went out to help them bring in their beds. They were amazed to hear the singing. At first they looked sour but in the end smiles of bashful gratitude appeared on their faces, as if the whole thing had been put on in their honor, to encourage them, and Hedgehog clenched his fist and waved it in the air a couple of times as if to say: *They won't break us!*

It went on until lights-out. The strains of the accordion and sound of the singing from 3 Platoon died down and Hegehog and Ressler completed their punishment. Muallem came to check all present in front of their beds and detail the guards. As I was about to fall asleep something in my heart told me that a certain thaw might be setting in there and the strangers surrounding me were growing less strange to me; but perhaps this too was only an illusion, and this ground would always be foreign soil to me.

Suddenly I was shaken awake.

"Micky?"

"No, it's Hanan. It's your turn to get up for guard duty."

Again I experienced the fall and oblivion of the silencing-a-sentry exercise; again the bitter taste came into in my throat. Hanan was one of the Jerusalemites, Hedgehog's friend. I let my eyes get used to the darkness. After a moment I sat up in bed.

"Okay?" asked Hanan.

"Yes, you can go, I'll come in a minute."

"I can't wake Avner, he doesn't answer."

"Leave him to me. Don't worry, you can go."

He left the room and went back to his post to wait for us. I went up to Avner's bed, which was next to my own, and called his name in his ear. There was no reaction. He was lying on his back, his legs stretched out in front of him, his arms at his sides, his head straight between his shoulders, and his face to the ceiling. He snored faintly, and stopped when I shook his shoulder and called his name again. But he still didn't wake up.

"Oh God, what a life," moaned Zero-Zero from his bed. "Every time he goes on guard duty I have to wake up." Despite the long, backbreaking hours of the day, despite his perpetual exhaustion, Zero-Zero slept very lightly. He woke up whenever anyone opened his mouth, and especially when the guards were woken. And the next day his eyes were red and he kept falling asleep in the rest breaks between training.

I gripped Avner by the shoulders, hauled him into a sitting position, and shook him until his eyes opened and looked at me. He covered his eyes with his hands and said: "I'm dead beat."

"So am I dead beat," cried Zero-Zero in a tearful voice, "and when are you going to let me go back to sleep? Why don't you get out of here already?"

"Stop moaning," said Avner. "If you don't shut your mouth, I'll give you a crack that'll shut you up forever."

Zero-Zero was silent.

"You can go and relieve them," Avner said to me. "I'll come in a minute."

I got dressed and put on my boots. My fingers had already learned how to lace the gaiters rapidly in the dark. I took my gun from its hiding place under the mattress and went outside. Hanan and Micha were waiting for me on the path outside the door.

"What's up with him?" asked Hanan.

"He's awake. He'll be out in a minute. You can go to bed."

"I don't want any trouble," said Hanan. "I'll wait till he comes. I only hope it doesn't take all night."

"All night oceans of flames seethed," gabbled Micha, "and tongues of fire leapt above the Temple Mount."

Hanan said: "He's probably gone back to sleep. I'm going to have a look." And he went into the barracks. Micha went on babbling. I moved a few steps away and turned my back on him. He fell silent. A few minutes passed and nobody came. I assumed that Avner had gone back to sleep and Hanan was having a hard time waking him up. The oppressive presence of Micha a few steps behind me filled my heart with loathing and rage against Avner, against his heavy, brutish sleep. I knew that this too was a question of decision: whether to wake up or not, whether to get up and do your duty or sink into oblivion and self-indulgence. That moment, even in the midst of sleep, maybe especially in the midst of sleep, was utterly clear and lucid and the choice between the command of the will and the seductions of the imagination was made in full responsibility. The wish to snatch one more moment of sleep was like every other form of self-deception. There was always someone who paid the price. Maybe that explains what happened later, on that night of betrayal. In any case, at that moment it was hard for me to see the Avner who had spent the whole evening helping Hedgehog and Ressler carry their beds, and risked being punished for it too, as the same person who kept putting off the moment of waking up and doing his guard duty as if he were waiting for some miracle to come and save him.

When I heard his boots creaking on the barracks steps, I turned my head and saw his black eyes glittering in the lamplight in a self-satisfied smile. Micha mumbled something and walked off toward the barracks.

"Idiot," I said.

"It's a kind of nervousness with him," said Avner, "a kind of fear that if he stops talking something bad will happen to him."

"I never know what to do with him, if I'm supposed to answer him or just ignore him. It's depressing."

"It doesn't bother me," said Avner. "Crazy people don't scare me either, maybe because I don't have any tendencies that way myself, so I'm not afraid of being infected."

As far as I was concerned, there were a lot too many things that he wasn't afraid of. Like on the first day on the base, when he stood whistling next to the tree and the three runners kept going past us with their instructor. And afterward too, in the race against time, with the pressure hanging over us like a well-aimed threat, to wash and shave, make our beds, tidy the barracks, and get ready for parade, he did everything at his own pace, ostentatiously calm and deliberate, as if he were trying to prove something; and the truth is that he usually made it on time, the same as everyone else. But in my opinion there was something provocative in this demonstration and the self-satisfied smirk that accompanied it. There was something irresponsible about it. I couldn't help thinking that if his gamble ever failed to come off, there would always be somebody to pay the price. And the thought that this somebody might be me was so savage and maddening that it overshadowed everything else.

According to our orders he was supposed to stand guard opposite the barracks door while my duty as patrolman was to make the rounds of the company every few minutes and then come back to stand next to him until the next patrol.

"I'm coming with you," said Avner. "If I stand still I'll fall asleep on my feet. I'm dead beat."

"You'll leave the place unguarded?" I asked.

"What's there to guard here, the rats?" He burst out laughing.

"I mean, if there's an inspection."

"There won't be any inspection," said Avner. "They want to sleep too."

I knew that if we were caught walking together we'd both be punished as accomplices in the same crime. Fear made me furious with him. His presence at my side was so oppressive that I felt as if I had to carry him on my back. His voice and Oriental, biblical pronunciation with its rasping gutturals, rolling *R*'s, stressed vowels, and glottal stops sent shudders of rage running through me. The best way to overcome and disguise these feelings was to be extra friendly. I said: "You knocked yourself out this evening, helping them carry their beds. It was nice of you."

He stopped to light a cigarette even though smoking during guard duty was prohibited, in case the guard would show his presence to the enemy lurking for him in the darkness. The lighting of the match sounded like an explosion in my ears, and the flame blazed like a bonfire in my eyes.

"I'm used to jobs like that," said Avner. "In Jerusalem I worked in a music shop. In actual fact, I was a porter. I even carried pianos upstairs to customers' houses."

He found a way of holding his cigarette so that his hand shielded its burning tip, but every time he took a puff his palm was illuminated with a reddish light, as if it were bleeding.

"Is that where you learned classical music?"

He said: "You think I didn't notice, on that first day when we were sitting there, that you were watching me whistling and wondering: *Where the hell did this black ape become acquainted with Prokofiev?*"

"That's not true," I lied, "I was just wondering how you managed to get it off pat, it's quite difficult."

"When there wasn't any work to do I used to sit there sometimes in the storeroom, down in the basement. There was an old gramophone there, and the boss let me use it. I listened to records. At first it was very strange to me. I listened out of curiosity and I hated it. But whenever I had any spare time I went and took a record and listened. And gradually it got into my blood. I got to know more and more works. Then I began to go to concerts at the YMCA, until in the end I was hooked. But then something happened. Something disgusting. That put a stop to it all and made me hate music. But I don't want to talk about it now. Maybe I'll tell you some other time."

He fell silent for a minute, reflecting perhaps on this disgusting thing that had happened to him. I was glad that the patrol was coming to an end, that we were approaching the platoon and for the time being the danger of an inspection had been postponed. Everything he said I had heard through a fog of fear. No one was waiting next to the abandoned sentry post.

"And now?" I asked.

"Now I'm not so involved. Then it was my whole life. Nothing else interested me. Now I occasionally hear a concert on the radio that still gives me a thrill. There are some works I've forgotten, that I can't whistle anymore, but I can still remember the feeling they gave me, I remember colors, shapes, something like that. It's a wonderful feeling. But it'll never be the same as it used to be, when it was the center of my life."

He lit another cigarette. I looked around anxiously. Everything was quiet. The shadows of the rats setting out on their nocturnal journeys, scurrying backward and forward as if in accordance with some mysterious plan, flitted past us where we stood, and I still couldn't overcome my horror at the sight. These were my first encounters with these night creatures, the plague carriers leading their subterranean lives by our side, hidden but undeniable, remote but powerfully present, as if they had been created for no other purpose than to embody some dreadful vision buried deep in the heart of the great night inside us, to give it a name and a form and a physical proximity perhaps in order to make it easier for us to hate it, to spew it out, to bear it.

"Yossie Ressler used to come to the shop with Daddy, to buy scores, or cello or violin strings. He plays the piano, his father plays the cello, and his sister the violin. They played chamber music at home. Sometimes I used to see the whole family at concerts at the Y, and they never even had the grace to nod when they walked past me. I can't begin to tell you how it made me feel. I was a kid. I thought we all belonged to one big family of music lovers, something like that. But now everything's changed and I don't really care anymore."

"Is that why you helped him carry his bed?"

"I wanted to prove to myself that I don't feel bitter about them anymore. And I know Hedgehog too, from the days when he was still called Yudeleh. I remember him in a cap with side locks tucked behind his ears. He's from a religious family in Geula."

"I thought he was from Rehavia or Beth-Hakerem," I said in surprise.

"No, the others are from there, Yossie and Micha and Hanan and the rest of them. But Hedgehog's from a religious home. He used to hang out in Zion Square with all the guys. Whenever there was a scuffle he was the first to jump into the fray, and he always got the worst of it. He likes fighting, but he's not cut out for it. He just wasn't in the same league as the guys from our neighborhood. But you never saw the little darlings from Rehavia and Beth-Hakerem sitting on the fence in Zion Square. They went to Boy Scouts, or stayed home with Mommy and Daddy to play chamber music and all that stuff. I've got nothing against them, they're not bad chaps, but I never had friends like them, I never had anyone my own age that I could talk to about my feelings about music. Sometimes I felt so full of it I thought I was going to burst. I grew away from my family and neighborhood friends because they had no interest in the thing that was most important to me. So you could say I was quite lonely. And that's what tripped me up and nearly caused my downfall. In that incident I hinted at before. Until my call-up came and I wasn't sorry when it did."

I had to go out on patrol again. "I'm coming with you," announced Avner. And again he walked by my side, but this time my fear of being caught subsided. Again we marched in the darkness, our boots creaking on the trodden path and Avner hooding his cigarette in his palm and everything quiet around us and less menacing than it had seemed at first. We had hardly advanced a few paces when we heard the tread of boots on the steps of our building. We stopped short and turned around. In the light of the lamp we saw Sammy's face. He descended the steps, looking from side to side until his eyes got used to the light outside after the darkness inside. We assumed he was going to piss. But he was fully dressed and had his boots on and he stood still for a moment as if considering his next move or examining the terrain around him. He must have missed us and thought that we were on the other side of the building because he turned to the right and started walking up the path toward us. When he saw us he recoiled, but didn't panic, skirting the place where we were standing and slipping past us like a cat, without a word or sign of recognition. Then he broke into a light run and disappeared behind one of the other barracks.

I gave Avner an inquiring look. He looked thoughtful and a little worried. "A shady character," he said in the end. "God knows what he's up to at this hour of night. He wasn't glad to see us, that's for sure. I hope this doesn't mean trouble."

"You think he'll get us into trouble?"

"He might, " said Avner. "I don't know."

I must have looked worried too.

"We mustn't tell anyone," said Avner. "We have to keep our mouths shut." He sounded very mysterious. He stood still for a minute, leaning his gun on his leg, then took off his helmet and rubbed his hair vigorously. "I'm tired," he said, "dead tired." We went on walking. "Did you graduate from high school?" he suddenly asked.

"Yes."

"I'll have to do it in the army. Depending on where they send me."

"What do you want to do after the army?"

"Study medicine," he said. "You think that's funny?"

"No."

"Well then I'll tell you something guaranteed to make you laugh: I want to be a gynecologist. That's my dream." He himself burst out laughing.

"And what about music?" I asked. Perhaps to escape the embarrassment into which his laughter cast me.

"I can't study music. I don't know how to play an instrument, and at my age it's too late to learn. Altogether it belongs to the past, to a period when I was lonely and shy with girls and music was the outlet for all my emotions. Later on I discovered that I was good looking and girls were attracted to me. Imagine," he said, "that PT instructress we saw today coming to me for an examination when I'm a gynecologist. And I say to her: *Take it off, take it all off, let's see all your secrets, let's see exactly what you've got down there, why you don't like men, what gets in the way of you liking them down there?* Oh God!" sighed Avner. "I want to know all the secrets of her body, all its hiding places. I want to teach her how to love men! Today before I fell asleep I couldn't stop thinking about her; it made me so horny I thought I'd go crazy. Not liking men is exactly what makes her so attractive, like a fortress you have to conquer by force. In order to distract myself I began to think about my girlfriend, and suddenly I said to myself: *Maybe I don't love her anymore.* She's a wonderful girl and she's mad about me. And she risks a lot for me too, because she's a married woman. She's older than I am. But never mind that. So don't I love her anymore? Is the drive to conquer, to break down resistance, stronger than mutual devotion? What kind of a lousy world do we live in? If you only knew what she sacrifices for me, what she suffers so that we can meet, so that we can be together. So all that doesn't count anymore?"

This question was addressed to me in all its severity and I didn't know how to reply.

He said: "I tried to explain to you why I want to be a gynecologist, because you asked me what I wanted to do after the army. The more you discover about women the more mysterious they remain. It's the only thing in the world that may be even more mysterious and beautiful than music."

Again we came to the end of the patrol and stood in front of the barracks. Avner dropped to the ground, leaned his back against the eucalyptus, laid his gun on his lap, and rested his elbows on his knees, his hands cupping his chin. He sat looking pensively at the night sky. The stillness was broken only by the symphony of sounds coming from our sleeping squad. Snores, murmurs, a cough, a groan, a sigh, and a sudden cry. Yes, something sickly emanated from that building, like a foul miasma, the contagion of the flawed, rejected bodies of the lost children of Sparta, left out on the bleak mountain to die.

His head slipped from his hands and dropped onto his chest. He had fallen asleep. I tapped him on the shoulder. He raised his head and gave me a sad-eyed look, smiled apologetically, and whispered: "I don't know what's wrong with me. I have to sleep for ten minutes or so. I can't keep my eyes open."

"What are we going to do?"

"I don't know. I feel as if I haven't had a cup of proper black coffee for years. That might help me. If you were really a good friend — you'd go and get me some black coffee."

"Waiter!" I said. "Black coffee, please."

"With cardamom."

"With cardamom, please."

His head dropped back onto his chest.

"Listen," I said to him, "it's no joke. You have to do something to keep awake. Pull yourself together."

"What's the matter with you?" He roused himself. "What kind of a way is that to talk? What harm have I ever done you?"

I was overcome by anxiety and couldn't find anything to say. The guilt was so violent, and so irrelevant, that it found me unprepared and vulnerable. I said to myself that this too, like the personal confessions, was his way of forcing intimacy and involvement on others, and that he had put his finger on the fiercest of all feelings of involvement, groundless hatred and its accompanying guilt, and was trying to bring it into play.

"You must have a lot of complexes," he said.

The darkness was still intense, but I knew that it would soon begin to grow light, and with the light the heart-numbing fear of inspection and being caught would fade.

"Okay," he said, "okay, okay," and he took off his helmet again and rubbed his hair vigorously. Maybe he thought it was a way of keeping awake. "I suppose I must be talking nonsense because I'm too tired and sleepy to know what I'm saying. Sometimes at night people say things they're ashamed of the next morning and they're sorry they said them. As if the night turns them into different people. It's a kind of power possessed by the night. Nights were apparently made for love and sentimentality and not for normal relations between human beings."

I interrupted his reflections. "I have to go out on patrol again."

"You can go," said Avner. "I'm staying here. If you see anything suspicious or any sign that anyone's coming — wake me up at once. If I can just sleep for about a quarter of an hour, I'll get over this crisis."

He hugged his knees and raised his face to me with an expression of impatience, waiting for me to go so that he could close his eyes. As if he didn't want me to catch him napping again and hate him more than ever.

"And what if they come when I'm on the other side and I don't see them?" I persisted.

He spread out his hands in a gesture of resignation to his fate. "Do your best anyway. Try to act like a friend."

I set out, this time alone. I really needed it. I marched like a model soldier, conforming to all the rules and regulations, but the fear did not fade from my heart. The responsibility imposed on me by Avner to secure his sleep weighed on me like incriminating evidence just waiting to be discovered, like a trap at the end of the road. Dawn would soon be breaking, and I hoped that on my own I would recover my spirits somewhat; I loved these moments and I was glad that I would have them to myself. But now, as I advanced, the nocturnal landscape was revealed to me in a new and hostile guise. I walked slowly, carefully inspecting the shadows stretching around me, pricking up my ears at every little sound. I knew with a bitter certainty that I would be caught, blameless as I was, however hard I tried to display my devotion and loyalty to the rules. This is the way I feel to this day when I go into a big department store, sure that all the hidden television cameras are homing in on me and the security men are watching me tensely from their hiding places, waiting for a give-away move, an incriminating tremor, and when they come and surround me, without my knowing how it got there, a stolen article will be found in my pocket. I have often wondered about this strange feeling and its possible origins, especially since I have never really desired any of the things offered for sale in such places, nor been tempted to take them, not even in my secret heart of hearts. I thought that if these were the pangs of a guilt not yet embodied in action, and if, indeed — like dread, sorrow, faith, and longing — guilt precedes the occasion or object that is supposed to arouse it, and the true sequence of cause and effect are the opposite of what they are commonly supposed to be, then perhaps I should be more faithful to it and perform the act that would put it into effect, thus transforming it from cause to result, from a restless ghost to an external, liberated, living reality.

And this bitter certainty regarding the imminent inspection that would catch me red-handed in some transgression might well be nothing but a wish that it would actually happen and cure me of my anxiety. The farther I advanced along the path between the dark buildings and the eucalyptus trees with their shifty, misleading shadows, the more certain I was that it would happen tonight. After a moment there was a sound of footsteps coming toward me, but I did not know from which direction. I stopped and gripped my gun with all my might; I knew that the first thing they would do would be to seize my weapon: They considered this the gravest dereliction of duty possible, the worst sin of all, except perhaps for treason and spying for the enemy. I mobilized all my strength to overcome the sluggishness that anxiety had spread through my limbs. I advanced along the path, turning to look back every few seconds, in case of a feint from the rear. My shoulders sent out warning signals behind my back. In the end I saw the figure coming from the end of the path and for a minute my heart stopped. A few seconds passed before I succeeded in pronouncing the command: "Halt! Password!"

The figure did not stop but went on advancing with light, confident steps, and for a moment it seemed to me from the movements of his hands that he was laughing silently to himself. I walked toward him and at a distance of a few paces recognized Sammy. I turned off the path to let him pass. As he passed me, I saw him putting his hand to his mouth, and he really was laughing, all his limbs shaking with irrepressible laughter. This time he walked quite slowly and deliberately, making no attempt at evasion or stealth, but on the contrary he looked right at me, his hand over his mouth, as if he was afraid his laughter might burst out, and continued on his way back to the barracks.

I stood still to let out a breath of relief. My hands gripping the gun with all my strength were cold and clammy. My whole attitude was one of insult. This was surprising: Was there any room for insult left; had an inch of honor, without my knowing it, remained untarnished — a leftover from the days before the sinking of the soul? I thought: *In a minute Sammy will reach the building and see Avner sitting asleep on guard duty,* and suddenly I was glad that there would be another witness. A wave of righteous indignation swept through me, full of resentment and gloating malice. *How dare he sleep on guard!* Toward this end I marshaled all the arguments at my command. Avner's compulsive need for sleep now appeared in the light of an ugly, brutish instinct, intended to destroy some enlightened social order, harmonious, egalitarian, and just. It was clear to me that he would have to pay for it. The night grew pale and gray, or perhaps my eyes were now able to look clearly into the darkness and await its messengers. I completed my round again, and when I approached the place where Avner was sitting I heard him snoring softly, his head on his chest, his hands resting limply on his knees, his gun propped up between them with the barrel leaning against one of his shoulders. I stood still for a minute and looked at him. The expression of sleeping people has always been a fascinating mystery to me. It seemed to me that his face expressed expectation, but I had no idea what it was that he was expecting. I wondered whether I should wake him up, since the quarter of an hour he had given himself was already up, or whether I should let him go on wallowing in his sleep, incriminating himself. I knew that the closer it came to dawn, the more remote the chances of an inspection became, but nevertheless, because of this faint chance, which like all hopes for righting a wrong is often more important in the promise than the realization, I overcame the immediate temptation to put an end to the scandal and shake the guard who had fallen asleep at his post.

The sound of snoring suddenly stopped. I wondered if he had sensed my presence and woken up, although his eyes were still closed. I went on standing next to him for a minute longer. His face twisted in a momentary grimace of pain, as if something had stung him; he seemed almost about to burst into tears. But the repose returned immediately to his features, together with the expression of expectation. I set out.

It was now clear to me that he would be caught and punished. Just as on similar occasions I had known what was about to happen with an uncanny certainty and vividness. I was overcome by the sensation that I was losing the possibility of hesitation and choice and control over my actions, and operating within the framework of some grand plan, step after step, according to a scenario that had been determined in advance. Thanks to this sensation, in all its extraordinary clarity and unexpectedness, I had been enabled, on these very rare occasions, to taste the taste of freedom, and to realize that it was not simply a wish and a promise but a real and actual event.

Even the possibility of being charged with seeing him asleep and failing to wake him up did not arouse any uneasiness in me. Like the night growing pale and clear and the trees assuming their final shapes and sizes around me, the sequence of events was set out with astonishing simplicity. Even the thudding of my footsteps sounded in my ears like the beat of a finely tuned mechanism, coordinated with all my movements and replying *Yes, yes, yes* to all my questions. The end of the fuse had been lit, its length was equivalent to that of my patrol, it was growing shorter with every step I took, the fire was rapidly burning it up, nothing would stop it now.

Right at the end of my round, not far from where Avner was sitting, I saw them coming. They were coming from the top of the road leading to the staff quarters and joining up with the path passing the company barracks. I recognized Raffy Nagar, the platoon commander, and with him someone I didn't know. They disappeared behind one of the buildings and I knew that in another moment or two they would reappear and advance toward us. I stationed myself behind one of the eucalyptus trees and peeked out at Avner. He was sitting as I had left him, his hands limp and his head bowed, without moving. This was the moment when I could have hurried toward him, woken him up, and resumed my patrol in all innocence before the two men reappeared on the path. This was the moment when, as at the touch of grace, my mind cleared. The preordained course of events came to a halt and allowed me to observe the action and myself, as if I was the one responsible and I had a choice in the matter. Even if it was only an illusion, since the die had been cast long ago, it had about it that beauty that cannot be mistaken, and a new happiness welled up in me in response, a happiness similar perhaps to that of mountaineers when they reach the jutting rock before the summit of the final peak. When I turned around and ran back part of the way along the patrol route, I seemed to myself like an animal that had broken out of its cage and was making a dash for open space. I stopped at a place where the path was no longer visible and waited. It never occurred to me that the two men would take a different route and not even enter the path. For a moment or two I heard nothing. I looked around and saw no movement. Morning was already breaking, and there was another half an hour to go before the company woke up. I set out with a firm, measured tread to see what was happening. A few minutes passed, and the path in front of me looked empty. I went on walking until I saw Avner standing up and looking around him, searching for something. When he saw me, he nodded sadly. I didn't know what was wrong with him. I couldn't see anything out of the ordinary. There was no one to be seen on the path. Everything was quiet and clear as the morning light. When I came closer, I saw how pale his face was and that his gun was gone.

"They jumped me, grabbed my gun, and went away," said Avner. "Raffy Nagar and the corporal from Four Platoon."

My astonishment was genuine. Despite all my certainty that it would actually happen, and despite the peculiar state in which I had been for the past hour, when I was confronted by the *fait accompli* I could hardly believe my ears. He sat down at the foot of the tree, in exactly the same place he had been sitting before sleeping, as if he wanted to begin again from the beginning and correct his mistake. He took his helmet off again and rubbed his hair, raised his face to me, and said: "You didn't have time to see them coming?"

"No," I said.

"I'm in trouble," said Avner, "this time I'm in trouble."

"What'll you do?"

"They'll court-martial me, that's for sure."

We were silent for a minute and suddenly he waved his hand and said: "Do me a favor and don't say what you want to say now."

"What?"

"That I shouldn't have done it and all that stuff. I can't take it."

"I wasn't going to say it anyway," I explained. "There wouldn't be any point now."

"There's never any point," said Avner. "In any case whatever has to happen — happens." He gazed at me with eyes full of bafflement and added: "Do you really give a damn about what happens to anyone else?"

"Of course!" I said. "I'm sorry it happened to you and that I couldn't do anything to prevent it."

I was speaking sincerely. Everything that had happened before now seemed to me like a dream. It had nothing to do with me, but with some ideal possibility, remote and hopeless. The intoxication of betrayal too, which only a few minutes before had given me such a thrill, had faded with the fading of the dream. The whole vision grew as pale and misty as the dawn light now breaking around us. Suddenly Avner smiled his self-satisfied smile, as if the whole thing had been worth it as far as he was concerned for the sake of one little drop of kindness and sympathy. I couldn't understand what he had to smile about.

"Never mind," he said. "I've already overcome all kind of things in my life. I'll overcome this too."

Was he trying to spare me, to soften the blow?

"What do you have to do now?"

"Nothing. Sit and wait. I expect they'll deal with me at parade."

About half an hour before reveille Nahum emerged from the building, rosy-faced as usual, and responded to Avner's "Good morning" with his habitual embarrassment, smiling his wondering smile and mumbling something unintelligible. Under his arm he had the bag containing his prayer shawl and phylacteries. He always got up early to say his prayers, so that he would be able to get back in time for the morning run. Nobody had to wake him up; his inner clock woke him every morning at exactly the same time. The strongest human relationship he had with the others was in the shower: The depilatory shaving cream he used in order to avoid the prohibited touch of the razor on his skin gave off a terrible stink. There was a strange contradiction between the silent, withdrawn youth and the terrible smell, sticky and aggressive and intensely physical, that he exuded in the shower room, as if he had vomited up something from inside him in order to stay pure and anonymous and purge himself for his prayers. All the insulting remarks about his religious shaving cream were greeted by the same shy, remote, wondering, embarrassed smile.

After Nahum had gone off to pray, Avner stood up and went into the barracks. Apparently he thought that after everything that had already happened, it would make no difference if he remained at his post to the last minute or abandoned it. I remained alone and tried to introduce some order into my soul. The events of the night, which I had almost succeeded in banishing from my mind, had left their mark on my body. The physical weakness was like a kind of abandonment to the artificial stillness that had descended on everything. The thought of the day's training soon to begin wasn't too terrible. More than the night had been a rest from the hardships of the day, the day promised to be a refuge from the delusions of the night. When I went into the barracks at reveille I found Avner sitting on his bed, somber and sunk in thought. I wanted to say something to him, but I didn't know what.

Not long afterward we were running on the road outside the camp. Avner's face had recovered its usual expression. In the shower room nobody spoke of anything else. The news of what had happened gave rise to a peculiar happiness and elation in everyone, as you sometimes come across in people when they hear of some catastrophe or death, and gleeful cracks appear in their mechanically assumed masks of shock and horror, and laughter trembles at the corners of their lips, and you know that it is not malicious delight in another's misfortune or the relief of the survivor that he has been spared, but something far deeper and more terrible. Avner himself replied laconically to their questions, avoided going into details, and glossed over everything with his self-satisfied smirk. However hard I tried to detach myself from the matter, I found myself at its center. My explanations that I hadn't been there when it happened did no good at all, but only aroused resentment against me, as if I were keeping all the goodies to myself so that nobody else could enjoy them. Only Alon, who was really sorry for what had happened, whether out of affection for Avner or due to soldierly principles stemming from some other source, went up to him and patted him encouragingly on the shoulder.

"You're lucky it didn't happen to you in the paratroopers," said Alon. "Over there they wouldn't have been satisfied with a court-martial. They would have expelled you from the unit in disgrace."

Avner gave him an ironical smile of thanks and said nothing. And

Alon added sadly: "But in the paratroopers nothing like this would have happened in the first place. No paratrooper would ever fall asleep on guard duty or abandon his weapon. Because there it's serious, it's for real! And here it's just a game. We're playing at being soldiers. And from that point of view, the instructors are no better than the recruits."

"I don't care," said Avner. He didn't look in need of any consolation or encouragement. If he was worried, he kept it very well hidden. His expression was as confident and complacent as usual. And as usual he did everything slowly, in defiance of the passing moments. Perhaps this time he really did feel that he had nothing to lose or risk anymore. I believed that it wasn't an act, a boast of toughness and indifference in the face of his misfortune. I believed that he felt as calm as he looked. He stood on parade without his gun, waiting for the storm to burst. His face revealed nothing of what was going on inside him, but I felt his unrealized fear being transferred to me. My heart filled with his fear. My shoulders shook and I didn't know how to hide it. Why did I want to save this fear, as if I were trying to stop some very precious fire from going out? Why did I make such an effort to fan the flames of this vital terror in my heart so that it would not die? I felt no regret or guilt for my part in his trouble. I felt no pity for him: I don't know what mountaineers feel after scaling the peak and starting back for home, or what wild animals feel after breaking out of their cages and making for the jungle depths or desert spaces; in any case the act I myself had committed now seemed very disappointing to me. Almost meaningless. After the fading of the sense of power and freedom that I had experienced in myself, rapt in a kind of dream, after the web of this dream had been torn, I no longer felt any desire for the act. All it had left in me was a feeling of dreariness, lowness, and wretchedness. No transformation had taken place in me or in my surroundings. The feeling of emptiness was now being filled by a fear not mine. Are the great treacheries really committed in thought rather than deed, against ourselves rather than others? All that was left of the intoxication of those moments of betrayal was a dim memory of a motiveless act, a kind of aesthetic gesture, like a ballet step. I couldn't ignore the beauty revealed to me at those moments by the possibility of betrayal and its realization, but I thought that perhaps its reward and its beauty would have been greater by far if it had remained as a possibility alone.

CHAPTER 5

Dry, deliberate, monotonous, his voice drones on and on. His face is the face of a bespectacled rat, self-satisfaction gleams in the myopic eyes, he is sweating even more than usual in the sweltering heat of the windowless hall. His stance is rigid, one hand leaning on the table behind him, the other digging the stick into the floor as if he wants to make a hole in it. The two sweat stains under his armpits grow. *Soon,* I say to myself, *those stains will spread. They'll cover his pockets and shoulders, they'll spread down his chest and his trousers, he'll stand there in his soaking-wet uniform and melt into a puddle in front of our eyes, and nothing will be left of him but his voice droning on in our ears.* He stoops over and leans on his stick, like an old man laboriously getting into gear to take his first step, straightens up, and sweeps the stick over the map behind him without even turning his head. Raffy Nagar and Muallem pass between the rows to wake the sleepers with a well-placed kick. My eyelids are heavy as lead, drooping and begging, if only for a moment, to close. My whole body yearns to succumb to the temptation of that heaviness and sink like lead into the depths. Again the alarm goes off, jumping out of some anxious corner in my mind and beating like a fist at my heart; my drooping head snaps back and my eyes open, braking the soft glide down the seductive slope. I find it harder and harder to resist the temptation. More than a victory, every arousal is only a reminder of the bestial, degrading heaviness overpowering me like everyone else, the same brutish heaviness that overpowered Avner on the night watch.

I peek at the glazed, tortured eyes of the people sitting next to me, catch the hint of a despairing smile from Hanan on my right, fighting a losing battle like me. It's not as late as all that. If we had the evening off, if we were in our barracks now, most of us would be sitting and talking, maybe Ressler would start strumming his guitar and we would sing, Micky and Alon would be conducting one of the endless arguments they've started having recently.

Why does the hand of sleep lie so heavy on us here? Is it the stuffiness of the air in the hall, the droning monotony of the intelligence corps captain's voice, or is it something that comes from inside us? *The power of the defeated,* I say to myself, *is the power of hatred.* This possibility occurs to me like a last hope of energy. The saving hatred begins coursing through me, the captain's voice sounding like an insect knocking against a closed windowpane. I welcome his voice: Let it come and buzz in my ears, let it send shudders running down my spine and fan the flames of my hatred and my glee. Even though I know that all this is nothing but an exercise to keep sleep at bay, I respond gladly to the warm rush of emotion and abuse the man in my heart: *Insect, miserable buffoon. Insect, who's going to listen to a clown like you? Crawl back into your rat hole, rat, and drone away, nobody'll hear a word you say.*

Soon he would stand in his sweat-soaked uniform in front of a blank wall of disobedient ears, ears that refused to hear, and even if they stood an MP next to every man in the hall the only response he'd get would be blank looks from expressionless eyes saying only one thing: *No, no, no.* While I was busy organizing this rebellion, concentrating my gaze on the captain as if trying to hypnotize him, there was a dull thudding noise. Zero-Zero, who had fallen asleep, had been given a hefty shove by Raffy Nagar, lost his balance, and fallen to the ground. The lecturer stopped talking for a minute; sounds of laughter broke out like little flames of rebellion, and immediately subsided. The instructors rushed in to find the laughers and punish them. The captain continued. Now, he said, he would keep the promise he had made at the beginning of his lecture and tell us the details of the action in Khan Yunis, secret details, he stressed, not for public knowledge. I could see Alon's profile in the row in front of me. He was eagerly drinking in the captain's every word. When the lecturer drew lines and circles on the map with his stick, Alon fixed his eyes on the spots indicated and saw things that none of us could see in them. Alon knitted his brows in concentration. The captain's deliberate voice droned on monotonously, and to Alon his words sounded like the glorious verses of an ancient epic, told by the elder of the tribe to the young warriors sitting in a circle at his feet, calling silently on the spirits of their ancestors to come and inspire their hearts and empower their arms for war. This is how Alon seemed to me as I saw him narrowing his eyes in concentration, his face tense, his head bursting with visions of heroism. Ever since his enlistment Alon had been cut off from his origins. On his kibbutz, he told us, officers and fighters who came home on leave would tell the other members and the younger generation about secret missions and heroic paratrooper raids, about special mysterious crack units that the public didn't know about. Alon knew the names of illustrious warriors the rest of us had never heard of, and he called them by their nicknames, as if he were one of their closest friends. Now I saw him return to himself from his inner exile, the exile that we, who were so different from him, had imposed upon him by the very fact of our difference. In these moments I saw him shaking off the dull weight of the cloddish earth, the savage and exhausting sadness of the interminable arguments with Micky, and soaring back into his true element, the bright blue skies and far horizons of legend. But there was no fear of Alon flying up too high and, like Icarus, plunging to his death in the ocean depths, his wings melted by the heat of the sun. It was enough to catch a glimpse of Micky's ironic smile to know that this moment of respite too, this sudden bestowal of grace, would be eroded by nagging arguments, dragged down by the humdrum daily reality of all the pettiness, the ugliness, the vulgarity, the selfishness, the sickness, and the diaspora mentality by which he presumably felt himself surrounded.

I couldn't understand what drove Micky to keep dragging Alon into these arguments and hurting him by what he said. I had no doubt that Micky formed and from time to time changed his opinions simply in order to be in a position to contradict Alon. Since the first day on the base, when he had extolled physical strength and regretted his inability to serve in the paratroopers, Micky had changed his opinion several times. For him, or so it seemed, these debates were no more than an intellectual amusement, whereas for his opponent they were a source of insult and pain. Perhaps Micky felt that the principles on which Alon's opinions were founded were sufficiently sturdy to serve as the anvil for his hammer, or perhaps they were far closer to Micky's own heart than he himself realized, and it was only their danger that he sensed.

There was about an hour left before lights-out. Micky and Alon were sitting on their beds getting ready to go to sleep. Peretz-Mental-Case's gang was for some reason in high spirits and their vociferous mirth infected the rest of the platoon, rousing them from the lethargy that had descended on them during the lecture. Alon said: "You hate everything. You don't believe in anything. In anyone. How can you be that way? Maybe for an old man it would be normal. But not at our age. Everything's out there waiting for us. Great things to be done. And what's left for you?"

"The trouble is that you don't listen to what I say and argue with things I never said," protested Micky. "All I said was that that intelligence captain, like everybody else, doesn't dream at night about the state of Israel and the Jewish people. What he really cares about is getting ahead in the army, getting promoted, getting more power, more prestige, making more of an impression on his mates, on the girls he likes. That's it. That's what makes people run. The source of their energy. It's true that this energy gets spent on important things too, I don't deny it, but that's not the main goal. What I can't stand is all this Zionism, the hypocrisy and the bullshit. All those ghastly phrases. I hate it. It's a lot of lies, hypocritical pretense. It's like poison."

"Anything anybody does for others, for society, looks to you like hypocrisy and Zionist bullshit. Because you're incapable of believing that anybody exists who doesn't think only of himself," said Alon. There was a smile of contempt and disdainful forgiveness on his thin, chapped lips. "You also said that the whole business with Uri Illan's suicide in the Syrian jail was hypocrisy and pretense. Bullshit. You don't believe in anything. You'd even be prepared to leave the country. You don't give a damn about it, do you?"

"You know what," said Micky, "if the whole nation becomes an army and the whole country a front, like you people want, then I'm not interested in staying here. I don't want to live like that. I'm quite capable of living somewhere else, it wouldn't be the end of the world for me."

"The question is," said Alon, forcibly restraining his feelings, his lips trembling with the strain of the effort, "the question is whether to belong to something big. Or not to belong. It's a question of the size of your world. That's the question."

The bed next to mine, empty and mattressless, suddenly made me think of Avner. We had all forgotten him. Nobody had mentioned him since he'd gone to prison. As if he had never existed. I felt no regrets on his account, but the fact that he had been forgotten was like an insult.

"After all the blood," said Alon, "after all the sacrifices? So much blood has been shed so that you can live here, so that we can all live here together."

"I don't want all that blood on my conscience; I don't want all those sacrifices on my back. You don't understand, Alon. I don't want to owe a debt like that to anyone or any country in the world."

"You don't want to, but you have to. They debited your account without asking you."

"You're saying something shocking," said Micky. "I don't know if you realize how shocking. What you're talking about is slavery. Slavery to previous generations, slavery to future generations. Debts, debts, debts. And when are you going to do your own thing, the thing you believe in and want because it's yours and yours only? And for your information, I didn't say anything about Uri Illan and I certainly didn't accuse him of hypocrisy. How can I judge him? I was talking about all the bullshit in the Knesset, the press, and the radio. All the hypocritical hue and cry against the Syrians. How dared they, and so on. What's that supposed to mean? He goes there on an intelligence mission in their territory and they catch him. So they throw him in jail like any other spy. So what's all the fuss about? What do they think, they can make fools of the whole world? And what would we have done if a Syrian soldier had entered our territory to spy or carry out some mission? His suicide and the letter he left are something else, that's his business, his conscience, his decision, and those are things I have every respect for."

"You're trying to get out of it," said Alon. "Uri Illan was sent there in your name too. And you definitely can judge him, and he did what he did because he took your judgment into account. A man commits suicide and leaves a note: *I did not betray.* Who is that letter addressed to? Himself? No. He does feel that he's got something to say to you. He does feel his debt to all of us. It's important to him to make it known that he didn't betray us. He owes it to us all."

"No!" Micky raised his voice. "No! Alon, you don't understand me at all. I didn't send him there and he wasn't there in my name. Whoever sent him — sent him. He doesn't owe me a thing and I don't owe him a thing. That's why I don't judge him. I have no idea what happened there. I don't know the details. If he was a traitor or wasn't a traitor is none of my business, and believe me I don't give a damn. It's his own affair. He doesn't owe me. He doesn't owe me a bloody thing!"

"You can't really think that," said Alon. "You're not living on the moon. You live here in a society that acts together, with mutual responsibility, you can't escape it. You can't get out of it. That's the way it's built, and your will can't change it. You can't get out of it, Micky!"

There was a kind of threat in Alon's tone. Maybe he knew that he should cut the conversation short before it turned into the kind of quarrel that left a residue of pain and hostility in both of them, but then a mean, brutal, ugly smile appeared on Micky's face, the same smile that always appeared there when the debate grew acrimonious and he directed his barbs at Alon.

A bad smell of something burning spread through the barracks from Peretz-Mental-Case's corner. Panic broke out among his pals. Zackie jumped up and shook a smoldering blanket. He threw the blanket on the floor and stamped on it. Then he picked it up and displayed it to the others: There was a big, charred hole in it. They burst out laughing.

"Ben-Hamo, look what you did!" cried Sammy.

"Take the blanket you burned and bring me yours quick sharp!" said Zackie.

"You're crazy," giggled Ben-Hamo, "it was you burned it with your match. You threw that match down and you didn't see it was still burning. What d'you take me for?"

"Ben-Hamo!" intervened Peretz, with all the weight of his authority as leader. "What kind of a way is that to talk? Didn't we see what happened with our own eyes? You pulling our legs or what? Go and fetch your blanket now and take that one!"

"What d'you want of my life?" sniggered Ben-Hamo, searching the eyes of his friends for a sign that the joke was over. "It was Zackie burned it with his match. I ain't got no match nor no cigarette neither. Have I got fire in my hands or what? How could I burn that blanket? Hey? Tell me that!"

"You heard him!" said Zackie. "You heard him say it was me! Just so he doesn't try and get out of it afterward. Did I do it?" He gave Rahamim a hard look.

"Yes," said Rahamim.

"There," said Zackie, appealing to the group at large, "you heard him! He says it was me that did it."

"Ben-Hamo, stop it!" scolded Peretz. "You playing with fire, boy!"

Ben-Hamo remained alone in his contention.

"Go fetch that blanket now before I get mad at you!" instructed Peretz-Mental-Case.

But Ben-Hamo persisted in believing that they were only having a joke at his expense. And he tittered and clapped his hands and wriggled his shoulders in the movement that never failed to elicit the delighted laughter and rude remarks of his comrades, but this time nobody laughed. They glared at him angrily. The suspicion that they wished him ill must have penetrated him at last. He stood up and looked at them for a minute, dumb with astonishment.

"We're all witnesses," said Zackie, "that you burned the blanket. So what're you going to do about it?" He immediately turned to each of the men sitting next to them, who one by one confirmed that it was Rahamim who had burned the hole in the blanket.

Peretz rose from his place, walked over to Rahamim's bed, took one of his blankets, and replaced it with Zackie's burned blanket. Then he put Rahamim's blanket on Zackie's bed, slapped his hands up and down against each other as if shaking off dust, and said: "Enough! Finished! Enough talking."

Now there was no longer any doubt in Rahamim's heart that they were serious.

"Why're you doing this to me? What've I ever done to you?"

"If you don't shut your mouth, I'll tell everybody what you want to do to me at night, trying to get into my bed all the time and make me let you hug me and kiss me and all that. And a lot worse too. I'll tell all that stuff to the instructors and they'll bring MPs and take care of you for good, like they do in the army to buggers like you."

An expression of relief crossed Rahamim's face. He tried to laugh, to take part in the fun, but was confronted again by a wall of accusing eyes. He went to his bed, sat down on it, crossed his legs, cupped his chin in his hand, and waited. When he saw that nobody was talking to him and his friends were all getting ready for bed, he asked them: "And how did I do it? Go on, tell me!"

Zackie explained: "Suddenly you felt like a smoke, and you dunno how to smoke, do you, 'cause you're not a man. So your fag fell on the blanket and burned it."

"Wise guy. You think you're clever, don't you," said Rahamim.

"When you come crawling into my bed at night you sing a different tune: *Zackie, oh Zackie, my eyes, my soul, please let me touch you down there*," said Zackie, mimicking Ben-Hamo's wheedling voice to the loud guffaws of his friends. He sighed and said plaintively: "Is it my fault I'm so handsome? What do I need it for? All it does is get me in trouble."

"Go to hell!" said Ben-Hamo. "You and your stories. Nobody believes you, everybody knows you're a liar."

He made his bed, spread out Zackie's scorched blanket, and contemplated the hole as if considering how he might repair the damage.

Zero-Zero called over to him: "You can darn it like a sock. I'll get you some thread from my wife."

"Thank you very much," said Rahamim.

Again there was a burst of laughter from his friends' corner, but he didn't hear the remark that had given rise to their mirth. "What now?" he asked. "What's the matter now?" But his question only made them laugh louder.

Muallem came in for lights-out, and Rahamim made haste to conceal the scorched part of the blanket under his body. Muallem, who had heard the laughter and noticed Rahamim's quick movement to hide the incriminating hole, said: "Up to your tricks again, Ben-Hamo? You'd better watch it. I've got my eye on you."

"Sir, I didn't do anything," said Rahamim.

"I told you to watch it, so watch it. This is the army here, and not what you might think."

After Muallem left there was silence for a while in the dark room, until it was broken by Zackie saying: "Never mind, Ben-Hamo, don't cry, if you behave yourself I'll give you what you want."

Rahamim made no reply. From my bed I could see his shadow turning from side to side.

"You hear me, Rahamim?" asked Zackie.

"Let me sleep," said Rahamim. "I have to get up soon to go on guard."

And he tossed and turned again, as if the scorched blanket were still on fire, burning around his body. Then I saw his shadow sitting up in bed, his arms hugging his knees and his head bowed, as if thinking. Perhaps he had decided to stay awake until his guard duty.

Zackie and his friends were still whispering in their corner, laughing softly, and I saw Rahamim's shadow leaning toward them from time to time, presumably trying to catch what they were saying, after which he immediately resumed his former position, as if his dignity depended on it.

Perhaps at that very hour a little group of paratroopers was crossing the border into Jordan or Egypt, stealing down the village paths, climbing up the mountain terraces and descending into the wadis, without dislodging a stone, without showing against the skyline. At the sound of a dog barking or a voice calling *Min hada?* in the darkness they dropped instantly, as one man, to the ground, as if the earth had swallowed them up, making a detour around the village and coming into the fields and orchards of that ancient, mysterious land beyond the border, where another moon shone, carrying explosives on their backs to blow up a police station or an army HQ, spreading panic and dismay in the enemy ranks. Then the attackers would immediately slip away and make their way home, fleet and light of foot, brave-hearted and full of enterprise, and they all looked just like Alon, their faces sunburned and resolute as his, bearing on their shoulders the stretchers with the wounded whom they would never, never leave in enemy territory.

Perhaps at that very hour a suicide squad of fedayeen was infiltrating into the country, stealing through the orange groves, emerging into the border villages and roads to ambush its prey, to throw grenades at buses, to murder people on their way to weddings, to stab a watchman in the back, the faces of the men masked by their keffiyehs, empty, blank, resembling nothing.

When Avner came back from detention he seemed embarrassed, as if he were facing a whole new group of people with a wall of strangeness standing between him and them. He came straight up to me and stood next to me, as if I were his only friend in the platoon, as if some kind of alliance had been cemented between us on that night of guard duty. His head was shaved and his eyes looked sad. He refused to talk about his imprisonment, or explain why he had been punished more harshly than was usual for his offense. To all the curious questions raining down on him from all sides he answered with a reserved smile. Marks of suffering were evident on his face. Being the center of attention was obviously not to his liking. He was determined to carry on where he had left off when he went to prison. Maybe this was why he stuck to my side, as if returning to his starting point, reattaching himself to the moment at which time had stopped for him then. He looked peculiar, presumably because of his shaven head, and there was a beaten expression on his face. After getting back his gear and making his bed, he sat down to write letters. From my place on my bed I inspected his face for signs of transformation. I was very eager to know the nature and extent of the changes wrought by suffering. There was no halo of heroism over his head. Everyone wanted to know what had happened to him in prison and what the conditions there were like. But I wasn't interested in the physical distress, the humiliation and harassment; what interested me was the dialogue he had had with himself. A new man looked out from the shaved head and sad eyes, the shoulders slumped in embarrassment and exhaustion. I envied him. I knew that even if after a while he apparently went back to being what he had been before, he would always retain these marks of trial by suffering and humiliation, of the hope of transformation. I couldn't contain my curiosity and eagerness to know how it happened, how the inner transformation took place, and although I saw that he expected me to say something to him, as if I owed him some sort of explanation, as if our last conversation had been cut off at a question that had not yet been answered — I was unable to overcome the embarrassment and strangeness that he cast around him. When he finished writing his letters he lay on his back with his hands behind his head and his eyes staring at the ceiling.

Micky and Alon were in the middle of one of their arguments again. However much Micky explained to the offended Alon that his sneers were not directed at him personally but at the principles in whose name he spoke, he could not make him understand, because these principles were no less precious to Alon than his own personal honor. And since

Alon was hurt, Micky tried to dispel the insult with a new explanation, even more outrageous and original, which only made the argument more acrimonious. Any pretext served as an excuse for them to get into an argument. Sometimes when I watched them I would try not to listen to what they were saying, concentrating on their facial expressions and gestures. I imagined that these arguments were an outlet for some other hostility, a hostility that other people, in different circumstances, would have vented in physical violence, perhaps even bloodshed. There was hatred there, or something close to it at least. But I didn't know what the nature of this hatred was or what gave rise to it.

The people sitting on the sidelines and kibitzing, mainly the Jerusalemites, would goad them and spur them on as if they were watching a cockfight. Sometimes they would even supply them with new arguments, encourage them with cries of agreement or oppose them with exclamations of disapproval. But the contestants hardly heard the cries of the kibitzers, they were so absorbed in the battle, they had so much at stake to win or lose, as if they were trying to settle some old score that would never be written off between them. So passionate was their absorption that they didn't even realize how ridiculous they looked, how out of place in the reality surrounding them.

Avner asked: "Do they carry on like this all the time?"

"Yes," I said, "ever since you left."

"If there are two things I hate, it's arguments and politics. I can't stand them."

Peretz-Mental-Case and his friends too were fed up by now with these noisy debates. Peretz even argued on their behalf that such things were expressly forbidden by General Routine Orders. He was a sight too fond of referring to GROs whenever it suited his needs, arousing the suspicion that despite his self-assured tone he was making it all up. He and his friends approached the debaters and their audience and demanded loudly that they stop it. They said they were worn out by the day's training and needed their rest. Peretz even referred to the famous condition of his nerves and shouted that if it didn't stop immediately he would lose his self-control. Micky and Alon looked at each other in embarrassment, and then resumed their argument in an undertone, almost in a whisper, waving their arms about emphatically to make up for the loss of volume. Hedgehog, who was a keen listener to these debates and frequently an active participant too, could not contain his umbrage at the interference of the new immigrants. He never tried to hide his contempt and dislike for them, and claimed that the only reason they resented the arguments was that they were outsiders and couldn't understand or take part in them.

"What are you interfering for?" he yelled at them. "It's got nothing to do with you! You can't even understand what we're talking about. So don't interfere. Just shut up and be grateful for being treated like human beings."

Peretz's face paled and his lips trembled. "Hold me down!" he cried to his friends, who leapt forward immediately to stand like a wall between him and Hedgehog, as if he was on the verge of some terrible outbreak. "Fighting's not allowed in the army," said Peretz, apparently referring once more to the GROs with which he was so familiar, "and I don't want to do something here that I'll have to pay for later." He looked around him as if to see where help might be forthcoming, or if there were any witnesses to the offense he was almost on the point of committing.

"You don't scare me," said Hedgehog, pushing the human wall between himself and Peretz aside and standing opposite him, his head thrust forward and his fists bunched up like a boxer's: "I know your kind, I've already had dealings with animals like you in the past. You'll pull a knife on me in a minute. You or one of your friends. You should be grateful for being here in this country at all, that they let you serve in the army, that they feed you and your families, that they provide you with free accommodations in transit camps, that they teach you to read and write. The least you can do is shut up and not interfere in what's got nothing to do with you. Just keep quiet and mind your own business!"

Peretz spat on the floor. His friends led him to the corner of the room while he made gestures of protest and attempts to break out of their restraining hands, but he yielded to their strength in the end.

Micky and Alon, who had fallen silent, looked at what was going on with a certain gloom, as if their polemical passions had died down. Hedgehog returned, breathing heavily, to the bed where his Jerusalem friends were sitting and kibitzing. He raised his eyes to Micky and Alon, waiting for them to go on now that he had successfully dealt with the disturbance. But the argument was over. Micky and Alon were tired. From the end of the room Zackie's voice suddenly rose in an Arabic song, and his friends responded with a drawn-out, quavering refrain that sounded like wailing. There was nothing that could better have illustrated to me at that moment their feelings of insult, their strangeness and helplessness among us, than this ugly, plaintive song with its note of whining, wheedling entreaty. Hedgehog looked at the corner with the singers, and the expression of revulsion on his face intensified. I remembered what Avner had told me about Hedgehog's fights in Jerusalem, about the way he rushed into battle and invariably got beaten within an inch of his life. His weak, skinny body was ill suited to his temperament. What was it that drove him to jump into the thick of the fray? What was the source of this courage and self-confidence? I imagined that people like him never felt like strangers on the face of the earth, treading it by sufferance and not by right, but that anyplace where they set foot was theirs: Wherever they went they would feel like landlords.

Avner made his bed slowly, as always, dwelling on every detail until everything was arranged precisely to his taste. Maybe this time he even exaggerated more than usual, prolonging the ritual in honor of his first night back in the platoon. Maybe this bed, chosen at random from dozens of others standing in two crowded rows on either side of the room when he first arrived, and which perhaps he even hated, as I hated mine with its stinking, scratchy blankets, now seemed to him like his own, and for the first time conveyed a sense of home.

After he finished making his bed, he sat down on it and lit a final cigarette. I lay down and covered my head with the towel that protected my face from the revolting touch of the blanket that served me as a pillow. This way I could keep my eyes open while remaining apart from everything around me.

There had been talk of leave on the coming weekend. The outside world still seemed more real to me than life on the base, in the platoon. I thought about Arik, my friend from school, the only sign of that other, outside reality, who was also on the base undergoing basic training in a different company. I hadn't had a chance to talk to him yet. Once I had seen him marching and drilling with his friends on the parade ground, looking as idiotic as the rest of them. He who had once been my guide and mentor, a fountainhead of knowledge and wisdom, now gave rise in me to resentment and hostility. Later I saw him standing in line for the mess hall. I didn't want to see him anymore. But now, for the first time since arriving on the base, I suddenly felt an urgent need to find a connection to my previous life. As if some vow had been broken inside me and there was no point in hoping for a new beginning. The promise of leave on the coming weekend made me want to go and look for him. I didn't know how to get to his company. I knew that we weren't allowed to leave the lines of our own company.

"Just a minute," called Avner, as if I were going someplace and he wanted to join me. His rasping biblical gutturals, like a snake's hiss, jarred on my ears, as foreign and affected as ever. I took the towel off my head and turned to face him.

"I broke down there," he said softly. "Once."

"What happened?"

"I began to cry." He turned his face from side to side, and to the bed opposite him, to make sure no one was listening. Then he looked at me again: "That's how people break down, no?"

And he fixed me with an impatient, even indignant, stare, as if he were afraid that this breakdown might not be considered significant enough in the eyes of the world.

"It was because of something quite trivial. It's always the trivial things that break you. One day I'll tell you how it happened."

The list of things he had undertaken to tell me about one day was growing longer. And the basic training wasn't going to last forever. I laughed and he seemed to understand why. "You must think I'm a queer customer. But everything has a reason, you know. I'm not trying to make an impression. You can trust me. Man! You can't know anything about it until you experience it yourself. Imagination is no use here."

Albert, the cheerful, optimistic Bulgarian, came into the room in a state of unusual agitation. He had been to visit a friend in 3 Platoon and heard something there that had shocked him profoundly. He muttered: "Crazy, plain crazy!"

The fatso from 3 Platoon had shot himself in the arm to get a discharge from the army. The fatso's friends in the platoon told Albert that he had been planning it for ages, but the right circumstances hadn't come up. That afternoon, during an exercise with live fire, he had done it. Naturally, he'd claimed that it was an accident, but they were going to court-martial him anyway and in the end he would, in fact, be discharged from the army.

Albert said: "How can a person do such a thing to his own body! What crazy people there are in the world!"

Hedgehog said: "It's simply a case of the diaspora mentality. Some people haven't yet realized what it means to live in a state of our own with an army of our own and all the rest of it. There's a guy in our neighborhood, a carpenter, deaf, and his mouth's so crooked it reaches all the way to his left ear. He was in Russia and they had to go to the army there so he took a big nail and drove it into his ear, and it made him deaf and screwed up his whole face. As long as he didn't have to go to the army. It's a kind of Jewish tradition, draft dodging at any price."

And once more that mysterious shudder of joy ran through the platoon, as it did whenever we heard of a disaster that had befallen someone, or some astonishing news that seemed to hold out a secret promise of riot and disorder, together with the bursts of choked, nervous, liberating laughter and a buoyant lifting of the heart, as if all the laws of gravity had stopped operating for a moment.

Micky said: "I respect that fat guy. Even though I can't understand how a person can reach that state, I take off my hat to him. You have to have faith in yourself to do a thing like that. He's got guts."

"If he'd shot himself in the guts instead of the arm I'd have respected him more," said Hanan. "Anyway, that fatso's a bad lot, with guts or without."

"If he'd shot himself in the guts he'd have had less guts now," said Micha the Fool.

"This is something new," said Alon to Micky. "This is the first time I've ever heard you admire someone for breaking. Do you really respect weakness so much? What if everyone who was having a hard time in the army shot himself in the arm or leg, got discharged, got better, and took care of his private affairs while the rest of us had to serve for him?"

"I'd call it a day!" said Hanan in English. He liked throwing off these witty quotes from his favorite detective story with a sophisticated, cynical smile on his face.

"You call that weakness?" said Micky. "You think anyone could do it? Whoever does it pays a price, and what a price! It's war, the war of the one against the many, and it's got a heroism of its own."

"If you were true to yourself and your opinions instead of trying to be so clever and original all the time," said Alon, "you would have called it sick, not heroic."

Suddenly it transpired that we had all seen the fatso from No 3 Platoon, even if we had only caught a glimpse of him. Apparently you couldn't miss him, and not only because he was fat. He was always isolated from the other men in his platoon, who hated him and picked on him and never missed a chance to poke fun at him. And he reacted by putting on supercilious and disdainful airs, which made him more of a laughing-stock than ever. He was said to regard himself as a young poet. I had seen him once or twice in the mess hall or the parade ground without paying particular attention to him. Now I tried to conjure him up in my mind's eye and imagine the reasons for what he had done. But my attempts were soon cut short. Avner said: "Have you seen that PT instructress again?"

"No," I said, "we haven't seen her."

"What a girl," sighed Avner. "Tell me, has there been any talk about me here? Did the little dears take the opportunity to gossip about me while I was gone?"

"No."

On Thursday we began getting ready for the CO's parade and the weekend leave. The floor of the barracks was washed again and again and the beds were moved to make sure no dusty corners were left. We went outside to shake our blankets, and the clouds of dust rising into the air sent our spirits soaring with them. Muallem came to supervise the work and make sure that everything was done in accordance with regulations.

When the room was spick-and-span Muallem set up an ironing board and showed us how to iron our uniforms and how to starch the collars and epaulets until they were stiff as pieces of felt. Then we took turns in ironing our uniforms under his guidance and making the proper sharp creases on the shirts and trousers. When he left us we sat down to polish our boots, brushing them over and over with spit, which according to Muallem was the way to make them shine like a mirror you could shave in. A few eager beavers even got a head start on cleaning their rifles, which would have to be cleaned all over again the next morning, until the minute before the parade, because the air was full of specks of dust that under the CO's scrutiny would take on the dimensions of rocks in a quarry.

That whole day had been devoted to exhausting foot drill on the main parade ground of the base in preparation for Friday's big event. In the terrible heat of the end of summer we marched back and forth, endlessly repeating the same movements over and over again, shouldering and presenting and ordering arms, closing ranks and opening ranks and closing them again in time to the commands yelled at us, abandoning ourselves to the robot inside us, and even afterward, when we were cleaning the barracks and getting ready for the CO's parade, we did not seem to feel the effects of the day's hard labor. But when I got into bed I felt how the weakness of my body was trying to seduce me and offer me solutions that had not occurred to me up to now: For how could anyone possibly become attached to a place like this? How could you feel any kind of relationship at all to it? I looked at the gray barracks walls, at the two rows of beds, the gray and brown blankets, the weak electric bulb shedding its dreary yellow light over the room and casting shadows on the men's faces, illuminating everything in the light of a bleak, gloomy transience that was frozen for a moment as if it were a reflection of eternity: This was how I had always imagined a prison or a German POW camp to myself. A place where the violent intrusion of sounds and movements and smells no longer even impinged on the mind — so far had everything that was most precious, most sensitive, most personal, eroded and disintegrated. And lo and behold, the mere possibility of approaching separation, if only for a day or two, was enough to recommend a different picture to the heart, full of the temptations of loyalty and the sorrow of loss, spoiling for a moment my happiness at the ancient memory promising to awaken and attach me to myself at the point where I had been disconnected before the sinking of the soul. And the closer the hour of departure approached, the heavier was the shadow cast by this picture over everything else — a picture that in all its sordid ugliness radiated a very tempting aspiration to a purity, perhaps a deceptive purity, that had been irretrievably lost. My voice said to me: *You have lost the most precious thing of all here. If you ever regret it, this is where you will have to begin everything over again, returning in your body or your mind to search for the traces.* And when I said to myself that I was falling asleep, I tried to teach myself to long for this place and time, as for a lost opportunity, and with the same heartbreak.

It was only the next morning, in the fever of preparation and excitement, of fear and happiness, that things fell into place. One by one the companies and platoons marched onto the parade ground and fell in around three of its sides. The process of marching on and falling in, although it was slow and complicated, became clearer and clearer as the parade ground filled up and all the companies and platoons took up their places. All the squares were gradually occupied and the general movement advanced and diverged with a marvelous logic, uniform, economical, and spectacular. It was early in the morning but the heat was already unbearable, with the sun blazing down on our heads and the asphalt ground looking as if it were about to melt, and I sensed a strange happiness taking hold of me and pride at being part of all this. *We're soldiers after all,* I said to myself, *soldiers despite everything.* And in the silence that fell when the flag was raised, to the muffled beat of the drums, I could hear the breathing of the men standing next to me frozen, rigid and solemn as they presented their arms, and I knew that they were feeling the same thing I felt, and what had been up to now surrender and renunciation turned into love. It flowed among us like repressed weeping, contagious and electrifying and full of beauty. When the drums stopped and the flag hung limply from the top of the flagstaff, without a wind to fly it, and the ends of the ropes were being tied, and we were still presenting arms, waiting for the command to shoulder and order them, there was a sudden thud in our ranks and immediately afterward a loud metallic clang, the sound of a rifle hitting the asphalt, and someone behind me whispered: "Miller's fallen."

No one moved. Not one of all the hundreds of recruits standing on three sides of the parade ground and presenting arms looked around. But we could sense that all of them, recruits and instructors and officers to a man, were directing their attention, their disgust, and their thoughts of vengeance at us, singling us out of all the other platoons standing there, because we had been caught out in something sick and ugly and our disgrace had been exposed in the middle of all that thrilling and unifying splendor. At that moment I hated Miller and cursed him in my heart. I imagined that all the others felt like me, because the unity of our feelings at those unique moments was as certain as our physical presence, as the furnace heat of the sun beating down on us, as the smell of our sweat and the boiling asphalt. No one made a move to see how he was and to free his tongue so he wouldn't choke. We wouldn't have cared if he did choke, as long as the disgrace he had brought on us was wiped out. Even after the command to shoulder and order arms was given, no one moved. It was almost possible to hope that in another minute the whole thing would be forgotten. And then, as if in obedience to some mysterious command, some secret conspiracy, there was another thud, this time from the wing on our left, from another platoon, where someone standing in the front row had fallen flat on his face and lay spread-eagled on the ground with his rifle underneath him. And a minute later someone else fainted too, also from the left wing. But none of this could remove the stain from our platoon. The disgrace had come from us. We were the source of the disease and I had no doubt that we were going to pay for it.

Only after the inspection of arms began did anyone find time for Miller. Muallem's face was flushed and strained when he bent over him. Another instructor came to help. When Muallem stood up with a friendly smile on his usually scowling face I realized how relieved he was and how unconcerned by the disgrace. Miller was still lying in our midst when the CO passed before us — lordly and ceremonious as a god who had stepped down for a moment from his pedestal to review us and inspect our arms — paused opposite the place where Miller had fallen, entered the ranks, and looked at the huddled body with no expression on his face but a kind of scientific curiosity in his eyes, and said to the instructors with paternal expertise: "You mustn't touch them when they fall. You have to let him come to by himself. It's not like those others who fainted." Then he said something in an undertone to Raffy Nagar, who stood there looking tense and nervous, saying, "Yes, sir! Yes, sir!" and the feeling of uncleanliness and untouchability, which had been so strong at first and grown somewhat fainter in the course of time, came back in full force. *You mustn't touch them when they fall.* It sounded to me more like some mysterious ancient commandment than a medical prescription or ordinary piece of superstition. So the previous moments of grace, with the pride, happiness, and identification they had aroused, were only a delusion, a hint at what might have been in some different, blessed, healthy dispensation. Our tracks on the ground, our mess tins, uniforms, and blankets, our hair and nails could no longer keep us from harm, turn the enforced isolation into a protective wall, because we had allowed ourselves to be seduced by dreams, we had aspired to great things and reached out to touch what was not intended for the likes of us.

It was as if a door had been slammed, a chapter closed. And the idea of going home took on an extra meaning, vital and urgent, because everything had once more become alien and accidental. The picture that had come into my mind before falling asleep the previous night disintegrated, like all the other delusions. Everything had to be begun from the beginning again.

When the companies and platoons began filing off the parade ground I turned my attention to my friends. I saw them withdrawn into themselves, into the image of home in each of their hearts. I imagined hearing them echo the cry in my own heart: *Home! Home!* A cry as seductive and dangerous as a call to mutiny.

Miller remained where he was, attended by the MO who had been summoned for this purpose. We left the parade ground at a close, coordinated run, but something in our feet kept urging us to break out and escape, to run for our lives, to leave the memory of the disgrace behind us and distance ourselves from the moment of shame. We entered the path leading to the platoon barracks. We had not been ordered to sing but something broke out of its own accord, savage, discordant, strange, several different songs thundering together and sounding like barbaric yells. Raffy Nagar shouted at us furiously to stop singing. Silence fell, broken only by the thudding of our boots. The sight of our approaching barracks suddenly seemed like a safe refuge instead of a signal to break into intoxicated holiday cheers. We fell to in front of the door, waiting for the command to fall out, and Raffy Nagar announced that the leave had been canceled.

There was a moment of silence. From the next building we could hear the sound of a different singing, united, triumphant: the song of men about to go on leave. But the news hadn't yet sunk in. Raffy Nagar looked at us without saying anything, as if trying to assess the effect of his announcement, and his look was like the look in the eyes of the CO when he gazed at Miller's body lying on the ground. What he saw was presumably rows of faces stupefied with misery. Then he began listing our sins, the sloppiness, negligence, and irregularities discovered by the CO when he had inspected the barracks room in our absence, the state of our weapons during the arms inspection on parade, and various transgressions against military discipline that he preferred not to go into at the moment. It all sounded cooked up, unconvincing, arbitrary. And it fit in with the way we felt. Raffy Nagar waved his hand at Muallem, who went into the barracks and came out again carrying Rahamim Ben-Hamo's scorched blanket. Muallem spread the blanket out in front of us, displaying the hole burned in it, and Raffy Nagar expressed his opinion on the destruction of IDF property and the punishment appropriate to those responsible for it.

I wondered why I should be surprised. Was this surprise a form of protest? The triumphant singing and cries of joy coming from 3 Platoon sounded exaggerated, artificial, like an attempt to convince themselves and a demonstration for the benefit of others. And it was precisely for this reason that there was something malicious and insulting about them. When the command to fall out was given and the instructors left we remained standing in front of the barracks, looking at each other, ridiculous in our turnout uniforms and the gleam of pride that had not yet been completely wiped from our eyes, ready and waiting for when we stood with the other soldiers at the Sarafand junction to hitch a ride.

Micky said: "I prefer not to know their real reasons. Because if it turns out that I've been screwed because someone else fouled up I might lose my self-control and do something I'll be sorry for later." And he gave Rahamim Ben-Hamo a look of loathing and warning.

We went into the building to change our clothes and return to the daily grind. I said to myself that the leave was over. It was the shortest amount of time I had ever known. But I knew that it would have finished more or less like this anyway. I had a whole Saturday in front of me to reconstruct it and fill in the details until the memory was right and complete. In the whole base the only person connected with my former life and my former surroundings was Arik. Meeting him now became an urgent priority. The last time I had seen him, in the queue outside the mess hall, we had exchanged a few words and he told me that they were about to go home on leave for the weekend. He would be able to tell me how it was to be home. I needed his memory now, his talk, his peculiar ideas. After too long I felt a vestige of this old, childish attachment stirring in me again, the memory of the admiration I had felt for him and my attempts to imitate him.

Micky said: "You have be able to take stuff like this in your stride. That's the trick. Not to make an issue out of it and carry on as if nothing happened. Go into reverse."

"The truth is I'm not too upset about it," said Alon. "I didn't feel like going home anyway. Putting in an appearance on the kibbutz as a recruit on Training Base Four. Answering questions. Explaining myself. Everyone takes an interest in you there. They're all a bit like your father or your big brother. And what have I got to tell them? I'd rather go home later. After I go up before the medical board. And maybe they'll agree to transfer me at last."

"It must be hell to live like that," said Micky, "to have to account for yourself to everybody all the time."

"Not a bit," protested Alon. "You don't understand. You don't have to give anybody an account. You feel it for yourself. You have an example. It's the kind of place you live in. People contribute their maximum. You're part of it. You don't want to let them down."

Avner, who was lying on his bed, made a face. "All those phrases make no impression on me," he said to me loudly enough for Alon to hear. "I wanted that leave to see my girlfriend. To go to bed with her."

"I've got nothing against that," said Alon. "I'm not stopping you. Believe me."

"But you're sure that any girl would prefer some paratrooper or combat fighter to a grade-B recruit from Training Base Four. Right?" said Micky.

"No, I wouldn't say that," said Alon. "But maybe. Maybe."

"On kibbutzim," said Hedgehog, "boys and girls take showers together until they get married. Nobody knows who his father and mother are, because everybody believes in free love."

"In Jerusalem you don't take showers at all," said Alon. "Ever since the siege you're too stingy with water."

"If I wash myself with snow water, and make my hands never so clean, Yet shalt thou plunge me in the ditch, and mine own clothes shall abhor me," said Micha the Fool.

Peretz approached them. Their lighthearted banter was not at all to his liking. "They've got no right to do it. According to GROs you're not allowed to screw a whole platoon because of one little shit like Ben-Hamo burning his blankets."

Avner sat up on his bed and called out to him: "Tell me, how did you get to be such an expert on GROs? Who told you all that rubbish? Why don't you stop shooting your mouth off?"

Peretz gave him a contemptuous look, paused a moment, spat, and said: "Go lick the Ashkenazis' asses. I suppose you think they'll accept you as one of them. You poor bastard."

Avner lay back on his bed, cupped his shaved head in his hands, and snickered to himself. But I could see that he was upset.

At that moment Miller walked in. There was a dead silence, as if everybody had been talking about nothing but him. But actually Miller had been completely forgotten; he and his wretched fall during the ridiculous parade had nothing to do with what had happened to us. At the most he was the comic element in the strange episode we were just beginning to digest. He looked tired and slightly embarrassed. He went straight to his bed and began occupying himself with his possessions. He opened the little brown suitcase and put a few articles of civilian clothing, which he took out of his knapsack, into it, and when it was full he shut it, picked it up, and made to leave the room. But before doing so he looked around him in bewilderment. His dark, parchment face looked in danger of disintegration and took on an expression of concern.

"Home?" he asked.

"No, not home," said Hanan, imitating his German accent. "Leave kaput! Kaput!"

"I yes to home, to Haifa," insisted Miller, "must go."

"No, you can't, verboten," said Hedgehog. "Verboten to leave. Everyone has to stay here."

"Why?" said Miller. "Why? They say home! Leave!" He tried to dismiss the bad news by appealing to logic, to his trust in good order and the moral obligation to keep promises.

"Punishment!" explained Albert the Bulgarian. He drew his finger across his throat as if to slit it with a knife, and unable to contain his laughter said again: "Punishment!"

Miller sat down helplessly on his bed, put the little suitcase down, and began shaking his head from side to side, as if commiserating with himself on his troubles.

The laughter bubbling up inside us at the sight of Miller boiled over. Our eyes gleamed as we sought each other's gaze. Perhaps because Miller reflected our situation and its consequences to us in the form of a caricature: the heartbreak and disappointment and helplessness. And however genuine and pathetic these feelings were in the wretched figure and grotesque speech of Miller, they were nevertheless ridiculous, superficial, and unreal to us, as if we were reacting to the situation in the way that was expected of us, according to the rules of a folklore we were beginning to learn instead of feeling our real pain, our real anxieties. Even Miller's fits now seemed less real and mysterious to us, for in the guise in which he now appeared before us, like some funny, touching marionette, his falls seemed almost like some charming, artistic flourish added to the phenomenon as a whole — like the part of the performance when the puppeteer lets go of the strings and the puppet drops crookedly and clownishly to the ground.

And there was still something uncertain, something unclear in our situation. An account that had not yet been settled. Even after we had changed our clothes and come back from eating our lunch, there was still a certain hesitancy about our movements, as if to protect ourselves from further surprises in store.

Micky and Alon found a soccer ball, put on their gym shorts, and went out to play on the open ground in front of the armory not far from our barracks. I tried to take a nap, to taste something of the rest I had been looking forward to so eagerly, of the promise of solitude whose taste I had almost forgotten. But my body refused to respond. I couldn't close my eyes. The others couldn't seem to find anything to occupy themselves with either. Boredom, the revenge of the automaton denied its necessary dose of routine, frustrated our attempts to rest. Books and newspapers were thrown to the floor in despair, letters left unwritten. Avner stood up and went to join Micky and Alon, followed by Albert the Bulgarian and a few others. In the end nearly all of us left the room — the minority to participate in the game and the majority to watch, shout encouragement, and relieve the agony of boredom. I sat down next to Yossie Ressler, and we watched the players. Two stones were placed on opposite sides of the field to mark the goals, and the game resembled a raucous free-for-all more than a soccer match. Among all the players yelling and running wild on the field Micky amazed the eye with his acrobatic feats and perfect goals and elegant feints to deceive the people milling around under his feet. Nobody counted the goals or cared who won or lost, and the whole game seemed intended to show off Micky's skill and brilliance. Hedgehog, who could not see a fray without throwing himself into it, even at the cost of emerging full of bruises and cuts, ran to and fro on his skinny legs, tirelessly crying foul against the other side, and more than taking part he looked as if he was preventing any kind of logical game from coming into being. And indeed, everything soon fell apart, and while the players were arguing and accusing each other of breaking the rules and ruining the game, Micky and Alon and Albert and Avner went into a huddle and emerged with the proposal that the four of them would take on all the rest, but this time they would play by the book and count the goals. The proposal was accepted as fair, an accurate reflection of the relative strength of the players, and soon they were all running over the field again, flushed and sweating, panting and yelling, four against ten, and while the four played with ease, efficiency, and coordination, the ten threw themselves furiously into the game to forget who they were and why they were there, to forget the hours and minutes staring at us with empty eyes and threatening to swallow us alive.

"Do you know any Negro spirituals?" Yossie Ressler suddenly asked me.

"Yes, a few," I said.

"If you like we can sing in harmony. I'll take the second part, it could sound good with the guitar. You know 'Nobody Knows the Trouble I've Seen'?"

"Yes, I know it."

"'Swing Low, Sweet Chariot'?"

"Yes, I know that too."

And he sang softly in my ear the second part he had composed to "Swing Low, Sweet Chariot" — not in ordinary tercets, which I also knew how to do, but something far more complicated and interesting — and as he sang I hummed the first part to myself to see how they sounded together. Yossie lowered his back to the ground and lay down, perhaps in order to avoid seeing the soccer players, and waved his hand in the air like a conductor, to emphasize the opposing stresses. He wasn't interested in dividing the people around him into superior and inferior, or testing his place in the hierarchy; his ability to mark off a little plot of beauty for himself protected him and enabled him to carry his home around with him from place to place, like a snail or a tortoise.

"That's really nice," I said.

"When I'm fed up and sick of it all, I compose second-part harmonies to all kinds of songs," said Yossie, "but I'd never try to do it with classical music. I wouldn't have the nerve, not yet."

"Are you going to study music after the army?"

"I think they'll take me for the IDF orchestra." He smiled, as if it were some kind if silly caprice. "But yes, I do want to go on with my music after the army. Maybe I'll go abroad to study. How about you?"

"Maybe I'll go to college, but I don't even know yet what I want to study."

"Naturally," he said, "after all those years . . ." And he sat up and surveyed the players on the field. A quarrel had broken out, at the center of which stood the indefatigable Hedgehog accusing Avner of touching the ball with his hand while Avner's three teammates vociferously denied the accusation.

"Hedgehog's crazy," said Yossie, "always rushing in to do battle for truth and justice — why should he care if he touched the ball or not."

"You can't have a game without rules," I said.

"Why didn't they let us go home for the weekend?" he asked, with a resentful expression on his face, as if I had something to do with the cancellation of the leave.

"I don't know," I said. "I've stopped thinking about it."

"Well I haven't," said Yossie. "There's something bad here, very bad. And you talk about rules. According to the rules they should have let us go. But that's just the point. There are no rules. They think they can do whatever they like. I was expected at home. I'm already beginning to feel like an animal."

So even his armor was cracking? He stood up. The soccer game had come to a halt. Micky was still kicking the ball into the air from one foot to the other, the argument died down, and they all lay down under the trees to rest.

After taking a shower I went to look for Arik's company. I knew it wasn't far from the staff quarters, but I didn't know exactly where. Recruits I didn't know were returning from the showers while others were sitting outside their barracks; a Sabbath quiet was descending on the base. A few hundred yards from our lines it was a foreign country, ostensibly identical to the landscape of our own company, but immeasurably different. I walked between the buildings, not daring to approach them and peep inside. I hoped that Arik would see me and come out to meet me. I wandered around like this for a long time and despaired of finding him. I marveled at myself for not being afraid. I had entered a forbidden area where I might be discovered at any moment by some orderly-instructor on the prowl. Rules and prohibitions, presumably, were not affected by the Sabbath calm. But I didn't see any officers around. *All this peace and quiet,* I said to myself, *is deceptive, a trap.* But I knew with intuitive certainty that I would not be trapped. I left the lines of the enlisted men and turned onto the dirt road leading to the staff quarters. I stood still to orient myself before making another attempt to reach Arik's company, and then I saw her again.

She was coming from the end of the road. In uniform, a knapsack hanging on a strap from her shoulder, a big bag in her hand. She looked as if she were on her way home. Her dogs weren't with her. Had they ever been? I strained my eyes to examine her while she was still far away. It was definitely her. She walked quickly, apparently in a hurry. Perhaps the vision of her as an ancient goddess of the hunt was only a figment of my imagination? I knew my tendency to escape from seeing things as they really were, from accepting them in all their dreariness. I knew that

I tried to deceive myself, to push everything toward the borders of legend, to compose my own second-part harmony to everything that was happening around me. Just like Yossie Ressler humming second parts to songs in his heart all the time to wrap himself in a protective covering of private harmonies.

Now I was afraid. My legs screamed *Run,* but an irresistible force rooted me to the spot, despite my fear, or perhaps it was precisely the fear, and instead of turning back immediately and returning to the lines of the strange company I stood at the side of the road and stared at her as she came rapidly toward me. It had nothing to do with courage or provoking fortune, or even the wish to prove something to myself, it was simply a need, stronger than fear or pain, to see her at close quarters, if only for a moment, and stand next to her face-to-face.

I stood rooted to the spot, transfixed to the ground by a force not mine, and there was no wild pounding of the heart and no moment of lucidity and regret. I could already see her face in the shadow of her beret more distinctly, exactly the same face as I had seen on the day of the silencing-the-sentry exercise, and exactly the same amazement, full of pain and longing, rose up in me again, as if it had never ceased, at her beauty and foreignness to this place. Even the uniform was like a disguise on her body, a deception; her whole being declared that she belonged in other spheres. My eyes fell on her shoulder badge with the picture of the owl on it. As she came closer the owl on her sleeve grew bigger and clearer and took on additional details lacking in the original schematic representation. I raised my eyes to her face with a frank, direct look, as if I wanted to address her. She walked past me, and I saluted without taking my eyes from hers. She didn't return my salute, and her eyes turned me to air, to a void in the vast spaces she surveyed. I remained rooted to the spot until she disappeared at the end of the road. Relief flooded through me and I filled my lungs with a different air, delightful and intoxicating, blending with the strange joy that gripped me at this accidental contact with the world of signs returning after so long an absence. I suddenly knew with the certainty of a blow that I should never have entered this part of the camp, that I was going to be caught and the price would be as high as the promise.

I heard steps behind my back, a hand came down heavily on my shoulder, and although I had been expecting it, or perhaps precisely for this reason, I jumped as if bitten by a snake.

I turned and saw Arik writhing in laughter at the sight of my panic. It had been so long since I had heard his peculiar, slightly hysterical laughter, such unintelligent laughter for Arik, of all people, who was the cleverest person I knew.

"What are you doing here? You told me outside the mess hall that your company was going on leave."

"They left us behind," I said. "Punishment. I've been looking for you for more than half an hour."

"So why are you looking here?" said Arik. "Our company isn't here. I'm on my way back from the showers and suddenly I see you standing here in the middle of the road staring into space with a dopey expression on your face."

We started walking toward his company barracks, not far off.

"A minute before you showed up," I told him, "I saw Ofra the PT instructress. She passed right in front of me."

"Ofra the PT instructress!" Arik burst into his disagreeable laughter. "You must be dreaming. There aren't any female PT instructors on this base. Allow me to remind you that until further notification you're stationed on Training Base Four, not Training Base Twelve. A fact that may be depressing, but you'll have to get used to it."

"You don't know," I said. "There is a PT instructress here, and her name's Ofra. I saw her once before, we all did, she walked past us in PT dress with her two dogs."

"With two dogs!" cried Arik gleefully. "But they weren't dogs, they were centaurs — how come you didn't notice?"

"You can laugh as much as you like. You just don't know."

"Is this a new thing with you, these hallucinations? When I saw you standing there like that, as if you'd fallen asleep standing up, I wondered if anything had happened to you since you joined the army."

"Never mind. It's not important."

"It's vitally important! You're suffering from hallucinations. Try to control yourself. It could get you into trouble, especially in the army."

We arrived at his barracks. He went in to put away his towel and toilet gear, and I waited for him outside. Had it been wise of me to seek him out? Had I forgotten his pontifical manner, his opinionated self-assurance, his sneering superciliousness? I had always drunk in his words with childish thirst, tried to imitate his way of thinking, so different from anything I was used to.

He came back and we went to a little square not far from the road to the mess hall. There we sat down on the ground and leaned against the trunks of the eucalyptus trees.

"Why did they cancel your leave?"

I told him about Ben-Hamo's blanket.

"Nonsense!" pronounced Arik. "That's not the reason. They just used it as an excuse. You don't understand. The real reasons are less clear. It's war. They're trying to break us. And however much we break it won't be enough for them. And one of their methods is to subvert their own code of justice, as soon as they think that we're beginning to understand it, accept it, and behave according to it. So we won't have anything to hang on to, so we won't be able to find any logic in anything, any connection between intentions and results. Any relation between reward and punishment. So we'll be dependent on one thing only: on their mercy. Because they've got the power here, they're the rulers and we're not even human as far as they're concerned."

He warmed to his theme. His appearance had changed since being drafted. The uniform gave his complexion a grayish hue. The sunglasses he wore clipped over his prescription glasses, by special medical permission, hid the main source of vitality in his expression. His face looked dead and uglier than it had ever looked before.

"When you look around and see all these bastards, the officers, the instructors, the PT instructors, the sergeant majors," continued Arik, "you begin to understand the secret of how power creates evil. I never really knew what evil was. You remember, we often talked about it and I said it was a myth, an invention of primitive people, to make things simpler, to find an explanation for all kinds of behavior that we don't understand. I always said to myself that even the people who do things we consider evil must think they're doing good, otherwise they wouldn't do it. Or else they convince themselves to think it's good, and that's something too, at least they feel the need to think so, or they do it for their own benefit and they don't give a damn for morality, any morality, okay? Even then their end isn't evil itself, but profit, and the evil is only the means. But here I discovered that evil exists for its own sake too, that people who've been given power — in other words, the possibility of forcing other people to do whatever they feel like — enjoy the very fact that they can make others suffer. That they can humiliate them and torment them, and be regarded as national heroes at the same time. You know what that means to them?"

"Don't you think they believe that that's the way to make soldiers of us?"

"Nonsense. Even if they thought so in the beginning, they forgot that goal a long time ago and became immersed in their power games. They must feel like gods. They can do almost anything they like to us; they can almost decide destinies. There are a lot of people here who might be broken for life, who'll never get over the wounds inflicted on them." *Is he talking about himself?* I wondered. Maybe this time it wasn't all theories and ideas he'd picked up in books, but a cry from his own wounded heart. Perhaps something had happened to him that I didn't know about. He had lost weight in basic training and his face had fallen. The dark glasses hid the glint in his eyes, which often modified his exaggerations and peculiar ideas with a measure of irony. Something of the old affection for Arik stirred in me at the thought of the defeats and humiliations to which he may have been subjected, which may have had an even greater impact on him given his intelligence and critical spirit.

I told him about the fat soldier from 3 Platoon.

Arik said: "It's terrible when people are pushed to such extremes. Perhaps he really is someone special, perhaps he's a great poet and we just don't know it. Imagine what he must have gone through. But you can take it from me that none of his instructors feels the least bit guilty or uncomfortable. As far as they're concerned it's nothing but a passing sensation to make life a bit more interesting and relieve the boredom of the daily routine."

"They're not all the same," I said. "Some of the instructors are better than the rest, more human."

"Don't you believe it!" said Arik. "There are all kinds of myths. The myth of the sadistic instructor, who behaves like a bastard because he's got psychological problems, because he's sick, and the myths about the officer who gets his own back on us for the humiliations inflicted on him by his own officers, or for what his wife does to him at home, and the myth of the good instructor who tries to encourage his men and help them behind the scenes. These are the typical myths that slaves have about their masters. They're universal. And since our status here is that of slaves we've developed the reactions of slaves to their masters. There's no difference between them. They're all obsessed with games of power and evil. Some of them may try to be friendly, smile, or say a kind word. But those are only differences of temperament or style, or tactics. And in many cases, they're simply more cunning than the others and they do more harm. You have to understand, what we're up against here is something that's stronger than they are, stronger than sex or money or status. It distorts them completely. All of them. The evil inside them takes over and controls them. It's like a pact with the devil: Before you know where you are you're acting on behalf of somebody else."

His face was red and flushed, and the deathly gray was gone. He smiled as if to soften the dire impression of his words.

"This war," I said, "between them and us, what's of the point of it? They've already won in advance. They're been given everything and we've had everything taken from us. What's left for them to conquer?"

"I don't know," Arik admitted. "I don't understand it so well. But it seems to me that in the process of making us dependent on them, they've become dependent on us in some way too. Perhaps the torturer is dependent on his victim. Perhaps he wants to control what happens inside here too" — he tapped his finger on his head — "thoughts, love, memory, I don't know what. Perhaps they want us to love them too?"

Both of us burst out laughing. Arik changed the subject. Perhaps he felt he had gone too far. He was breathing strenuously. "What are the guys in your squad like?" he asked.

"Okay," I said. "Most of them are nice guys."

"You're got an epileptic too," said Arik, "that guy who fell on parade this morning. What a collection! But on the whole we're lucky to be in the August intake. At least most of them are high school graduates and people like us. You don't know what went on here before we came — knife fights in the barracks rooms, hashish, real underworld characters. Just imagine, the officers were afraid of the recruits!"

"How was your leave?" I asked.

"What do you think?" replied Arik. "I spent the whole time in a depression at the thought that all this was real and I had to come back to this hell. When you look at it from outside it's even worse than being in it, because outside your mind's clearer and calmer and more alert, and crueler."

"Did you see anyone from our class?"

"No. Eli's in Camp Number Eighty. You know. I imagine he's recovered by now from the shock of not being accepted for the academic reserves even though he's such a genius, and soon we'll hear that's he's being sent to a Squad Commanders Course, or an Officers Course, or the Nahal Paratroopers. I wouldn't be surprised if he makes it his life's work. If you think about it, you can see that an army career would suit him. If I know him, he's got no intention of burying himself on the kibbutz for the rest of his life. Rachel Heiman's here on Training Base Twelve. Once on our morning run our platoon met a girls' platoon running opposite us on the road, and she was one of them. We saw each other and waved. And I'm damned if I know why I was so glad to see her. You can't imagine how happy I was. I could hardly breathe from that bloody running, but I felt as if I'd just been given a fantastic present. I don't know why. I was never particularly crazy about her, as you know. "

"Naomi?"

"She's on a kibbutz outpost on unpaid premilitary service with the movement group. There was a letter from her waiting for me at home.

The usual nonsense. But I think she's happy there. Over there she can contribute to everybody in general without expecting anything in return, not even a thank-you. She's probably running everything already, cultural committees, social welfare committees, all that nonsense. Hoping that Eli will turn up on leave between one course and the next, and she'll be able to worship him from a distance. What more does she need?"

Arik spoke rather quickly, but with more frankness than he had ever displayed on such matters before; as if the disconnection and distancing from old attachments and affairs had robbed them of their sting, deprived them of their secrecy, and transformed them into the subject matter of casual remarks.

"How are you coping?" I asked.

"What do you mean?"

"You said it was hell here."

"And don't you think that it's hell?"

"I don't know, there are moments, sometimes —"

"You've already been brainwashed," Arik interrupted. "You believe all that crap about how they turn babies wet behind the ears into men, about how you shed your lousy skin here like a snake and emerge a new man, a hero ready to conquer the world. Believe me, there's no resurrection from this death. Look at your mates, because nobody can see themselves. What do you see? The generation that took Canaan by storm? You see human wrecks, beaten animals. There are people here who'll never get over it, who'll be emotional cripples for the rest of their lives, traumatized forever. The only thing you can do is try to keep your head clean, to chuck out all the rubbish they keep throwing into it all the time."

"And how do you do that?"

"I try to lead a double life. I tell myself to imagine I've been thrown into a madhouse, even though I'm sane. A madhouse where the madmen are in charge and the patients are the sane ones. The only way for me to believe in my own sanity is to cooperate with them, to do everything they tell me, not to resist, not to make waves, to let it all pass over me on as superficial a level as possible, to try not to let it pollute my inner life, my thoughts, my opinions about myself and about them."

"First it was hell and now it's a madhouse," I said.

Arik laughed his unpleasant laugh: "It's not hard in the least to see them as madmen. Isn't that what they look like? What are they shouting about all the time, screaming their heads off like a bunch of madmen? And that famous sergeant major, the one with the monstrous mustache that we're all supposed to be so terrified of, does he even look like a normal human being? If you manage to overcome your fear, even for a minute, and look at him from the side, you see a demented clown and nothing more. Look at their movements, that swaggering walk, all the ceremonies, the parades, the rules and regulations they invent — they're not normal. I don't know how to cope with evil, but I can cope with madness, so I prefer to see them as madmen. Sometimes I have a hard time not bursting out laughing. You'd be surprised, I've learned to keep my big mouth shut, to keep my opinions to myself, not to poke fun, not even to smile, but to myself I never stop repeating: *Don't believe them, don't be converted, don't identify with anything connected with them, don't be seduced by the bait they hold out to us like a bone to a hungry dog, don't surrender to the sick, perverted beauty they sometimes try to display with their flags and weapons and parades, or the illusion of power they think a recruit should feel when he stands there doing the same thing at the same second with a few hundred other second- and third-grade soldiers.*

"God! You don't know how much I hate it, and how hard I try to do everything by the book, however difficult it is for me, anything to avoid friction with them, because friction is a form of closeness, and that's the worst, the most dangerous thing of all. Every time I fail and get it in the neck the temptation arises to identify with the torturers, and resisting it is hell. And hell, among other things, means living in a permanent state of half-truths and half-lies. Sometimes I wonder how the Marranos felt in Spain, if the double life they led was only a technical problem of camouflage and secrecy, or whether it was an emotional problem too: Didn't they ever feel a true inner attraction, like love, to the Catholic Church? And how about spies, don't they sometimes begin falling in love with the countries they're living in under false identities? I don't know, but it's the only way I can keep from breaking here and avoid being influenced by them."

"And if you were living in Europe during the war, in a Nazi-occupied country? Would you have cooperated externally then too, done whatever they told you to so as to keep sane and maintain your true inner identity?"

"And then I would have been one of first to be hung after the liberation," said Arik. He moved away from the eucalyptus trunk and lay flat on the ground, took off his glasses, and rubbed his eyes with the back of his hands. There was a tired expression on his face. "I don't know, I really don't know. Do you know what you would do in those circumstances? Does anyone know in advance? But there's a difference, no? There is a difference. In any case, if it's a question of treason, which it probably is, then I'd say that there are situations in which a man has to choose between two conflicting loyalties, the loyalty to himself and his private

identity and the loyalty to the group, to society, to country, to his obligations toward others. So whichever way you look at it, he has to betray
something to be loyal to something else. In other words, it's a dilemma."

"Yes," I said, "and in any case we're always betraying something. You
remember? *Growing up means betraying your dreams?* You said that once
to Eli."

"I said that?" Arik sat up, all amazement and disbelief. "No kidding!"
he cried. "What a disgrace! And you mean to tell me that you still
remember all the nonsense I once sprouted?"

"Yes," I said, "because I haven't grown up yet. The child refuses to go
away, he doesn't want to forget. He still remembers everything."

"Your irony sounds almost like blackmail," said Arik.

The day began to turn. A murmur ran through the eucalyptus branches,
a wind trembled in the leaves, a hint that autumn would soon be here. The
summer days too were getting shorter. The guavas were ripening in our
yard at home, and soon their smell would spread giddily through the
house. And after them would come the tangerines and the new oranges,
every scratch on their still-green skins oozing with drops of a burning,
intoxicating alcohol, full of the promise of new beginnings. And the smell
of new notebooks and textbooks at the beginning of the school year, which
would never come again. The first pages of the notebook clean and tidy,
written in a fair hand, optimistic and full of goodwill, like new resolutions.
And both going to rack and ruin — and who could tell their end? And
Rosh Hashana and Yom Kippur and Sukkoth and my father and mother
and little brother. Every autumn would always remind me of home.

I stood up and so did Arik. We brushed the earth and the prickly eucalyptus fruits off our clothes. Arik was silent and I said: "It's Rosh
Hashana soon. I forgot all about time."

Arik said: "I told you, it's hell. In Dante the souls in purgatory know
what's going to happen in the future but they have no idea what's happening now."

We walked down the road to his barracks. Before we parted Arik said:
"Be strong!"

And for some reason it sounded like: *Manage without me.* How unnecessary to have said it.

I covered the way back to the platoon at a run, and as I ran, to the rhythm
of my boots and my breathing, I heard a kind of humming inside me: *I won't
fall into that trap again! I won't fall into that trap again!* As if I were running
from a dream to the threshold of waking. When I reached the barracks, I
turned off the road onto the path leading to the armory, opposite the field

where the soccer game had taken place. There I stood for a few minutes to collect myself and order my thoughts. Something had broken inside my heart and I didn't know if I was sorry for it or not. Arik and his world were becoming alien to me. I didn't want any connection with them. I wanted to be myself, to start thinking for myself. This farewell was formulated in my mind long after it had actually taken place inside me. I wasn't going to fall into that trap again! Was this a certainty, a wish, a vow?

I turned around to return to the barracks. When I approached the door Nahum came out on his way to Sabbath eve prayers. He was carrying his prayer book under his arm, like a gift to a lover. His steps were more hurried than usual, as if he was afraid of being late. This haste, so reminiscent of a first lovers' tryst, amused me, because it reminded me of the Sabbath song "Come My Beloved to Meet the Bride" and gave me a moment of malicious glee at his expense: His strange dumbness was nothing but an unfair trick. Nahum would stand alone at the trysting place, confounded and ashamed, looking anxiously around him and glancing at his watch, trying to suppress his doubts, and the longer he waited the more apparent it would become that the other party was not going to keep the date. And he too would learn to live in this exile and make it his home. He would no longer lift up his eyes to the mountains, for his help would not come. There was no favoritism.

When we came back from supper, the walls of our building gave off the dank smell of old wooden planks that had been standing all day in the sweltering heat and humidity. Rising to join it was the smell of male sweat and pulled-off boots and clothes still sour with the vapors of the body. I thought that I was already insensible to these smells, but suddenly they assailed me again with all their violence. My face must have betrayed my revulsion.

"What's the matter with you?" asked Avner. "You look as if you've been trodden on."

"It's the smell," I said. "It's ghastly."

"It's the smell of living people. We all stink. You too."

"Yes," I said. "I know."

"You hate that smell because you hate people."

This piece of patronage sounded so insulting that it filled me with anger and hatred. I knew that I had to keep quiet. I took off my clothes and lay down on my bed. Around me I saw downcast faces, closed or half-closed eyes, even though it was still early. Hardly anyone spoke, and there were none of the usual groups clustering round the beds. Everyone felt it differently, but I would never have imagined that so many people could feel so lonely in such crowded conditions.

Miller opened his little suitcase. The click of the metal clasps sounded like the cocking of a gun in the silence. All eyes turned to him, more in boredom than in curiosity. He leaned his back against the wall, raised his knees, laid his notebook on them, and began to write. This was a sight that had accompanied us ever since our arrival, but now it was the only thing happening in the room. Miller wrote line after line without noticing the eyes fixed on him from all sides. What had at first been accidental, because of the noise of the click, quickly turned, by means of winks and eye signals rapidly communicated from bed to bed, into a siege. The eyes encircled him, threatening in their sleepy indifference. For a moment or two he continued writing without noticing anything. In the end he lifted his head from the notebook, as if awakening from a trance, and looked around him, and his brown, parchmentlike face twisted in alarm. Slowly he lowered his head and inspected his body to try to discover the cause of the stares. And since nothing unusual met his eyes, he decided to take no notice, resuming his writing. He wrote a word or two and his pen came to a halt. He sat like this, afraid to raise his head from the notebook, apparently trying to make up his mind what to do next. The silence continued; nobody laughed. The eyes remained fixed on him. When he finally decided to raise his head his face was trembling with terror and rage. Again he looked from side to side to see if the staring had stopped and again the eyes closed in on him from all directions. With shaking hands he removed the cap from the bottom of the pen and screwed it onto the nib end. He closed the notebook and laid it on the side of his bed, with the pen on top of it. And then he sat there with his knees raised and his suitcase shaking on top of them. Until he made up his mind to speak, and the expression of anger on his face turned into one of supplication. "What is it here? What is it?" he mumbled. Nobody answered him, nobody opened his mouth, nobody took his eyes off him. The prank was only beginning to bear fruit, and no sign of the laughter already tickling the pranksters' stomachs was permitted to show on the frozen faces. He must have imagined a ring tightening around him, for he suddenly thrust out his hands as a warning not to come any closer, closed his eyes, and uttered a brief, choked, animal cry: "What is it?"

Alon was suddenly on his feet in the aisle between the two rows of beds. For a moment he stood there looking distraught, and then he went up to Miller's bed and said to him: "It's nothing. It's only a joke. Don't be frightened." Then he surveyed us with narrowed eyes, from one end of the room to the other, and shouted: "Stop it! Bastards! Bastards! Bastards!"

Miller put his suitcase carefully on the floor, bent down, opened it, and put his notebook and pen away inside it. Then he put the case under his folded blankets and walked out of the room. The silence continued until it was suddenly broken by Avner, who sat up in bed, opened his eyes in astonishment, and asked: "What's wrong with him? Why's he shouting?"

The question echoed in the air and triggered a delayed reaction to the joke set up so patiently only to fall flat in the end. The laughter exploded and thundered around the room. "I fell asleep," he said. "I suppose I must have missed something." He lay down again, rubbed the stubble beginning to grow on his shaven head, yawned, and looked at me. "Is everything okay, Melabbes?"* he asked. "Has the stink stopped bothering you?" And my laughing face presumably answered for me that my bad mood was over. Before the hilarity evoked by Avner's question had subsided, Miller returned, his head stuck out like a tortoise's, and a sly smile on his old man's face, like a participant in the joke, laughing with the laughers.

Micky opened the chessboard on his bed and he and Alon set up the pieces. Avner took *The Elements of Hebrew Grammar* out of his knapsack and settled down to make yet another attempt at preparing for his matriculation exams. The book, he said, was so boring that he had never managed to read more than three pages of it. Peretz-Mental-Case and his friends were debating the question of whether an officer was obliged to obey an MP private on duty, and Peretz was irate because they weren't prepared to rely on him and his familiarity with military law. He informed them that they had the brains of donkeys, lit another cigarette, and, although the expression on his face announced that he had no further desire to discuss this or any other topic with them, immediately plunged back into the finer points of the debate, silencing them with dismissive gestures and demanding his right to hold the floor. And Zero-Zero, who had recovered from the pains that had attacked him in the mess hall, and from his dread of developing an ulcer, resumed his favorite occupation of abusing Rahamim Ben-Hamo three beds away. At first Ben-Hamo ignored Zero-Zero's cries, and then he stopped his ears and announced that he couldn't hear a thing. Then he took his hands off his ears and said: "All your rubbish goes in one ear and out the other." In the end a sly twinkle came into his eyes, as if he found the whole thing highly amusing. He said: "You must have a shithole for a mouth to talk like that."

"You better be careful, Ben-Hamo," said Zero-Zero, "I've got friends in your transit camp and they know you. Everybody knows what you do. The whole of Ramle knows your dirty ass."

---

* The name of the old Arab village originally adjoining the site of the town of Petah Tikva.

"My ass's cleaner than your mouth," said Ben-Hamo triumphantly, his eyes gleaming.

"They gonna chuck you in the calaboose," said Zero-Zero. "The CO knows all about you, even the CID's investigating you already. Here in Israel we don't want pieces of shit like you turning the country into one big casbah. In Ramle there's a few guys waiting to grab you and pour boiling tar down your asshole and stop it up for good, so you won't be able to use it to spread your dirty diseases anymore."

Yossie Ressler's guitar suddenly broke into this dialogue. He was tuning the strings. I couldn't see him from my bed. His bed was at the other end of the room, where the Jerusalemites were concentrated, and they were sitting on Hedgehog's bed, hiding him. I knew the expression that came onto his face when he tuned his guitar. The tuning took a long time, because there was always some string whose pitch didn't satisfy him, and he would raise and lower the pitch again and again, testing it in chords with his head bent over the guitar, his eyes wide open and staring off to one side, as if he were trying to look at his ear, his mouth slightly crooked, all concentrated attention and seriousness. At such moments this delicate boy sometimes looked like a violent maniac. When he finished tuning his instrument his face resumed its usual ascetic mien, with only an occasional gleam of restlessness flickering in his eyes. The six-string chord struck clearly and confidently from the corner of the room, and then there was a silence, the sign that the tuning had finally been accomplished to Yossie's satisfaction. After a moment I saw him coming toward me and I knew what he wanted. Behind him Ben-Hamo and Zero-Zero continued their mutual abuse, to the amusement of the people lying in the beds next to them, but Ressler paid no attention to them. He was listening only to himself, to his second-part harmony. Like someone afraid of losing the thread of a thought at the end of which trembled an important and elusive idea, he closed his eyes and shut his ears to all outside disturbances.

Rahamim tittered with a peculiar kind of enjoyment. "You're the one who'll go to prison if you talk like that. That's how criminals talk. Your poor wife, I feel sorry for her."

Yossie said to me: "Do you feel like singing now?"

I said: "I'm not in the mood."

"Your poor mother, who taught you your dirty tricks. And your poor sisters, who go and bring you customers. How much do they pay you, the Arabs who come to you?"

"'Sometimes I Feel Like a Motherless Child' — you know that too, don't you? Remember you said you liked my second-part harmonies? Come on, let's have a shot at it."

"And you," said Rahamim, "when you go to your wife at night you can't even get it up because of all your diseases. Poor woman, I feel sorry for her being married to you."

"All right," I said, "later."

Ressler stood and waited.

Avner said to him: "Can't you see that he doesn't feel like singing? Why don't you leave him alone?"

Ressler said: "I'll play a for a few minutes first, until the atmosphere's right. And then we'll sing. I know a nice bit of Telemann, listen."

"I'm engaged, if you want to know," said Rahamim. "All the filth and rubbish that comes out of your mouth doesn't mean a thing to me. Not one lousy little thing."

"I wonder they don't get sick of it," I said, "going through exactly the same routine every night."

Yossie looked at me questioningly, and I jerked my head in the direction of Ben-Hamo and Zero-Zero. He looked over his shoulder and said: "Nonsense. So are you coming? I'll wait for you over there."

"Engaged!" cried Zero-Zero gleefully. "Congratulations, Ben-Hamo! Who's your fiancée? Muhammad?"

Yossie returned to the Jerusalem corner, where he could immediately be heard striking a few complicated chords on his guitar strings. Then he began to play the Telemann piece.

Avner said: "How do you like his nerve? When he wants something, the rest of the world can go to hell. He's a real maniac, that Ressler. The only thing that interests him is music."

"And later on, in the middle of the night," said Zero-Zero, "you try to sneak into people's beds and get them to do it to you. What kind of scum are they taking into the army today? God help our poor country . . ."

"Don't worry," said Rahamim, "nobody's going to sneak into your bed, someone as ugly and stinking and sick as you, you make even your poor wife sick to her stomach."

"But he plays well, that's true," said Avner.

"He's okay," I said, "even if he is a bit weird."

"And what a snob!" said Avner. "Like his whole family."

I stood up and went over to the corner. Yossie's Jerusalem friends were gazing at him admiringly. Hedgehog sat cross-legged at the head of his bed, and like a natural leader, used to commanding others, he nodded his head in time to the music as if he were conducting. Micky and Alon, absorbed in their chess game on the next bed, sent sidelong glances at Yossie Ressler's fingers, dancing over the strings and producing such beautiful harmonies, while waiting for the other to make his move. Slowly there came into being that invisible, magical circle of light that I had once wished would envelop us and isolate us, like a wall of grace, to protect those delicate and fragile moments in which friendship takes shape and barriers of loneliness and embarrassment and shame are broken. And the people sitting there were suddenly very dear to me. I forgot my vow to be a stranger everywhere, not to strike roots. Ressler finished the Telemann and played another piece of classical music. Alon and Micky finished their game of chess, folded the cardboard chessboard, and put the pieces back in their little wooden box. They sat down opposite us, and when Avner came and sat down next to Micky, the circle that had formed around the two beds was closed.

I hoped that Yossie would become so absorbed in his playing that he would go on and on and forget about the singing — that he wouldn't break the spell that descended on us during those moments, the enchantment shining at us from the faces of the people in the circle, quiet and pure and contained. But Yossie finished the piece he was playing and immediately struck the introductory chords and said in English: "'Nobody Knows the Trouble I've Seen.'" My voice was weak and hesitant at first, and Yossie gave me a surprised, disappointed look, as if I had betrayed a promise and was spoiling and undermining the alliance coming into being around us. The vestiges of dejection and childish pride were still constricting my throat and chest and I had to suppress them before my voice cleared and Yossie's face broke into a thankful smile. I felt that I was performing an act of vast significance in entering as a partner into the creation of this beauty. As if I were being controlled by a force more powerful than me, like a medium in a circle of spiritualists. The words of the song, which I had not heard or sung for so long, came back to me in full, and Yossie's second-part harmony answered them like an echo, at unexpected intervals, against the background of the chords full of tenderness and sadness flowing like an infinite promise. I couldn't believe that it was my voice coming out of my mouth, so full was I with the sensation of beauty, unfamiliar and unlooked for, like a blessing I did not deserve.

CHAPTER 7

We finished the first song and Yossie Ressler quickly struck the opening chords of the next one, "Swing Low, Sweet Chariot," trying not to leave an interval between songs in case the flame died down. Did he too feel what I had been feeling for the past few minutes? At the end of the second song Yossie went on strumming on the guitar, and Alon suddenly croaked in his hoarse, broken voice: "'For Me Each Wave Bears a Souvenir,'" and we all joined in with the guitar and with Yossie's second-part harmony, and before we came to the end of the first verse there was a long, loud moan from the other end of the room, a wail that increased in volume until it sounded like the muezzin calling the faithful to prayer in a long drawn-out, throttled, sobbing tremolo. Zackie had broken into an Arabic song and his friends responded with rhythmic clapping, cries of encouragement, and groans of pleasure. Yossie stopped playing, and the rest of us, feeling extremely foolish, fell silent. Hedgehog leapt from his place at the head of the bed, his face flushed with the joy of battle. He ran over to the corner where the disturbance was coming from.

"What's the matter with you?" he yelled. "Why do you have to spoil everything?"

"We want to sing our songs too," said Peretz, "and if you don't like it you can shut your ears." And he motioned to Zackie to continue, joining in with a wail of his own.

"We don't want Arab songs in the army!" shouted Hedgehog. "We don't want to hear that shit here!"

"We don't like your Ashkenazi songs either," said Sammy.

"But why do you have to sing right now, when it disturbs us?" demanded Hedgehog furiously.

Zackie stopped singing, smiled sweetly, and said, "Because your singing gets on our nerves, we can't stand it. It makes us sick."

"Okay," said Hedgehog. "We'll see who gives in first." And he came back to us and announced, "We'll carry on singing until they give up and stop. They'll see who's the boss here."

"Give it a break, for God's sake," said Yossie Ressler and put his guitar down on the bed. "Let them sing their songs if it makes them happy."

"No!" cried Hedgehog. "They can go back where they came from and sing those disgusting songs there. Not here! Pick up the guitar and play!" But Yossie shut his eyes and took no notice of Hedgehog's command. "Play, play!" screamed Hedgehog.

"I can't play like this," said Yossie. "What do you want of my life?"

"Okay," said Hedgehog. "Then we'll sing without an accompaniment." And he extended his neck, took a deep breath, and started clapping his hands and singing at the top of his voice: "And on the Sabbath day two lambs of the first year, two lambs without spot, and two tenth deals of flour . . . ," gesticulating to us to join in. A few people who knew the song joined in, and Peretz's crowd raised their voices. Sammy went outside and came back a few minutes later with a large empty tin, apparently from the kitchen. He sat down and began drumming on the tin, inspiring Zackie and the rest to new heights of enthusiasm. The volume of their singing rose and Hedgehog saw that the battle was lost. His camp had lowered the flags.

"They've got the right to sing their songs," said Alon sadly. "It's not only our army. It's their army too."

"One day it'll really be their army," said Micky. "They'll be the majority here. They have lots of kids."

"And your Ben-Gurion hasn't got anything better to do than give prizes to families with ten children, so they'll have even more," said Hedgehog.

"Their children will be just like us," promised Alon.

"Or our children'll be like them," grinned Micky, "and in the end it'll be just another Arab state and there won't be any more wars and there'll be peace and quiet in the land."

"Why don't you say anything, Avner?" said Hedgehog. "Haven't you got an opinion? You have to decide what side you're on."

"When your grandfather was still in some hole in Poland," said Avner, "or wherever it was, my family was already living in Jerusalem. So it's not my problem."

"It is your problem," said Hedgehog, "if you give a damn about this country. It all comes from corruption. From the politicians. They bring all this trash here to drag them to the ballot box in elections, to shove a slip with the right letter on it into their hands, and to stay in power. You saw what went on in the last elections. And so they fill the country up with invalids and welfare cases and lunatics and criminals. All so that the Labor Party can get their votes. And by the time Ben-Gurion's famous Yemenite chief of staff gets to command the army, there won't be any soldiers in it. It'll be an army of Ben-Hamos."

We all laughed at Hedgehog's exaggerations and he pointed at the singers and said, "Listen, just listen to that disgusting, degenerate moaning, like a lot of bitches in heat."

"Tell me," said Avner, "what have you got against bitches in heat?"

"Oho!" cried Hedgehog. "That got you where it hurts!"

And breaking through the guffaws accompanying these remarks, Avner's voice rose, serious and thoughtful: "Perhaps there's a beauty in these songs too, and you simply can't understand it because you're not used to it?"

Yossie Ressler said, "It may be a failing in me. It may be. But I'm sure that Bach and Mozart and Beethoven wouldn't have been able to discover the beauty in this music either, because they weren't used to it either. So if it's a failing I can live with it."

"Beethoven wouldn't have been able to hear it anyway, because he was deaf," said Micha the Fool.

"The army," said Alon, "is our only hope. Only the army can educate them, turn them into Israelis, until they're like us. They don't know the country outside their *maabarot,* they don't know its history, its beauty, its culture. When they bring them to their new settlements, they don't want to get off the trucks. They're not used to hard work and living in the country and farming. So how can we expect them to like our songs? The army has to educate them — at least the young ones because the old ones may as well be written off. The generation of the wilderness."

"I wouldn't agree to go to those settlements either!" said Hedgehog. "Not everybody has to be a socialist!"

"You see!" said Alon. "So why should they agree to go? Why should they go and be pioneers when they see that the veteran population don't want to do it and all they want is to live in town and make money and have careers."

"Students of Israel!" cried Micha the Fool in an imitation of Ben-Gurion's shrill, jarring voice. "The history of the Jewish people in our time confronts you and all the youth of Israel with a fateful question: Career or Zionist Mission?"

"When we were at the Sheik-Munis meeting with Ben-Gurion," said Micky, "I said to my classmates: In another year, two years, he'll be back as prime minister and defense minister. Mark my words. Politicians can't change, it's in their blood. He won't sit there on a kibbutz in the Negev forever and give up his power."

"I was watching Dayan," I said. "I saw him sitting there on the ground, in the first row, and it looked to me as if he were falling asleep, as if he weren't listening to a word Ben-Gurion was saying, as if his expression was one of demonstrative boredom."

"Stop it!" Hedgehog suddenly yelled in the direction of the singers. "Give it a rest! How long are you going to keep it up? I can't stand it anymore. Zackie, for God's sake, do us a favor!"

"Come and sing with us," said Peretz, and he and his friends laughed at the suggestion.

"It's no good asking them to stop," said Micky. "It's their way of fighting back. You've got to let them get some satisfaction."

Avner said to Yossie, "Your singing before was great. It was really great."

"Aha!" cried Hedgehog. "So you've finally decided where you stand."

"No," protested Avner. "I didn't say I don't like what they're singing now."

Micky said, "In the end you'll drive yourself crazy with schizophrenia."

"We all will," said Hanan.

"In jail there was one guy shut up in a cell by himself," said Avner. "And he did nothing all day long. They never gave him any work to do like the rest of us, I don't know why. They didn't want him to mix with the others. So he lay there all day in his cell and sang. He never stopped singing. I think he made up his songs by himself, and every song had a refrain, always the same, *Oh, Mother! Come and take me away from here. They're eating my heart out, Oh, Mother!*" And Avner sang the refrain softly, very carefully, *"Oh, Mother! Come and take me away from here. They're eating my heart out, Oh, Mother!"* Suddenly he burst out laughing as if he had remembered some incident of prison life that he hadn't told us. And then he grew serious again. "He sang it over and over again, at first it was funny, then it was irritating, and in the end I remember that I said to myself: *Maybe there's something in it?* Like folk songs, like the songs you were singing before, that the Negro slaves made up about their fate. They weren't any more cultured or educated than that fellow. I said to myself: *Don't sneer at it, maybe he knows things that you don't know, maybe he's been through things that you've never been through. Maybe all this is like a language that has to be translated for you to understand it.* In the end I found myself singing with him: *Oh, Mother! Come and take me away from here. They're eating my heart out, Oh, Mother!* And tears nearly came into my eyes. I felt I was beginning to identify with him, beginning to understand the beauty in his song. I hoped that I would get to see him before I was released and be able to say something to him, perhaps thank him, but I never saw him. I only knew his voice, but I knew that voice the way you know a whole person. Two days before my release they transferred him somewhere else and suddenly it was quiet. Terribly quiet. And those were my two worst days. Today I don't know myself whether it was a joke or a nightmare."

Avner examined our faces, as if to make sure that we had heard his story. A silence fell. I thought that it must be late and looked at my watch. But it was still early in the evening. Avner said no more and appeared embarrassed at having exposed himself to us. At that moment I knew that one day I would tell him the truth about our guard and ask his pardon.

Suddenly Rahamim Ben-Hamo got out of bed and spread out his arms, like someone stretching himself after a nap. He went on standing there, moving his arms up and down, and his intentions were unclear. But the singers understood, and Sammy called out to him: "Come to us, sweetheart, come to us!"

And Rahamim glided toward them, stamping his feet and wagging his behind, with a provocative smile on his face, and when he reached them he stood still and looked down at the floor, as if choosing the exact spot where he would stand, and closed his eyes. His face was grave. Zackie's wailing voice rose higher and higher, the drumming paused until he choked for lack of breath, and his friends groaned with him and cried out thanks and blessings in Arabic, and then the drumming began again and the singing was renewed. Rahamim opened his eyes and smiled and wriggled his plump body in a kind of caricature of a belly dancer. His torso was naked and hairy, and the frayed edges of his working pants almost entirely covered his childishly small feet.

Gradually a circle formed around him and the singers, and the circle grew until there wasn't a man left sitting on his bed. Everyone came to watch the performance, some clapping in time to the singing to encourage the dancer, some expressing contempt and shouting insults, and others reacting with violent revulsion and disgust. But no one remained outside the circle. Rahamim responded to the laughter and catcalls with a smile of complicity and amused protest. He didn't leave a single member of his audience out. His smiles flew in all directions, obsequious, fawning, almost tortured with effort. He shook his body and swayed his shoulders in coy, ingratiating movements, raised himself on tiptoe, spread out his arms invitingly and immediately drew them protectively back to his chest, bold and timid by turns, dashing forward only to recoil in alarm, stroking his hips and thighs and winking at his audience and then shrinking back and covering his face with his hands, as if ashamed of his own boldness and afraid of its consequences. Finally, moving around the circle with tiny, mincing steps, he held out his hands in supplication and let his head fall back in a gesture of acceptance of the verdict and resignation to his fate.

Gradually we receded from his eyes and he no longer looked at us, as if he were sure of our attention. Now he struggled with himself, as if locked in combat with hostile forces inside him. Zackie's wailing voice sent tremors through his body, and amid shudders of fear and alarm he stamped his feet while his hands strained as if to tear the invisible cobwebs of a dream, cobwebs strong as chains — not to extricate himself from the dream but to enter into it. The expression of concentration on his face grew more acute, and the chains were us, his spectators, our faces observing him, our eyes barring his way. His body writhed and twisted, refusing to surrender to the hostile forces trying to paralyze him, straining to snap the chains and escape far away from here. The Arabic song, so ugly to me in its tearful tone, its wet, guttural consonants, its dissonant trills, its repulsive moans, took possession of the room and everyone in it. No longer a beggarly outcast, its foreignness and ugliness were transformed into a source of strength. The laughter and catcalls died down. We stood in a circle around the dancer and the singers, watching silently, not knowing what all this had to do with us. Rahamim Ben-Hamo danced as if possessed by a demon, increasingly liberated from the forces connecting him to us, increasingly given over to the demon inside him; he closed his eyes and writhed like a rearing snake, his hips and thighs and belly and chest and neck and arms and head all at the mercy of a strong inner tide sending waves rippling through every inch of his body. His eyes were closed and his face looked as if he was on the point of tears, or in the throes of some terrible, ecstatic expectation. Zackie fell silent and only the drumming on the tin can was heard, with Sammy accelerating the beat. Rahamim opened his eyes and glanced at Zackie as if to obtain his permission for going on with the dance although the singing was over. He went on dancing with his eyes open, and there was a different expression now in those big, black, stupid eyes, beaten and long suffering and resigned, an expression such as I had never seen before. I remembered what Avner had said before about the prisoner in solitary confinement, and I thought that these eyes too might have seen things that we never would. He went on dancing without a pause, and now that the singing had stopped the only sound was the drumming on the tin can and the sound of Rahamim's breathing. He was bathed in sweat and the waist of his pants was soaked, and from time to time he blew onto his upper lip to get rid of a drop of perspiration that had splashed off his nose. Suddenly a throttled cry escaped from his lips. A shriek of pain or pleasure, and then another, and his face flushed darkly, and as his body went on writhing he stretched out his hand as if in a cry for help, as if the intensity of the pain or the pleasure that was producing one moan after the other from his mouth was too much for him to bear. The ugliness of the animal-like writhing and the moans that accompanied it, of the savage beating on the drum, was so powerful, dark, and fascinating that it hardly seemed ugly at all. Rahamim must have sensed our feelings from the way we stood there, silent and suspicious, momentarily defeated. A happy smile spread gradually over his face, a smile of gratification and relief. He went on shouting, rhythmic shouts, and the sounds emerging from his throat now sounded like cries of victory. The dull stupidity and resignation to disaster had vanished from his eyes, just as the heaviness and tension had vanished from his movements. His feet began to skip and stamp, and his torso followed as if all he wanted was to disappear, as if his whole being was bent on disappearing without leaving a trace.

At that moment Nahum came into the room, unnoticed by everyone but Rahamim, who stretched out his arms to him and made inviting gestures with his head. Under Nahum's arm was the velvet pouch containing his prayer shawl and prayer book, which he had taken with him when he'd left earlier in the evening for the evening prayers. He was in the habit of staying with his religious friends for the Friday-night meal and singing so as to avoid coming back to the room and watching us smoke and desecrate the Sabbath. His usual smile of embarrassed detachment was now enhanced by a special touch of solemnity, in honor of the Holy Sabbath Queen. He stood next to us, looking first at the dancing Rahamim and then at us watching him, unable to understand what was happening. For a moment he deliberated, then he walked over to his bed, put his ritual apparatus away, and sat down on his bed with his back to us. A smile of exaltation illuminated Rahamim's flushed, perspiring face. With mincing little steps he left the confines of the circle and advanced toward Nahum's bed. He glided around it until he was standing facing Nahum, and once more he stretched out his arms toward him and quivered as if an electrical current were passing through his body, his shoulders twitching and jiggling as if in search of their wings. Nahum's face blushed a deeper red than usual and he said: "What do you want of me?"

"What do you want of me?" Rahamim's arms came closer and almost touched him.

He recoiled and said: "Leave me alone. I'm asking you to stop it."

But Rahamim took no notice. He came even closer and touched Nahum's shoulder, inviting him to join in the dance.

"It's not right!" For the first time Nahum raised his voice, a tone we had not heard before. "It's not right! Please stop it. It's Shabbat!"

Rahamim seized his hand, pulled him to his feet, and succeeded in dragging him behind him for a few steps. Nahum freed himself and escaped to the other end of the room, where he sat down on somebody's bed, his shoulders slumped and his hands clasped, looking frightened and upset, the shy, wondering smile no longer on his face. Rahamim refused to give up his prey. With dancing steps, with suggestive movements and saucy winks, to the accompaniment of laughter and cries of encouragement from the rest of us, he advanced toward the place where Nahum had fled. Our shouts and guffaws returned the dance to its grotesque beginnings, making us forget the moments of danger when it had seemed like a struggle with death or the devil, like some ceremony of invocation and sacrificial dedication. Nahum called out to the approaching Rahamim, "Keep away from me, I don't want to see you!" Rahamim smiled with the generosity of a victor, a grotesquely forgiving, fawning, ingratiating smile. The fascinating power of the ugliness no longer worked on us, his sweat-soaked body was indefatigable, he seemed to have forgotten the secret of stopping, and if he had not been stopped by force he might have gone on and on until he wore himself out and fell to the ground, to the insistent beating of the tin drum with its cruel, stubborn demand to finish the dance to the end.

Muallem came into the room and surveyed the scene with angry little eyes. We spread out on either side of him as he advanced, but Rahamim seemed neither to hear nor understand, and perhaps he was incapable of stopping. The drumming stopped but he went on.

"Ben-Hamo!" called Muallem.

Rahamim froze, wet with perspiration, puffing and panting, barely able to keep on his feet, his body swaying backward and forward. With every breath he took he leaned over as if to fill his lungs from some invisible reservoir in front of him, and when he breathed out he straightened up, closed his eyes, and let his head fall back.

"Ben-Hamo! I'm talking to you!" yelled Muallem.

"Yes, sir," gasped Rahamim.

"Stand like a soldier when your commanding officer's talking to you!"

Rahamim tried to stand steady on his feet, his eyes clouding with their habitual glaze of dull stupidity. His hour was over.

"What the hell do you think you're doing?" inquired Muallem.

"We were having a bit of fun, sir," said Rahamim, gasping for breath. "I was making the boys laugh."

"I don't want any more of that kind of fun here, understand? Go take a shower and calm down."

"Yes, sir," said Rahamim, and went to sit on his bed to recover his breath.

The wrathful expression on Muallem's face relaxed slightly. He paced thoughtfully up and down the aisle for a moment and then sat down on

Alon's bed. "Come here and sit down," he said in a friendly tone. We gathered around, some of us sitting on the neighboring beds, others on the floor. Muallem evidently had something he wanted to say to us, but he didn't know how to begin. Rahamim took his toilet kit and walked to the door.

"Where do you think you're going?" shouted Muallem.

"To the showers, sir," said Rahamim.

"Wait for your sweat to dry first," said Muallem. "Look at you, wet and panting like a whore."

Rahamim returned.

"You'd be better off thinking about your trial," said Muallem. "You'll have plenty of time for your bloody dancing in the calaboose."

"Yes, sir," said Rahamim.

"What's new, guys?" said Muallem in the friendly tone he sometimes adopted toward us. I remembered what Arik had said about the evil that cloaked itself in cunning disguises, and tried to discern this evil concealed somewhere on Muallem's blank face, in his thick eyebrows, his small, sunken eyes, his long, hooked nose, his drooping upper lip with the thin mustache above it, which almost covered the lower one and made him look on the point of bursting into tears. But all I could discover was a certain embarrassment in the hands fumbling on his knees and the eyes that always avoided meeting those of the person he was speaking to.

"Sir," said Hedgehog, "why did they do it to us? The real reason?"

"There were reasons," said Muallem. "The CO found a shocking mess in here. And his blanket." He indicated Rahamim. "You know what it means to destroy army property? You know what a serious offense it is?"

"So why does everybody have to suffer because of him?" asked Peretz. "How come we get screwed because of his blanket?"

"In the army you're all like brothers," said Muallem. "Everyone's responsible for his mates. One for all and all for one. For good and bad. Anyhow, that's what the CO decided, and whatever he decides is right. What's all the fuss about? Why all this whining? I was supposed to go on leave too and I stayed behind because of you. Am I whining?"

"I've already forgotten what home's like," complained Zero-Zero. "And I live right here next to the camp. I don't even know what it feels like to be human being anymore."

"This is your home now!" cried Muallem. "And a good home too, believe me. What have you got to complain about? They give you food, meat three times a week, beds to sleep on, they educate you to be men, to succeed in life. A lot of people would be grateful to get what you're getting."

A few suppressed smiles appeared on the surrounding faces. Muallem shook his head contemptuously. "You're a bunch of spoiled little kids. What do you know about anything? You don't know how people live in this country, in the transit camps, in the new villages. You don't know how soldiers live in the army. You think you're soldiers? This is a vacation camp. Real soldiers do things in training that you lot don't even dream about, they get sent out on missions, they shed their blood for their country. And with your profiles you'll never see combat in your lives, you'll never get a whiff of live fire. And you complain. What's the big deal? You didn't get to go home for the weekend? So you'll go next week, or the week after. What's the big deal?"

For a moment there was silence. Muallem looked at Yossie Ressler's guitar lying on its side and surveyed us appraisingly. "Why don't you look on the bright side? Have a bit of a singsong with his violin — it'll do your hearts good. Instead of Ben-Hamo's belly dancing. Get it into your heads that this is your home. Once you understand that you'll be a lot happier, believe me. Your instructor isn't only your commander, he's like your father, and he wants you to be happy and turn out men."

He was about six months older than us, maybe a year. But the gap between us was so wide that his words didn't sound ridiculous to us. Even the cynics among us found them natural. He belonged to another generation, with absolute control over our fates.

Rahamim sat on his bed, not far from us, waiting obediently for his sweat to dry so he could go and take a shower. Then he lay flat on his back, panting for breath, pale and exhausted, with his hands at his sides. Suddenly he raised his knees to his stomach as if stabbed by some sharp pain, curled up in a ball, and buried his face in the folded blanket at the head of his bed. His back shook spasmodically.

"You'll be happy here," said Muallem, "as long as you don't step out of line. Soon it'll be winter. You know what life's like for most people in this country, for the people in the camps? Have you ever been in a transit camp when it's raining? Have you ever seen what happens when the wind blows people's tents away at night and their beds get wet and everything they own gets ruined? And what can they do about it? Families with old people and children without a roof over their heads?"

He looked around his audience and his eyes came to rest on the Jerusalemites, as if waiting for a reply. But there was none. His words had not struck a chord in the hearts of his audience. Albert the Bulgarian and Zackie and Peretz and all the other residents of the new immigrants' transit camps in the platoon had never spoken of their lives there as of some terrible misfortune; on the contrary — they were full of stories about their neighbors and friends and all the laughs they had and tricks they got up to. It was a different country, new, not quite ours. On the radio, in the newspapers, in the newsreels they spoke about the *maabarot* and showed pictures. Volunteer women went from house to house collecting old clothes and toys for their children. We even heard about families who took kids from the camps into their homes during the winter floods. But none of this seemed an actual part of real life; it was more like a kind of symbol, a metaphor for the disrupted world of our childhood, which would never be the same again.

"You think you've finished high school, you know all there is to know about life," said Muallem. "But life isn't books. Some people who never went to school and never read any books have got a lot more sense and understand more about life than all the professors in Jerusalem."

He looked at Rahamim lying curled up on his bed, his face buried in the folded blanket and his shoulders shaking.

"Go on Ben-Hamo, cry! Cry!" he called. "You've got a lot to cry about, believe me!"

Then he turned to us again. "The trouble with you is you've got no team spirit. No morale. Look at the other platoons in the company. They're always singing, always in good spirits, you don't catch them moaning and complaining all the time. With you guys everybody thinks about his own problems and nobody cares about anybody else. Come here, Ben-Hamo, come and sit with us."

Rahamim did not react. Everyone looked at him and smiled. His performance was over. It had happened so long ago that it was already hard to remember the details. It was hard to connect him to that strange hour of glory when he had pranced before us, confident of his power, intent on his purpose.

"Take you head out of your blanket when your commander speaks to you!" Muallem called to Rahamim.

Rahamim turned his face toward us. It was expressionless, and his eyes were dry, as dull and stupid as ever.

"Come over here and sit with us," repeated Muallem.

"Sir, I feel sick," said Rahamim, and his voice sounded choked, as if with suppressed laughter.

"So why were you carrying on like a whore?" asked Muallem.

"I wanted to make them laugh," said Rahamim, "because it was my fault they had to stay behind. It was because of my blanket the officers took their leave away."

"It's not funny, Ben-Hamo, it's bloody disgusting!"

Rahamim said nothing but kept his face turned toward us. A silence fell. Muallem stood up. "Go to sleep, Ben-Hamo, maybe you'll wake up with a clear head in the morning."

On that night at the end of the month of Elul I became aware of the absence of the voice that had shattered the nights of my childhood with its screaming. For as long as I could remember this voice would break into my sleep just before dawn, so regularly and vehemently that I would wake up a moment before the scream and wait for it to come and go, and sometimes I would go on sleeping and only a part of me, the part always alert to the changing shapes in my room and the sounds of the night outside, would tense and convey to me as I slept both the dread and the relief when it was over. On the winter nights, when the windows were closed, the voice would reverberate in the distance, dim and muffled, and I would have to assist the cry flung again and again into the darkness and complete it myself: *"Hatzi — lu! Hatzi — lu!"* — "Help! Help!" But on the summer nights the cry thundered stubborn and angry, full of wrath and vengeance, shaking the walls of the house. Even when I grew older and allowed myself to be convinced that the screamer in the night was only the beadle of the synagogue in the Yemenite quarter, calling the faithful to prayer in his Yemenite accent, *"Tefi — lo! Tefi — lo!"* my ears refused to depart from the version that had been implanted in them during so many hours of dread and mystery. No matter how hard I tried to overcome my fear and repeated the cry to myself and even moved my lips in the Yemenite pronunciation: *Tefilo! Tefilo!* I heard only *Hatzilu! Hatzilu!* — as if the two words had been stuck one on top of the other with the latter invariably triumphing over the former, and thus the desperate cry for help was repeated night after night, and nobody came to the rescue. I would concentrate all my powers of attention on the attempt to dismember the cry into its separate syllables, to peel off the extraneous layer, but it was no use. When the echo of the last cry died away, I would pull the sheet up over my head and try to hide from the danger as I had learned to do on the nights when robbers prowled outside and my mother and father took turns guarding the window of my room. Until the September nights came and the cry that rose from the Yemenite quarter called *"Sli — hot! Sli — hot!"** and there was no more ambivalence in the cry and no more rough, vehement, vengeful anger. The call to penitential

* The penitential prayers recited early every morning in the month preceding the Day of Atonement.

prayer rose in a chorus with the barking of the dogs and the crowing of the cocks and the creaking of a cart and the whistling of a pump from one of the orange groves, all the sounds of the night that stole into my room on the delicate currents of a soft, new breeze holding out the promise of autumn.

On that night at the end of Elul in the room gradually filling with the sounds of its sleeping occupants, it struck me with a kind of physical certainty that the New Year was really around the corner and autumn was truly on its way. I listened attentively to the mute night outside, which had no voice to cry the fears of the heart or its pity when the hour of penitence came, and for the first time in many weeks I realized that I no longer heard that voice.

CHAPTER 8

Breakfast in the mess hall was shrouded in a Sabbath gloom, transient and desolate as a house up for demolition, bleak and grim as a cheerless awakening. The hall smelled of the stale, lukewarm tea that had gone sour during the night, and the cold, hard-boiled eggs stared up at me like murky, jaundiced eyes. I looked at the mess tin in front of me and the food piled on it and I couldn't touch it. The faces of the people sitting next to me fell too and Hedgehog said, "Every Saturday it gets worse. It's revolting." He tipped the contents of his mess tin and the tea in his mug into the big, empty tin can standing in the middle of the table for leftovers. He smeared margarine on two slices of bread with the handle of his fork and we all did the same. A gleam of rebellion flashed in our eyes as we ceremoniously performed the demonstrative act. A sergeant in the chaplain corps looked at us reproachfully as he passed our table. Hedgehog said, "How I hate them, all those religious maniacs who think they've got the right to tell us what to do. You saw that fatso with the ugly mug — that's how they all spend their time in the army, prowling around the kitchens and guzzling their heads off, supervising meat pots and milk pots and driving everybody crazy. Why should we suffer because of them? Why can't we eat on Saturdays like normal human beings?"

"And what about at your own house?" asked Hanan. "Don't you observe the Sabbath and keep kosher and all the rest of it?"

"So what!" said Hedgehog, for whom this was evidently a sore point, indignantly. "So what? Am I married to my family? The minute I finish with the army I'm leaving home. Getting out for good. I've got my own ideas about how I want to live. Who says I have to live like them?"

"I still remember you when you had side locks, and you used to hide them behind your ears and come to Zion Square to sit on the railings and look for fights," said Avner. "You weren't such a saint then either."

"They made me do all that stuff," said Hedgehog. "They're primitive people. From the day I remember myself, I hated it. And later on, when I saw how they sold things on the black market in their shop, I began to realize that there was no connection between honesty and justice and all that religious bullshit. I saw that it was all hypocrisy and I hated it. But to this day I can't eat on Yom Kippur. I swear. I tried, when there was nobody at home, and I couldn't put a bite of food into my mouth. They really brainwashed me, boy! That fear's so deep, it's become part of my nature. I just can't do it. Every year I say to myself, *This time I'm going to eat on Yom Kippur and get it over with,* and every time I can't do it. I'm so scared, my stomach just turns right over inside me!" He laughed in amazement at himself and added, "And I don't even believe in God and all those stories. But Yom Kippur is stronger in me than God and the whole Jewish people."

After we returned to the room, Zackie said to Hedgehog, "I heard what you said in the mess. You've got no shame. Anyone who eats on Yom Kippur isn't a Jew, it makes no difference what he believes or doesn't believe."

"What do I care if I'm a Jew or not a Jew?" said Hedgehog angrily. "I'm an Israeli. And when you're Israelis, you'll feel the same way."

"And what are we now?" demanded Zackie. "Jew? Arab? Dog? What?"

Hedgehog did not reply.

"What kind of a way is that to talk?" said Zackie. "And the way you talked last night when we were singing?" The merry, good-humored Zackie's face was taut with tension and his eyes flashed. "Who d'you think you are anyway? A king? A professor? What do you know about us anyway, to talk about us like we're shit? We're good enough to go to the army, but we're not good enough to sing our songs or say what we think? You think I don't know how you talk about us behind our backs? How you make fun of us with your mates, copying the way we say things in Hebrew, making jokes about it? What d'you think? You think we can't hear you? And you — what's so great about you? All you've got is a big mouth. You're like a matchstick. One *foo!* and anyone could knock you over. So where the hell do you get off laughing at other people?"

There was an uneasy silence after Zackie's long complaint. His friends stood around him as if he were their spokesman. Hedgehog was embarrassed: "What's the matter? Can't you take the truth? Why're you always getting so insulted all the time? Did anyone touch you? You're got an inferiority complex, that's your problem. You think people want to insult you all the time. When you get rid of your inferiority complex, maybe you'll begin to be Israelis like us."

"If being an Israeli means I have to be like you," said Zackie, "you can shove it up your ass. I'd rather be an Arab."

"Do me a favor," said Hedgehog, "leave me alone. I don't want to argue with you."

Zackie turned his back on Hedgehog, and he and his friends retired to their corner of the room. Hedgehog was left standing by himself in the middle of the aisle, and Hanan called to him, "You're not normal, Hedgehog. What do you have to argue with them for?" He added in English, "I wouldn't give a tinker's damn."

"What does he want of my life?" said Hedgehog. "Do I owe him anything? Is it my fault they lumped us all together in one platoon? Am I supposed to solve his inferiority complex for him?"

"What are you so mad about?" asked Avner. "What harm do they do you?"

"I'll tell you what I'm so mad about! I love this lousy country, I want it to be a terrific place, a place where it's great to live, I don't want everything that was built up here to go down the bloody drain! Maybe that sounds like slogans and Zionist propaganda to you, but I'm thinking about myself, about the kids I'll have one day, I want this to be a decent, modern, civilized place. Why shouldn't I? It's what any normal human being wants."

"You know how many new immigrants were killed in the War of Independence — the battle for Latrun, for example?" said Alon. "They took them off the ships and threw them straight into that terrible battle. Most of them weren't Israelis according to our lights. They didn't know Hebrew, they didn't know anything about the country. They didn't even manage to see it. They didn't understand the commands. They didn't understand each other. Everyone spoke a different language. There were sabras and new immigrants there. Ashkenazis and Sephardis. Students and workers. And the blood they shed was the same blood. There was no difference."

"What kind of example is that?" asked Hedgehog. "An example of a total screwup? What's so inspiring about Latrun? The blood that was spilled in vain? It doesn't inspire me. Every time you say the word *blood,* you sound as if it turns you on. When I see blood I nearly faint. I'm not against wars; on the contrary, if something has to be done by force, then the quicker the better. I want us to be strong, but not because the thought of blood gives me a thrill. We have to be strong so that we can live a normal life here, like in any other state in the world."

"Love sanctified by blood, you will blossom between us again," Micha the Fool quoted solemnly.

"I don't understand you, Alon," said Hedgehog.

"There are things you don't understand," said Alon without elaborating.

Hedgehog shrugged his shoulders. But he couldn't bring himself to let Alon have the last word, and after a pause for reflection he said: "And there are some things that even you don't understand."

"I didn't mean to hurt your feelings," said Alon.

"You didn't. I agree with you that each of us knows certain things and doesn't know other things, depending on his point of view, education, background, and so on."

"My father fell in the War of Independence," said Alon, "and when I say *blood,* I mean something real, something true and deep. Not everyone can understand it like I do."

"With all due respect," said Hedgehog, "I didn't mean to mock, God forbid. I, for your information, grew up in Jerusalem under the siege and our house was quite close to the Jordanian Legion. I saw people getting killed. I know what it means. But I'm talking about the goal, the purpose of it all. The blood is the price, not the goal. The goal is for us to be a normal state, where people can lead a good life."

"What's been created here up to now," said Alon, "isn't yet the state. It's only the beginning. This whole country will be ours one day. And there'll be more wars. And more blood spilled. Maybe it'll take a hundred years, I don't know how long. That's the way normal states always came into being. Read history. You don't understand. Something much bigger and grander than you imagine is being created here."

Avner said, "You're upsetting Hedgehog with your historical visions. All he wants is to get through the army as easily as possible and begin to make money. As much money as possible. He'll buy half Jerusalem first and then the whole country. You can trust him."

"What have you got against it?" cried Hedgehog. "What's wrong with making money? Does it hurt anyone, is it at anyone else's expense? Does it harm the state? Sure I want to make money. Lots of money. And how! I'm going to put everything I've got into it. So what? I'm not a kibbutznik, I don't think money's dirty. What are you looking down your nose about all of a sudden, Avner, don't you want to make money?"

Avner did not reply. He hated arguments. He smiled and sat down on his bed.

Suddenly there was a cry from Miller's bed. He lifted his knapsack and displayed it to us: There was a hole the size of a fist in it, and when Miller shook it slightly scraps of material and paper fell out of the hole onto the floor at his feet. There was an expression of horror on his face. "What is this? What happens here?" he mumbled. He dropped the knapsack onto his bed and shrank from it as if he were afraid to touch it. We all gathered to inspect the marvel. There was a look of suppressed glee on the faces around me; nobody imagined that it might happen to him too.

"He must've brought food with him, a piece of bread or something," said Sammy. "They smell it and they want to get in to eat. Take everything out," he added to Miller. "Empty it out, so it doesn't get back in."

"No," said Miller. "Perhaps she is inside?"

"Who?"

"The mouse," said Miller. "Perhaps inside, eating." And he recoiled in horror from his bed.

"Let me," said Avner. "I'll open it for you. There's no mouse. He was only there in the night. He ran away long ago."

"No," said Miller. "No open."

"What have you got in there?" asked Alon.

"Nothing," said Miller. "I have nothing there."

I wondered if he had transferred his diaries from the little suitcase to the knapsack, where they had fallen victim to the rat's teeth. Or perhaps they were cherished letters, which he carried about with him wherever he went? I looked at the flakes of white paper heaped up in a little mound on the concrete floor, and I didn't know why this thought gave me a feeling of satisfaction. Did I hate his foreignness, his refugeedom? Did I see him as a messenger from another world, dark and inimical, the world of the walking dead who had come to spy on us and record every detail of our daily lives in his notebooks? It sometimes seemed to me that he was storing up damning evidence against us there, and beneath that ludicrous disguise, that foreignness and anonymity, that marionette leaping and falling on the brink of the abyss between life and death, I sometimes tried to discover the open eye observing us in secret, penetrating every hiding place, ruthless and uncompromising.

"No! Leave knapsack alone!" cried Miller. "Mouse inside knapsack!"

But Avner took no notice. He opened the knapsack and emptied its contents on the floor at the foot of Miller's bed. Miller shrank back in alarm, and the anxiety in his small, dry eyes revealed that it was not only the appearance of the mouse he feared, but the exposure of his privacy, bundled up and hidden away like a bad dream, encrusted with layers of soiled underwear and socks and a few crumpled articles of civilian clothing and old newspapers and books and a flat tin box and various other unidentifiable objects. And there, in the middle of the pile, lay the remnants of an old sandwich, wrapped in tatters of gnawed, greasy, disintegrating paper, which he must have brought with him when he arrived at the base weeks before and forgotten. Crumbs of black bread and bits of broken crust were all that was left of the sandwich, spotted with dark mouse droppings and tatters of gray-white paper, like a shameful souvenir of some ancient, squalid gluttony. All the spilled baggage that we inspected with curiosity, disgust, and a terrible glee, searching for clues to the solution of Miller's mystery, lay exhibited on the concrete floor like the ripped-out guts of some living creature, still quivering secretly in the longing for a lost warmth it had once possessed.

Actually there was little difference between Miller's things and those in our own knapsacks, but the violence of their exposure was like the revelation of some strange, disgraceful secret. We had long since ceased to feel any shame in displaying our nakedness to each other, but there was something in this sight incomparably more shameful and stinging than any nakedness. The diary wasn't there. It must have been left inside the little suitcase and saved from catastrophe.

Miller stood to one side, in fear of the mouse or in the attempt to deny any connection with the squalid spectacle of his possessions spread out on the floor, wringing his hands and shaking his head, nodding sadly as if in acknowledgment of a disaster that had overtaken somebody else, mumbling, "No good, no good."

After a few minutes he was left alone next to his exposed disgrace. Standing at a little distance from the pile he poked it gingerly with the toe of his boot, and after satisfying himself that the mouse was not hiding somewhere among his possessions, he squatted down next to them and began examining them one by one to assess the damage. And every time he picked a pair of underpants or a sock or a piece of paper from the pile and held it with the tips of his fingers he would nod his head sadly, as if confirming to himself the inexpressible extent of his loss, and repeat, "No good. No good."

Alon said in a lowered tone, almost a whisper, so that Miller would not overhear him, "At home on the kibbutz there was a woman who came from the camps. She seemed fine, she didn't talk much, and she never spoke about the war. She fit in. She was well liked. An excellent worker. Well educated. Cultured. Wonderful Hebrew. Everything. After about ten years she got sick and died. They found bread in her room. In the drawers. The closet. Tins under her bed. All over the place. All those years she'd been taking bread from the dining room. Hiding it in her room for a rainy day. It was something that stuck in her head from over there."

"Everyone who comes from there," said Micky, "has got to have something wrong with him. It stands to reason. Nobody who went through that could come out physically or mentally normal. The strong ones manage to hide it. But when they're alone and there's nobody to see they break down, I'm sure." In the meantime Miller finished sorting out his possessions, transferring part of them to the little suitcase and leaving the rest lying on the floor with the damaged knapsack. He pushed the pile cautiously to the foot of his bed and sat down to think. Over the past few days his cup of suffering had apparently brimmed over.

Micky returned to his book. Alon took out a bundle of newspapers he had been sent from the kibbutz, laid them on his bed, and began leafing through them.

"You're playing against *Hapoel* Petah Tikva today," he said to Micky.

"They are, you mean," said Micky. "And no miracle's going to save them either. They'll be demoted to the second league with Balfouria. But I don't give a damn, believe me. I've finished with all that."

"What do you mean?" exclaimed the shocked Alon. "How can you just walk away all of a sudden, and after everything you've achieved?"

"It wasn't all of a sudden," said Micky. "When the medical examinations began and dragged on and on I had plenty of time to think about it. And then came the verdict. It took nearly a year. Don't think it wasn't a crisis for me. It was bloody tough. I was in a real depression. But I decided not to fight lost battles. I don't have the least desire to be a Don Quixote. If they decided I'm an invalid, that's it. The only thing I could do was cut off all connections until I began to feel that the whole thing was a mistake from the word *go*. And believe me: Today I can't even work up enough interest to go and see a soccer match or read about it in the newspaper. I'm not interested in meeting the guys from the team. Before it was almost my whole world. And now it's over. As far as I'm concerned it's over. I'll find something else I can be good at without fears or restrictions."

"Yesterday, when we were playing, I thought you seemed happy, as if it reminded you of something," said Alon.

"Yes, my childhood."

Yossie Ressler began tuning his guitar. As usual, a slight pressure on the key, tightening or slackening one of the strings, would result in a kind of screech, like a shriek of pain. As if pain was the price that had to be paid for being in tune. Then a sequence of chords followed one close on the heels of the other, bathing the sweltering air of the room in the heat of the approaching noon with cool, exquisite waves.

"'Begin says that Israel should have occupied the whole of the Strip on the night we attacked Khan Yunis. In his opinion it was a missed opportunity to kick the Egyptians out of the Gaza Strip for good,'" read Alon from his newspaper.

"And you think he's right?" asked Micky.

"Are you crazy?" said Alon. "Me — and Begin? All those places are ours by rights. They're part of this country. We don't need Begin to lead us there."

"But you do need Gaza. It has to be part of the state of Israel."

Alon did not reply. He went on reading the newspaper, but it was obvious that he was hurt by Micky's irony.

"You hope it'll happen in the second round. Everything depends on us. If everybody thinks like you do we won't stand a chance in the second round," said Alon and went on turning the pages of the newspapers. "Are you interested in archaeology?"

Micky pursed his lips as if considering his reply. "Not particularly."

"If I was going to college that's what I'd want to study. But I'm not going to college."

"What makes you ask?"

"Do you remember the epic of Gilgamesh?"

"I remember learning something about it at school."

"Imagine — a shepherd from Kibbutz Meggido goes out with his flock in the vicinity of the ancient tel. And suddenly he finds a tablet written in cuneiform. He passes it on to the archaeologists. They decipher it. And they discover that it's part of the epic of Gilgamesh. A story someone wrote more than three thousand five hundred years ago. And they read part of that story, the part about Gilgamesh's friend Enkidu. Enkidu is sick, dying. And the fragment from the Meggido tel is about Gilgamesh's sorrow for his friend, who's going to die. Can you understand that? A story from Babylon. From over three thousand years ago. Suddenly it comes to light here. In Israel. Next door to where you live. And in Hatzor they discover Herod's palace. And in Nahal Lever, next to Ein Gedi, a cave. Near the ruins of the Roman camps. A cave full of skeletons. Apparently women and children who died of starvation under the Roman siege. And next to the skeletons, sandals. Shreds of clothing. Remains of food. And a big potsherd with Hebrew letters on it. As if it all were waiting for us. For us to come and discover it. And now it's all bursting out all over the place. As if this faithful earth preserved it all for us. Our roots. When you see the antiquities — when you feel them — it's amazing. It's not like reading the Bible or Josephus Flavius. Bar-Kochva's warriors. Maybe they were like Arik Sharon's and Meir Har-Zion's guys today. Men who know every wadi, every bush. Who can smell out every path, every ruin, from miles away. Who don't know the meaning of fear. Three, four guys stealing up on a whole enemy company and taking them out."

"I'll tell you something that'll probably shock you rigid," said Micky. "The story of Gilgamesh grieving for his dying friend moves me more, much more, than the skeletons in Bar-Kochba's caves."

"Sure!" said Alon bitterly. "Because you feel closer to the Romans than to the Jews. You hate the defeated, the failures, even if they're your own people. You hate your own little nation. Which revolted against the strongest state in the world. Fought and fought and didn't give up. But failed in the end."

"Not at all," said Micky. "That's simply not true. The important thing is that I can imagine it, I can feel what it must be like for a good friend to be sick and dying, and you can't save him, all you can do is sit by his side and wait for it to happen. That's a feeling I can understand, I can live it in my imagination."

"*Nation* is just a word to you. You don't believe in it at all. If you can believe in friendship between two people, why can't you understand the bond between a lot of people living together, which is what constitutes a nation?"

"That's too big for me," said Micky.

"Haven't you got any dreams?" asked Alon.

"Why?"

"Nothing big begins without a dream. Everything begins with a dream, don't you understand?"

A shout of "Attention!" came from the door. We all jumped to attention in front of our beds. Muallem came in. He gave the command "At ease!" The smile, which resembled a tearful grimace, appeared on his face. "I hope you're all taking advantage of the opportunity to rest and get your strength up for next week," he said. "If you behave yourselves, you'll get an after-duty pass to go out for a couple of hours this evening, until eleven o'clock."

Cheers broke out. Muallem's face darkened. At his shout of "Attention!" an instant silence fell. "This is the army, not a bloody vacation camp. What's all the shouting about? What are you — a lot of little kids? To repeat: If you behave yourselves there'll be an after-duty leave this evening. I'll hand out the passes after supper. Two of you stay behind on guard. Are there any volunteers? . . .

". . . No volunteers," he concluded. "Okay, I'll volunteer you." He looked down the two lines of men and said: "Ressler, Yossie, and Gabai, Avner."

Muallem left the room and everybody clustered round in groups, arguing about how to spend the evening out. Avner lay down on his bed again. I thought he was depressed about having to stay behind on the base, but he must have read my thoughts, because he suddenly sat up and said: "I don't give a damn. What can you do in a few hours? By the time you get out you have to start coming back again to make it to the base in time. I don't have the least desire to cruise the streets with all these characters or go to a movie with them. It doesn't interest me. Right now I need something else and this after-duty isn't it."

"Maybe we'll get leave next Friday?" I said.

"We have to," said Avner. "We have to." And he sank into thought, frowning and rubbing the stubble on his head with the palm of his hand. Then he looked at me again and said: "Someone has to stay, so why the hell not Gabai, Avner?" But I knew that he was really upset and that he was actually dying to go out with everyone else.

Hedgehog cried: "Zero-Zero, we're all coming with you to visit your wife!"

"Go visit your sister!" said Zero-Zero.

"I'm starving," said Avner. "This morning I couldn't eat a thing." The book *The Elements of Hebrew Grammar* was lying next to him open at the first pages. He hadn't made much progress in preparing for his exam. He lit a cigarette, lay down on his back, and stared at the ceiling.

At the end of the room near the door a commotion broke out. Peretz and Zackie and their mates were playing at throwing a matchbox onto the floor, points being awarded or lost according to the way it fell. They often spent their leisure hours at this game, but this time they were playing for money, despite the fact that it was expressly forbidden in GROs. For a long time the coins passed from hand to hand, until Zackie suddenly jumped up and accused Peretz of cheating him out of his win by deliberately blowing his cigarette smoke onto the matchbox — which had landed standing upright on its shortest side, gaining him the whole kitty — and making it fall onto its broadest surface, which meant losing points. At first Peretz denied the charge with an indignant expression and shrill laughter, intended to demonstrate his offense and astonishment. But Zackie refused to withdraw his accusation, swearing on his eyes and the lives and honor of his family that he had seen the matchbox standing and Peretz blowing hard onto it and making it fall.

Peretz lost his composure. He shouted: "Zackie, you know me! Just don't start with me. You dunno what the fuck you're talking about. The money's making you crazy in the head. I don't care about the money, I care about my honor. Just don't call me a cheat! What am I, a thief?"

"Yes!" cried Zackie. "You're a thief! I saw you do it!"

"My nerves're starting to go crazy, Zackie, I'm telling you, I can feel it. Leave off or I dunno what'll happen here."

"I'm not afraid of you and your nerves!" yelled Zackie. "You Moroccan thief!"

Zackie got off the bed where the players were sitting and stood confronting Peretz, his eyes boiling with rage and his face pale. His torso was covered with black hair, like a furry pelt, as were his arms and shoulders and the top of his back, all the way up to his chin. For a moment they stood very close to each other, their lips trembling and muttering words in Arabic. "Go on, touch me," said Zackie, "let's see you, hero. You're a thief! Let's see you, Mister Moroccan knife. You won't take my money. Nerves, nerves, I'm sick of hearing about your bloody nerves. You think I don't have nerves! Everybody saw what you did, I'm not scared of you or your bloody knife. Take it out, go on." He flung out his hand and let it hang in the air over the head of his opponent, who remained rooted to the spot, only his cigarette trembling between his lips — the cigarette that was an accomplice in his crime, that was growing shorter and shorter, the lengthening cylinder of ash about to drop at any minute. Zackie's hand was still waving in the air over his head.

Peretz said: "You won't take the money. It's not yours. It belongs to everybody."

"I will take it," said Zackie. "It's my money and I'm taking it." And he drew in his arm and squatted on the floor, reaching for the coins. Peretz squatted too and slapped his hand down on the coins before Zackie could get there. He spat the cigarette out and crushed it with his heel, then thrust his face into Zackie's with a menacing expression. Zackie tried to shove Peretz's hand off the money, and they began to fight. Peretz leapt to his feet, clenched his fists, and yelled: "Come on, shitface, come on, put 'em up, let's see you fight like a man, come on, come on, put 'em up!" Zackie stood up, but before he had time to hit him, Peretz landed a punch in his belly that made him crumple up, his face twisted in pain. Peretz brandished his fists again, taking a step backward to increase the power of his punch, at which point Rahamim Ben-Hamo suddenly jumped off the bed where he was sitting with the rest of the players and faced Peretz, interposing his plump body between Zackie, who was straightening up to resume hostilities, and his assailant, who yelled: "Get out of the way, you whore, take your nose out of my business, this is between men here!"

But Rahamim did not budge, and even after Zackie shoved him violently out of the way he resumed his stance between the opponents, crying in his ridiculous, plaintive whine: "You're a liar, you crook! I saw you. You cheated him, you're just a crook!"

Peretz spat out a few sentences in the Moroccan dialect under his toothbrush mustache in a quiet, very dangerous voice, and Rahamim replied in Hebrew, so that we would all understand: "I don't care what you do to me, I'll say what I saw."

In the meantime most of the platoon had gathered around, but no one tried to separate them. Peretz fell on Rahamim and hit him. Rahamim collapsed on the floor, protecting his head with his arms while he went on crying shrilly: "I don't care what you do. You can hit me as much as you like."

Zackie jumped on Peretz from the side. They fell to the ground in a clinch and lay there wrestling. When Rahamim realized that he was no longer in danger, he stood up and, after looking at the wrestling pair for a moment, again tried to pull them apart. This time both of them set upon him together, whether because he was preventing them from settling the score between them or because he provided an easier target on which to vent their rage than each other was hard to tell.

Albert the Bulgarian now intervened and with one hefty shove sent them both flying. "You're crazy," he said, "because of you they'll cancel our after-duty. Come on, break it up," and he began to laugh at the sight of them panting and sweating, still seething with rage. Zackie's black fur was dripping with sweat, and Peretz lit another cigarette with shaking hands. Rahamim lay on the floor with blood trickling from his nose. Slowly he rose to his feet, his painful movements and twisted face giving rise to general laughter. With every step he took he tottered grotesquely and almost lost his balance. Even though we had all seen him take a severe beating, it was impossible not to sense the exaggerated, ludicrously theatrical nature of his attempts to arouse our sympathy for his sufferings and admiration for his heroism. He went on limping, swaying, and tottering, spreading out his arms as if groping for something to hold on to, until his hand encountered one of the beds in his way, and thus he tottered from bed to bed, looking around him with dreadful eyes. And this pantomime of a Via Dolorosa came more and more to resemble his dance of the night before. Until I seemed to see in his beaten face, splattered with the blood pouring from his nose and contorted in an expression of anguished pain, a kind of brightening, some shadow of a smile of satisfaction, and perhaps even of complicity and response to the laughter of those enjoying his performance.

When he reached his bed he sat down slowly, took off his torn undershirt with heartbreaking groans, rolled it into a ball, and pressed it to his nose, gasping for breath and sighing deeply as he did so. Then he tried to lower himself gradually into a recumbent position but could not manage it until he flung the upper half of his body backward with one violent jerk. When he laid his head on the end of the bed his face twisted again, and a piercing birdlike shriek escaped his lips. The laughter died down. Now he lay still and silent on the bed. From time to time he removed the blood-soaked T-shirt from his nose, inspected the spreading stain, found a clean, white bit, and put it back again.

Peretz and Zackie turned their backs on each other. Their mates tried to effect a reconciliation, urging them to shake hands like good sports, but they took no notice and continued with their mutual recriminations.

"Take the lousy money, go on, take it, Moroccan thief," said Zackie.

Alon went up to them: "First you play games for money, which you know is forbidden in the army, and then you start a roughhouse. The whole platoon'll get screwed because of you. Give it a rest, for pete's sake."

"You mind your own bloody business, " said Peretz. "And don't you try and teach me nothing. I don't take no lessons from you about what to do and not to do. Who d'you think you are anyway, God? You think you're the only one around here knows what's right and wrong?"

Alon retreated. Peretz looked at Zackie and muttered something under his breath in Moroccan. Zackie said: "Go on, take my money, go on, take it." And Peretz began collecting the coins, which had been scattered round the concrete floor during the fight, and putting them in his pocket. He said: "It's all of ours. And I'm keeping it."

Zackie went up to Rahamim's bed and looked at him with disgust. "Get up, whore," he said. "Fix your clothes and stop putting on an act. Unless you want the whole platoon to get fucked again because of you." Rahamim did not reply. Zackie lifted his leg and gave him a light kick. "Stop it. Get up and fix your clothes. Go wash your face, so's they won't see the blood. Watch it, Ben-Hamo, I'm telling you. Just watch it."

"Okay," said Rahamim. "Don't worry."

Avner lay on his bed, his fists clenched and his whole body tense. "Have you finished laughing?" he asked me when I approached my bed. "It's a big laugh, isn't it, to see the little savages fighting and cursing over a few pennies and that degenerate Ben-Hamo putting on his dirty act."

"Yesterday, when he was dancing, you laughed and clapped too," I said.

"Man, I'm ashamed," said Avner. "I'm really ashamed. When they started hitting Ben-Hamo instead of each other, I suddenly had an urge to get up and lay into him too. I could hardly control myself. He's beginning to get on my nerves. I would have torn him to pieces, beaten him to a pulp, believe me. I would never have thought myself capable of it. Where does it come from, this hatred, this evil? I don't know. But there's a lot of evil inside me. And the strength it gives me! I felt that I could move mountains. And now, when he was limping to his bed with blood dripping from his nose, I hated him even more. Suddenly I began feeling furious about not going out tonight. As if that were his fault too. What do I know about him at all? What right have I got to hate him so much? I don't know. I felt as if I had a murderer I couldn't control inside me. And you all stood there laughing."

"I don't think I'm better than anyone else."

"Liar. You do think so. That's exactly your problem. You observe the rest of us as if we were animals."

"Why does the fact that we laughed bother you so much?" I asked.

"If it had happened between Micky and Alon or between them and Hedgehog or any of the other little darlings, would you have laughed then too? Or maybe you think it could never have happened to them, they're too civilized, too refined — such things only happen between dirty, primitive Oriental scum, right?"

He spoke in a whisper so that the others wouldn't hear, and the undertone imbued his words with a kind of pale, bitter rage.

"I thought you weren't interested in that whole business of Sephardis and Ashkenazis. Yesterday you told Hedgehog that it wasn't your problem."

"Then I was lying," said Avner. "It is my problem, why should I hide it? Hedgehog said to Zackie that it was all an inferiority complex. Okay, so I've got an inferiority complex. At least as far as this is concerned. Why do you think I was so mad about classical music? And why do I hang around you guys all the time? And it's not easy, believe me. So what — Hedgehog's got an inferiority complex too, because he's so weak and skinny and he hates his family. Okay, so that's his problem. And I've got my problem."

"And is that what made you so mad at Ben-Hamo? That he was letting your side down?"

"It's not only that," said Avner. "Look —" He paused for a moment to gather his thoughts and find the right formula, despaired, flattened his hand, held it up in front of his face, and hit himself on the nose with it, saying: "*Bzzzz . . . Wham!* Slap into the glass again!"

"What are you doing?"

"Did you ever see a hornet flying into a room and not knowing how to get out? Next to our house there's some sort of hornets' nest. Sometimes one of them gets into the room. When it wants to get out again it keeps banging into the windowpane, because it thinks that it's the outside. Then it retreats, zooms around the room, back to the window, and *wham!* it crashes into the pane again. And the other half of the window is open right there next to it, an inch away, but it can't tell the difference between the transparent glass and the open window and the real outside. It simply makes for the direction of the light. And so it keeps on coming up against the glass, without ever reaching the open window. Unless by a lucky chance it flies in that direction. Or maybe it suddenly senses the air coming from outside, I don't know, I'm not an expert on hornets. Anyway, the whole performance drives me mad, I can't stand watching it. In the end I get up and grab hold of something and crush it against the windowpane. And believe me, it's not because I'm afraid of getting stung. It's their blind stupidity that makes my blood boil. It fills me with hatred, with a terrible cruelty that makes me kill it."

"In the Luna Park," I said, trying to take up his metaphor, "there's a kind of labyrinth of mirrors where people get lost. They can't get out because of the optical illusion. You keep thinking you've found the exit, and then suddenly you find yourself confronting your own face in a mirror blocking your way out."

"It's been happening to me too often lately," said Avner. When he saw the incomprehension on my face he added: "But you don't know about that, it's something between me and myself." He blew his cigarette smoke out in rings and watched them rising and expanding and disappearing.

When we went to the mess for lunch Rahamim had already recovered, except for a pinkish bruise on his face and a slight limp. As usual after his performances he retreated into himself, withdrawing from his friends and going to stand alone at the end of the line. Zackie suddenly approached him and without any superfluous preliminaries said: "I'm warning you, just don't make any trouble —"

Rahamim cut him short: "Okay, okay, don't worry. If anybody asks I'll say I fell in the dark when I went to take a piss."

"Yes, you say that," said Zackie. "Act like a human being." He looked at Ben-Hamo coldly for a moment and said: "You're nothing but trouble, Ben-Hamo, nothing but trouble."

We picked out whatever was edible from the revolting Sabbath meal on our plates and Avner said: "For God's sake bring me something when you come back tonight, pita if you can and maybe falafel. One of these Saturdays I'm going to die of hunger here. I'll begin chewing up the knapsacks like that rat."

I didn't know yet what I was going to do in the evening or whom I should join. Hedgehog and the Jerusalemites intended to go to the next-door *maabarot* where — so they had heard — there was a cinema, a café, and pretty girls. In the café, they said, there was music and dancing. Hanan hoped that the radio was tuned to Ramallah, where there was a *Saturday Night Hit Parade.* He was an admirer of Frankie Laine's, knew the words of all his songs, and could do a good imitation of his sentimental voice. Micha the Fool announced in the Arab announcer's English: "The Brrroadcasting Serrrvice of the Hashemite Kingdom of Jorrrdan . . ." to the delight of his friends, who were all devoted fans of the broadcasting station in question.

In the middle of the excitement and anticipation Sammy, who had not been seen since that morning, came into the room and went straight up to Avner.

"There's a girl waiting for you next to the Jerusalem Gate. Maybe she's your big sister. She says her name's Aliza. She's asking everyone who goes past if they know you. Lucky I met her. She's come from Jerusalem to see you. Lucky for you that I passed there."

Avner leapt off his bed and stood there for a moment with a furious, distraught expression on his face. I imagined that he was angry at the unexpected, unwanted visit.

"Come with me," said Sammy. "I'll show you a hole in the fence that'll lead you straight to the Jerusalem Gate."

"Wait a minute," said Avner. "Just give me a minute."

He rubbed his head, bit his lips, and sat down on his bed. He began to get dressed. And all the time his eyes were narrowed in an expression of painful concentration. In the middle of lacing his boots he suddenly straightened up and beat his fists on the bed: "Godammit! Why can't I go out tonight? What am I going to do with her now?"

He looked at me as if consult me on his plight, but I had no suggestions to offer. Sammy stood opposite him with a knowing smile on his face. Unlike me, he had apparently grasped that the girl was not Avner's sister.

"If I didn't have that bloody guard tonight, I could go to her now and tell her to wait for me somewhere and meet me later on this evening. What am I going to do with her now?" He raised his face and fixed me with his eyes, which were a more piercing black than I had ever seen in my life, under the thick black eyebrows that met over the top of his nose; perhaps these were the eyes of the murderer who according to him was hiding inside him and over whom he had no control? He did not take his eyes off me, but gradually the look in them cleared and turned into a pleading smile, full of gratitude in advance, leaving me no option but to say: "I'll stay in your place."

He stood up, his face shining with solemn joy, placed his hand on my shoulder, and said: "You're a real friend! I'll never forget it, never!"

"No problem," I said. "I wasn't crazy about going out anyway. I don't mind staying."

"No!" he cried in a hurt tone, as if I had spoiled this exalted moment. "Why do you say that? Say that you're dying to go out but you're prepared to stay behind for my sake, because you know how important it is to me."

"I'm in a hurry," said Sammy. "Are you coming with me?"

"Yes," said Avner, but suddenly his face clouded over. Some detail was evidently not yet taken care of to his satisfaction. He said: "I'll talk to Muallem and get him to agree to the swap. Don't worry."

"I'm not worried," I protested. "What's the problem?"

"I don't know," said Avner. He looked intently into my face, perhaps trying to account for the sourness and discontent that were presumably only too evident in my expression.

"Then what is it?" he asked. "What's wrong?"

I flattened my hand, raised it in front of my face and banged it against my nose: *"Bzzz . . . Wham!"* I said. "Bang into the glass."

Avner grinned in embarrassment and impatience. "If you just think about what you're missing tonight, then maybe you'll begin to understand what it means."

After he left with Sammy, I did think about it. I couldn't come up with a single reason for regretting what I was missing, except for Avner's conclusions about the depth of our friendship and the extent of the sacrifice I was making on his behalf, which had been thrust on me like some disagreeable burden. Even the thought that I was now making amends in some way for what I had done to him on that other guard did not lighten the imposition. I knew my behavior then was something I had to come to terms with and resolve in my own way, and at the moment the possibility of doing so seemed extremely remote.

"I hope they don't catch him crawling through that hole in the fence," said Micky. "It could screw us all."

"And you don't want to suffer for him?" asked Alon.

"Me?" said Micky in astonishment. "All of us! And you, do you think it's fair? I don't want anyone to suffer for me. I couldn't live with the feeling."

The feeling he referred to was familiar to me, so familiar that it filled me with self-disgust and resentment against Micky.

"Listen," said Micky, "I hate hypocrisy. If they catch him and it screws up our after-duty, no one will be crazy about Avner, I promise you. Even though most of them will pretend they don't care. Because Avner's one of us. But you saw what happened with Ben-Hamo, after they canceled our leave because of his blanket. It didn't win him any popularity contests in the platoon. Nobody felt the need to pretend in his case, because he's nobody's friend, he's God's orphan. People say things to his face they wouldn't dare say to anyone else. So that's not hypocrisy in your opinion? Why's it okay for Avner and not for Ben-Hamo? Because Avner's one of us? So that means he can screw us all and we have to take it?"

"Yes," said Alon. "That's right."

Micky was not surprised. He smiled and kept quiet, waiting for Alon to go on.

"You remember our argument on the first day we came here?" said Hedgehog. "I didn't know you and I was really shocked by what you said. I thought you'd changed your opinion since then."

Micky reacted with anger to this remark: "What the hell's going on here? What are you being so bloody pious about all of a sudden? If we all get screwed because of Avner I suppose you won't get mad? You won't think he's a shit?"

"No," said Hedgehog. "Because in his place I'd do the same thing. If my girlfriend was waiting for me outside. And if I was caught I'd want my friends to understand me and even be prepared to suffer for it. If they're my friends. When me and Ressler had to drag our beds to the company office for that parade, Avner got up and came to help us without anyone asking him to. And he knew that if he was caught he'd get it in the neck too. But that didn't stop him."

"With you everything's simple," said Micky. "You're prepared to suffer for your friends and for someone who once helped you and you owe him. As if it were a question of returning a loan. But you don't owe anything to Ben-Hamo and he's not a friend of yours, so you can curse him because he screwed up your leave?"

"Absolutely!" said Hedgehog. "What do you think? You think I feel the same about everybody in the world? Of course I've got friends and people I owe favors to, and other people I don't give a damn about and don't want to suffer for. So what? That's natural isn't it? I'm not a saint. What's hypocritical about it?"

"I once read in a zoology book," said Alon, whose chapped lips were parted in a strange smile, exposing his pointed teeth that looked like a beast of prey's, "about the philosophy of the frog. For a frog the world is divided into three categories. Creatures smaller than it is. Which it eats. Creatures the same size as it. With which it mates. And creatures bigger than it is. From which it flees. Everything's simple. But human beings sometimes sacrifice themselves, even for people they don't even know. That's the whole point. To help and suffer even for someone you don't like and don't owe anything to."

Sammy came back to the room with the same secretive, mysterious smile on his face. There was a pause in the conversation. After a few minutes Micky said to Alon: "I could agree with everything you said, if it had any connection to the real world we live in. But it's connected to a dream world."

"I've already told you," said Alon, "everything begins with a dream." And his face suddenly grew grave.

"Zero-Zero!" cried Hedgehog. "Have you got girls who don't make a fuss about opening their legs over there in your camp?"

"Go ask your sister," said Zero-Zero.

"But I don't have a sister! " cried Hedgehog plaintively. "What can I do?"

"Go ask your mother," suggested Zero-Zero.

"She can't stand me. She only wants my old man."

"So go ask Ben-Hamo, maybe he'll help you out," said Zero-Zero.

Sammy approached the corner where the Jerusalemites and Micky and Alon had their beds. "If you want a fuck, go to Gita. I can take you there," he said in the gruff voice that was in such contrast to his childish face.

"Who's she?" asked Micky. "A whore?"

The fresh-complexioned face with the ugly scar running down one cheek and the dead, sky-blue eyes twisted in a gratified smile. The was something revolting and horrifying in that smile, and in the bass laugh that followed it, something coarse and sinister. It represented something that was still beyond our comprehension.

Avner did not return until just before supper. As if he were tempting time, playing with the last moment like a loaded gun. He looked as if he were trying to hide some anxiety or excitement, and even made an effort to suppress the panting from his run.

"Is everything okay?" he asked.

"Yes," I said, "I'm glad you finally made it."

"Irony," he said, "irony. I always make it."

"Did you fix something up for tonight?"

"Yes. You haven't changed your mind?"

"No. Don't worry."

He smiled and said nothing. The Jerusalemites gathered around him as if they were waiting to hear how the meeting had gone, and Hanan, after referring humorously to Avner's hordes of "big sisters," crooned "My Little One" under his breath, imitating Frankie Laine's moaning voice, as if he too were a partner in Avner's secret and his amorous exploits. Avner looked at them with a politely skeptical smile, and at those moments, as we were putting on our uniforms and getting ready to go to supper, it was possible to sense a subtle but definite change gradually taking place in the vortex of faces and desires and small talk and shifting moods: This was the second time it had happened. The first was when Avner came back from jail, but this time it was clearer. All eyes were fixed on him, waiting for some word to fall from his lips, examining him for something with which to feed their imagination, their hopes, their longings. He sat on his bed like a victor, a tired smile on his lips, still panting and sweating slightly from his running, and I had no doubt that with that strange sensitivity of his, whose nature I did not yet understand, he was fully aware of what was happening around him, flowing like some subterranean current, seething secretly behind the smiles, the looks, the expectation, the protest, the pleading, and the insult. The skeptical smile never left his face. Perhaps he already understood that this terrible thirst demanded fantasy no less than water for its satisfaction. Was he enjoying his victory? I could not tell from the expression on his face, but he did not respond to the signals. It occurred to me that the spectacle I was witnessing, a dumb show of looks and gestures, was like the story of a poor family who had saved and scrimped for years to send a son out into the world to study and make his fortune, and when he comes home many years later to share his bounty with them, even as they finger the clothes he bought in foreign lands and wonder at his changed appearance and unaccustomed manners, they are already testing him, scrutinizing him, and their eyes are already crying: *Betrayal!* As if afraid their sacrifices have been in vain, as if despairing in advance of finding a way to the heart of this foreign guest; as if betrayal were a precondition of this deal. Avner wanted no part of this game; he refused the part assigned to him in the charade. He removed himself from the group that had collected around him and went over to Sammy, put his hand on the shoulder of his benefactor, and squeezed it with friendly warmth. He said something to him, maybe, *You're a real friend, I'll never forget this, never,* and his new, sinister ally responded with a wink and a muttered word or two.

When we went to the mess for supper Avner was quiet and looked worried, reserved, and tense. Only when the passes were handed out and Muallem had agreed to the substitution did an expression of relief and undisguised happiness appear on his face: "I was sure it wouldn't work out at the last minute. Until I had the pass in my hand I was sure he wouldn't agree. My lousy luck, you know. And then she would have waited and waited. I would have sent you to tell her not to wait, that there'd been a screwup. And now everything's all right! You know what it means — you know what it means to me? And to her! She told her husband she had to go to Lydda to visit her aunt who'd suddenly been taken ill. On Saturday! The stories she tells! She's really crazy. She left the house at the crack of dawn and hitchhiked here. At least she'll go back by bus. I'll take her to the bus stop in Ramle myself. Just pray for me that I'll get back to the base by eleven o'clock."

"Yes," I said. "You'll need it. And we've both got the first guard tonight."

"Don't worry. I'll get back on time."

He must have seen my skeptical smile.

"I won't get into trouble this time and I won't get you into trouble either." He was silent. For a moment he was thoughtful, his face darkened, and he gave me an appraising look as if wondering whether he could trust me. In the end he smiled and said: "It makes me into a good person, believe me."

"What does?"

"Her love. Being so loved that I don't even know if I deserve it at all. So many sacrifices. You have no idea what she does for me."

They left the room with singing, rousing cheers. The cries of joy and anticipation mingled with the message of desolation and gloom that could already be heard, as in all such obligatory performances, welling up from the depths in a strange harmony, shadowy and accidental, like a soft pizzicato on the basses gathering strength until it overcomes the melody of the main theme. A miasma of Aqua Velva shaving lotion and the stench of unwashed socks and rifle oil hung in the air of the empty barracks for a long time afterward, and a sudden silence fell, blessed as solitude, sensuous as an unexpected caress. I wanted to sleep. I lay down and closed my eyes, and I opened my ears, as I was in the habit of doing every night before I fell asleep, to listen to the rats gnawing away incessantly under the foundations of the barracks. I took the sound with me, as a lover setting out on a long journey might take a token of his love as an amulet or nourishment for the voyage, to feed his longings and ensure his safe arrival at his destination. But the rats, whose nibbling had in recent weeks become my beloved and appalling lullaby, were now silent, either because of the earliness of the hour and the light in the room, or because they missed the sounds of the sleepers protecting their nocturnal activities like a crumbling, breathing, moonstruck wall.

My call for sleep was not answered, but my happiness at not having gone out with the others was enough to keep me lying there without moving, my eyes closed, pretending to be asleep. The moment I felt my weight dissolving and it seemed to me that my inner wakefulness was at its height, even though I was already half asleep, I experienced something that sometimes happens to me when I wake up suddenly to find my ears full of snatches of speech, like the echoes of some feverish conversation I've conducted with someone else or with myself in a dream I've completely forgotten, or perhaps the dream was a radio-dream from the outset, as opposed to the usual movie-dream. Just as I had clung to the last fragile threads of the dream images on recovering consciousness after the silencing-a-sentry exercise, so on these occasions I cling to the fading fragments of words and snatches of sentences echoing in my ears, trying to understand their meaning and place them in the context they've lost. But this time it was an entire sentence that reverberated clearly in my ears, the echo of my voice demanding of some nameless person, in an aggrieved, resentful, sarcastic voice full of self-righteousness and disagreeable self-pity: *And how many sacrifices, in your opinion, are necessary in order for one man to be loved?*

This argument, however hypocritical and ludicrous and pathetic it sounded as I repeated it to myself in the light of a graver and far more demanding and critical point of view, must have stemmed from something deep and dormant inside me; I could not banish it from my mind and cast it into oblivion together with all the other rubbish. There was something beyond the literal meaning of the words or their context; for it was all too easy to assume that they were simply a continuation of my conversation with Avner that had been interrupted not long before. It was as if there were a beauty in the sound of the words, their melody, their rhythm and meter, and the way they were combined together that had nothing to do with their literal meaning. A poetry lover, perhaps, might feel something like this when listening to the reading of a poem in an unknown foreign tongue. Perhaps the magic worked like the whisper of a vow, whose words are banal and indifferent in themselves, but charged in the saying with all the weight of the vower's eagerness and awe. But none of this was sufficient to account for the moving beauty that arose from the mysterious meeting between the speaker and the words rising unbidden to his tongue and ears, formulated by some other mechanism of which he knew nothing: *And how many sacrifices, in your opinion, are necessary in order for one man to be loved?* Today I cannot imagine attaching any beauty, musical or otherwise, to this sentence, and all I can remember is the wonder and addiction to which it gave rise in me then. The thought flashed through my mind that perhaps it had been sent to me like a secret transmission through the air. Again and again I repeated the sentence to myself, trying to ignore its contents and to concentrate exclusively on its sound and music, and once more I congratulated myself on having stayed behind on the base, because I had gained something far more valuable in my eyes than anything that might have awaited me outside.

The sound of heavy footsteps dragging across the concrete floor fell on me like an ice-cold shower. I knew that I was still not alone.

CHAPTER 9

I opened my eyes. Miller was pacing to and fro with a worried expression on his shriveled face. When he saw that my eyes were open he approached my bed.

"What happens?" he asked.

"I don't know," I said. "I fell asleep for a minute."

"Where is platoon?"

"They've all gone out for an after-duty leave," I said. "Didn't you get a pass?"

"Pass?"

"Didn't you know we were getting the evening off?"

"I in Haifa must be. Friday kaput, Saturday kaput, what now happens?"

"It's only a few hours' after-duty. Everybody has to be back by eleven o'clock."

"Eleven o'clock?"

"Yes, till eleven o'clock."

"Not possible Haifa?"

"No, just around here. Not far. Haifa's far."

"Yes," he said and frowned. "Haifa far, far." His small eyes tried to estimate the distance to Haifa and stuck at an imaginary point not far from the tip of his left ear, measuring infinity. Yossie Ressler entered the room. He had gone to see his friends off at the gate. Miller turned to him at once, with new hope: "What happens, please?"

"What does he want?" Yossie asked me.

"He didn't know about the after-duty and now he wants to go to Haifa."

"Haifa far, far," said Miller.

"Nahum didn't go either," said Yossie. "He's sitting with all the other religious guys and they're all singing 'Shavua Tov' and 'Eliyahu Hanavi' and all that stuff."

"Where have platoon go? " inquired Miller.

"Those two could have stayed and done the guards," said Yossie, "if they were staying anyway. We could have gone out with the others."

"I don't mind," I said.

Yossie sat down on the edge of my bed and looked absentmindedly at Miller pacing helplessly to and fro, anxiously rubbing his parchment chin, seeking a way out of an impossible predicament, until he finally retired to his bed, where he turned his back on us, undressed, and put on his turnout uniform.

"I hope he's not going to Haifa," I said to Yossie, lowering my voice.

Miller combed his hair, tucked his shirt into his trousers, rubbed the toes and ankles of his boots on the calves of his legs, right boot on left calf, left boot on right calf, as I had once seen Charlie Chaplin do in one of his films. Then he inspected the shine on his boots and, satisfied, nodded to me and Yossie Ressler and walked out of the room.

Yossie said, "If Kafka had come to Israel he would probably have seemed like him."

I didn't understand what he meant by this remark. "It's not that he doesn't know Hebrew," I said, "and it's not only that he doesn't understand what's going on, he also seems a bit mad to me."

"Once you begin thinking along those lines, " said Yossie, "you'll start seeing madmen everywhere. In the end there won't be anything special about it."

Yossie sat on the edge of the bed with a thoughtful expression on his face, as if he were trying to make up his mind whether to say something. Stooped and frowning, he stared at the hands spread on his knees, the hands of the musician-to-be, as if hoping to discover the answer to some question in them. In the end he raised his head and looked around the empty room.

"This place is even worse when it's empty. Just look around you. Have you ever thought how ugly it is? God, what ugliness!"

"I thought you managed to ignore it, that your music protected you like a coat of armor."

"It doesn't always help," said Yossie."I suffer horribly here. You can get used to the physical suffering in the end, to all that insane running, to the harassment, but you can't pass through the filth and stay clean. I try not to see too much, not to get to know too many people, not to listen to all the rubbish people talk here, not to get close to all the dirt. To absorb only what's essential to survive this nightmare and afterward to forget, forget it all, all this ugliness, like washing filth from your body."

He fell silent, apparently exhausted by the effort of talking. But he didn't look in the least embarrassed by what he had said, by the personal, confessional note of his words. There was a kind of arrogance in him that penetrated the screen of his hesitant, colorless voice — an aura of weakness and timidity that always surrounded him as he hid behind his friends. This arrogance seemed to me to hint at some hidden strength.

"I sometimes feel like that too," I said, "but I want to fight it. I want to live with people, in all the ugliness and loathsomeness. To get to know people, to be on equal terms with them, to feel the same worries and joys as everyone around me, to fit in with them, never to forget that

I'm not superior to them in any way at all. That I'm no better than anyone else."

"Balls," said Yossie. "You don't really think that. Nobody does. It's some kind of ideal people aspire to. I can't understand it at all. What does it mean to be like everyone else? It's terrible! As far as I'm concerned, as long as I can remember I've only had one ambition: Not to be like everyone else, to be an artist."

He pronounced the word *artist* as if it were a chord of astonishing beauty that he played arpeggio, carefully stressing each separate syllable, the sounds flowing together yet barely touching, like three lofty peaks looming on the horizon and vibrating there in the sonorous reverberation that filled the air. "An artist . . ." His voice almost broke as he pronounced the word, as if the emotion it contained were too much for him to bear.

When I heard this word coming out of his mouth I shrank in shame and embarrassment. As if I had been forced to witness a crime, as if he had confessed something disgraceful to me and made me an accomplice by taking me into his confidence. The disgrace lay not in his ambition to be an artist but in the way he announced it so simply, bravely, and proudly. I felt my body contracting, I could no longer bear to have him sitting next to me on my bed, I was ashamed of myself for having heard it. And there was no way of getting rid of the oppression, the anxiety at having transgressed against some mysterious prohibition; it was fluttering in my stomach and threatening to break out in terrible laughter.

"You understand," said Yossie, "my ambition to be an artist takes precedence even over my love for music. If it wasn't music, it would have been something else. I don't know if I'm worth much as a musician, but even if I can't be a famous performer or composer or conductor, then at least I'll be a pianist in a café. I won't give up. Until I succeed. And if not in music, then in some other art — never mind what, painting, dance, poetry, it doesn't matter. I believe I'll make it somehow. I can feel it inside me. So I don't have the least desire to be like everyone else. To be equal to them. It terrifies me."

He was speaking to himself more than to me. Why had he chosen me for this confession? I hoped that it was only the coincidence of our being left alone together in the barracks, and not that he thought I was like him. I hoped there was nothing in my appearance or behavior to encourage him to think we had anything in common. I was horrified by this possibility; I wanted to say something that would refute it immediately. But I couldn't think of anything, and besides, as soon as I had succeeded in suppressing the evil laughter and overcoming it inside me, I found myself beginning to respond to something in his words — not to their content or manner, but to the sense of confidence and deep inner strength they exhuded, the strength of obsession and single-mindedness.

Suddenly he smiled nervously, got up, and went over to the entrance to the room, where he stood leaning against the doorjamb, looking out pensively into the gathering darkness. After a moment he returned and stood opposite my bed with an expression of tension and suffering on his face. There was something accusing about his attitude. He said: "I can't live with brutes and animals, in ugliness and filth. I have to be surrounded by beauty and refinement, otherwise I can't survive. Sometimes I feel that I'm choking. When I was conscripted, it never even occurred to me that I would find myself among animals like these. The kids I knew were from the neighborhood, from school, they weren't capable of understanding my dreams either, but at least they weren't hostile to them in advance. I've know Hanan, for example, ever since grade school, he lives not far from me, and the same goes for Micha and the rest. Not Hedgehog. I only met Hedgehog at the induction center, but I can get along with him too, he's a nice guy and he's got a lot of good qualities despite his vulgarity. But I've never in my life been exposed to the things we see here. Their voices, their language, their faces, those ghastly songs of theirs.

"When they were singing their songs yesterday and that disgusting Ben-Hamo danced, I felt really frightened: if that's art too and it has a kind of beauty of its own that we're simply not used to — like modern art, say — if everything's relative, then maybe there's no point in my life at all. If this ugliness is also art, than nothing's worth a damn. Nothing! Then it's a fight to the death. I began singing Handel's Largo in my head. You know it —" He hummed a few bars to remind me. "— and I went on singing it to myself, with the harmony, and it was bloody hard. So much external noise and excitement against one inner voice. I saw how much strength they had, how much violence. It's a deceitful strength, a fraudulent, destructive strength, and I knew I mustn't give in to it. I felt like the Jews in the Inquisition shouting *Shma Yisrael* when they were being burned at the stake. And I kept on and on, and that Largo sounded so sad to me, like a funeral in my soul. Until I managed to blot out their wailing altogether and all I could hear was the Largo. And I had a feeling of victory. I felt that I wasn't alone, that even if I'm only a kid of eighteen I'm still a continuation of some other life. Not that I believe in reincarnation or any of that stuff. But I'm not alone here, I'm not only my body, which is really only eighteen. Being an artist means inheriting a kind of spirituality that's handed down from generation to generation, a kind of feeling for beauty, together with a steely determination not to give in to the majority, to the mob, to stupidity, to brutishness. And to keep the sacred flame of beauty burning in some secret shrine that only the very few know about. I know I'm completely insignificant in myself, but the thing that connects me to this covenant is much bigger than I am. Anyone who feels this knows that the years he's lived and all the years he'll live his whole life long are only zero-point-zero-zero of the great life that he partakes in, a life that goes on for hundreds and maybe thousands of years and has no limits."

"I imagine that it must give you a feeling of power," I said.

"Not at all!" protested Yossie. "It's not a question of power. An artist is like a delicate flower growing on a pile of manure with all kinds of flies and insects flying around, and he has to be cultivated and loved and protected, otherwise he won't survive. But most people are more attracted to the manure than the flower. Everything depends on his faith in himself and his willingness to suffer for it and to lead a lonely life."

I didn't know what put me off more: the ludicrous pretentiousness, the shameless conceit, the narcissistic posturing, or the forced, insulting, egotistical intimacy in his words. He stood opposite me like an accuser: I felt that I was one of the manifestations of ugliness that he found so upsetting. What had appeared at first to be a feeling of inner strength that aroused my admiration now seemed to me as brutal and violent as the power he attributed to ugliness. I tried to find the most wounding thing I could say under the circumstances: "Artists are usually people with complexes."

"Is that so?" said Yossie humorously, as if he were talking to a backward child. "Have you ever read books by composers about their lives? Did Mozart have complexes? Did Bach have complexes? Some of them did and some of them didn't. Like everybody else. What about you? Haven't you got complexes? You should hear what Avner says about you. He's says he's never met anyone with so many complexes in his life."

"What on earth made him say that?"

"I don't remember. You expect me to remember everything somebody says here about somebody else? Everyone talks about everyone else here behind their backs, like a bunch of old women. What do you think? That Avner's any better than anyone else? He's not a saint."

"Look, I don't care if people think I've got complexes or not," I lied. "I just never imagined that that's what Avner thought about me."

"Don't think Avner's any different from the rest of them, even if he knows a bit about music and talks fancy Hebrew to make an impression on us and thinks himself so clever and cultured. He's exactly the same as they are. We know him from Jerusalem. We know all about him and his women. He'd sell his mother and father to get laid, and all his friends into the bargain. I happen to know his mother, she used to work as a cleaning lady for Hanan's mother, and she's a good woman, primitive but intelligent. You should hear the way she talks about him."

"I don't admire Avner," I said. "What are you trying to convince me for?"

"No," said Yossie, "I'm trying to warn you to be careful of him. He can get you into all sorts of trouble."

"What kind of trouble do you mean?"

"He's out of control, he's got no sense of responsibility, he's selfish, all he cares about is getting what he wants the minute he wants it, he wouldn't think twice about putting the blame on you for some screwup of his and making you suffer for it, and afterward he'll smile a saintly smile and sprout a lot of phrases about friendship and loyalty and all that stuff."

"In other words, you're not crazy about him."

"He's corrupt, rotten. You know what he did? He got one of the girls at school pregnant, and when he found out about it he buggered off, just buggered off and didn't want to have anything more to do with her. She had a breakdown, she went crazy and tried to kill herself and she had to go to a psychologist. He ruined her life."

"Yes, but when they gave you that extra night parade he was the only one who helped you carry your beds, despite the danger to himself."

"He didn't do it for nothing, you can trust that. We'll still pay for it. It's all part of his game — he puts on this noble act to get you to trust him and like him, and make you feel obligated when he comes to ask you for a favor."

Yossie fell silent for a moment with a sour expression on his face. Then he curled his lips in a kind of sneer: "There are other things too. Much worse things that I don't want to foul my mouth by telling you. Altogether I hate gossiping, I really hate it. But you ask him once, just out of curiosity, where he got his interest in classical music from. Who taught him to listen to music. See how he reacts. He won't tell you. But maybe his reaction will give you a clue about what a dirty bastard he really is."

"He doesn't interest me to that extent," I said. "I don't need to know any more about him than I know already. He's not some important personality whose life history I have to sit and study."

"For him it was the most natural thing in the world that you should stay behind and do his guard for him so that he could go and meet some woman."

"Boy, you really hate him. What's so fascinating about him that you have to talk about him all the time?"

"Nonsense," said Yossie. "You're right. He's nothing. Just a big fat nothing. All his big talk about life and all the ideas he's always going on about come from the movies. In Jerusalem he spent most of his life at the movies. He'd see one movie three, four times, and then go and see another one the next day. Everything he knows about life comes from those crummy movies. That's where he gets all his profound ideas. He thinks he's making an impression on someone. The truth is that he's ridiculous. You can't even hate him."

"Maybe you just don't like people in general?" I said.

He gave me an ironic look that was not, in fact, brimming over with the love of humanity, and without deigning to reply went to his bed, where he removed his guitar from its case and began tuning it at length, as usual. Once more the look of furious, almost demented attention distorted his face as he closed one eye in intense concentration and aimed the other at his temple like the barrel of a gun. With his back hunched, his right thumb plucked the strings as his fingers held the key and turned it imperceptibly, tightening and slackening until the sound matched the one inside his head. I knew that I was watching the process of his metamorphosis into another person. In a moment or two the person sitting on his bed would turn into the silent, withdrawn boy who took no interest in what was going on around him, but only in the melodies and harmonic combinations that gave him no rest until he played them on his instrument. And he began to play.

He began playing Handel's Largo, which he had sung to himself the day before, when Ben-Hamo was dancing to the strains of the Arab songs. I didn't take my eyes off Yossie in order not to miss the signs of the transformation. But some things are presumably not meant for human eyes: At that moment there was a sound of footsteps entering the room. I turned my head and saw Nahum, his cheeks flushed, still radiant with the light of the Sabbath Queen, whom he had just finished seeing off. He mumbled *"Shavua Tov* — May you have a good week." Ressler went on playing. He may not have noticed Nahum at all. When I turned back to him, he was already the other person, of whom only a small part was visible while the rest of him could not be seen, as if his portrait had been left unfinished and the missing lines would never be those that the eye filled in by force of habit. There was no connection between him and the ridiculous, pretentious boy with his speeches about the sacred flame, his disagreeable conceit, and his nasty, self-righteous gossip. The whole conversation of a few minutes before was now a vague, blurred image, perhaps a figment of the imagination, perhaps a dim memory of other people in another place and time. Everything was bathed in the melody produced by his fingers on the guitar in its clear, radiant sadness, so different from the dull, heavy gloom that can sometimes be produced by relations between human beings. I lay on my back on my bed and closed my eyes to concentrate on listening to the music. His playing was unsure; perhaps a long time had passed since he had played the Largo, and perhaps this was the first time he had tried to play it on the guitar. In any case he was less practiced than in the other pieces I had heard him play, like the Telemann, for example. Occasionally he made a mistake and went back and corrected it, repeating the passage over and over again until he imposed his will on his fingers and instrument. Sometimes the harmony, which he was apparently improvising as he went along, insofar as the limitations of the guitar allowed, failed to satisfy him. Again and again he would try other possibilities until he found what he wanted. Gradually his fingers learned to overcome the obstacles, but they still lacked sureness and fluency. And wonder of wonders, so far from detracting from the beauty of the music, this hesitant quality gave it the kind of pristine charm that belongs to things coming into being by a process of trial and error, in front of our very eyes. I felt very moved as I lay there listening with my eyes closed. I said to myself that even if such grace was sometimes bestowed on those who were least worthy of it, it didn't matter. Ressler played the piece again, and this time it sounded more confident, fuller and more fluent, progressing at the right, even pace, for his fingers — which had overcome their stumbling uncertainty — were calmer now and no longer hurried as they had before. Thus the Largo was given its correct tempo and final form, and its beauty, which had been so moving in the first rough drafts, froze into a last, perfected version emptied of the unique sadness, so clear and radiant, that had come upon me like a kind of revelation. The innocence and mystery of the first meeting, the hesitant progression, full of suspense in anticipation of the unknown, the striving to get it right despite the difficulties and disharmonies, the fear and relief that accompanied it, had all disappeared from the final version. The playing had become mechanical, cold, measured, haughty as an artificial smile. I wondered if this was really so, or if perhaps my own response to the music had become blunted after having listened to it several times in succession.

After Yossie finished playing the piece for the third time, he stood up, put the guitar down, and came up to me. He stood facing me defiantly, his hands on his hips: "Do you still think I don't like people?"

He sounded pleased with himself and proud of his achievements. I didn't tell him about my disappointment with the third version. "It was a lot better than going to sit in some café in a transit camp," I said.

"Do you think they really went to that prostitute?" he asked.

"I don't know. Did they say anything to you about it?"

"That Sammy went with them and made them all kinds of promises. They looked quite enthusiastic to me."

I hoped they would all come back soon and the melee of voices and smells would fill the room again, and bring it back to life. Nahum had fallen asleep on his bed. He was lying on his side and the pressure had drawn his cheek into a ghastly mask: The stretched, gaping lips exposed his teeth and gums, and saliva dribbled from his mouth onto the folded blanket under his head. Yossie saw me looking at him and turned to look too. When he looked back at me his face was full of revulsion and despair. He hunched his shoulders and drew in his head, as if he had received a blow or was trying to protect himself from an impending avalanche: "Like an animal," he said.

And he went straight back to his bed, placed the guitar on his knees, and played the Largo again. Presumably he wanted to practice it and polish his performance. Pleased with what he had accomplished so far, and intent on deepening and consolidating his achievements, he was soon oblivious to his surroundings. Perhaps the truly strong are those who can shut themselves up in their own world, where if only for an hour or two they can pursue their dreams, utterly identified with their self-imposed task, detached from the disintegrating, leveling, lowering forces outside, unafraid of being ridiculous, pathetic, or weird, true to themselves and willing to pay the price. This did not fit in with the picture of the elite and the poor family that I had painted previously. It was impossible to belong to both of them at once. The picture was becoming too complicated for me to encompass. But I remembered that the moment of power, fullness, and confidence could take place only in circumstances of renunciation, of detachment and alienation. It was the old dream betrayed again, the resolution kept for no more than a few days. A feeling of urgency and panic suddenly overcame me: Every hour removed me farther from myself, every minute was a missed opportunity that would not return, and I still didn't know what I wanted. The sounds of Handel's Largo filled the room, Yossie Ressler entrenching himself in them like a blind mole behind its wall of earth; and like the mole he would dream his life instead of living it. Was this good or bad?

He returned again and again to the same passage, raising the key and, dissatisfied with the results, lowering it again. Quietly I stole out of the building, trying not to attract his attention. I sat down on the bottom step and looked into the darkness. I said to myself: *At these very moments I'm becoming and I have no influence over it. We're all becoming now, and maybe that's why we've been incarcerated here, like plague carriers or criminals serving their terms.* I tried to unite my gaze with the darkness, to mold it like some soft material into the remembered shapes I was accustomed to seeing from my present vantage point. My eyes began introducing order into the phantasmagoric chiaroscuro in a sudden thirst for objectivity. Inside the barracks the guitar stopped playing. Between the eucalyptus branches an old acquaintance who had known happier nights than this, the thin, sickly crescent moon of the end of Elul, peeped out, pale and miserable. The sound of traffic came from the distance, maybe from the road to Jerusalem, a subdued roar rising and falling — and silence reigned again. For a moment I thought that I heard the sound of a radio coming from somewhere, playing a Hebrew song I couldn't identify. The sound of nailed boots on a concrete surface approached and receded into the distance. And the sound of the rats gnawing incessantly in the silence, which I may have been only imagining as a kind of background music to the flitting of the patches of shade at my feet over the whitewashed stones marking the sides of the path — they too, perhaps, only an illusion of the night. A silhouette appeared at the end of the path. Someone was approaching with slow steps, one hand in his pocket and the other holding a glowing cigarette. When the light outside the next building fell on his face I saw that it was Avner.

When he reached the step where I was sitting he said: "You were sure I was going to be late this time too, right?"

"What happened?" I laughed, as if the fact that he was on time meant that something had gone wrong with his plans.

"I saw her onto the last bus to Jerusalem, and right after that I hitched a ride all the way to the base. Aren't the others back yet?"

"No. You're the first."

We went inside the barracks. He winked at Yossie Ressler, who was lying and staring at the ceiling, glanced at Nahum sprawled on his side like a dead man with his face distorted in the same bestial mask as before, and sat down on his bed with a bleak, forced smile, as if to cover up some anxiety or sorrow. Then he took a small package wrapped up in newspaper out of his pocket and held it out to me.

"Here, this is for you."

It was a foreign-language newspaper, covered with oily red spots. A damp, disgusting warmth touched my hand and my heart was full of foreboding. He kept his eyes on my face, anticipating the expression of surprise and delight soon to appear there. I unwrapped the newspaper and a sour, nauseating odor of tahini and pickled cabbage, soggy pita, and stale oil mixed with the acrid stench of newsprint; it flooded my head and shrank my stomach. The foreign print had come off on the decomposing sides of the pita. The opening of the pita, soaked in the red pimiento sauce, like the mouth of an open, bloody wound, had spewed part of the tahini onto the crumpled newspaper, where the white paste mixed with the red sauce and black print had hardened into a dry, wrinkled crust. The squashed balls of falafel, with their greenish yellow contents sticking to the shreds of pickled cabbage, looked like potbellied beetles trodden into the grass.

"Terrific! This is great!" I cried and began carefully rewrapping the precious little packet as if to cherish it and keep it safe from harm.

"Eat it! Why don't you eat it?" said Avner in a voice I had never heard him use before, low and quiet, hoarse with suspense and suppressed rage.

"I thought I'd keep it for my guard —"

"Man, eat it now!"

Yossie Ressler sat up on his bed and looked at us with an amused, curious expression on his face. Nahum woke up and turned over onto his other side, looking as if he were still half asleep. He covered his eyes with his arm, as if to shield them from the light.

I examined Avner's face in the fatuous hope of discovering a sign that he was joking, but his face was like a blank wall, stiff with hatred and pain. I tried to breach this wall with a friendly smile: "What's up? What's the matter with you? What are you making such a fuss about?"

"I'm telling you for the last time," he whispered in a tired voice, pale with rage and menace: "Eat it now, before it gets cold."

I wondered why, after weeks of eating the nauseating mess dished up to us in the mess hall, I was unable to overcome the disgust aroused in me by this accursed portion of pita and falafel. Did even nausea require an individual address in order to realize itself fully, some intimate and familiar target that was lacking in the anonymous mass production of the kitchen on the base?

I opened the newspaper wrapping, took the pita in my hand, forced a smile of enjoyment to my lips, and began to chew. "It's great, just great!" I said, but the words were not convincing. The flaw was deep in the heart of things, like a preordained fate.

"Just eat and shut up," said Avner.

He looked at me with narrowed eyes, clenched his teeth, and spat out: "You're a shit, a shit, a shit!"

The demon of laughter began seething dangerously inside me. I looked at Yossie sitting and watching the little drama with an expression of amusement on his face. I signaled astonishment and humorous helplessness and shrugged my shoulders, and Yossie responded with a satisfied smile and a nod of *I told you so!* Avner noticed this exchange and called out to Yossie: "Come on, come and help him finish the falafel, you're a sissy just like he is, I suppose it would disgust you to eat it too, after it's been in my filthy black hands, in my filthy pocket, next to my filthy balls. What are you waiting for? Come on, come and join in the feast!"

Yossie did not reply. The smile did not fade from his face. He sat back, leaned against the wall, and folded his arms with an air of waiting to see what would happen next.

"Look," I said to Avner, "this is ridiculous. I had no intention of —"

"Man, shut up and eat. And chew. You're swallowing it whole so as to get rid of it as quickly as possible and not taste it. Go on, chew. Chew slowly and taste every chew."

The demon of laughter was running riot in my stomach; my whole body was trembling in the attempt to suppress it. Avner kept a close watch on my mouth to supervise my chewing. I chewed slowly, to appease him. The pita with its falafel and tahini and pickled cabbage tasted bland and insipid and slightly smoky, but not in the least disgusting as I had imagined it would from the softness and suspect warmth of its touch, or its revolting appearance when I opened the newspaper. This discovery brought an unlooked-for relief, a sudden release from fear grounded in error or prejudice. The relief surged through my limbs, arousing dormant sources of childish mirth that I did not know I still possessed. The only way to control the laughter shaking my belly and clutching my chest was to cooperate with it: Once more I began to observe myself from the side. I turned the whole thing into a joke, a performance: I crossed my legs, took little bites of the pita, licked my lips, closed my eyes as if drunk with pleasure, and murmured: "Wonderful, fantastic!"

"You bloody clown," said Avner. "In a minute you'll go outside and vomit it all up, don't think I don't know."

At the thought of this possibility the imprisoned laughter burst out. The mash in my mouth sprayed in all directions, my body convulsed and folded over, and the laughter that broke out of my mouth had an ugly, bestial sound. I couldn't stop it. From behind me I heard Yossie, and even Nahum, joining in. I must have looked grotesque, but I didn't care. Tears came into my eyes, I was laughing so hard, and through them I saw Avner's face. The corners of his eyes and mouth were tense with the effort not to smile, not to make any concessions where his honor was at stake. But the battle was already lost. Opposite the crude, anarchic, destructive force of the laughter subtleties of feeling and honor had no chance. With the back of my free hand I wiped my eyes and saw his thick, black eyebrows contract, his lips tremble, and his face give way. Before being forced to acknowledge surrender, he stood up and snatched the remains of the pita from my hand, wrapped it in the newspaper again, and went to the door, where we saw him throwing it with all his might in the direction of the eucalyptus trees. Then he came back and clapped his hands as if shake off the crumbs and announce the end of the affair.

He sat down on his bed, his face relaxed. I was still gasping for breath and Yossie and Nahum sitting on their beds were still smiling, perhaps in anticipation of a continuation of the performance. The first group of returnees arrived. Avner made his bed, took off his boots, got undressed, and lay down to wait for lights-out.

"We've got guard duty, "I reminded him.

"Damn, I forgot!" he said and put his hand on his forehead as if to check his temperature, closed his eyes for a moment, opened them again, shook his head, sat up, rubbed his scalp, and grimaced in a forced smile. He moved slowly, dragging time out as much as he could, as if to find a refuge and a hiding place from himself in it. Slowly he got dressed again, this time in his fatigues, putting on his boots and lacing up his gaiters. His face resumed its usual expression, the rage gone; only his eyes looked beaten and embarrassed, perhaps in shame for his outburst. He was silent, keeping his eyes on the door, where additional groups of men were arriving. Soon no one was missing, and even Miller, who had apparently grasped the time limit, arrived with fifteen minutes to spare, sweating and panting and beaming with a strange and feverish joy. He gave off a strong smell of alcohol. For the first time I saw him smiling, at ease, bubbling over, his crumbling parchment face bright and animated by a kind of intensity and gay intelligence. I studied him in the light of the adventure stories of men at war and buccaneering sailors I had read as a child. His ideas of soldiering, I imagined, must be taken from this culture, where soldiers spent all their free time in bars and pubs, getting drunk and going to bed with barmaids and dockside prostitutes. The idea appealed to me in its literary exoticism. He felt my eyes on him, and came up and held out his hand as if in greeting. We shook hands. Although he was bathed in sweat and full of animation, his hand was as icy as death.

Perhaps I looked to him like some old acquaintance from a previous incarnation, he was so free and friendly. "Haifa far," he said, "far, far," and he winked at me and burst into a laughter that was almost soundless, his chest heaving violently, enjoying a joke known only to the two of us, which needed only the utterance of its code name to spring back to life.

There was a mean smile in Muallem's eyes when he came into the room for stand-to-your-beds before lights out. His drooping upper lip twitched as if enjoying some secret taste. "Tomorrow you'll meet your new instructor, Corporal Benny. For your own good, you'd better keep on the right side of him. Carry out your orders properly and do everything a hundred percent by the book. He'll take you for your morning run." He smiled again, as if trying to ascertain if the message had been understood. "Remember what Corporal Muallem tells you and in the end you'll say thank you. Tomorrow morning after parade Ben-Hamo goes to the company office for his trial."

"Yes, sir," said Rahamim.

"There'll be an inspection tonight," said Muallem. "And any guard that makes a screwup knows what to expect. Remember the password I gave you?" He lowered his voice, as if the walls had ears, and repeated the password: *"Open pin,"* and the answer: *"Shooting star."* There was something ominous in his words and behavior that night, which made even the passwords sound dangerous, menacing, charged with interstellar dynamite.

CHAPTER 10

I had a terrible dream. It was only the pain that woke me up," said Avner. "It was so unbearable that I woke up."

We had gone around the hill crowned by the company office a few times and were standing at the end of the path with its border of white-washed stones leading to the flag square and the entrance to the building. There was a light on in one of the rooms and we didn't know if it had been left burning deliberately — if someone was still sitting there and working late at night, or if he had fallen asleep without bothering to switch it off. A number of lamps illuminated the offices from outside, and the whole hill was exposed like an island in the surrounding sea of darkness. We were easy prey for a surprise inspection, from either inside the building or outside it.

We didn't speak, afraid of breaking some sacred unwritten military rule or of being overheard by the person sitting in the room with the light on. Avner didn't seem eager to communicate anyway. Even before, when we were patrolling around the hill, he had said hardly anything. In the shadow of his helmet his face was quiet, tired, and inscrutable, his back slightly stooped and his head lowered, as if he were trying to distract himself from anything that might interfere with his concentration. When we set out on our round again, he suddenly roused himself and said: "I'm dying for a smoke but it's too dangerous."

"You'd better not smoke now," I said.

"If I don't have a smoke I'll go crazy."

In the bitterness of his heart he attempted to communicate his pain: "I had a terrible dream," he said. "It woke me up. It was so unbearable. I dreamed that I brought you a falafel from Ramle, as a token of gratitude for your staying behind in my place, and I dragged it all the way back to the base for you. And when I give it to you, instead of being glad and enjoying it, you're disgusted by it and pull up your nose. And I think to myself: *What, am I so filthy, so tainted, that it disgusts him?* The blood rushes to my head. I feel as if someone's spat in my face, because for me it was a gesture of friendship, and I don't think of myself as disgusting or dirty or sick. So I lose my temper and begin yelling at you to eat it. You're frightened and you begin to eat. You force yourself to eat it just to shut me up, but you make a whole performance out of it, to emphasize the fact that it's torture for you. And then I can't control myself any longer and I begin to hit you. I go berserk and I beat you within an inch of your life. But you just sit there looking at me indifferently as if it doesn't touch you at all, as if you don't feel a thing. And every blow I give you hurts me, as if in some strange way the blows are turning back on me instead of being transmitted to you. And the pain is terrible. I hit harder and the pain increases . . . I woke up. And up to now, something of that pain is still with me."

He fell silent and I didn't know if he had finished the story of his dream or if this was an interval before the next chapter. It seemed to me a reasonably fair and intelligent way to put an end to the affair. Better than apologizing and asking me to forgive him, which would have embarrassed me and involved me in the sticky sentimentality usual in such circumstances. I was grateful to him for it.

We walked on in silence for a moment, and when I realized that this was the end of the story and he was waiting for my response, I said in a tone that I tried to make as light and humorous as possible: "It seems to me that we won't get through this basic training without you beating me up — but this time for real."

"Why?" he asked, "Why does it happen?"

"I don't know. Maybe it's my fault. Maybe there's something about me that annoys you, something that offends you."

"I bet you've never fought anyone in your life," said Avner.

"Right. I don't know how to deal with physical violence. It's like a foreign language I can't understand or speak. Whenever I see people fighting I manage to get away in time and disappear. I'll do anything to avoid a fight — give in, lie, betray, run away. When it comes to running away I'm an Olympic champion. I've learned to run fast for short distances. And I don't know if it's the fear of getting hurt, because I know I don't have a chance and I'll always get the worst of it, or the fear of the close physical contact, which I can't endure."

"I've spent half my life fighting and getting beaten up," said Avner, and a nostalgic smile suddenly illuminated his face in the shadow of the helmet, "first my father hit me, my big brothers hit me, the tough guys in the neighborhood hit me, and later I fought my friends and beat up the kids who were younger than me, and in the end our neighborhood gang fought another neighborhood. It was the way to show who was stronger, because strength was the only thing that counted. If you were strong you were admired, you were loved. The girls ate you up with their eyes, dreamed about you at night. I suppose it must sound childish to you now, silly, but who knows, maybe it's a stage you have to pass through. Maybe one day you'll miss not having passed through it. Not knowing that outburst of anger and feelings and hatred, although at the beginning it may be just for the sake of the sport, or even in fun. It's true that there's a kind of intimacy involved. Only love has that kind of closeness of body to body.

And you begin hitting to kill, no less. You go flat out with everything you've got. You're stronger than you thought you were. And the pleasure of victory, when you're barely breathing, barely alive, but the guy who's lying there on the ground, the one who dared to challenge your superior strength, is nothing now. He's your possibility of being a king. He's the sacrifice, because in order for there to be a king there has to be a sacrifice. Perhaps it's important to have those fights at the right age? Maybe they immunize you against the blows that life deals out later, strengthen you for other, more important battles?"

I said: "When I stayed behind with Ressler tonight, he played a piece by Handel on his guitar. I think it was the first time he ever played it. Because at the beginning he groped for the chords and his playing wasn't so confident. I felt that something wonderful was happening at those moments, when he was gradually mastering the piece, as if his effort were turning into a revelation of beauty. Beauty was born, a beauty so great it made you want to cry. I admired Ressler and I envied him terribly. I thought: *Maybe that's the true strength.* It was like a declaration of war against the whole world. I forgot all the rubbish he was talking before about himself and art and all kinds of other unpleasant things about him. I would have given anything to be in his place at those moments. It seemed to me that I was beginning to understand something I once heard about primitive tribes, that when they kill someone they believe the power and spirit and talents of the dead person enter the soul of the murderer, as if murder is the height of identification. At those moments Ressler was a sure candidate for murder."

Avner's face darkened again: "Did you see how he took all the little darlings aside and told them about the way I flipped my lid? And they stood there giggling and whispering like a lot of little schoolgirls. If there was anything farther from beauty and power —"

"Guards! Guards!"

The call came from behind us, low, dry, sleepy, flat, the voice of a man accustomed to being swiftly obeyed without any effort on his own part. The voice was unfamiliar to us. We had just finished rounding the hill and were passing the facade of the building. We turned around and saw him coming toward us, strolling over the concrete paving in front of the entrance, barefoot, wearing short gym pants and over them a uniform shirt with two corporal's stripes and paratrooper's wings carelessly buttoned in the middle. I had never seen him before. But he had emerged from the company office building — the person who had been sitting in the room with the light on. He was tall, dark, and bespectacled. His face was long, his brow high, and two bays of premature baldness had already bitten into the hairline over his temples. When he came closer we saluted. He did not return our salute, but asked in a sleepy, apathetic voice: "Have you got a cigarette?"

My heart sank. I stole a sideways glance at Avner and saw the moment of hesitation and danger trembling on his cheekbones. Very slowly he inserted his hand behind his pouch webbing and unbuttoned his shirt pocket, as if he were trying to gain time to think and put off the moment of doom, took out a packet of cigarettes, and offered it to the corporal like a criminal handing his revolver over to his captors. The corporal removed a cigarette from the packet and gave it back to Avner.

"Matches."

Avner took the matches out of his pocket. The corporal took them from his hand, turned around, and strolled back to the building, closing the door, which he had left open when he came out, behind him.

We stood staring at the building and the lit window but we couldn't see anything, not even a shadow or sign of movement inside the room. Avner took off his helmet, rubbed his head, and frowned, as if trying to solve a mystery.

"That's the corporal who gave me a lift back to the base," he said.

"What are we waiting for?" I asked. My voice was still shaking with fear, and all I wanted was to run for my life, to start making the rounds again as if nothing had happened. The corporal's appearance had given rise in me to a shrinking feeling that went beyond fear, as if he were connected with some personal memory of a disagreeable nature.

"I want my matches," said Avner. He put on his helmet with an obstinate, offended expression, as if he had made up his mind not to budge until his property was returned. But the corporal did not return.

"He could have lit the cigarette and given you back your matches on the spot," I said.

"Don't you understand?" said Avner "It's not for him. He's not alone in that room." Avner said this softly, his face rigid, as if whispering a curse through clenched teeth "He's got a woman in there with him. He's been busy necking with her. Now she wants a cigarette. He himself doesn't smoke, so he went to look for a cigarette and matches for her."

This explanation sounded impressively logical, like the deduction of some experienced detective, but there was nothing to prove that it was correct.

"And you think that after she's lit her cigarette he's going to come back here to return your matches?"

"I don't know. But I do know that if I don't have matches and I can't smoke to the end of guard duty I'll go crazy."

"So what are you going to do? Stand here for another three hours? We have to get back on patrol."

He sighed. We set out. His expression was sullen and I wasn't sure if he was sulking because of the matches or because of what he assumed was going on in the room between the corporal and the girl. He resumed his previous attitude, staring silently at the ground. We completed another round, and when we passed the facade of the building again, the light was still on in the window and there was still no sign of life behind it. After another time around we took up our positions in front of the flag square, occasionally turning our heads to look at the lit window. After a few minutes of this we heard the door open; the corporal came out again. Once again we saluted, and this time he returned it. He looked at us for a minute, narrowing his eyes behind his glasses as if intent on exposing some hidden design, and said in his monotonous voice: "What the hell are you up to, standing here all the time? You want to fall asleep on your feet or what? Get on with your patrol!"

"We've just finished patrolling, sir," I said, "and taken up our positions here, as per orders."

"Bullshit!" said the corporal. "You're lying." He pushed his face up to mine and scrutinized my face "You're a liar. I don't want to hear your lies." He patted his shirt pockets, looking for something, perhaps a pen and paper to take down our particulars so he could put us on a charge. Then he looked behind him with a certain impatience, inspected the open door, looked back at us. and said: "You're making a screwup of your guard, and you don't know how to talk to your superiors either."

Avner suddenly gave me an anxious look, as if I had made some terrible mistake and brought disaster on us both. My heart pounded, not only because of what the corporal had said but also because of the expression on Avner's face, which foreboded complications without end. I therefore made haste to set out again, but Avner, instead of joining me, turned to the corporal and said: "Can I have my matches back, sir?"

The corporal turned on him, smiling sarcastically.

"So you want your matches back do you? And what, may I ask, do you need matches for when you're on guard?" And so saying he landed a vicious kick on Avner's behind, the force of which propelled him forward at a run for about ten yards, until he came to a halt and almost fell. The door of the office slammed behind us. I went up to Avner and when we were about to set off around the hill, we heard footsteps crossing the concrete paving in front of the building. We stole a look backward and saw the corporal with a little soldier girl slipping around to the right wing of the building, where they disappeared down the slope of the hill, and at the same time we heard her laughter ringing out with a clear, sweet sound, as if in response to some amusing story. We didn't see her face, only her back as she hurried down the hill with the corporal and disappeared. The light in the office was off.

We marched side by side in silence, and when I looked at Avner out of the corner of my eye he averted his face and walked a few steps ahead. Then he stopped and stood still for a moment, as if he had lost his way and was wondering where he was and which way to go. Suddenly he dashed into the darkness, came up against a solitary eucalyptus tree at the foot of the hill, and began kicking its trunk and beating it with his fists. I stood still and watched him. The pounding of fists and boots against the tree went on for a long time, reverberating in the silence like wild, muffled drumbeats coming from far away to summon help, tirelessly, interminably repeated. He was standing on the brink of the darkness and from where I stood I couldn't see his face in the shadow of his helmet or the movements of his hands and feet clearly, only his silhouette swaying to and fro like a Jew at prayer. When the blows stopped, his hands dropped to his sides and he bent over as if he wanted to vomit, straightened up, raised his arms and removed his helmet, threw it to the ground at his feet, and covered his head, which had fallen onto his chest, with his hands. In the end he went up to the tree, put his arms around the trunk, and rested his forehead against it. He stood like this for a few minutes, which seemed to me like eternity. I looked around anxiously. All that was missing now was a sudden inspection. I walked down to the road leading from the hill to the staff quarters, doubled back to the facade of the office building, and returned to the patrol route without seeing any figures emerging from the darkness. When I came back to my previous position, Avner was still standing embracing the tree trunk and leaning his forehead against it. The sound of my footsteps must have startled him, for he suddenly jumped back and looked at me. He bent down, picked up his helmet, put it on, and came slowly forward to join me, breathing rhythmically as if he were sleeping. For some time we walked side by side in silence, and when I turned to look at him I saw tears streaming down his cheeks. Only a faint tremor, which made his lips and chin twitch for a moment, betrayed the straining of his facial muscles to maintain the frozen composure of his expression. As soon as he realized that I had seen his tears, he moved a few paces ahead and walked in front of me. The sight of that frozen face with the tears pouring down it, as if from some mechanism that had suddenly broken down, was more terrible than any weeping I could remember. From time to time I saw him from behind wiping his eyes and nose with his wrist, hardly making a sound, and he sniffed slowly too, as if he had a cold, so as not to make a noise.

A furious hostility took hold of me at the sight of Avner broken and weeping, at the thought of that bloody box of matches, of his childish stubbornness, his damned addiction, his humiliating dependency on the needs of the moment, on cigarettes, on sleep, on the lusts of his body. For these were the things that led him astray and brought punishment and pain in their wake. I understood then for the first time, with great clarity, that he was immeasurably better than his weaknesses, than the flaws in his character, than his nature from which nobody could save him.

After a few minutes he stopped and waited for me to catch up with him. He pulled the helmet down to shade his face and said: "It's okay now."

I didn't dare look at him for fear of seeing the traces of the tears on his face. I didn't dare open my mouth in case I said something wrong.

"It was inevitable," said Avner in the end.

"The hornet crashed into the windowpane?" I tried to make light of what had happened and cheer him up.

"Tonight was the hornet's big night," he said. When he saw that I was averting my face from him he added: "Man, you can look at me now, it's all over."

He even tried to smile, but the stillborn grin twisted his lips in a peculiar grimace, as if he were about to burst into tears again.

"This guard isn't ending any better than the last," I said.

"Somehow they both ended with a kick up the backside for me," he said. "Last time I got one from the CSM, when he pushed me into the CO's room for my trial."

"Maybe I bring you bad luck," I said jokingly, although I felt that it wasn't too far from the truth.

"The bad luck's been inside me from the day I was born," said Avner. "I don't know if there's a God, but one thing's sure — he hates me. Everything that happened tonight, from the moment I met her on, was predetermined. It was all aimed against me, and you got the ricochets." He paused and looked at me, wondering whether to say something or not. In the end he said: "I apologize for the way I carried on tonight, when I came back to the platoon. I thought I could get through it without apologies. But now the words have to be said. They may not be worth much, but they're the only ones I've got. Now that you've already seen me standing there next to the tree, broken and crying, there's no room for hints and allegories and dreams anymore. I apologize."

He fell silent and looked at me expectantly.

"Haven't you got anything to say?" he said impatiently.

"I don't know," I said, "I don't know what one says in these circumstances. Nobody's ever apologized to me before, except when he trod on my foot by mistake or tried to push past me in a crowd. But like this, seriously — I just don't know what to say."

"If you ever feel the need to apologize to anyone," said Avner, "you'll know what to answer too."

"I'm a minor detail here. You didn't do me any harm."

"What were you staring at me for all the time I was standing next to the tree? You think I didn't see you staring?"

We had come around to the facade of the building again and took up our positions in front of the flag square. The whole ritual now seemed pointless and ridiculous. I knew that if somebody decided to screw us he would find a way to make us look bad no matter what we did, but at the same time the need to do everything strictly by the book was more vital than ever. The building, which was now completely dark, was like a protective wall against the surrounding lights. Avner took off his helmet and rubbed his head with the palm of his hand. "If there were any water around here and I could wash my face I'd feel better," he said. "Can you see anything?"

He raised his face to mine. His eyes were still slightly red. "No," I said, "I can't see anything. Do you think I shouldn't have looked at you then? That it was wrong of me?"

"No, but it doesn't matter now. What did you think?"

"I thought it was beautiful."

"Beautiful?" He frowned in disgust. "Beautiful like a picture? Like a movie? A play? Are you normal?"

"The blows on the tree sounded like jungle drums calling for help. And I didn't know how to help."

"You think there's something beautiful about a person breaking down?"

"Yes, I think so."

"I stopped understanding you a long time ago." He looked at his watch. "An hour and a quarter to go. I'm dying for a cigarette."

He sighed so heartrendingly that I felt I should rush off immediately to find him some matches. I said: "It was all because of those cigarettes that it happened in the first place."

"You're talking rubbish," said Avner. "It was only the last straw that broke the camel's back. Never mind, I'll get used to kicks up the backside in time. It seems to be my fate. There's nothing to be done about it. It's like a relay race. One catastrophe sends me to the next and they never stop running. This whole evening was the same. I had a terrible quarrel with her. You know why she came here all the way from Jerusalem? To find out if we got leave or not. She thought I came home on leave and I didn't want to see her. She went to look for me! Understand? She doesn't believe me. She spies on me. As far as she's concerned I'm a liar, a cheat, running away like a thief in the night. It began as soon as I met her this afternoon at the Jerusalem Gate. We began quarreling and she cried and we made up and I thought it was over. And in the evening we met again and took a bus to Ramle. She went to her cousin to tell her about the lie she told her husband, in case he asked, and she invented a new lie, for the cousin, why she had to keep the trip a secret from her husband. And all the time I'm waiting for her outside, because they're not supposed to know about me. So I stand there in the street like a dog, wasting that precious after-duty. By the time she comes out almost an hour's gone down the drain. And then we start looking for somewhere to be alone together. We wander around the back alleys of Ramle like the children of Israel in the wilderness. And by now it's already dark. We wandered around like that for about an hour and I was getting really mad, after waiting for her outside her cousin's place for an hour before that. I didn't think too much about what I was saying and I let her have it, I wanted her to understand that I was getting sick of the whole scene, and that it couldn't go on like this much longer. I've had enough of clandestine affairs. And she explained what a sacrifice she's making for my sake, and how much harder it is for her. Which is true. And we made up again.

"Until we found an abandoned building not far from the cemetery, a dirty, stinking, derelict ruin that people probably use for a public lavatory. We could hardly find a clean bit of floor in the darkness to put our clothes on. And then for the big surprise: I couldn't get it up. I'm telling you, that story about the soda they put in our tea and food's no joke. In the end it apparently really has an effect. It's never happened to me before, and I've had a lot of experience with women, believe me. I couldn't understand what was happening, I was stunned, I felt as if someone had knocked me on the head with a hammer. And nothing helped. We rolled around like a pair of animals in that stinking shit and it was dead, useless.

"I remembered how I used to think about that PT instructress, the one with the dogs, before going to sleep here on the base, and it drove me crazy. A few times, after everyone was asleep, I even went out to the latrines to off-load. So I began to pretend that I was necking with that PT instructress instead of Aliza, that it was her body and her face and her hair, like I used to see them in my imagination before I went to sleep. And gradually it began to have an encouraging effect. I had my eyes closed all the time, so as not to interfere with my imagination. At a certain moment, I was lying on the ground with her on top of me. And suddenly, I don't know why, I opened my eyes. And I saw the sky and the stars above me. I couldn't understand how they got there. When we went into the building I'd never even noticed that the roof was missing. It struck me like a blow. A terrible fear that God in heaven could see me now, like this, and there was nowhere to hide. I felt as if I were falling from a high cliff straight into an abyss. The fall lasted a moment or two and gave me terrible vertigo. And I couldn't get it up again.

"Suddenly we saw an old man coming in, he must have come to take a shit, at first he didn't notice us and we didn't move, but suddenly he stumbled into Aliza's leg. He saw us and he got a terrible fright and began to scream. We got up and got dressed as quick as we could and got out of there. For me he was the prophet Elijah sent straight from heaven to get me out of the shit. He went on screaming and we ran for our lives. We went to the bus station to get her bus to Jerusalem.

"When we were standing waiting for the bus I told her about my detention and my suffering there and I saw that she was looking at me and nodding her head without taking in a word. Her eyes were like two glass marbles. All she was thinking about was herself. About her fear that I didn't love her anymore, about how she'd come all the way from Jerusalem for nothing, about her problems at home, and God knows what else. But not about me. And this made me mad, really mad. I decided to tell her what I thought of our hole-in-the-corner affair. She has to make up her mind what she wants. It can't go on like this much longer. I have to think about my own future too. I want to get married one day, have a family; I'm not a child. Naturally she began to cry, and say that she'd known all along that I didn't love her anymore, and that's why I couldn't make love to her properly, and I must have someone else, and that she knew it would end like this, and that I'm incapable of appreciating everything she's done for me. All the usual stories. When the bus came, she got in without even saying good-bye.

"I stood there watching the bus drive out of the station and I was boiling with rage. She didn't even look at me. And when the bus disappeared I breathed a sigh of relief and said to myself: *That's over.* I felt as if some nightmare had come to an end, as if a difficult decision had been taken out of my hands and made for me. I went to the main road to hitch a ride back to the base. I had fantastic luck: A van stopped immediately and brought me all the way back to Training Base Four. With that goddamned corporal driving it. I thought it was a good sign, that maybe my luck was beginning to change at last. But gradually I began thinking about her and what she'd said again, and it hurt me terribly. I felt that I really had treated her badly, that I was unworthy of such love, such sacrifice. That maybe I'd lost her forever, that if she had any sense she'd throw me over and get rid of me for once and for all, because I bring her nothing but trouble and danger, without any security or loyalty. I knew that I couldn't live without her and that no other woman could mean what she'd meant to me. And all kinds of other thoughts that began eating my heart. And the fear that this time she wouldn't forgive me. And the pain of what's over, dead, of parting, ending. And then I came back to the barracks and gave you that goddamned falafel that I bought next to the bus station in Ramle. And you really were so irrelevant, so guiltless. But it all came out on you, because you were the last drop that filled the cup to overflowing."

We set out to patrol around the hill again. This time the patrol passed very quickly. We had about twenty minutes to go before one of us went to wake up the next two guards. At last Avner's face began to brighten and relax and he smiled. I was as glad as if I had accidentally met an old friend after a long separation, with all the embarrassment, disappointment, and surprise that usually accompany such meetings. He saw the gladness on my face.

"I had to tell you, you understand? To get it off my chest. Now I feel about a hundred pounds lighter. Perhaps the nightmare's over. I think I can see the end in sight. Oh, Mother! I'm dying for a cigarette!"

"How does that song from the lockup go?" I asked him.

"Oh, Mother! Come and take me away from here. They're eating my heart away!"

The sudden feeling of relief made him cast fear and caution to the wind. He sang loudly into the darkness, and immediately pulled himself up short: "I'm waking up the whole base!" He looked around him with an exaggerated pantomime of panic. "I told you all that," he said, "to make you understand that it's not the matches or the cigarettes or the falafel or the kick in the pants. It's something deep down in my lousy fate. It's my lust for life. I've got such a huge appetite for life that the world may not be able to satisfy it at all. And so I keep tripping up, like that hornet flying into the windowpane. I don't really know what it is. It's like a thirst. A thirst that can't be quenched, and I'll probably spend all my life running like a lunatic to look for something to break that thirst. It's a tremendous thirst for love, for friendship, for feeling. If I don't break it, it'll break me. And that's what'll probably happen. Once I thought that everyone felt like me, at least at our age, when we're young and strong, on the brink of real life, the life of men. But more and more I've come to realize that most people live according to what they've got. They adjust their thirst to the amount of water in their glass. They restrict their ambitions, cut their wishes down to the size of what they can achieve. And I've never tasted satisfaction in my life, only thirst. Especially in the last few years I just can't get rid of it, it sticks to me and follows me around like a dog. Don't you know that feeling? Aren't you thirsty for something?"

"I thirst for thy waters, O Jerusalem," I sang wittily.

But Avner was unimpressed. "Don't take offense at what I'm going to say to you now," he said, "because I'm saying it out of friendship. Sometimes I look at you and I think that you're half dead. You don't attach yourself to anything, you're afraid of intimacy, of commitment, of failure, all you want is not to make a fool of yourself and look ridiculous. You don't really give a damn about what happens to the people around you. It's as if you were a visitor in the world. A guest who's come on a short visit, and in a few days time he'll pack up his bags and move on somewhere else, and all he really cares about is leaving a good impression behind him. You're not alive, because you've got a cold heart," he said "A cold heart."

It was the old, familiar Avner again, singing the tune I had grown accustomed to hearing over the past month, when he recovered his composure between one blow and the next, with all the self-righteous personal criticism, the confidence in his own rightness, the belief that you could reform people and baptize them in what he called "Life," so that they would be reborn with new souls, open and full of feeling, fearless and free of "complexes." His words hurt me, and I didn't know if it was because they were unfair or because they were true.

I said to him: "Go and wake the others up, it's time. I'll wait for them here."

Without a pause or a word he broke immediately into a run, galloping like a racehorse when the starting gate goes up, hoping perhaps in this way to banish the vestiges of the evil spirit of that ill-fated night. He left the circle of light, and was instantly swallowed up in the surrounding darkness.

After the two guards arrived I walked slowly back to the platoon.

There was something seductive in the stillness of the dark paths, something that tempted me to stay outside and not to go into the barracks. When I finally went in, I saw the tip of his cigarette glowing over his bed like a tiny lighthouse helping me find my way in the dark. When I got into bed, he leaned toward me and whispered: "Good night, I'm off to my date with the PT instructress now."

CHAPTER 11

For a few minutes he stood and inspected us one by one without moving from his place, without uttering a word. We stood tensely at ease in our dark gym shorts, our eyes blank with sleep, staring at the dull morning air, which was getting colder and cloudier, wondering how this latest development was going to affect our lives. He looked at us as if he had bought a job lot for next to nothing at an auction, and was now asking himself what the ill-assorted contents were good for and how to put them to some sort of use. The moments before the morning run dragged out for longer than usual. Apparently he knew the secret of these moments. Something in the previous order of things began to creak. At the end of the first row I saw the back of Avner's neck and his left eye; I knew he was looking for me behind him, trying to make contact with me without turning his head, in order to share the flavor of the surprise with me.

The new instructor with the parachutist's wings suddenly smiled a thin, bitter smile and began moving along the ranks. He proceeded with extreme slowness, his shoulders slumped, his eyes sleepy behind his glasses. Occasionally he paused between the rows and sighed. When he was behind us, on the point of completing his review, he was heard to murmur in his dry, tired voice: "Heaven help us!"

We emerged from the gate of the base and ran along the wide road, as we had done every morning for the past month. When we reached the intersection, where we usually turned back, the new instructor ordered us to keep on running in the same direction. We entered new territory. After a few minutes the road became narrower, turned, and encompassed a corner of the base I had never seen before. And as we penetrated farther into this foreign territory, a strange sensation arose from the noise of the running boots thudding rhythmically on the asphalt, from the smell of the bodies steaming in the morning air, the picture of the place whose distances could not be guessed, and the new man running next to us. The sensation of the first days returned and grew clearer, like a dream already dreamed before, surprising as a new beginning, poignant as the delusions of memory. Did things really repeat themselves over and over again, but each time in shapes and circumstances so different that their underlying structure was difficult to discover? If so, then everything that had happened over the past few weeks was nothing but running around in a closed circle, always returning to the same starting point in a frantic, never-ending race to reach the eternal beginning. This possibility did not seem in the least depressing; on the contrary, it was an inexhaustible source of opportunities for correction, full of meaning, a finality that never came to an end, like the promise I had tasted years ago when I was lost in the labyrinth of mirrors in the Luna Park.

By the time we returned to the main road leading to the base, the rhythm of the drumming of our feet had lost its uniformity and our ranks had grown ragged. The new instructor did not seem put out by this. He went on running rhythmically and lightly, hardly sweating, and showing no signs of fatigue. *The road back to the base has just begun. It is longer than we remembered it. The threes are disintegrating. The first casualties are falling and remaining behind. He gives the command to close threes. New threes are formed. A few more men fall by the wayside. The moment of choice looms. No breath left. Feet no longer feeling the ground. Heartbeat wild, erratic. Pounding violently. Booming fit to burst. Thumping against my nape. Blocking my throat. Weighing like a rock on my shoulders. Clutching my neck. Pulling me down. Down. A tremendous weight pressing down. Everything pales and dims. Only a strip of black asphalt. Ex-black asphalt. Gray asphalt. Ex-gray asphalt. Rings of road. Ex-road. Turning, gliding, spinning. Disintegrating. Dissolving. Vanishing. An inner alarm goes off: The moment of choice.*

Time suddenly stopped and I was flung forcefully forward. Like screeching brakes. Like a car crash. Falling on my face. Part of me went on running with them, the five or six threes receding in the distance. Another one dropped out. I didn't know who. And the new instructor ran alongside them, waving his hand like a conductor, urging them to keep it up, not to break down, not to lose the horizon line. Behind me I saw the others who had fallen by the wayside, puffing and panting as they walked. It was still a mile or two to the base. What was a mile or two? The light cloud that had covered the sky began to melt, exposing scraps of the metal heating up for a blazing noon. Someone else dropped out of the group of runners turning the bend in the road and disappearing from view. And with the gradual evening out of my breath and slowing down of my pulse, the awareness of my body returned and with it the yoke of time. The minutes allocated for the morning tasks, for washing, shaving, eating, bed making, tidying the barracks for inspection, weapon cleaning, getting ready for parade, gaped ragged, threadbare, lost.

To run, to retrieve whatever little was left, to try against all odds to get there with them. A race against the odds. Cocooned in the web of the dream, the stupid, recurrent dream that still came back, sometimes even in the daytime, after all these years. In the morning, on the way to school, it's late, and I'll never make it. Suddenly I realize that I'm naked, or barefoot, or in my pajamas, in front of all the passersby. I have to go home and get dressed. But all kinds of obstacles and hitches appear on the way. The nakedness, or the barefootedness, or the pajamas, are also a technical hitch, like the house that is locked. I go to look for my mother, to get the key; the first class must be over by now. I find her in the market with surprising ease. I take the key and go home. Get dressed. The second class is already under way. I leave the house fully clothed at last, looking for my bike in the yard, to get to school as quickly as I can. It isn't there. I realize I must have left it at school the day before, because I walked home with my friends. Who knows, maybe it's been stolen. I set out. Not far from the school I realize that I've left my satchel at home. Back home again. Running all the way, frantic, refusing to give up, against all the odds, striving again and again to reach the eternal beginning. And never getting there.

On the road, next to the entrance to the base, stood the few who had run all the way to the end of route and were now performing various exercises under the direction of the new instructor. The fallen gathered on the sidelines, arriving one by one, and watched the gymnasts sullenly, with seething, mutinous despair. Zero-Zero supported his stomach with his hand and closed his eyes in agony and dread. Peretz-Mental-Case looked ominous and menacing. Hedgehog gripped his skinny thighs and bent over to recover his breath, muttering: "Bastards, bastards." Our ranks swelled. And opposite us, Micky and Alon, Avner and Albert the Bulgarian, with another seven or eight, as if under some magic spell, radiating something unclear, something like the exhausted calm and supreme equanimity one sometimes sees in the eyes of people burning with fever. They performed the exercises he instructed them to as one man, relaxing their strained muscles, jumping up and down, flinging their arms sideways and raising them above their heads, bending and straightening, breathing in and out to the rhythm he dictated, together, with perfect coordination, a team of well-drilled child prodigies.

From time to time the new instructor glanced in our direction with a look that was unmistakable. When he calculated that the last of the stragglers had arrived, he instructed us to join the little group of the elect, as if graciously bestowing upon us a favor of which we were manifestly unworthy. The platoon formed up again, and we marched into the base.

In the showers the mutiny broke out. Zero-Zero was standing next to the door when he saw Micky and Alon come in. "You crazy bastards!" he said. "What did you want to run like that for? You want to kill us all? Now he'll make us run a hundred miles every morning! Why did you do it? Why?"

Peretz-Mental-Case grabbed hold of Avner's arm and shook it as if he wanted to tear it off. "Who the hell do you think you are?" he yelled, his narrow toothbrush mustache quivering electrically on his lip. "What d'you bastards want anyway? You want it to be like Germany here?"

Micky couldn't restrain his laughter. A strange hilarity seized hold of him, as if he had been freed of some oppressive burden. Peretz let go of Avner and turned to Micky: "What're you laughing at? You think you're God? You'll laugh on the other side of your face when we get through with you!"

"What do you want of me?" asked Micky, still laughing. "What harm have I done you?"

"You want to kill us?" continued Peretz, his fury fanned to boiling point by Micky's laughter. "Who're you trying to impress? What the fuck's going on here? We ain't combat soldiers, we're job soldiers. This ain't a paratroop commando. So don't try to be a fucking hero. We ain't combat-fit here, everybody here's Medical Grade B. Defective Combat Ability! You know what that means? And there's some of us here deserve to be Medical Grade C. Limited Combat Ability! You know what that means? So what the hell's going on here?"

Micky said: "What do you want of my life? Go and file a complaint against the new instructor. What did you want? For me to fall flat on my face too? For me to put on an act?"

"Don't pretend to be so innocent, Micky," said Hedgehog, who was taking his time brushing his teeth. He could afford to: He shaved once every three days, and that was only to encourage the meager growth of his facial hair — a shadowy patch on the tip of his chin, a few wisps under his sideburns, and the faint, downy mustache that had never been touched by a razor. "Don't pretend, Micky," said Hedgehog in a quiet, somber voice. "You did a terrible thing. You betrayed us."

Zero-Zero, who was busy working his shaving soap into a copious lather, in the vain hope that this time his daily ordeal would end without bloodshed, approached them and declared: "There's some platoons would know what to do with rats like them who screw their mates to suck up to the instructor and laugh with him at their expense. They'd be walking around with their legs in casts already and not running no more. But there's no mates here, just shit. Everybody worries about himself, everybody hides behind the other guy, everybody's glad when the other guy gets screwed."

"Fellows!" cried Alon, shocked, surprised, hurt, and as always when he addressed us like this I felt a pang of shame and pity for him. "Fellows! But nobody did you any harm. Nobody screwed you. Everyone ran as well as he could and in the end we waited for you all to catch up. He didn't even bawl you out. So what's the problem? Dammit all, this is the army isn't it? We obey orders here, don't we?"

"Army?" The savage shriek escaped the lips of Zero-Zero, whose long, beaky nose, red as a piece of raw meat, and bulging, bloodshot eyes burst like signs of life from a face that resembled a death mask in its thick, white coating of shaving cream. "Army my ass!" he cried and turned his backside to Alon. Then he examined Alon's face with animosity and a look of concern in his eyes, as if trying to assess the intentions of the enemy, and said: "And you just don't try and be a hero, you hear? You can take your army and your whole fucking state with your kibbutzim and your Palmach and stick it up your ass! You hear? Maybe on your kibbutz they bring you into the world to be soldiers. I suppose that's how they bring you up there, drilling and running and playing soldiers and getting ready for the big day when you go to the army. So you can go on running there as much as you like, till you don't have a drop of air left in your bodies for all I care. But this here ain't a kibbutz, this here is Training Base Four, not the fucking Palmach. If you want to be a paratroop commando, then go to the paratroops, but not here, not if my heart and my health have to suffer for it. I want to stay alive, you hear? I got plans for my life; I want to get through this shit in one piece. How much is he gonna make us run tomorrow? Hey? He's not normal, that corporal. It's gonna be murder with him, I'm telling you, murder!"

Zero-Zero lowered his head and took a deep breath. The long, vociferous outburst had left him weak and breathless. Avner, Albert, and the other runners did not intervene in the argument, keeping a low profile and trying not to draw attention to themselves. They were happy to leave the conduct of the debate to their representatives, as were those who had fallen by the wayside. Both camps sent their delegates into the field.

"But he didn't do anything to you, did he?" said Micky "That's a fact."

"Wait," said Hedgehog. "It's only the beginning."

Micky thought for a minute, and then raised his face with a resolute expression. "You know what," he said, "I'm not interested. It's not my problem. It's your problem." After that he muttered, as if to himself, and perhaps in order to remind himself of some golden rule that he might forget unless he repeated it over and over again: "I'm not going to adapt myself to anyone else's needs. I'm not going to burden myself with other people's weaknesses. I don't owe anyone anything."

"You'll be the first one to get it in the neck," predicted Hedgehog. "And no one'll come to help you. You're not as strong as you think you are, that you can afford to be so conceited and egotistical and high-and-mighty." And although he had already cast off the yoke of Orthodoxy, Hedgehog remembered the traditional version of this thought from his religious schooldays and saw fit to add a warning: "There's a saying of the sages: If anyone cuts himself off from society, let him not expect the consolations of society either."

"I'm not afraid," said Micky. "No favors. I can take care of myself."

"No one's asking you for favors." Hedgehog tried to speak reasonably and reduce the tension. "But there's a certain code of behavior. No one's saying that you have to get into trouble and put on an act and not run. But you don't have to excel either. The golden mean! That's what I'm saying. Just stay in the middle. Society doesn't like outstanding excellence any more than outstanding backwardness, you know. You have to be average. Not stand out in either direction."

"That's not the society that I want to live in," said Micky. "I want to live in a society where the minority sets the standards for the majority, like a goal to be strived for. I don't have the least desire to sleep my life away on the middle ground with all the average citizens. And if I can't be on the top I'd rather be right at the bottom, pulling everyone else down, anywhere rather in the middle."

Albert the Bulgarian, to whom life seemed a simple and comfortable affair, and who perceived every complication and abstraction as a threat to the peaceful, optimistic integrity of his existence, was alarmed at Micky's words: "What's all the philosophizing in aid of?" he said. "Why frighten the boys for nothing? Why upset everybody? What's the big deal? It'll all settle down in a few days' time. You'll see. Everyone'll run the new route, they'll get used to it, and there won't be any problems."

"They can get used to it or not," said Micky, refusing this offer of compromise and standing firmly on his principles. "I couldn't care less. I'll run as fast as I like and as much as I can and I don't need advice or criticism from anyone."

Peretz could not longer restrain the rage that had been mounting up inside him during this discussion, which he regarded as a dangerous deviation from the urgent, fateful matter at hand: "What d'you mean you couldn't care less? I'll give you couldn't care less!" he yelled, trying to grab Micky by the arm. But Micky shook his hand off with demonstrative disgust, and for the first time I heard him shout: "Don't touch me, you hear! Don't ever touch me!" And he punched Peretz so hard on the shoulder that he stumbled backward against the wall, wide-eyed in astonishment. Alon immediately stepped in between them and spread out his arms. "That's enough, fellows knock it off," he said, and then he looked at Micky: "What happened to you?"

Micky bit his lip, obviously ashamed of his outburst. "I don't know," he said, "I couldn't help it."

Zero-Zero swore in Romanian and looked at us in wordless accusation, displaying his face as mute evidence of our guilt. Blood tricked from his temple down his cheek, which was still covered with lather, and every time he scraped the razor over his face additional rivers of blood appeared amid the snow. He gazed at his face in the mirror and closed his eyes in despair. "You'll pay for it!" he cried. "Ass lickers always have to pay for it in the end!"

"By the three hundred men that licked the water will I save you, and deliver the Midianites into thine hand; and let all the other people go every man unto his place," said Micha the Fool.

Nobody laughed or reacted. A strained silence fell, gloomy and embarrassing.

Something had happened, but was not yet clear enough to be defined. Something had been broken, something that had been built gradually, secretly, heedlessly, without our consciously sensing it, until now, when it fell apart and we saw how delicate and fragile and very superficial it had been. And there was nothing to take its place. We evaded each other's eyes and withdrew into ourselves. The silence was broken by Sammy, one of the little band of runners who had reached the base without dropping out. He said: "Shut up, you fool."

"Shut up, you fool, you're talking bunk. You yourself are just a punk," declared Micha.

"Stop it, fellows, that's enough," implored Alon.

On the way out of the showers Rahamim approached Micky and, seeing his glum expression, said: "Don't take any notice of them. They're just jealous because you're so strong."

Micky stopped, looked at him, closed his eyes, and said: "Do me a favor and get out of my sight. I can't stand the sight of you. Shove off!"

Raffy Nagar presented the parade to Benny, the new instructor, and went away. There was an atmosphere of impending doom. Nobody would escape unscathed. Benny stood looking at us in the same way as he had looked at us previously, before we set off on the morning run. And after the furious barks of Raffy Nagar, which over the course of time we had come to regard as a kind of stylized performance, the new instructor's voice sounded sleepy, dry, bored, mean, and dangerous.

"I don't understand why they take scum like you into the army in the first place. But that's not my decision," he said in a slow drawl, dragging out every syllable. "My job is to turn this scum into men, into soldiers. And for your information, that's exactly what I'm about to do. The vacation camp is over. The army begins for you today. You'll begin to understand through your feet what the past month didn't succeed in getting through your thick skulls. What's that on your face, don't you know how to shave yet?"

He went up to Zero-Zero to inspect his face and neck, a mosaic of scratches and cuts, black islands of unshaved stubble and freshly dried bloodstains. The frozen poker face, calm and utterly lacking in any emotion, could not prevent a drooping of the corners of the mouth and a thrusting-out of the lower lip in an expression of revulsion and disgust. Hie eyes gleamed behind the lenses of his glasses as they examined Zero-Zero's face with a pseudoscientific interest, like the eyes of a doctor upon first encountering some rare clinical phenomenon.

"Did you hear what I said?" he asked Zero-Zero in an ominously quiet voice.

"Yes, sir," said Zero-Zero.

"Why do you cut yourself like that? Are you trying to commit suicide? Forget it! You're IDF property now. Any attempt to destroy IDF property is an offense against General Routine Orders."

"My skin's bad, sir," said Zero-Zero, "it gets cut when I shave."

"Have you got a skin disease?" inquired Benny. "A skin disease!" he announced like the same doctor, having hit upon the correct diagnosis and solved the mystery of the rare phenomenon before him. He took a few steps backward, as if alarmed by what he had discovered. "But why don't you go for a medical examination? Don't you know that it's infectious? You want to infect the whole platoon? Aren't they sick enough already? You want to make them even sicker? Go on sick parade and get yourself examined."

"Yes, sir."

"Are there any other men here suffering from infectious diseases?"

His question was greeted with silence. He put his hand in his pocket, extracted a box of matches, threw it up in the air and caught it, threw it up again and caught it again.

"Do these matches belong to anyone?"

I saw the hesitation trembling on the back of Avner's neck, until he stepped forward, jumped to attention, and said: "They're mine, sir." Benny threw the matches at Avner, who caught them.

"Where's the other man who was on guard with you?" He scanned the ranks as if seeking the second guard. I stepped forward, jumped to attention, and said in a breaking voice: "Me, sir."

"You stayed in the same place all the time without patrolling. You slept standing up instead of guarding. The bullshit's over. Tonight you're on guard at the same place, and this time you'll do it right, as per orders, and I'll see to it."

He took a slip of paper out of his pocket and looked at it: "Ben-Hamo, Rahamim."

Rahamim jumped to attention and called: "Yes, sir!"

"After parade you'll report to the company CO on a report."

"Yes, sir."

"The route you ran this morning will be your regular route from now on. Anyone who doesn't finish the course tomorrow morning will run it again in the evening, until he's fit enough to do it. Is that clear? Any questions?"

"Sir!" called Alon, jumping to attention.

Benny stared in the direction from which Alon's voice had come in surprise. Presumably he had not meant his invitation to be taken seriously. "What is it?"

"Most of the platoon have medical problems, sir, and they can't run so far."

Fear fell on us all. Benny looked at Alon as if he couldn't believe his ears. He dragged the moment out excruciatingly.

"Is that how you were taught to identify yourself to your NCO?" he asked at last.

"Alon, sir."

"What?"

Alon identified himself properly, giving his serial number, surname, and first name in that order.

"And are you somebody's representative here?" asked Benny with a polite, sly, ironic smile, as if he were trying to trip him up. "Did they choose you to represent them?"

"No, sir," said Alon.

"So why are you speaking for them?"

Alon said nothing.

"You know what you just did?" asked Benny. "You said something that in the army is considered incitement to mutiny. You know what mutiny means in the army? You miserable nonentity! You know what they do to people who incite to mutiny in the army?"

"I was wrong, sir," said Alon. "I shouldn't have said what I did."

"You shouldn't have thought it!" said Benny. "Since when do you have the right to think for yourself here? You're here to obey orders! What do you think this is — a vacation camp?"

"I take it back, sir," said Alon.

"Who gave you permission to speak? You'll speak when you're spoken to, and when I give you permission to. How dare you burst out like that in front of your NCO?"

Alon was silent. We stood tensely in the ranks, eyes forward, and I couldn't see Alon, but I knew that his face, which was always flushed and looked as if he were suffering from permanent sunstroke, was even redder now with shame and defeat, and that his downcast eyes were ready to endure more and more humiliation, to take his punishment like a man.

"This time I'll let you off without having you court-martialed and sending you to jail," said Benny, "because I can see that you lot don't know your ass from your elbows. You need to be taught the ABCs of military behavior and I'm here to teach you. You'll have plenty of time today to take back everything you said and thought and try to understand what I've explained to you. After parade you'll report to the CSM for latrine duty. You'll find everything you need to satisfy your interfering soul there and you'll be able to snivel over the problems of the weak to your heart's content in the perfect place for it. Are you satisfied?"

Alon said nothing.

"I asked you a question, why don't you answer when your NCO asks you a question? I asked you if you were happy now?"

"No, sir."

"Why not?"

"They said we were going to have bayonet drill, sir, and I don't want to miss it."

"Bayonet drill? Is that what you deserve, in your opinion? You think you're worthy of it? Rifles and bayonets aren't for the likes of imbeciles like you. You have to graduate from the shithouse stage first. If there weren't any shithouses they would have to invent them for you. Wake up from your dreams, children, Mommy isn't here anymore. Corporal Benny's in charge of you now, and he's going to turn this scum into men, into soldiers. It won't be easy. You're going to wear your asses ragged, you're going to be drilled and trained to within an inch of your lives, but in the end you'll be soldiers. And you'll like it and you'll say thank you to your instructors for making men of you. And then you'll begin to understand what miserable worms you are now. The fact that you're high school graduates, that you're so cultured and intelligent, doesn't impress anyone. Any more than the famous medical problems you think are going to protect you and make things soft for you and let you go on sniveling and whining and degenerating together. Forget it. It won't help you. It'll only make it harder to break you. Your only hope is to break as quickly as possible and turn into soldiers."

He gave us a long, doubtful look, and muttered again, as before we set out on the morning run: "Heaven help us."

Then he announced: "You've got eight minutes exactly for an extra parade with clean weapons, neat turnout, barracks spick-and-span, everything tip-top ready for inspection. Spector, Micky!"

"Yes, sir," cried Micky.

"Are you the one from *Hapoel* Hadera?"

"Yes, sir."

"On the command *Move!* you'll all run to your barracks on the double and get ready for the extra parade. Apart from those who received a different order. Spector, you'll stay here. I want to talk to you. You've got eight minutes exactly. Dismissed! Move!"

As in an anthill kicked by a child a commotion immediately broke out, with everyone rushing in all directions, apparently without aim or plan, each ant fleeing for its life, running around in circles, joining its friends and milling around with them and getting nowhere. But only apparently. A closer look reveals the shifting pattern in the chaos, a complex and highly sophisticated plan in which every detail plays its own unique role in perfect coordination with hundreds of others, like a single note in a great and complicated harmony. And what was previously two miserable, straggling rows in a column marching interminably backward and forward opened out like a bud suddenly turning into a flower, transformed into a crowded, frenzied, mass ballet, precise, compulsive, and emotionless as clockwork.

It was the beginning of something, like the beginning of falling in love. Something was imposing a new order and new relations into matter that had lost its form, promising to fill the void that had opened up with the sinking of the soul. It stamped an image of fear and longing indelibly on the heart, seeping like glad tidings into the depths of the mind. The game was familiar, but the spirit was new. Again and again we leapt to obey the shouted command of the orderly student to fall in for parade, our actions governed by a different logic, the logic of a machine gone mad, its operations becoming less and less practical, more and more poetic. And he stood there in front of us, relaxed, his shoulders slumped, his eyes looking sleepily at the watch on his wrist, counting the seconds like a scientist in a routine experiment, impervious to the cry of the heart rising from this Sisyphian labor and calling to him, especially to him.

I felt that we had lost some happiness we had possessed without being aware of it, a communal happiness that had now been taken away and replaced by some obscure promise, involving new sufferings, and standing at the end of the road was the new instructor whose face I refused, with the vestiges of whatever strength remained to me, to recognize.

Between one parade and the next Micky returned and said he had been asked to join the soccer team of the training command. This would mean long absences from the base for practice and games. The gloom that had descended on him in the morning, during the argument in the showers, had vanished; his eyes were sparkling with suppressed delight. Everyone congratulated him on his good fortune, but the eyes surrounding him cried *Traitor!* He said little and played down the importance of what had happened, as if he had resolved to resume the caution he had been neglecting of late. I knew that he wanted to share his happiness with someone, but the only person he considered worthy of his confidence was not with us: Alon had gone to clean the latrines, punishment for inciting to mutiny. While we ran to and fro from the barracks to the parade and the parade to the barracls, at diminishing intervals of time, Micky's heart was already somewhere else, on his soccer field, as if he knew that from this moment on he was immune to harassment. And Hedgehog, who had argued that excellence, like failure, did not win any prizes in a society whose ideal was the golden mean, looked at Micky going indifferently through the motions, unaffected by the terrors of the repeated inspections and parades, and nodded sagely as if to say: *Let's wait and see.*

When Rahamim came back from the company office he refused to reveal his sentence to his friends. And when they pressed him he began to giggle, as if enjoying their anxiety. Their faces fell. Had he told his judge the truth about who had burned his blanket? Peretz and Zackie threatened to hit him, but Rahamim was unconcerned. Did he too feel that he had been granted some kind of immunity? Zackie spat an Arabic curse at him and stuck his fist between his ribs, and suddenly he found himself accosted by Miller, holding up an admonitory finger: "No. No fight, no more fight!" Zackie recoiled. Miller's presence was mysterious and threatening to them; they avoided him like the plague. Rahamim too was taken aback and even horrified by this unexpected salvation, his body shrank at the sight of the German rushing to his rescue, and the air of mischievous glee with which he had met the inquiries of his friends on his return disappeared, as if he saw this intervention on his behalf as an ill omen full of dire foreboding.

We lifted our bayonet-armed rifles into the air, drove them vigorously into the stomachs of the invisible enemy in front of us, pulled down, and twisted hard. But we couldn't yell. We looked into each other's eyes, surprised to discover a residual as yet unvanquished shame. For otherwise, why couldn't we yell? The sounds that came out of our mouths were more like groans of pain or cries of surprise and disappointment than the murderous yells required. Benny commanded us again to yell with all our strength, but the yell refused to come. His look said: *I'm losing patience.* He got ready to demonstrate the way a battle cry should sound during a bayonet assault. For the purposes of the demonstration he took Micky's rifle. From the slightly slack, slump-shouldered body, from the apathetic face, from the sleepy eyes behind the glasses, a new figure leapt: its legs tensed to spring, its taut neck out-thrust, its shoulders hunched like the wings of a bird of prey, its eyes wide and gleaming. And from his wide-open mouth burst the shriek of a terrible animal tearing its prey to pieces. A terrifying shriek that was repeated several times with the movements of the bayonet rising and stabbing and slashing and mauling. Who would have believed that such a shriek could be summoned at will, simply for the purposes of demonstration? When it was over his face resumed its sleepy expression and his stance slackened. "That's how I want it," he said and looked at the long line of men standing in front of him, their faces still showing the effects of his performance. He went up to the end of the line with the intention of going through it one by one until he achieved the right yell. At the end of the line stood Nahum, his baffled smile anguished and full of dread.

"Action!" cried Benny.

Nahum brandished his bayonet and let out a couple of peculiar bleats, giving rise to tentative, experimental bursts of laughter. We were afraid to laugh out loud, uncertain of the new instructor's reaction.

Benny looked at Nahum in silence. Then he said: "Don't you understand what I say to you? That's not a broomstick you're holding, that's a bayonet-armed gun! And you're sticking it into his belly" — Benny pointed at the air in front of Nahum — "and you're going to yell the way you yell when you're killing someone, and if you don't yell you won't be able to kill him. Do you understand now? I want you to yell — not sing like a cantor in the synagogue. Is that clear?"

"Yes, sir," mumbled Nahum.

"What?"

"Yes, sir."

"I can't hear."

Nahum raised his voice: "Yes, sir."

"Louder!" Benny too raised his voice.

"Yes, sir!" Nahum yelled at the top of his lungs.

"Louder!"

"Yes, sir!" Nahum's face was red with effort and the vein on his neck swelled to bursting.

"I can't hear!" yelled Benny.

There must have been no air left in Nahum's lungs, because now he yelled in a voice that was not his own, a harsh, throttled voice, hoarse and fierce, like a man fighting for his life.

"Yes, sir!"

"At the command *Action!* you'll do the bayonet assault exercise and yell at every stage like I told you."

"Yes, sir!" Nahum yelled again in his new voice, apparently still surprised to hear it coming out of his throat, not yet used to its sound and straining his ears to accustom them to it. "Yes, sir!" yelled Nahum again without moving from his place, still stunned by the shock of the encounter with his voice. His face, which had lost its smile, looked naked. His eyes stared as if hypnotized. Benny sprang at him and punched him in the stomach. Nahum jumped, stood still for a moment like a sleepwalker who had bumped into a wall, and when he heard the command "Action!" repeated again he yelled, brandished his bayonet, and was about to drive it into the new instructor, who immediately jumped aside and looked at him with a certain satisfaction.

Nahum closed his eyes and breathed hard as if after a strenuous run. His eyes were wet with tears from the strain. When he opened them, he tried without success to resume his habitual smile. He woke from a dream and looked around him, presumably hoping that nobody had seen his dream.

The man standing next to him found less difficulty in executing the exercise. *Soon the whole thing will stop being ridiculous and shameful,* I said to myself, *because the shame is rooted in the performance and not in the idea behind it, and now we're beginning to understand that it's not a performance. It's a moment of truth. Like the moment of death in silencing a sentry, and the empty space we shook with our shouts and stuck our bayonets into isn't the empty stage of a performance — it's inside us, behind the barrier of our last secrets, like a refuge for fears and memories that hasn't yet been destroyed.*

And so each of us waited for his turn, for the moment of recovery, to spew out his yell. And when my turn came, I embraced it eagerly and rapidly mobilized all the forces of memory and hatred at my command, but I was unable to come up with anything to match the depths of the scream I wanted to spew out of myself. Until the command: "Action! — *Pa'al!*" thundered in my ears and I heard the hidden echo of the voice of the child whose name I had forgotten and who had saved my life in the train on the way to Jerusalem. Maybe because of the similarity in the sound of the words. His voice was hoarse, because it had already begun to break, and at the end of a fraction of time in which I had apparently lost consciousness, I heard him yelling in my ear: "Lucky! Lucky! — *Mazal Mazal!*"

We were traveling to Jerusalem by train on an end-of-the-year school outing. They said that a section of the tracks passed through Jordanian territory. Rushing past the windows were hills and wadis and terraces and orchards and shepherds, and I didn't know if they were still our Arabs or their Arabs already, but the sight was ancient and it thrilled my heart. From where we were sitting I couldn't see any of the details properly, because it all rushed past in the square of the window and changed from one second to the next. Although it was forbidden, I stood up and went over to the window and stuck my head and shoulder out. I looked to my right at the open countryside the train had left behind. The wind blew onto my face and from my vantage point I could see the land of Canaan spread out before me in a semicircle as far as the horizon. Suddenly I was pulled and thrown violently backward into the coach, someone was holding me by the throat and pulling my head inside and a heavy darkness suddenly came down on everything, the windows disappeared, and I couldn't see the people sitting on either side of me. I thought I had blacked out. A deafening muffled roar filled the dark compartment, as if ears blocked up for a long time had suddenly opened, a monotonous roar, drawn out like a siren. And the voice of the child, whose name I had forgotten, yelled to overcome the noise and cried in my ear: "*Mazal! Mazal!*" in a hoarse voice that had already begun to break, and as I said to myself: *Where have the windows suddenly disappeared to?* I lost my grip on reality and sank for a few split seconds into a strange dizziness, and when I recovered I could still see the side of the rounded wall a hair's breadth away from the window. The train emerged from the tunnel and was bathed in the noon light again and the boy went on holding on to me, as if loath to let go of his prize. He was beaming with happiness, and the children sitting on either side of us shared in his delight and he went on crying: *"Mazal! Mazal!"* At that moment I felt the pain on the nape of my neck where he had taken hold to drag me from the window and the burning of the insult, and the rage boiled up in me. I extricated myself from his grip and from his excited story, repeated over and over again, how he had seen and decided and jumped and pulled, right at the very last minute, and if he hadn't been so quick it would have been all up with me. I went to the other end of the car, with him behind me, still obsessively reciting his story, reliving over and over the moment at which he had pulled me out of the eternity of the dark tunnel and saved me, like a rebirth into the light of the world.

He only stayed with us for a year. The next year they refused to promote him to the next grade and he changed to the agricultural school in Pardes-Hannah. And after that I never saw him again. But the memory of the trick he played in the classroom, whose results we saw on the last day of school when we came to get our report cards, before the long vacation began, went on exhilarating me inside with intoxicating laughter for years, besides giving rise to a certain admiration, which I had been ashamed to admit at the time.

Was it only the similar sound of the words that brought back to me after so many years the cry of *"Mazal!"* and the picture of the thin, dark child with his faint mustache (he was a year or two older than the rest of us), dressed in a khaki shirt and shorts far too big for him, whose name was impossible to remember? And when I fell on his memory with my bayonet I yelled as if I wanted to settle a long account, to free myself of a debt that could never be paid off, like an incurable illness, in the same way as I had tried to free myself from the excited grip of his hands, from his eager, pressing joy, hungry for a slice of the big win. I strained my voice to the utmost: *"Aah! Aah! Aah! Aah!"*

Perhaps my zeal was too great. My voice sounded artificial. It was a performance, but it satisfied the instructor. He passed onto the next man. And all that time the cries rising into the air sounded to me like an echo in anticipation of the real scream that had not yet come into its own. Only when we were about to execute the exercise together, each man against the transparent reflection opposite him, and the few score voices combined into a really mighty roar, savage, fierce, intoxicating, I sensed something like relief passing through our ranks again, as if one more passage in the labyrinth was concluded, one more secret revealed, one more pact coming into being.

During the rest break the new instructor moved a short distance away and stood looking at us as if trying to make up his mind about something,

until he walked off and we looked after him until he disappeared from
view, feeling that our fate in some way depended on his mystery.

Everyone wanted to know about Avner's matchbox. We told them
about the girl soldier who had been in the office with Benny at night, and
who had apparently wanted a cigarette. Who was the girl? Sammy, our
usual source of information about activity on the base, didn't know, or
perhaps he didn't want to tell what he knew. He told us that until
recently Benny had been an instructor in the paratroops, until something
happened and he had been transferred to Training Base 4. What had happened? He didn't say. Maybe because of the glasses? someone suggested.
Maybe they had discovered he suffered from some medical problem? To
judge by the way he'd run that morning, he was amazingly fit. The runners who had reached the end of the long road with him said that he'd
showed no sign of effort; he'd hardly even perspired.

"That corporal will be the death of us," Zero-Zero sighed.

"Just so they don't give us too much of him," said Hedgehog, "and just
so certain people in the platoon don't start getting any big ideas that he
brought from the paratroops from him."

"You see," said Peretz, "this new one's one of yours, a German. Soon
he'll start talking in your words too." And he dropped his eyelids and
drawled in a tired, sleepy, monotonous voice: "The psychology of the
sociology of the scumology."

"Don't worry boys," said Albert the Bulgarian. "Listen, it'll all work
out, we'll get used to him, he'll get used to us. It's only now, at the beginning, he wants to make an impression. He knows what he's doing; he'll
make men of us all. He's confident, he's intelligent, he's well educated,
he's not a sadist, why talk nonsense for nothing?"

"He's a German," Peretz repeated. "Listen to what I'm telling you. I
understand types like him. In the end they come to the Sick Fund Clinic
to go see the psychiatrist and sit with all the crazy people. Like animals
he wants us, with our throats on the ground yelling: *Aah! Aah! Aah!*" And
he imitated the battle cry, squatting down and hopping like a frog and
shouting: *"Aah! Aah! Aah!"* to peals of laughter from his audience. "He's
a German just like all of you. He's got no heart for people, I bet he's got
no friends. And he wants to make us suffer for his problems. It makes
him feel good to put us down." He raised his foot a few inches from the
ground and stamped it down hard. "Like this."

These speculations about Benny's character continued unabated for
the next few days. We had never talked much about any of the other
instructors. Sometimes we would be content with a curse, an abusive or

a humorous remark after some incident, and sometimes we would try to analyze what had happened. But their personalities and motives didn't interest us all that much. Avner said: "He really is different from the others. He's a different type. The type that spells trouble." Did I understand what he was getting at? With Benny it was more dangerous, he touched something deep and devious in us, he attached us to him with ties of hatred and admiration, hope and fear. We sat next to the road, in the shade of a few meager eucalyptus trees, and the sun approaching its zenith beat down on us mercilessly. The shade of these trees was more symbolic than real, like the reference point of a possible settlement in the heart of the desert. There were five minutes left to the end of the break and he had not yet appeared. Micky suddenly broke a long silence by saying, as if to himself: "Maybe we'll get leave on Rosh Hashana?"

Nobody knew the answer. There was no way of guessing at their intentions.

"What are you worrying about?" said Hedgehog. "You're going to get leave all the time anyway."

"So why does it bother you so much?" asked Micky. "Is it any skin off your nose? Will it cost you anything, will it cost the platoon anything?"

"Why should it bother me?" cried Hedgehog, insulted. "Go ahead and enjoy yourself! That's life — ups and downs. And everyone has his moment. This is your moment, so take advantage of it and enjoy it."

Rahamim's nervous giggling intervened: Zackie had grabbed him by the throat and announced that he would not let go until he told them what he had been sentenced to. When the grip began to hurt Rahamin stopped giggling and tried to remove Zackie's hands from his throat. "Will you tell?" demanded Zackie. Rahamim nodded and Zackie let go. Rahamim hung his head and shook it with an agonized expression, as if trying to recover his consciousness. He must have gone on too long with the performance, for Zackie kicked him and yelled: "Talk! Talk!"

Rahamim looked gleeful again. "Confinement to barracks," he said.

"What?"

"Confinement to barracks. That's the punishment they gave me."

"Is that all?" shouted Peretz indignantly, holding his head in his hands as if lamenting some disaster. "What an army, what an army!"

Rahamim laughed in enjoyment of his victory. Everyone else looked disappointed.

Zackie said: "What did you tell them?"

"I didn't tell them nothing! I swear on my mother!" said Rahamim.

"They didn't even ask me anything. They just read something out loud so quick you couldn't understand a word and told me my punishment."

The lightness of the punishment seemed to many like a conspiracy against us, a provocation against the collective sense of justice we had developed over the past month, a further step in the direction of frustrating any attempt on our part to understand the logic of the army identify with its spirit.

On the hill opposite us a number of greenish figures appeared. More and more came up behind them, a few score men marching three abreast, their knapsacks on their shoulders, until they came to a halt and formed up in front of the soldier commanding them. They lowered their knapsacks to the ground and, in response to a command inaudible to us, all sat down at once. Their instructor went away. They sat without moving, waiting for a command to come from somewhere, and after a moment Sammy's voice suddenly broke out from among us, as if giving a signal: "Raw meat! Raw meat!"

And other voices immediately joined in the chorus: "Raw meat! Raw meat!"

We couldn't see their faces clearly, only their clumsy shapes in the new uniforms, sitting uneasily on the hill with their possessions at their feet and the sun beating down mercilessly on their heads. I didn't try to understand the meaning of the hatred that flooded me at the sight of them. I had long ago forgotten my vow to observe things from the sidelines, to try to explain them to myself exempt from the burden of belonging. The feelings of anger and hostility aroused in us by the new recruits sitting on the hill were stronger than anything else. As if something precious to me, precious to all of us had been desecrated, as if their very presence constituted some new threat, some humiliation worse than anything we had known up to now. They were tainted, contagious, a caste of untouchables who had come to infect us with the very thing we had been struggling so long and at the cost of so much suffering to cleanse ourselves of. Our voices grew louder and we all chorused together: "Raw meat! Raw meat!" like some magic formula that would rid us of the taint, remove the invaders from our borders.

And suddenly he was standing there. We had scarcely recovered from the intoxication of the catcalls when the orderly-student cried "Attention!" signaling the end of the rest break. Silence fell and only Micha the Fool went on shouting "Raw meat! Raw meat!" to the laughter of Peretz and Hedgehog. Benny stood looking at him. The orderly-student, pale and silent, silenced him and formed us up into threes, saluted, and mumbled something. Benny stared at us in silence. From the opposite hill came the sound of rhythmic shouts: "Hup, hup, hup!" and the thud of boots on the ground. Their instructor had apparently returned and was taking them somewhere else.

When the noise died down Benny said in a quiet, menacing voice: "In the army, when the NCO allocates time for rest, the orderly-student forms the platoon up in threes in readiness for the moment of the NCO's return. And everyone stands at attention and keeps quiet. Dead quiet." He fell silent and looked at us with an expression of disgust and almost of pity, nodded, and said: "And the army isn't an abattoir or a butcher shop." His voice was now charged with an anger we had not imagined him capable of: "What do you mean by yelling *raw meat*? If they're raw meat, you're rotten, stinking meat, full of worms. Carcass meat. Those recruits you saw are going to a combat regiment, to Golani, and they're only here temporarily. They'll be combat troops, not jobniks like you lot. How dare you, how dare you call them raw meat? You're not even worthy of the honor of washing their feet. When they're shedding their blood for their country, you'll be sitting in your cushy jobs. And you!"

He pointed at Micha.

"Yes, sir!" cried Micha.

"Your NCO's standing and waiting and you go on shouting like an idiot! Step out of the ranks and stand here!"

"I didn't see you, sir," said Micha, stepping forward and standing in front of Benny.

"How dare you speak when I'm talking to you? I didn't ask you a question!" He stared at the Fool with disgust, examining his mumbling lips.

"What's wrong with him?" asked Benny. "In addition to all your physical diseases and epilepsy and sexual problems, have you got nutcases here as well? Where did they pick you up — the national garbage dump of the state of Israel?"

Micha mumbled to himself without stopping and without making a sound; there was no knowing if he was repeating verses from the Bible, a selection of classical poetry, historical dates, or logarithmic tables.

"Stop that, stop it at once, that's an order!" said Benny sharply.

Micha said with a dumb smile: "Yes, sir, " and went on mumbling soundlessly, his face pale and his smile fixed. Benny looked at him for a minute and then turned away from the revolting sight.

"You!" he cried and pointed at Hedgehog. "The one who laughed!"

Hedgehog stepped out of the ranks.

"And you!" He pointed at the orderly-student. "The three of you will now run to the platoon and return with full equipment and knapsacks. On the double, I want you back here in two minutes flat. Move!"

The three of them set out immediately at a run toward the platoon barracks, and we returned to the bayonet drill. And while Benny was busy explaining the various stages of the assault to us, there was a sound of thudding boots shaking the earth in time to cries of *Hup! Hup! Hup!* Immediately afterward we saw the platoon of Golani recruits reappearing at the end of the road, loaded down with their equipment. Their instructor assembled them at the edge of the ground where we were standing. At a distance of about two hundred yards from us they sat down, formed up in threes. Two soldiers arrived carrying big piles of fatigues and put them down in front of them, and at their instructor's command the recruits stood up and fell on the piles of uniforms, holding them up against their bodies and measuring them for size. Then they got undressed and put on the fatigues, exchanged their berets for peaked caps, doing everything at great speed, and in the end they sat down again in threes and listened to something their instructor was telling them. The latter went off again, and left them sitting there.

Benny finished his explanation and just as we were about to execute the first stage of the assault, Hedgehog, Micha, and the orderly-student arrived in full equipment with their knapsacks on their shoulders. Benny looked at his watch. They were late.

"You will now begin to run," he said and pointed out the route, "from here, down to the end of the field, to where they're sitting, and left, to the corner in front of the armory, and back, and then around again, and without changing your pace. I'll be watching you from here. Until you get the command to come back here. Move! Hup! Hup! Hup!"

Hedgehog and Micha and the orderly-student ran off side by side, three abreast, and we immediately commenced the bayonet assault, yelling the battle cry as we had been taught, while opposite us, at a distance of about two hundred yards, still, shapeless green patches, blurred to the point of merging into the surrounding landscape, watched the performance, unaware of the fact that it was into their bodies that we were sticking our bayonets, against them that we were yelling our cries of passionate fury and hatred. Hedgehog and Micha and the orderly-student ran past them. If they looked closely at the three runners, and presumably they had nothing more interesting to do during those moments of waiting, it must have been evident to them — raw meat though they might be, arrived here straight from the induction center, without any military experience — that they were looking at a few pieces of filth that had been collected from the national garbage dump of the state of Israel. And we made every effort to deny any connection with them, and to hide behind the war play directed by our combat instructor, throwing ourselves into our roles with all the powers of illusion and identification we could summon.

The three of them came up at a run, their faces red and sweating, while Benny watched them with a suspicious, critical expression and cries of *Hup! Hup! Hup!* until they ran past us, the sound of their groaning, rhythmic breathing still loud in our ears, and approached the new recruits again, a few of whom stood up to get a better view. And there, there of all places, Hedgehog fell, his knapsack rolling on the ground. He tried to get up and failed, and the orderly-student, who had already run a few steps forward, turned back and helped him up. Hedgehog stood up, the orderly-student hoisted the knapsack onto his back and gave him a push, and then he set off again with Hedgehog bringing up the rear and trying to catch up with him and Micha the Fool. But Hedgehog couldn't make it, and the two of them ran in front of him until Micha looked back and saw him stumbling behind them, and stopped and started running on the spot until Hedgehog caught up. The orderly-student closed ranks with them and they went on running straight ahead and then turned left until they reached the armory corner. Benny observed all this without any change in his expression. But when they had completed another round and ran past us again, he called out to them: "Every fall — two more rounds. Hup! Hup! Hup!"

After they had receded some distance down the road Benny ordered us to sit around him in a semicircle. "You can smoke if you like," he said. He tried to introduce a more relaxed atmosphere. He had a little stick in his hand and he kept tapping it on his hand. "In the end you'll be soldiers, I promise you. It'll be hard but you'll see that it will happen." This time he said it not as a threat but as a statement of fact. "Who's that nut who can't stop talking to himself? Where's he from? Is there anyone here who knows him from civilian life?"

Hanan stood up to reply. Benny said: "You can talk sitting down, it's okay." His sudden liberality and relaxation began to seem more menacing and humiliating than his previous aloofness, harshness, and contempt.

"He's from Jerusalem, sir," said Hanan. "I've known him for years."

"What's wrong with him? Is he sick in the head? Why did the army take him?"

"He's a genius, sir," said Hanan. "We were in the same class at school."

"A genius?" sneered Benny. "What's he a genius at?" The faint smile that appeared at the corners of his lips suddenly alerted my attention without my understanding why.

"Mainly in mathematics," said Hanan, "and all the sciences. But also in history and everything else. He's got fantastic memory and a mathematical mind."

Benny smiled. The smile that had suddenly alerted me like a warning cry. My heart hammered like a pendulum rapidly striking three beats: the first beat, the happiness of discovery and recognition; the second beat, insult and dejection; the third beat, uncertainty. It was a difficult smile to forget. He smiled with half his mouth, as if the left half of his face were not taking part in the act. The right-hand corner of his lips stretched upward, giving his face an expression of obscene pleasure, as if he were relishing some particularly dirty joke or cruel, disgusting trick. His eyes behind their glasses grew damp, as if wallowing in the pleasure afforded by such thoughts, as if conjuring up the picture of some filthy memory, and one of them even half closed, as if to aid him in the effort to remember. And from the parting between his lips one of his incisors peeped out, the right one, which was broken diagonally and ended in a sharp point. The fourth beat: I remembered this smile, I remembered this broken tooth, but I felt as if part of my resources, the essential, major part, refused to cooperate in retrieving the circumstances, the time and place in which I first seen this loathsome smile. My heart contracted in pain, and I couldn't remember why.

"Hup! Hup! Hup!" cried Benny to the three runners coming up to us again, tottering after each other, close to the breaking point. "Together, close ranks, keep in line!" They tried to narrow the gaps between them but they seemed to have been overcome by a kind of giddiness, which upset their sense of direction. Benny stopped smiling. He watched them receding and tapped his hand with his little stick, drumming some tune.

Alon came running toward us, his rifle with bayonet fixed hanging on his shoulder, stopped opposite Benny, and saluted. "Sir! I finished my detail and the CSM told me to report back to you." He was breathing heavily; his face was radiant with happiness and excitement.

Benny asked: "What do you think now about what you said on parade?"

"I think that I shouldn't have said it and I shouldn't have thought it, sir. I understand that now. I thought about it all the time."

Benny ordered us to get up and form up again in a line facing him. Alon saw us brandishing our bayonets and stabbing and slashing and twisting to the accompaniment of the famous savage yells. Then he joined our squad and executed the exercise with us, doing it with sureness and precision and the proper battle cries, as if he had practiced it for a long time.

Benny said to him: "Why are you on Training Base Four, what's your problem?"

"Heart, I think, sir," said Alon, shamefaced, as if he had been caught in the act of committing a crime.

"Have you got some heart disease?"

"No, sir, I don't know. There was never anything wrong with my heart. I don't know why they saddled me with this section."

"So what are you then, a malingerer?"

"No, sir. I wanted to go to the paratroops. I was already accepted for paratroop recruit training but then they sent me here."

"Where are you from?"

Alon gave the name of his kibbutz.

"And you still want to be combat, you want to go back to the paratroops?"

"Yes, sir, very much."

"You want to put in a request from here for a medical board reexamination?"

"Yes, sir," said Alon, "that's what I want to do."

"Come to me, I'll tell you how to go about it."

"Yes, sir," said Alon with a grateful smile.

The combat recruits at the end of the field stood up and shouldered their knapsacks. Their instructor formed them up in threes, apparently in order to move them somewhere else. Benny looked over at them, inserted two fingers in his mouth, and whistled loudly and shrilly. The other instructor immediately looked around, and Benny signaled something with his hand. The three runners reached us again, exhausted and breathless, groaning under the burden of their equipment and knapsacks, and under the burden of their bodies falling off their feet. Benny looked at them with satisfaction and told them to join the squad.

"So who's raw meat here?" he asked them. "Raw meat. And you!" He turned to Micha. "You won't make a fool of your instructor anymore!"

Micha said nothing; he bit his lips to stop them moving and strained to get his breath back.

"They tell me that you're a genius. Maybe you'll make an atom bomb for the state of Israel?" And again Benny smiled his obscene smile, as if enjoying some sick, perverted pleasure. "All your genius isn't worth a shit here, you understand? It doesn't impress anyone. Here you're all raw recruits and there's no difference between you. All that counts here is your distinction in training and discipline and in whatever you're taught here. Is that clear? Don't let there be any misunderstanding. Because in case you don't know, misunderstanding doesn't save a soldier from punishment. Is that clear, genius?"

"Yes, sir," bleated Micha, biting his rebellious lips.

"Watch out that you don't get into trouble." He assigned time for an additional break, cautioning the orderly-student to form the squad up properly and on the dot this time. Then he ran off toward the new recruits standing in front of their instructor at the end of the field. Our three runners lay on the ground, put their knapsacks under their heads, and tried to get their breath back. After a moment they hurried off to the barracks to put their gear away and be back in time for the end of the break. All eyes turned to the end of the field, watching Benny talking to the instructor of the combat recruits. Some even strained their ears in an attempt to overhear what they were saying. As if it were us they were talking about there, our fate that were being decided. We sat in silence until Alon said: "An RP just told me about the new instructor. Until not long ago he was a paratroop-training instructor. He was going to be sent to an Officers Course. Then he got into trouble with his CO and they transferred him here. As punishment. He's got balls. I can imagine how he must have felt. Having the red ground removed from his badge."

"What are you getting so excited about him for?" said Hanan. "After he screwed you like that for nothing."

"What do you mean for nothing?" retorted Alon indignantly. "He had a good reason. Saying what I said is forbidden in the army. It's incitement. He was right! He could have had me court-martialed. So what's the big deal? I cleaned some shit. Is it beneath me? Am I too good for it?"

"Because of you we'll all eat shit here," said Peretz.

The three runners came back. They were in good spirits despite their gray, drained looks.

"Where is he?" asked Hedgehog in an undertone and looked around, afraid he might be hiding next to him. "I thought we'd come back and find him looking at his watch and counting the seconds."

Someone pointed in the direction of the combat recruits. Hedgehog said: "He's a sonofabitch, that corporal. And anyone who thinks it'll do him any good to lick his ass is making a big mistake. Types like him hate ass lickers worse than anyone."

Avner lit a cigarette and gave a despairing smile. "He really is a bastard," he said. "We disgust him, all we do is make him sick and tired. He can hardly move his lips to say anything to us; he's so bored he can hardly keep awake. He's too good for us. He belongs with the combat troops, the ones with red grounds to their badges! The ones whose feet we should wash, only we're not yet worthy of the honor, all we can do is dream about it."

"But as far as raw meat is concerned," said Micky, "he's quite right. It really is stupid and disgusting. What right have we got to yell it at them?"

"And you didn't yell I suppose?" said Hedgehog angrily.

"Yes I did," said Micky, "and I admit it was disgusting."

"Sure!" said Hedgehog. "Whatever he does and says is right as far as you're concerned. What's the big deal? When we came here, didn't they call us raw meat? It's part of basic training. Everyone goes through it. It's like the sergeant major's mustache and the whitewashed trees, it's like 'You'll call me sir and I'll call you scum.' It's what the veterans call the rookies. So what's all the fuss about? If those new guys weren't from Golani he wouldn't have said anything and he wouldn't have given a damn. And their NCO's a friend of his on top of it, so altogether they're too good for this world."

Zackie broke into a heartfelt song whose Persian words I did not have to understand to know that they were very dirty indeed: "Golani, Givati, *ananinamu* . . ."

Avner said: "When the older guys in the neighborhood reminisced about army life in basic training, it all sounded so frightening, so unreal, so fantastic."

"Don't worry," said Micky. "When you talk about this time to people younger than you, it'll sound the same to them. You'll dress it up a bit and add some spice and a few exaggerations and a bit of imagination and it'll sound great, an experience you wouldn't want to miss."

"Raw meat, " said Albert the Bulgarian wonderingly, as if to himself. "The Communists say cannon meat."

"Cannon fodder," corrected Micky.

"Do me a favor," said Zero-Zero, "don't start talking Communism here. That's all we need now, for someone to hear."

Micky burst out laughing.

"What's so funny?" asked Zero-Zero angrily. "When you've buggered off to play soccer we'll get it in the neck here for stuff like that. You know what they do to Communists in the army? I heard about a case like that once. A guy they found out was one of them Communists. They brought in the CID and made a proper song and dance, they questioned him and all his platoon and there was no end to it."

"Quite right!" said Hedgehog. "Those people are spies for the Russians and the Arabs. You have to watch out for them, to keep them from infiltrating the army."

"Everything here's just a game, " said Alon, "nothing's for real. It's pathetic. In real units there's folklore, there's group spirit, morale. People are prepared to die for each other."

"The stories I heard about basic training . . ." Hedgehog sighed nostalgically, as if remembering some distant past. "In our neighborhood most people didn't go to the army at all, they got out of it with yeshivas and all that stuff. And there was this one guy who stopped being religious and went to the army and he used to tell me all these stories. He said, for instance, that in every platoon of recruits there was one sexual pervert, one who went crazy and one who tried to kill himself. We've got our pervert and we all know who he is. And we've got more than one crazy here already. So all we need now is the platoon suicide."

"Don't worry, " said Rahamim Ben-Hamo from his corner. "Maybe our suicide will be you."

All Ben-Hamo's mates burst out laughing and called out: *"Mabrukh! Mabrukh!"* to congratulate him on his wit.

The orderly-student shouted at us to fall in. The time assigned for the break was over. We stood and waited. The orderly-student kept looking nervously at his watch, afraid to turn his head around in case Benny was standing behind him. Was he in the wrong again? The failure was unavoidable, incomprehensible, its consequences hard to predict, but it hung over our heads nevertheless, as suffocating as the air in room left shut up for too long. A few more minutes passed. The orderly-student gazed at us, guilty and embarrassed. From where we were standing, formed up in threes, we could see Benny talking to the combat recruits' instructor at the end of the field. He showed no signs of being in a hurry. The resentment began building up. First in undertones, hints, and mutters, and then in outspoken indignation at the precious time wasted, the betrayal of the common goal.

He had plenty of time. What did he have to talk about to that instructor that was so important? While the new recruits stood behind him — and waited. Benny shrugged his shoulders and spread out his hands as if to say: *What can you do?* This gesture usually came at the end of a conversation, as a conclusion or summing-up, something along the lines of: *That's life,* et cetera. But he went on standing there, his hands on his hips, listening to his friend talking and shaking his head. The minutes passed slowly, more slowly than usual. As if even our watches had entered into a conspiracy with him to sink into this scandalous idleness, to cover up the outrage. Over our heads was a blazing, colorless, artificial sky, an unchanging noon covered with a dull film of dust and humidity. Apart from the flies, nothing moved around us, nothing changed.

"What the hell's going on here? What does he think he's playing at?" said Hedgehog indignantly.

"What are you crying about?" asked Alon. "What's your problem? Everybody's always complaining that the breaks are too short, and now all of a sudden you can't wait for it to be over? He met a comrade-in-arms, they must have been through all kinds of things together. So they're having a bit of a chat. We can wait a few more minutes."

"Stand straight, for God's sake," implored the orderly-student. "Is he coming?"

No. He wasn't coming. He actually took a few steps backward, waved his hand, and sprang around as if to break into a run, but then he changed his mind, perhaps remembering something important he still wanted to say, and he went back to his friend and continued talking.

And Avner, standing next to me, suddenly said to himself: *"Cannon fodder."* He repeated the expression, which he had apparently come across this day for the first time, several times, as if to test the way it sounded, *"Cannon fodder.* What a terrible expression. Only the Communists could have invented it."

CHAPTER 12

What's that you writing there, my eyes?"

"What d'you care?"

"Go on, show me, I want to see," said Zackie and leaned over his shoulder.

Rahamim covered the page with his hands to hide the writing. Zackie tried to pull his hands away. The paper crumpled up. Rahamim burst out laughing, grabbed the page in one hand, and clenched his fist around it. Zackie tried to pry his fist open and Rahamim laughed and cried: "You won't see, you won't see!" When Zackie succeeded in forcing his fingers open and the corner of the page appeared, Rahamim suddenly bent down and seized the paper in his teeth, crammed it into his mouth, and began to chew. Zackie looked at him chewing the paper in astonishment. "Now swallow it! Go on, swallow it!" he shouted. And Rahamim pretended to swallow, but his cheek was still bulging.

"Why do you hide things from me, my eyes?" said Zackie in the lewd tone he sometimes humorously adopted in addressing Rahamim, a curious mixture of a plaintive whine, an ingratiating whisper, and a menacing growl. "You mad at me? What have I done? You keeping secrets from your handsome Zackie now? What were you writing there?" And he laid his arm on Rahamim's shoulder and wound it around his neck in what might have been a stranglehold or an embrace. Rahamim removed his hand and turned away from him, sitting on the side his bed with his knapsack on his knees. "Leave me alone," he said. He wasn't laughing anymore.

"I just want to see what you're writing there."

Rahamim put his thumb into his mouth, took out the lump of chewed-up paper, and offered it to Zackie.

"Read it," he said.

Zackie recoiled in exaggerated disgust. "What's the matter with you? Why're you treating me like this?"

"Leave me alone," repeated Rahamim.

"You can write, I won't bother you, I promise."

Rahamim looked at him, his eyes smoldering with hatred. He sighed resignedly, placed his writing pad on his knees, and began to write. Zackie looked over his shoulder.

"What's this? You writing in English?"

"You said you wasn't gonna bother me, so why're you talking?"

"No, no," said Zackie sweetly. "Just tell me if it's English, that's all."

"No," said Rahamim, "it's French."

"Why don't you write in Hebrew or Arabic then?"

Rahamim shut the pad and closed his eyes impatiently. "Get off my bed!" he said.

"Why're you talking to me like that? What's the matter?" Zackie tried to put his arm around Rahamim's shoulders again, and Rahamim removed it angrily. He had stopped enjoying the game.

Zackie kept it up, but now he could no longer contain his laughter. "You've got somebody else!" he cried and his voice broke with laughter. "You've thrown me over! And now you're writing him love letters in French! And you won't even let me see. I only want to see the letters is all. What d'you care? Anyway I can't understand French. Go on, let me see."

We lay on our beds, worn out. The spectacle of Zackie tormenting Rahamim, which repeated itself almost every evening, had long ceased to amuse us. Nobody laughed, nobody heckled; even Zero-Zero, who usually never missed the chance to say what he felt, in length and in detail, about Rahamim's habits and personality, was too occupied with his own affairs, lying curled up on his bed, his knees under his chin and his hands over his head, absorbed in his own thoughts and fears.

"Who're you writing to?" asked Zackie.

"If I tell you, will you leave me alone?"

"Yes."

"Honest?"

"I swear. On my mother's eyes."

"I'm writing a letter home, to my sister."

"Why don't you introduce me to your sister, my eyes," whined Zackie. "If she's anything like you, I'll marry her on the spot."

"Go to hell," said Rahamim.

"What're you writing to her there? You telling her about your handsome Zackie?"

"You said you'd leave me alone, you swore on your mother's eyes!"

"I'm not doing anything! What do you want?"

"Get off my bed and go away."

"Just tell me what you're writing. I'll go. But mind you. don't tell me no lies."

"How'll you know if I'm lying or not?"

"You swear on your mother's eyes too."

"And then will you leave me alone?"

"Yes, I swear."

"Okay then. I'm writing her that I'm not coming home on leave. Yesterday I told them maybe I'd get leave for Rosh Hashana. And now they took my leave away and if everybody goes home I'll have to stay here."

When he said this Rahamim's face suddenly fell, and instead of the relief he had felt on hearing his punishment in the morning, his mood darkened. For the first time, presumably, he now saw things clearly. The possibility that he would be confined to the base on Rosh Hashana, while everyone else went home, suddenly seemed so real that a shout broke from his lips: "You burned the blanket! Why do I have to stay behind? Why should I get the blame?"

He was close to tears, his lips trembling. He sighed deeply and made an effort to control his face. Zackie raised his finger and brought it right up to Rahamim's face, almost touching his nose: "You watch it, Ben-Hamo. Just watch it. Say that again and you'll pay for it. Everybody saw. The whole platoon saw that you did it." Zackie turned his face toward the rows of beds on either side of the room, as if requesting confirmation. Then he flung out his hand and looked at Rahamim as if to say: *There, see for yourself. They're all witnesses.*

"Leave me alone, please, " begged Rahamim. "Just go away and leave me alone."

Zackie returned to his friends. The game was beginning to pale on him too. Rahamim put his knapsack on his knees again and tried to write his letter. But the agitated state of his emotions apparently prevented him from concentrating. He bit the end of his pencil, wondering how to begin. Then he glanced sideways at Zackie and Peretz and the rest of the gang, and his eyes narrowed in an expression of pain and accusation.

"Don't worry," Alon consoled him, "there won't be any leave anyway. Nobody promised us leave."

"The new instructor'll make sure we stay here over the holiday," said Hedgehog.

"Muallem said there was a chance," claimed Yossie Ressler.

"Muallem!" cried Micky scornfully. He was no longer impressed by instructors of the old school.

"So there'll be some other leave," said Rahamim. "And you'll all go home and I'll have to stay here. That's what I got — confinement to barracks. Why? Why should I have to stay behind? I didn't do nothing wrong."

Avner sat up and said: "Time to get dressed for our guard." He smiled his despairing smile, sat on the edge of the bed, and looked down at his boots, as if wondering whether he had the strength to put them on.

Last night's guard seemed remote, as if months had passed. The things that had happened on it seemed to have taken place somewhere on the borderline of reality. Avner's weeping next to the tree, his story about his encounter with his girlfriend in the roofless ruin, the appearance of the corporal we were to meet again the next morning: Those hours had been pushed into some forgotten corner by the pressure of later events. They were enveloped in a nightmarish atmosphere, full of terror and mystery, and when we reached the brightly lit hill with the little office building on its summit I felt as if I were standing with my feet in the still, illuminated waters dividing memory from memory. There were no lights on in the building; everything around it seemed quiet and sleepy, waiting for surprises.

"He won't come," I said to Avner. "He just wanted to put the wind up us."

"As long as you're on guard with me," said Avner, "you can be sure something bad will happen. Trust my rotten luck. If it weren't for me, you wouldn't be guarding here again tonight."

"His mind's on other things," I said. "You saw how we had to wait for him while he was standing there talking to his mate, and when he came back he probably didn't even realize he was late. As if he doesn't even take his own orders seriously."

"Then something else'll happen. Something has to happen. It's bloody unfair." Suddenly he remembered the injustice of it all. "We guarded the way we were supposed to, we did everything by the book, what does he want of our lives?"

"It's not because of you," I said. "It's because of me. He knows me."

"Don't think I've forgotten," said Avner, sunk in his own thoughts. "I was crazy last night." He was silent for a moment and then he said: "What a night it was!"

"And now we've been given an opportunity to relive those hours from the beginning and correct our mistakes."

"You can't correct anything. It's impossible to turn the clock back and begin all over again. You can only be sorry, ask the people you hurt to forgive you, be ashamed, and suffer — that's all."

Someone came toward us in the dark, and by the time he entered the circle of light we already knew, by the glint of his eyeglasses and his sloppy, slouching walk, who it was. The route of our patrol around the hill had brought us to the place where he had stopped. He made no attempt to hide and ambush us from the darkness, to bide his time and take us by surprise. He stood out in the open, deliberately attracting our attention.

"Halt! Password!" we called in unison.

"Open pin."

"Shooting star."

"Evening, boys," said Benny.

"Good evening, sir."

"Everything all right?"

"Yes, sir."

"You carry on with the patrol," he instructed Avner, "and you stay here."

Before setting out Avner managed to flash me a look of helpless apology, as if to say: *I told you so.* And then I saw his back and I knew that I was trapped.

Benny said: "They call you Melabbes here."

"That's right, sir."

"Is there anyone else from the town in the platoon?"

"No, sir, I haven't seen anyone."

"Do you remember me?"

"Yes, sir, you saved my life on the train to Jerusalem."

"Me? What the hell are you talking about?"

"Sir, it was on the end-of-the-year excursion to Jerusalem, on the train."

"Actually I remember that trip, but I didn't save you from anything."

"I was standing with my head out of the window, the train entered a narrow tunnel, and you pulled my head back in, at the last minute, and afterward everything went dark and the wall of the tunnel was right next to the window."

"No, you're wrong," said Benny. "Maybe it was someone else. I don't remember anything like that, and I've got an excellent memory."

I was silent.

"You must have just made it up. You're lying. You were always a liar. And a sissy, you were always a sissy too."

"Sir, may I carry on with my patrol now?"

"You'll carry on when I tell you to. What's the matter, are you tired of talking to me?"

"No, sir."

"Melabbes" — he sang the word, taking pleasure in every syllable — "you like it when they call you that?"

"No, sir."

"Why not? It's a good name for you."

"If you say so, sir."

"You know what I remember about you, after all this time? You used to blink your eyes. You don't do that anymore. Why did you stop, actually there was something quite nice about it?"

"It stopped of its own accord, sir," I said. I stood with my head lowered, so as not to see his obscene smile, which I imagined he must be smiling now, the smile with half his mouth and the broken tooth peeping out between his lips.

"And do you still play the violin?"

"No, sir."

"Did that stop of its own accord too?"

"Yes, sir, you could say so."

"So many things get lost along the way. Listen, I still remember how you once brought the violin to school, to play for the class, and the way you sawed! Remember? What a laugh!"

"Sir, I think you're mistaken. It wasn't me, it was Zvika Prager. I never played the violin at school."

"You're lying again. Can't you stop lying?"

"Sir, why do you keep calling me a liar?"

"Because I know what I'm talking about. I've got a good memory. And there are some things you never forget, silly things that stick in your memory forever."

I raised my head. There was a silence and I didn't have anything to say. It was strange to hear this man, whose rank and role made him much older than the year or two of actual difference in our age, talking like this about childhood memories. Not only was it incompatible with the new instructor's character, but it didn't connect with the child I remembered either. And although seven or eight years had passed since then, with all their boundless possibilities for development and change, it was inconceivable that it was the same child. But there could be no doubt that it was.

"Maybe you blame me for something I didn't do then," I said.

"And what have you done since then?" he asked.

I looked straight at him. His face was triumphant, gloating in his own power, proud and reserved.

"I graduated from high school, sir."

"You passed your exams."

"Yes, sir."

"And after the army, you'll go to the university."

"Yes, sir, I think so."

"I did my exams at a cram college," he said, "and after my service I'm going to study law in Jerusalem." He examined my face, perhaps to see if I was surprised.

"Maybe we'll meet again in Jerusalem, in a few years' time," I said.

"And you'll tell me that I saved your life in basic training."

Avner appeared at the end of his round, approaching us with slow, careful steps, like an obedient child. For some reason this made me want to burst out laughing.

Benny said: "Don't fear and don't hope."

"I don't understand, sir."

"Don't fear revenge and don't hope for favoritism," said Benny. "You're just like any other recruit to me and you won't get any special treatment, neither better nor worse."

"Yes, sir."

Suddenly he put out his hand and it was clear that he wanted to shake hands with me. In the whole embarrassing conversation, this was the most embarrassing moment of all. I shook his hand. When our hands dropped, I saluted him, but he had already turned his back and didn't return the gesture. A moment later he had vanished into the darkness surrounding the hill.

Avner came up and gave me a questioning look.

"We were in grade school together," I said, looking around apprehensively in case he was listening.

"So you were reminiscing about your schooldays?"

"Something like that," I said.

"Man, I'm dying to smoke."

"You're starting again!"

"He seems a decent enough chap," said Avner. "Yesterday he must have been in a bad mood because of that dame he had in there, or maybe he wanted to make an impression on her."

"It seems to me that his moods change all the time. From one minute to the next. He's going to give us the Scotch shower treatment."

"What's that?"

"I heard once that the Scots have a special method of taking a shower. They jump from a boiling shower into a cold one, and then back again from boiling hot to cold."

"Maybe it's because they're stingy with the hot water," suggested Avner.

"I don't know. Maybe they think it's healthy."

"So how does he want us to do the guard?"

"He didn't say anything about it. If you ask me, he's not interested."

"He won't come back to check up on us again," said Avner hopefully. "I'll wait another twenty minutes for a cigarette."

He looked at his watch to begin counting the extension he had afforded himself as a safety margin. The laughter, which had started to rise inside me earlier when I was standing with Benny and saw Avner coming toward us, welled up again, and this time I knew why. I couldn't hold it in; it burst out like water rushing from a broken dam.

I couldn't talk. In a gasping voice I indicated that I would satisfy his curiosity soon. I couldn't go on walking; I collapsed onto the ground and laughed soundlessly. Avner stood next to me and looked at me with an offended expression on his face, as if he thought I was laughing at him. When I recovered and got my breath back, I stood up and resumed the patrol.

"It's something about him," I said, spurts of laughter still disrupting my voice, "when we were at school together. It's really silly, but I don't know why, I remember it as vividly as if it happened yesterday, and whenever I think about it, I can't stop laughing. After all these years, it's as if I'm still the child who saw it then, and it makes me so happy, I can't explain it."

"Keep your voice down," said Avner. "He may be lurking in the dark to hear what we're saying about him."

"Yes," I whispered, "that would be just like him." The mere possibility helped me to pull myself together and control my laughter.

He was a wretched child, neglected, lazy, dirty, and rather stupid. The children called him Benny-trousers, because he always wore outsized khaki trousers that belonged to his father. He was in our class for a year or two, having been kept back a year. At the end of the year he was told that the school would not be keeping him on. On the last day of school, before the summer vacation, we came to get our report cards, and there was supposed to be some kind of ceremony in honor of the end of the school year. When we walked into the classroom we saw that someone had shat on the teacher's table, a big pile, with pieces of white paper next to it that the culprit had used to wipe himself with. We had barely had time to recover from the sight when our class teacher came into the room with a beaming face, and when she approached the table a scream burst from her lips, one loud, fantastic scream, and her face paled. She stood on the platform and looked at us, her eyes wide with accusation and despair. The whole class was there, except for Benny, who had not come to get his report card. She looked from one child to the next, and we sat facing her silently, like suspects in a police lineup. We knew who it was: the child who had not come to get his report card because he had been expelled from school! She looked at the table and what was on it again, and her eyes fell on the pieces of white paper. Then she stepped off the platform and went over to look at the map of Eretz Israel on the wall, and she shrieked: "The map! The map of our country! He used the map of Eretz Israel!"

This was the map the whole class had drawn together on a large sheet of stiff, glazed drawing paper, in colored crayons, with decorations, a modest offering to the Motherland. And indeed, a part of the Negev and a part of Haifa Bay had been torn off the map, leaving two big, gaping holes. These were the pieces of paper now lying on the table. A number of children who could no longer restrain themselves burst out laughing. She was astounded:

"What are you laughing at? Shame on you! Shame on you! This is the map of our country, the map of Eretz Israel!" And I, who had clothed my face in an expression of revulsion and moral indignation, filled with a strange, gleeful happiness and a wild wish to laugh. My whole body shook with the desire to laugh; it was all I could do to choke it down.

She sent someone to call the janitor, and in the meantime she pulled the map off the wall, folded it against her stomach, three times over, and walked toward the table, apparently intending to lay the desecrated map upon it, but when she drew nearer, she remembered that it was already occupied, and recoiled in horror. She nearly fell over backward. At this point I lost all control and burst into laughter with the rest of the class. She held the desecrated map against her bosom, like a mother protecting her baby, but it burned in her hands, like live coals. She didn't know where to put it, how to get rid of it. Everyone was laughing, the good with the bad, and amid the peals of laughter thundering in the room, we heard her cry: "Oh! He'll pay for this! He'll pay for it!"

We all knew who she meant. I didn't ask myself then why I was laughing and why this laughter was so exceedingly enjoyable. But I can still remember that glee, and especially the glee at what he had done to the map. The laughter was so strong, so liberating; destructive and purifying. And I remember that I admired him for what he had done.

"And was it really him who did it?" asked Avner.

"In the summer vacation, a few weeks later, I met him in the street and he asked me what the last day of school was like and if anything in particular had happened in class. I told him about what had happened, as if I didn't know who'd done it, and he showed a lot of interest in how it had gone over, what the reactions were. Like an artist. You know? And when I told him how she screamed and how we all laughed, he smiled that crooked smile, like he smiled today at training, the same smile that stayed stuck in my memory all these years."

"But he never actually said that it was him who did it?"

"I didn't have to ask him, it was obvious."

"But maybe he only heard about it from someone else, the one who really did it?" Avner persisted.

"What is this? Are you his lawyer or something? Trust me, he did it."

"And in the end, did anything happen to him because of it?"

"The school administration got in touch with his parents and told them. It was already in the middle of the long vacation, but the school was still busy with the scandal. The kids in his neighborhood heard him yelling when his father took off his belt and laid into him. And then they still made him go and apologize to the headmaster and the teacher. And he went. Don't worry, they didn't send him to jail for it."

"And you" — Avner continued his interrogation — "did you tell the other kids that you'd met him and that he admitted doing it?"

"I don't remember, but anyway nobody had any doubts about it. Maybe I did tell people."

"And perhaps that's how it got back to the school authorities that he admitted it, and that's why they contacted his parents — in other words, the incriminating information came from you, and you yourself say that he never admitted it in so many words."

"He may have met other kids from the class and told them. Look, I understand what you're trying to prove, but it won't work. It's a small place, everybody knows everybody else. There aren't any secrets. Why does it bother you so much?"

"Because I know only too well how it feels to be blamed for something you never did. When I was a little kid, they accused me of stealing from a neighborhood store, and I never stole anything. It's true that before that I stole a bit, but during that period I became religious and I was afraid of God and I never touched a thing. Nobody believed that I was telling the truth. Including my parents and the whole family. It's a terrible feeling, something you never forget. Like a wound that never heals. I wanted to die of loneliness and despair."

These words astounded me and filled me with fear. Maybe this was what Benny was getting at when he accused me of being a liar? But why had I gone and told Avner the whole story in the first place, with all my idiotic interpretations? From the minute that things had been placed on the firm ground of the moment coming into being between us, the moment of injustice and wanting to die of loneliness and despair, I felt like an idiot for not keeping the whole episode to myself. I looked at Avner marching silently beside me and I saw an enemy.

We stood silently opposite the flag square in front of the company office. A night at the end of Elul with a moon as slender as a silver thread. In the rain forests of South America, I had once read, there was a lethal strain of wild hornets that fell on anyone they encountered and stung him to death. The only way to save yourself was to lie flat on the ground without moving and play dead. Then they lost interest in their victim, abandoned him and flew off somewhere else. Perhaps because they realized that he was no longer dangerous. Perhaps they had no interest in the dead. And the man whose life had been given him as a gift had death to thank, for lending him its form for a moment.

"I can't smoke now," said Avner suddenly, as a result of lengthy reflection. "He'll come back, I promise you." His words sounded accusing, as if I had implicated him in something that was none of his business.

"He doesn't want us to stand here for too long. Let's patrol again."

We set out and Avner said: "That was the first time I wanted to kill myself. I didn't know how to do it, and anyway it was terribly important to me to see how they reacted, how sorry they'd be, how they'd regret it, how they'd realize their mistake, blaming me for something I didn't do: *Why didn't we believe him? He was telling the truth!* It was a form of revenge. To die and remain alive, and make them come and beg my pardon, make them suffer."

"When he finished talking to me," I said, "he put out his hand and we shook hands. As if he was glad to meet me here. I don't think he's got anything against me."

"Maybe he was just giving you that Scotch shower treatment you mentioned before?" said Avner.

"Maybe, but everything here's one big Scotch shower anyway — what was right yesterday's wrong today, we're getting leave, we're not getting leave, we're good soldiers, we're bad soldiers."

"And every day you forget what happened the day before," said Avner. "Every minute you have to readjust yourself." He changed his mind and lit a cigarette, shielding the dull glow with his cupped hand, which reddened bloodily. When he inhaled the smoke, holding the cigarette between both hands, his eyes darted in all directions, keeping a lookout for anyone emerging from the darkness.

"What pleasure can you get out of smoking when you have to hide it and be frightened of getting caught all the time?"

"It's not a pleasure, it's a necessity. I suffer when I'm not smoking. You'll probably never smoke in your life. Because it binds you, it enslaves you. But those are exactly the things that make life worth living, all those things that once you've tasted them you can't do without anymore. There's only one form of slavery I refuse to submit to: the slavery to fear. Being a slave to fear paralyzes you, it stops you from doing what you want to do, anything that isn't offered up to you on a platter, anything that involves risk, difficulty, pain, and sometimes dishonesty too. As far as I'm concerned, I'm open to any pleasure that life can offer me, and that includes what has to be taken by force. I'm not afraid! I'm not afraid!"

And he put his cigarette between his middle and index fingers, without bothering to hide the glowing tip anymore, lifted his face to the sky and inhaled long and pleasurably, after which he shot out his arm, holding the cigarette in front of him as if he were flying a flag in the darkness. "I'm ready to pay the price, take whatever's coming to me for it!"

And as if in response to his declaration and outstretched arm we suddenly heard a loud shot, with an immediate echo that was even louder than the shot itself, making the ground shake under our feet and the air tremble. And then there was silence again. Avner instantly dropped the cigarette and stamped it out, as if his pursuers were closing in on him and he was quickly getting rid of the incriminating evidence.

"What the hell was that?" he asked.

We had never heard a shot so close up in this part of the base. He looked into the darkness surrounding our circle of light, waiting for the answer to his question to emerge from it.

"Someone's gun must have gone off by accident," I said. "Probably one of the guards." I tried to hide my alarm.

"Maybe it's the platoon madman or the platoon suicide," said Avner with a guilty smile. "You heard what Hedgehog said about the folklore of Training Base Four."

We stood quietly and listened for a follow-up to the shot, the sound of shouting or some kind of activity. But there was nothing to be heard. Avner regretted the cigarette he had ground underfoot for nothing, and lit another, cupping his hands around it again. We continued our patrol. A soft, light breeze began to caress the back of our necks, another vain promise stealing across the autumn borders. For a moment the rustling of the eucalyptus leaves sounded like the brushing of birds' wings, passing overhead in the night sky, circling, receding, and dying away, and then silence again, and the sound of wings coming back from the same direction, from behind us, passing over our heads and receding into the distance. And during those moments, with the soft, fresh breeze caressing the nape of my neck and giving rise to a new, tense stir in the night air, I felt something sleeping and forgotten inside me move, as if something there was stirring and stretching a numbed limb in its sleep, turning over onto its side, unconsciously calculating, to the rhythm of its breathing and the beating of its heart, the hours and days remaining until the final awakening, and the long summer sleep was growing light and brittle, like the sleep of a sick man before daybreak.

"There are a lot of people here who should never be allowed to handle a gun," said Avner. "It's really dangerous, you know that?"

CHAPTER 13

The sound of the guards talking in front of the barracks reached my ears fitfully in a muffled, incomprehensible murmur that merged with the voices of the sleepers — the chorus of breathing and snoring, sighs and mutters and shifting bodies into which I had been trying for hours to fit the rhythm of my own breathing, the sensations of my own body, in the vain hope that the grace of togetherness would accept me too into its sleeping ranks. But something in me over which I had no control kept obstructing my efforts, rebelliously refusing to be seduced and deluded. Perhaps it was a leftover from the child who could never sleep a wink the night before a trip, tense with excitement, or fear of oversleeping and being left behind, or perhaps with the hope that morning would delay its coming until the threat was removed and it all turned out to be a bad dream. The heat lifted at night. The sharp smell of a new chill in the air came from the windows and blew down the aisle between the rows of beds, giving the room the feel of a ship borne on gentle waves, rocking to and fro like a cradle, and there was nothing in this slow, gentle, dignified motion to make one think of flight, except for the crowds of birds darkening the sky above. We saw them in the break during arms drill on the parade ground. They almost blackened the sky from horizon to horizon. Alon shaded his eyes with his hand and watched the migrating birds, his face breaking into a happy smile: "They don't mess around. When the time comes — they're off. Like clockwork." As if he needed this confirmation that the old patterns still existed.

"It's frightening," I said. "It looks like a mass flight from a disaster area."

"Not at all!" protested Alon. "Look how marvelously it's organized, how beautiful it is. It's a perfect formation. Each bird knows its precise place. Nothing's left to chance. Each one knows its function. And the communication among them. It's fantastic. The spearhead passes on commands. And that whole huge flock carries them out exactly. They change the formation according to need. They maintain a uniform speed. Uniform gaps between them. They inform each other about dangers on the way. Changes of direction. Weather problems. Look at the fantastic navigation. It works better than the most detailed maps. Better than the most precise radar and compasses. They never make a mistake. It's all in those little heads of theirs."

Micky intervened to put the record straight: "It's instinct, they're born with it. They don't understand what they're doing. They don't even know why they leave one place and fly somewhere else. And they don't know where they're going either. They're just little machines. They've got no concept of past or future. They're propelled by some blind force that directs them."

"I don't know what they understand and what they don't," said Alon. "Nobody knows. But just imagine the strength they need to fly such distances, the planning. If it isn't their intelligence, then it's their instinct. It understands. It directs them. It gives them their strength. The instinct to stay alive. To reach a warmer climate. To survive the winter. To go on living. But most human beings don't know what impels them either. You think everyone understands why he's alive? Why it's so important to him to stay alive? Why he's prepared to do anything, anything, just to stay alive?"

"If you start thinking about it," said Avner, "you can go crazy."

"So nature took care that we wouldn't have to think about it," said Alon. "That it would be automatic. If everyone began thinking there'd be no end to it. Look, a lot of them will fall by the way and not reach the warm climates. But the rest will carry on until they reach the Arab peninsula. Or Africa. Or the equator. And that's the main thing as far as they're concerned. One bird can't make that whole journey by itself. Without all the others. It hasn't got a chance of making it alone. It's a huge enterprise! In the army you need a whole staff to plan and organize something like that. And here it happens of its own accord. Because they all pull together. Like one great, efficient machine. That's the only way they have a chance. A chance of living. Surviving danger. Getting food. Reproducing. Perpetuating their species. So it won't become extinct. If they could think, they might think that that was their ideal. But they don't have ideals in their heads. They live their ideal automatically. The way we breathe or sleep. And that's what's so wonderful. It's only with human beings that there's no real connection between life and ideals. They talk about ideals. And the more they talk about them, the farther they get from realizing them."

Nevertheless, there was something terrifying in the sight of the birds blackening the sky, in the mass flight from disaster. The fear to which this sight gave rise in me disrupted the inner automaton directing my movements. When we returned to the drill I stumbled over one of the complicated turns and fell behind. And although I was in the middle of my three, Benny saw.

"Come here, Melabbes," said the sleepy drawl. The lips parted in their lopsided smile and revealed the broken tooth. "Come here, you little clown."

"Sir!"

"Have you decided to put on a clown show for us?"

"No, sir."

"Do it again, for everyone's benefit this time. It's a shame to waste a performance like that on two or three people. Stand here in front of us and show us again how you get your legs entangled like that and nearly trip yourself up. I want to get a better view. Maybe you can put your act on later for the Army Entertainment Troupe and make the whole base laugh." And he barked out the previous series of commands again, this time for my benefit alone.

I stood rooted to the spot. I didn't know what I was supposed to do, but a strange calm descended on me, as if the worst was already over and I was now entitled to breathe a sigh of relief.

"What are you standing there for? Jump to it!"

"I can't do it again, sir. It was an accident."

"Repeat that accident!"

Again he barked out the drill commands and again I couldn't move.

"Are you disobeying an order?"

"No, sir, I just don't know how to do it again. It was a mistake."

"Try."

"I don't know how to begin, sir. I've forgotten how."

"You've forgotten," he said quietly. "You'll have to forget a few other things too."

The smile vanished from his face. He looked at me, narrowing his eyes behind his glasses. In the dull, calm indifference that had come down like a screen between me and the rest of the world, I thought about his eyes scrutinizing me and wondered if I could really see in them the reflection of the evil that Arik had described to me. All I could see was something like a maturity and responsibility that I was not yet able to measure up to. Arik would no doubt say that this was simply one more of the masks that evil donned to deceive and trap us, but he had shaken hands with me that night and said, *Don't fear and don't hope,* and the words had sounded sincere.

"Step back," said Benny, "and remember that I've got my eye on you. Watch it, Melabbes." He pronounced the ugly name with a special emphasis, as if he were savoring the sound. "You're pushing your luck." He was silent for a moment and then added: "The name of the second man to stay behind on duty during your leave hasn't been decided yet."

This was the first hint at the possibility of our getting leave the next day. Nothing had been said the whole week and we had nothing to base our hopes on. Why had he picked on me? Was he looking for an excuse to leave me behind on duty with Rahamim Ben-Hamo when the platoon went home for leave over the holiday? To my surprise this possibility was less of a blow than might have been expected. If this was my fate, I would endure it, I promised myself. In any case the whole thing seemed unreal: the image of home, the world outside, Rosh Hashana — these were words that had almost lost their meaning, retaining only a pathetic, childish sound, like a dream that refuses to go away, anachronistic and pitiful.

The guards approached the door of the barracks. Now I could hear their voices clearly.

"What kind of crap is that? Would you marry a girl who wasn't a virgin?"

"Sure I would. If I loved her, I wouldn't care."

"How're you going to love her, if she's already done it with somebody else? It's disgusting."

"I could even fall in love with some whore, if she turned me on. What do I care? If she gave it up, if she kept herself for me, I could love her."

"You're sick. I'm telling you, you're sick. Fucking a girl who's already done it with somebody else, that's like getting into bed with her and all the guys who were there with her before. So okay, if it's just a whore, you do it and it's over and you wash yourself and forget it. But your wife! What kind of a life is that?"

"Today people don't worry about it so much."

"What's that supposed to mean — today? Today! Anyone'd think you were the most modern person in the world. If you knew that your sister —"

"If he was serious and he wanted to marry her, I wouldn't care if before they got married —"

"I'm not talking about a bit of necking, kissing and that, I'm talking about actually opening her for God's sake!"

"Let him open her. If he's going to marry her anyway, what's the big difference if he does it before the wedding or after it?"

"Why d'you think a girl's born closed, if it makes no difference?"

"Once it was important."

"And what about today? A man's not a man and a woman's not a woman? Today everything's different? Everybody's a whore?"

"A girl who does it a couple of times before she gets married isn't a whore. Maybe it was a mistake, or maybe she thought he was going to marry her or something like that. That's not a whore."

"So what's a whore? You're a baby, you are. You don't know anything about women. As long as she lives a woman remembers the man who opened her. Even if she gets married to somebody else afterward and has his kids and keeps in line, she goes on waiting for that guy, the first one, as long as she lives, she dreams about him at night. When you're on top of her she'll shut her eyes and think about him. And if he ever shows up again, even if it's years later, the minute she sees him she'll drop everything and go after him, like a dog goes after the person who gives him food. And that's what's to blame for people getting divorced and families breaking up and kids on the street and becoming criminals and all the rest of it. Is that how to live?"

"You think the Ashkenazis live any worse than we do? Today things are different. In Israel it's different. Not like it was in the old countries."

"What kind of crap is that? What are you — more Ashkenazi than the Ashkenazis? You think her father'll keep quiet when you open his daughter?"

"For your information I do want to marry an Ashkenazi girl, and I don't care if she's open or closed."

"Any woman who marries after she's already been opened, the same way she carried on before she was married — she'll go on doing the same thing afterward too, because she doesn't care anymore about right and wrong. The minute she feels like it, she'll find someone. She won't have any respect for her husband. And what kind of education's she going to give her kids? Hey? Do what she did before to give an example to her daughters?"

"My father took my mother when she was twelve years old, she didn't have a clue. She never had a moment's peace, she never had a minute to herself. She worked like a donkey from morning to night, and the children came one after the other. Today she's always sick. It hurts her here, it hurts her there, she can hardly breathe. She looks a hundred and fifty, and she's no more than forty-five or -six. When I see an Ashkenazi woman of that age in the street, young, healthy, all dressed up and looking good, I feel heartsick for my mother."

"You don't know the first thing about women, mate. That's her pride, having kids, looking after the house, making food, keeping everything nice for her husband. And another thing, a woman who never gets a crack or a bawling out from her man, she's miserable, she can't see any point to her life, as if nobody needs her no more . . ."

Zero-Zero jumped out of bed as if bitten by a snake. For a moment his silhouette remained standing in front of the bed, as if uncertain which way to turn, and then he ran to the door of the barracks and disappeared into the darkness.

"What the fuck's going on here? What d'you think this is, a bloody café?" His voice rose in a scream from outside.

"Okay, okay, keep your hair on. We'll stop talking. You can go back to sleep."

"How'm I gonna fall asleep now? I've been waiting for an hour already for you bastards to stop, but did you? Where from! *Brr-brr-brr-brr-brr,* on and on like a couple of bloody old women."

"Okay! We forgot. We'll stop now. Go back to bed."

He came back into the room and got back into bed. I heard him tossing and turning and groaning. He kept it up for a long time. He too was trying in vain to fall asleep. I saw his silhouette sitting up in bed, writhing about, curling up into a ball, his hands rhythmically beating the mattress, sitting up and then lying down again, and suddenly a sharp little shriek rose from his bed, high and thin as a mouse's squeak, and then another one, making a grating noise like the last turns of a tightening vise, one shrill squeal after the other in abrupt, excruciating succession. Zero-Zero sat up. I saw him cover his face with his hands. He sighed heavily, removed his hands from his face, pounded rhythmically on his mattress, and squealed shrilly. I got up and went over to his bed. He rubbed his eyes with the backs of his hands.

"What's wrong with you?" I whispered.

"Those two bastards" — he pointed to the door — "fuck their mothers, woke me up and now I can't get back to sleep." He whimpered soundlessly. "I feel so bad. Why can't I just die and get it over with already."

Suddenly he seized my hand and laid it on his chest. Through his sweat-soaked undershirt I could feel his heartbeat, rapid, rhythmic, and nervous, like a signal in Morse code I was unable to decipher. I tried to pull my hand away, but he replaced it firmly, scanning my face in the darkness to see whether I had understood the seriousness of the situation. Trapped between the heat of his hand and the heat of his chest, my hand began to lose its sensation, as if it had been detached from my body.

"Yes," I whispered, "I see." And his hand loosened its grip.

"I can't go on like this," groaned Zero-Zero and his lips twisted. "I can't go on." He turned his head away, bent down, and buried his face in the mattress. And again the squeals of the tightening vise rose into the air. Sensation returned to my hand, which was still damp with his sweat. I touched his shoulder. He didn't react. I patted his shoulder encouragingly a couple of times and whispered: "Go outside, have a drink of water, and get a breath of fresh air, it'll do you good."

He raised his head and turned it toward me: "When I want your advice I'll ask for it. Who d'you think you are, my goddamned doctor?"

He stood up slowly, pushed his bare feet into his boots, and went outside into the night. I returned to my bed, closed my eyes, and listened to him cursing the guards. Until silence fell again.

The ship sailed on, borne forward by the waves, as passive and drowsy as its passengers, and above it the multitude of birds blackened the eye of the sun. These birds, who knew the secrets of eclipses and earthquakes, before whom the folds of the earth were spread out like the palm of a hand, little creatures of nature propelled by a wise life instinct to the south, to the south, flew before the ship like a black cloud, directing us to the continent of a new, pure beginning, far from the sick, polluted coast, minutes before disaster struck.

"I don't have to tell you who's going to be the second guy to stay behind on duty. There isn't a doubt in my mind. Especially now, when it's so important for me to see her, to make it up with her, to apologize, to explain. After everything that happened on Saturday night. It's inevitable. That's the way my luck operates."

We had been shaking our blankets outside the room, and Avner had just broken an unspoken conspiracy of silence regarding the possibility of leave.

"You know what," I said, "trying to trick fate the way you're doing doesn't always work: Sometimes we're left with nothing but the doubtful satisfaction of being able to say *I told you so,* which isn't much of a consolation. Why do we imagine that fate is so vain as to change its decisions just because we boast of being able to guess them right?"

"So there's no way of fighting fate?" said Avner indignantly. "Is that what you're saying? What are we supposed to do then?"

"Maybe accept the outcome in advance, never mind what it is, even try to love it. Or maybe be indifferent to it in advance, cut it off completely from our emotions. That's two possibilities."

"What you're saying is terrible," muttered Avner. "I hope you're only saying it to put me down and that you don't really believe it yourself."

"Why should I invent things I don't believe in just to put you down?"

"I don't know," said Avner. "Sometimes I have the impression that whatever I say or do you try to pick holes in."

"I'm sorry you feel that way. It isn't true."

"Never mind!" Avner tried to cover up the bad impression made by his words with an optimistic smile. "Forget it. I'm strong. I can take it."

There was a sound of shuffling at the door to the building. Zero-Zero was climbing the steps, pausing for a moment in the doorway, trying to find his way in the passage from darkness to darkness. Then he began slowly shuffling forward, his boots dragging over the concrete floor again. He was puffing and panting, as if he had been running. The skinny silhouette, stooped like an old man's, in the outsized underpants that seemed to be kept up by a miracle, stopped next to his bed. He sat down and took off his boots. Again he rubbed his eyes with his hands, the permanently bloodshot bulging eyes with their inflamed lids. Then he rose slowly to his feet and busied himself with something on his bed, perhaps smoothing out the blanket covering the mattress, straightened up, put his hands on his hips, and looked round at the sleepers. It seemed to me that his eyes rested on my bed, perhaps trying to ascertain if I had fallen asleep. Maybe he needed some kind of help. I held my breath. Someone coughed suddenly and Zero-Zero turned his head in the direction of the cough, a sharp, animal movement, startled and alert. He waited a moment longer, listening attentively in the darkness, until he gave up and got into bed. He sighed bitterly again, and then there was silence.

The announcement of the second man to stay behind on duty with Rahamim on the base over the Rosh Hashana leave was postponed until after parade on Friday. Benny couldn't hide his satisfaction as he informed us of this arrangement and studied our faces one by one to see its effect. And again nothing was said about going on leave the next day. Not during the training sessions in the afternoon nor that evening, when we were busy cleaning and tidying the room for the CO's inspection. None of us spoke about our plans for the leave, about the rest and pampering and home-cooked food awaiting us, about the anticipated meetings with friends. In contrast to the previous occasion, everything was done energetically but joylessly. This too was a trick, a stratagem to avoid arousing the anger of the fates.

Zero-Zero sighed again. He began hitting the iron frame of his bed. For a few minutes he kept up the rhythmic banging, and suddenly I heard a sound coming from his direction, at first like a sigh, that went on and on without stopping, very softly, no louder than breathing, a soundless voice, a kind of lazy hum, like someone humming a tune in his sleep.

At first I couldn't believe my ears. I raised my head slightly and listened: He was lying in bed and humming a song to himself, as if he were sure that nobody could hear him, as if he were all alone in the world. Was he singing a lullaby to himself, to put himself to sleep at last? The sound was very soft, dragging out slowly from sigh to sigh, but there was definitely a tune to the song. Maybe it was a song in Yiddish or Romanian? The humming went on for a long time in the darkness.

Someone suddenly shouted: "Quiet!"

Zero-Zero stopped singing abruptly.

Not long afterward Nahum got out of bed and began putting on his clothes. One of the guards came into the room: "I came to wake you up," he whispered. "How do you know when to wake up by yourself?"

"It doesn't matter," said Nahum.

The guard returned to his post. Nahum got dressed slowly, sat down to lace up his boots in the dark. A pleasant coolness spread through the room. I wrapped my blanket around me. The darkness outside was suffused by a gray-blue radiance. He had woken early to say the penitential prayers. The only one in the whole platoon. I looked at the phosphorescent figures on my watch. I didn't mind lying awake until morning, and as this clear, consoling thought crossed my mind a pleasant lassitude spread through my body, like a reconciliation after a bitter quarrel. Nahum tucked the bag with his prayer shawl and phylacteries under his arm, glanced at his bed as if to make sure that he hadn't forgotten anything, and walked slowly out of the room, trying not to make a noise with his nailed boots.

When one of the guards came in to wake the next pair of guards, I knew that I was already asleep, even though I could hear the noise of the comings and goings clearly. I didn't open my eyes. Everything was happening a long way away.

The amused expression disappeared from Benny's face and an alert, worried look came into his eyes, as if he scented danger, as if things were slipping out of his control. Alon did not look at the corporal scrutinizing his face, trying to get to the bottom of his hidden intentions. He lowered his eyes, protecting himself from the anticipated barbs of mockery and humiliation. Was he so ashamed of the decision that for some reason he felt impelled to make? Raffy Nagar's rebukes were still ringing in our ears: However accustomed we were by now to this speech, with its set formulas and vocabulary, its clipped, deliberate pronunciation, the words still held something of the deceptive sharpness of the first days. Our miserable achievements in training, our standards of discipline that were beneath contempt — all this came out of the platoon commander's mouth with the ring of bitter personal disappointment. With all these generalizations it was hard to know what specifically he had in mind, but of our deep guilt there was no doubt at all, the guilt that had preceded our coming here and brought us together, that we dragged with us wherever we went. When Raffy Nagar had gone away and left us with Benny, we knew that the hour of reckoning had come.

He looked at us with the expression of loathing we had grown familiar with in the past week. The hour of reckoning was the hour of sacrifice, the means by which we would obtain the leave we did not deserve. Although any of us was liable to be chosen for the role of sacrificial victim, regardless of his conduct or actions, there was a profound truth in the need to choose him, which none of us dreamed of questioning. The expression of loathing thus changed gradually to one of amusement, even of joviality, and it was fair.

"Before I assign one of you to stay behind on duty during the leave, is there a volunteer?"

The interval of silence after the fading away of the last syllable in Benny's sleepy drawl was slightly longer than expected. As when something deviates from the plan and threatens to upset the existing order of things.

"Yes, sir, me!" called Alon.

Benny narrowed his eyes behind his glasses, clearly resentful of this interference: "You want to give up your leave and stay here for two and a half days on duty?"

"Yes, sir."

"You deserve to go on leave," said Benny. "You deserve it more than all these craphouses. But if you volunteer you'll stay. And no one will thank you for it. Is that clear?"

"Yes, sir."

We went back to the room to wait for our passes. Micky sat next to Alon in silence. His expression was sullen and hostile. Alon said: "Bring me the holiday newspapers, okay?"

"Okay."

Alon looked at him in surprise: "What's up, why are you in such a bad mood?"

"Nothing."

"Good."

"Tell me, are you crazy? What's going on? Why did you volunteer to stay? Why didn't you tell me about it?"

"I don't want to go home to the kibbutz as a recruit on Training Base Four."

"What's it got to do with them? You have to give them a report on what you're doing in the army?"

"You were never on a kibbutz. You can't understand. The kibbutz is my family."

"And what does it matter to your family what you do in the army?"

"It matters to me. It's my problem. Micky, do me a favor and leave it alone."

"Your girlfriend's expecting you."

"She understands."

"You could have come to stay with me. We've got a big house. My parents would have been glad to have you. I could have shown you around the town, we could have gone swimming in the sea, you would have met my girlfriend. You could have relaxed and had a rest at our place."

"I never thought of it."

"Why didn't you tell me before what you were going to do? Why didn't you ask my advice?"

"It came up at the last minute. Until the parade I couldn't decide. But it's okay. Don't worry. I won't be bored. And I can rest and think."

"If at least you were staying here alone — but having Ben-Hamo around all the time!"

The last remark gave rise to laughter in their audience. Ben-Hamo too was sitting on his bed not far off and heard what Micky said. In contrast to his usual habit of enduring the obscenities and ridicule directed against him with forbearance, or reacting with stupid laughter or playing along and responding in the same coin — he stood up and went over to Micky. His face was serious and seemed more mature than usual, as if this time he bore the brunt of a grave responsibility.

"Why did you have to say something like that about me? What harm have I done you?"

"I've told you a thousand times not to talk to me!" Micky yelled at him. "Don't you understand Hebrew?"

Rahamim looked at him for a minute and his lips quivered. Then he turned away and went back to his bed and sat down. His face, which had suddenly grown older, looked right and left, as if to familiarize himself with some new place into which he had just been cast.

Zackie, who had also laughed, now took it upon himself to come to Rahamim's defense: "He's right! Where d'you get off talking to people as if they were dogs? Having a bit of fun is one thing, okay, I make fun of him too, but you think yourself so bloody high-and-mighty, as if we were all under the sole of your boot. What's the big deal? What makes you so great? That you play soccer? What are you, a professor or something?"

Peretz called to Zackie: "Leave them alone. Thank God we won't see them for two days. We'll have a bit of peace and quiet."

"I don't understand you," mumbled Micky, "I swear to you, Alon, I don't understand."

"Do me a favor, give it a rest," said Alon. "What difference does it make now?"

"It doesn't make any difference!" Micky gave up in despair. He went to pack his knapsack. Rummaging in the bag he encountered a book he had brought with him from home, and he turned to Alon. "Here's a book for you," he said with a sour, offended smile. "You've have plenty of time to read."

Alon grinned in embarrassment, took the book, and glanced at the cover. "I don't know it," he said.

"It might interest you, it's a historical novel. The end of the Second Temple period, the revolt against the Romans and so on."

Alon paged through the book, a skeptical look on his face: "I've never heard of the writer. He's not Israeli."

"He's Swedish," said Micky. "He got the Nobel Prize. I've only managed to read thirty or forty pages since I was drafted. Usually I can polish off a book in a few hours."

After handing out the passes, Benny called Rahamim. "Mommy's come to see you," he said, "and she brought your sister too. I don't know how the hell they got past the main gate. But that's not my affair. Go and find them and tell them that this isn't a kindergarten or a vacation camp. I don't want anything like this to happen again. The RP at the gate of the base has instructions to let you through. For fifteen minutes and not a second more. Is that clear?"

"Yes, sir," said Rahamim, with a long face. He stepped back into the ranks.

Benny looked at us, waiting perhaps for us to laugh, but we were afraid of his unexpected reactions, his volatile moods. We stood in silence. For some reason Benny decided not to march us to the gate of the base in regulation three-file and at the command "Dismissed!" we stampeded to the barracks to collect our packs.

Avner's nostrils quivered, his eyes gleamed like the eyes of an animal scenting blood. "Hurry!" he whispered in a parody of terror. "Let's get out of here before they change their minds. They'll never let us go without any problems. That's not their style."

I burst out laughing. Ever since I'd woken up that morning I'd felt drunk. Maybe because I'd hardly slept the whole night. I knew that I was capable of doing something stupid and I had to exert myself to keep my movements and my tongue under control. Now, as we made our way to the gate, the controls suddenly slipped.

"You know what," I said to him. "I didn't sleep at all last night. It was the fear, the excitement. The doubt: *Will I go on leave or not.* It wouldn't let me sleep. And all the time I kept saying to myself: *I don't care if they don't let me go. It makes no difference. I accept the verdict, whatever it is.* But the doubt drove me crazy."

"And now?"

"The way I feel at this minute makes it all worth it. Like a gambler: It doesn't matter how much you won and whether you'll actually get to pocket the winnings — the main thing is that the gamble came off. Even if they called me back now before we reached the gate and told me my leave was canceled, I don't think I'd care."

"Don't talk nonsense," said Avner, as if he were afraid I was tempting fate. "Hurry! Hurry! In the movies," he said, "you sometimes see the Germans or the crooks letting a prisoner free. At first he can't believe it, he starts walking and all the time he keeps on looking behind him, to see if they really mean it, and suddenly he starts to run, not to miss the chance, and then, the minute he begins to be convinced it's for real, that the miracle is really happening to him — *wham!* He gets a bullet in the back and falls. Don't laugh. That's how I feel now. I've got a funny feeling in my back, I'm walking slowly, as if I don't give a damn, I keep saying: *Hurry! Hurry!* and I'm afraid to look back."

We got past the gate without any trouble. As we stepped onto the road where we ran every morning, Avner said: "My legs want to run now, but I won't let them. Not until we walk through the Jerusalem Gate. When we reach the main road, I'll know we're free."

At that moment our eyes fell on the woman and the girl with her and we knew who they were. Rahamim's mother and sister were standing a little way off, watching the recruits approaching the gate. His mother, a fat, heavy woman in a black dress with a black kerchief around her head, was holding a large basket and mopping up the sweat running down her face with the corner of the kerchief. His sister, who looked about two or three years older than him, resembled him greatly, but while he was short and plump, with a round, vague, characterless face, she was tall and shapely, her face finely drawn, her expression decisive, and her black eyes quick and suspicious. We looked at them. Avner's eyes took in the sister and the ground stopped burning under his feet. By now most of the platoon had passed through the gate. The Jerusalemites joined us and stood staring at Ben-Hamo's mother and sister. The mother, who was obviously suffering from the long wait in the sun, squatted on the ground and rested her arms on the basket, while the sister remained standing, ignoring the stares of the soldiers standing on the other side of the road.

In the end we saw Ben-Hamo approaching. He must have been waiting for the whole of the platoon to leave through the gate, but as he came closer he saw us standing and staring at his mother and sister. He turned away from the gate and approached the fence. From behind the fence he waved at them to go away. His sister called him to come out to them and his mother made several attempts to stand up and failed, until her daughter came up and took her by the elbow and helped her up. Rahamim's mother called to him in their language, but he glared at them and shouted in Hebrew: "Go home, go home! Why did you have to come here?"

His mother called out to him again in their language and laboriously lifted up the basket, to show him what she had brought. His sister called in Hebrew: "What's wrong with you, Rahamim? Why don't you come outside? What's the matter?"

"I can't come out!" called Rahamim.

A puzzled, suspicious expression crossed the sister's face. She looked in our direction, and when she saw us observing the scene and laughing, she crossed the road and came toward us.

"Are you from Rahamim Ben-Hamo's platoon?"

"Yes," said Avner, flashing her his most ingratiating smile. "You're his sister, right?"

"What's wrong with him?" she asked Avner. "Why doesn't he want to come out to us?"

"I don't know," said Avner. "You know, you look alike, I knew immediately that you were his sister."

"He came home on Saturday night, and we said that if he didn't get leave we'd come to him. Then we got a letter to say he had to stay on duty. So we brought him some treats for the holiday. We were lucky they let us through the main gate. I did my service in the military police and I do my reserve duty here, I know the guys here and the officers. They did us a big favor and let us in. So what's the matter with him now?"

She returned to her mother, said something to her and pointed to us, apparently telling her that we were in the same platoon as Rahamim. The mother turned to look at us, trying to see us despite the sun dazzling her eyes. Then she straightened the kerchief on her head and set her hands on her hips. It was hard for her to stand. At the same time the sister tried to approach the fence at the place where Rahamim was standing, but as soon as he saw her coming closer he cried: "I don't want you here! Go away! You can't come here. I'll get into trouble. Because of you!"

Zackie was one of the last of the platoon to leave the base. When he approached the gate and saw what was happening, he went up to Rahamim to persuade him to go out to them.

"Go away," said Rahamim. "Go to hell."

"Rahamim!" called his sister. "Go to the RP and ask him to let you out for a few minutes. He won't make any problems."

"I can't come out!" replied Rahamim. "I'm not allowed to!"

"That's not true!" cried Zackie. "They gave him a pass especially to come out to you."

"What d'you want of me, you bastard?" screamed Rahamim. "Haven't you made me enough trouble already? Go away, go home!"

Zackie burst out laughing. "No, my eyes!" he shouted at the top of his voice, so we could all hear. "You have to go out to them, what's the matter with you? Are you crazy? You want them to go away after coming all the way here to bring you treats for the holiday?"

"Go away! Go home!" yelled Rahamim at his mother and sister. "I don't want you here, go away! I'm going back to the barracks."

Zackie walked out of the gate and crossed over to us. Rahamim's mother and sister gave up trying to communicate with him from the other side of the fence. They stood and waited. His mother grew tired of standing and squatted down again on the pavement. His sister kept a close watch on Rahamim in case he slipped away and vanished into the camp. Zackie said in a whisper: "Did you get a load of his sister?"

"She's Avner's!" said Hedgehog. "He's already got her eating out of his hand."

"What babies you are," sighed Avner. "Tell me, Hedgehog, haven't you ever spoken to a girl in your life?" Everybody laughed at this piece of wit. "Have you ever seen such babies in your life?" he asked me. "She's certainly cute, Rahamim's sister, I'm not saying otherwise." He looked at her again, narrowing his eyes, appraising her with an expert expression. "Not bad at all," he murmured.

"Are you coming, or are you going to wait for Ben-Hamo's sister?" Hanan asked Avner to a chorus of laughter from his friends. "It'll be hours till we get a ride home."

"Nonsense!" said Avner. "If you stand next to me, you'll get a ride straight away." His belief in his good luck had apparently returned over the past few minutes.

Rahamim's sister came up to us again. She asked Zackie: "If he got permission to come outside, what's he afraid of?"

Zackie said: "Maybe he's upset because he's not going on leave."

Rahamim's sister called to him: "I'm going to the RP, I'll fix it with him for you to come out to us."

"I don't want to! I don't want to!" cried Rahamim.

His sister took no notice of his protests. She approached the gate to talk to the sentry, or at least she pretended that this was what she had in mind. Rahamim waved his arms in helpless rage. He took a few steps toward the gate and immediately changed his mind and turned back again. He paced to and fro distractedly. The Jerusalemites lost patience with Avner and walked off. Micky and a few others who were standing with us joined them. Only Avner, Zackie, and I were left standing in front of the gate. We heard the old woman calling to us: "What's the matter with him? Rahamim's a good boy. Why he won't come? What's the trouble with Rahamim?"

Avner and I shrugged our shoulders to indicate that we were ignorant of Rahamim's motives. His sister came back from the gate and called to Rahamim: "It's all right, go to the RP, he'll let you out, I fixed it up with him."

Rahamim stayed where he was, shaking his head obstinately. Zackie said: "What an idiot! Okay, you coming?"

Avner wanted to get going, but Rahamim's sister came up to us again. "Why didn't Rahamim get leave like everybody else?" she asked.

"That's how it is in the army," explained Zackie. "Today it's him, tomorrow it's me, next time it's somebody else."

"Why's he so mad?" she asked. "What did they do to him? At home he's always laughing, like a little boy. The army's not for him, I'm telling you."

"It's not for nobody," said Zackie.

Rahamim came out of the gate onto the road.

Avner asked: "What are we waiting for?"

"I want to see," I said.

Zackie parted from us with a "Happy New Year" and walked off. We saw Rahamim go up to his mother and sister and talk to them in their language, waving his arms furiously while his sister tried to calm him down. His mother rose laboriously to her feet and showed him what she had in her basket. Rahamim stood still for a moment and looked into the basket, and then he gave it a violent kick, sending a few of the dishes flying. When he saw the dishes lying on the road, he went berserk. He picked the basket up and shook it, scattering the contents on the ground and kicking the little dishes and parcels wrapped up in paper and pieces of cloth. His sister hurried to pick up the dishes and parcels, replacing them in the basket without a word. Then she turned away and looked into the camp. A new bunch of recruits and soldiers came out of the gate, calling out to each other: "Happy New Year!" The air filled for a moment with happy cries and commotion and the thud of army boots on the asphalt. Rahamim's mother stood where she was and looked at her son with uncomprehending eyes. She did not seem shocked or alarmed; there was no anger or reproach on her face. He approached her and dropped his eyes. His face was red and quivering with rage.

"Come on, let's go," said Avner. "It's not nice."

"Just a minute," I said, "I want to see something."

Rahamim turned round and looked at us. Avner said: "You see, it's not nice."

We began walking away, and after ten or twenty paces I turned around and stood still. Rahamim was kneeling in front of his mother, embracing her thick waist and burying his head in her belly. I retraced my footsteps and stood opposite them to watch. The sister saw me and smiled in embarrassment: "I don't know what's gotten into him," she called across the road to me.

Rahamim's mother stroked his head, murmuring something in their language, and tried to make him stand up, but she couldn't detach him from her body. His shoulders shook. His sister picked up his beret, which had fallen on the ground, shook off the dust, and looked at it and at the recruit's badge attached to it. His mother went on murmuring to him, and he raised his head slightly, shook it from side to side as if to say *No, no,* and let it fall onto her belly again.

Avner turned back and came up to me. "What's going on?" he said. "Have you gone mad?"

"I want to see," I said. "Just hang on a minute."

"So what if you want to see? There's a limit, you know."

This piece of patronage filled me with rage, insult, and detestation, and brought me to the brink of losing my self-control. I knew that I was about to say things I would regret. The air between us was tense with suppressed violence.

"Okay," he said. "You can do what you like. I'm going." And he turned away.

After a minute I joined him. We walked for a while in silence, and then he said: "There are some things you're not supposed to see."

"Who says so?" I asked.

Avner ignored my question. "There are some things you're not supposed to see, don't you understand, man? There are some moments when a person should turn aside and avert his eyes."

"I wasn't looking out of any kind of malice or ridicule," I said. "I was looking at them because I thought there was something beautiful about it."

"You know what? There are sexual perverts who cruise the public parks at night to see couples making love or peep through windows to see a woman undressing, and in the end they also think they're looking at something beautiful. If you asked them, they'd probably say there wasn't any difference between them and people who go to see art exhibitions or sunsets or ancient buildings or plays or movies. Don't you understand that what happens to living people at moments like the one you were just watching isn't a play or a movie?"

"For God's sake, Avner, stop preaching at me. I can't stand it. You think I did something bad, I don't think I did anything bad. Okay, we're each entitled to our own opinion. What do you think of his sister? I could see you took a shine to her."

"Sorry, but I have to talk about it. It bothers me. I'm not preaching. I just want to explain my position to you, so that you'll understand why I think you're wrong."

He clenched his fists, as if in a strenuous effort to concentrate, but said nothing. Another group of soldiers and recruits came up from behind us, passed us, shouting, joking, swearing; military vehicles drove past on the road, a few stopping to pick up soldiers. And in the middle of the merry, boisterous stream only the two of us proceeded at a leisurely pace, carrying on a conversation that soon ceased to interest me and whose seriousness grew more and more tedious to me, less and less to the point. Avner took off his beret and rubbed his head vigorously.

"Look," he said, "there are moments that an outsider shouldn't intrude on. It's a question of respect, perhaps. Respect for pain, for the tears of a broken man, respect for the mystery of those moments. Moments like these, like moments of love, should be protected, wrapped in mystery, in solitude. Let's suppose that you're right, and the moments of pain and weeping and collapse are moments of beauty, not that I agree with you, but just for the sake of argument — then what's more beautiful than a pair of lovers in bed? That's the most beautiful thing there is, the most beautiful thing in the world. So just imagine that somebody's standing next to the bed and watching. However much he admires and worships that beauty, by the very fact of his being there and watching, he turns it into the ugliest, most disgusting, bestial, obscene thing in the world. Because it's not the same thing anymore. It's beautiful and true only if it's closed off and isolated and no one intrudes on it."

I knew what he was driving at and I said nothing. He continued: "Let's assume that moments of weeping and breakdown are beautiful too, as you say — not that I agree with you, but assuming they are — here too, by the very fact of looking at them you rob them of their mystery and beauty, you turn them into a caricature, something sick and despicable."

"You're not talking about Ben-Hamo," I said, "you're talking about our guard on Saturday night, when you stood next to the tree and cried and I watched you. I didn't know it would upset you so much. You're the one who's always talking about friendship and sharing, you told me the most intimate details about what happened between you and your girlfriend — and I'm supposed to be out of line when all I did was stand there waiting for you, and I could hardly see you in the darkness anyway. How do you tell where the dividing line is? Where friendship and sharing and sympathy stop and intrusion into someone's sacred privacy and spying on his mystery begins? How am I supposed to know?"

"For your information," said Avner, "I wasn't crying. I went off by myself to get rid of the pain, it was suffocating me, and not only because of the way he kicked me, but because of the whole damned evening. I didn't have enough of a hold on myself to analyze myself, the world, the hell knows what, I had to do something aggressive, physical, irrational. I went a bit berserk. And you stood and watched the performance. How I hated you then, how I despised you; if only you knew how miserable and petty you looked then. If there's any kind of beauty in such moments, and God only knows what it could be, then let me tell you that you didn't rise up to it. On the contrary, you brought it down, you made it ugly, you turned it into a ridiculous, degrading, pitiful spectacle."

"You're not answering my question: Where do you draw the line between desirable friendly participation and ugly intrusions into your private mysteries?"

Avner looked at me in surprise and disappointment: "What kind of a question is that? What do you think, that you can see a line, signs? A true friend should know, he should be able to feel it. The real line is drawn in your heart."

At the end of the road the Jerusalem Gate came into view. The traffic of people and vehicles grew denser and noisier. On the main road, beyond the gate, we could see crowds of soldiers, boys and girls, waiting to take a bus or hitch a ride. The conversation seemed highly inappropriate to the atmosphere, to the holiday eve bustle that had infected even this strange place.

"That's your trouble," said Avner. "Behind all your talk about beauty, you have no true respect for pain, for the tears of a man breaking down and crying by himself, for the mystery of those moments."

"That's not true," I protested. "I love those moments, their pain and mystery."

"Don't love them! Nobody's asking you to love them. Respect them!

Make way when you come across them, turn aside, disappear if you can, until they're over."

We passed through the Jerusalem Gate and saw Hedgehog and the other Jerusalemites standing in a long line of male and female soldiers at the side of the road. Avner looked at them for a minute, stopped in front of the gate, and said in an undertone: "I hoped they'd be gone when we got here. I really don't have the patience to listen to their cackling now. I want to forget them now that I'm going home on leave. God!" Suddenly he beat his chest with his fist. "God! I'm really going home on leave! I'm not dreaming! I'm going home for two days! Which way are you going? Via Lydda?"

"No, I think I'd do better going to Tel Aviv and taking a bus from there."

I accompanied him to the line of hitchhikers to say good-bye to the Jerusalemites again and wish them a happy New Year. They were standing in a row a few steps away from us and suddenly my heart contracted in a strange pang of longing, as if I were parting from them forever. A feeling as unaccountable as the vision of what was going to happen next, when I would walk off by myself while they remained together — like an image of betrayal. But before we reached them, Avner suddenly stopped.

"Melabbes, before we go up to them, I want to ask you not to take what I said to you before too seriously. It's only my opinion. I could be wrong. Accept it in a spirit of friendship. And forgive me if I hurt your feelings."

"No, of course not," I said. "I've often thought about the same thing myself, even before you said what you said today. Maybe it's necessary to know how to disappear sometimes. I'll have to give it a try. Maybe that's the only way to change."

• PART TWO •

A NIGHT OF ATONEMENT

"Y ou're not going out to meet your friends," asked his mother. She was standing at the entrance to the room, leaning against the doorjamb, with the old, familiar smile on her face, the smile he could no longer bear to look at: worried, inquisitive, complacent, reproachful, apologetic, sarcastic, concealing more than it revealed. Too many qualities for one strained smile, embarrassingly close yet so very strange. "You're not going out to meet your friends." The question, as always, was formulated as a negative statement, in her own unique syntax, cautious, pessimistic, ingenuous.

His room was exactly as he had left it, and nevertheless he could not rid himself of the strange, disturbing feeling that something had been changed, been added or removed, perhaps something had been moved, perhaps something had changed in him, there was no knowing what.

"I don't know. I haven't decided yet."

Why should he care if something in his room had been changed? He had never taken any interest in such details. So why was he so disturbed by this feeling, nagging away like an unsolved riddle? A few pages from the holiday newspapers lay scattered on the floor, at the foot of his bed. He had no idea how long he had been sleeping, but the light in the window was already beginning to fade.

"Oded came this morning to ask if you were coming home for the holiday. He's been home since last night."

"Yes, you told me before. It's all right. I know."

The afternoon sleep had left him feeling dull and despondent. His textbooks were still standing on the bookcase by the desk, next to a few old favorites he had been meaning to reread. On one of the shelves, in a glass frame, stood a fairly recent photograph of the team. He remembered vividly the occasion on which it had been taken, the game that had preceded it, the victory celebrations afterward, but he could on no account remember his place in the picture. He got out of bed and went over to the shelf, to examine the photo from close up and find himself in it.

"Your father will get up soon and we'll have coffee."

"I want to shower first."

He felt a pang of pity at the sight of the face smiling at him from the group photograph, as predictable and logical as the knowledge that nothing had changed, as ugly as the illusion that it might. He examined the faces of the friends standing next to him, feeling no curiosity as to what they were doing now, no need to see them, as if he had met them only yesterday and they had nothing new to tell him. There was a sound of footsteps in the passage.

"We'll wait for you," his mother said and left the room.

Suddenly the age difference between his mother and father was striking, surprising. Was it because it had been so long since he saw them? Perhaps he had only just began to notice it? There were only a few silver strands in his mother's dull blond, sand-colored hair. Her broad face with its broad nose, slitty blue eyes, and fair eyebrows, all the features that so resembled his own, showed no signs of age. But it was already possible to discern the ruin waiting to pounce when the time came, suddenly, like a raid. His father, on the other hand, wore his age like a robe that had been made to measure for him. Dignified, chilly, remote — as opposed to her self-effacement, her wiped-out, hesitant face, always hiding something as if she were ashamed. He did not have a single one of his father's features, his tall, slender body, his refined face with the proud, pale, calmly determined eyes, the nobility of his slow, sure, precise movements. He knew that he would never be able to imitate him; nobody would. Old age had brought out his beauty. The contrast between the full mane of white hair and the tan of the brow and face, a gleaming bronze tan, stressed the wrinkles on the cheeks and chin, the jawline that had lost its firmness, the scragginess of the neck, but these curves and hollows too were soft and subtly modulated, cast in a strange, harmonious mold, like the contours of the earth from a bird's-eye view.

His mother said: "So you're not sorry now that they didn't take you for the paratroops."

"It doesn't make any difference now," said Micky.

"So you're not having a hard time in basic training, right?" said his father, and Micky was aware of the note of impatience in his voice and the wish for a immediate and optimistic summing-up of the situation, so that he could get the duty of showing an interest over as quickly as possible and return with a clear conscience to himself, the only subject that really interested him.

"From the physical point of view it isn't hard," said Micky.

"What do you mean?" asked his father with a certain resentment, as if to rebuke him for the ingratitude implied by his words.

Micky said: "In Sparta they solved the problem much more efficiently."

"What did they do?" asked his mother.

Micky said: "They left the weak and crippled babies to die on a mountain, so they wouldn't be a burden on society. Because they weren't capable of bringing any benefit to society."

"That's terrible, you don't mean what you're saying," said his mother.

"Once I told you about the wine test they gave the babies in Sparta," said his father. "You were about nine, or ten. I told you that in Sparta the women would bathe the newborn babies in strong wine instead of water. They believed that the wine killed the weak sickly babies and strengthened the healthy ones. And you listened without showing any signs of pity or protest or indignation. As if it seemed quite right and just to you."

"I don't remember," said Micky.

"I was very surprised at your reaction," said his father.

"I remember the story about the Spartan boy who stole a fox cub and hid it under his shirt. The fox clawed and bit him and the boy didn't make a sound or show any sign of pain. All that mattered to him was not being caught in the theft and being mocked by his friends. Because his honor was at stake. But I never asked you why he stole the fox in the first place."

"To eat!" exclaimed his father with a certain show of surprise at his lack of understanding. "To slaughter and cook it. He was hungry. All those boys always went hungry. They fed them sparsely on purpose, to immunize them against hunger, to accustom them to go on fighting even when they were hungry. And also to teach them to look after themselves. To make them develop cunning, agility, resourcefulness, to sharpen their wits. That's why stealing wasn't considered a disgrace there, but on the contrary, a sign of success, of nimbleness and quick wits. But if anyone was caught he was flogged. He was whipped on his bare flesh and he had to endure it in silence and show no signs of pain. And it was clear to everyone that he deserved his punishment because he had failed in his task. In Spartan society, which strove for excellence and perfection in everything, failure was considered a terrible disgrace. The bad thief was whipped just like the bad pupil who failed an exam."

His father's face was flushed as if with some hidden source of vitality, some revival of the soul, as he held forth to his wife and son about the education of the children of Sparta. It could have been any subject under the sun, as long as it wasn't personal, connected to his life or theirs, to what was going on in the country, but to the protected sphere of books, history, and classical philosophers. Only distant things could bring him close to them, and there seemed to be nothing at all that could bring them close to him. I'll probably never understand you, thought Micky, and all because you were once a teacher and you remained a teacher, despite everything that's happened and all the years that have passed since then. And I'm incapable of understanding a person who's a teacher. They were sitting on the porch overlooking the little garden in front of the house. It was twilight. The air was still hot from the blazing day; only the lawn and hedge and flower beds and the paved path leading from the gate to the porch, which had been watered shortly before, gave off a fragrant freshness and an illusion of coolness. Their house was on the outskirts of the little country town, and only an occasional family was to be seen, dressed in their best, making their way to the big synagogue. Sometimes a little cart harnessed to a donkey passed, its owner, returning late from work, pausing in his conversation with his donkey to greet them and wish them a happy New Year. And then they were alone again on their little island, with its flimsy, fragile, artificial tranquility.

Micky's mother said: "In the Palmach they used to steal chickens on the kibbutzim too and cook them over campfires. It's not the same thing, of course."

His father looked at her with sad, forgiving eyes and said: "No," then fell silent. She smiled triumphantly. She always leapt to the defense of Eretz Israel against what she regarded as disdain and hatred of the country and its sons. Micky used to follow her example, because he couldn't stand his father's attitude toward these things, which was annoyingly different from everyone else's. Perhaps because he sensed, without actually knowing, the reason behind this attitude.

It was only in the past year that Micky had begun to really love him and to try to convey the signs of this love to him. He didn't know how this had come about. It had happened so gradually that it was hard to chart its course. It had taken years for forgiveness to mature and bear fruit, for his honor to be restored, for the strange beauty radiating from his old age to be understood, a lost, superfluous beauty engendered by loneliness and despair, alienation, the attempt to escape, and misunderstanding.

His mother smiled her triumphant smile and his father examined his empty coffee cup, as if seeking something suspect in it. Micky said to himself: If I wasn't an only child, if I had brothers and sisters, we would all have surrounded you like a wall, protected you from the world, hid everything ugly, crude, vulgar from you, cocooned you in love and agreement, kept you in the hothouse of an artificial world where everything was done according to your wishes. But there's only one of me; it's not enough for you.

"Why were you surprised at my reaction when you told me about the Spartan babies being washed in wine? What did you expect of me?"

"I don't know," said his father, "some moral indignation, perhaps, in the name of the sanctity of life." He paused for a moment; the conversation was getting too personal for his liking, too pertinent. "By the way, putting the sick or crippled children out to die was customary in the other

Greek cities too, not only in Sparta. But in Sparta they were particularly harsh." The flush of enthusiasm returned to his cheeks. "Their criteria were far stricter. Their society was structured so as to leave no room for the maimed. That's why they put the babies through that test. I thought it would shock you. But children are generally more egocentric, crueler, and more callous than adults are. Contrary to what is commonly believed, perhaps due to the influence of Christianity, romanticism, who knows. Growing up only refines the child's feelings, develops his sensitivity, his consideration for others, his ability to put himself in someone else's place and even identify with him. A child is apparently incapable of that."

And again, silence and withdrawal. His mother went inside and came out onto the porch again. She was carrying a thin cotton jacket to cover his father. The old man did not react, or even turn to look at her, when she placed it on his shoulders. As if it were part of a daily routine, something to be taken for granted. But it was new, a new expression in the repertoire of family gestures. The heat had lifted slightly, but there was no hint of a chill in the air. Micky in his undershirt and shorts tried to feel the change in the weather. The laying of the jacket on his father's shoulders was performed slowly, like a gesture of love, like a hesitant but meaningful embrace taking place behind his back.

His father said: "We can't get inside the skins of those people and see the world as they saw it."

A shiver ran through Micky's heart. He had never seen his father wearing anything over his shirt on summer evenings. Was this simply a new idiosyncrasy of his mother's, or had something happened to his health? His father had never been sick. He had always cultivated his body and been grateful to it, lived with it on terms of a kind of friendly, mutually beneficial alliance, which had seemed narcissistic, if not effeminate, to Micky, and given rise in him to shame, revulsion, and hostility.

The garden was already dark. His mother switched the porch light on. Micky quickly examined his father's face, as if this stolen glance might discover the secret of the jacket. Other sons, he thought, would have asked their father straight out, unhesitatingly, about his health, and why he had suddenly taken to wearing a jacket on a summer night like this; other fathers would have been glad of the opportunity to tell their sons about their aches and pains, real and imaginary. *Don't go. Don't leave us now, when I've just begun to love you.*

His mother sat down by the table. "Something terrible happened to the Droris," she said. "Amos's jeep drove over a mine and he was very badly hurt. He's been unconscious for a week. I met Yael, she'd just come back from the hospital and she said they didn't know if he was going to live or die. And if he lives, he'll be in a shocking state. They've already amputated both his legs, and that's not the end of it yet."

Instead of shock and pain the terrible news gave him a feeling of urgency: I have to see her. And shame: Maybe, maybe, there's a chance now? Maybe there's an opening? Would the curse be lifted one day? And what if the shadow of the dead filled her even more intensely, forever, with longing, memories, adoration? What was she going through, so far from him and from thoughts of him, in this pain, in the fortitude demanded by this tragedy? If only he could go and help in some way, get some gratitude in return. Maybe guilt: Hasn't someone been sacrificed here, the best and most beautiful of us all, who's paid the highest price of all? Pity: Maybe there's some wretched fate that ties all three of us together?

His mother said: "It didn't even happen in action."

"What difference does that make?" his father exclaimed indignantly.

"He was going to Nahal Oz to see his girlfriend," added his mother.

"Did he have a girlfriend in Nahal Oz? I didn't know," said Micky.

"He *has* a girlfriend in Nahal Oz," said his mother. "Don't talk about him as if he's already dead."

Micky had never understood the relations between brothers, let alone brothers and sisters, and especially adolescents, people his own age. When he was a child he had envied his friends for having brothers and sisters; he had felt angry and deprived. When he grew older he had come to accept it. But when his interest in Yael began to deepen and to take on its bitter, and what he regarded as its fateful, character, he became obsessed with the desire to know the nature of her relationship with her brother. The more he thirsted for her love, and the more he despaired of obtaining it, the more fascinating, painful, and mysterious this question became. Amos was two years older than he was, always two years ahead of them at school, always within her sight, always within range of her smile. When Micky's heart was bitter and the certainty of never being loved descended on him again and again, as if by order, he attributed his failure to her relationship with her brother. He knew that the ties between brother and sister could not be measured in terms of that other, new, true, burning love for which he so yearned, and that this tie would not be able to compete with it for any length of time, but it was no longer clear to him whether he had been tempted to invent this forbidden relationship between Yael and her brother and feed it with a larger-than-life intensity and dread in order to excuse the failure of his love as respectably and painlessly as possible, or whether perhaps he had been so powerfully attracted to Yael precisely because of what had seemed to him from the beginning a dark, morbid tie between her and her brother Amos. And like someone driven to destroy something of which he had been cheated, he wanted to interfere in their lives and destroy as much as he could.

"There's no point in going to visit him in the hospital," he asked-stated in his mother's style.

"No," said his mother. "In any case they wouldn't let you see him. In his condition, they only let the family in. What a tragedy. Amos Drori, such a sweet boy, kindhearted, good looking, noble."

"Now you're talking about him as if he's dead," said Micky.

"What kind of life will he have if he lives?"

What would be more natural than going to see her now, saying a few kind words to encourage her. Like friends. I'm kidding myself. It's ridiculous. It should have all ended long ago, as soon as I understood I didn't have a chance, and accepted it as a fact. But I never accepted anything and I'm just looking for an excuse to go around there, hitching a ride on her tragedy. What does she even know about my feelings for her? Everything happened inside me, almost everything. The pride, the shame, the fear of failing, of making a fool of myself. They all worked together to make me miss every chance. She doesn't know anything. And if I did try anything, it probably wasn't so different from what other guys tried. Her attitude to me is much more natural than mine is to her. When she sent me her regards, she was acting like a friend. And when I heard that she'd sent me regards, I acted as if I'd received some sort of secret message, with a thousand intentions, a million possibilities. Nothing's finished.

His father was silent, and from the expression on his face Micky could not tell if he had been listening to their conversation at all. What stupidity to have invited Alon to spend the holiday with them! It would have created a vast gulf of strangeness. Keeping the different spheres apart was the first law of hygiene in personal relationships.

His mother said: "Don't you think it's a good thing that they're letting you carry on with your soccer in the army, that way you'll be able to keep your standard up, or don't you care about it anymore."

"Soccer is over as far as I'm concerned," said Micky, "but for the army it's a good deal. It'll give me a chance to get away every now and then, not to see those characters all the time. It was lucky for me that one of the instructors recognized my name."

"You don't get on with the other boys in the army," said his mother.

"I've got one friend there. A kibbutznik. I nearly brought him home for the holiday, but he preferred to stay behind on duty on the base, he volunteered. He's ashamed to go back to his kibbutz because he's a Medical Grade B recruit on Training Base Four, and where he comes from they all go to combat units and it's a huge big deal for them."

"The kibbutzniks symbolize our society," said his father.

Something of the old resentment against his father stole back into Micky's heart: "That friend of mine is a first-class guy."

"I can imagine," said his father.

"You need at least one friend in the place where you're stationed, don't you," said Micky.

"Yes, yes, I imagine you do."

"I can't understand your reservations," said Micky.

"My reservations are linguistic: the word *friend,* the word *friendship.* What exactly do you mean when you use these words? I think I know what they mean to your generation. A kind of alliance to escape from loneliness, from boredom, from looking inward. Because people are afraid of looking into the abyss inside them. It's a kind of agreement based on mutual aid or mutual exploitation or mutual stupidity. Two people, or more, agree to compromise and give up the most important thing of all in order to preserve everything that's most pointless and insignificant. And however shallow the relationship is, and it's usually the product of circumstances or chance, the partners to it invariably give up something of themselves, and it's usually the most important thing, the thing that makes them different, unique. Most people are always trying to escape from themselves, from their true, essential selves. They run away from the depths inside them in order to float up to the surface and be swept into the shallow waters, where everyone wallows together. There they help each other forget the experience of the depths, the pain of their unique individual identities. Because not everyone can endure it, and not everyone can forget it."

"And what have you got against people wanting to help each other, to overcome their difficulties together?"

"I've got nothing against it, I wish them well of it! But for God's sake, don't exalt it, don't make it into some great human and moral ideal, don't attribute nonexistent qualities to it. Whenever I hear the word *friend,* the word *friendship,* I immediately think of Montaigne. I can't help thinking of him. I've often asked you to read his essays. But you never wanted to. I don't know — something frightened you. Or perhaps it was my pressure that put you off. You must read Montaigne. As opposed to the experience of friendship he knew, the common ties between people, what you in your corrupted language call friendship — seem pathetic, pitiful if not contemptible. The friendship Montaigne talks about is a sublime unity between two human beings, a kind of supreme spiritual pact. It's the real thing, an act of grace, a gift of the gods to the elect."

"That's no reason to sneer at the friendships between ordinary people, at the ties that come into being between them, if they don't happen to be members of the elect."

"If you saw two infants throwing a ball of rags at each other, you wouldn't call it a soccer team. And yet it would resemble a soccer team far more closely than what you call friendship resembles true friendship."

"Perhaps you're talking about love," said Micky.

"Yes, it's a form of love," said his father. "Love that is all spirit, pure soul; love that is not dependent on the flesh. It has nothing to do with sensual pleasure. It has no ups and downs because it's not subject to the dictates of time. Youth, age, beauty, ugliness, have no effect on it. It's completely uncalculating, no promises or commitments, no rights and no obligations, no thought of expediency. And the main thing — it has no mutuality, because anyone who enters into such a union between souls is really returning to himself, but to his full selfhood, his complete, double selfhood, which includes both possibilities, of being the self and the other at one and the same time. And therefore it involves no compromise or renunciation, because the two wills are two voices of one common, comprehensive will. It involves no mutual aid, because when one friend does something for the sake of the other, he does it to exactly the same extent for himself. If you like, I'll read you a passage from Montaigne's essay on friendship."

Micky nodded. Although his father saw that there was no great enthusiasm on his face he got up and went inside the house. His mother gave him a miserable look, as if asking him to forgive his father. But Micky said to himself: I never imagined how lonely he was, how little we fill even a small part of his need for love and friendship, how incapable we are of filling that role, her and me both. The way he talks about friendship it sounds like something religious. He misses it so much. He's lives with us like an exile, longing for a lost homeland that he'll never see again.

His father returned with the book in his hand. He leafed through it until he found the passage he wanted to read to Micky:

"'As for the rest, those we ordinarily call friends and amities are but acquaintances and familiarities, tied together by some occasion or commodities, by means whereof our minds are entertained. In the amity I speak of, they intermix and confound themselves one in the other, with so universal a commixture that they wear out and can no more find the seam that hath conjoined them together. If a man urge me to tell where-fore I loved him, I feel it cannot be expressed but by answering, Because it was he, because it was myself.'"* He fell silent and looked at Micky. "How beautiful it is," he said.

Micky smiled to indicate his understanding and agreement. To himself he said: All this is aimed against ordinary, simple, natural friendship. All this is aimed against the world around him. When he was still a teacher, he used to meet his colleagues often, and on the face of things at least he seemed to enjoy the company of some of them. After he stopped teaching he retired into this proud, disdainful, wounded solitude. He cultivated it like a sign of distinction in a sordid, vulgar world. This whole lecture about ideal friendship is meant to justify his attitude — everything or nothing.

"Just one more passage, it's very fine too," said his father. "'For truly, if I compare all the rest of my forepassed life, which although I have, by the sheer mercy of God, passed at rest and ease and, except the loss of so dear a friend, free from all grievous affliction, with an ever-quietness of mind, as one that have taken my natural and original commodities in good pay-ment without searching any others — if, as I say, I compare it all unto the four years I so happily enjoyed the sweet company and dear, dear society of that worthy man, it is naught but a vapor, naught but a dark and irk-some [night]. Since the time I lost him . . . I do but languish, I do but sorrow. And even those pleasures all things present me with, instead of yielding me comfort, do but redouble the grief of his loss. We were co-partners in all things. All things were with us at half; methinks I have stolen his part from him. . . . I was so accustomed to be ever two, and so inured to be never single, that methinks I am but half myself. . . .'"**

Had tears really come into his father's eyes as he read the last lines? In any event a tremor choked his voice slightly, as if he had to cough and clear his throat. He stood up immediately and hurried inside to return the book to its place in the bookcase. I know nothing about him, said Micky to himself, and I don't want to know any more than I know now. His father did not come back to the porch right away. Micky thought: That's definitely a symptom of old age, that sudden, treacherous weakness, like incontinence. It's a kind of emotional incontinence. Not being able to stop your feelings in time. Some muscle in the soul weakens, things begin coming out, like tears, like dribbling from the corners of your mouth. All the old dreams, the regrets, the shames, the longings.

---

* Quotation from *Selected Essays of Montaigne,* translated by John Florio. Boston: Houghton Mifflin Company, Riverside Editions, p. 62.
** *Ibid.,* pp. 66–67.

"Your father hasn't been feeling so well lately," his mother whispered. "But you're not supposed to know. He doesn't want me to tell you."

"What's the matter with him?"

"Weakness, occasional giddy spells. It's apparently got something to do with his heart. He's going to have tests next week."

"Has he been to the doctor?"

"Yes. He has to rest more now, not to get upset or exert himself. After the tests they'll decide what to do."

He didn't have to exert himself at all. He did what he pleased. He walked to the beehives, which was quite a long way, but he liked it and he thought it was good for his health. He spent a lot of time with his bees. When he'd retired from teaching, he'd decided to keep bees. All his knowledge on the subject came from one of Virgil's Georgics; to be on the safe side, he'd found himself a partner and loyal helper, a taciturn young man from one of the surrounding farms, who was an experienced bee-keeper. After a few years the partner left, because the income from the bees was very small. Micky's father was left alone with the bees, to his heartfelt relief. He found a sense of vocation in the beekeeping almost commensurate with the sense of vocation he had found in teaching before he gave it up as a bad job and retired. They didn't live off the bees, but from his wife's family property. But they let him believe that they lived on the proceeds from the honey; there was no knowing if he actually believed it or not. In any case he took no interest in the bookkeeping and left it to his wife. Perhaps he was afraid of putting his dream to the test.

The wavering light of a lamp appeared at the end of the road between the two rows of little houses. Someone was riding a bicycle, coming to their garden gate, stopping. Oded got off his bicycle, waved to them, leaned the bicycle against the fence, and came in at the gate.

Micky was surprised to realize how glad he was to see him. When his mother told him that afternoon that Oded had asked about him, he had hoped that the two days' leave would pass without their meeting. But now, as soon as he saw him waving and leaning his bicycle against the fence, as he always did, it seemed like the most natural and self-evident thing in the world. And Micky felt a kind of consolation in the fact that things continued faithfully to take their natural course, as if in contempt and indifference toward what had happened in the meantime.

Soon, after sitting with them for a moment out of politeness, his father would get up and go to his room. His mother would bring out some refreshments and then she too would go inside. They would stay on the porch and talk and tell each other about their experiences in the army.

Later his parents would go to bed and Micky would bring out a bag of sunflower seeds and they would sit cracking them and talking until late at night, and when Oded left Micky would accompany him to the center of town. There they would part and Oded would ride home to his house on the outskirts and Micky would run back to his own house on the other side. That's how it always was, how it had been for years.

After they had all wished each other a happy New Year, Micky's mother went inside, and his father asked Oded where he was doing his basic training. Oded said proudly that he was on the Nahal training base, with a number of other friends from town, from the youth movement and school. Micky's father smiled benevolently and added a few perfunctory words, until his mother appeared carrying a tray with saucers of honey and sliced apples in honor of the New Year. She placed the tray with "our honey" and the apples on the table, and after they had dipped the apples in the honey, his father asked them to excuse him and went inside. After a while his mother went inside too.

"You heard what happened to Amos Drori?" said Oded.

"Yes. It's terrible. And all he was doing was going to visit his girl on Nahal Oz."

"It can happen anywhere," said Oded. "To a civilian going for a walk in the evening in some new settlement in the Lachish district or in an orange grove in Rishon LeZion or traveling in a bus in the Negev. Nowhere's safe."

"How's Yael taking it?"

"I haven't seen her," said Oded. "I expect she's in the hospital all the time, at his bedside. You know how close they are."

These words stabbed Micky's heart like a knife. Oded went on talking, and Micky answered him without listening to what he was saying. He imagined the room in the hospital, the bed on which Amos Drori lay unconscious, with Yael sitting by his side. But for the fact that it was so terrible, he might have permitted himself to wonder at the moving beauty of the stillness enveloping the two of them, the stillness of fate hanging in the balance, of the transience of their bodies, of their unspoken thoughts. She was listening for the sound of his breathing, and his breathing was very quiet, quieter than the breath of a person sleeping. Oded was talking about his friends on the training base, about a show put on by the Nahal Entertainment Troupe, and Micky blurted out something about the imbeciles in his platoon, and suddenly, for the first time in his life, he felt something like a hole opening up inside him, giving way beneath the unbearable weight of fear and pity for the breaking of the body, its vulnerability to sickness, to old age, to lovelessness, to the terrible estrangement from others, from ourselves.

Oded talked about the team, about the next day's game. Surprised at Micky's indifference, he suddenly stopped and looked at him closely. There was an insulted expression on his face, as if Micky had betrayed something precious to them both, as if he had betrayed the relationship itself. Micky could not endure this look. He averted his eyes and, on the pretext of going to get the sunflower seeds, went into the house. His father couldn't stand the noise and the sight of people cracking the seeds between their teeth, and Micky never did it in front of him. He went into the kitchen and paused for a moment before reaching out for the bag. I've stopped understanding what's happening to me. Soon I'll probably start wishing I was a child again. Everything's falling apart around me, and salvation won't come from inside me, it will come from other people. I have to accept it. Begin everything from the beginning again.

You only have to turn your head and they change things behind your back. Something had been changed in his room and he didn't know what it was. He had sensed it the minute he woke up from his afternoon nap. And now, as he stood in the kitchen, reaching out for the bag of seeds, he suddenly remembered the dream he'd had that afternoon. It wasn't a proper dream, at any rate; all he remembered was one picture, vague and incomprehensible. A man seen from the back, from the waist up, the bottom half of his body in the dead space between two folds in the earth. Sitting on his shoulders was a baby or perhaps a dwarf. He was barely moving forward. His invisible feet were trudging through a difficult terrain, deep sand, perhaps, a swamp, or water. His body bent under the weight of his load. And the only sound was the sound of weeping, a high-pitched sobbing sound — no doubt about it, it was the voice of the baby or the dwarf sitting on his shoulders, whimpering in fear.

Micky returned to the porch. And he and Oded began voraciously cracking the sunflower seeds. The bowl was quickly filled with shells, Micky emptied it, and it filled up again. When they had polished off the whole bag, Oded got up to leave. As always, they took the dirt road behind the row of houses, Oded pushing his bicycle and delivering his opinions about the political situation and Micky listening in silence. They passed opposite Yael's house. Despite the lateness of the hour there was still a light on in one of the windows. Micky stopped and looked at the house.

Oded whispered: "Yael's not sleeping yet. There's a light in her window."

"Are you sure that everything that's going on here is a struggle between sanity and insanity? I don't trust our leaders blindly, I don't believe that everything they do is out of wisdom and idealism. Can you see yourself, Dedi, going to fight and die for the Motherland?"

"It's impossible to think about it honestly," said Oded. "Nobody imagines that he's really going to die."

"Why?" demanded Micky resentfully, almost furiously, "why is it impossible? You have to! You have to learn to live with the idea. Maybe a combat soldier in a fighting unit should say to himself: I'm like a person with a serious illness, our chances of dying young are the same. Both of us bear the seeds of death within us, him because of his illness, and me because of the statistics that such-and-such a percentage fall in battle. Maybe that would be the healthiest approach?"

"Keep your voice down," said Oded. "They can hear you in Amos's house. For them it's not theoretical anymore."

Micky stared at the light coming from Yael's room, the same anger on his face as there had been in his voice when he spoke of the need to learn to live with the thought of death. The shutter was closed and the light broke through the slats. Was she in bed? If there's anything in the world she's not thinking of now — it's me, said Micky to himself, without bitterness; and if I wasn't an outstanding soccer player admired by her brother, she probably wouldn't have paid me even the little attention that she once did. Maybe that's a good enough reason on its own to give up soccer, to put things to the test of truth. To be me myself, without any additions, any decorations. What I really am. So what's left? The rotten face I got from my mother, the sad mind I got from my father, and the heart murmur, which it turns out I got from him too. All the things I was born with and I can't change, all the things that can't be improved or influenced. Is that the truth? She admires her brother, her brother admires me, and the end result is that I'm left with nothing, with my hands empty.

Oded said: "For God's sake let's get out of here. You're talking out loud, I don't know what's gotten into you."

They continued on their way and Micky was seized by a feeling of pointlessness. Everything they had said to one another that night was so far from the heart of the matter, the essential point that he was seeking. And even though it wasn't clear to him precisely what this crucial thing was, it was evident that it had nothing to do with what they had been talking about. This waste of time filled him with resentment. This was not the way he always felt when he set out to accompany Oded after talking far into a Friday night about politics and sport. So something really had been broken.

True strength was perhaps the ability to concentrate on the main thing and not to bother too much with the inessential, to ignore them, and if necessary — to crush them. Ruthlessly. But first of all you had to be sure what the main thing was. It was becoming increasingly urgent. In any case it was clear that this strength was within ourselves and not in the ability to change things or influence external events. The way the strength of a clock lay in its inner mechanism, and not in the movements of its hands and the intervals it made between the minutes; the way the strength of the wind was not in the swaying of the branches or the sound of its blowing, which were only the results of friction or resistance to the true strength of the wind. But how was it possible to love love, and not a specific Yael, how was it possible to fear fear, and not a specific danger, how was it possible to befriend friendship and not a specific friend? Perhaps the strength needed the cogs of the clock and the hands, the markings on the clock face, in order to move and measure distances with them, no less than they needed it in order to live? It was impossible to remain alone with all that strength.

For a while they walked in silence, passing the dark, locked youth movement building. It was late. Oded gazed at the dark barracks, as if searching for something. A kind of gloom clouded his face, which was as clear and honest and straightforward as his thoughts.

They reached the town center, and Oded mounted his bicycle: "Hang in there, Micky. Don't let them change you."

"You too, Dedi, and regards to all the gang. We all change, there's nothing we can do about it."

Old habits slowly lose their strength and wither away, the life's blood drains out of them. Oded disappeared into the darkness, and only the sound of his whistling could still be heard somewhere. He always whistled when he was riding alone on his bike. Micky walked slowly down the dark, empty street, a pleasant coolness caressing his neck. The stillness brought with it a sense of great spaces and loneliness. The road, which his feet knew so well, lacked some dimension, as if it were denying him. He always ran home, and the echo of his bounding steps would ring rhythmically in his ears until the place where the asphalt ended and gave way to the dirt track leading to his house. But this time Micky preferred to walk slowly. The light in Yael's house was off. He stood facing her window and for the first time since hearing of the catastrophe his heart was wrung with a true, searing pain for Amos. He would die tonight, a voice said inside him; there was no doubt that he would die tonight. It was inconceivable that he would come back to life without any legs, in a wheelchair. This is the first time it's happened to somebody I know. The time comes when it has to happen. Perhaps it's a question of age. The older you get, the more cases you know personally. And then, perhaps, your heart learns to harden and adjust, and the agitation subsides. But the first case is a revelation, a terrible warning.

In his room he had the same disturbing feeling that something had been changed and he didn't know what. He looked around the room, counting the furniture and things in it one by one. He went up to the open window and gazed out at the night. The afternoon sleep had been so long and deep that he had no desire to go to bed now. He had not felt so alert for a long time. There was nothing to engage this feeling, nothing to satisfy it. No one to share it with. What was the dividing line between this alertness and the restlessness he felt all the time, like disturbing background music? Had the era of betrayal begun? His room was already betraying him, hiding secrets from him. His father's health. What had happened to Amos Drori? As if the edge of a curtain, behind which things changed ceaselessly, had been lifted. Someone outside was whistling in time to his footsteps on the dirt road; soon his shadow would appear in the darkness and then too it would be hard to tell who he was, for there was hardly any moon. His left elbow sought its habitual resting place in front of the window, and found nothing there. The movement was so deeply ingrained in him that he could not explain the nature of the lack that was upsetting his balance, the sudden uncertainty of his stance, the empty space that stubbornly met his arm seeking a resting place in vain. When he drew back from the windowsill he discovered that the folding bed, which had always stood between the window and the corner of the wall, was gone. This bed was kept for guests. From the day he remembered himself in his room, it had stood there, folded up, leaning against the wall, covered with a long, faded white tablecloth, embroidered with blue and orange hexagonals and edged with an orange fringe. Lying in bed he always saw this tablecloth in front of him, spread over the folding bed, with its embroidered hexagonals surrounding each other in a pattern that seemed to repeat itself endlessly. He sat down and contemplated the empty corner and it seemed to him that the whitewash on the wall was whiter there in the protected corner, which had suddenly been exposed, pale and painful as a secret.

The folding bed had apparently been moved into his parents' bedroom. Perhaps it had something to do with his father's condition. Perhaps his mother hadn't told him everything. The usual patronizing stupidity of trying to keep things hidden, as if he were too weak to know the truth. They had always slept in a double bed. Now they had separate beds. No doubt she was sleeping on the less comfortable folding bed, loyal to her role as always, depriving herself for his sake, devoted and suffering in silence, although not without a certain emphasis. The components of his security were coming apart and receding from each other. The first signs of the final separation. Presumably there was a certain age at which circles began to close. Was this the first circle closing in his life, or at any rate the first circle to whose closing he was paying attention? The new love he had lately discovered in himself for his father, after years of resentment and contempt, like the return to an early, dormant, animal love, did it presage the pangs of separation to come? The warmth that flooded his heart at the thought of this possibility seemed to melt the vestiges of the restlessness that had been troubling him for the past few hours. Ah, he thought, he was beginning to learn the art of acceptance and reconciliation.

His breaking voice, his eyes that had suddenly grown damp when he was reading the passage from Montaigne, the dream of ideal friendship that had burst through the walls of his cold, arrogant isolation, like a cry of alarm at the sudden realization of the magnitude of what had been lost. It was necessary to understand those moments well. *Children are generally crueler and more callous than adults, contrary to what is commonly believed* . . .

Micky thought of his own callous, selfish, unforgiving childhood. What had made him go that day to the big boys' classes and stand opposite the blue, oil-painted door, behind which warlike noises rose? He was then in one of the first classes of grade school. They had told him he wasn't allowed to go there, and they had never told him why. But he had already begun to sense, if not to understand, the reason for the prohibition. The jokes and catcalls that came his way from the big boys in the higher forms, the looks they exchanged when they saw him. But for them it might never have occurred to him to go that day and wait for his father next to the door of the class where he taught. His own lessons finished at noon, and instead of going home, as he did every day, he went to the high school, passed the closed doors, and listened to the voices behind them until he heard his father's.

One of the boys shouted: "Bread and circuses! Bread and circuses!" and loud bellows of laughter rose from behind the closed door. His father's voice implored: "Students, quiet, quiet please, students!" The laughter gradually died down, giving way to a loud, constant buzz, with his father's voice rising in an effort to overcome the noise. He looked up and down the corridor to see if there was anybody there, because the sense that he was doing something wrong suddenly grew acute, intoxicating him with its terror, temptation, and exhilarating danger. But the corridor was empty and he was alone. He tried to peep through the keyhole but couldn't see anything. The need to see for himself what was happening in the room and what his father was doing was unendurable. He touched the handle of the door and was about to turn it very slowly, to open a narrow crack. But the minute he touched the door a terrible grating noise rose from the room, like the creaking of a great, unfamiliar machine. This new noise drowned out the buzz that had filled the room up to then. A kind of deafening, rhythmic screeching like the noise of a train. His hand fell from the handle in alarm, for it seemed to him that it was his touch that had triggered the noise, but it went on even after he had taken his hand away and now it was possible to guess that it was made by the scraping of dozens of pairs of shoes on the floor of the room, uniform, merciless, without a pause. From time to time loud bursts of laughter broke out, apparently in response to some gesture of his father's, or something he said that was drowned out in the terrible din.

Something told him exactly what was going on in the closed classroom, but his heart was not yet ready to understand it. The rhythmic noise now split up into a medley of noises, shouts, running footsteps, peals of laughter, and strange bangs and thuds. Like objects falling on the floor tiles or thrown at the blackboard. His heart pounded. His instincts told him to run away, to run home as quickly as he could. At that moment the door opened, the volume of noise doubled, and the boy who was pushed outside bumped violently against him. Micky stepped back and stood aside and let the boy run down the corridor. It was Haim M. Micky knew him well from around town, but Haim didn't even notice him, he was so elated. Haim M., of the rumpled curls and the khaki shorts rolled up almost to his groin, animal lover and practical joker, ran down the corridor doubled up with laughter, shouting the mysterious slogan: "Bread and circuses! Bread and circuses!" looking for someone to share his hilarity with, and not finding anyone, shouting at the blue doors of the closed classrooms: "We're ragging Spector!" on his way to the headmaster's study, where he had been sent by his teacher. He was happy and content and he knew no fear.

Micky went up to the door, which Haim M. had left half open, stood opposite it, and saw his father. Mr. Spector was leaning with his back against his desk, covering his face with his hands. Little paper airplanes, sent flying in his direction from the invisible part of the classroom glided through the air and dropped slowly at his feet, one by one, with a strange, gentle sadness, like white birds arriving at their destination with the last of their strength, falling to the ground and dying. His father took his hands from his face and walked over to the door to close it. Micky wanted to pick up his heels and run, but his legs refused to obey him. Their eyes met.

His father stood in the doorway and bent down slightly toward him: "Michael."

To this day the tone of his father's voice as he said *Michael* echoed in his ears with astonishing precision and substantiality. And he still didn't know what the voice expressed — surprise, rebuke, threat, relief, helplessness, supplication, despair, love?

The man's face was bathed in perspiration, and when he lifted his hand Micky thought he wanted to wipe the sweat away. But the man placed his hand on the child's head, as if he wanted to keep him there, and not let him run away until he had found something to say to him. Micky recoiled from the touch, extricated himself, and started running. He ran for his life down the deserted corridor, crossed the school playground, and came out into the street. The satchel strapped to his shoulders hit his back in time to his running, like a punishment, until he no longer knew whether it was his running that caused the blows on his back or he was running away from the blows, like a cat from its tail. His feet did not carry him home, as he had expected them to, but to an abandoned little field, not far from the school. When he reached the field, he stopped and looked around him, wondering what he was doing there.

There was nobody in the field. He found a big stone to sit on, took his satchel off his shoulders, and put it down next to him, panting to recover his breath. But the panting went on longer than it should have and suddenly became suspect in his eyes. Something inside him commanded him to fight against it and not give in. This was not the first time he had struggled against the soft, liberating temptation. In order to prove something to himself or to his surroundings. But up to now he had never felt it to be of such fateful importance, capable of influencing the whole course of future events. The question now was not how to stop the tears threatening to spurt from his eyes and the spasm trembling in his chest and threatening to spread, the question was how to uproot this need from his heart. Was this the reason his feet had carried him to the deserted, isolated field? To be tested there, as if he had been called upon to respond to a new, unfamiliar voice.

"Bread and circuses! Bread and circuses!" he murmured to himself like a whispered invocation that had it in its power to awaken all the forces latent in him, to abolish all the stumbling blocks and weaknesses, for these words, which it was apparently forbidden to speak, were full of magic and mystery, giving rise to thoughts of rebellion and exhilarating lawlessness and the hope of power.

From his parents' room he heard his father groan and his mother asking something in a whisper. And then silence again. Micky opened his eyes. The light was on in his room and he was lying fully clothed on his bed. He must have fallen asleep. He got up, stretched, and went to the kitchen to have a drink of water, for he was very thirsty. The short sleep had done him good; at last he felt that he had really come home. When he returned from the kitchen, he got undressed and got into bed. He picked up one of the newspapers he had bought for Alon and glanced through it, looking for something to read until he fell asleep again. The failure of the UN mission to Cairo. The new government had completed the formulation of its program. The Arab Foreign Ministers' Conference had been canceled. The end of the year 5715.* In the shadow of Asia — when and how was the idea of the Bandung Conference conceived? From Khan-Yunis to the Gulf of Aqaba. Failed campaigns and dead illusions. New horizons for Israeli science. Agriculture and settlement in the year 5715. In the literary supplement his eyes fell on a poem: *"Standing on the road at night this man / Who was once my father. / And I have to go up to him where he stands / Because I was his oldest daughter . . ."*

His eyes scanned the newspaper columns; he threw down the pages he had finished and took up new ones. He didn't know what he was looking for. He didn't feel like reading a single one of the articles. Suddenly he realized that instead of reading what interested him, he was trying to imagine the way Alon would have read the paper, the way he would read it when Micky gave it to him. But the newspaper was alien to him. He couldn't read it through Alon's eyes. Even Alon was alien to him.

After putting out the light he didn't close his eyes but smiled at himself in the darkness. The figure of Haim M. loomed up in his memory, confronting him vividly, the way he had looked that day when he had been expelled from the class and sent to the headmaster, shouting in the empty corridor: *Bread and circuses! Bread and circuses!* And then: *We're ragging Spector!*

Haim M. had fallen in one of the battles in the Negev, in the War of Independence. In the notebooks he had left behind him, his parents had found notes about the habits of various animals, and nature observations at the changing of the seasons, and a few verses he had composed about

---

* 1954–1955.

love and loneliness, anger and unhappiness. In the years that followed, during the Memorial Day services in the school playground, there was always some girl from the top form, with an emotional voice and proud eyes, who would stand at the foot of the flagpole with the flag at half-mast, in front of the assembled school, pupils and teachers formed up in a U, and read the poems and nature notes of Haim M. They had been published by the Defense Ministry in the anthology *Scrolls of Fire*. Some of the women teachers would wipe away a tear. The memories were still quite fresh. During all these years Micky was never struck by the absurdity in the overlapping identity of the two figures of Haim M., the one he saw that day running down the corridor yelling "Bread and circuses!" and the one commemorated with high-flown solemnity at the Memorial Day parades, the one whose black-framed picture hung in the Nature Room named in his honor at school. But now, with the events of that distant day suddenly so fresh in his memory, so concrete in all their details, Micky smiled to himself in the dark, not without a certain malice, as the riotous image of the laughing, shouting boy made a mockery of the hypocritical, bombastic monument erected by the teachers and the headmaster in their ceremonies and speeches, smashing the big bluff of solemn faces with their obligatory gloom, wiping a tear from the corner of their eyes, listening grief-stricken to the reading of the wretched poems and the pathetic notes on the life of the lizard and the autumn crocus in the spring and the fall. Thus Micky felt his ancient pact with Haim M. reviving, the pact that came into being during the moments when he sat alone in the field, muttering *Bread and circuses!* and drawing comfort for his pain from the strange words and strength to declare war on the thing that was dearest to him of all.

He had no idea how long he'd sat there on the stone, struggling with himself and the temptations of weakness and compromise beckoning him from every side, until he'd finally stood up, confident of his mastery over his feelings, wondering what was going to happen to him now. When he came home his father had already returned. His parents looked at him with worried, accusing eyes, but they didn't say anything or ask any questions. They must have discussed him and the incident at the high school before he arrived.

His father had said only: "Go and wash your hands and come to the table to eat."

Micky had felt his father's eyes examining him, but he was still incapable of saying to himself that these were the eyes of a guilty man. He refused to meet his father's eyes, responding curtly to his mother's questions about what he had learned that day at school, and why he wasn't eating, and what he was sulking about. His father told her to stop it and leave him alone, he understood that something had been broken, and despaired of forgiveness. So it went for a number of days. Micky hardly spoke to his father and his father didn't speak to him, waiting for the evil spirit to leave them. And Micky didn't forgive his father, although the sharpness faded from day to day. It was then that Micky heard the terrible word *purgatory* for the first time, when his father used it to describe his work as a teacher. For many years afterward Micky did not succeed in finding out what this word meant, and he did not dare to ask his father. It was the end of the school year. And it was his father's last year as a teacher. It was then that he turned to beekeeping, and grew more remote from Micky and his mother. Micky never stopped judging him in his heart, lying in wait for every word, every gesture that could be saved from the silence and withdrawal of the man growing old beside them in stillness and inexplicable beauty. Every word and every gesture, precisely because they were so rare, were like warning signals, arousing his contempt, his accusation.

Now, at a distance of years, with the feeling of the closing circle striking him so vividly and forcibly, Micky wondered what this unforgivable weakness was; what was the Achilles' heel that had turned his teaching into a "purgatory"? Because he wasn't a weak man at all, there was nothing ridiculous or strange or peculiar about him that children could sense and attack. He had always been an impressive figure of a man, with his height, his face radiating self-confidence, authority, calm and pride, his speech compelling, full of knowledge and wisdom. So what was it that the children sensed in him and because of it decided to make his life hell? It was something that children were never wrong about. His father himself had once told him that children were like dogs, they sensed who was the master and obeyed him, they smelled out the weak and bit him. This instinctive knowledge revealed something to them. What? And what was it about Benny the instructor that made such an immediate and compelling impression on them, so that they never stopped talking about him, guessing his intentions, and wondering about his private life? What was it about someone like Benny that made people admire him, try to imitate him, long to hear a kind word from him, need to know that he approved of them? Obviously it wasn't simply a consequence of military discipline and the fear of punishment. The fact was that with other instructors it was different. Was Benny crueler than the others? No, but there was a certain hint of a possible, theoretical cruelty in everything he said and did, in every movement he made. What was this cruelty? What was this power? On the surface of things he was unimpressive, even repulsive. The sloppy way he stood, that face with the little eyes behind the glasses, his bored, drawling, nasal voice, a certain lack of seriousness in all his behavior. But none of this detracted from his power. What exactly was the thing that the instructor Benny possessed and the teacher Spector didn't? What had happened? Where did the weak spot lie?

The answer to this question might never be found. We didn't know much about the people closest to us, perhaps precisely because they were the closest; they were the last people we wanted to know about. Perhaps we were right not to want to know, because the knowledge would be unbearable. But one day, when we least expect it, after all the compromises, all the forgiving and forgetting, who knows, maybe suddenly some distant, long-forgotten memory, like a planet that everyone thought had been snuffed out somewhere in infinity and died, would come back and reappear, according to the complex laws of the astronomy of the soul, an old-new point of direction for measurements and calculations, and all would be explained. Wouldn't it be too late?

I was unkind to him in his most difficult hour. And today it seems he doesn't need anyone. Today he's a different person and nothing can be mended anymore. It hurts, but it seems you can live with it. Maybe you carry a pain like that with you all your life, you get used to it. The pain turns to guilt, the guilt turns to love, the love turns to longing, the longing turns into an idea, and the idea turns into a dream. Everything begins in a dream, like Alon says: Everything begins in a dream and ends in a dream.

CHAPTER 15

Dearest Dafna,

Ten o'clock in the morning — Sabbath, Rosh Hashana. I
stayed behind on the base on duty. The whole platoon went on
leave for the holiday. I volunteered to stay. It probably seems
strange to you. Like a lot of other things I've done and said
recently. This time too I'm sure I'm doing the right thing. And
don't think I don't miss you awfully, and home too. I do. But
my problem overshadows everything else now and I have to
solve it. These two days alone are awfully important to me. To
try and find some way of dealing with it. From a certain point
of view, this is the major problem of my life now. I have to concentrate all my strength and attention on it. You see, like the
religious, I'm using Rosh Hashana to make a reckoning. I've
been a bit on edge lately, I know, I took offense at everything,
I answered questions impatiently. Socially speaking, my situation isn't easy. The atmosphere in the group suffocates me.
That's why Yuval's remark was the last straw. I never imagined it would come from him of all people. I'm sorry it had to
develop into a quarrel, with insults and everything. But maybe
there was no alternative. It had to explode. After all the things
people said behind my back, the jokes, the hints, the digs, the
winks. I can't stand it anymore. I'm positive that it was all a
mistake, simply a mistake. And I have to do everything to get
it sorted out and fixed up as soon as possible. I won't stay on
the sidelines like Yuval said. That's for sure. One day Yuval
will understand how wrong he was. I'll never forgive him as
long as I live.

"I'm shoving off for a bit," said Ben-Hamo.

Alon looked at him for a minute uncomprehendingly.

"I'm sick of sitting here all the time. It's worse than being alone. I'm
shoving off."

"You stay here and do what you're told," said Alon.

"What's the matter with you? You're not my bloody CO." Rahamim's
voice was trembling with rage.

"So what are you telling me for? If anyone asks me I'll say you took off.
I can't keep you here by force."

"Who'll ask? " said Rahamim. "There's nobody here. Everyone's gone
on leave."

"There are officers on duty, there's an instructor on duty, and they'll come to check. I'm not going to lie for you, I'm telling you in advance." Rahamim went and sat on the steps of the barracks.

> I'll never forgive Yuval. How could you have said that it was all my imagination? As if I had a persecution complex or something. I know you wanted to encourage me or something. I expected another kind of encouragement. I expected you to have faith in me. To stand by my side. I was going out to fight a battle, and I thought that you would stick up for me in front of everyone and boost my morale, not say that it made no difference to you where I would serve. Because to me it matters very very much, it matters terribly! So how can you, the person who's closest to me and who I love most in the world, say it doesn't matter? It's as if you're belittling my struggle. My suffering, my hopes, my will not to give in. As if you loved somebody else and not me. Because to me it's the center of my life now. How can you say to a warrior going into battle that his war is of no importance? It's like a betrayal. I know you did it out of tact and the purest of good intentions. But you know that we've agreed to be honest and sincere with each other, and you shouldn't treat me like some invalid who everybody keeps in the dark about his condition because they don't want to upset him. I'm sure that you're with me in my struggle. And that you know how important it is to me. How important it is objectively. I'd like it a thousand times better if you told me that my worth's gone down in your eyes because they put me "on the sidelines" instead of pretending that it isn't important and that it doesn't matter. Because it matters terribly. It goes against my whole way of life, all my dreams, for as long as I can remember. If I give in — I won't be myself, and you won't love me but somebody else. Somebody I despise from the bottom of my heart. Who doesn't deserve to be loved by someone like you.

The silhouette next to the door stood up. Rahamim came inside and began slowly pacing to and fro. Alon raised his eyes from his writing pad, looked at him for a moment, and then put the pad down on his bed.

"What's the matter with you?" he asked.

"I can't stay like this," said Rahamim. "Without anybody talking to me, without seeing anybody. I'd be better off in jail."

"What do you want?" asked Alon. "Is it my fault they confined you to barracks? Go and complain to your friends who burned your blanket, whose fault it is that you're here now."

"Don't talk about my friends," sighed Rahamim. "They're not my friends. They're a bunch of crooks, garbage, they're not human beings."

Rahamim sat on his bed and covered his face with his hands, as if he were tired and wanted to sleep, took his hands away, glanced at his watch, and sighed again. "I'm gonna go crazy by the time this leave's over, I'm gonna go off my rocker, I'm telling you right now."

He lay down on his bed and closed his eyes, apparently trying to fall asleep.

> Yuval's remark was so insulting and hurtful because it was gloating too, supercilious, as if it was clear to him in advance that he would get his place and I would get mine. Everyone was getting what they deserved. After all these years. Yuval and I always shared the same point of view, the same private and general experiences, the same mutual respect. Everything was always equal, mutual. That's what I thought at least. Until he came home on his first leave. I hardly recognized him. He was another person. Maybe something that was always there hidden inside him suddenly came out. As if putting me down would raise his own status. And then you say that he didn't mean anything by it. That I'm imagining things that he didn't say and doesn't think. My dear Dafna, I understood exactly what he was getting at. I know Yuval better than I know myself. It still hurts me. The pain of betrayal. Like being left behind wounded in enemy territory. But now there's hope. One of the instructors here, who couldn't understand what I was doing here, told me I should put in an application for a reexamination by the medical board. I'm positive they'll discover their mistake. I know it. I know my body. Its strength and its endurance.

"Just my lousy luck," said Ben-Hamo, sitting up in bed. "Just my lousy luck that you wanted to stay behind. What d'you have to volunteer for all the time? Otherwise they would've made somebody else stay here with me. Even if they would've made that shit Zackie stay, even Zero-Zero. At least he would've cursed me and picked on me all the time. The time would've passed quicker. This way I'm gonna go out of my mind!"

"I don't talk to you? Why do you say that?" said Alon indignantly. "What have I got against you? Of course I talk to you all the time."

"Like hell you do! " said Rahamim. "The whole day yesterday and the whole evening too either you ran around the room or you slept or read your book or stood outside and thought by yourself, and you didn't talk to me one bit. As if I was some sort of stone. Even a stone you go up to, push it around with your shoe, pick it up, and throw it someplace. Something! But me, excuse me, maybe I get in your way just by being here? What do I want of your life?"

"What kind of nonsense are you talking? If I didn't talk to you, it's because I've got problems and I have to think about them."

"I got problems too. Everybody's got problems. So what? They don't talk? As if there's nobody here, no human being? Air? It's all air?" And he waved his hands around in the air to illustrate his words. Then he closed his eyes and his face darkened. "What do I want of your life? I'm just shooting off my mouth. Don't do me any favors."

> That whole story about my problem doesn't mean a thing. You'll still be proud of me, Dafna, and the kibbutz won't have any reason to be ashamed either. I love you, and when things are bad I feel as if you're there next to me, right up close. I think about you all the time, I want you terribly. Maybe my mother's right. Maybe in years to come I won't even be able to understand myself why I got so upset over this business. Okay, but that doesn't help me now. I'm living now. In these years. Living my own age. My ideals. With friends my own age. That's the field I'm playing on. And I don't want to stand on the sidelines and watch other people play. It's important to me that you have faith in my strength to get through this hard time. Until I realize my ambitions. I don't care how the others react or what they say about me. I've given up on that already. I've learned my lesson. But it's terribly important to me to know that you're on my side. Loving, confident, in other words, close. Even when we're not together. Don't give my regards to anyone. Not even to my mother.

"I suppose you think if you're from a kibbutz you're too good to talk to Ben-Hamo. I was on a kibbutz too. Six months."

"Is that so? Where?" asked Alon with exaggerated interest.

Rahamim mentioned the name of the kibbutz. "It was right after we

came to the country. My big sister was there first and she fixed it for me
to go there too. In the kibbutz boarding school. With the outside kids,
like they call them."

"Why didn't you stay?"

"It was hard for me. I'm not used to that kind of life. I didn't even
know Hebrew yet. In the middle of the year they sent me home. For not
fitting in. They didn't give me a chance, that's the truth. But I wasn't so
sorry. A kibbutz is no place for me. You people are too conceited. You
look down on the whole world, as if you're sitting up in the sky and
everybody else is lying in the mud, in the shit. You know what, in the old
country everybody knew our family. Wherever you went everyone knew
the Ben-Hamo family. We had a shop and a big house with Arab servants. We only spoke French. Not Arabic. People came from all over to
ask my father's advice, they came to ask him to settle arguments between
people, Jews and Arabs both. Everybody knew my father. He died before
we came here. His grave stayed there. Who knows what the Arabs did to
it? I dunno why we came here. It's all because of my big sister, who was
here before, the one on the kibbutz. She kept on writing letters all the
time, telling us to come, saying it was so great here. Now we're in Ramle
and it's no good for us. We had to leave all our money behind, the shop,
the house, everything. They didn't let us take it. And the little we did
bring, my uncle in the transit camp took, damn his soul. We were left
with nothing."

"You speak Hebrew better than all the . . . than the rest," said Alon
insincerely.

"That's because I was on a kibbutz at the beginning. They were all
sabras there except me. Every word I said, they'd laugh at me and copy
my mistakes, so's to make each other laugh. It was awful. All the time
they laughed at me. They talked all kinds of nonsense. They made up
shows and jokes about me. The outside kids more than the kibbutz kids.
The outside kids are mean, meaner than anyone. No one pays no attention to what they do to a person. Even if they kill a person, no one'll take
any notice. That's how I learned Hebrew."

"In the Negev, in the Lachish district, in all kinds of places there are
new villages for new immigrants now. You should have gone there. That
way you would have been able to begin a healthy, new life, not like the
lives you lived abroad."

"It was good abroad!" said Rahamim. "It was very good! You people
don't know nothing about it. Sabras think that over here it's better than
anywhere else. You think we lived like Arabs there. You don't know

nothing about the way we lived there. We had everything we wanted. We should never of come here. This country here's not for us. What d'you think, that my mother should go and be a farmer now? Cows, chickens — what? We ain't used to it. That's not our life. Maybe it's good for you. You've got the strength for it and you get taught it. Our life's different."

Alon looked at him without knowing what to say. His conversational repertoire was exhausted, and he stole a glance at his writing pad. Rahamim said: "What do I want of your life? You want to write a letter and I'm talking your head off. Why should I shout at you? You're the nicest guy in the platoon. You help everybody and never insult nobody. Never make no trouble for nobody. But I can't be alone all the time, without a human being to talk to. I ain't used to it. I ain't got nothing to do. It's gonna drive me crazy."

"That's quite okay," said Alon. "You don't bother me."

"If someone else'd stayed, some other trash like me, it would've been better for me. You're too good to talk to me. Ben-Hamo's like shit under your shoe. Don't think I don't know my place nor yours neither. We ain't the same, we ain't in the same world. Why don't I leave you alone?"

"If you would have stayed longer on the kibbutz, you would have known that according to what we believe all human beings are equal. You shouldn't talk like that. It isn't nice. It offends me."

"Don't make me laugh," said Rahamim and laughed bitterly and demonstratively. "In all my life I never felt like I was such shit as I felt on the kibbutz. Even here in the army I've got more respect than there."

"What about your sister? Didn't she help you to fit in?"

"She didn't have no time for me. And she was ashamed of me being her brother too. After all the trouble, and all the jokes they made about me. And in the end, when that business happened, that they threw me out for, she didn't want to have nothing to do with me. Maybe she was scared she'd get into trouble too because of me. I dunno. In the end she left there herself. It wasn't so great for her either."

Rahamim got up and went to look out of the window, with his back to Alon. Perhaps the memories of those days had upset him and he wanted to collect himself and hide his face.

> And definitely not to anyone from the group, if any of them come home on leave. I'll come when my problem is solved, and it won't take too long. I'll come holding my head high, with a red beret, like everybody else. And not what Yuval thinks I deserve. For the time being I want to be as nonexistent

as possible. I'm in a transition period. I've got a lot to tell you about life here and all kinds of characters in my platoon, but this isn't the place for it. It's a whole new world, a world we only hear about in the newspapers and from stories. But I've got at least one good friend here. Micky Spector from *Hapoel* Hadera. Yes, he's here too! They found some problem with his health too. And he promised me that he'd come to the kibbutz for a visit once, on our next leave maybe. And you'll meet him. In any case I intend keeping in contact with him after my transfer too. Write to me, dearest Dafna, I need your letters, I wait for them every day. Write as much as you can. And go on sending me the papers too. They're very important to me. They're my connection with what's happening on the outside, with all the things that are closest to my heart.

"There was one girl there, Batya, an outside kid from Tel Aviv. In my group. Her father married another woman, her mother married another man, do I know? They sent her to the kibbutz. They should of sold her for a whore. Then maybe she'd have done somebody some good in the world."

Rahamim was standing with his back to the window. The expression on his face was determined, proud, confident, accusing. There was something in the way; he was standing barefoot against the window that recalled his appearance when he had danced before them on that Friday night the week before. Alon put the pad down on the bed next to him and tried to look interested and sympathetic. A feeling of despondency and weariness spread through his heart, a feeling of pointlessness and futility, like the beginning of waking up.

"From the first minute she hated me, that Batya. What harm did I ever do her? Wherever I go there's always someone who hates me, really hates me. That's my luck. Now that I'm already used to people hating me, what do I care? I laugh inside myself. But then I was still a child, fourteen, maybe fifteen. Something like that. I couldn't stand it that she hated me for nothing. I wanted her to like me, even if she had a face like the back of a bus and she stank and everyone hated her too. But she hated me. All the time: Ben-Hamo, Ben-Amo, Ben-Bumo, Morocco, Morocco-Knife, Morocco-Nigger, and all kinds of curses. And they'd all stand around and laugh, not only the outside kids, the kibbutz kids too. They'd laugh in my face and afterward they'd talk all kinds of nonsense behind my back. And I wanted to be friends with her. It's only now that I really hate her. I hate her like hell. If I ever see her in the street with nobody looking I'll strangle her on the spot. As true as God."

The sense of obligation and responsibility, said Alon to himself, is like a tangled ball of string, with only one end in my hand, and the other hidden deep inside the ball. I know more or less what my duty is to my society, my movement, my country, to my people, to mankind, but I can't find the connection with the problems and troubles of some Ben-Hamo, someone who can't be my friend, who's got nothing in common with me. But I know, instinctively, that somewhere at the far end of the thread, the one that's buried in the tangled ball, the connection exists between his problem and my responsibility. Am I being hypocritical when I listen patiently to the rubbish he talks, pretend that it's important and interesting, instead of asking him to leave me in peace to think about my real problems? One thing sure is that it's impossible to hold the thread at both ends. Maybe only special people, maybe only saints, can. If you let go of the end in your hand and begin to look for the far, buried end, you have to give up too much for something uncertain. It's dangerous. But if you hang on to the end in your hand and you don't delve into the knots to look for the buried end, you stay with the ideas and lose contact with the real person, you lose the vital glue that turns us into what we are, men in society, moral beings, with common goals and mutual concern. Perhaps the instinct that tells me that at the end of the thread there is a connection between Ben-Hamo's problem and my responsibility, is like a scout's sense of direction and orientation. The defined duties of responsibility are like a topographic map with reference points and scale and all the rest. Between the one and the other you find your way.

"She used to play the guitar," said Rahamim and gave a bitter snort of laughter. "It was something awful the way she played. Not like that Yossie here who plays really musical. She used to just knock you on the head the whole day long. No one could stand it. They were busy getting ready for some big party in your movement. Initiation ceremony or something. I wasn't at that party because they already threw me out by then, so I dunno what it was exactly. They were going to play together, one guy on the accordion, another girl on the recorder, and her on her guitar. And some others were supposed to sing your songs, from the war, with them. It was all in aid of this initiation ceremony, I think you call it.

"One day Batya was having a fight with another girl, about some magazines called *She* and *Movies*. They weren't allowed to bring them there, because children on the kibbutz aren't supposed to read *She* and *Movies*. That other girl, that one who was fighting with her, she was also from Tel

Aviv. She had a big bunch of those magazines, which her mother used to bring her. She used to hide them and only read them when the house-mother or the teacher wasn't looking. So they wouldn't catch her and throw her out. She read under the blanket. So no one would see. Batya was always asking her to let her read them too, because she also liked reading *She* and *Movies*. But that other girl didn't want to give them to her, she was scared they'd find out, and maybe she didn't want to do her a favor, because they all hated Batya too. They fought about those maga-zines every day. And then they began to curse and call names and all that. And then everyone went to the dining hall for supper and Batya stayed behind alone in the room and cried. And even though she hated me so much and said mean things about me I was real sorry to see her crying like that. She didn't see me standing behind the door and watching her cry. I was sorry for her after that other girl called her *you stinking bitch*. And it was true too, that Batya was always stinking, I dunno why. Everyone used to hold their nose not to smell her stink. So I thought I'll do something for her, so she'll stop hating me and begin to like me instead. Like I feel sorry for her because everybody hates her, maybe she'll feel sorry for me too, because everybody hates me. But I didn't know her. I never knew what a stinking bitch that Batya was. I used to look from behind the door to see where that other girl hid her magazines. And one day, when there was nobody in the room, I went in and opened the closet and took a big pile of magazines out of her hiding place, I put them under my shirt and then I hid them in my bed. And when Batya was by herself, I gave her the mag-azines, so she could read them and be happy."

This isn't the letter I wanted to write to her. I wanted to write her a love letter, and something else came out instead, all the arguments, the resent-ment, the bitterness. I can't listen to his stories. It's maddening. It demeans everything. I can't think seriously. Like in an archaeological excavation, you have to destroy a layer from one period to reach a layer from a previous period. You can't spread all the layers lying one on top of the other out like a fan so as to preserve them intact and see them all together. If you choose one possibility, you have to destroy the others, or leave them buried in the ground. How can you live without one clear, central goal, without direction and justification? If you don't break any-thing you can't decide on one important thing. You can't find a clear direction, strive for a goal, there's no point or purpose. So what then? Be like the birds, get up and fly to the end of the world according to a fixed, natural, automatic program? Is that the true call of nature inside us?

"She just looked at me for a minute, and then she took the magazines and never even said thank you. She went straight to the housemother and said: *Look what Ben-Hamo stole.* And then they held an inquiry. They all sat there, the whole group with the teacher and the housemother and talked about me. Like a big bloody court case they made against me. Doesn't fit into the group, rotten, corrupt, all those words. And her too, Batya, she joined in with all the rest. It was only later I found out what she was up to, that she wanted to get that other girl who didn't want to give her the magazines in trouble, for them to find out she was hiding them, but for it to come out because of me, and not that she went and told on her. As if she wasn't to blame for anything. Only that Ben-Hamo stole. They told me I had to go. They went and talked to my sister too. She said to me: Go home, the kibbutz isn't for you. It's too good for you. Here there's people with education, refined, Ashkenazis. The place for you is the transit camp, with the gangsters. You go there. That's what she said to me. She was mad as hell. And then after two, three years, she got out of there too, she couldn't live with them. When she said that to me I wanted to cry, I was so ashamed. I was a little kid. I told her what happened with those magazines, how it wasn't my fault and I just didn't know enough Hebrew to tell them how it happened. But my sister didn't want to listen, she just said go home, the kibbutz isn't for you, the transit camp with the gangsters is the place for you, you'll never know how to live with the Ashkenazis. I went back to the room and they were already taking my things off my bed and putting them in a corner, and the whole group was standing looking at me and making their jokes about me like they did all the time. Even my sister didn't come with me to help me, because she's ashamed that I'm her brother. And the other kids are standing there saying bad things about me and making rude movements. Until the housemother came and told them to leave me alone and they went away and left me alone. I had about half an hour for the bus to come. So I sat in the room by myself and thought and suddenly I felt happy. Because I was going away from there already. Like a person let out of jail. Before then I didn't even know how shitty it was for me there. And now that it was over I was as happy as if I'd had too much to drink. I was like some drunk, I couldn't sit still. All our songs from the old country that I like so much came back into my head, and the taste of food from home came into my mouth, and how I wouldn't have to eat their food I couldn't stand so that I never ate there and I was thin as a string no more. And how I wasn't ever going to see those kids no more and those kibbutzniks who think they're sitting up in the sky with God. I was so happy I was nearly crazy. There was still a bit of time left for the bus. I went to those girls' room. There wasn't nobody there and Batya's guitar was standing next to her bed. I put it on the floor and stamped on it with my shoes hard as I could. Again and again. The strength I had in my feet then, I dunno where it came from, like I could of run twenty miles without even getting tired. All the wood broke and the strings tore and in the end that guitar was flat as a pancake on the floor!"

Rahamim burst out laughing; he laughed so much that he had to lean against the windowsill so as not to fall down. He clapped his hands and cried: "Like a pancake! I swear on my mother's life! Just like a pancake! I grabbed my things and ran to the bus. I sat and waited for it to go. I was happy but I was scared too that they were coming to get me because maybe somebody already saw what I did to the guitar. But nobody came. The bus started and I sat on the backseat and sang softly to myself, all my old songs I always loved and then I forgot and suddenly I remembered them again, I was so happy, I was just so happy."

Rahamim returned to his bed and sat down. He looked at his watch.

"Soon it'll be time for chow. What did I have to go and tell you all that story for? I messed up your whole morning with my talking."

"No, not at all," said Alon.

"It was just because you said that on the kibbutz everybody's equal to each other."

"No, I'm not saying there aren't personal and social problems, sometimes there are problems."

"Everybody should stay in his own place," said Rahamim. "Everybody should look at his own plate and not make trouble for other people."

Rahamim stood up and went outside to sit on the steps.

Alon stretched and thrust himself forward until his feet projected from the foot of the bed, laid his head on the folded blanket, and closed his eyes. To lie like this, without moving, and let time pass slowly by, aimlessly, pointlessly, hopelessly. How disagreeable was the thought of having to go back to the letter. Perhaps the whole thing was nothing but self-deception? Mistakes like that didn't happen in the army, the medical examinations had been long and thorough. At all kinds of civilian clinics, with all kinds of instruments. Why cling to this fatuous, misleading hope? Wouldn't it be better to think of the other, realistic, humdrum possibility, to try to give it meaning and content? To destroy one layer in order to expose the other one, which was really yours, good or bad, but yours? To resign yourself, despair, surrender, and begin all over again? But what did it mean exactly? For years everything had been geared to getting ready for this supreme test, this climax, nothing had been prepared for the other possibility. For years you prepared yourself for a journey, and at the last minute they told you that the destination had been changed, and you didn't have the right equipment or the necessary expertise. And you weren't like the birds, who migrated according to a predetermined program, at the right times, in obedience to the inner call of nature. This wasn't nature. It was fate.

He opened his eyes, sat up and looked at the writing pad lying next to him. What sadness! What terrible sadness covered everything, like desert dust. That letter had been written by someone else, some conceited child playing at make-believe. Nothing in it was true. Nothing was going to change. Why did I stay here over the leave? Alone in this sad, empty building? Without anyone I can talk to. Instead of going home, seeing her, seeing my mother, the friends I love? Confronting them and being what I really am. With all the defects. Instead of facing up to the problem I ran away from it, I escaped to an army stage set to play at soldiers. Between the truth and the pretense, I chose the pretense. How long will I be able to keep it up? One day the act will have to come to an end. And the worst thing is, that I've begun to believe in these lies, these false hopes, myself.

He picked up the letter and began to read what he had written. After a minute he put it on his knees. What sadness covered everything? What misery! Paralyzing muscles, will, thought. This must be the way you resigned yourself to your fate, as if hypnotized. Any movement might break the spell of the illusion. He put out his hand to take hold of the sheets of paper, and it was unbearably hard, as hard as if heavy weights were hanging on it. He tore the pages out of the pad and began to rip them up. A shadow crossed in front of him, and when he raised his eyes he saw Ben-Hamo standing and looking at him. Now he had to go on tearing up the pages slowly, calmly, indifferently. Ben-Hamo stayed there and watched him tearing up his letter.

"What do you want?"

"It's a shame," said Ben-Hamo. "A waste of all your work. I bet it's because I got on your nerves and it didn't come out right."

Alon's hand was full of the scraps of paper and he didn't know where to put them. This was his chance to get up and go outside, to be rid of that worried, disturbing, interfering look. But he overturned his helmet and threw the scraps of paper into it.

"It doesn't matter," said Alon.

"I'm nothing compared to you," said Rahamim. "You've got a good heart. Too good. That's why you put up with me. There're good people on the kibbutz too. But I'm no good. Don't think I don't know what I'm worth."

"What are you going to do after the army?"

"I got uncles in France. Maybe after the army I'll go there. Here in Israel's no life for me. But maybe I'll get married. How should I know?" And he burst into embarrassed laughter, as if he were suddenly ashamed of revealing his private affairs.

Alon looked at him expressionlessly. It was impossible to tell by his face if he was listening to him and taking in what he was saying, or if he was thinking of something else entirely, and his eyes were only fixed on him by chance, as they might have been fixed on some spot on the ceiling without seeing anything. It was time to go to the mess for lunch. Rahamim sat down to put on his boots. After he left the room Alon was seized by a feeling of urgency. He stood up and stretched his limbs and began pacing up and down, trying to put some order into his thoughts.

In ancient times, when the armies were drawn up for battle, if two birds were seen fighting in the air the armies would disband and wait for another day, for different signs. They saw it as an evil omen, as if something had gone wrong in the natural order. This image, for no evident reason, was very strange and compelling. Two birds fighting in the sky and two armies facing each other on the ground, looking up at them, watching this aerial battle, as if the fate of their battle were being decided there, in the sky, before it even began. And there was no point in beginning the battle. In defying the omens and going to certain defeat. Why were the signs so important to them? Today they calculated risks and probabilities, made assessments of the situation according to intelligence reports, the size of the opposing forces, the numbers of weapons, the command of the terrain. The method had changed, but we went on looking for signs. You didn't go to war simply in obedience to an inner call if you thought you didn't stand a chance. But the chances weren't only a matter of calculations. They depended too on your will, your dream. You created them. Even when the chances were zero, the struggle was justified. Everything was a question of making a decision, and the decision preceded all the calculations. Because it came from the depths, from the inner call of nature and also from the terrible fear of losing point and purpose and direction.

And I have to listen to this inner call and not give in. If there's a one percent chance, the battle's worth it. So I have to mobilize everything. Hope and self-confidence and faith. To proceed on the assumption that there's a possibility and that it's real. To shelve the doubts, the hesitations, the proposed assessment of the situation, in other words, the signs. And if that's called living a lie, then I have to live a lie, so as not to lose even the one percent chance that can only be gained by fighting. And what was perhaps previously a lie will turn into the truth. To be loyal to the dream, because even at the cost of illusion and self-deception it's the only chance to turn the illusion into reality, into the truth. And not to think about what'll happen if not and what'll happen afterward — anything that's not relevant to the struggle has no place. It has to move aside, get out of the way, and be shelved until after the test. Single-minded concentration on the goal, like partial blindness, so as to see only what's important to the maximum effort, and ignore all the rest. To forget, otherwise everything fills with sadness and a feeling of futility that can paralyze you. And just look — now that I've reached this point, look how relieved I feel, what a wonderful feeling of relief. Filling my heart, spreading throughout my body, like dry summer soil drinking in the first rain. Like someone saved at the last minute from falling into an abyss, finding something to hang onto and saving his life.

SOMEWHERE IN ISRAEL, ROSH HASHANA, 1955
Dearest Dafna,
Saturday afternoon and the beginning of a new year. I stayed behind at the base on duty. The whole platoon's gone on leave for the holiday. I volunteered to stay. It will probably seem strange to you. Like a lot of other things I've said and done lately. But I'm sure I'm doing the right thing. Believe me that I'm sure.

CHAPTER 16

That's all that was missing now. Those eyes. Those obscene eyes. Like the stench of a rotting carcass suddenly carried by the wind from a place you swore never to go near again. Little eyes sunk in their sockets, and dead, murky pupils hiding in corners like thieves or frightened mice running to their holes until the danger's past, eyes hiding behind a cover of death to save themselves. They cross the street next to the Interior Ministry building and suddenly encounter his eyes, over the heads of passersby dressed in their best on their way home from the morning synagogue services. Those eyes of all the eyes in the world, and their look falls on him like a blow. He quickly crosses the street in the opposite direction, hastening his steps, turns the corner and slips into an alley, where he looks around him, frowns, and asks, almost out loud: What's happening to me?

If I was superstitious, I wouldn't have much to look forward to in the New Year. Am I superstitious? Is there anyone who isn't? In which case, all this New Year holds in store for me is more obstacles and disappointments, running around with my tongue hanging out, expecting, expecting, expecting — what? While the precious hours, the precious days, pass, and the whole year will pass that way too. Running around like a rat in a trap. Do other people invest so much for so little? However hard I try, I'll never be able to free myself of the cruel, maddening feeling that everything's always much harder for me than for anyone else.

"Have you only just arrived in town?"

"No, I got in yesterday evening."

"Because you're still in uniform."

"Yes, these are the nicest clothes I've got." His smile did not succeed in covering up the pain and resentment in his voice. She was evidently right. All the others, the moment they got home, the first thing they did was to take off their uniforms and put on civvies. She looked him up and down and he felt that the expression on her face showed the satisfaction of someone who knew something he didn't, something very important to him, and she wasn't going to tell him anything in order not to lose her position of power, not until she had squeezed the last drop of advantage out of it, not until she had had her fill of seeing him hanging on her every word in a torment of uncertainty. A slightly mocking smile appears in her eyes as she raises them to the recruit's badge on his beret. Talk, you fat little cow, get it out already. The best friend, her ugly shadow. Sometimes I don't know who you envy more — her for having me, or me for having her. But one thing I do know, you didn't agree to play the role of pimp out of pure and simple friendship and devotion. Maybe I should have done it to you once, to break you, so you wouldn't be so bloody superior. But just thinking about it gives me the cold shivers. And you wouldn't have missed the chance to use that too to make trouble between us. Who knows what you're saying to her about me now, when I'm not here, what kind of advice you're giving her. You'll do anything to destroy it — and what you won't do I'll do myself anyway. But I'm being burned in this fire. And you, people like you destroy anything good that happens to others and will never happen to them. What did she say to you? What kind of games are you playing with me now? I don't have the patience for it.

"So how are you? How's life in the army?"

"Listen, Yaffa, go to her and tell her that I'm here on leave and I have to see her."

"I can't now. In a little while they'll be coming back from prayers and I have to help at home. I don't know if I'll be seeing her over the holiday at all. There's so much to do."

Her hand was already on the door handle.

"Go now, before her husband gets back from the synagogue."

"I told you, I can't."

"What's the matter with you?"

"Nothing's the matter with me." Her face took on a look of pretended innocence, announcing her victory, full of mystery. His heart filled with foreboding. How can I soften up this stupid cow? He smiled his most captivating smile, bent down, and whispered in his most seductive voice: "Why do you hate me, sweetie, what harm have I ever done you?"

Not a muscle moved on her face, nothing melted inside her, or so it seemed at any rate, and everything took on the aspect of an immutable, inevitable doom.

"I'm getting out of the whole affair," said Yaffa. "I don't want to have anything more to do with it, you hear? I told her too. Go and see her yourself, if you've got the guts, if you love her so much, like you want her to think. Leave me out of it. I've already gotten mixed up enough in something that's none of my business. What do I get out of it? It's madness. All I need is for her husband to find out about it, and he's sure to find out soon, all I need is for my family to find out what I've been doing. You know what kind of trouble I can get into on your account? Have you ever even thought about it?"

"Yaffa —"

"Leave me alone, I'm telling you. I don't want to have anything more to do with it. Find someone else."

"What happened, have you quarreled with her?"

"I haven't quarreled with her and I haven't quarreled with anybody. And don't tell me that I hate you, because that might mean I once loved you. And you know that's not true. So stop exploiting people. Stop exploiting me and stop exploiting her . . ."

A slight tremor of anger entered her voice; emotions were breaking through the mask she was trying to hide behind, vague and dim, but sufficient to provide a certain degree of relief and inspire a modicum of confidence that she would give in to him again and deliver the message. Stupid fool, he said to himself, feeling a little better, stupid fool, it's the best thing that's ever happened to you in your miserable life, you'll never come any closer to this fire, you won't give it up so easily, the warmth that reaches you from this fire, however stolen and indirect it is.

Her hand was already turning the doorknob and in a minute she would disappear inside the house. The seconds that were left had to be put to immediate, effective and decisive use, like a command: "Five o'clock this afternoon at my brother-in-law's shop —"

"I'm not interested," said Yaffa. "I don't want to know about it, I didn't hear what you said."

"Five o'clock at my brother-in-law's shop!" he cried again, to impress the message on her memory, separate it from the rest of the conversation, "Five at the shop!" The door closed behind her. As his feet carried him toward Jaffa Street, he said to himself that there was no point in racking his brains with attempted interpretations of her hints and calculations of her motives and his chances; all he had to do was wait until five o'clock and see if she came. He would have to get hold of the key and then go there without any hopes or expectations, to be prepared for the worst and let whatever happened happen. He always made up his mind to follow this course, but he never put his decisions to the test.

There's no doubt that she's doing what Aliza told her to do. After the wretched meeting on Saturday night Aliza must have made her calculations and come to her conclusions. Yaffa would never have behaved like that on her own initiative. She's got no will of her own, no opinions on the matter. Like the parasites that live on the bodies of other animals, she fed on the love and dreams and dangers of another woman. Without them — she would have no life at all. Strange that it's never occurred to me to pity her. I really do use her as a means to an end, I never try to see things though her eyes. And now she's accusing me of being an exploiter. If you look at things from a deeper perspective — she's the biggest exploiter in the whole affair. And maybe I am an exploiter. Maybe sometimes I only think of my own good. But it's not out of any great abundance of good, because everything comes to me the hard way, everything that others take for granted I always have to fight for, me against the world and my own rotten luck.

There's no doubt that she'll run around right away to tell her. The test will be if Aliza comes this afternoon or not. She has to come, I'll break if she doesn't. I'll go berserk. Now of all times, after what happened on Saturday night, things can't be left like that. And now when it's so clear that it really is love, true, fateful love. I can't go on without her. She won't come after that quarrel. She's sick of me. She saw what kind of person I am. I've never shown her how much I appreciate the greatness of her sacrifice, the suffering I cause her, how much easier my situation is than hers. I really proved my selfishness. I don't deserve you, I know it now, I'm not worth even one minute of the love you've given me. You pampered me, you spoiled me, and I kicked you like a spoiled brat. If you come today, I'll prove to you that I can be different. That I can be worthy. I'll change. I'll overcome my shortcomings and perhaps we'll find a way of solving the problem and living together. I'm torturing myself. There's no reason on earth why she shouldn't come. We've quarreled before, it's nothing new. The bond that unites us is stronger than all those things. Like a blood tie. I haven't reached the stage where I can be thrown over like that. Not yet.

If she came all the way to Sarafand to see me last Saturday, why shouldn't she come this afternoon? Unless something's really happened that I don't know about, that that little bitch doesn't want to tell me. Sometimes I feel that I can transmit my thoughts to you, call you. But I've never received your thoughts, your calls. It's a one-way transmitter, apparently.

I'll go there and wait. Now the expectation begins. There's nearly five hours left. To get hold of the key to the shop and get home in time for lunch. Slipping away in the middle of the service isn't going to be passed over either. All the arguments and quarrels and lies. For something that is perfectly natural, after all, that should be taken for granted, the minimum a man of my age needs. Always the hard way. Does someone up there ever feel sorry for Avner? How much do you have to pay for a bit of joy? Why do I feel persecuted? And if there's nothing up there, then why the fear, the secrecy, the shame, the anxiety? And who decides what's a sin and what isn't? What's good and what's bad? What's selfish and what's unselfish? If there's no one there, then why am I so bound and why is she so bound?

In Jaffa Street his self-pity became so intense that he couldn't bear it any longer. The sight of the uniform in which he had gone to the synagogue that morning with such pride now gave rise to revulsion and self-hatred. It's grotesque, really grotesque, to wear a uniform when you come home on leave, especially a recruit's uniform. She was right, the fat cow. But it's true, these are the best clothes I've got. And there, opposite the Interior Ministry, those eyes fell on him like a blow, like an evil omen overshadowing everything that was going to happen to him today, tomorrow, perhaps all year long. Those blank, loathsome, obscene eyes. Even the look in the eyes of the blind was clearer, more alive, more lucid.

What's happening to me? Why am I running away?

He emerged from his hiding place in the alley and returned to Jaffa Street. He scanned the passersby and the eyes were no longer among them. For a moment he stood still, as if he had forgotten where he was going. Music is the language in which the soul speaks to itself. His inner ear had not yet forgotten the sound of the voice saying that, the stifled sob in the words, giving rise in him to an unendurable loathing.

His sister opened the door. A smell of festive dishes rose from the interior of the house. Shaul had already come back from the synagogue service with the children and they were sitting at the table. His sister asked: "What happened, why aren't you eating at home?"

"I only dropped in a for a minute, to say something to Shaul."

"Oh yes." His sister smiled nastily, turned her back and went to the kitchen. Did she know what was going on? Shaul must have told her. That soft, kindhearted man was incapable of hiding things, incapable of withstanding pressure and pleas, just as he hadn't been able to withstand Avner's pleas to give him the key to the shop, just that once, and afterward to give it to him at regular intervals, after closing hours, and on Saturdays and holidays. Shaul didn't ask any questions, but Avner saw it as his moral duty to explain what use he was making of his shop, and promise that he wouldn't do any damage and would lock up properly and return the key on time. It was a secret between men, but Shaul was not the man to withstand the pressure of his wife's pleas to tell her the secret. This time Shaul did not seem keen to cooperate; perhaps his sister had already managed to undermine his confidence in Avner's sense of responsibility, because of his weak character, his selfishness, and the fact that when he wanted something he had to have it right away, and he didn't give a damn about the rest of the world, his father, his mother, or anyone else. Nobody was worth the sole of his shoe, all he cared about was getting what he wanted, and quickly. That's what he was like, because their mother had spoiled him rotten and never allowed their father to raise a hand to him. She had done everything he asked and killed herself for him, and now they all had to suffer and pay for his whims. As the youngest of the family Avner had grown up with the criticism of his brothers and sisters, which he interpreted as jealousy, and often compared to the jealousy of Joseph's brothers. In the end he had learned to ignore it.

"Shaul, don't do this to me, you have to give it to me, after all this time in the army, after all the torture and the humiliation, this was my only consolation, my only hope, I'll never ask you again, this is positively the last time."

"Last time you said it was the last time too," smiled Shaul, and Avner saw from his kindly, easygoing smile that he would get the key this time too.

"Man," said Avner, "it's all changed now, from the minute I was drafted my whole life changed. This is the time to get out of all kinds of entanglements and open a new leaf. Don't break me, please."

At home he was greeted by his father's sullen, hostile face, his mother's careworn eyes, and, next to them, the brothers and sisters who were still living with their parents, staring at him with expressions of contempt and despair. All except poor Benihu, who was never part of anything, his body with them and his spirit in other worlds. They were all sitting around the table and they had already begun eating the holiday meal. Avner knew that sooner or later they would find out that he had gone to his sister's house to look for Shaul and there was no point in inventing some excuse to satisfy them. In any case they would hold any lie or excuse he made up against him, as new proof of his irresponsibility, his frivolity, his lack of consideration. His father said furiously: "You couldn't even stay to the end of the service, where are you running like a lunatic all day?"

Avner said nothing. He went to wash his hands, sat down at the table, blessed the bread, and ate in silence. His brother Avishai said: "He's got ants in his pants, that one, can't sit still for five minutes, running around from morning to night, even on Rosh Hashana he can't stop his dirty little affairs."

Avishai, who was the closest to him in age and with whom he had even had a certain intimacy at one stage, had recently begun telling their father tales, and Avner could not help connecting the change that had taken place in Avishai's attitude toward him with that day two or three years ago when their mother had said to Avner: "Now you look exactly like your father when I married him, so big and handsome he was, just like you are now." She had said this jokingly, and even added a loud laugh, perhaps to correct the immodesty of what she had said, but the words stabbed Avner's heart like a knife. And Avishai, who was standing and listening, said to her: "It'll be your fault if he lands up in jail, for talking to him like that and doing everything he wants. He'll come to a bad end, you'll see."

"That's enough!" his father said now. "Don't talk like that. And on Rosh Hashana too."

"I promise you," said Avishai, despite his father's request, "that even in the army he hasn't stopped his dirty tricks, and that he smokes on the Sabbath too, and doesn't keep up any of the observances."

Avishai had become stricter in religious observance than anyone else in the family. Their father was no more punctilious than he considered his role as head of the family demanded.

Once, a few years ago, Avner had felt eager to confide everything that happened in his life to Avishai. It seemed to him that his brother's hostility toward him had grown together with his increasing religious strictness, and there was no knowing which was cause and which effect, or if there was any connection between them. If only Avishai knew how hard it was for Avner not to smoke when he was with the family on the Sabbath. Even outside the house he refrained from smoking on the Sabbath, he hadn't even brought his cigarettes with him so as to avoid temptation. They would never appreciate any effort he made on behalf of the family; all his attempts to please them, to conform to their ideas and prejudices, were doomed to failure. They already had a fixed image of him in their minds and no force in the world could change it. Whatever he did would be interpreted in terms of this formula in which they had imprisoned him, and as far as they were concerned he would always be guilty in advance.

"Enough!" his father cried to Avishai again, and he even pounded his fist on the table for additional emphasis. "That's enough of speaking evil against each other. The ten days of penitence are beginning now and soon it will be the Day of Atonement, Yom Kippur! Every day I pray for Avner too in the penitential prayers, for God to forgive him. Because Avner isn't a bad person, God forbid, there's only something wrong in his head. He's not to blame. He hasn't got the strength to fight the evil instinct."

Avner knew that his mother's opinion of him was no different from theirs. Her love for him did not mean that she found him not guilty; it was bestowed on him as a grace that had nothing to do with his real nature and deeds, as if she consciously allowed herself the indulgence of this weakness, this single deviation from the norm of her life, which was otherwise governed by logic, expediency, caution, and responsibility. This was her whim, which sweetened the travail and heavy load she bore, and she jealously guarded her right to indulge it. Avner had never been able to understand her, or the reason for this discriminating love. He knew that she was incapable of understanding his true nature. She knew nothing of his activities, his suffering, and his hopes. There was a gulf between them, and only this thread of grace, arbitrary and mysterious, spanned it. When he was a boy, he had sometimes wished that she would love him less out of forgiveness and indulgence and weakness, and more for his merits and virtues. But when he brought his end-of-term report home from school and read out his grades, he never saw any admiration, any vindication on her face, only the same soft look in her eyes and the same sober, long-suffering smile of a servant-queen, invariably forgiving, forgiving in advance, for both the good and the evil, as if there were no essential difference between them, at any rate, not according to her criteria, which were based on a different logic. Later on, and sooner rather than later, he learned that beggars can't be choosers. When he compared the immensity of his hunger for love to what it appeared that life was likely to offer him, which was heartbreakingly little, he realized that he would have to be grateful for every smile of affection, every gesture of love that came his way. He thanked her in his heart and stopped insisting on his due as a grown man. He pardoned her reluctance to see him stepping outside her circle of light forever, and he forgave her for passing sentence on him in her heart before she granted him her grace. For he assumed that his guilt was exceedingly great in her eyes, as great as her forgiveness and her love. And when his sorrow overwhelmed him, he would sometimes kneel at her feet and press her hands and kiss them, and he would do this with an exaggerated flourish, as a kind of mad, humorous parody, in order not to embarrass anyone, but something inside him wanted to cry and couldn't. And Avishai, watching the display with demonstrative displeasure, would say over and over again: "Avner will come to a bad end. You mark my words: He'll come to a bad end!"

Avner and his father did not speak much to each other. There was no need for it. They could read one another like the pages of an open book. His father had long ceased complaining to his wife that she was "spoiling Avner," and he was no longer interested in listening to Avishai's tales. The conspiracy of silence that came into being between them, like a common destiny without a drop of closeness or affection, was a function of weariness and sadness rather than the acceptance of a new order: Nothing could be guaranteed in advance.

As usual his mother had saved the best part of the holiday meal for Avner. Everybody took this for granted and it passed without comment. Only his father's eyes wandered from the head of the table to his plate for a second, without a hint of curiosity or concern, as if merely to confirm what was already well known, after which he immediately looked at his wife as he said: "Eat, eat, you have to build up your strength for the army."

God knows where she got the money to pay for the meal. The family income, which was meager enough anyway, had grown even smaller when Avner was drafted and stopped working, and now he would still need their help from time to time, since he would not be able to support himself on his army pay. She would find what he needed. She had ways of her own of managing. And the lazy old bugger never inquired too closely as to what they might be. Still, Avner would have preferred her to give him the same as his brothers, and to set the most generous portion in front of his father. Because in his father's silence he sometimes heard not his resignation but his entreaties not to let the truth slap him in the face.

How could he avoid resenting his father bitterly, how could he not hold him in contempt? The man was so obvious to him, so familiar and predictable in every detail, so terrifyingly similar to him, not only in his features and physique but also in what they concealed. He showed him the quintessence of everything he hated in himself, everything that terrified him and screamed out for forgiveness and atonement. Like a mirror presenting him with the inevitable image of his own future, of the lousy luck in which he believed more than any other possibility.

For a moment he thought of saying to them: "I've already been in jail, too," in order to give Avishai some satisfaction. Avishai, the good son, the hardworking conformist, Avishai who helped his father when the old man made his way home in the evening, drunk and vociferous, while the neighbors stood watching with glum, pious faces from their doorways, and the children ignored their mothers' strictures and laughed. Avishai who never allowed himself the luxury of a single minute that wasn't full of seriousness and responsibility and self-righteousness. Avishai who could have been his friend, if things hadn't turned out the way they did. Okay, I've already been in jail, too. And what now? What next? What else is waiting down the road? But what would be the point? This was his time out, a couple of hours' rest between one race and the next, and this afternoon he would have to slip away from the synagogue again and listen to all the scolding and criticism. And in the meantime his father announced that he was praying for him too, because he didn't have the strength to withstand the evil instinct. Silly old fool, how could anyone not hate you? All your big and little lies, your pretense, your cunning, your smokescreens, the moments of black despair in your bleary red eyes, your grotesque standing on your dignity, how well I know them all, like a familiar old tune wanting to play its notes inside me, as if I've already experienced them all, even though I've hardly begun to make their acquaintance. They're there inside me, all of them, biding their time.

One day, he knew, he would love him too. In his world full of love he would find a place for his father. And that day, he felt, was perhaps not far off, but in the meantime it was hard, very hard. The memories were too fresh, too personal. One day he would presumably be able to forgive him for everything he had done to him, every day of pain and suffering he had caused him, every hour, every minute, for his laziness, his tyranny, the way he had humiliated her in front of her family, in front of her neighbors. No, all this could not yet be forgotten, his affairs with other women, the way he left home for three months when he was running after some Yemenite girl and thought he'd found the love of his life, that she would save him from the old age that was beginning to defeat his body. His miserable, broken homecoming and the beginning of the big bouts of drunkenness, the real and imaginary pains, the unemployment, the beatings he gave her, after she had forgiven everything and tried to help him, to get him back on his feet, to restore his self-respect. One day Avner would forgive him everything, but it was not yet possible. The similarity between them was still too disturbing; it made them into rivals, into deadly enemies fighting for a single, common shadow. One day he would forgive him too for the miserable heredity he had bequeathed him, and for the sermonizing, the denunciations of the evil instinct. One day, he knew, all his grievances would disappear, fly away like dust in the wind, vanquished by another love, by the opening of the heart to unconditional forgiveness. He wouldn't say a word, but in his heart he would forgive him and love him, because he owed it to himself, not him, and perhaps, perhaps, after the love and forgiveness he would be at peace with himself too, and perhaps this consuming fire he had inherited from him would die down, and the terrible thirst would leave him at last, the thirst that never stopped raging in his blood, was deterred by nothing, never relinquished an opportunity, and refused to come to terms with the fact that it was a bottomless pit that could never be quenched. Perhaps he would find a way of living with it in peace, in dignity. Just so he didn't lose all self-respect! Just so he didn't degrade himself like him! Just not that! And perhaps after he forgave and loved, he would attach no importance to honor either, he would understand that it had no meaning. And then he would be exactly like him. And he would have nothing left but grief for missed opportunities and bitterness and grievances and self-pity and resentment against the whole wide world, which had robbed him of his due. Indignation at the injustice of it all would serve as a justification and a cover for every vileness, every degradation, every grotesque pretense, for putting an end to all lucid, critical, tormenting thoughts, like consciously and resolutely switching off a radio. And then he would live like him, in silence, immune to disturbances, alone and free in a world of shadows. But not now. Not yet. That day would come, but for the time being they were still enemies and the battle was still raging. There were still so many things left to do. There were no shortcuts.

What was the meeting going to be like? The doubts and fears made it so precious that it was impossible to envisage. He walked down Jaffa Street in his civvies and felt his self-confidence returning. I'll hear the light knock on the back door of the shop, I'll open it and she'll be standing there, frightened of somebody seeing her as usual, and she'll slip quickly inside, into the darkness. Even before I get a chance to see her face in the light outside. Oh God, this is my chance! If she comes, I'll begin to believe in you. Seriously. Just this once, just this once! I'll never ask again. After the quarrel on Saturday night, it's so important, I need her forgiveness. For my lack of consideration, for my selfishness, for my unfairness.

The possibility of sitting and waiting for her, of her not coming, doesn't bear thinking about. If it happens, it happens, I don't have to prepare myself for it. The infinite beauty of the passing moment, that's the thing itself, the thing that mustn't be missed. Not to get distracted by worries and anxieties, by the outside world. A light knock on the back door, I'll open it and she'll be standing there, frightened as usual, and we can wipe the whole of last week out, take up from where we left off, just bring her to the shop this evening, that's all I ask, all the rest will be up to me. But I can't bring her; that's outside the bounds of my possibilities. If only I'd left the synagogue earlier, maybe I'd have had time to drop in on the cow and ask her what's happening. But I always leave everything to the last minute, I never have time for anything. And now all I can do is wait and see.

"Avner!"

Hanan stopped next to him, on his bicycle. For the first moment or two Avner refused to recognize him. Do I look like him too, like a child in my civvies, after we're grown used to seeing each other in uniform?

Hanan said: "You're not looking where you're going."

"I was thinking about something else," said Avner.

"What's up?"

"Nothing much."

"One day of the leave's gone."

"I've managed to forget that I'm in the army at all."

"What are you doing tomorrow night?"

Avner could not help recoiling, as if he had been caught red-handed. He narrowed his eyes beneath the thick eyebrows that met over his nose, frowned and looked at Hanan with a worried, inquiring look — and said nothing.

"We're having a party at my place tomorrow night, all the guys will be there, and a few other friends of ours, who you may not know. And girls too, some of the greatest girls in Jerusalem. Dancing and all that. It won't be boring."

"You're inviting me," said Avner.

"Yes, I'm inviting you," laughed Hanan. "Do you want it in writing? What's the problem?"

"What would you have done if you hadn't met me by chance in the street?"

Hanan looked embarrassed. "I don't know. What's the matter with you? Why do you ask? We did meet, didn't we?"

"Maybe you didn't plan on it," said Avner.

"Give it a rest, do me a favor. What's your case?"

"All right, all right, I'll come," said Avner and slapped Hanan's shoulder to show there were no ill feelings. "Thanks for the invitation. But tell me, aren't you worried about your girlfriends? You know my reputation."

"On the contrary! You're the star of the evening. We're bringing you as bait, to attract the girls to the party. If they know that you'll be there, they'll show up in droves! Don't you understand?"

"I can be as cynical as you," said Avner. "Okay then, it's your funeral. But you needn't worry, I'll behave myself."

"Nobody expects you to behave yourself. Just come and have a ball. That's what it's all about."

"See you tomorrow night then."

"You know the address?"

"No problem. My mother will remind me."

Hanan smiled in embarrassment. Avner watched him riding away on his bike. The sense of urgency suddenly left him. He knew that even if he arrived at the shop after five he would not be late. He didn't even look at his watch. Everything seemed easier and simpler now. The trouble with me is that I think I'm worth exactly what I'm worth at any particular minute. When the wheel turns, I can't or won't believe that the next

minute it can turn again. And I never learn from experience, I never take
into account the possible changes that the next minute may bring, for good
or bad, I behave as if every minute is a life sentence. Two people keep
changing places inside me, one on top of the heap and the other at the
bottom, each of them manages to persuade me that he's the only true one,
to make me identify completely with him and disown the other one. I've
never tried to bring the two of them together, let them argue it out
between them, to come to some kind of agreement, because you never see
both of them in action at once, only one of them, the one and only, true,
final one. The eternity of the moment.

He opened the lock hanging on the back door of the shop. The alley
was dark and deserted: She hadn't arrived yet. Nobody could expect her
to be punctual, in her situation, with all the dangers and complications
attendant on the simple act of going out of the house. He locked the door
from inside, sat down on the packing crate standing against the wall,
delved into his shirt and took out the packet of cigarettes and box of
matches hidden there, lit his first cigarette for hours, inhaled deeply, and
sat and listened to the silence outside. Perhaps she couldn't come, through
no fault of her own? She had no way of letting him know. This possibility
hurt less now than it had a few hours before. Was it a sign that she would
come? Or a sign that he cared less? No! I want this moment, I want it
desperately. To see her standing in the doorway, coming toward me. To
fall on her, make love to her. God! Even if I have to wait here in this hole
for three hours, alone in the dark. With the rats. I'm not worth much, if
an invitation to a party at Hanan's made me so happy and gave me such
a good feeling. I can't stand them or their girls. No, that's not true, I'm
lying to myself. I want to conquer them, especially them, all of them. The
sound of footsteps outside. God, let this be the moment. No, they're not
her footsteps. They're a man's footsteps, coming closer, passing the shop.
Going away. And silence again. He looked at the phosphorescent numbers on his watch. They held no answer to his question; they were irrelevant. When a man was alone, what was the point of looking at his watch?
If she doesn't come by six, it means she can't come. He crushed the cigarette under the sole of his shoe, stood up, and opened the door to throw
the stub out. If this evening's screwed, I've still got tomorrow. Someone
entered the alley. An old man in holiday clothes, limping on a stick, with
a woman hurrying a few steps behind him, her head wrapped in a scarf.
The old man turned his head and grunted something, apparently in reply
to a question she had asked before they turned the corner. Avner closed
the door and sat down on the wooden crate again. He heard their foot-

steps approaching, and waited for silence to return so that he could begin listening again. The footsteps stopped in front of the shop, lingered there a moment, the old man muttering something unintelligible, and then they began again, receding into the distance, and silence returned.

After a while there was a knock at the door. Heavy and hesitant, not like hers. His heart skipped a beat in surprise, incredulity, and relief. He hurried to the door and opened it. On the threshold stood a thickset youth in shorts and sandals, who examined him for a moment in the dim light of the room, then averted his eyes and called into the shop: "Shaul? Shaul?"

"It's okay," said Avner. "Shaul's my brother-in-law. He gave me the key. Don't worry, I'm not a thief."

The thickset youth called again: "Shaul? Shaul?" into the darkness of the room, as if Avner weren't standing there next to him, as if he couldn't see or hear him. When no reply was forthcoming from Shaul, he turned his attention back to Avner. "How do I know you're telling the truth? I don't know you," he said. "If you're not a thief, what are you doing here in Shaul's shop?"

"He asked me to fix something up for him," said Avner.

"So why are you in the dark?"

Avner switched on the lightbulb dangling from the ceiling: "Here's the key, see? Where do you think I got it from? What do you want? " There was anger in his voice, and the youth withdrew slightly.

"Actually, maybe I do know you," he said.

"Of course you do! " said Avner. "I used to come to the shop often. Shaul's married to my sister. Don't worry."

"Okay, okay, I recognize you now. I know you're Shaul's brother-in-law. I'm not worried." But his voice did not carry much conviction. Avner was afraid that he was trying to get away from him in order to come back with reinforcements, neighbors or police. The boy remained where he was. "Lately two shops in the neighborhood have been broken into, and we have to be careful. Keep an eye out for each other. What's your name?"

"Avner, Avner Gabbai."

"Oh yes, of course, Avner Gabbai. I know. Happy New Year!"

"Happy New Year."

Avner left the light on in the little storeroom. He sat down on the wooden crate again and looked around him. In contrast to that ghastly place in Ramle, this cubbyhole was a little palace. Even the old blanket still lay untouched where he had left it so long ago, before he went to the army, folded on top of one of the crates in the corner. He went up to it and undid one of the folds, buried his face in it, and breathed in its smell. Something in the denying, resistant smell infuriated him. His mood grew sober and bitter: No, no, don't do it to me this time! Not this time! It became quite clear to him that she wasn't coming. His heart froze inside him.

He could have known it in advance, last week, the minute he saw her getting onto the bus in Ramle. The moments when something is ending have a special, unmistakable color all their own. The sound of the finale in a Brahms symphony. You have to know how to listen. He knew that one day it would happen, and now it was happening. And he was stunned. His heart felt like ice. What did he mean to her, if she could throw him over like this, because of what had happened last week? Just a piece of meat? Fresh meat? Stolen fruit to sweeten the tedium of her life with her husband? And maybe she had found someone else in the meantime? The cow knew something, and she was hiding it. It was obvious. He wasn't the first and he wouldn't be the last.

He rested his forehead on his hands, his elbows propped on his knees, and closed his eyes: I'm not budging from here until you come. God, I don't know if you exist, but I'm sure you can't stand me. That's why there has to be forgiveness in the world. And I'm the first in line. I only want one thing: for her to come now, for everything to be like it was before, before last week, like it used to be, like it was in the beginning. Are there people who know how to preserve the happiness of the beginning? Is there anyone who knows the beauty of the eternal beginning?

He raised his head and looked at his watch. Twenty to six. The numbness of his heart had clouded his thoughts; he had lost track of time. He no longer remembered how long he had decided to wait. Was this a sign? Like a rhythmic hammering on the back of his neck he heard the voice inside him: It's my fault! It's my fault! I'm not a human being. I don't know how to be worthy. I don't think ahead. I don't think about what happens to other people. I had it coming. It's my fault! I did it to myself. He shrugged his shoulders, took a deep breath, stood up, opened the door, stood on the threshold, and looked outside. The darkening street was deserted. Most of the buildings in it were shops, closed for the holiday. He lowered his eyes and examined his body. In the end I'll be thin as a stray dog nobody wants. Always dependent on the goodwill of the world. Unable to exist without cooperation from outside, without other people. Always the hard way, always having to steal what's mine by right, reduced to getting what I'm entitled to by cunning, by flattery, by charm, by humiliation. And always deceiving myself. This damnable dependence on others. The redemption that can only come from others. Suddenly people in the alley. Apparently on their way home from some neighborhood synagogue. But she isn't among them. What's happening to time? A day and a half already gone. Wasted on expectations. And the day that's left will be even worse: There won't be anything to expect anymore.

He returned to the cubbyhole, shut the door, sat down on the crate, raised his eyes to the ceiling as if hoping to find some sign there, and looked at his watch again. It wasn't six yet. He stood up, took the blanket, spread it out on the floor, lay down on it, closed his eyes, and tried to fall asleep for a few minutes to restore his spirits.

Within the patches of darkness that entered him, changing shape ceaselessly, lightening and darkening, contracting and expanding, like oil stains on black water, he tried to find the elusive path leading to the final forms. Flickering lights occasionally signaled to him from the thickets of the dark forest, and he knew that they were the memories of the light from before he closed his eyes. Phantom lights luring him backward. He directed his steps into the heart of the darkness, but when he came closer to the dark mass he saw that it too was only a screen of gray smoke swirling and spreading and narrowing, and behind it, like trees in the wind, swayed more patches of shade and more phantom lights, the last flicker of moments that had faded and died thousands of years ago, and found no resting place. The entire landscape was suspended on a slender thread of intense concentration, neither to wake up nor to fall asleep. If he stopped walking, it would all be lost and turn into dense mist, flat and opaque. He strained his will to the utmost and went on walking. He had made the journey so many times before, it held no dangers, only hopes and unfulfilled promises, unintelligible signs and shapes, and if he could only keep on advancing steadily, and not take any notice of the will-o'-the-wisps, if he could only overcome the seductive weariness drawing him back into himself, if he could only focus his attention properly perhaps he would reach the place where she stood, virginal and fair, with her two dogs, next to the electric water. Suddenly he found himself facing a high net, the first physical obstacle on his way. His eyes were tired of the effort of gazing into the heart of darkness, of the task of freezing the shapes and lines lest they were lost in colorlessness, in formlessness, in endlessness, within the dazzling blackness, and he knew that if he looked through the net and his eyes conquered the landscape behind it, he would be able to pass through it, even though its holes were smaller than his own fist. Soon the fair girl with the pair of dogs at the end of the road, in the depths of the wood, would appear, at first in the distance, like a cool, inner spot of light, the true, unmistakable light of dreams, standing in the shade of a great tree not to be found in nature, her outlines gradually growing clearer as he struggles against the temptation to go back and fall asleep, his feet no longer treading the ground, gliding between the dark spots to land on the banks of the water, if only he could see her face, if only he could come close enough to imagine the feel of her skin and her hair, their touch and smell, on the thin borderline between sleep and waking. If he concentrates exclusively on the line of sleep, or the line of waking, even if only to measure his distance from them so as not to stray from the middle line — everything might be lost. He strains his eyes and advances. She has not yet sensed his closeness, only the twin dogs raise their heads, sniff and growl to warn their mistress, who has just bent down to stroke them, but now she straightens up, in her scanty PT outfit, leans against the tree trunk, arches her body, closes her eyes, and raises her arms to the sky, as if in thanks to some invisible deity, basking in her marvelous, fresh, pure physical being, secure from any touch. And he knows that now the decisive step in this journey is about to be taken, when everything is liable to disintegrate and collapse, because of the excess of will that kills every possibility. He has to ignore the dogs, in other words, he has to identify with them, to turn into a pair of dogs and look at her through their eyes. Suddenly her glance fell on him, and she was alive and real and precise, just as she had been that day on the base, for a split second she was revealed in full, close and unattainable, and he knew that he was beginning to dream. Like an alarm going off inside him the message came: His wakefulness had betrayed him, he had no control over the change, the whole journey had been in vain, all was lost, for the dream was the way back. This knowledge was so painful and bitter that a scream tried to escape from his heart, and its unexploited power assailed him like an enemy.

The hesitant knocking on the door reached him as through a fog, so similar to the certainty and the anticipation that it didn't sound real. He opened his eyes without moving, testing the signs, the door opened slowly and he saw her behind him, upside down, coming inside, standing on the threshold, closing the door and lingering on the top step before descending the other two. Her inverted face smiled nervously and anxiously at the body prone on the floor. He jumped to his feet, her figure righted, and her smile, which had previously seemed disappointed and anxious, now looked radiant with joy and promise. She came down the two steps and he, holding his breath with difficulty, did not hurry toward her, as he had imagined the moment, and say to her *Don't talk, don't talk,* but rubbed his head and said in a stunned, defeated voice: "I fell asleep."

"I have to hurry back home, I can't stay even a minute, I just wanted to fix something for tomorrow evening —"

"Don't be so nervous."

He locked the door from inside, smiling and saying to himself: You'll stay as long as I want, at any rate, longer than you can afford.

And when he felt the warmth of her body straining into his arms, the smell of her hair and clothes, her whimpering surrender, and all the walls of memory fell one by one so that he and she could forget each other, and enter like initiates into the coordinated movements and rhythms of the mysterious dance, the ever-renewed secrets of mutual revelation came, and the murmurs of wonder and the depths of breath and the depths of the dream and the depths of the longings bursting and straining toward their goal, toward their annihilation, and again he knew that he had missed something important, and again the bitter reminder struck him, like a second of intoxicating breathlessness, the scream he hadn't screamed: You've missed the moment! You've missed the moment! The first moment when she appeared in the doorway, standing upside down, the first moment with all its infinite beauty, which nothing could ever bring back, which was lost to him forever, and all the rest was only compensation, a consolation prize for the scream he hadn't screamed, which had stayed stuck in the depths of his chest until it sank, until it died. *The moments of love are moments of loneliness; the moment of climax is the climax of loneliness.*

CHAPTER 17

Who said that? Did I think of it myself or did I hear it from someone, or read it somewhere, or take it from some movie? Where did it spring from all of a sudden? It isn't true, I don't believe it, but why is there something so seductive in the rhythm of the words, in their cadence, in the pauses between them, something that makes me want to believe it and hold fast to it?

As usual she made haste to hide her nakedness, as if she were ashamed and regretted it. Maybe she was afraid of making herself cheap. And he, as usual, revealed it again, with a gentle, soothing hand. Everything repeated itself with a kind of obstinacy, giving these moments the regularity of a ritual, reassuring and permanent, promising that there would be no need for further sacrifices, covering up what had been lost in the meantime.

He lit a cigarette, as usual, and put it in her mouth, looking at her expressionlessly. At these moments he always said to her *Beloved,* in order to express in both gratitude and distance at once in the high-flown word.

"What's wrong with you, why are you looking at me like that?"

She took a drag on the cigarette, hollowing her cheeks as she inhaled and looking reproachful. Then she closed her eyes and exhaled intently, returned the cigarette to his hand, and looked at him.

His voice sounded false and hollow to him: "Beloved."

She got dressed slowly, carefully, as if her clothes were made of a very delicate and fragile material, liable to tear with any abrupt movement. He turned over onto his stomach, raised his head, and contemplated the dainty, delicate movements of her body as she put on her clothes, the beauty of her body as it covered itself and distanced itself from what she had been only a moment before. He tried to revive the mystery in which he might find certainty again. Gradually the girl turned back into a woman. Again the worried, anxious, embittered expression, the petty daily cares enveloping her together with her clothes. She took a comb out of her bag and combed her rebellious hair without looking in a mirror, and then she rubbed her face with her hands as if she were washing it with invisible water. I'm ruining your life and I'm not even sure that I love you. It's gotten so that sometimes I don't even know what draws me to you more, the drive to destroy or the desire to love. Maybe it's the same thing?

"I want you to stay longer."

"I can't. There's going to be trouble anyway."

In the whining tone of her voice, in her sullen expression, her despairing gestures, she resembled a woman who had nothing left to lose. Do I really love her?

"You're staying."

"Stop nagging."

"Beloved."

"Tomorrow."

"Last Saturday, after you left, I wanted to die. Seriously. And later, when I was on guard duty, I longed for you, I asked you to forgive me. I started to cry. The friend who was guarding with me saw me crying."

"I don't want to talk about what happened last week." She gave him the look that sometimes worried him, a look that seemed to hint that behind the pettiness and sulks, behind what looked like dullness, was a natural intelligence that saw straight into his heart and that without his being aware of it, she was the one who was leading him in the direction she wanted. To satisfy his childish pride she let him think that he was the master, and at any rate she probably understood him much better than he understood her. And now she had already decided about tomorrow, as if there were no question about it and it was all up to her. At moments like these, her beauty reminded him of what he had seen in her in the beginning: her big, limpid, dark eyes gazing at him, asking something. The way she stood there, as if she wanted to turn around and leave, but at the same time she held her ground, arms folded on her chest, as if she were waiting for something, maybe for a confirmation of the doubts in her heart. Her brown dress, her arms in the short sleeves, her ripe, soft, proud body under the thin stuff of the dress.

"You don't love me."

"Why do you have to give me problems all the time? It's hard enough as it is. And you still say you love me. If you love me, you should want me to be happy, right?"

Why didn't he let her go? What devil got into him to make him torment her like this, as if he was fighting her for his freedom, for his hope of finding true love.

"Tomorrow," said Aliza, "tomorrow night, later on, he won't be at home. I've arranged with Yaffa to come and baby-sit. We can be together for a long time. Today I really only came to tell you that. I wasn't even going to come inside. And now I'm going to get into terrible trouble."

Avner lit another cigarette. His nakedness suddenly bothered him and he got up and quickly put his clothes on. The trap was open in front of him; he would neither advance nor retreat. There was no way he was going to give up tomorrow night. Why should he? For what? It didn't make any sense. He had to look out for himself.

"What does Yaffa say about me, why does she hate me?"

"She doesn't hate you. She's just worried about me. She says the truth, which is that the whole thing's going to end badly, that in the end I'll be left with nothing, without him or you or the baby either, and everyone'll call me a whore. That's what she says. The trouble is that I can't see the truth, because I've got you in my blood."

"I'm your madness, eh?" He asked and smiled complacently behind the cigarette smoke.

She smiled back, a submissive, despairing smile. This was the way he saw her in his imagination when he longed for her; this was the way she aroused his pity for himself and her and his wonder at the strength of this ruinous tie between them, when she stood before him defeated and pleading for her life and he could not help her.

He went up to embrace her. The trap: For someone to be happy someone else had to suffer; for someone to have hope, someone else had to give up and resign himself to his fate. The hornet smashed into the pane of glass, and the swifter its flight, the more passionate its desire for the blue spaces, the more painful the blow. She tried to evade his arms: "I have to go, he'll kill me."

"One day I'll kill you," said Avner and tightened his embrace. Between his arms he felt the start of terror that silenced her resistance — maybe she really believed him, maybe she thought he was going to do it right now. He continued, whispering into her ear: "If you ever stop loving me, and if you listen to Yaffa and leave me."

When he relaxed his grip she rushed to the locked door and rattled the lock. Avner burst out laughing: "No exit!" She sat down on the steps, rested her head on her hands and waited, looking as if she had been sentenced to torture.

Was he keeping her there because he hadn't made up his mind yet? But he had: Tomorrow night he was going to the party at Hanan's. She gazed at him with sad, accusing eyes.

"Why are you so nervous and cross?"

"I'll tell you tomorrow night."

"But tomorrow night I can't make it, beloved. I'm busy, I have to be somewhere and I've already promised to go."

"Where?"

"Friends from the army."

"What's so important about that? You see them all the time anyway. You don't see me at all. I've already made all the arrangements especially for tomorrow."

"No, beloved, I can't make it tomorrow, it's impossible."

"Because I put out for you this evening. I shouldn't have put out," said

Aliza. How vulgar and shameful it sounded. "I suppose there'll be girls there and you're going to try and make it with them."

Every word she added would only strengthen his desire to be rid of her and to establish a new freedom for himself. Every word she added would put him off her more.

"Please don't talk like that, it's not nice, it makes the most beautiful thing in the world cheap and bestial. I can't stand listening to you talk like that."

"What's wrong? Since when are you such a saint? You think I'm stupid? If you don't love me anymore why do you send Yaffa to come and call me? What do you need me for, to kill time when you've got nothing better to do, until you can go and enjoy yourself somewhere else? For that I have to take all these risks? And you don't know what's waiting for me at home!"

"Do I still have to prove to you that I love you?"

"All the time you have to prove it."

"Beloved."

"Stop calling me beloved, stop making a fool of me. I know when you're lying, I know you too well."

"If I tell you I have to go tomorrow, can't you believe me? You can't always come either, and I don't blame you for it."

"How can you even compare it?"

She stood up, rattled the lock again, and said in a firm, decisive tone: "Open the door, Avner, I have to go. I'll never forgive you as long as I live for having treated me like a whore."

He unlocked the door, opened it wide, and looked at her in astonishment. She climbed the steps, stood in the doorway for a moment with her back to him, turned around and shut the door behind her, sat down on the step, put her head on her knees and burst into tears. "I knew this would happen, I knew this would happen," she moaned between her sobs.

He stood opposite her, looking at her without taking a step toward her or saying a word. What was it that was hardening his heart, strengthening him in his determination not to give in? Apparently she was right, he didn't love her anymore. This was not what he so yearned for, this was not what would quench the thirst for love burning in his bones. And nevertheless she was very dear to him. You're the victim of my excess of will, he said to her in his heart. Believe me, it's not selfishness, it's just excess of will. I don't control the dream, the dream controls me, plays with me, leads me wherever it likes, it's far stronger than I am. I don't control anything. He felt very sorry for her. He bent down to stroke her abundant, curly, rebellious hair. She pushed his hand away: "Don't touch me!"

He was so sure that he was in the right that as he walked up the street to return the key he was still arguing with her in his head and justifying himself to her, as if it made any difference which of them was right. When the question of right and wrong appeared on the agenda — it was a sign that love was finished. Love had nothing to do with right and wrong. If there was any need of proof, here it was. The more eager he was to prove to her, and himself, that he was right, the more deeply it was borne in on him that their love was over. This was a dangerous time: It was called loneliness. You detach yourself from your family, from your parents' home, but you don't have a family of your own yet, and luckily for you the army gets you out of it, rides your loneliness so you won't go berserk. Why had he decided to go straight to his brother-in-law and return the key, even though the next day was a holiday too, and the shop would be shut? In order not to leave himself a loophole for retreat, not to allow any room for second thoughts and doubts. Perhaps longings and expectations were better than fulfillment. But there was something dangerous about them, something barren.

Next to the King David Hotel he stood and looked over at the Old City. The stones of the wall were a darker gray in the twilight, and there were already lights going on behind the wall. Perhaps at this very moment one of the Jordanian soldiers was aiming his gun into the dusk and the barrel was pointed directly at him. It wasn't impossible. One shot and all the dreams of love and excess of will would turn into a bloody lump of flesh on the pavement. I never think seriously about death, as if I'm somehow immune to it. Maybe I'm still a child? But when I was a child I was afraid of death. During the siege, under the shelling, the terror would suffocate me, every explosion would come as a relief: It had fallen somewhere else. I'm eighteen years old and I feel as if my whole life's already been wasted. If someone wants to take a potshot in the dark — let him! I'm here, standing and waiting for a stray bullet. Shoot, maniac, shoot! Here I am, a sitting duck, what are you waiting for? I'm here waiting. I don't have anything better to do at the moment. If someone told me I only had an hour left to live, what would I do with it? I would wait. At long last without dreams and excess of will, without flattery and lies and pretense, without a seductive smile and a dark gleam in my eye, without this never-ending battle to conquer people's hearts. Perhaps it would be the finest hour of my life. The hour of truth. To be Avishai.

The moments of love are moments of loneliness; the moment of climax is the climax of loneliness. Where did this nonsense spring from? But it really is one big loneliness. I've got nothing to do with myself. I don't have a single friend I could meet, talk to, tell things to, share things with. I've got no one. How did I reach this point? Avishai can't stand me, but I can't help loving him. Maybe I'd be better off if I was like him? Keeping to the straight and narrow. Looking after our father. Thinking small. Satisfied with little. If I was like Avishai, I would find a friend in him, even though he is my brother. But we don't have anything in common anymore. And I don't really want to be like Avishai. Friendship is no less important than love. Only when the two of them exist side by side, nourishing each other, fertilizing each other, can each of them exist in full. Otherwise, something gets spoiled in the striving to transcend the boundaries, to invade the other's territory. How did it happen? Why am I so lonely? What's wrong with me? Is it all because I set my sights too high? Obviously, it's my fault. No doubt of it. And there's nobody to ask to forgive me.

The YMCA building was dark, the terrace deserted. He hadn't listened to music for a long time. His heart ached to hear something beautiful again. So much time had passed, it seemed the circle had closed, the score was settled. He was ready to stand the test again. That evening, going home in the pouring rain, something had broken inside him, and he had made up his mind to cut himself off from this sickness. Those moments were moments of crisis, which he bore in his heart in the form of a vow: If I don't get into trouble I'll cut myself off from music, because music belongs to a world in which I have no part, a world forbidden to me. Those moments were also moments of wonderful tranquility. As if he had been revealed to himself, made the acquaintance of his true self. Whereas now, in the bitterness of his heart, he felt as if that break had been mended and his vow had been canceled. A light breeze touched the nape of his neck, suddenly sending cold shivers down his spine. If only he could have listened to some music now, how it would have sweetened his sadness, his sense of insignificance in the world, his loneliness and the guilt for this loneliness, for which he blamed himself alone. *Music is the language in which the soul speaks to itself.*

He well remembered when this had been said and who had said it. It was the beginning of the awareness that this dark spell had to be broken, the addiction ended. What happened afterward, inevitably, strengthened his decision in a burst of insult, hatred, and violence. The break was easier than he had imagined. There was no way back. But despite all the efforts at forgetting and denial he had made since then, the words came back to him now, final as a verdict. Other sentences popped into his mind when he least expected them, some of them sentences he had heard, some his own invention, and some whose origin he had already forgotten, but all of them resonant with the same strange, feverish intensity, more seductive in its form than its content. Like the urgent, ingenious improvisations of a thief caught red-handed, standing in the burgled house with his loot in his hands, quickly making up all kinds of strange, contradictory stories and explanations to account for his presence there, each one more fantastic and incredible than the next. Anyone taking the trouble to listen to the words as such, detached from the time, place, and circumstances of the act, freed of the restraints of the accidental, material facts of the situation, anyone paying attention to the pure voice speaking from the words themselves, might find it to be as persuasive, if not more so, than the circumstantial truth, which is subject to the specific, ephemeral context and to the technical laws of logical probability. True, there is not much practical or theoretical profit in this truth; but did the thief caught red-handed really believe in his ability to persuade his captor of the contents of his arguments? Since the brunt of these arguments presumably depended on outlandish coincidences, on a chain of fateful mistakes and unique disruptions of the familiar causal connection between intentions and consequences, did he think even for a minute, however naive and primitive he was, that his audience would agree to accept the hypothesis that some supernatural, cosmic conspiracy existed against him on the part of the laws of nature and logic, which had departed from their usual course and upset the natural order in order to trip him up? Anyone who knew how to listen to the pure voice of the words — words charged with the force of the urgent, pressing need to talk and talk and gain time; or even better: arrest time until some trick or stratagem for extricating himself occurred to him — would hear in them an appeal to the elements of nature and the laws of logic to deviate, if only this once, from their normal course and repair the damage, a invocation to time to turn back and undo what had been done. This urgent appeal was only too familiar to Avner, from the times when he himself had held forth, moralizing, rationalizing, defending himself against imaginary accusations, fighting for the love and affection of the world, stopping gaps and putting up barricades, conducting the dialogue with himself and others in this code of seduction and invocation. He believed in the truth of the code more than its meaning, because in the code he recognized that pure, mysterious power, the intensity of form that gave it an independent life and that, he sensed, held out his only possibility of understanding, if not of saving, himself.

Music is the language in which the soul speaks to itself. The words came back and confronted him now in all their original power, the power they had when they were first spoken, but the effect was the opposite of what it had been then. Today he knew how to listen to the power of the melody of the words, the rhythm of their breathing, the beating of their heart, and even though the message was not to be deciphered in terms of the literal significance of the words, their meaning nevertheless welled up and broke out of the ostensibly opaque skin of the code, like beads of sweat from pores, like something self-evident, as if it were his own invention, and not something somebody else had said to him. And now it was calling him to retreat into himself, to find his home inside himself, to lay his head on his shoulder and cry. To make his peace, surrender, and renounce the world.

But no! Something inside him protested, his natural health, it seemed to him, refused to allow him to retreat into these thoughts of surrender. He could confront, that rainy evening, the decision he had come to as he made his way home, on foot, weighed down by water. The horror that had seized him this afternoon, when he saw those obscene eyes in the crowd crossing the road next to the Interior Ministry and went to hide in the alley, returned even now to haunt him. But on that evening, when he walked home in the rain, he had known a wonderful serenity of detachment and reconciliation with himself. What do they know about it, the little darlings, who were given everything on a platter, without complications, without humiliations? Everything clean, clean. The obscene eyes, which would always be associated in his mind with the second, marvelous movement of the Beethoven violin concerto and sully it for him, had indeed cursed his day. How could he not be superstitious?

That evening it had poured. It wasn't late, he could still have taken the bus. But he couldn't have endured the proximity of other people, and so he went by foot in the rain. Apparently he needed the rain. It was a long way and there was no point in running. Besides, he didn't want to run. He wanted to walk slowly and let the rain cover him, flood him, seep into the marrow of his bones, come what may, even if he got sick and died. Was it a need to purify himself? He was not yet able to provide a satisfactory explanation. And as he stepped out now with the cool autumn breeze chilling his neck and arms, and his light, short-sleeved shirt swelling as if to escape the touch of his skin, he whistled the second movement of the Beethoven violin concerto, trying to recapture those moments of walking in the rain, to relive them, as if it was a mission from on high, as if the way back to those moments would cancel out all the mistakes he had made since then, defeat the cunning of time. He bowed his head and thought of the water that had washed over him then, his clothes heavy with the water, the streams of it running down his face, the noise of the rain that he had never heard so close before, so personal, filling his ears with a loud, angry roar. The downpour fell on his back like a hail of arrows pursuing him, but he didn't run. A strange and marvelous calm descended on him. His fists were still numb from the blows. Perhaps he had hit him until he bled, perhaps he had killed him? His eyes had seen nothing. Who knows what he had left behind him there, in the room, where the Beethoven violin concerto was still playing, the second, slow, sad, resigned movement, as if nothing had happened. The equanimity he had felt then, the justification of his violence that appeared to him in biblical terms, the belief in his power to save himself and control his fate, he could not retrieve now these things now — some memory of them still thrilled his heart, but not much. Much had been lost on the way.

There were no lights on in his sister's house. He knocked again. Nobody at home. Perhaps they had gone to visit his parents. The key was in his pocket. He stopped whistling Beethoven. The key lying in his pocket was an annoying reminder that the decision was still up to him. This worry had been nagging at him relentlessly despite all his efforts to ignore it; the decision had not yet been taken and it stood before him unresolved, painful, shameful, as if some role reversal had taken place here and Aliza was only an instrument for satisfying his lust; all the rest was coarseness and deceit.

I'll never forgive you as long as I live for having treated me like a whore. Why did she say *having treated* in the past tense? Was it all in the past now, was everything over between them? Here was the real, true fear of these actual moments, unlike those moments in the distant past that existed now only in his memory and thoughts — what, has she decided to throw me over?

Our decisions, future, fate, set their stamp on the way we speak, our facial expressions, our body movements, but it is a faint, subtle stamp that becomes apparent only after the fact, recognizable in small, marginal details, in things that seem absentminded, that are less deliberate and therefore truer. If only he could go back and see the exact expression on her face when she said *I'll never forgive you as long as I live . . .* the way she stood looking at him for a moment without saying anything, the way she climbed the steps, the way she turned her head toward him, the way she walked away as he watched her from the door of the shop, breathing a sigh of relief. If only he could have brought back all these things, watched them like a movie, observed the details, listened to the nuances of her voice, he would have known what her intention was. If he knew her intention, it would have been easier for him to answer to himself the question of whether he loved her. And in the meantime all the certainties were disintegrating. Should he send Yaffa to ask her to come tomorrow night, as she had offered? Why was it so hard to give up the party at Hanan's for her sake? Surely she was worth it! But the party seemed like a heaven-sent opportunity to give him a way out of the trap, a chance to set his life on the right track. Who knew what lay in store for him there, what new love — the right love, with a future and stability and rest. Would he finally find rest? From the heights of his eighteen years he looked down on his life as on a long, long trail of wanderings, of false enthusiasms and sad disillusions, of vain hopes and sinkings into despair. How long would his bad luck go on riding him? Her tearful protest, her voice choking as she spoke, different from her usual voice, her downcast eyes — there was something so very close to him about her then, like a part of himself, perhaps the best part, a shiver ran through him at the thought that he was willing to give this up. Everything depended on her intentions. It was like a problem in algebra with one unknown factor, and however much he turned it over it would always defeat him. The simplicity of the problem and the impossibility of discovering the unknown and finding a solution demonstrated his situation as the victim of a malicious trick.

Going around and around in circles like this was exhausting his body and depressing his soul. He began to feel hungry. He made his way home. Since the beginning of his leave, more than twenty-four hours ago, he had almost forgotten that he was a soldier. Now for the first time the pictures of his life on the base came back to him. He had plunged back into his old, premobilization affairs, as if his civilian life had never stopped, but at this minute — even though he still refused to admit it, even to himself — he would rather be back on the base than in Jerusalem. He would be better off enduring the common hardships of army life with the others, being broken with them, participating in the camaraderie and carefree laughter with them, hoping for leave with them, being part of that togetherness, forgetting the insult of his damnable loneliness, the sense of his nothingness in the world, rubbing all that out with the frantic, stupefying activity, the physical exhaustion, in the constant company of others, living from one minute to the next, obeying orders without the need to make decisions, without the superfluous involvement of imagination and soul searching. One day outside the base was enough to sweeten the humiliation and the rage, Benny the instructor and the evil spirit pervading everything, the nights of guard duty and the unbearable craving for sleep, the hours of depression and hatred. The evil spirit turned them into animals. Now it seemed to him that all those weeks he had been in some kind of trance, semiconscious, walking around like a zombie.

At home he was received with the usual complaints, and his mother said: "Leave him alone, what do you want of him? He's on leave from the army, he wants to make the most of it."

She knew nothing about his life, she was incapable of understanding his life, but there was no doubt about it, she heard the voice of his heart, thanks to some mysterious bond between them that was beyond knowledge or understanding. Hearing his inner voice was her special gift. When he sat down at the table with his brothers and sisters, his brothers-in-law and sisters-in-law and their children, and the whole room was filled with merriment and commotion, too small to contain its occupants, he caught her look, saying plainer than words: *Don't fall. Don't fall.* Like the look in her eyes on that rainy evening when he came into the house. He was afraid then that she would be alarmed, that she would scold and yell. But she opened the door as if she were expecting him at that moment precisely. Without a word she brought him a change of clothes and placed a towel on his head and began to dry his hair, rubbing and massaging with all her strength. He took her hand away and dried his hair and neck and face himself, and for one short moment he held the towel over his eyes, while the cold, hard armor of his indifference on the way home cracked and his gratitude for the hour that had granted him mastery over his fate burst forth. He had had many occasions to doubt it since; but when he had covered his face with the towel while his mother stood waiting silently beside him, an unwitting accomplice in his silence and the hiding of his face, he had felt the calm indifference melting inside him, and everything suddenly becoming astonishingly clear, as if he had entered into an alliance with the world for good or for ill, and thus, silently and directly, her approval reached him, the inner voice of her blessing. This gave rise to a new strength in him, to eagerness for battle and to a sense of freedom. He said to himself then that he had become a man. And his mother's eyes said to him: *Don't fall, don't fall,* without knowing anything; she only heard his inner voice reaching her through his silence, and she answered him wordlessly: *Don't fall, don't fall.* How far those moments were from him now, and how full of power.

His father was already drunk, although not disgracefully so. His eyes were red and watering, and he broke into song in his hoarse, ugly voice. Everyone joined in the refrain, the little ones piping up too. The eldest brother, poor Benihu, who was sitting next to Avner, grunted something in a throttled voice, like the moan of a beaten animal. His brother-in-law Shaul sat with Yoel, whom Avner loved best of all his nephews and nieces, on his lap, bouncing him in time to the singing. When would he have children of his own, he wondered; up to now he had never thought about it seriously. She wasn't prepared to understand it. She was trying to pull him toward her, to remove him from the children he would have one day, to enclose him with her in this accursed, barren circle. It was insanity, it was an illness. It had gone on for far too long already, longer than any relationship of this kind should go on, could go on. How could he ever have believed that this was the great love of his life! It was more like a curse, a spell he had to learn how to break. To get out of the cursed circle, to free himself of it, meant freeing himself from the seductive pains of guilt, freeing himself from the longings for the figure endlessly transforming herself in his heart, from the spell of the images that had mostly been created in his imagination, and very few of which had any real relationship to her. Freeing himself meant not allowing the dream to control him anymore, but controlling the dream. Getting back his control over his fate. That was the way to come into his own and find peace at last. For a moment he felt full of energy and resolution to do what had to be done. (The key was still in his pocket, and he knew that the sooner he returned it to Shaul, the better it would be for him. But he would have to do it discreetly.) But then his heart shrank in fear of the threatening, devouring emptiness gaping ahead of him. He had to give the key back as soon as possible. He had so little faith in his ability to change.

They were singing Rosh Hashana songs. His mother did not take her eyes off him, as if none of the others interested her. Her eyes examined him and he had no doubt that she was listening to his inner voice, perhaps trying, without success, to guess what was happening to him. He couldn't guess the contents of her thoughts either, he could only hear the tone of her voice, its sad, encouraging, wordless question. Poor Benihu swayed at his side, his strange big brother, who was still living with his parents. He was about thirty-five years old, his face, in contrast to his fat, clumsy body, was boyish, and his once coal-black hair had been rapidly invaded by a ghostly gray, making his face seem more and more transparent and giving it an air of transience and formlessness, a kind of gradual parting taking place before their very eyes, as if he were already halfway gone from them. His mind had not developed as it should have, apparently as a result of an accident at birth, and he accompanied them like a shadow all his days. He had not learned to speak either, and the sound of his soft groaning filled Avner's ears, giving the singing a different beat, strange and wild.

And opposite him was the smiling face of little Yoel sitting on his father Shaul's lap. His big, heavy-lidded eyes shone like two black lamps. Avner called him to come to him. Shaul took him off his lap, and the little boy circled the table to come to his young uncle, but Benihu stretched out his hands and grabbed him on his way to Avner, hugged him and tried to seat him on his lap. Little Yoel burst out crying. Shaul stood up anxiously and his wife said: "Don't worry, he won't hurt him. He's got a good heart." But Avner couldn't stand the child's frightened tears, and got up to rescue him. Benihu would not let him go. The singing stopped as everyone watched the struggle. Avner had to exert all his strength to pry Benihu's arms apart; then he gave in, hung his graying head, and Avner sat Yoel on his lap and hugged him. Avner's father rose from his place at the head of the table, and with drunken, bloodshot eyes and a slight lurch to his walk approached Benihu.

"What's the matter with you?" he shouted. "If you can't behave like a human being we won't let you sit with everybody anymore!"

Did Benihu understand the meaning of his father's shouted words? In any case he went on sitting with his head lowered, and suddenly a strangled wail escaped his lips, one long, heartrending wail, and after it silence — expressing regret or protest or anger, there was no telling. This was the way he moaned at night too, in his sleep, one long strangled moan, and then silence.

His father returned to the head of the table. Yoel gradually stopped crying, but Avner could still feel the trembling of the thin little body between his arms. He closed his eyes and buried his face in the baby's head. The smell of the silver-embroidered skullcap mingled with the pure smell of the soft, silky black hair. Avner kissed Yoel's head and his heart murmured, in lament or consolation: *Everything's up to you, everything's up to you.* And from the end of the table his mother's eyes fell on him again, and her face, which up to now had been immobile, heavy and pensive, suddenly moved, as if to say: *Yes, yes, yes.* They were singing again. And perhaps this really was the auspicious hour for a reckoning, for New Year's resolutions? Perhaps there was truth in this belief? Perhaps it really was possible to turn over a new leaf? And his mother went on nodding at him from the other side of the table, as if to say: *Yes, yes.*

Later that night, when he was alone with Avishai, he asked him to lend him a little money: "When I get my first quarterly leave, I'll work and pay you back, don't worry."

"Sure," said Avishai. "I can trust you. Like I can trust anything else you say."

"Listen, man, I haven't even got the money to buy cigarettes in the canteen, I swear!"

"So stop smoking. Do what the other guys there do."

"They get money from home, Avishai, their folks give them money. What do you think, that they can manage on their army pay?"

"When I was in the army, I managed. I didn't have anyone to ask at home. I didn't ask you. But I'm sure Ma puts something aside for you; she'd take the bread out of our mouths to give you money to spend on having a good time."

"I don't want to take money from her," said Avner.

Avishai looked at him with an amused smile, and Avner didn't know why. Avishai was short and sturdy, he always wore a shabby black beret on his head, and he looked like their mother. His arms were too long for his body, his hands large, his fingers thick and very hairy. They were sitting on the doorstep after everyone else had gone to bed. They always sat there, because there was nowhere else where they could talk. The street was deserted and a cool breeze blew through it, like a new beginning. The last days before the beginning of winter.

"You've already gone to ask Shaul for money!" said Avishai with a triumphant expression.

"No I haven't! Where did you get that from?"

"You think I didn't see, when they went home, how you took him aside, and he gave you something, or you gave him something. I saw. I saw everything."

"No," said Avner, "that was something else."

"You, what do you care about the family? All you care about is yourself. When you earned money you could have saved. But you spent it all on the movies. And on girls. Now you want us to fork up. You think you've got everything coming to you?"

Avner assumed that in the end Avishai would give him the money, but first he would have to undergo this ordeal, bow his head and listen to his brother's lectures, complaints, and sarcastic remarks. That was the price and he could afford to pay it. Avishai had to prove that he had justice on his side. Justice, that was all that was left to those who were unloved. In love there was no justice, it wasn't needed. The test of love was different. All Avishai had was to be in the right. And he had to be allowed to feel this.

"I'll need your bicycle too tomorrow night," said Avner. "I hope it's not too much to ask."

The irony in his voice was apparently not lost on Avishai. "And don't think," he said, "that people don't know you're carrying on with married women. That's how much you care about the family honor. And you don't care if you destroy other families either."

"What?" cried Avner in alarm, so horrified that he was afraid his face would betray his secret. Apart from himself and Aliza the only person who knew was Yaffa, and her loyalty to Aliza was beyond question. "Are you crazy? Who told you that?"

Avishai laughed. Avner smelled danger. Where had he found out? Had he been following him? He had never felt more bound to defend her, her honor, her well-being, and who knew — maybe even her life.

"It's not true," said Avner. "It's true I once knew a divorcée, but that was ages ago, it was over long ago. And I've never touched a married woman."

"What do you need the bike for tomorrow night?"

"Forget about it," said Avner bitterly.

What had to happen for Avishai to be friendlier toward him? There were about three years between them; about six months between Avishai's demobilization and his own enlistment. And the distance between them was so great, there was no way of bridging the gap. And now that he had smelled danger, the need to get Avishai onto his side and be liked by him was more pressing than ever.

"And you, always talking about the family, the family, you think you behave toward me like a brother? Sometimes I feel that you treat me like an enemy."

"As your elder brother I worry about you," said Avishai. "I can see you going off the rails, and instead of sticking to the straight-and-narrow you're going downhill all the time. You think you're so clever because you went to school a few years longer and read books. But that doesn't make a person more clever or more honest. True wisdom comes from the heart, from the way a person behaves. You think if you know how to talk like an Ashkenazi you're an Ashkenazi already and you can do what you like? Soon you'll start being ashamed of your family because we're not Ashkenazis. You've got no respect for yourself, for your home, for your place in the world. So naturally I worry about you. You think I don't want you to be happy? The same blood runs in our veins, the same nerves, the same heart! But I can see farther than you, I can see the end, and it's bad. You can only see one step ahead and you think you're a king and the world owes you a living, money, love, kind words, the lot! Pull yourself together and start looking out for yourself."

"For God's sake, what's all that got to do the fact that I need a bit of pocket money in the army? You know that I gave most of what I earned at work to our parents, I had hardly anything left for myself."

"Why was the army pay enough for me?"

"I don't know. I don't waste money."

"Of course you do. You spend it all on girls and married women and whores."

"You're just saying that, Avishai. You know it's not true. And if I have a date with a girl once in a while, so what? Do I have to live like a monk? What's wrong with it?"

"Don't think I'm some loser," protested Avishai. "Don't think I don't know anything about women. I may not be as handsome as you, but I understand more about women than you do, I just don't talk about it and brag about it and carry on about it all the time. But you listen to what I'm telling you now, and when you get into trouble, remember that I told you so: All the trouble in the world comes from women. A real man doesn't let women turn his head, he knows how to keep them in their place. There's no limit to the pleasures women want for themselves. There's no limit to their fantasies and lust and the demands they make of a man. Anyone who doesn't know how to say *This far and no farther,* anyone who doesn't know how to stop a woman sliding downhill, falls into the abyss with her. So don't think it's such an advantage for a man to be handsome; a man has to be strong, clever, but not handsome, and then a woman knows her place, what's permitted to her and what's forbidden, and she doesn't get all kinds of lustful thoughts into her head. And if the man's handsome, the woman forgets her place, her role, and instead of doing what the man tells her, she teaches him all kinds of things, plays her games with him, she turns him into her female, as if the roles were reversed. And then after she's done whatever she likes with him, after she's tired of him, she chucks him onto the rubbish heap, like some used-up whore, and goes to look for somebody else. Just remember I told you, and when it happens, you'll know I was right."

"Is that what you think of me?" said Avner.

"That's the way you're going," said Avishai.

"No," said Avner. "I'm actually planning to get married as soon as I get out of the army, maybe even at the end of my service, and have a family and settle down."

"I'll be the first to congratulate you," said Avishai, "but it's hard to believe."

"You should help me, if you want what's good for me."

"Sure!" said Avishai. "Everyone has to help you, only you. Everyone has to worry all the time about how to make Avner happy. Nobody else is important, only Avner. And who's going to help me? When will I get married, if I have to worry about everyone, support the family, look after our father, help our mother, take care of everything? They're old, you know. They don't have the strength for anything. When he drinks, I have to bring him home to save the family honor. When she's sitting down and she can't stand on her feet it hurts her so much, I have to be there to lift her up. And soon they won't be able to do anything for Benihu, and that'll fall on me too — who else? You? And with all that, I have to work and earn money to feed the family. So when will I be able to get married?"

"You'll get married too," said Avner, and his heart bled for Avishai, as if he really had sinned against him. "Everybody gets married. You're such a kindhearted, hardworking person, I'm sure you'll find some good girl who'll know how to appreciate you."

"Don't think girls aren't interested in me. Some girls look for character and strength in a man, not just looks. And those are the good, serious girls, who can be relied on, the good mothers for our children. You think our mother was such a glamour girl, you think that's why our father chose her? No, even when she was a young girl he saw that she had a good character, and that she would bring him honor."

"I don't know what she looked like when she was young," said Avner. "I've never seen a photograph of her when she was young. She hasn't got any photos from then, not even a wedding photo, like everyone else."

"Why should they have wasted money on getting themselves photographed? They had more important things to think about."

"It's a pity," said Avner. "I'd really like to see what she looked like when she was young."

"Because that's the only thing that's important to you, what people look like. But beauty passes with the years, you know? It passes like a dream, like the wind, and what remains is character, behavior, honor."

"A trace of the beauty remains, in memory," said Avner.

"Oh sure!" said Avishai. "Father told me once that she wasn't pretty at all when he met her. She had a sister who was more beautiful, Sara, who was sickly and died young, but from the first it was her he wanted, because he could see her character."

"He was handsome," said Avner, "and that didn't stop her marrying him."

"He wasn't handsome and he wasn't not-handsome, he looked like a normal man. You think that if you look like him, than he had to be handsome too. You think I don't understand what you're getting at? But okay, supposing he was handsome. So what came of it? All he got out of it was trouble and he's regretted it all his life. All it brought him was sorrow, and now he gets drunk to forget it."

"I don't consider myself handsome," said Avner. "I don't know why you're making such an issue out of it."

"Otherwise you wouldn't carry on the way you do! It's because they chase after you; for them you're a plaything for the most corrupt pleasures Satan put into a woman's heart. When she says *Oh, Avner darling, oh Avner!* you can be sure she's thinking only of herself, of her own pleasure, and she doesn't care if she ruins you. But you delude yourself, you think the whole world was created for your convenience, to serve you and pamper you."

"Does our mother think I have affairs with married women, like you do?"

"Of course! Everybody knows. What did you think, that you could keep it a secret? There are no secrets in Jerusalem, everybody knows everybody else."

Again he felt himself longing for Aliza, afraid that she was going to leave him, afraid that he had caused her downfall, blaming himself for the exposure of their secret, ready to stand beside her in this catastrophe, until the bitter end. All his hopes and new resolutions froze in the distance; there was no substance to them.

"I don't know who invented that story, but why did they have to go and tell Mother, why make her miserable for nothing, when it's not even true?"

"As if you care," sniggered Avishai.

"Of course I care."

"If you cared, you wouldn't have disgraced our family."

"They put me in jail in the army," said Avner suddenly, without even meaning to.

"What happened?"

"I fell asleep on guard and they took the gun out of my hands. They charged me with sleeping on guard, abandoning my weapon, and impertinence. I got jail for the impertinence. They dragged the gun out of my hands by force. I was already awake when they grabbed it and I couldn't stop them."

"So what's it like in a military prison?" asked Avishai. In the dim light coming from the window of one of the houses Avner couldn't see if he was gloating or really curious.

"Terrible," said Avner, "it's hell. I suppose you never got into any trouble in the army."

"A clean conduct sheet," said Avishai proudly. "I don't go looking for trouble."

"I envy you," said Avner. "Believe me, I envy you."

"You don't envy anyone, you're so pleased with yourself, so sure you're a king, it's only when something doesn't work out exactly the way you want that you immediately start crying and asking other people to help you, instead of helping yourself. You don't envy me, kid, you feel sorry for me. You think I don't know? You say to yourself: *Poor Avishai, what a miserable life he leads, working from morning to night, without any girls, without anything, wasting his youth on the family, on our parents, on Benihu, while I, Avner, have a ball.* Don't think I'm stupid, but you needn't feel sorry for me, I'm not poor Avishai. You'll still see whose life turns out better, more settled, more respectable. When you went to listen to their music at the YMCA, I was still busy cleaning the shop and going to drag our father home. When did you ever come to help me?"

"I was working myself. You know what it's like to work as a porter all day?"

"You used to sit there in the basement for hours listening to the gramophone, you think I didn't see you?"

"That was only sometimes, until they called me to come and carry something."

"Whenever you've got a problem you suddenly remember your family, your brothers, and you suddenly come and tell me you envy me. What's there to envy? But I'll tell you what: In the night you pissed in your bed, and now you think that the sack I'm sleeping on is better. It's like the story our father used to tell us when we were small, about the sultan who couldn't sleep at night and envied the straw-stuffed sack that the peasant slept on, because he thought that it would make him sleep well —"

"— and the flea that sucked his blood all night long explained to him who the real king was," said Avner. "I remember. But I don't think I'm a king. I really do envy you, for your character and the kind of life you're going to have. I'm not just saying it, believe me."

"Who's stopping you?" Avishai spread out his hands in a gesture of incomprehension. Strange to think of those thick, hairy fingers holding a razor, snipping with a scissors, nimble, careful, precise. Now they looked rigid, dead. "Pull yourself together and you won't get into any more trouble."

"Haven't you heard that people have different characters, a different fate, that they're born with it, that it's impossible to change?"

"That's something for old people to believe in, not young ones."

"Don't you believe in fate?"

"I believe in God, not fate. I don't know what fate is."

"And I don't know what God is," said Avner sadly.

"Nobody's asking you to know what he is. All you have to do is believe. Our fathers and our fathers' fathers believed in him, and if it was good enough for them it's good enough for you. We're not more clever than they are. You're definitely not."

"If there is a God, I'm sure he hates me. My life's not easy, Avishai. Sometimes it gets so bad I want to die."

"What have you got to cry about? You're doing cushy basic training for jobniks on Training Base Four. What do you think it was like for me doing combat training in Golani?"

It was late and the air outside was growing sharp and chilly. Avner wearied of trying to persuade his brother. Better to give up, forget, go to sleep, try to dream, and stop trying to squeeze water out of this stone. After all the events of the day and its mood swings, with the signs of tiredness touching his body like a caress, he was finally granted an hour of equanimity. As if he had detached himself from his worldly affairs. And this suspension gave him wings to float as light as a feather, almost bodiless, above the flat, clean, objectless spaces in which the soul could finally speak to itself. He felt no grievance against Avishai, no grievance against man or God. He felt no grievance even against himself. The oppression weighing on his heart lifted and the space freed in his chest soared upward, flooding him with a gliding sensation, far from the struggles and obstacles, far from the contradictions and the traps. At moments like these of reconciliation with himself he felt that he had certain things to say, and that he might even say them with a degree of eloquence that would astonish his audience. But he had no audience, and there was nothing left for his soul but to speak to itself. But even the longing to find someone to open his heart to at these moments, or to listen to music, did nothing to dispel the blissful sense of floating and detachment that had descended on him like an unlooked-for grace.

In their room, when he got into bed, he heard Avishai whispering "Hear O Israel." Avner's eyes grew accustomed to the dark and gradually painted in the details of the room in which he had slept ever since he could remember. Once they had shared the room with two other brothers, who had married in the meantime and moved into homes of their own. Since then each of them had a bed to himself. Until he closed his eyes he let them wander over the beds of the two brothers who were still sharing a bedroom with him. Poor Benihu, like Avner himself, slept with his body stretched out and his face to the ceiling, occasionally mumbling broken and unintelligible words in his sleep, as he did when he was awake. One day, and it was not too far in the future, they would have to worry about finding a solution for Benihu who could not care of himself, who could not exist without them. And there was no knowing how long he still had to live.

So little attaches me to them, a thread so slender that you can hardly tell when it breaks. What exactly is the thing that Avishai calls the common blood in our veins, the nerves, the heart, and all those things that are supposed to connect us to each other? I don't know what it is. And Avishai too talks about it without thinking, just repeating the clichés he's always heard, perhaps despite what he really feels. But he'll always do what's expected of him, without examining anything too deeply, without thinking for himself.

Avner lost the sense of time. Out of a deep sleep he was suddenly cast into the twilight of consciousness, half awake and half asleep, and then he suddenly woke up. The sound of the strangled cry from Benihu's bed was still echoing in his ears, one long cry, until there was no breath left, and then silence. It seemed to him that it was the silence falling after the cry that had startled him into consciousness and not the cry itself. After his long absence from home these wails were more terrifying than ever, like a siren suddenly going off. Pardon me, Benihu, for taking the baby away from you so rudely, without it even occurring to me that you too, like me, feel that emotion, those longings. When I was a child, I thought of you as the guardian spirit of the family who watched over us and took care that we didn't break any rules, sin against the covenant, turn traitor. I never loved you, and I never pitied you either. I wasn't afraid of you. But you were always here, the representative of something unclear, of some world in which the family was everything, a constant reminder that as long as you were with us there was still hope of some glue to hold us together and we were not lost. And even today you go on playing that role, the mission you were sent to perform among us, like a souvenir of other days, like an ancient copper vessel our ancestors brought from over there, which we've grown so used to we never look at it anymore. And if we did look at it, we wouldn't see anything. In a few more years you'll become a burden to us, and all of us will wish in our hearts for you to be taken back to the strange place from which you were sent to us, and for your sufferings, too, to come to an end; each of us will try to avoid the burden and impose it on his brother or his sister. That's the way of the world. Except perhaps for dutiful Avishai, who'll look after you devotedly, just like he helps our parents now, because that's what he knows, that's what he wants, and when Father and Mother are no longer with us, he'll have you, you'll justify his life, you'll be his private life. But even he will never understand this plaintive cry that suddenly breaks out of you, and you'll never know how to thank him or understand what he gave up for you.

After he dozed off again an alarm suddenly went off somewhere inside him, and together with it the old, familiar, caressing temptation to give in, to welcome it, not to be afraid, not to resist the promise. But a moment later Avner didn't know where he was, if he was awake or asleep. Strange hands were around his throat in a nervous, clumsy, uncertain grip. A grip more dreadful than if it had been efficient, painful, and truly suffocating. It was no dream! He opened his eyes and saw the white hair against the background of the opposite window, illuminated in a strange glow coming from the bluish darkness outside. He heard his heavy breathing but he did not see his face, which was bending down, close to his own throat; all he saw was the forehead and white hair glowing in the night. In the seconds that passed before he seized the hands and removed them from his throat, he wondered if he should let him be and pretend to be asleep, since he was sure that no harm would come to him, and he still wasn't certain that he was awake. But as the seconds passed and the grip grew tighter, he knew that he had no choice but to play his part in the mime. When Benihu felt Avner's hands loosening his grip, he raised his face and saw his brother open-eyed, he took fright and suddenly tightened his stranglehold with all his strength. Avner's body jerked violently. Now they were equally matched. As he struggled to free his neck it occurred to him that it had to be done in silence, so as not to wake Avishai. After prying the hands apart, he held on tight and prevented Benihu from getting up, examining the face right next to his and listening to their heavy breathing in the silent room. Benihu's body suddenly began to shake, and Avner was afraid that he was going to scream. He let go of his hands, got out of bed, put his arm around his brother's shoulders, and led him slowly back to bed. As he did so he implored him silently: *Don't scream, don't scream, for God's sake keep quiet, don't let Avishai hear, don't wake him up.*

Benihu didn't make a sound and allowed Avner to lead him back to bed, obedient and submissive, shaking all over and breathing heavily. Avner covered him with his thin blanket and patted his shoulder to calm him. Then he went back to bed and lay listening to his brother's breathing grow calmer. His neck hurt, especially his Adam's apple, which had been squeezed hard, making it painful for him to swallow his saliva.

He tried to fall asleep again, but something prevented him from doing so, an inner agitation that was even stronger than the fierce pain in his neck. He stood up and tiptoed over to Benihu's bed, which was next to the window. For a moment he stood at the head of the bed and looked down at his quiet face, illuminated by the dark glow. He had never thought before about how handsome this face was, how similar to his own face and his father's face before he'd grown old, and how different from theirs. The crown of whitening hair lent it an air of great purity, and the thick brows, which were still coal black, met over the bridge of his nose, casting a shadow over his closed, sunken eyes. Like a prince sent into exile to serve his term of punishment, so he had been born and lived among them, alien and unloved. The ragged blanket covering his shoulders lay exactly where Avner had placed it and his face was immobile, riveted by some inexplicable force to the point on the ceiling where his eyes had been fixed before they closed. His breathing was even and rhythmic, and so quiet that Avner hardly heard it as he bent slowly over his face and kissed his brow.

CHAPTER 18

The cat stared at them with worried, curious, suspicious eyes, rearing its head to show readiness for battle, while its whole body said: *What are your intentions? What are you trying to prove?* It ran its eyes over the people sitting in a row in front of it, then turned to face the place where the sound was coming from, back and forth with tiresome obstinacy. From time to time it would recoil from the bursts of laughter, as if they offended some deep fastidiousness in its nature in addition to alerting its sense of danger, after which it would stand still for a moment, turn around, look at the row of people sitting behind it with an expression of skeptical disdain, and then begin picking its way slowly out of the circle of danger, only to be halted in its tracks by the sound again. An expectant silence would fall. The cat would sit down, turn its head in the direction where the sound was coming from, sink its head into its neck, half close its eyes as if trying to concentrate, to solve the mystery, watching them warily at the same time. Whenever the laughter exploded around it, in response to some remark or some movement it made, it would raise its head and glance nervously from side to side, examine the faces of the laughers, and turn around, until the noise of the laughter subsided and the sound came again and the expectant silence surrounded it once more. Once or twice it went to the door, stopped, changed its mind, sat down on the threshold, and waited with them, sharing in their secret, riveted by the magnetic force of their stares; it had become the center of a story it could not understand. The alternating laughter and talk with the moments of silence in which the sound was heard, like alternations of fullness and emptiness, threat and promise, changed the rhythm of its movements. Its safe territory had suddenly turned into a battleground where unclear forces confronted each other, everything in it was out of joint, and thus, drawn by their company and repulsed by it, appeased and alerted to danger, it entered the circle and withdrew from it, a demented gleam in its eyes.

"Maybe the cat's been castrated!" said Rina. She was a pretty, vivacious girl, and in the greenish eyes flashing behind her spectacles, too, there was something catlike. She looked restless, always trying to ingratiate herself with everyone. Avner said to himself that this feverish gaiety was a cover for embarrassment or fear; girls like her were capable of doing all kinds of crazy things, which would only increase their embarrassment and fear. Judging by the way she made herself at home in his parents' house, she was apparently Hanan's girlfriend. She burst into laughter at her own words, and the girls sitting next to her giggled too, except for Ziva, whose posture and expression made it evident that she wanted to dissociate herself from this childishness and crudeness. Ziva looked like a girl who had taught herself to behave in a manner she considered aristocratic: Laughter too was apparently evidence of coarseness and vulgarity in her opinion, and accordingly, like those Oriental women brought up to believe that showing their teeth is equivalent to exposing their nakedness, and who cover their mouths with a corner of their headkerchiefs or their hands when they speak, Ziva placed her hand over her mouth and dropped her head, while a delicate blush spread over her pale, fair face. She even closed her eyes as a sign of weariness and rebuke. Everything about her signaled reserve, together with a noble, exhausting effort to renounce her natural superiority in order to grant them the favor of her company. Her eyes were narrow and very light, cold as steel, her hair was fair, short, and straight, combed back behind her ears with a severity that made it quite clear she had no need to worry about the way she looked. She was one of those girls who are so sure of their own beauty that they sometimes tend to dull it with what might seem like carelessness, or even blasé indifference, like wealthy people who play down their wealth and even put on airs of poverty in order to show that they did not have to work for their money but grew into it naturally, and also perhaps because they know that the idea of wealth is more powerful than anything that money can buy, and they would like to elevate their money to an abstract plane.

Avner was already there when Ziva arrived with her friend Miri, a dark, too-tall, rather ungainly girl whose face he remembered, although it seemed to him that when he'd last met her she had been less tall and less ungainly. When the two girls entered the room Ziva could not stop herself from stealing a quick glance at the row of boys, and in the fraction of a second that her eyes fell on him Avner said to himself that the expression on her face changed, but he could not decide if it was one of disapproval or pleased surprise. Immediately he felt sure that it was because of her that he had come to the party. Whenever he looked at her he was aware of her efforts to cover up the fact that she sensed his eyes on her. There was much charm in these efforts of hers to control her facial expressions and movements, but he was even more impressed by the delicacy and beauty with which her face betrayed her for a second, under the pressure of the curiosity and discomfort caused her by his stares. He couldn't tell if she was the girlfriend of anyone present; he couldn't see any signs of a special relationship between her and one of the boys in the room. They all knew each other. Except for Avner and Hedgehog, who were new to their crowd. They sat in two rows facing each other, seven boys opposite four girls, looking at the cat looking at them, and waiting, like it, for something to happen.

Hanan protested indignantly at his girlfriend's speculations about the castration of his cat, almost as if she were casting aspersions on his own virility. The cat was a male in every respect, he insisted, and Raffy's theory was based on superstition and old wives' tales. But Raffy insisted: "If there's anything wrong, it's not the theory but your cat."

"Maybe it's like those stories about the red rag and the bull," said Ruthie, a plump girl with fair hair curling over her head like wool: "Bulls are color-blind, and it makes no difference to them what color the rag being waved in front of them is."

"Ressler, do it again!" called Hedgehog. "This time I think it's going to work!" Perhaps he had seen something in the cat's body or behavior that nobody else had noticed. Yossie struck the piano key again, and again nothing happened to the cat.

"I'm still a doubting Thomas," said Hanan, in English.

"What exactly are we supposed to see?" asked the tall Miri, and twisted her face in a puzzled smile.

"When it happens," said Raffy, "you won't need anyone to tell you."

Everybody burst out laughing, except for Ziva, who began to show distinct signs of impatience, making Avner wonder: What exactly is she waiting for?

"Hanan's cat has got sexual problems," said Uri, Raffy's friend from the ROTC.

"Or else it's tone deaf, and it doesn't know that it's the third E above middle C," said Ruthie of the woolly hair.

"Nonsense," said Raffy, the future scientist. "It's been proven in scientific experiments. That note should stimulate it sexually. It should drive it so wild that the effects would be apparent to everybody. More than that I can't say."

"But maybe its rutting season's already over," said Hedgehog. "At the beginning of summer, when they want it, you can hear them howling like banshees all night long."

"Do you intend discussing the subject all night?" said Ziva, with a disdainful expression on her face. "If so, then say so now, because there are a number of good movies showing in town."

"Have you seen *Don Camillio* at the Studio?" asked Uri. "It's fantastic!"

"Nobody's going to the movies now," said Hanan firmly.

"Why shouldn't we talk about it?" said Hedgehog indignantly. "What's all this hypocrisy? What's wrong with talking about it? In the whole of history that's all they talk about. What do you think the driving force behind the history of the world is if not sex?"

Ziva ignored this remark. She stood up, walked over to one of the pictures on the wall, and examined it with exaggerated attention, her back to the company and their childish, vulgar games, waiting for them to change the subject.

Micha the Fool cried loudly, in the deep, pompous voice he used to imitate a well-known radio quizmaster: "And now, children, who knows how the sexual passion of the horse elevated Darius to the throne? Two points for the right answer!"

"Oh Micha, not that!" A chorus of protests greeted him. "For God's sake, not now!"

But Micha ignored their protests, he was so accustomed to them by now, and his compulsion to continue was so great: "Who knows, children? No one knows? So two points to me . . ."

Ziva concluded her examination of the picture, went up to the cat, which was now sitting in the doorway leading to the passage, knelt down, and began stroking its neck and back. Avner could not help thinking that this performance was being put on solely for his benefit. Even the way she knelt down was different from other girls, more aristocratic, more refined and feminine. What was she trying to tell him? Her position emphasized the narrowness of her waist, the beauty of her white, outstretched arms, her long, slender neck. Her breasts were only hinted at in the embroidered blouse that billowed as she knelt. And suddenly he saw something sad and moving in her supplicant posture, in her outstretched neck as she stroked the cat, something that wrung his heart and awoke the feeling of estrangement and profound loneliness from which he had been trying to distract himself all evening.

Micha kept up a steady patter: ". . . What did the groom do?" he asked and answered: "He took Darius's stallion's favorite mare out of the stable, led her out of town, and tied her to a tree, not far from the place where all the candidates were supposed to meet the next day. Then he brought the stallion and began leading him around the mare, closer and closer, until the sun began to rise, and then he let the stallion mount the mare. The next day, before dawn, Darius's groom went to the stable and rubbed the mare's vagina with his hand and put his hand in his pocket, to preserve the smell. Then he took the stallion and rode it to the place where the king was to be chosen. All the horses were supposed to start galloping at sunrise and were already assembled. The owner of the first one to neigh would be crowned king. A moment before sunrise, when Darius was already seated on his horse, waiting for the first light of dawn, the groom took his hand out of his pocket and rubbed it on the horse's nose. The stallion took one whiff of the vagina of his favorite mare and immediately began to bolt and neigh. At that moment the sun rose. All five contestants dismounted their horses, bowed down to Darius, and declared him king of Persia. So you see, children, how the sexual passion of a horse changed history?"

"Babies," said Ziva with a sigh, "What babies you are." She stood up and began circling the room, examining the pictures on the walls and the books on the shelves. Now it was the turn of the other girls to express their disgust both at the story and at the guffaws of laughter with which it was greeted by the boys, and they hid their faces in disapproval and shame.

You and I are allies here, said Avner to her in his heart. We mustn't miss this opportunity. You know everyone here, everyone here knows everyone else, you've probably been living in each other's pockets since school, the youth movement, God knows where else. And I'm the only outsider. And I have to take advantage of my position and exploit it. Turn it into a springboard, use it to fascinate you, to conquer you.

The way they were sitting in two rows, boys and girls facing each other, was highly unpromising, and as long as they were occupied with the cat and the musical experiment they were performing on it, the whole thing seemed like a lost cause to Avner. But at last they abandoned the cat, and the latter, sensing their disinterest, turned its back on them and went away. Avner said to himself that in the few hours left until the party was over everything was possible, if only he chose the right strategy and employed it with shrewdness and patience. The assessment of the situation, the available modes of action, the various possibilities, and the best way of reacting to them — all of these sprang up before him with such astonishing clarity and sharpness that he said to himself: Maybe this time I'm really falling in love. From that minute on he no longer needed to think and worry and plan; the whole program of the campaign seemed to have become part of his innermost being, so that all he had to do was attend to its signals and act accordingly, without fear of mistakes. He was inspired: He knew exactly who she was, and who he had to be for her to respond to his call.

Uri and Raffy, the two friends from the ROTC, told the latest dirty jokes, Ruthie of the puppy fat and woolly hair went to the kitchen with Nira to make sandwiches, and the tall, dark Miri, Ziva's friend, suddenly smiled at Avner, a shy, timid smile, and said: "How are you, Avner?"

Establishing a relationship with the best friend was a good idea, even though it always ended up badly. When Hanan had introduced them at the beginning of the evening, Miri showed no signs of recognizing him, and Avner made no attempt to refresh her memory. He was immediately captivated by Ziva, and afraid that any diversions would distract him from the main thrust, or even sabotage the new relationship. But now that he knew the campaign was going to be conducted along indirect, ostensibly passive lines, every marginal advantage became important. He also knew that it was vital to make a dent in this ridiculous lineup of boys opposite girls, and he set about doing so, discreetly and casually. He got up and went across to Miri: "Okay, how're you doing?"

"You're together in basic training?" said Miri.

"Yes," said Avner, "that's how it turned out. And what about you, have you been drafted yet?"

"No, I'm at the teacher training college too," said Miri, nodding at Ziva, who was sitting next to her, staring at some invisible point on the other side of the room and deliberately ignoring Avner's presence beside her. "I've got a deferment."

The demonstration of indifference boded well. It was definitely a defensive gesture, unnatural and completely illogical. Unless she had been seized by a sense of danger, threat, or weakness. From now on everything depended on him. It would be done quietly, maturely, sincerely. If that moment of inspiration was right, she would fall into his hands like a ripe fruit. She would take the first step toward him. It was important for her to take the first step, he had to remember that.

Guffaws of laughter rose from the dirty-joke audience, and Hedgehog's voice rose above the rest. "Come and listen," he called to Avner, "this will interest you."

"What do you know about what interests me and what doesn't interest me?" said Avner crossly under his breath, but within hearing of the two girls sitting in front of him, one oblivious and the other surveying him with interest and a hint of irony. Hanan and Nira brought in more refreshments and invited the guests to partake of them. Micha recited something, the commotion grew. This was the moment Avner had to build on. He parted from Miri with a smile and retired to the far end of the room, where a large brown armchair, its back covered by a white antimacassar, stood next to a standard lamp with a kind of little table upon which reposed a marble ashtray projecting from its stem.

Avner sat down in the armchair, took his cigarettes out of his pocket, lit one, and contemplated the rising smoke and the cigarette in his hand. Ziva's head was situated between the heads of the two officer cadets, who had their backs to him. He looked at her, an expression of reserve and faint melancholy on his face. From time to time he looked intently at the cigarette in his hand, as if measuring its length, and sometimes he shook the ash off into the marble ashtray, tapping longer than necessary with his finger, as if he were so wrapped in thought that he was in another world entirely. His heart was flooded with an ancient joy, unlike anything he had felt for a very long time, the joy of new beginnings, and the intoxication of returning to the starting point. At moments like these he had no doubt that he was the master of his fate, that nothing could stop him from attaining his goal, that even his rotten luck would not be able to trip him up. He did everything with deliberate slowness, but with no need of concentration, effort, or calculation. Sometimes he leaned his head against the back of the chair, closed his eyes and straightened his head again, took a slow drag on his cigarette and blew the smoke out sideways, before directing his gaze back to the face of the girl between the two heads. His gaze was as empty and indifferent as possible, but constant, resolute, and patient. Miri and Ziva put their heads together for a moment, and then Ziva looked him up and down for a second, dropped her eyes, and straightened the pleats in her skirt. There was no knowing if they were talking about him, but if they were, it made no difference at all if Miri had said something to his discredit. The important thing was for them to talk about him. She had to be rescued from the demonstration of indifference and refusal to notice him in which she had entrenched herself without knowing how to extricate herself. He had to rouse her interest, force her to take the first step, make the first gesture, say the first word. After that everything would go smoothly and naturally. And if the things Miri was saying to her were the kind of stories he knew people told about him, about his attitude to girls and his promiscuity, as Miri knew to her cost — all the better! It would awaken more interest, more curiosity, more mystery, more desire to respond to the challenge.

Hanan came up to him with the tray of refreshments: "Why so solitary?"

"No, no, I'm just resting in the armchair for a minute and dirtying your ashtray. Don't worry. Everything's okay."

"You can take the ashtray over there if you like. Are you in a bad mood?"

"No, not at all." Avner smiled to show that he was in a good mood and between the two officer cadets' heads he saw her face looking at him, right at him, with a smile at the corners of her mouth, in response to the smile with which he had answered Hanan. "But there's no point," he added, "in sitting in two segregated rows and not budging from them."

"You're right," Hanan agreed. "Afterward we'll move the chairs out of the way and dance a bit. There's dance music on the army program soon, and there are a couple of girls here who're probably dying to dance with you. Believe me, I know what I'm talking about."

Good grief — the thought suddenly crossed Avner's mind — did they bring me here to play the role the cat played before?

He took a bunch of grapes from the tray. Hanan turned away and Avner ground his cigarette into the ashtray, looking at her again from his observation point, but one of the officer cadets moved his head and hid her face. As if sunk in reflection he rose slowly to his feet and stood leaning against the wall, eating his grapes. He saw Yossie Ressler abandoning the group telling dirty jokes and going to sit next to Miri, in the place vacated by Nira when she went to take care of the refreshments in the kitchen. Ressler spoke to the two girls and again Avner said to himself: Go ahead and gossip, pal, slander me as much as you like, it'll only do me good. Avner knew that everybody was talking about him; the whole party was nothing but a mise-en-scène for his personal story, the story of his falling in love, and all the other people there were secondary characters, extras, accessories to the main plot. I'm sweating, I'm all worked up, I think I'm really falling in love. All these coincidences that brought me here aren't coincidences. She was sent to me. I was sent to her. Everything else is decor.

Yossie Ressler concluded his conversation with the two girls and got up. For a moment he stood to one side as if wondering what to do next, a weary expression on his thin, ascetic face, his whole person exhuding boredom and contempt. Avner saw him coming toward him in his corner at the other end of the room.

"How's it going?" asked Ressler and sat down on a chair next to the armchair.

"Okay," said Avner. "Our leave's over, it's back to base tomorrow."

"I'm trying to forget it. That's why I came here. Do parties bore you too?"

"No, the opposite. But you all know each other. You've got memories in common, experiences in common, your own folklore, and I'm a stranger here."

"Look around you," said Yossie softly. "I grew up with all these people, except for Hedgehog, of course. We were in kindergarten together, at school, in the movement, in the neighborhood. I can't remember myself without them. All these guys and girls are part of my life. And I feel like a stranger among them too. The strangeness is inside me, in my depths.

The shallow, external part of me joins in with them. The inner, deep part of me is a stranger to them, and they're strangers to it. They don't know anything about me. They don't really interest me."

"What are you trying to prove?"

"That the feeling of being a stranger isn't a social problem, it's an individual stance, a way of looking at the world."

"Not my way," said Avner. "I came here by chance, I met Hanan in Jaffa Street yesterday afternoon and he invited me to come. If we hadn't met by chance, I would be somewhere else now."

"And what are you trying to prove?"

"Nothing," said Avner. "Play something nice on the piano."

"Are you out of your mind?" exclaimed Yossie. "You can see what's going on here. It's the wrong atmosphere."

"What kind of atmosphere is it?"

"A party atmosphere. The stupidest thing in the world."

"Be a sport, go on, play something. Someone has to create the atmosphere. Someone has to introduce some order into this evening, some idea of beauty, of love. Listen, maybe this evening's special for me?"

"I'm not sure they'd be so interested."

Miri crossed the room to them.

"Do you mind giving Ziva a cigarette?" she asked Avner.

"Of course!" Avner caught himself showing too much enthusiasm.

"She suddenly feels like smoking and she hasn't got any cigarettes."

He turned to look at Ziva and she smiled at him apologetically in confirmation of the request, but there was something else in the smile too, something Avner was a past master at deciphering, something that said: *I know you and your kind, you're not making an impression on me. But the game amuses me nevertheless, so don't run away.*

Accordingly, he rejected his original intention to get up, go over to her, offer her a cigarette and light it for her, and then remain casually in her company. He smiled back at her, a polite, reserved smile, gave the pack of cigarettes and box of matches to Miri, and asked her: "Why didn't she come and ask for herself? Do you usually run her errands for her?"

"She was too embarrassed," said Miri, ignoring his sarcasm with the smile of a person who had already resigned herself to every possible insult and surprise. "She hardly knows you, and you're the only person here with cigarettes."

Miri left them and Yossie Ressler said: "She's just a snob, and she's trying to make an impression on you."

"Why?"

"What, don't you understand?" Yossie burst out laughing. "You really don't understand? She wants you to make a pass at her."

"Is she the kind of girl that anyone can make a pass at?" asked Avner.

"Is that what you think about yourself? That you're anyone?"

Avner saw his pack of cigarettes passing from hand to hand, with most of them taking one. He was annoyed.

"What do you want me to play?" asked Yossie.

"What kind of a girl is she?" asked Avner.

"Ziva?"

"Yes."

"I told you, a snob. And a bitch too."

"Before you sat and talked as if you were friends."

"If I told everyone what I really think of them — I wouldn't be able to go out of the house," said Yossie. "I told you that my superficial side, my external, buffoonish side, plays the game by their rules. You probably think it's hypocrisy, two-faced, but I think it's quite okay. Because it serves a more important end."

"In other words, you're quite capable of bad-mouthing me behind my back, and it wouldn't prevent you from talking to me like a friend."

"Right."

"And who do you keep the deep, inner, true part of yourself for?"

"You're talking to me but all the time you're looking at her," said Yossie Ressler. "Forget what I said to you about her. I'm not objective, not in relation to her or anyone or anything. But do me a favor, don't ask me any more questions about her."

"You still haven't told me who you're keeping the deep part of yourself for."

"I don't know, but maybe one day I'll meet a girl who'll understand me, who'll really love me and be able to participate in that part of me. But I don't have any illusions. I know it isn't simple."

Miri brought back the half-empty pack of cigarettes, smiling apologetically: "All of a sudden they're all addicts." Avner sat down in the armchair again and Miri rested her hands on the back of Yossie's chair. From close up Avner saw that her face was pockmarked, as if scarred by a bad case of acne. This added a touch of unexpected pathos to the pleasant expression on her face. Her eyes were dark and slightly slanting, and her mouth was small. She was more elegantly and maturely dressed than the other girls in the room. Her uncommon height gave her an air of sadness, as if she didn't know what to do with her surplus inches, and sometimes it seemed that all her unhappiness gathered at the corners of her small lips in a wry, defensive, ironic smile, and melancholy veiled her slanting eyes, which announced that they could see right through you and that you would never be able to pull the wool over them. "What are you talking about here all by yourselves?" she asked archly. "I want to join in the conversation too. Micha's holding forth there and they're all sitting and laughing. They're still not sick of it after all these years. It's terrible, they just don't want to grow up. It depresses me."

"Don't you like parties either?" asked Avner.

"Not at all! I love parties. That's why I'm here. Ressler hates parties, but he never misses a single one, it gives him an opportunity to spread his misanthropy around. Just a minute, I'm going to go and fetch a chair. Don't say anything interesting until I come back."

"Misanthropy," sniggered Yossie. "She gets those big words from Ziva and repeats them without understanding what they mean. "

"Play something, Yossie, do me a favor and play something."

"What should I play?"

"Something sad," said Avner.

"Sad? At a party?"

"What's happier than sad music?"

"There's something in that," agreed Yossie. "What, for example?"

"The saddest thing you know."

"You're so happy now, are you?"

"Yes."

Avner saw Miri and Ziva talking, Miri standing and holding the chair she intended to drag over to them, and Ziva sitting opposite her and making defensive, refusing gestures with her hand. Miri returned, bringing the chair with her, and Avner looked at Ziva, who had remained seated in her place, and saw her avoiding his eyes.

"How could you leave your friend all by herself? Why doesn't she join us?"

"What do you think we are, Siamese twins?" asked Miri. "She feels like sitting there. Don't worry about her, she can look after herself."

There's something rather nice about you, said Avner to himself. You're not stupid and I quite like you. But be careful: The roles appointed us in the story won't turn us into friends. If everything goes according to plan, and for the time being that's what it looks like, there'll be no peace between us. My role is always to be the best friend's hated enemy, maybe because in order for two people to love each other, someone else has to lose everything, to be the sacrifice. It hurts me to think that it will be you, because I've already treated you like a bastard once.

Yossie got up and went to the piano. Miri said to Avner: "Going by the stories you seem to having a high old time there. It sounds more like an army joke than real basic training."

Avner smiled without saying anything. Yossie began to play. In the din in the room Avner heard the notes of a tune he did not know.

"You've changed," said Miri.

"How?"

"You're much more relaxed. Once you were so nervous and restless."

"Maybe I had good reason to be."

Gradually the music overcame the noise. The voices died down to a quiet murmur. Avner looked round the room, as if to see the change wrought in it by the music. How the soft, slow, restrained, seductive sounds of the melody dominated the atmosphere, the facial expressions, the rhythm of people's movements. All heads turned toward the piano and suddenly Hedgehog's voice cried: "Ressler, play something everybody knows and we'll be able to sing along, like on the base."

"Idiot," muttered Miri in Avner's ear. Without seeing her, he sensed her eyes fixed on him, examining his face, looking for some kind of confirmation. Hedgehog looked around him uneasily, refusing to believe that his leadership was slipping out of his hands. He sniggered in embarrassment, regretting his cry, realizing how much of an outsider he was here. Avner looked at Yossie, hunched over the keyboard, the strain of his concentration distorting his face, giving it an expression of anxiety and anguish. At that moment Avner saw her getting up and crossing the room on tiptoe so as not to make a noise, not to disturb the playing, stopping next to the piano, and leaning against it with her profile toward him. Now she was no farther away from him than a few paces and he could examine her face at close quarters without betraying his interest. And he saw that even from close up her face looked distant, mysterious. Her attempts to appear older than her age had given her a mask that had become part of her, no less natural than her true nature. Only her out-thrust neck, her slumped shoulders, and her slightly stooping back, as when she had knelt down to stroke the cat, betrayed her and signaled something like sadness and loneliness. Something in the appearance of her nape and slumped shoulders revealed weakness, vulnerability. The way she was leaning on the piano and inclining her body toward the player made an arch that joined up with Yossie Ressler's bowed back and created an imaginary dome uniting the two of them in a bond of belonging and fraternity. Whatever the two of them might say about each other, and like them the other members of their crowd — the memory of the pact that had once bound them deeply and directly together, and lasted for years like a common dream that was now coming to an end, still hovered protectively over them. Avner knew that anyone daring to intrude on that dream would pay the price in full. This realization gave him a sense of power and calm, but a certain inner tremor, forgotten and familiar, reminded him that he was taking his last steps in an area where he was in control and that soon he would enter the domain where other forces would take over, sweep him away, destroy his identity, and there would be no way back to himself.

Suddenly, as if she had been stung, Ziva turned her head toward him for a split second, perhaps sensing his eyes fixed on her, and immediately turned back to the piano again. But in the second that their eyes met, her expression conveyed rebuke at the intrusion, or astonishment, and once more her profile inclining toward the player described the common dome enclosing them, and her half-closed eyes resumed the silent dialogue that Avner had been caught eavesdropping on, disrupting.

There was something in the beauty of the melody that suggested the beauty of partings, the sadness of endings, cold as a sober assessment, arrogant and withdrawn and in love with its own impotence, something that said to him *You're excluded,* just as Ziva's eyes had said to him in that split second when she turned to look at him, a blank, light blue look. Were they really beginning to wake up from their dream? Was it possible that each of them in their own way felt, at these very moments, that they had come to the end of their road together, and it would not be long before the memory of the old bond between them hardened like a scar? Now, however, that the music had brought not a promise of liberation and melting of barriers and opening up to new relationships, as Avner had hoped, but instead sounded a lament for the pain of being torn apart, they clung fiercely, unconsciously, to the remnants of the dream, with a desperation and despair whose likes they had never known as long as the dream itself had sheltered them, taken for granted and self-evident as everything else.

Yossie Ressler suddenly stopped playing and silence fell. He covered his eyes with his hand and muttered to himself, with the silence in the room making his words sound like a cry of complaint against the world: "It's ridiculous, ridiculous! Why am I playing it at all?"

Ziva straightened up, bowed her head, laughed soundlessly into the palm of her hand, looking at Avner again as she did so, and her light, steely blue eyes filled with a mischievous animation that might have seemed malicious but was actually a shrewd understanding of reality, without pretense or patronage. Avner smiled back at her with his saddest smile, and when she came and sat down between himself and Miri, on the chair previously occupied by Ressler, things began to happen outside his control, as if he were watching a movie in which he himself was acting, and the thread connecting the actor to the spectator was extremely fine and taut, every moment making it tremble with a new, different tremor, bringing him closer or sending him farther away from the role he was supposed to play, alternately recalling or suppressing his hopes, and although he had experienced this feeling before, it always felt like the first time, it always held mystery and the intoxication of playing with danger and the irresistible urge to give way to compulsion, to go full speed ahead, and to forget about everything else.

Yossie Ressler came back and stood next to them, his face flushed and his expression impenetrable. Avner lit a cigarette and offered the pack to Ziva, who shook her head, closing her eyes as she did so. Miri said to Yossie: "What's the matter with you?"

Instead of replying Yossie turned to Avner and said: "I don't know why, but you always give me the feeling that I owe you something."

Avner suppressed the tremor of surprise that ran through him. His inner mechanism, finely attuned to his role, called for silence and with-drawal. He smiled his saddest smile again and gazed at the cigarette in his hand.

Miri said: "You're just a problem child, Yossie."

"And spoiled," added Ziva.

"You don't know what you're talking about!" said Yossie.

"Never mind, never mind," said Ziva, and Avner knew that whatever she wanted to say to Yossie she wouldn't say in front of strangers, in front of him.

Hanan switched on the radio. The army program had already begun to play dance music. Yaffa Yarkoni was singing the first waltz. They pushed the chairs out of the center of the room and the people who had been sit-ting there moved to other places. Hanan and his girlfriend Nira began to dance. Raffy the officer cadet took the floor with Ruthie, and for the first time in the last hour or so a doubt awoke in Avner's heart: Would he dare to ask her to dance? Why was this the hardest thing of all? Was he afraid of breaking some spell that had been working perfectly up to now without his direct intervention? He looked at Hanan and Nira dancing the first waltz and he knew that he could do it, although he had never danced in his life. That wasn't the problem: It was all inside him, waiting to be put into practice, all the knowledge and the words and smiles and movements and reactions — but the possibility of losing, the dread of failure was even stronger now than the role being dictated to him from his depths. And since the whole scene seemed to him like a movie he was acting in and watching at the same time, he sometimes wanted to take his eyes off the screen, so as not to see the hero fail, for there were many things that he knew and the hero didn't. The memory of the hornet taking flight into the vast blue spaces and crashing into the windowpane, and the ugly little thud of the crash, a sound as dry and blind and abrupt as the split-second transformation of the quick into the dead, injected a sense of reality into his dreamlike state.

Now that she was sitting next to him he could not stare at her as he had before, and his eyes had not yet had their fill of her. For this was the joy of beginning he had so longed for, the hope of the looks before the words, before the battle. And so despite himself he turned his head to look at her, and met three pairs of eyes, hers and those of the other two, three looks that asked: *What do you want?* But hers was the saddest, the most understanding and sympathetic of the three.

"What was the piece you played?" asked Avner.

"Schubert," said Yossie.

"It was beautiful," said Avner. "Too bad you stopped."

"It was idiotic and ridiculous," said Yossie.

"I'm sorry you feel that way, I suppose you blame me for asking you to play."

"He's always like that," said Miri. "Like a prima donna. He thinks none of us deserves to hear him play. He saves his treasures for himself. Yaffa Yarkoni's good enough for us."

Yossie did not reply. He left them and went over to where Hedgehog and Micha were sitting.

"He's a strange boy," said Ziva. "You must know him by now from the army." Avner sensed how hard it had been for her to produce this sentence. She spoke as quietly and softly as she could — one of the grown-up airs she put on for effect. The sleeves of her blouse were puffed, slightly blurring the shape of the stooped shoulders that had so moved Avner's heart. In contrast to her friend Miri, she was dressed like a little girl. There was something strange and striking in the contradiction between her desire to look and sound like a grown-up and the childish clothes and femininity that had begun to blossom without yet finding its final form.

"Will you dance with me?"

Ziva blushed and immediately started raising her hand to her mouth, to hide some smile of embarrassment or shame, but the hand stopped halfway, and Avner could see the decision taking shape in her eyes, and her thin, transparently fair face tensing, sharpening, concentrating with increasing determination on setting its features into an expression of responsiveness that had something oddly cruel about it. She stood up and drew herself erect, her whole being proclaiming with an exaggerated flourish *Here I am!* But the sporting, would-be humorous smile did not disguise her profound disinclination for this, or any other, test. They walked over to the center of the room, where three other couples were already dancing. The radio was playing the tango "Jealousy." Ziva raised herself on tiptoe and said in the lowest voice she was capable of producing, right next to his ear: "I have to warn you that I don't know how to dance. I've never danced ballroom dances before."

He caught his breath at the sensation of her warm breath blowing onto his ear and cheek, spreading all over his back, seeping rapidly down to his depths, intoxicating him, almost making him weep tears of empathy and gratitude. The closeness he had so thirsted for found him unprepared, melted the defenses he had built up during the course of the evening, and threatened to return him to himself and turn off the movie.

"Neither have I," he said, "this is the first time I've ever danced in my life."

Her face darkened with apprehension, surprise, and disappointment. She stopped next to the dancers and asked: "So what will we do? I was relying on you to lead me."

"We'll do fine, don't worry."

"No. We'll look ridiculous. I don't want to."

Fear sometimes takes on irrelevant forms: For the first time in many hours, after all his determined efforts to forget the day before and Aliza's insulted feelings, and after it seemed to him that he had succeeded in shaking off the heaviness and gloom, the memory of the scene came back to him in all its details, the argument, the expression on her face as she climbed the steps on her way out of the shop, filling him with anger, hatred, and self-pity. Something inside him cried out: None of you is worth her little finger, I'm not worth her little finger! And this cry seemed to tell him that he was about to lose everything, that his excess of will had been his downfall again, and he was going to end up empty-handed.

Ziva took a step back toward her chair in the corner, and Avner grabbed her slender wrist and held it hard.

"What's the matter with you people that you're always frightened of looking ridiculous? Do you put on an act for each other all the time or what?"

His voice was audible all over the room. Everyone looked at them in surprise, embarrassment, and amused curiosity. And again the thought flashed through his mind, stunned by the sound of his voice thundering in the room, the thought about the cat: I did what they expected it to do, and it didn't do. Ziva's face turned bright red, he had never seen anyone blush so red, her eyes widened in fear, astonishment, pleading, but she made no attempt to free her hand from his. He lowered his voice, inclined his head toward her, and although he knew that everyone was watching them and they could all hear him, he said: "There, you see, I've just made myself look completely ridiculous. So what? Am I any the worse for it?"

"You're hurting my hand," said Ziva, and only the steely blueness coming at him from her wide-open eyes could rival the dry, decisive, cutting coldness of her voice.

At that moment he sensed that the hero of his movie had conquered the heart of the girl.

When he let go of her hand she glanced at him for a moment, examining his face with a searching, ironic, puzzled look, narrowing her cold eyes as if trying to see into him, refusing to believe the evidence of her eyes, wondering if it were possible that all this had seriously happened, how she could have gotten herself into it, where she had gone wrong. The intensity of her expression sharpened her features, etching shadows and angles on the smooth, fresh skin as if the source of light falling on her had suddenly changed. This intensity together with the vestiges of the blush lingering on her pale face, the narrowing of her eyes, and the lines of a sly, wary, suspicious, cruel, and provocative smile gave her an astonishing beauty that froze his heart and revived the sense of his utter insignificance in the world, the futility of his life, the dubious longings that had tempted him the night before when he had felt Benihu's hands tightening around his neck and called him to give up, to surrender, to be still.

She placed her hurt hand on his shoulder. The dance was in his body, waiting like a trained animal for a sign. He felt the touch of her hand on his shoulder, a sure, strong, intelligent touch, telling him something, seeking him, finding him, understanding him, wishing to calm and appease him. And he put his hand on her waist, and his other hand clasped her other hand, which was suspended in the air, in warning or self-defense. The warmth of her body flowing to him from her hand, her shoulder, her waist, her strange, new, intimate smell, the joy he had so yearned for,

burst the barriers that had been restraining his imagination since the
beginning of the evening, forbidding it to soar to the land of the pits and
snares of hope, that had sentenced him to absolute passivity, forcing him
to wait until she took the first step. He knew that he must not think about
his dancing feet and he had no doubt that he was dancing well. The hand
encompassing her waist exerted a gentle pressure to make her come
closer, and she offered no resistance.

He was just about to rest his chin on her shoulder when he heard her say
in a soft, husky voice: "And you said that you didn't know how to dance."

"I said I'd never danced before in my life," said Avner. "It's true, I don't
know how to dance. My body knows, when it feels happy. There are
some things you don't have to learn, that you know in advance. This
dance was waiting for you. It's been waiting a long time."

Her hand tightened slightly on his shoulder, squeezed and let go, as if
asking him to stop talking. He couldn't see her face, only feel its warmth.
The burst barriers allowed his imagination to picture various possibilities
in different places and times, in circumstances that he had never yet experienced. His inner mechanism refused to accept that its role was over and
went on signaling restraint, mystery, withdrawal, like a radio continuing
to send out routine instructions from a distant coast to a ship wrecked at
sea and abandoned by all its sailors, monotonous, detailed, logical, and
meaningless: Carry on according to plan, don't lose the advantage of
being a stranger, the battle isn't over yet, it's only begun, don't open your
heart, don't be grateful too soon, don't reveal the depths of the passion,
the hope, the eagerness, and the generosity burning inside you. All is not
yet lost. Nothing is certain. Don't let the illusion of certainty spoil the
plan. But his whole being rose up in rebellion. That emotion that may be
called the voice of life flooded him with a sensation of freedom and naturalness that could not be denied, banishing thoughts of pretense, caution, tactics from his heart: The joy of beginnings for which he had so
longed was here at last, the hour of purity, of mutual discovery and
making contact, of dreams.

Suddenly she raised her face and asked: "What's wrong, why are you
angry?"

"I'm not angry, what an idea!"

If he could have seen his face at that moment, he would have been
astonished at its gloom, its surliness, its air of suffering. Almost like
Ressler's face when he was playing. As if seeking a mirror in which to
examine his face he looked around him at the other people in the room
and discovered that they were all staring at him and Ziva. There was an

atmosphere of suspense in the room, of anticipation. Why weren't they staring so curiously at the other couples dancing with them? The tension and suspense surrounding him gave rise to a vague memory of some proud but joyless victory in the past.

He said to her: "All I want is for this dance never to finish." She looked at him with a smile of secret complicity, a reckless smile. "I didn't mean to shout before," he whispered into her ear, "somehow it came out like that. Out of panic. I was afraid. I thought I was beginning to lose you. From the minute I set eyes on you this evening I've been waiting to be alone with you. I don't have a bad temper. I'm not a difficult person. I'm much nicer and softer than you think."

"Why are you telling me all this?" asked Ziva.

"I love you."

"You don't even know me!" She blushed again and bit her lips so as not to burst out laughing.

"What did Ressler tell you about me?" he asked. "Did he run me down?"

"Not at all, he said very nice things about you."

The dance came to an end. Another dance began. Ziva removed her hand from his shoulder, took her other hand out of his, and stood facing him with a chastised smile, her arms hanging white and slender by her sides, looking as if she wanted to shrink to nothing and disappear. And again the sight of her narrow, slightly stooping shoulders under the puffed sleeves of her blouse moved him greatly, like something extraordinary and full of mystery, some graceful negligence of nature.

"One more dance," said Avner.

"Better not," said Ziva, "we're already the sensation of the evening. Look how everyone's staring."

He knew that she was testing him and he gave her an understanding, conciliatory smile, as if he were a past master at the art of compromise. Then he looked directly at her, as if to say: *You see, I'm not angry.*

"Ask Miri to dance, she likes you," said Ziva.

Her words stabbed him to the heart. He curbed the anger exploding inside him and repeated to himself that he was being tested. "You don't understand me, sweetie," he said. "I'm not a dancer! I told you I don't know how to dance. I can only dance out of love, when it comes of its own accord, naturally. Like what happened now, with you, for the first time."

"Your trouble is that you're too romantic," said Ziva. "I can't say that it hasn't got a certain charm, but be careful. Listen to me. You'd better be careful not to act like the hero of some trashy romance or some cheap

Hollywood movie, because then you'll simply be ridiculous. And there's nothing more off-putting, believe me."

She's trying to make me lose my temper, said Avner to himself. It's war, and whoever controls himself better will win. She's going for my weak spot. There's something really detestable about the way she's talking, as if she's trying to get out of it, to deny what happened a few minutes ago, a kind of vindictiveness, an attempt to dismiss the past with cowardly lies. And yet, instead of putting him off, her words seemed to hold out a promise of possible intimacy, if only he could overcome the obstacles she was setting in his way.

He stood where he was and watched her going back to her friend Miri. Was she really as beautiful as she seemed to him? Was she as attractive as he imagined her to be? He was too far gone by now to be able to answer these questions objectively. In any case it was clear to him that she was different from any of the girls he had had up to now, much more unattainable, and that she would make him eat his fill of gall. Maybe that was what he needed now.

She stood next to Miri with her back to him, her head slightly bowed, as if she were confessing something or apologizing, but it may have been only her narrow, stooping shoulders that gave him this impression: the shoulders he so yearned to embrace, as if they were some entity independent of the rest of her body, belonging and not belonging to the figure as a whole, revealing vulnerability and fear and innocence.

What were the two of them talking about? Maybe she was saying: What does he want of my life? He came here ready to fall in love with the first girl he set eyes on, as long as he didn't have to go home empty-handed, and for some reason he decided on me, and began bombarding me with those soulful looks of his, those mysterious smiles, those cheap Hollywood tricks he learned from the movies, thinking he could hypnotize me with his black eyes, make me feel sorry for him, make me feel guilty, as if the world owes him a living, as if somebody's to blame for his loneliness, which isn't a social problem but his own personal problem that he drags with him wherever he goes, and he wants instant gratification, he wants it on the spot, and if he doesn't get it — he'll scream and yell, he'll throw a temper tantrum, he'll make a scene, he'll make me look ridiculous, he'll make a spectacle of me in front of everybody.

Even from the distance, with her back to him, he thought he could make out the redness tingeing her ears. What was so scandalous about him, what was it that caused the embarrassment and the blushes, the fear of being made to look ridiculous, and the whispering behind his back?

He looked around him and did not know where to turn; there was no one in whom he could confide, no corner where he could seclude himself for a moment and introduce some order into his thoughts. He stood rooted to the spot in the middle of the room, trying to understand: What did they invite me for? Why did I come? What part am I expected to play in this childish game? What am I supposed to do now? Do I have to make some sort of decision?

Ziva knelt down at the foot of Miri's chair, bending her head and leaning on her arms with her hands on the floor. From behind she looked exactly as she had when she had knelt to stroke the cat. It had been a captivating spectacle, full of beauty and sensuality. He had no doubt that it had been put on for his benefit alone. The memory of those moments still thrilled him, instilling him with the confidence, the feverish optimism and impatience so familiar to him as the signs of falling in love. In these signs he found more encouragement than in her response to his closeness when they were dancing together. He didn't have much time left. The party would be over soon, everyone would go their separate ways — would he succeed in remaining alone with her and accompanying her home? That one dance couldn't possibly be the end of the story! He looked around and said to himself: These people came here to pass the time together, I came like someone trying to save his soul.

He went over to the two girls, sat down on the empty chair next to Miri's armchair, and offered them his almost empty pack of cigarettes, and Ziva took one with a polite smile. He lit a match and when he leaned forward to light her cigarette he looked closely at her face, at the intentness with which she gazed at the flame, as if drawn to its magic, at her lowered lids, at the thin, precise eyebrows that seemed to express strength and ambition. She did not breathe the smoke into her lungs but sucked it between her lips as if she were whistling something soundlessly, her eyes looking pensively sideways.

He took a sandwich from the plate on the table projecting from the stem of the lamp and began to eat it, more out of nervousness than hunger.

"That Hedgehog of yours," said Miri, "doesn't stop shrieking like a backward child. What made you take that vulgar creature to your bosoms?"

"He's not my Hedgehog, he's your pals' Hedgehog. He's your Yossie's best friend. When I was a kid I used to beat him up on Zion Square, and that was the last I saw of him until the army. Then he still had side locks curled up behind his ears. He had some neurotic need to be beaten up, and I satisfied it for him."

Ziva burst into soundless laughter, put her hand over her mouth, and bowed down to the ground, prostrate with mirth. When she straightened her back her face was red, and her eyes expressed gratitude for the pleasure afforded her by his witticism.

"Ressler," said Miri, "always needs somebody to hide behind, somebody to protect him from the filth of the world, somebody to get dirty instead of him — every Narcissus needs its toad."

"He's a very unique person, you must know that by now," said Ziva. "One day we'll all be proud of having known him."

"You're all so unique," said Avner, "that it's difficult for an ordinary, nonunique person to understand you, or behave naturally in your company."

He finished the sandwich and the cigarette, stood up, and said to Miri: "Will you dance with me?"

Why was she so surprised? She shot a glance at Ziva, as if seeking advice or approval, but Ziva who was sitting kneeling on the floor, her skirt encircling her body and covering her legs, turned her head in the other direction as if she hadn't heard a thing. Even when Miri walked from the corner to the center of the room with him, there was still a confused expression on her face. He hadn't taken the surprise into account: She, who was always tensed to meet failure by belittling the value of the prize in advance, she who was always ready to adjust herself to frustration with bitter repartee, with an old lady's sour, knowing smile, had been caught out in hesitation, in astonishment. Avner wondered if it wasn't a trick played on her by her best friend, with him as the instrument. He couldn't believe that she simply wanted to get rid of him and distract his attention from her.

"What's this dance called?" he asked.

"I think it's a slow foxtrot," said Miri.

"I'll dance it the way I feel it, okay? You're not afraid of looking ridiculous?"

"Nobody here knows how to dance, if that's what's worrying you. Dance however you like. I'll follow your lead."

He looked at the feet of the other dancers for a minute, clasped her around the waist, and began the slow dance. She was wearing high heels, which made her even taller than she already was, her eyes were a little higher than his, her body was soft, she smelled good, and something in her expression, her doubtful, apologetic smile, strengthened his feeling that he was retreating to familiar positions, going back to the security he had sought to escape, to the well-trodden paths, the landscapes that no longer had anything left to hide from him. His heart refused to accept it.

He clasped her body to his, he felt her breasts against his chest, he felt her thighs, her neck, he squeezed her hand in his as hard as he could, as if calling out to her: *Forgive me and help me!*

"What are you looking for, Avner?" He heard her voice, cutting and ironic, in his ear.

"You. Do you like me?"

"When people ask me that question, I know that I'm going to have to do somebody a favor."

"Okay, never mind."

"What's eating you? Go on, pour out your heart to Auntie Miri."

"You can't stand me, can you?"

"Say what you want."

"Tell me about her."

"What do you want to know?"

"Has she got a boyfriend?"

"Yes."

"Who?"

"A student."

"So why didn't he come with her?"

"He went to Tel Aviv for the holiday, to his parents."

"A student," said Avner.

"And an officer in the paratroops," added Miri.

"Do you think I interest her?"

"There are certain things about you that might interest a girl," said Miri.

He moved his cheek closer to hers and tried to kiss her but she averted her face and said: "There's no need to exaggerate."

"He's better looking than I am," said Avner.

"I don't think that's what interests her," said Miri.

"So I don't stand a chance with her."

"Why ask me? Try."

"I want to try and see her home after the party."

"I wish you luck," said Miri. "I won't get in the way, I promise."

He glanced at the place where they had left Ziva, but she wasn't there.

"You've changed, Avner," said Miri. "You've lost some of your sparkle, your self-confidence. What's happened to you?"

"Soon my hair will go gray, in our family we go gray early, gradually I'll go out of my mind, and in the end they'll send me to sit in Jaffa Street and sell peanuts next to the bus station. And when you walk past with your children you'll drag them away as quickly as you can so you won't have to stop and look me in the eye —"

"Stop it, for goodness' sake, I don't want to hear any more," said Miri. "The trouble with you is that you see too many movies."

"Not anymore," said Avner. "I've stopped going."

His eyes searched the room. Ziva was standing next to the group around Hedgehog and Micha, who were apparently still telling jokes, judging by the occasional bursts of laughter coming from their corner. No one was paying any attention to the dancers. Avner was no longer creating a sensation; the sensation was standing there next to the laughers, her head slightly cocked, as if someone were whispering a secret in her ear, but no one was whispering anything in her ear. Yossie Ressler, who was sitting behind her astride a chair, hugging the backrest and leaning his chin on it, was staring into space. And again an invisible dome seemed to rise up and encompass the pair of them, a circle of secret stillness within the din of dance music and laughter, within the pools of light and shadow in the big room, and Avner paused in the middle of a turn in order to go on looking at her and said to himself: If she catches my eye and looks at me, it's a sign that I stand a chance. But it seemed that nothing could rouse her from her thoughts. Not even Yossie Ressler, who said something to her, causing her to turn her head toward him, and then immediately turn back to her previous position, for no more was needed, a word was enough between these two. Avner twirled his partner blindly, while the picture etched too deeply in his heart for him to bear went on disturbing him, the picture of the two of them next to the group and set apart from it, sheltering beneath the wings of some dark, secret grace. The bond between them seemed to him suspect, repelling, threatening to the natural order of things.

"What's going on between Ressler and Ziva?" he asked.

"Why?"

"Something really upsets me when I see them together, and believe me, it's not jealousy. What is there between them?"

"I don't know. They've always been like that, all these years, ever since I've known them, maybe ever since they went to kindergarten together."

"Like brother and sister," Avner ventured.

"I don't know. Maybe."

This was the thing he had not dared say to himself before. Like brother and sister, like incest. Now, for some reason, he had the courage to face it. It was this that had painted the picture in such dark, menacing colors, made it repellent and fascinating, arousing destructive impulses and forbidden longings. He did not know what would be easier to bear: finding out that there had been something between them, or not. Both possibilities seemed equally hateful, equally tainted by a curse that excited and horrified him, banishing the bittersweet melancholy in which he had been wrapped for the last hour or so, passive, groundlessly optimistic and full of self-pity. As if he had now found firm principles in whose name he could set out to do battle.

Avner and Miri turned again, and again he saw them. Still as statues, sunk in their sick, damned world. Again he concentrated his eyes on her, and immediately she raised her head and looked at him from the far end of the room, as if waking from a trance, responding to his sad, under-standing, forgiving look. He knew that this was the true beginning. Things had begun to happen in the real world. He had emerged from the watery world with its vague, floating images, ambiguous and ceaselessly changing, calling on him to sink, to forget, to merge. The tall girl dancing with him, her body so close to his, so alive inside him, took him back to the precise, shameful hour in his life that he had been trying to forget ever since he first set eyes on her this evening. Her closeness now felt good and human, demanding empathy and identification. Again he put his cheek against hers — this time she did not avert her face — and he whispered in her ear: "Don't think I've forgotten, please forgive me."

"What are you talking about?" asked Miri. "I don't think I've got any-thing to forgive you for." Her voice trembled as she spoke, as if she were begging him not to remember, not to remind her. But he was imbued with a spirit of renewal and sense of mission: He wanted to purify him-self before he set out to fight the monster.

"For what happened that night, the first time we met, and I behaved like an idiot and a swine."

"No," said Miri, "I don't remember anything, I think you must be con-fusing me with someone else."

"Please, I beg you to remember so you can forgive me."

The dance ended, their hands loosened, and he followed her to the corner where they had previously left Ziva and which was now deserted. His eyes went on imploring her.

"What's the matter with you?" asked Miri. "You want me to relive it all again now so that you can get your forgiveness?" She spoke as if she couldn't believe her ears. "Why are you doing this to me?"

"Please, you can't just leave things like that alone."

"You're a strange boy, Avner. Really strange." She looked at him for a moment, examining his face, trying to understand his intentions, afraid of some new trick. "What do you think, that there's any difference between what you're doing now and what you did then? With you it's always the same basic principle: You use people like instruments. Then you used me to make an impression on the others and show them how easily you could pick up a girl and make a fool of her, and this evening you're using me to get Ziva, and God knows what your real aim is in wanting Ziva. But as you see, I don't care. I was prepared to cooperate with you. I don't have anything against you. On the contrary, I like you. I even feel sorry for you. But don't think I didn't understand what you were up to right from the start. Your head's full of scenes from the movies, and they taught you that the best way to get a girl is to flirt with her best friend and make her jealous."

"That's not true, Miri," said Avner, "it really isn't true." His heart was flooded with a strange, liberating happiness, at last he was standing on the real battlefield, aiming at the target.

"What you don't understand, Avner, is that as far as I'm concerned you're a baby. You don't know me. You're knocking your head against a stone wall. Those Hollywood tricks don't have any effect on me. Don't you understand that?"

"You hate me."

"Are you crazy? I knew from the start what you were using me for, and I did it gladly, out of true friendship, to prove to myself and to you that I'd gotten over that business, that I'd wiped the slate clean, scraped it off like a bit of mud from my shoe, and that now I really like you, as if nothing had ever happened between us. But up to now I hoped that you would be decent enough not to drag it up. It seemed to me that it was in both our interests to forget it and ignore it. I never imagined that you would suddenly start with this kitschy forgiveness act, against all common sense and minimum decency. And now do me a favor, Avner, take me out of your movies."

He stood next to her listening with downcast eyes and a chastised smile to her whispered words, which came pouring out in a rather monotonous flood like a speech prepared long in advance, ready and waiting for when the right opportunity came along. He was grateful to her for the thrill of reality she sent shooting through him, the tension and conflict promising a world of openness and mutual relations.

"So why is it so hard for you to say that you forgive me, if you like me and even feel sorry for me, and I tell you that it bothers me so much and makes me ashamed of myself?"

"Because I don't forgive you! Can't you understand? I haven't forgiven you and I don't want to forgive you. I've simply vomited it out of my system. As far as I'm concerned the whole thing never happened. I relate to you now like another person, not the one from that night in the past, and I'm not the same person that you remember either, but someone else, someone you don't know. We met here tonight for the first time. We danced, we talked, tomorrow or the next day you'll forget me, I'll forget you, and life will go on. And I don't want to talk about it anymore."

And she stood up and walked away, very calmly and deliberately, as if trying to hide her agitation, and went over to stand next to Ziva and Yossie Ressler. The radio stopped playing. The dancing was over. The party was coming to an end. All evening he had been too preoccupied with himself to engage in any social contacts, to take an interest in anything not connected to himself and the goal he had set himself. Like a man possessed, as if it were not his own battle alone that he was setting out to fight, as if he believed that the eyes of all the downtrodden of the world were upon him, all those who had no hope of salvation, and whose blessing was vitally important to him, so full of a sense of vocation was he.

"Did you enjoy yourself?" asked Hanan. "You see that it was worth your while to come?"

"I never doubted it. Thanks for inviting me. Your girls are really cute."

"The fruit's ripe for the picking," said Hanan.

"Really?" exclaimed Avner. "You really think it could be serious?"

Hanan retreated somewhat in the face of the eagerness in Avner's voice, as if afraid of taking the responsibility: "Look, you're the expert. You don't need me to give you lessons."

"Listen, she's fantastic," said Avner. "She's not just some girl to spend an evening with. And now even the evening's gone." He sighed.

Hanan sang: "Heigh-ho, heigh-ho, it's back to work we go . . ."

Avner shuddered at the thought that tomorrow, early in the morning, they were all going back to that terrible place, and this evening would turn into a memory, to an obscure pang in the heart. People began to leave, Ziva hung her sweater on her back, and the empty sleeves dangling from her shoulders like two limp arms caressed her breasts. Outside nobody wanted to break up the party yet; they all stood around the street lamp opposite the house. Hedgehog came up to Avner and said: "Are you coming? We're going in the same direction."

"No," said Avner, "we're going in two different directions."

The sound of Ziva's laughter, closer to him than he thought, rose strong and confident in his ears. He turned his face toward her; her hand was no longer covering her mouth and her eyes told him that her appreciation of his wit was no less warm than her pleasure at Hedgehog's discomfort. He approached her, looked into her eyes, and was not embarrassed to say in front of everyone: "I'm going in your direction."

Yossie Ressler said: "The third E above middle C, Avner, remember the sound! On some tomcats it works," and he broke into terrible laughter. This laughter devastated his face. As long as his narrow, monkish, bony, ascetic face preserved its relative calm, or wore an expression of gloomy anger, it hinted at a delicate, spiritual, unfinished beauty, like an intention not yet realized; but his strange, rare laughter seemed to break some inner mechanism that held his features together and united them into a whole, coordinating their movements, imposing order, discipline, and cooperation on them. Ressler's face was in terrible disarray, like a battlefield in the wake of a massacre. His lips grinned and pursed alternately, the corners of his mouth jerked in nervous spasms, his eyes darted around as if seeking something to hold on to, to stop them falling out of his head, his nose twitched and sniffed like a hare, various little muscles and bones in his temples, his forehead, his cheeks and jaws rebelled against their covering of skin, straining to break out of hiding and take part in the hilarity.

Avner looked at him with narrowed eyes, concentrating all the power of his insult and hatred on him, as if conjuring them to strike him down. If only he could have knocked him down there and then with the power of his look, if only he could have made him scream with pain and fury, a scream that would break the surrounding silence, reverberate from house to house, from garden to garden, from street to street, like a public admission of his disgrace, his defeat. The spectacle taking place on Yossie's face filled him with loathing and the lust for revenge, the wish to hit him sent new energy rushing through his body, tensed him like a spring, but when he looked at Ziva, he saw that she was smiling the same smile at Yossie she had smiled before, in response to his reply to Hedgehog. This impartiality, this smile that showed no favor to anyone, cooled him down and made him understand that Yossie's hatred was no less important to him than his wish to hurt him.

Ziva said: "It's late."

This was the signal to say good-bye. Yossie said: "Good night. See you tomorrow. Everything's over now." His voice was still unsteady after the convulsion of laughter that had raged through him previously, but his face was gradually recomposing itself. There was a look of embarrassment and regret in his eyes, as if he were sorry to have demeaned himself in so degrading a fashion.

They exchanged good wishes for the New Year and broke up, with one group turning off into a side street. Avner stayed with the group walking in the direction of King George Street. Hedgehog was the first to separate from them, striding alone up the street until he was swallowed up by the darkness. Ziva said: "Good riddance!" Next to Gaza Street Raffy the officer cadet and Ruthie, the girl with the woolly hair, said good-bye. When they reached the Terra Sancta Monastery building, Avner and Ziva and Miri stopped at the foot of the steps leading to the entrance, and Miri laid her hand on his shoulder and said: "Happy New Year. Hang in there." Then she took a few steps with Ziva, exchanged a few words with her, waved at him again, and walked away. Her tall, gawky silhouette strode off briskly, her head bowed, her body leaning forward as if she were advancing against some invisible tide in the dark, deserted street.

A bell chimed in the distance, one single chime of a church bell, deep, muffled, and explosive as the sound of a dish shattering to pieces, echoed for a few seconds and was not repeated, a lost moment escaping by mistake from the system of hours and half hours and quarter hours. And silence fell again.

"You don't have to see me all the way home. I live here in Lincoln Street, just around the corner," said Ziva.

"But you don't mind if I walk with you anyway?"

"No, not at all."

"Because I've been waiting all night for these few moments. It was because of you that I came to the party."

"Really? I thought it was because of Miri."

"Why did you think that?"

"When I saw you dancing together I thought there was something going on between you."

"Is that what it looked like?"

"Definitely."

"But you asked me to dance with Miri, I only did it because you asked me to."

"Thank you," said Ziva. "Nobody's ever done what I asked them to so enthusiastically before. From where I was sitting it looked as if you were about to rape her right there in the room."

So the cheap Hollywood tricks worked anyway. They were stronger than all the sarcasm and cynicism and superiority.

"I didn't know who was going to be at the party. Nobody told me who was coming."

"So how can you say you came because of me? That sounds like Hottentot logic to me."

He had never heard the word before, but it had a gay, exotic, tuneful sound that filled his heart with joy.

"You're angry with me," said Avner. "And I thought that I was punishing myself for your sake."

"Look," said Ziva, "I also knew from the minute I saw you at the party that in the end you would see me home and we would be alone together; I knew that that whole infantile, idiotic party would only be a long, boring introduction to the few minutes that would come afterward."

"Seriously?" he cried, with excessive enthusiasm.

"Yes. But don't think that means that something's going to happen between us. It doesn't imply that these last minutes will have any special importance. It doesn't mean that anything's going to happen now that didn't happen before."

They began to walk, turned right along the Terra Sancta wall, crossed the street, and continued in silence until they came to a corner that was flooded with the scent of pines. Ziva stopped, leaned against a low stone fence, took hold of the sleeves of the sweater hanging from her shoulders, and tightened them around her throat, as if she wanted to strangle herself. Avner came closer to her and put his face next to hers, as if he were trying to examine it in the darkness. She recoiled and drew her head back. The expression on her face was once more alert, intense, concentrated, inquiring, and hostile. Her eyes narrowed as if in an attempt get to the root of his intentions, suspicious eyes, bold and challenging and slightly amused, while her lips were parted with a certain slackness, as if to express astonishment, irony, perhaps sadness.

"You're the most beautiful girl I've ever seen in my life," said Avner. He put out his hand to stroke her straight, fair, short hair and the nape of her neck, and she let him, she offered no resistance at all; only her hands tightened the sleeves of the sweater around her neck, as a last line of defense. Her eyes remained fixed inquiringly on his, showing no signs of embarrassment. A car drove slowly past behind them, its headlights suddenly illuminating Ziva's eyes with a strange, electric glint, like the glint in the eyes of a cat.

"What do you feel about me?" asked Avner. He put his cheek against hers, closed his eyes to abandon himself to the smooth softness of the touch, breathing in her warmth, her unknown, subtle, promising smell.

"Liking, curiosity, surprise, fear," said her voice in his ear, a distant, mature voice, as if she were standing apart, critical and appraising, not the girl whose hair he was stroking and whose cheek was brushing his, the girl who was tightening the sleeves of the sweater around her neck like a lost little girl.

"Is that all?"

"Isn't it enough?"

"Depends for what."

"What do you already expect to happen?"

"Give me some hope, at least," begged Avner.

She let go of the sleeves of her sweater, took his face in both her hands, moved it away from hers a little, and looked at it, as if she were scrutinizing some object whose nature was not clear to her. Her eyes contemplated his sloping forehead, his thick brows meeting over the bridge of his nose, frowning in an expression of anxiety and pain.

"Why so depressed? What's wrong?"

"Look, we met at a moment when I'm beginning my life as a man and my whole world is collapsing under my feet."

He couldn't understand why he said this to her. Perhaps because her two hands holding his head, impressing his cheeks with a soft, new, unique warmth that flowed through his whole body, forbade him to avert his eyes from the questioning look that was trying to penetrate the opaque shell separating one person from another, the reality from the dream. For a second he had the peculiar feeling that he was both self and other at the same time, and that what she saw in him was no less true than what he really felt or thought about himself. And although it would never have occurred to him that he looked depressed, in his opinion nothing could have been farther from what he was feeling at these moments than depression; he believed that the expression on his face, or the forces shaping it and changing it from one moment to the next, were already aware of how it would all end, already experiencing the disillusion of the awakening, while he was still crawling after the will-o'-the-wisps of the dream.

She removed her hands from his face. Her eyes swiveled around in their sockets, as if trying to look inside herself, full of resistance to anything that might distract her from her thoughts. He was silent, looking at her as if his fate were hanging in the balance, and after she raised her eyes to him again, as if she had taken some sort of decision, he said: "I thought that you felt it too, something strange and wonderful about our meeting."

"What?" Her voice was tired.

"That we met this evening for the first time, that we don't know each other, and nevertheless something deep, spiritual, connects us to each other, as if we should have met a long time ago, as if we've known each other for a long time without meeting, as if we were waiting for it, preparing for it. Or does that sound Hottentotish to you?"

"It's late already," said Ziva.

And he didn't know if all she meant was that it was late at night and she wanted to go home to bed, or if she was trying to tell him that they had met too late for anything to come of it. In any case the dread of missed opportunity was hanging in the air, accompanied by the dismaying knowledge that early the next morning he was going back there, perhaps defeated and empty-handed.

"If only I had something that was worth not going back to the base for tomorrow, going AWOL, getting in trouble, getting court-martialed, going to jail, even just for the sake of the hope; if anything depended on me, on my will, my strength, my readiness to pay with suffering, humiliation, danger, I wouldn't give it a second thought. If there's nothing like that, then what's the point of living?"

"Is that what you meant when you said that the world was collapsing under your feet?"

No, he didn't know what he meant when he said those words, he felt that he was losing control over what he said to her, as if the words were being dictated to him from outside, foreign even to his own ears.

"Yes," he said, "if only I knew that I had some sort of chance with you, that we would meet again, that there would be some sort of relationship between us, I wouldn't go back to the army tomorrow. I would go into hiding somewhere and wait to hear from you, to see you, to love you. I love you, believe me, it's not just the natural attraction to a girl as beautiful as you. My longings for you are like longings for some part of myself that hasn't yet had the opportunity to emerge, to live. It's like returning to yourself after wandering in foreign lands. I don't know if you understand what I mean."

Ziva sighed very faintly, almost inaudibly. She took his hand and held it soothingly, as if trying to calm a sick, feverish, delirious person. There was encouragement in her grip and the promise of friendship but not real love. Above all, perhaps, it conveyed her wish to conclude the meeting in a spirit of goodwill.

She said: "You don't know me at all, you don't know what kind of a person I am. I don't believe in love at first sight."

He refused to give in. "Just like you felt the minute you saw me that in the end we'd be alone together and I'd walk home with you, I felt straight away that I'd met a kindred soul. I'd never heard of you, I didn't know there was this girl called Ziva in Jerusalem, but really and truly I knew that I was going to meet you at the party tonight. That's why I broke off a long affair I've been having with someone who's madly in love with me.

I hurt her. I had no choice. I knew that I was going to meet you there, even though I didn't know who you were. And when I saw you, I recognized you, I knew it was you that I'd been waiting for all this time. Didn't you feel it when we danced? As if we'd known each other for a long time, in a common dream perhaps, as if we were both waiting for this meeting?"

Where did these words come from, words that weren't his, words that didn't even express what he imagined he felt? They came out of his mouth without any prompting on his part. Were they the words that would move her to return his love? He didn't know. A force not his put the words into his mouth, and as soon as he said them they sounded more sincere and persuasive and true than the truth itself.

"When people fall in love, or think they're falling in love, or want to fall in love, they always feel like that, don't they?"

"Look," he said to her, "I don't know what you know about me, what you've heard about me. I've had some experience of love. But it's never happened like this. I was always attracted to the mystery, the secret, the strangeness. When I fell in love with someone, I always fell in love with her enigma, her secret. What attracted me was always the wish to break into her mystery, to find the solution, to destroy her secret. Now I know that it was really a destructive love. Because the minute it seemed to me that there was no secret and no mystery, or that I was coming close to a solution, the disillusionment began and it was the beginning of the end for me. And then all that's left is habit and bitterness and lies and power games and the need to hurt. With you it's the opposite. I'm attracted to you precisely because of the feeling that we know each other, that the secret is one we have in common, like a page out of a book torn in half lengthwise, with each of us possessing one half that's impossible to read or understand. Only if we put the two halves together will we be able to read and understand what's written on that page. Separately, neither of us will be able to live our secret. That's how I feel. I suppose you think that everything I've just said is rubbish from Hollywood movies or trashy romances."

"No," said Ziva, "I believe that you're sincere in what you say. But, how shall I put it . . ."

She let go of his hand and gripped the sleeves of her sweater again, dropped her head, and said: "It sounds fine but it's not relevant to me at all. I don't know what to do with it. Do you understand?"

"You don't feel the same way I do about our meeting?"

"Maybe I do feel it, and that's the problem. That's why it's hard for me to say what I have to say to you. And I have to say it, I have to tell you to stop before you begin to charge full speed ahead and fall flat on your face. I don't want to hurt you. I have feelings for you too. Feelings of closeness, of friendship, even though we don't even know each other. But I don't want to lead you on. I don't want to feed a fire that will be impossible to put out afterward. What I really want to say to you is that you're like someone offering a gift, the most precious gift imaginable, and I don't even have anywhere to put it. I don't know what to do with it. And how can I return such a gift, how can I refuse to accept it without destroying something very precious, perhaps even holy? I don't know. It's always impossible. But the alternative's impossible too. So if you really love me, I beg you, in the name of that love, to stop loving me. If you love me and want to help me, it's not as paradoxical as it sounds."

The international words she used, with their non-Hebrew roots, words like *alternativa, paradoxali,* intoxicated him, filling his heart with a new, thrilling, Hottentotish tune, promising unimaginable possibilities of new love and happiness.

"Go back to the base tomorrow without problems and crazy ideas. Promise me. I know you meant it seriously. I can feel your temperament, and I know you're quite capable of doing mad things. You have to prove all kinds of things to yourself and others all the time. One of the reasons I like you is your temperament."

He put out his hand to embrace her, but she was too quick for him. She seized both his hands and locked his fingers in hers and smiled at him like a generous, understanding, sympathetic victor. This smile confirmed what he had said to her earlier, reciting words he felt were being dictated to him by some external source, about the deep, mysterious bond between them. He had never felt so revealed, so understood by another; he had never felt the other with such simple, direct, definitive clarity before.

"There, see how nice you are when you smile at last. You see that no tragedy is happening. We've both gained something. We're both conceding something. That's all."

He didn't know that he was smiling. Their interlocking fingers joined them in his imagination into a kind of circle transmitting their respective feelings, thoughts and even facial expressions to each other, while at the same time defining them as two separate poles with no direct contact with each other.

"I know you've got a boyfriend," he said, "and I know who and what he is. Miri told me. Don't think I don't understand what I am in comparison to him: Nothing. A miserable creature. A stupid black monkey. A primitive buffoon, an ignoramus —"

"Why do you feel a need to humiliate yourself?" asked Ziva. "So that I'll have to deny it and tell you that you're handsome, charming, intelligent, sensitive?"

"No," sighed Avner, "that's not it. I wanted to tell you that underneath all those things, which I know are important and which I don't take lightly, deep down at the roots of our beings this special bond exists which we both feel, the voice of life drawing us to each other, calling us to follow it to the end, and maybe that's the most important thing of all —"

"No," pleaded Ziva, "please don't go on talking like that, it won't help."

And once more she averted her face, as if examining something in the mass of darkness on the other side of the street. He tried to free his fingers from hers, gently, as if casually, in order to get closer to her, to try to embrace her again, to make her submit, but he couldn't do it, he was a prisoner in her hands.

"You're on the defensive."

"Yes."

"I won't do anything you don't want me to."

"I know."

"Tell me about him."

"It's not necessary. You said yourself that you already know about him. Why drag him into it?"

"You make me feel as if I'll dirty him if we talk about him."

"Nonsense, whatever gave you that idea? What do you want to know about him?"

"For instance, what's he studying at the university?"

"Economics and philosophy."

"He must be really tough. An officer in the paratroops, who took part in raids across the border, faced all kinds of dangers."

"He crossed the border on his own to go to the red rock at Petra too," said Ziva dreamily, "and anyone who's been there and seen it and come back alive is marked for life."

"How marked?"

"It's hard to explain. It's like a special kind of beauty."

"How long have you been dating?"

"About two years."

"That's a long time."

"With you does it usually last less?" asked Ziva, and in the even tone of her quiet voice there was no way of knowing if she was really interested or if she was trying to be sarcastic.

"I'd like to meet him," said Avner.

"Are you a masochist?"

"Am I at such a disadvantage?"

"You don't have a chance."

"You're so patient with me. Another girl would have sent me packing long ago."

At this she let go of his hands. He put his hands in his pockets, took out his cigarette pack, extracted the last cigarette, crumpled the empty pack, tightened his fist around it and crushed it hard, and threw it into the street, as far as he could, in a sudden fit of blind rage that signaled the beginning of surrender.

"I want us to be friends," said Ziva.

For a moment he was silent. The insult burned in his heart. He looked at her face, at her slender shoulders, at her neck encompassed by the sleeves of the sweater. "Friends?" he asked. "That sounds great, but what does it actually mean? Do you really think that a boy and a girl who're attracted to each other, like we are, can be friends without love and sex coming into it? What kind of friendship can there ever be between a boy and a girl? Unless they're attracted to each other like a man and a woman, and then it's the sexual attraction that interests them in each other and keeps them together. Friendship can exist between members of the same sex. And that's something else entirely. And I, for your information, have dreamed all my life of friendship. Of love and friendship. I've had love, as I told you before, but never friendship. I don't know yet what friendship is. I dream about it. But I haven't lived it yet. Where friendship is concerned, you could say that I'm a virgin. But how can I have a friendship with a girl? You can't mean it seriously."

"I certainly do," said Ziva. "I'm not ignoring the problems, but I'm positive that if they really want to, then it's possible for a boy and a girl to have a friendly relationship even if they're physically attracted to each other and all the rest of it. In any case it's worth trying, it could be really nice."

"Nice?" exclaimed Avner. "In my opinion it would be hell on earth. Give me hope, hope at least," he pleaded.

"Why do you keep talking about hope?" asked Ziva. "I can't tell you to hope, it would be like giving you an IOU due at some date in the future, and judging by the way I feel now I can't see the situation changing in the future. But how can I tell? Who knows what can happen, how things may develop, how our attitudes may change, how we ourselves may change? All I know is that I want to stay in touch with you, and be able to see you and meet you again. And that's it. As for hope, we'll have to leave it to its own devices and let it fly where it likes, free as a bird. I'm offering you a corner of my life, inviting you to come in and share it, but you keep insisting on taking over the living room, or, to be more precise, the bedroom. You have to understand: Those rooms are occupied. Full stop. I'm offering you friendship. Are you afraid of the difficulties? Let's try and overcome them. Where's your sense of adventure? Crossing the border and going to Petra is more dangerous, I promise you. I don't want you to disappear from my life now. Now that I've met you, I don't want to give you up, don't you understand, Avner?"

"I don't want to give you up either. But look, you're offering me a gift now, the most wonderful gift you're apparently able to afford at the present moment, and I don't know what to do with it, I don't know what's inside the wrappings, perhaps it's something so fragile that it'll break the minute I touch it and all that will remain is suffering and pain?"

"You're afraid," said Ziva.

"Yes."

He jumped up and sat on the stone wall, gave her his hand, and pulled her up to sit beside him. He put his arm around her shoulder and gave it a squeeze: "Is that permitted between friends?"

She laughed softly.

"I am afraid, you're right. I'm attracted and frightened at once. I don't want to be like Yossie Ressler. I can't bear to even think of it."

She was silent. For a minute neither of them spoke. He smoked his cigarette and looked into the darkness, as if seeking in it release from his distress, a way out of his predicament. Suddenly the silence was broken by the chime of a bell, and immediately after it another, and then another, more distant, responded, the chimes of the midnight hour followed each other in swift succession, filling the night air with a proud, solemn reverberation, striking and shattering and disappearing into the distance, falling and breaking. Ziva put her arm around his shoulder, squeezed his arm with her hand, and said: "Listen to how beautiful it is. After so many years I still haven't grown accustomed to how beautiful it is, I haven't grown indifferent to it. It still sends shivers of excitement down my spine when I hear the bells chime."

He said: "You know, I don't understand why this memory is coming back to me now of all times, after I'd forgotten it for so long. I can see it now as if it happened yesterday. I was a little boy, maybe ten years old. I was sitting in my room and I looked out through the window. It was winter. The sky was gray and heavy and it hadn't yet snowed. All winter I'd been waiting for the snow and it had betrayed me too. I had already given up hope of snow that winter. And then, as I was sitting at the table opposite the window, I saw the white feathers beginning to float in the sky. I ran to the window to look, and slowly everything turned white. The pavement, the street, the rooftops. And the stillness, that strange stillness that always accompanies the falling snow, as if the world has stopped breathing for a moment in honor of the occasion. And I wanted to be happy and I couldn't. I stood opposite the window and felt the tears coming into my eyes and I didn't know how to stop them. Tears of disappointment. I began talking to the outside, softly, almost soundlessly, just moving my lips, and I said — I remember the first sentence exactly — *Snow, snow, if all this is especially for my benefit, then you needn't bother, it's not worth it.*

"I don't remember exactly what else I said but it was more or less this: It's not worth the effort. It's wasted on me. I don't need it. Go to other children, maybe they'll get something out of it, maybe they'll be happy. It's a shame to waste all this beauty on me. And then, I think, I understood for the first time that beautiful landscapes and red sunsets and flowers and nature and starry skies, all that wasn't for me. It was wasted on me. That I would always look for living people. Their voices, their faces, their smiles, the bad or good things they did, the things they said, the things they felt. The smile of a girl I don't know, of some pretty girl passing me in the street, is more beautiful to me than all the bells in the world, than all the sunsets and the flowers."

"But you love music. Yossie told me that you know classical works. The bells are like music, aren't they?"

"For me they're like the wind, the rain, the thunder. To me it sounds like nature, like a machine. Someone once said to me: *Music is the language in which the soul speaks to itself.* I can't forget it. It's the farthest thing from nature and the closest to our inner voice, to the voice of life. That's the difference. You see, once I thought that music was an escape, a call to dream, like getting into bed and pulling the sheet up over your head, as if you haven't been born yet. But today I feel as if it's an invitation to a journey into yourself. It's frightening and very compelling and real. Because my red rock is inside me. I have to reach it. And it's farther away than that red rock in Jordan. The way there is no less dangerous. And if anyone reaches it, the beauty stays with him all his life. I don't know if I'll ever get there, and if I do get there, I don't know if I'll get back safely. But sometimes, at rare moments like these, moments of reconciliation, peace, I think I can catch a glimpse of some edge, some shadow of something that belongs to it, beyond the mountains, beyond the desert, beyond the dust and the fog. And then I feel that everything's worth it, and I wouldn't be prepared to give up any of the pain, any of the humiliation, any of the suffering that I've suffered all my life."

The chiming of the bells stopped. For a few seconds the tremor in the air went on echoing plaintively. Ziva removed her arm from his shoulder, looked at her watch as if to ascertain that it really was midnight, since the musical beauty of the bells was presumably unconnected in her mind to their technical, social function. But she could not see the hands of the watch in the darkness.

She said: "Strange that you ignore the beauty outside human beings, the beauty around them. A French writer once said that beauty was a promise of happiness. Ever since I read it, every time I see something beautiful I ask myself: What happiness does this beauty promise? If a man sees a beautiful woman, it's obvious what her beauty promises him. But what about a beautiful sunset, the chiming of the bells in the Old City at night, the sunrise over the Sea of Galilee? A moment ago, when you were talking about the red rock inside you, I thought: Perhaps the beauty of nature is the promise of metaphysical beauty? I don't know exactly what metaphysical beauty is, but it seems to me that it exists and that we can catch glimpses of it but never know it, only the promise of it's possibility."

"And what does your beauty promise me?" asked Avner, in a half-serious, half-humorous tone: "What happiness does it promise me?"

"It promises you possibilities that may never be realized, and in fact most probably won't be. It's late. We both have to get up very early in the morning. And you'll get up and go back to the army tomorrow like a good boy and not make any problems. Otherwise it's all over between us. And now it's time to say good-bye." She laid her hand on the back of his neck and began to stroke it, slowly drawing his face toward hers. Thus encouraged, he moved in eagerly to embrace her, but she immediately seized his face in her hands and held it there, as if to say *This far and no farther,* evading his arms with calm confidence and practiced skill. He gave in. Slowly she drew his face toward hers until their lips touched, a light, brushing contact, soft and delicate as the flesh itself. He tried to get between her lips, but she pursed her mouth, pushed his face away, and then drew it slowly forward until their lips touched again, and when she saw that he was willing to submit to her authority, she kissed him on his closed mouth as if sending him some mysterious blessing, a kiss that was a little more than a token of friendship, and less, a lot less, than the love he desired. He gave her back the same kind of kiss, spread out his arms, embraced her, buried his face in the hollow between her neck and her shoulder. If only he knew even a little more about what attracted her and what repelled her, what she expected of him, what kind of men she preferred, how he appeared in her eyes, what he could do to arouse in her the love he desired — if only he knew all this, he might have wept on her shoulder, appealed to her pity and groaned his complaint: Why, why does everything have to be so difficult, involve so much pain?

She leapt lightly off the wall and he accompanied her to the gate of the house in Lincoln Street. When she turned into the garden gate, he said to her: "I'll stand here and you, before you go into the building, turn around and look at me for a minute. That's all. I want to remember it. Okay?"

He knew that this night and the chiming of its bells, the dark street flooded with the scent of pine trees, the stone wall running from the corner to the gate of her house, the paved path leading from the gate to the building entrance, and the darkness into which she was about to disappear — he knew that all these things would be engraved on his heart with an unbearable beauty, heavy and conclusive as the burden of a solemn responsibility. Her pale shadow stepped slowly up the paved path, stopped at the entrance, and turned to face him. For two or three seconds she stood there as he had requested, and he saw nothing but a blur against the darkness, no feature of her face, not even her hair or the gleam of her eyes. No power of imagination or memory could help him retrieve the lost lines of her face. He started up the path, intending to advance only a few steps until he could see her face, but she immediately slipped away into the darkness and disappeared.

The thought that he was going home now to sleep seemed exceedingly strange to him. When had he last known such wakefulness? His senses were sharpened to catch the sights and sounds of the night, its scents, its touch on his arms and neck like a cool, strange hand. He felt powerful and triumphant, resolute and at the same time lost in a void. His brain transmitted a rapid, disconnected stream of images, voices, words, sentences, and he did not know what to take hold of; in which of them he would find himself now; in which of them to anchor the terrible need for hope thrusting up in him like a naked physical urge, such as hunger or cruelty, unrelated to any calculations of possibility, without any illusions, uncompromising.

He passed Terra Sancta and continued up King George Street, the echo of his footsteps in the dark, deserted street filling him with a vague, undefined sense of loss; so disconnected and suspicious that they sounded like the footsteps of someone else pursuing him with patient, animal-like persistence. And he didn't even have any cigarettes.

If only he had one cigarette to revive his spirits, he had no doubt that he would be able to find a train of thought and take off on it, extricate himself from the whirlpool that was making him pleasantly giddy while at the same time imprisoning him in a suffocating impasse.

The pool of light shed by the lamps of the Knesset building resembled an aquarium, and like a solitary fish sailing slowly through it a weird-looking woman advanced toward him, thin and pale as a corpse, wearing a black skirt that was too big for her, the black bag hanging from her arm swaying to and fro like a pendulum and threatening her tenuous equilibrium, as if she were walking on a tightrope. The watery ambience of the light lent an unnatural slowness to her movements, to the objects flickering around her like reflections, as if he were about to enter a different dimension of time, nocturnal, transparent, elusive, which would vanish the moment he stepped into it. Standing in the shadow of the large apartment block on the corner, he saw her stop on the brink of the hollow of the little park behind the Knesset building, open her big handbag, take a little mirror and a lipstick out of it, examine her face, stretch her lips, and repaint them with a rather sullen scowl, like an artist sick and tired of his painting. When she saw Avner enter the pool of light, she quickly put the mirror and the lipstick back into her bag, took out a pack of cigarettes, lit one with a trembling hand, and looked at him through the smoke. One of the Knesset sentries who was standing a few paces away stared at her with a bored smile.

Avner slowed down. He could already see her white, skinny legs, the yellowish socks rolled down over her black, high-heeled sandals, the demented makeup on her dead face, her hand holding the cigarette, trembling as if appealing for help, groping for the greasy red smear of lipstick invading her chin and cheeks. She gave him an accusing, defensive, inquiring look, to which the crude black arches of the eyebrows painted high on her forehead added a terrible, panic-stricken astonishment, as if they had frozen in a moment of horror, fixing them into a perpetual mask of dismay.

"What time?" a voice emerged surprisingly from the mask. "What time now?" the voice repeated, shrill and squeaky as a baby's.

Avner stopped and looked at her. He had often seen her here before. The Knesset sentry, standing about ten paces away from them, called out to him suddenly, warning him: "She's not a whore, she's just crazy."

"Not true," the voice squeaked indignantly from the lips immobile in the middle of the big red smear, "Not true, not crazy, only whore."

He had seen her many times before and never sensed such revulsion at her appearance; on the contrary, he had often pitied her. But this time he felt personal hatred, a desire to hit her, to hurt her, and a sense that at this moment everything was permitted, everything was possible. The smoking mask of her face tautened, exposing swollen gums and tiny teeth, like newly grown milk teeth. And again the babyish squeak demanded, this time in a tone that was tearful and commanding at once: "What time!"

Avner stared at her and said nothing. Suddenly the cry echoed in his head: *The third E above middle C, the third E above middle C!* and a peculiar certainty descended on him that he too was now the subject of a scientific experiment, like Hanan's cat.

He turned away and walked a few steps, and he heard her calling after him: "One minute! Why you run? What time? What time now?"

He turned his head and waited. She approached him mumbling: "What time? What time now?"

"I don't have any money," he said. "Leave me alone."

"Never mind money. I love your eyes. Thief's eyes," she piped.

"Give me a cigarette," said Avner.

She looked at him suspiciously for a moment, as if she did not understand his request, as if suspecting that he meant something else. In the end she opened her bag, took out the pack. and was about to extract a cigarette and offer it to Avner when he cried: "No! Don't touch! I'll take one out myself. You've probably got all kinds of disgusting diseases."

She offered him the pack and said: "Not true. Not sick. Lots of strength in my legs. I give you lots of strength. You be able to kill everybody in the world. Everybody scared of you."

"Where do you get the money to buy such expensive cigarettes?" He examined the pack, took out a cigarette, lit a match from the box in his pocket, took a deep drag, and absentmindedly put the pack into his pocket.

"Cigarettes," she said.

"Wait," he said.

"What the matter with you?"

He didn't know. He was the pursuer and the pursued. The cigarette smoke flooded his head with a new, unfamiliar aroma, calmed the anger of his body and sharpened the sense of the moment. He was sure of nothing; if they had been somewhere else, in some dark, secluded corner, and not in this aquarium of light casting an air of unreality over everything, he might have responded to her invitation. He might have tortured her with a cruelty he would never have imagined himself capable of, he might have given her all the force of his love in return for her pity. All in obedience to the sense of the moment, toward which his whole being streamed as if in response to the greatest of promises. Something told him to run and he walked slowly, like a thief whose flight might betray him. He heard the tapping of her heels on the pavement and her voice calling after him: "One minute! One minute!"

From time to time he turned his head and contemplated the figure tottering behind him in the dark, struggling to keep up with him even though he was walking so slowly. Like a person dedicated to some obscure mission he dismissed the temptation to ask questions, to weaken his resolve: What did he want, why was she pursuing him, what had brought them together in this street, at this moment, and what was it that made all this so real and inevitable? And every time he turned around to face her, he sent her his thief's smile, and when the distance between them grew too great for him to see her outlines distinctly, he waited for her to come closer before walking on. When he reached the corner of Jaffa Street, he saw her leaning against a tree trunk, exhausted. He turned on his heel and stood not far off and waited. She groaned at him: "Where you go, where?"

When he finished the cigarette he immediately lit another, waiting for her to interpret his standing still as a sign of hope and to continue her pursuit. She left the tree and began walking toward him, and when she was close enough for him to hear the sound of her breathing he set off again. When he reached the Jaffa Street intersection he waited around the corner for her to appear, and then he crossed the street and waited in the shadow of the pillared portico for her to cross it after him.

She called to him again in a plaintive, childish whine: "I'm tired. I want to go home." And he went on walking, holding back his legs that were begging to run, keeping pace with the tapping of her heels behind him. An occasional car drove past, casting shadows on the pillars and disappearing up the road. A man and a boy came toward them, prayer bags under their arms, a father and son hurrying to the synagogue for the Penitential Prayers. Next to the bus station an army jeep was parked with a few soldiers sitting in it. A radio crackled something. One of the soldiers put on earphones and said something unintelligible into the mike in his hand. His friend sitting at the wheel next to him started the engine. When Avner passed them he caught himself looking at them in the way he used to look at soldiers before he went to the army, when he longed for conscription and the thought that he would soon be a soldier himself filled his heart with excitement and hope. But he still didn't feel like a soldier, he said to himself, he felt no connection with these men, with the aura of quiet skill and confidence surrounding them without the fear of a commanding officer, without the disgrace of humiliation. The jeep moved off, made a U-turn in the empty street, and drove back toward the intersection. Avner looked after them and saw them stop with a screeching of brakes next to her silhouette. She was alarmed and withdrew to the far end of the sidewalk, where she cowered against a shop window. They called out to her to come with them, made obscene remarks and laughed in enjoyment. She didn't even turn her head in their direction, but went on walking toward Avner, afraid of losing touch with him in the dark, as driven and possessed by some mysterious sense of mission as he was. We're speaking to each other, said Avner to himself, and I don't know what we're saying, we're holding each other by the throat, we can't let go. Oh God, the mysterious bond that I was talking about to her all night is pursuing me now, taking its revenge like all the other lies. He saw her lurching from side to side in the effort to quicken her steps, to prevent the distance between them from growing and making her lose sight of him. *Come, my sister,* he whispered almost audibly, *come my sister,* and he couldn't help smiling to himself at the sound of the words. The jeep drove off, leaving the dark, empty street to them and their game. When she was close enough to him he turned quickly left into Rav Kook Street, and when he heard the tapping of her heels behind him he broadened his stride, turned left into the Street of the Prophets next to Café Patt, crossed the street, passed the shops on the corner, opened the gate of a walled courtyard, went inside and closed the gate behind him, walked a few steps along the wall, faced it, opened his fly and pissed.

After buttoning his fly, he looked behind him. In the depths of the yard he saw the house with a few trees in front of it; not far off was a cistern surrounded by a stone ring, like a little fence, which was capped by a metal lid gleaming dully in the darkness, with an unclear shape on top of it. He turned back, stretched his arms out in front of him, and advanced toward the wall until his hands were touching it. The chill touch of the stone, like the breath of life suddenly passing through an inanimate object, roused him as from a dream. He came closer to the wall and rested his forehead against it. Like a flicker of daylight the chill flashed through him, like the hope of purification, and he asked himself: What's happening to me? Have I gone out of my mind? What am I doing here?

Were his ears deceiving him? It seemed to him that he heard someone singing inside the house. He turned his face toward the yard and saw a very faint light coming from one of the windows, presumably from the wing farthest from him. The voices of two or three women singing together, a monotonous foreign song, long sentences with silences between them. He strained his ears in the attempt to make out the nature of the tune, the language of the words, and heard the sound of tapping heels on the other side of the wall, advancing down the Street of the Prophets. After a few seconds the tapping grew so loud that he could no longer listen to the alien voices rising from the house in the recesses of the courtyard. Now he could hear the groaning, rhythmic gasps for breath. The steep ascent of Rav Kook Street had apparently exhausted the last of her strength. The footsteps stopped. The panting sounded so close that he guessed she must be standing right opposite him, with only the stone wall between them.

"Hallo! Hallo!" her voice called to the empty street, broken and gasping, but with the same shrill, piping, babyish tone as before: "Hallo! Where he gone? Hallo?"

And once more a prolonged silence fell and he could hear the low female voices rising from the house, repeating the long, monotonous, mysterious sentences over and over again. He did not know if she was still there, opposite him, on the other side of the wall, whose coolness his forehead and hands were thirstily drinking in. She must be holding her breath in some sudden terror. What could have terrified her so?

The sound of the gate creaking startled him and he pressed his body against the wall, as if he wished he could disappear inside it. He saw two figures enter the courtyard, two old women dressed in black. They walked quickly up the paved path to the house and knocked on the door. After a moment the door opened and they went inside.

And again he heard her voice, this time not calling into the street but talking to herself in bewildered disappointment, as if trying to understand how such a thing could have happened to her: "Oy, Mammaleh! Boy gone, cigarettes gone! Mammaleh, Oy my Mammaleh!"

And immediately afterward a shrill, whistling shriek rose from behind the wall, long and strained, followed by a rising and falling wail, like the howl of an animal. Avner closed his eyes and said to himself: Now I'm merging into this wall, becoming a part of it, soon I'll disappear into it, in fear, in love, transformed not only in soul but also in body, in body! Take me, take me into you, I beg you! Now his hands were sinking deeper and deeper into the plaster and stone, being swallowed up by the material substance, with his forehead and his head and his whole body sailing after them in a slow, gentle voyage into the material responding to him, opening up to him, embracing him, enclosing him. The pounding of his heart imposed a repetitive inner movement on his body, a movement with a rhythm like swimming, like bowing and rising, thrusting and resting, charge and withdrawal, conquest and surrender, and this movement filled him with a sensation of wide-open spaces and the promise of peace until it came to a climax in a groan of relief and the yearning to take off and float, in a passive, continuous glide, without moving a muscle, to the end of the journey, to the starting point, to the opaqueness of matter, to the sadness of time, to the numbing dullness of weight, to the strangeness of the earth on which he stood.

Behind the wall the wailing continued, and in the midst of the slumberous heaviness he noted, as a surprising but evident fact, how closely this wail resembled the weeping of his brother Benihu in his sleep at night, despite the difference in the pitch and cadence of the voices, the weeping of these two lost creatures who had arrived here by mistake, who had been sent here on some unclear mission and been forgotten, but who had not themselves forgotten or ceased to long for and strive to return to the place from which they had come, their place, to go home at last.

"Oy, Mammaleh, Oy, my Mammaleh!" the babyish voice moaned again behind the wall. He heard her blowing her nose and breaking into harsh, convulsive coughing, rising from the depths of her body. And the tapping of her heels on the pavement again, and a renewed outbreak of coughing. He withdrew a few paces from the wall, took a deep breath, and rubbed his hair. It's not so terrible, he said to himself, I could have taken her money too, but I only took her cigarettes. This thought, instead of easing his heart, repelled him. He turned around and surveyed the courtyard. The singing had stopped. There was still a dim light in the window of the house, coming from some from some other source. He went up to the cistern, looked around him, and then walked over to the trees in front of the house until he found the tap. He crouched down in front of it, opened it, wet his face and hair, closed the tap, stood up and shook the water off his head. Then he went back to the wall, and when he was about to make for the gate he saw the door of the house opening. Five or six women in black emerged, and in the dim light of the house he saw that they were nuns. They took their leave of a man and a woman standing in the doorway. He clung to the wall, hiding in its shadow. He heard the voices in the doorway speaking Russian, apparently saying good-bye after some mysterious midnight rite, perhaps a prayer for some sick person, or for a barren woman? The man was tall and thin, his face bony and sad, the woman, presumably his wife, plump and smiling. The nuns left the courtyard, the man and woman went back inside. After a moment the faint light went out in the window. There was silence behind the wall. He approached the gate stealthily, opened it quietly, and peeped into the street. She wasn't there. He stepped outside and saw her not far from the intersection, dragging her feet, the big black bag swinging to and fro on her arm threatening to upset her tenuous balance.

Quietly he shut the gate behind him and stood close to the wall, watching her silhouette receding until she turned left, in the direction of Jaffa Street, and disappeared from view. He waited a moment or two, in case she changed her mind and came back to look for him. Next to one of the buildings on the left side of the dark street, not far from where he stood, he suddenly noticed a group of shadows that up to then had been standing in silence, without moving. A stir, an agitation, passed through them, a cry broke out and shook the street, followed immediately by the thud of a falling body. A young girl cried: "Father, Father! Can you hear me?" Someone said: "Water, fetch some water!" There was a sound of hurrying footsteps, of a woman sobbing softly; someone else came running from the direction of Strauss Street, approached the group, and was swallowed up by it.

Avner proceeded up the street, hugging the wall. When he passed the group on the other side of the street he averted his eyes; he wanted to flee for his life but something inside him would not let him run. The man who had fainted regained consciousness. Two of the shadowy figures raised him to his feet and supported him. "I want to see her," he said in a broken voice, "to see her." The young girl's voice responded: "It's impossible, Father, everything's closed now." Someone standing to one side sighed with a certain relish: *"Blessed be the true judge, the Lord giveth and the Lord taketh away."*

When he reached the intersection, Avner put his hand absentmindedly in his pocket to take out a cigarette. When the pack was in his hand he looked at it in astonishment for a moment, and he didn't know what to do. What's the big deal, he said to himself, I didn't take her money, only her cigarettes. It wasn't serious, more like a joke, a kind of game we were both playing. Oy, Mammaleh, boy gone, cigarettes gone. Where did it all come from? Was it always there inside me and I didn't know? Don't I know myself? Well, I'm beginning to now. What else awaits me? What other surprises are in store for me from myself? Nobody else took possession of me, nobody else told me what to do. It's me, the real me, taking over from the depths of my being. Beauty, you say, is the promise of happiness. And ugliness, what does it promise? And he swung his hand back and hurled the pack of cigarettes as far as he could in the direction in which she had gone.

I threw it away for nothing, he said to himself, it's of no importance. I didn't throw anything away, everything's still there inside me, I'm still there.

The farther he walked up the street, the more lights of little synagogues were scattered like garlands on his path. Because of the chill of the night their windows were closed and it was hard to hear the prayers clearly. This secret, nocturnal muttering sounded like a conspiracy against those sleeping soundly in their beds. He stopped for a moment, spread out his arms, and tried to take a deep breath, to loosen the dark knot of pain in his chest. I don't know myself, I don't know anything about myself, he thought. And there's nowhere to bang my head against and cry.

Let's be friends, you say, soul mates. If you could look into my soul, you would prefer the body you're so anxious to avoid. What have you got against my body? It's the best thing about me. I really and truly thought I'd fallen in love with you, but when you're in love you can't hate like this, you can't be so mean. When you're truly in love, you want the whole world to share in your happiness, you want to dish it out like a gift. There was no happiness. Only great misery and lies and hypocrisy all the way. *We have sinned before Thee, have mercy on us*. It's impossible, Father, everything's closed now, everything's closed. Oh, God, have mercy on me and forgive me. As a father forgives his children. Everything's closed now, Father. Boy gone, cigarettes gone, Oy, my Mammaleh. Forgive me, God, have mercy on me, I can't take any more. I can't. I'm thirsty for your forgiveness, God, I'm choking for it.

In Ezekiel Street the shadowy figure of bowed man dragging a cart approached him. With the creaking of the wheels he heard a kind of panting grunt, as if the man were humming to himself as he dragged the cart, in time to the rhythm of his breathing. As if he were alone in the world on this terrible night of penitence. When the distance between them narrowed, Avner could see the wooden cart with its shafts under his armpits, their ends gripped in his hands. The cart was covered with canvas or sacking. The man had a squashed cap on his head, and his face, which closely resembled Avner's father's face, was covered with the gray stubble of a beard unshaven for several days.

The man was not very old but his body was bowed, apparently from the load of the cart, and his face lowered to the ground, as if he were counting his steps. Where was he dragging this load so late at night? What did he have in the cart? When the distance between them shortened, Avner heard the tune the man was grunting to himself more clearly, apparently a song in Yiddish. He saw the ragged sheet covering the cart. The man was evidently unaware of Avner walking on the pavement, or else he ignored him, for he went on grunting his song even when no more than a few paces separated them. Avner stepped onto the street and confronted him.

"I'll pull it for you. Where do you want to take it?"

The man was unable to stop the cart at once, was impelled forward a few steps and stood still. Avner, who had drawn aside in order not to bump into him, hurried up to him. The man let the shafts fall from his armpits.

"What do you want?" he asked in alarm.

"I want to help you. Let me pull it for you."

"Don't start with me, boychick, you hear? I'm stronger than you think."

"Let me help you, I mean it."

The man narrowed his eyes to see Avner's face: "Leave me alone, you hear? Go away and leave me alone."

He fixed his eyes, sullen and anxious, on Avner.

"Please," said Avner, "do me a favor. I want to help you."

The man looked around him as if seeking help.

"Don't be frightened," said Avner. "Trust me. It's for the mitzvah, soon it'll be Yom Kippur. You remind me of my father. I'm strong, I can help you."

"You one of them Urfalis?" the man asked.

"No, I'm Bukharian," said Avner.

"I know you. You'll be sorry if you do me any harm. I know your family."

Amazing how he resembled Avner's father, even though he was an Ashkenazi.

"Don't do me any favors. Go look for mitzvoth somewhere else."

Avner did not move. A terrible rage welled up inside him, a helpless hostility toward this revolting man and his stupid obstinacy.

"If you don't leave me alone, I'll scream and people will come running, the police too!"

The man tucked the shafts under his armpits again, gripped the ends in his hands, and began to pull. Avner tried to put his hand on his shoulder, but the man shook it off with a sudden sideways jerk, and said almost imploringly: "If you want to do me a favor, if you want to do a mitzvah, just leave me in peace. What do you want, I should shout for people to come and rescue me?"

"You don't understand," said Avner. "You've got no sense."

"You are an Urfali. I know you and your whole family too. You better be careful, Yom Kippur's coming up, you want to get into trouble for trying to rob me? Bugger off!"

Avner stood aside. The cart moved off, creaking noisily as the man made haste to get away. From where he was standing Avner saw his back arching like a coiled spring, straining with a harsh, stubborn, crushing power. Until he turned into a shadow in the distance, Avner heard the panting grunt of his song accompanying the creaking of the wheels, a Yiddish grunt, monotonous and rhythmic as the wheels themselves, and suddenly a silence fell, and the man's voice called out in the dark: "Come here a minute, boychick!"

Avner ran toward him.

"You got any cigarettes, maybe?"

Avner did not reply. He looked inquiringly into the man's face, as if he found difficulty in understanding what he said.

"You ain't no Urfali," said the man. "I dunno. Maybe I don't know you. Understand? Maybe you're crazy? Maybe a robber? How should I know? This is my living I got here. If I let you pull, a strong young man like you, maybe you run away with the cart and leave me here to tear my hair out in the middle of the night? You understand what I'm saying to you? A person can get into trouble in the night. Maybe you got a cigarette for me? You a good person or not? It'll be a big mitzvah for you on Yom Kippur!"

When Avner reached the outskirts of the neighborhood he could no longer hold back his tears. He bit his lips to prevent the cry from breaking out. He walked slowly, to give his eyes a chance to dry before he got home. And in the meantime the tears poured silently down his cheeks and neck, bringing the promise of a certain relief. Gradually the night grew calmer and more merciful. Gradually he recovered his strength.

He didn't have a chance to open the door, he had barely touched the handle when the door opened quietly and his mother was standing on the threshold, a blanket around her shoulders, bareheaded, her graying hair loose, her eyes panic-stricken. His heart cried out inside him: *Something's happened to Father!*

She took his hand and closed the door without saying a word. She seemed unable to open her mouth.

"What's wrong? Where's Father?"

She raised a finger to her mouth to hush him.

"What's wrong?" He lowered his voice with an effort.

"I thought I would never see you again."

"Why? Tell me what happened."

She gazed at him and squeezed his arms with her hands.

"I dreamed someone was killing you."

His heart trembled in relief and gratitude. She had always spoken of death, the possibility of it and her fear of it, directly, called it by its name, without a screen of words and euphemistic phrases, in a very straightforward, secular style, incompatible with her piety and religious way of life. She spoke of death as of a cruel and powerful foe over whom even God had no control; its sentence could not be averted by prayer, by pleas or merit, but only perhaps, perhaps, by a trade-off that would satisfy its terrible hunger with another, comparable victim, from the world of strangers and foreigners instead of the near and dear on whom he had first set his sights. And in dealing with death, she considered herself a negotiator of no mean skill.

"I had a dream," she said, "I saw someone killing you. I woke up and went to look at you in your bed and you weren't there. It was so late already and you hadn't come home. I was afraid the dream was true. I waited for you at the door. I couldn't sleep for fear, for the sorrow that dream caused me."

"Why should anyone kill me?"

"How should I know? Do I know what you get up to all night long, when everyone's asleep? What do I know? You never tell me anything. Maybe you're a gangster and I don't know? My heart is sick from you already. Believe me. I saw you being killed in that dream. With my own eyes, as clear as I'm seeing you now. And I couldn't scream. I told him to take somebody else. To take me, even. If you're killed, I don't want to live anymore. What have I got if you're not here? Let him take me. What do I care? I woke up in great fear. Maybe he really speaks through dreams? Maybe it was true? I stood next to the door to wait. Until you came home safe and sound."

"Nobody's going to kill me. I've never done any harm to anyone."

"People can kill for nothing too," she said, "and what are you doing wandering around at night? Who do you go with? Where do you go with them? You're not happy, I know you're not happy. So why do you go with them? They're no good for you, they're bad, very bad. All the time I worry about you, all the time."

He knelt down at her feet, and took her hands and kissed them, as he sometimes did in a lighthearted, jocular fashion. But this time he did it with a solemn, fateful air, as if he really had risen from the dead.

"Go to bed," she scolded. "Go to bed already. How are you going to get up in the morning to go to the army?"

• PART THREE •

INFILTRATION

His arms sank up to his elbows in the gigantic pot and made waves in the murky water. His rolled-up sleeves hung in loose rings round his skinny arms, like sails flapping loosely around their masts. "Can you see how he's looking at us all the time," muttered Hedgehog in a whisper.

The cook's assistant sat on a low, ramshackle stool on the threshold of the room next to us, taking little sips of coffee from a little glass. It was hard to tell if he was really looking at us or if he was absorbed in some pleasant daydream, and one of his squinting eyes had remained fixed on us out of absentmindedness and forgetfulness. Shortly before this he had come over to inspect us, and burst out yelling: "What the hell d'you think you're doing? I'll have you on report! You think it's a joke or what? You're chucking out half the potato with the skin!" And he extracted first one and then another example from the basin of peels, two pale wet snakes, and waved them in our faces. Then he snatched the knife out of Hedgehog's hand, squatted down next to us, and began rapidly peeling a potato that he pulled out of the water-filled pot. Within a few seconds half the potato was peeled, and he displayed the peel, dangling like a thin strip of paper, and again illustrated the proper angle of the knife on the potato, the movement of the thumb and finger, a lore that had to be learned, step by step, like dismantling a machine gun, like firing at a moving target. We tried to emulate him, and he stood over us to supervise and criticize our efforts. "If you carry on like this, it'll take you to next week!" he shouted. "Where do you think you are? In kindergarten? I'll have you on report, I swear I will!"

Hedgehog looked at him as he sat down on the stool with demonstrative displeasure, his lips still muttering something in an undertone, probably a curse in Arabic. When we were alone Hedgehog whispered to himself: "Yes, sir, whatever you like, enjoy yourself, you're the boss." And then he said to me in a worried tone: "I only hope I can keep my big mouth shut and not get into trouble with him. We're better off here than running with that sadistic madman."

Hedgehog's face was small, his bristling rebellious hair stood up on his head, his nose was pointed, his eyes were very close set, and his lips were narrow as two thin lines. Even when he was joking his face had a suspicious, belligerent expression. Now he took his arms out of the vast pot and shook the water off them.

"Why's he looking at us all the time?" he muttered in a low voice.

"What do you care? Can't you see he's cockeyed? He isn't looking at us at all."

Someone switched on a radio in the next room, or in the kitchen, and the wailing of an Arab singer spread out around us. The staff sergeant rose from the stool and disappeared into the next room. He was short and fat, his stripes were pinned to his sleeve with safety pins, and his beret was pulled down so tightly it looked as if it were keeping his head in place. The squint gave his face an expression of sensual pleasure, a pleasure that was capable of driving a man out of his mind, but at the same time made him easy to get along with.

"That's not a squint," said Hedgehog, "it's an expression. It's their expression. I always see it on their faces. The expression of people who're waiting, who're prepared to suffer in silence for a long time, because they know their time will come and everything will blow up like a volcano."

I laughed, and Hedgehog, although he sniggered with me, did not renounce his vision.

"Seriously! Just take a good look at those guys in our platoon, when they're sitting there in the corner and talking Arabic so's we won't understand. Look at their eyes. Those are the eyes of people who're waiting for something, getting ready for something, like a rebellion."

"You just hate the Sephardis, that's all," I said.

"Are you crazy? Me hate the Sephardis? You know how many Sephardis there were in the IZL? And how many of them were hanged by the British? And how many fought like lions in the War of Independence? I admire them! But these new ones, the ones who've arrived here from Arab countries over the past few years, they're a danger to us. They didn't go through those years with us, the struggle and the underground and the war. They're not capable of fitting into what's being built up here. Their idea isn't our idea. They think about different things. Look at them, they seem quiet, apathetic, they do what they're told, but you can see the expectation in their eyes. They're got patience, a kind of Oriental patience. They're waiting. But when the moment arrives, the knives will come out. And they'll destroy everything. Don't kid yourself. Everything we love, everything that's dear to us and they can't fit into, they hate. And they'll destroy it. Because it'll keep reminding them that they're strangers here. Gradually they'll establish themselves, more and more of them will come to the country, they'll grow stronger and stronger, without standing out too much. They're waiting, biding their time, and one day it'll happen. Blood will be shed. After they've destroyed everything, maybe they'll build something else, something new, according to their own ideas, I don't know. But it won't be for us anymore. And the Arabs won't have to worry about a second round anymore. Everything will collapse of its own accord, like a rotten fruit falling off a tree, they'll do the job for them, they'll be their fifth column. They'll march in and find an Arab state ready and waiting for them."

Someone turned the radio off and the Arab singer was silenced. We set to work with redoubled energy, afraid that now he had turned the radio off the staff sergeant would come back to sit in the doorway. But he did not reappear for a long time and it seemed that our work would never end.

There was a sound of footsteps approaching. Hedgehog fell silent. We peeled potatoes with a vengeance. The cockeyed staff sergeant came in with two recruits from 3 Platoon. I knew them by sight but I didn't know their names. The strains of community singing accompanied by an accordion often rose from their barracks, and we sometimes saw them romping like children around the door, fighting, laughing, and swearing. The CSM approached the giant pot and leaned over it as if he couldn't believe his eyes. He gave us a menacing look: "What the hell have you been doing all this time? Is that all you've done? I'm taking your particulars! I'm going to your CSM right now! There won't be any lunch today!"

He ordered the two strange recruits to carry the pot with the peeled potatoes to the kitchen and when they came back he told them to help us finish the job. After concluding his shouts and threats he left.

As soon as the staff sergeant was gone the two of them burst into shy, suppressed laughter, like a pair of little boys caught red-handed and allowed to go unpunished. Hedgehog glared at them angrily: Even though they were there to help us with our work, he saw them as uninvited guests intruding on his territory. For a few minutes we worked in a tense silence. The two newcomers kept exchanging significant looks and bursting into suppressed, rebellious laughter, as if to remind each other of some prank they had perpetrated. One of them was squat and broad-shouldered, with a full, square face and a rather dour, skeptical, adult expression. His friend was a redhead with a sharp, sly face who wore a ring engraved with a skull on the third finger of his left hand, as an expression of originality, a special brand of humor, or artistic or Bohemian tendencies. (Afterward it transpired that the redhead had dropped out of high school and worked as an apprentice window dresser in Tel Aviv until he was drafted, and that he intended to go abroad to pursue his studies in this field after completing his army service. His friend of the square, adult face was a radio ham who had operated a radio station called the Voice of Youth from his backyard in Rehovot before being drafted. He expressed surprise at the fact that we had never heard of this station, and told us that he and his friends had broadcast records, greetings, and jokes on it, until the police discovered it about two months before the draft and closed it down. He hoped to serve in the signal corps and continue with his hobby in this way.)

The redhead waited for his friend's eyes to meet his over the giant pot, narrowed his eyes, curled his upper lip, and barked in a hollow voice with a heavy German accent: "Malingerers, *raus!* March! Back on parade! Here is zee Izrael army, not zee bordello!" And the two of them burst out laughing again.

Hedgehog was losing his patience: "What's the matter with you, are you quite mad?"

This only increased their laughter. They dropped the potatoes they were peeling and bent over the pot, doubled over with laughter, as if they were about to puke into it.

"We went on sick call to that woman doctor," said the one with the adult face, after he had regained his composure and powers of speech. "It was the first time we saw her. What do you know about it?"

"Not much," said Hedgehog. "We're not in the habit of going on sick call."

"You don't know what you're missing," said the radio ham.

The redhead tried to improve the atmosphere: "She's tall and skinny as a broomstick, with a captain's insignia, a little head, and a man's haircut; she shaves her face and she's got a voice like a dog. The Germans did experiments on her in the camps. They must have tried to turn her into a man and never managed to finish the job. She's got this terrible wolfhound lying next to her, it's huge, it takes up half the room. People say they live together like husband and wife, but I don't know who's the husband and who's the wife. It lies there next to her, guarding her, trembling all over, as if it's going to jump on you at any moment and eat you alive."

Hedgehog looked shocked. I didn't know if he was putting on an act in order to maintain his rivalry with the two newcomers or if he was really unable to restrain his anger at this speech.

"How can you talk like that? You're not normal! That woman was in the camps. Haven't you got any respect for what she went through? How can you laugh about it? Who are we to even imagine what people experienced there? Haven't you got any respect for that suffering, that nightmare?"

"You don't understand," said the redhead. "If you saw her you'd understand that she's some kind of freak. She's not a woman, she's not a man, she's weird, she really does look like something out of a nightmare. And she's evil, boy is she evil! She hits the sick recruits who come to see her. She curses in German and Romanian. Once she slapped one of the guys from our platoon who had a fever of one hundred and four and he fainted on the spot. And after that she actually put in a complaint about him for not leaving her room when he was lying there unconscious in a faint. Afterward he said that when he saw her he was sure she was a kapo, a Nazi who came to Israel disguised as a woman, because the Nazis can't live without the Jews. You have to see her to believe that such evil exists in the world. Even the instructors are afraid of her."

"You're not normal," said Hedgehog, "you don't hear what you're saying. What's evil is the way you talk, the way you make fun of a woman like that, after everything she's been through. And they say she volunteered to come and be a doctor here. You're a couple of twisted, spoilt brats."

There was a short silence. The two newcomers were taken aback by Hedgehog's reaction: Perhaps they thought that his family had been exterminated in the camps, or even that he himself had been there as a child, and they stopped laughing and made no further mention of the doctor. But the barriers fell, and the awkwardness and tension disappeared. The horror softened something. It was important to know that it existed and operated with impunity, larger than life, the supreme justification for all the evil spirits, all the malice, all the lost regrets, the ultimate redress for all the victims.

The four of us ate our lunch at the cooks' table before the recruits arrived for lunch. The cross-eyed staff sergeant forgot his anger, sat down with us, and urged us to help ourselves to more and more food. To let us know that we were in good hands, he said, "Anyone who does right by Staff Sergeant Mantzur won't be sorry, and anyone who makes a balls-up will curse the day he was born."

Sammy suddenly came in from the next room, looked at us for a moment as if surprised, gave us a nod, and retired to confer with the staff sergeant in the other room. The two recruits from the other platoon looked at us and then at the door, behind which rose the sound of their voices, at first softly and then increasingly loudly.

"Give me back my money!" said the voice of the assistant cook.

And Sammy's voice: "What are you getting so excited about. Wait till tomorrow."

"No! I'm not waiting till tomorrow! I'm fed up. Now! I want my money back now!"

Sammy: "Shhh. Don't yell."

The staff sergeant: "Tell your mother shhhh . . . What am I, a dog, for you to shhhhh me?"

Sammy lowered his voice; by the tone it sounded as if he were trying to calm his the staff sergeant down, but he would not be pacified. For a moment they spoke softly and it was impossible to hear a word they said. Then suddenly there was a brief, smothered cry from Sammy, a dull thud on the floor, the sound of blows and nailed boots stamping on the concrete. We raised our eyes from the plates in front of us, exchanged glances, and listened in silence to the noises coming from the other room. The wrestling went on for a while until the staff sergeant's voice said: "As soon as I finish here I'm going to the CID," and Sammy's voice bellowed with laughter. We heard their footsteps leaving the room by the back door.

When the staff sergeant came back to the table his hair was wet and combed and his face looked tired and resentful. His squinting eyes, which earlier that morning had seemed to me to be absorbed in daydreams so delightful they could drive a man out of his mind, now spoke of disintegration and defeat. His good mood had vanished and he began shouting and threatening again, and would not let us finish our meal.

After the staff sergeant left the room, the adult-faced recruit said: "Do you realize what was going on there?"

"Those people," said Hedgehog, "that's the way they talk."

"Don't make me laugh," said the radio ham. "That guy is a really dirty character, he's notorious all over the base, he belongs to the underworld."

"He's in our platoon," said Hedgehog proudly.

"I know he is, and you probably know more about him than I do."

"He's a nice guy," insisted Hedgehog.

The two men from 3 Platoon burst out laughing.

"What do people say about him?" I asked.

"I'd rather not say," said the radio ham, and his redheaded friend added: "You'll find out for yourselves soon enough. Be careful of him, he can get other people into trouble too, without them even realizing what's happening."

"You two are a mine of information," said Hedgehog. "I suppose you spend all your time gossiping like old women about everyone on the base."

I tried to understand what they were getting at. I thought of Avner, and how Sammy had helped him that Saturday to get through the fence to see his girlfriend Aliza, and speculated on the kind of complicity that could have come into being between them as a result, laying a trap for Avner. I also remembered the night of the guard, when Avner warned me not to say anything to anyone about what we had seen, as if he already understood what it was all about. I began to feel nervous about the consequences of Avner's friendship.

"The army's turned into a branch of the Jaffa underworld," said the adult-faced recruit; "the whole atmosphere's changed. A year ago I was still dreaming about Nahal, going to some new kibbutz in the Negev or outpost in Lachish. We had a great group from the scouts. We'd been together for years and we wanted to build something new. A little while before we were drafted everything fell apart, everyone went off in a different direction, everyone suddenly discovered some problem or other. Only four or five of the old crowd joined a different settlement group. Maybe in a few years time it'll all seem like ancient history anyway, and the whole country'll be one big Dizengoff Street. Ginger's dream is to be window dresser in Tel Aviv. Some profession. Have you ever heard of anyone wanting to be a window dresser?"

Ginger burst out laughing. The subject was apparently one they had discussed before.

"Is there any money in it?" Hedgehog asked doubtfully.

"Sure there is!" said Ginger. "It's a branch that's only just beginning to develop. Once I thought of learning to paint stage sets, I've got a flair for it, but to my profound sorrow and regret I discovered that the theater bores me stiff. I went to see a few productions, I tried to read some plays, but I was so bored that I started to look for some other profession. You can make a very good living window dressing, believe me."

The staff sergeant burst violently into the room. "The restaurant's closed!" he cried furiously. Suddenly his eye fell on Ginger's ring. He leaned over and examined it closely, and then he yelled: "Why're you wearing that thing? What's wrong with you? I don't want to see it, take it off! Hurry up, take it off!"

Ginger looked at him uncomprehendingly.

"What are you waiting for?" yelled the staff sergeant. "You want me to put you on report? Have you got permission from the army to wear it?"

Ginger took the ring off his finger and was about to put it in his pocket when the cook's assistant cried: "Give it here, I want to have a look at it."

Ginger gave it to him. Staff Sergeant Mantzur raised it to the side of his face, holding it at an angle from which he could submit it to the scrutiny of his crossed eyes, and a peculiar kind of smile appeared on his face. "Where did you get it? You shit! How much do you want for it?"

"Sorry, sir," said Ginger, "I can't, it's a keepsake."

"Who gave it to you for a keepsake? The Angel of Death?"

The staff sergeant focused one of his eyes on the ring, trying to solve its mystery. He tried to get it onto his little finger but it was too small for him. He began to titter in embarrassment, annoyance, and a certain excitement: "I bet it's a whore's ring," he said. "Who gave it to you, motherfucker?"

Ginger blushed and said nothing. He held out his hand for the ring. Unwillingly the staff sergeant placed the ring in his hand, and as he did so he gave him a violent punch on the shoulder and muttered a string of curses in Arabic with a hostile expression on his face.

Ginger put the ring in his pocket, out of harm's way.

From the place where we were standing and scrubbing the huge black pots, we could hear our CSM yelling in the mess hall. The wall must have been very thin, because we could hear him perfectly. It wasn't difficult to imagine his perpetually red face and his small, mean eyes, his short, thin body so tense it seemed on the point of exploding as he rolled his *R*'s and hissed his *S*'s in his Romanian accent, every *R* like the scraping of a knife on a whetting stone, every *S* like a spray of water spitting on red-hot steel. The four of us stopped working and listened to the shouts on the other side of the wall. If we had been in the mess hall with our friends we would probably have exchanged glances with the people sitting next to us, to try to make a joke of it, to neutralize the terror, to tame it: the great, abstract terror that we had managed to transform into a small, private, practical worry about how to save our skins, how to keep out of his sight, how to escape the beast unharmed. But now, as the four of us stood listening to the CSM yelling in the mess hall, we felt something like the primordial terror, the sense of great personal danger, a danger measured not by its practical consequences but by the dimensions of its manifestation as a force that needed no assistance. It was a reminder of the unchanging world behind the phenomena and illusions, like a return to some elemental order where the system of power relations was such that even the strongest didn't have a hope. We looked at each other sheepishly, as if we had been found guilty of something shameful. Our ears were riveted to the wall and we didn't have the strength to go back to work and forget about him. The physical barrier between us and the mess hall acted like an amplifier, transmitting the pure, crushing power of the danger, stripped of any bodily presence, we even stopped hearing the meaning of the words being shouted on the other side of the wall, only the hissing of the *S*'s and the spitting of the *R*'s and the stresses of the voice and its jarring discords, which sounded like the screeching of a bird of prey in the night.

Was it really only yesterday? I said to myself: *Incredible, it's all for real!* The fences and the MPs at the gate and the whitewashed tree trunks. Amid the commotion of the crowds gathering on the way to the gate, early in the morning, I saw Albert the Bulgarian and Micky and Miller and Peretz-Mental-Case and Zackie, and a few minutes later the Jerusalemites arrived. There was no reasonable explanation for the happiness we felt, the happiness of the return and reunion. I could see it in their eyes, in their beaming faces; I could hear it in their voices, when they began complaining about the leave that had passed as quickly as a dream, about everything they hadn't managed to do, and everything that was waiting for us now. And even Micky, who kept himself a little apart and was careful to preserve his silence and remain aloof from the muttered words of welcome and friendship and the backslapping, could not prevent a certain smile of satisfaction from appearing on his sealed face. Once again there was something so fresh and familiar in the warm, cloudy autumn morning, like the promise of new, better beginnings, like the hope of forgetting and being changed. At first everyone was hesitant, as if we were unprepared for the meeting, and perhaps we were ashamed of the happy sense of camaraderie that had suddenly seized hold of us; perhaps we even refused to admit to ourselves how much we had missed it in the last couple of days. The farther we advanced along the road from the Jerusalem Gate to the gate of our base, the louder and more personal the cries became. Zackie suddenly fell on Hedgehog, lifted him into the air, and slung him over his shoulder like a sack of flour. Hedgehog, whose notions of his own weight were highly exaggerated, choked with laughter and fear: "You're my witnesses, everybody, if he does himself any damage I'm not responsible!"

"Up! Down! Up! Down!" Peretz-Mental-Case yelled in Zackie's direction, and Zackie began running in time to his yells as if he were possessed.

On the road to the gate of our base other groups and individuals from the platoon joined us. It was the first time that we were walking through the camp together as if we were at home. Nothing that happened from now on, however bad, would be able to make us forget this feeling of belonging. An army truck stopped opposite us and an MP officer got out and began shouting at us to behave like soldiers. Zackie put Hedgehog down and they both stood to attention in front of the MP, hanging their heads and listening to his yells with downcast eyes and mumbling "Yes, sir," at the appropriate places. After taking down their particulars the MP officer got back into the truck and from where we stood we saw him smiling with the corner of his mouth at the sergeant sitting next to him, a sardonic, spiteful smile. The truck drove off and we continued on our way.

"Don't worry, Hedgehog," said Zackie. "He can wipe his arse with it."

"The only thing you know how to do is get people into trouble," said Hedgehog. "That's all I need now, for him to put me on report."

Zackie was still panting from the effort. He turned away from the group and walked along the side of the road, bowed and worried. We had forgotten the fear, the unexpected pitfalls lying around every corner. And nevertheless I had no doubt that we were making our way back to real time, to our destiny. Soon we would be returning, as to a meeting with a forgotten childhood realm, to the sourish smell of the wooden barracks, the smell of the rifle oil, the smell of the dried sweat on the fatigues we left in our knapsacks before we went on leave, and these smells would bring back the old resentments, the loneliness, and the moments of hatred and longing. And all these would be swallowed up initially in the hullabaloo, the laughter and the shouts of friendship, the pressure of time and the preparations for parade.

"How was it?" asked Alon.

"Okay," said Micky, "it was fantastic." Was there a faint note of irony in his reply?

They went into the building and while Micky was putting his gear down on his bed, taking off his uniform and putting on his fatigues, Alon sat on the bed and paged through the newspapers he gave him.

"Thanks for remembering the newspapers," he said.

"Why should I forget?" said Micky with a hint of indignation.

"Why not?" said Alon. He folded the newspapers and put them away in the little cupboard next to his bed.

"Are you crazy?" said Micky. "It was the first thing I did when I got home."

"How much do I owe you?" asked Alon.

"They're already used," said Micky. "Me and my parents have already read them. They're a present."

"But I asked for them. Why should you spend money on me?" asked Alon.

"What do you know about money, kibbutznik?"

"I've got enough money, you needn't worry," said Alon.

"How did you pass the time?"

"I read a bit, I thought. I talked to Ben-Hamo," said Alon.

"Great," said Micky. "It must have been thrilling. What did you talk about?"

"He's not so bad, poor guy. He hasn't got a clue."

"I went to the beach," said Micky. "It was terrific. If you'd have come with me, we could have had a great time."

"Never mind. I needed the time for self-examination."

"You're a lost case, Alon," said Micky. He stood up and smiled incredulously.

"Listen," said Alon in a low voice, "I need encouragement, you can't imagine how badly I need it."

Micky bent down and leaned over, put his hand on Alon's shoulder, squeezed it in a kind of mute promise, and smiled at him with the smile of one who has to compromise and realizes the advantages of compromising: "Look, maybe you know what's best for you. Who knows how far you might go?" This was the extent of the encouragement he was capable of producing at that moment.

It was almost time for inspection. We began going outside and forming up in threes. Yossie Ressler said to Hanan, as if he had won some previous argument between them: "Avner's not here!"

Hanan shrugged. "That guy's looking for trouble. He needs trouble like other people need air."

Hedgehog said: "Last night he stayed with the tall girl and that other one, he didn't want to go home. He had plans. I bet he managed to get rid of the tall one and spend the night with that girl. When I said good-bye I saw it on his face. I swear! He looked like a real sex maniac!"

"It's none of my business," said Hanan. "Let him look after his own problems."

The orderly-student asked everyone still in the building to come outside and form up.

Avner arrived a few minutes before the parade began. He tugged at my sleeve and said between pants: "I had lousy luck with getting rides. But at least I made it on time."

"Hurry up!" I said, "You'll be late for inspection—"

"Don't worry," he said, "everything'll be all right. Listen, man, I'm in love —"

"For pete's sake," I said, "go and get ready. In any case you're not going to make it. Do me a favor. You can tell me later."

"What 's the matter with you?" asked Avner indignantly. "Did you get out of bed on the wrong side today or what? What are you shouting at me for?"

"I'm nervous for you," I said. "Do me a favor, hurry up, maybe you'll still manage to put on your fatigues and clean your gun."

He smiled scornfully and walked nonchalantly into the barracks, whistling gaily. I couldn't help thinking that he was doing it on purpose, thumbing his nose at time and at the rules of behavior that applied to everybody except him. But perhaps it was only my fear and anxiety that made me think so. I never wanted to understand people who weren't bound by time, who didn't live with the tension of the last minutes, who never knew the anxiety of being late, the pain of that failure. Often they seemed to me like blind men groping their way among us, bumping into every obstacle in their path, as if on purpose, as if to punish us. Often I blamed them for lack of consideration, for spite. But above all I hated their somnambulistic optimism.

The orderly-student shouted "Attention!" Muallem came into view, approaching down the path. Avner pushed into the line in the nick of time and stood behind me, still fastening the webbing equipment on his chest. I turned my head and my eyes asked him if everything was okay.

"Don't worry about me," I heard him muttering behind my neck. "You worry about yourself."

Muallem was not satisfied. He sent us angrily back to the barracks and gave us a few seconds to form up again. Once again the orderly-student yelled "Attention!" and once again we heard Muallem forcefully expressing his opinion of us and what was in store for us, and once again we were sent back to form up again, with the number of seconds allocated us decreasing all the time.

"What are you so nervous about today?" asked Avner as we ran toward the building, the same scornful smile in his eyes, as if he himself weren't running back and forth with the rest of us. As if he were standing apart, watching in amusement as we, like a lot of panic-stricken mice, were sent scurrying backward and forward, while he — was in love! And therefore exempt from these trials and tribulations.

"You're out of touch with reality," I said to him, and so as not to sound self-righteous, added immediately: "I was only afraid for you, that's all."

We ran from the building to the ranks continuing the conversation.

"What's there to be afraid of?" asked Avner. "Don't worry, everything'll be all right. You'll see that everything'll be all right, all right, all right . . ." He went on mumbling to himself "It'll be all right" a few more times, and smiled pensively, as if contemplating some secret memory, distant and delightful, that gave him the assurance that everything would be all right.

Again the orderly-student yelled: "Attention!"

Muallem inspected us with a scowl and glanced at his watch: We were late again, and again we were sent running back to the barracks. And Avner, as if determined not to allow this nonsensical hullabaloo to distract him from the main issue, continued.

"Man, I'm in love. This time it's serious. This time it's the true love of my life. I've fallen in love with a princess. You hear? A real princess!"

The sound of footsteps approaching the room roused us from the terror and returned us to the reality of the moment. Again we fell on the filthy pots and cauldrons. Staff Sergeant Mantzur stood in the doorway for a moment, as if he were inspecting our labors, but he seemed sunk in other thoughts, as if he had forgotten why he had come. Something was disturbing him. He didn't say a word, and after a minute he went away.

Ginger said: "Ze'evik knows how to get in touch with spirits, to talk to the dead, to hypnotize people, to transmit thoughts telepathically and all that. Why the hell don't you use all those powers on that swine bawling his head off over there and shut him up for once and for all?"

"What are you shooting your mouth off for?" said Ze'evik angrily and gave his friend a rebuking look, apparently annoyed at him for revealing his secrets to strangers. His big face that was far older than his years looked despairing and exhausted. But like the headlights of a car driving in the dark, vanishing around a bend in the road and a moment later reappearing in a different direction after emerging from the dead zone, his face suddenly lit up and took courage. As if to confirm Ginger's story, he gave us a forgiving look, like the possessor of occult wisdom who could see into the distance, and said: "Why should I do anything to him? It's simply pathetic. Listen."

We listened for a minute in silence to the continuing shouts on the other side of the wall.

"What do you hear? Strength? Power? Arrogance? That's only because you don't know how to listen. Those are cries of suffering! The pleas of a soul in agony begging for mercy, for salvation. We have the key to the solitary cell in which that soul is confined, crying out to us to open the door and release it from its prison."

"For God's sake, stop it," said Hedgehog, "in a minute I'll start crying. You're making me feel so sorry for that bastard."

"Nobody's asking you to feel sorry for him," said Ze'evik. "Only to try to understand what's behind it."

"I told you!" cried Ginger. "He can communicate with people's souls. He went to a Yemenite rabbi next to Rehovot to study the Kabbalah, which explains about all those things. Sometimes I'm really scared that he's going to start casting spells on me or God knows what!"

And the lights went out again on Ze'evik's face, like a car vanishing into a dead zone at night.

CHAPTER 20

"They've found oil in the Negev! There's oil in the state of Israel!"
Hedgehog burst into the building, an urgent expression on his face,
red with excitement and panting for breath. There was something about
his excitement and his yells that suggested the announcement of a catastrophe. "How about that? They've found oil in Israel!"

"Someone's having you on," said Hanan.

"No! I saw it in the paper! Someone from Three Platoon got hold of a
newspaper and everyone's standing around reading it. They've got pictures. You can see a huge black jet bursting out of the ground."

"Where did they find it?"

"In the Negev, at a place called Hulikaat."

"That's next to Gvaram," said Alon. "If they've already hit on the place,
from now on they'll find more and more. It changes everything. This is a
great day!"

A soft, cloudy light filtered into the room from the silence outside, and
although it was still early in the afternoon, this light blunted the sharpness and angularity of the faces. It gave them certain airiness, grayish and
sensitive, as if an increased spirituality smoothed the transitions from
light to dark, concealing the personal, the particular, the characteristic,
and imposing a vague uniformity. After the last meal before the fast we
all lay down on our beds and a lazy calm descended on us. The stillness
outside was solemn and confident; the quiet before the holy day began.
Nahum and two other religious recruits had already gone to the synagogue or to meet their friends from other platoons who had gathered
somewhere on the base. Peretz and Ben-Hamo and a few more of their
Iraqi and Moroccan friends got dressed, their faces stern and grave,
casting looks of rebuke, contempt, and resentment at the other recruits,
especially at Zackie, who had decided not to pray or fast, because it was
"all a lot of nonsense," and remained lying on his bed.

"You think you're already like them," said Peretz-Mental-Case,
"ashamed of being a Jew."

"Pray for me too," said Zackie.

"I'll pray for you," said Ben-Hamo, "for God to forgive you for all the
trouble you make for other people."

Zero-Zero roused himself from his semicomatose state: "Look who's
talking! God'll never forgive you, that's one thing sure. People like you
they send straight to hell, they hang them up by the balls and pour boiling
oil and tar down their arseholes."

Rahamim couldn't restrain his laughter. His eyes lit up in mischievous
glee. "Shame on you," he said, "talking that way before Yom Kippur,

instead of asking forgiveness for trying to kill me with a grenade, for trying to kill everybody. I forgive you for what you did on the firing range and for all the things you said about me with your dirty mouth."

"Listen to the saint!" cried Zero-Zero. "He thinks if he goes to the synagogue and doesn't eat on Yom Kippur he'll get off scot-free. You shouldn't be allowed inside the synagogue, you make it dirty."

Peretz grew angry. "You shut your mouth!" he shouted. He advanced on Zero-Zero, who was sitting on his bed, and threatened him with his fists: "Don't you know what Kippur is? Are you a Jew at all?"

"Did you hear that?" laughed Zero-Zero. "Am I a Jew? And you, are you Jews? You're Arabs, that's all you are. There aren't any such Jews. When we were in the new immigrants' depot and we saw you people for the first time my mother started to cry: *They've put us with gypsies,* she cried. All the time she was afraid of those gypsies. She said: *I never knew there were Jewish gypsies.* Now I can see that she was right. There aren't any such Jews. You're just Arabs who're afraid of eating on Yom Kippur. That's all."

Peretz trembled with agitation: "And you, you . . . What kind of a Jew are you? You're a murderer. It's lucky that what's-his-name, Alon, jumped up and caught the grenade and threw it down. Otherwise you'd have killed us all. They shouldn't give you weapons, you want to kill Jews. Where do you get off talking about other people?"

Hedgehog intervened: "Give it a break, for God's sake, go to your prayers already. I'm sick and tired of listening to it!"

Peretz gave him a look of demonstrative loathing, turned his back on him, and went outside with his friends.

Hedgehog said: "They've brought their disgusting, primitive ghetto mentality here with them. Jewish, not Jewish, who the hell cares? They'll turn the whole country into one big ghetto before they're through."

Yossie Ressler laughed. "This is the first time you're not fasting on Yom Kippur yourself. Who're you trying to impress?"

"Do I believe in all that nonsense?" said Hedgehog indignantly. "Did I want it? They forced me! I had no choice. You can't keep fighting your family forever. I live with them. It would have made my father sick if I didn't fast in his house on Yom Kippur, it would have killed him. I'm telling you! They really are the generation of the wilderness, those people, our parents, the old folks who came from over there. Once I thought that after that generation died off, we'd be left here with a new Israeli nation, healthy, authentic, a nation of native-born Israelis. But now they arrive and bring the diaspora here all over again. How long will it take until they or their children are Israelis? Our generation may not live to see it."

Hedgehog got up and stood in the aisle between the two rows of beds, as if wondering what to do and where to go. He was restless, alone in the battle raging inside him.

"Don't worry, Yudeleh," said Avner, "it's still early. You've got plenty of time to get washed and dressed and make it to the synagogue before Kol Nidre. You haven't ruined your chances yet. All is not yet lost!"

"Really!" cried Hedgehog with sullen irony. "What do you say? And what about you? Anyone would think you'd been born to a family of atheists or on a left-wing kibbutz and none of it had anything to do with you."

"I don't have a problem with it. Apart from which, I haven't committed any sins to atone for. I haven't done any harm to God or man. My conscience is clean."

"Sure," said Hedgehog. "You're pure as the driven snow. Altogether, this platoon is full of saints."

Hedgehog frowned, as if concentrating for a moment on his thoughts, then an expression of decision appeared on his face and he walked out of the room.

"He's afraid," Avner said to me. "He's not sure. Maybe, maybe, it actually is serious. You understand? Why take the risk of losing? Anyway with him everything's a question of profit and loss. How much to risk and when and how much and when not. So then the doubts begin to nag: *Maybe there actually is something in it?*" A smile suddenly illuminated Avner's face, as if he suddenly felt affection for Hedgehog and his doubts, and he added in a low voice: "Don't think I really meant what I said, that my conscience is clean, that I haven't done anyone any harm. It isn't true. There's a lot of evil in me. Sometimes I feel like diving into it, to see how deep it is, if I can reach the bottom, where the limits are. But I don't have the guts for it. Sometimes I think that there is a God, that he sees all this, that he's testing me, trying me. And sometimes I think that it's all empty up there, that nobody's listening, nobody's taking pity, nobody's forgiving. And I don't know which is better — for there to be a landlord or not. But all this business of praying and fasting seems to me irrelevant, not serious. You don't have to be born on a left-wing atheist kibbutz to feel that way."

Avner fell silent and the platoon settled into the same lazy, sleepy calm again, as if not wishing to provoke the quiet coming from outside, the different, special quiet. Alon settled down to reading the newspapers Micky had brought him after Rosh Hashana, which he had not yet exhausted. Micky and Micha set out the pieces on the chessboard and began to play. Ressler took out his guitar and played a few quiet, strange, hesitant chords, trying out new harmonies and unfamiliar modulations. Hanan read a tattered English paperback, one of the Peter Cheney detective stories he admired so greatly. A faint, sad snoring rose from Avner's bed. There were no limits to his prodigious capacity for sleep, under any circumstances, at any hour, in any position. Now he was lying on his bed still as a board, his arms at his sides, his legs together, and his feet at right angles projecting from the bottom of the bed, as if he were standing to attention on parade.

He stared at the ceiling. On the mute, expressionless severity of his face there occasionally appeared a kind of grim, vengeful satisfaction, as of one parting forever, after painful doubts, from bad company. And sometimes the sleep-fuddled face suddenly twisted convulsively and a shudder passed through his body, like an electric shock, his bottom teeth biting his upper lip with an expression of resolute determination to survive despite everything. This lasted for a split second, and then his face was still again, with the stillness of a long-distance traveler. His sleep was like a great flow, as if all the rivers of his life were streaming into this dark, infinite sea, and he, like a raft borne swiftly on the current, without a detour or a pause, was being swept toward the place where all things go to be fulfilled. Even when he was awake you could see his obsession and his eagerness to return; often you sensed that only a part of him was walking by your side, mechanically doing what was demanded of him, without joy or fear, while the other part, the feeling, struggling part — remained over there, with the flow.

Zero-Zero groaned, whispered a couple of curses in Romanian, hoisted his knapsack onto the bed, and buried his face underneath it, hoping to find the peace he wished for there. Ever since target practice he had been depressed, and he had not yet recovered. Even his vociferous arguments with Ben-Hamo had lost their vitality, turned into a monotonous game, bereft of content and true excitement. "I felt death jumping into my hand!" he said to anyone prepared to listen, after the practice was over. He never stopped explaining why it had happened, trying to mobilize a little sympathy. His explanations were grotesque, he went compulsively from one to the other, he was so desperate for understanding, for pity. The true nature of his role evaded him completely. Everything had happened with tremendous speed, and it still lacked reality.

He had stood before his potential victims as if he were facing a firing

squad. A dull gray pallor covered his face like the hood of a condemned
man, with two eyeholes cut into it, two big, empty circles, dark and red.
His chest jerked convulsively with every breath, his hands trembling
without stopping. The platoon commander Raffy Nagar came running
to join the squad commanders. Everything happened as in a formal ceremony. The sound of the shots coming from the other squads deepened
the tense, horrified silence enveloping that moment. Raffy Nagar's voice
sounded more mature, and full of a fury we had not heard from him up
to now. A dry, personal, very dangerous voice. No longer the fierce
barks, the grotesque obscenities, the strange threats. Like a merry-go-
round suddenly stilled, the folklore stopped, the mad operetta stopped,
and a new reality began. A terrible seriousness descended on every face.
We knew that we were returning to real time, but our legs were not yet
accustomed to the weight of our bodies, to the redoubled force of gravity
of the earth. At moments like these we were capable of believing anything that was said to us.

Raffy Nagar accused Zero-Zero of an attempt at mass murder, of
trying to murder his comrades in the platoon. They would decide what
to do with him later, after his case was brought before the highest eche-
lons. The IDF had special ways of dealing with people like him.

Zero-Zero waited for the announcement. Several days passed and
nothing was said. This delay did nothing to calm his agitation or arouse
his hopes, but only increased his anxiety, magnifying the dimensions of
the affair that required such lengthy discussions at the highest level of the
army. He looked like a ghost. He couldn't eat a thing and claimed that
the ulcer was spreading through his body. The panic in his eyes was like
a sad, quiet madness, like an admission of guilt.

"Don't worry," said Alon, on seeing him pacing next to the trees one
evening, as if he were trying to get out of a trap. "Don't worry. Nothing's
going to happen. You're not to blame. They're not interested in letting it
get out. They're the ones who'll get into trouble. They were at fault. It's
their responsibility. They made a balls-up and didn't supervise us
according to the rules. Believe me, they want everyone to forget the
whole affair, they want to scare us and make us keep our mouths shut."

Alon was the only one who understood this. Maybe because of the slap
in the face he'd gotten from Benny for what he did. Maybe he understood
it from his conversation with Benny, when he took him aside afterward.
He knew more about the army than any of us; he had less need than us
of the story about Zero-Zero's murderous intentions, the story that we all
wanted to believe so much.

"Why on earth should I want to kill my mates?" whispered Zero-Zero, taking hold of Alon's hand, as if afraid that he would slip away before hearing all his arguments, before being completely convinced of his innocence. "Tell me," he whispered, "why should I do it? You think I don't love them, even if I sometimes lose my temper and curse and all that, and make problems, I love the guys like my own family, believe me. Isn't it enough that everyone hates me and laughs at the way I look? All I need now is for them to think I wanted to kill them."

"Don't worry, it'll be okay," said Alon.

"They shouldn't put things like that in the hands of a sick man like me. They shouldn't take people with a heart like mine in the army. I've got a weak heart, it's no joke. Maybe now they'll understand that it's dangerous, that my body's not made for these things. Look at me — do I look like a soldier?"

"Everyone can contribute something to the country," said Alon. "After basic training they'll find something easy for you to do, in an office or something, that won't endanger your health."

"Listen to what I'm telling you," pleaded Zero-Zero. "I'm gonna die young. I know it. But before I die, I want only one thing, to have kids. Not to leave this lousy world like some piece of shit. You're a good guy, I'll remember you as long as I live. You know how to behave like a human being and to help people and say a kind word. But believe me, in our world things don't work that way. Life isn't a kibbutz. I know something about life, take it from me. All people want is to eat each other up. The strong have only got one thing in their heads — how to trample on the weak, and get more power and respect in the world."

His hand had been shaking so badly then, you could see it from a distance. After he pulled out the safety pin and started counting, as required, before throwing the grenade toward the trench at the bottom of the slope, a terrible tremor seized his hand. It was the kind of tremor that comes from a great effort. From the certainty that no effort will be enough. His hand strained to press the lever onto the grenade, lest it explode in his hand, and this effort, which was concentrated in his wrist and the muscles of his fingers, was too great for his fear to bear: Death itself, as he argued later, was starting to jump inside his hand. In the end he swung his arm back, in order to hurl the grenade forward with all his might, and the grenade fell far in his rear. But Zero-Zero dropped to the ground and hid his head in the shadow of the sandbags of the parapet, as he had been trained to do. Presumably he thought that everything was as it should be. Before anyone understood what was happening, Alon leapt from his position, rushed up to the grenade, picked it up, ran to the sandbags, and hurled it down the slope. Then he stood and looked over the sandbags to see the explosion, ignoring danger and breaking all the rules and procedures practiced in training and repeated over and over again: *Lie down immediately and cover your head until the grenade explodes.* And this was the moment that remained as a heroic picture in our hearts, this rather than the resourcefulness, courage, and swiftness of the removal of the grenade: Panting and erect, like a priest mounting the altar, he stood facing the divinity it was forbidden to see, looking it boldly in the eye. Benny pounced on him and pulled him down, and as Alon collapsed at his side the grenade exploded. They rose to their feet. Benny looked at him furiously and slapped him in the face. Alon, whose whole appearance resembled that of a man acting in obedience to some inspiration coming from outside himself, looked around him in astonishment. Benny grabbed his arm, dragged him outside the emplacement, moved out of earshot, and said whatever he had to say to him. Zero-Zero, forgotten in the emplacement, went on lying on the ground until he received the command to move. When Alon returned he refused to talk about what had happened and confined himself to the following remark about what Benny had said to him: "He thinks I don't know that in the paratroops they actually make them look at the grenade when it explodes, they want to force them to get used to it." He did not seem overly excited by what he had done. Nor did his friends convey full appreciation of his deed to him.

Muallem conferred with Benny, and one of the other instructors hurried to summon Raffy Nagar. And in the meantime they refused to allow Zero-Zero to join the platoon, as if he had contacted some dangerous disease. He remained in the emplacement until Raffy Nagar arrived and kicked him out. Target practice was halted. The platoon was ordered to line up in parade formation. Raffy Nagar made Zero-Zero stand facing the parade and told us about his dreadful designs and the massacre that had been averted thanks to the alertness of our instructors and the resourcefulness of Alon. "You can thank your lucky stars that there are a few men in this platoon."

Zero-Zero was still convinced that he threw the grenade into the trench and thought we were pulling his leg. He couldn't understand what happened and put all the blame on his old enemy, his long-suffering body.

Miller was sitting on his bed with his back against the wall and the notebook in which he wrote his mysterious notes on his knees. Since the beginning of basic training he had become less comprehensible to his comrades in the platoon, but also less worrying. The terror of his fits had long ceased to haunt us, except for Ben-Hamo, who superstitiously avoided any contact with Miller, to everyone's mirth. The young man with the brown, shriveled, parchment face spoke little and kept himself apart, obviously not wishing to cause any awkwardness by his presence. Gradually he had learned the ropes of life on the base, what was permitted and what was forbidden; his Hebrew had improved somewhat, and he no longer made a nuisance of himself with his questions. Sometimes a kind of clarity appeared on his face, his small eyes suddenly waking up as if becoming known to themselves, as if he had discovered his place at last. He raised his eyes from the notebook and looked with rather amused curiosity at Zero-Zero, burying his head under his knapsack. For a long time he didn't take his eyes off him, trying to understand something. Then he turned his face to Yossie Ressler playing chords on his guitar, and there was no telling if it reflected reproach or bewilderment or an appeal for pity, but something had disturbed him in his writing, troubling his former serenity. Slowly he screwed the top on his fountain pen and sank into thought.

Albert the Bulgarian, as was his habit, lay on his bed naked as the day he was born. Only thus, he argued, did his body get the airing required for perfect repose, refreshment, and naturalness. There was something ostentatious and ridiculous in this habit, something shameless, bizarre, and rather repelling in the attention he devoted to cultivating his body, the concern with which he examined every pimple and spot that appeared on his skin, in the way he stroked his stomach and chest whenever he lay down to rest, carrying on a mysterious dialogue with them, flexing his muscles in order to arouse admiration for their achievements, encouraging them and egging them on as if they were performing animals in a circus. But his easygoing, invariably optimistic nature, his ringing laughter, bursting with health and generosity, his funny accent and the familiarity that came with time, all these had their effect in dispelling the strangeness. "Quiet comes from the head," said Albert, "and noise comes from the nerves." He was pleased by this saying, which more or less covered his philosophy of life and was true, at any rate, of these particular moments. He pressed his chin into his throat and let his eyes wander lovingly along the prospect of his body stretching down from the heights of his head, like a panorama of fields and hills and valleys and woods suddenly spread out before the hiker scaling a peak, his reward for all the rigors of the road. He turned his head to the right and the left, to change the vantage point, not to miss a single view, to expose the dead zones, to gain the horizons, and smiled to himself with satisfaction, a man richly rewarded for his pains.

"I'm spoiling his country for him," said Zackie in a low voice, perhaps to himself, perhaps in defiance of the drowsy calm that had descended on the platoon, covering up the angry words that had reverberated in the air shortly before, covering up all their sins. "He's crazy. He doesn't know what he's talking about. He doesn't know how many Jews we need here in the country against all the Arabs. What does he know about the Arabs anyway? Millions of Arabs, millions and millions. He thinks he's doing me a favor by letting me live here in his country. If he could have seen the way we lived there, he wouldn't talk like that. If we're such trash, why did they come there to fetch us? Why did they get us out? Maybe they thought we were needed here in Israel, that we could do something to help?"

"Don't take any notice of him," counseled Albert. "Hedgehog's all right, he just talks too much. He likes annoying people, it makes him happy."

"He thinks he's clever," said Zackie, "but he's not a man at all. He's a child. He doesn't even have to shave. The only reason he shaves in the morning is to make the hair on his face grow."

This sally made Albert laugh loudly, and the noise of his laughter roused Sammy from his reverie. He gave the naked Bulgarian a threatening look and turned his eyes back to the ceiling, where he went on staring at an invisible point. He too did not need to shave yet, and there was no knowing if it was this that had aroused his wrath or whether his spirit was troubled due to some other cause. His childish face with its little blue ice-cold eyes exuded suppressed anger and hatred. The ugly scar on his fair cheek, whether it was really a souvenir of a knife fight, as people said, or a birthmark or the result of an accident, seemed to hold a threat that nothing would stand in his way and stop him from getting what he wanted. What he wanted was hard to say. Behind the facade of tense, repressed stillness on his face, his forehead frowning in concentration, his blinking eyes and angrily clenched fists, you could see a trapped animal prowling around its cage, circling the bars for the umpteenth time in search of a loophole, possessed by a dybbuk of desperate hope, refusing to learn from experience.

And again nobody spoke, and apart from Ressler's chords reverberating and dying away at unexpected intervals, and Alon's rustling newspaper, and the brief exchanges between the chess players, which were no more than a murmur of surprise or disappointment or a breath of suppressed laughter, there was nothing to disturb the atmosphere of tranquility and friendship descending on the room, welling up in harmony with the silence coming from outside, until the sound of footsteps came running toward us and Hedgehog burst in shouting: "They've found oil in the Negev! There's oil in the state of Israel!" yelling as if the world had collapsed around him.

In the midst of the revival that greeted this news, like the signs of some impending individual salvation, Zackie's voice sounded childish and absurd, still settling some old score.

"My uncle," he cried proudly to Hedgehog, his liquid black always smiling eyes with their curtain of long lashes, dense as a brush — the eyes that always lent an air of falsehood to anything he said, however true — challenging Hedgehog: "My uncle worked for an oil company abroad; he can teach the Israelis a thing or two about it."

"My friend," said Hedgehog, "nobody's interested in Iraqi methods here. Here they'll bring the most modern machinery, the most up-to-date methods. If only Israeli brains are given a free rein, they'll work miracles. But who knows — with those Laborites in power? They're capable of ruining anything."

"You don't know what you're talking about," retorted Zackie. "The oil company in Iraq is English."

"Eenglish!" gloated Hedgehog, who never missed an opportunity to mimic Zackie's accent. "Here they'll operate with American methods. The Eenglish don't count anymore."

"What are you all so happy about?" inquired Albert the Bulgarian. He sat up in bed, arched his back, and massaged his thighs. His face expressed astonishment and contempt, in contrast to his usual light-hearted optimism that dismissed every problem, smoothed over every contradiction. "What are you so happy about? The workers won't get anything out of that oil. The capitalists'll grab all the money, they'll build villas, buy motorcars, go for trips abroad. All that oil will go in their motorcars and the ships that take them on their vacations abroad. Anything left over will go on the machines in their factories that we'll have to work in and wear our arses ragged so they can have even more money. Our lives won't be any better, only harder. That's how it is in life. You're still babies."

This was the first time he had spoken so seriously and weightily about the state of the world, the first time he had shown that he had any opinions, for which his good-humored optimism had acted as a cover. Now he had revealed a small part of his views, and there was no mistaking their nature. His words gave rise to shocked surprise, and more than that —

not so much on account of their content, which might have been accepted as realism or cynicism, but because of the vocabulary he employed. Even the way he pronounced them, in his Bulgarian accent, was different and special and extremely suspect: *the workers, the capitalists.* If these words had come out of the mouth of a sabra, a kibbutznik, or appeared in a local left-wing publication, they would have sounded like naive, idealistic, old-fashioned slogans, or like a parody of the Founding Fathers of the Second Aliyah, but in the mouth of a foreigner they sounded doubly foreign. There was something dark and violent about them, something menacing and subversive, that threatened to overturn what was closest to our hearts, inimical to the integrity of the childhood that had only just been concluded and begun to turn into a memory. (I felt something like this some years later when I heard Hebrew spoken by a man selling Christian tracts in a little bookshop in Jerusalem, an ageless foreigner, whose smile was too polite and whose books gave off a dubious smell of strange drugs, strong disinfectants, and the stifling odor of a closed space that had not known fresh air or sunlight for many a year; a different Hebrew, suave and suspect, which apart from the fact that it was correct and intelligible Hebrew was a foreign language, inciting to sin, touching on old, for-gotten terrors.)

"What are you talking about?" said Hedgehog angrily. "What's the matter with you? Where do you get all that Communist rubbish from? Do you know what you're saying?"

"He's lost his temper already!" Albert burst out laughing, but now the laughter was unnatural, an attempt to wipe out the impression made by his former words, to pretend he wasn't really serious. "You're still a child. When you grow up you'll understand too. You don't even shave yet. What are you so cross about? You yourself said that the Americans would be the bosses. It's got nothing to do with Communists or non-Communists. What do you think, that the Americans will help us because they like the way we look?"

"I don't talk the same language as Communists," said Hedgehog. "As far as I'm concerned all that stuff is a bunch of fairy tales."

"I'm not a Communist," laughed Albert. "Are you crazy? I come from there, I know what it's like. But there are things you don't understand."

Hanan said: "Now they'll start with all those ceremonies and pageants and speeches and songs about the first oil after two thousand years. What a bore!"

Micha raised his head form the chessboard and barked in the shrill voice he kept for imitations of Ben-Gurion: "We expect you to serve as an

example of a new generation of Jews, untainted by all the ills of the diaspora, creative, enterprising, bold, courageously facing every enemy and
foe, capable of mastering the elements of nature, making the desert
bloom, conquering the sea and air, working and creating for the glory of
the independence of Israel and molding a new Hebrew society, one that
will not shame our past or disappoint the messianic yearnings for
redemption of the generations . . ."

The sound of community singing rose from 3 Platoon. Beginning soft
and low, growing louder and more enthusiastic, their voices thundered,
accompanied by hand clapping and foot stamping. I had no doubt that
they were celebrating the news of the discovery of oil in the Negev. Song
followed song and their enthusiasm did not abate. Alon stretched his
neck, turned toward the direction from which the singing was coming,
and looking straight ahead of him said as if addressing the company in
general: "Those men are a cohesive group, with high morale and group
spirit, the way it should be."

"Most of them are high school graduates from Tel Aviv, gilded youth
from Dizengoff Street cafés," said Hanan.

"I bet you that most of them are from pioneering youth movements,"
said Alon. "If they sing like that, at a time like this, they're not gilded café
youth."

Avner, whose sleep had been disturbed by Hedgehog's shouts and the
argument that followed, looked for a moment like a solitary sailor
swaying on a raft on a stormy sea, without aim or direction. In the end he
frowned and said in a whisper: "Will that oil change your life? Why are
they singing as if the Messiah's arrived, as if all their problems have been
solved?"

Something turned over inside me with hatred and rage. The false
naïveté, ironic, supercilious, denying, selfish, ostentatious, held up like a
banner of originality, independence, freedom, honesty, echoed in my ears
like the creaking of an old machine repeating the same stupid, automatic
operation ad nauseam. How thin and mean this irony was compared to
the happy, uninhibited camaraderie, compared to the liberation from
individual bonds, filling the heart with goodwill and hope and identification with something bigger than all of us, with the power uniting us into
one body, with history. How disgusting I suddenly found all Avner's stories of his loves and sufferings, in all their minutest details, accompanied
by his would-be profound reflections, his aphorisms about life, coated
with his eternal self-pity. The hostility his words aroused in me did not
make them foreign to me, however: How could I hide my participation

in this heresy, which infected me like an ugly disease? How could I forget
the hopes and resolutions that were not always successful — not to
become attached, to keep apart and live among them like a stranger, to
maintain my independence of thought, not to be tempted by this sticky
sentimentality? When I heard the words in Avner's mouth, they rang in
my ears like an accusation. I felt an urge to say something hurtful,
insulting, and humiliating to him; to make him feel his nothingness compared to the thing he was rejecting with such arrogance and dismissing
in contempt. But it was impossible to ignore the moments of regret and
guilt that would come afterward, the embarrassment and the self-hate,
the inability to understand why, how it had happened, whether it was
really necessary.

So I said: "If there are circles here like there are in hell, then we're in
the lowest circle and Three Platoon is high above us."

"Rubbish," whispered Avner. "We're both in the same circle, only they
don't know it yet. That's why they can sing like that."

We said no more on the subject. But Avner heard the words left
unspoken too. His face darkened; his eyes reflected suspicion, disappointment, and sorrow at what he invariably regarded as betrayal of friendship, as gratuitous hatred: as one who detested arguments about anything, especially politics or public affairs, he couldn't see any disagree-
ment except as a failure of friendship, a breaking of vows on one of the
sides, a malicious pretext for causing pain and offense. He couldn't
believe in the possibility of an argument that wasn't personal. He was
prepared to understand and forgive two bosom friends who quarreled or
even came to blows over the love of a woman or over material gain. (The
agonies of body and soul, the struggle for survival and the need for love,
were real enough in his eyes, justified by his picture of the world, which
resembled a cinematic drama about the struggle between hostile forces,
full of pity and cruelty, forgiveness and desperate needs.) But in the holy
of holies of personal relations there was no room for arguments about
politics, society, or morals. He saw himself as an aristocrat of feeling,
despising in his heart the benighted masses with their vain beliefs in the
common good and similar abstract ideas, which generally served, in his
opinion, as a self-righteous pretext for fabricating artificial quarrels in
order to hurt the other person not out of any real distress, and without
any justification. Perhaps he had this in mind when he once spoke about
"coldhearted hatred" — which was like death — as opposed to "warm-
hearted hatred," which could sometimes rise to the level of love.

He lit a cigarette and smoked it lying on his back, contemplating the spiraling and dispersing smoke with a kind of tragic concentration, looking almost like the Bible illustrations of Cain contemplating the smoke of his offering that God did not accept.

The mess hall looked like a disaster area whose inhabitants had fled, leaving it clean and neat for those who would come after them, ready to begin again. On the table in one of the corners stood an aluminum basin full of hard-boiled eggs, a tray with loaves of sliced bread, leftovers from the meal before the fast, a big tin of jam and a big pot of cooling tea. At the foot of the table were a few cardboard boxes of battle rations, in case of need. We were among the first to arrive. Gradually the hall filled up, and precisely because the arrivals did not enter in the usual orderly fashion but straggled in any how, in groups and one by one, and sat down where their fancy took them, with no one standing over them to supervise and give orders — they seemed to be getting ready for a festive ceremony about to commence. I saw Arik come into the hall with a few other recruits. I stood up and waved until I caught his eye. Arik said something to his friends and came over to my table.

"Is anyone sitting here? Keep a place for me, I'll be back in a minute," he said and went to get food. After a while he returned, sat down, and began to eat without saying a word. Everyone seated at the table was waiting to see Hedgehog eat on the eve of Yom Kipur for the first time in his life. But Hedgehog, with his mess tin in front of him, containing a hard-boiled egg, bread, and jam, looked at the mess tin and at the people sitting next to him with an expression of despair on his face. Slowly he peeled the egg and, before biting into it, looked at it compassionately. As if he were about to torture a defenseless animal. He closed his eyes, sighed, filled his lungs with air, and returned the peeled egg to the mess tin. Everyone burst out laughing and Hedgehog laughed too, as if taking part in the fun. Arik didn't understand what was going on. I explained to him, but he wasn't amused.

"I don't know what to say to you, guys, I really don't," Hedgehog apologized, "but I can't, I simply can't put it in my mouth. I want to but my body's afraid. Look, drinking for example isn't a problem." He gripped the mug of lukewarm tea and, lifting it to his mouth, took two small sips, looking around triumphantly. "But eating, that's something else. Just thinking about it makes my stomach shrink. I'll get over it in a minute."

"Your body's still Jewish," said Hanan. "It doesn't know that you've become an Israeli."

"Laugh, go on, enjoy yourselves. I don't care," said Hedgehog, and a strange laugh shook his body, as if someone were tickling him. "You just don't understand what education does to a person, how it brainwashes him! All those years of believing, of fear, you've got no idea what it's like." Again he picked up the smooth egg and looked at it as if it were an insect.

Arik said to me: "Have you heard about the oil they found?"

"Yes, just now."

"If there's a lot of it, if they find more — it's serious business."

The people sitting around the table cheered loudly: Hedgehog had bitten into the egg and eaten half of it. He chewed and chewed, and in the end he swallowed what was in his mouth with an exaggerated movement of his head, trying not to choke on his laughter. He was beginning to enjoy the performance more than his spectators.

"How was your leave?" asked Arik.

"I met Ilana," I said, "she told me about what happened to Ginger Pesach. Have you heard about it?"

"No," said Arik. "I've already forgotten that he exists. What happened to him?"

"He ran away from his unit in the army and stowed away on a ship in Haifa port. They only discovered him on the high seas, when he came out of his hiding place to look for food. They kept him on the ship as a prisoner, and when they returned to Israel he was court-martialed. They decided he was off his head and discharged him from the army. And now he's in Geha, in the loony bin."

"What do you say!" cried Arik. "He really was crazy, we just didn't realize it. You remember him on that night after the party at the school cadets camp?"

"When he ran past the girls naked?"

"After he roamed around outside in the dark pulling up all the saplings we'd spent three days planting. And the shock we got in the morning — you remember? When we came outside to drive home — hundreds of saplings lying all over the ground! And that religious instructor's face, when he saw it."

"You said then it was the most beautiful thing that had happened to us in all the three days we were there, that it was the most right thing that had been done there."

"What do you say! Did I say that?"

"Yes."

"I don't remember. You go on remembering every nonsensical remark that comes out of my mouth. Tell me, haven't you got anything better to do with your memory? But when I think about it now, then I really do think it was beautiful. Don't you think so? There was madness in it, but a beautiful, liberating, rebellious madness. Admit that there's something in destruction, a kind of poetic, moving, imaginative beauty that no construction can match. So now he's in Geha. I wonder if Naomi knows."

We washed our mess tins and walked away from the mess hall. "I'm on guard duty this evening," said Arik. "Let's walk around a bit, I've still got some time to kill. A person can breathe here at last. Everything's full of holiness and quiet."

I too felt that this evening was dispelling a certain claustrophobic oppression, as if I were returning to myself after a long absence. It wasn't only the serene stillness and the darkness descending early on the camp and as if emptying it of its inhabitants, nor the autumn breeze shaking the leaves of the eucalyptus trees, sending a soft, consoling rustle through them like a sweet, deceitful promise that the nightmare was over, that this stillness would last forever, but also something in the rhythm of my body's gait, the movements of my legs, the inclination of my head, something so familiar, slow and deliberate, trying to arrest the passage of time, as on the days when we would dawdle home from school, dragging the time out as long as we could, talking for hours.

Arik took a breath as if he wanted to say something, but stopped himself, let the breath out as a sigh, and was silent.

I said: "Maybe Naomi does know. I think she and Ilana correspond."

"Who doesn't she correspond with?" said Arik. "Did I tell you that she's planning a class reunion next year? She can't stop being a busybody. She's not prepared to let go of a single relationship, a single memory, a single thread that seems to her to connect her to the world, to what she thinks is her world. What a revolting idea: a class reunion!"

What was it that drew me again and again into these conversations with Arik? After our last talk I had been oppressed by the sense of disconnection and estrangement that he and his peculiar ideas aroused in me. I said to myself: *Our ways have parted, I've parted from my childhood,* and a kind of happiness mingled with curiosity, like embarking on an adventure, dispelled the pain of this parting, sounding a call of independence in my ears: *I won't fall into that trap again! I won't fall into that trap again!* And here we were strolling together again, and although we were silent now, we were continuing something that had not stopped inside us, and even the tread of our nailed boots, knocking into stones, crushing grains of soil on the paved path, sounded that forgotten rhythm, the rhythm of setting forth on those interminable conversations, and just like then the creaking of the speaker's shoe was different from the creaking of the listener's shoe, and like then I walked a step ahead of Arik and turned my head slightly backward while Arik dragged his feet and kept his eyes on the ground as if seeking the right word there.

"You remember the red tape hanging from the lightbulb in the grocer's? That paper covered with sugar and glue that attracts the flies and they stick to it and can't move anymore, and when they've eaten their fill of sugar they flap their wings and try to fly and they can't — their feet are stuck to the sugar, and more and more of them come and stick to each other, and the paper grows black with flies, and they're stuck there forever, it's all up for them. Well, clinging nostalgically to memories, trying to stop them from disappearing, hanging on to the past so it won't slip away from us — that's a kind of trap too, a kind of glue covered with sugar. That whole period at high school was a disgusting period, so why all these longings for it? How can you long for everyone? I can understand having some sentiments for two or three people, for people who played some kind of role in your life, who leave you with something, who go on existing somehow in your present too, but a whole class! With most of them I had nothing in common even when I was at school, I couldn't stand them, and they weren't crazy about me either. So why on earth should I take any interest in them now, why should I take the trouble to go and meet them?"

"Once you talked about loyalty, loyalty to the dream, loyalty to friends, to the past, to memory. What other way does a person have of being loyal to himself? With Naomi it's a kind of loyalty."

"Our loyalty to ourselves is a choice we make, what to throw out and what to keep, to live with the selection of memory. There are some things that memory pushes deep down and leaves dormant, and other things that it leaves on top. Being loyal to memory means being loyal to its game. But with Naomi it's not that kind of loyalty. She's obsessed with the past; it's only from the past that she can hope for anything good. And it always seems to her that once upon a time she was happier. In the present she can't cope, the future terrifies her, all she's got left is the past, a safe refuge, from which she can still hope for something good. Imagine if we had to spend all our lives on memories and class reunions from primary school, from high school, from basic training, from army units, from places we'll be in afterward, from all the periods when we met all kinds of people in all kinds of circumstances. We wouldn't have time to live! And so, we simply forget. I know that I'll forget. I choose to forget and go ahead. Naomi's place in my life, and Eli Shapiro's, won't be what it was either after one or two years without contact between us. I'm not talking about letters or two or three meetings a year, that's nonsense, it's not natural, it's an artificial connection. Not much will remain of it, apart from a certain embarrassment and a slight bad conscience. And now, you think there aren't a couple of good guys in my platoon, whom I feel friendship for, whom I'm together with all the time, going through this hell with them — so what? After basic training each of us will go to his unit and there won't be any contact between us, we'll become strangers and the memories will sink and grow dormant and fade. And after being discharged from the army? Another parting and everyone will go somewhere else and forget the people from his unit and form new ties. And you, what do you think, that you'll remember that ridiculous character who's afraid of eating on Yom Kippur forever? And the other one, who kept looking into his mouth and yelling: *Chew, chew!* And the others who laughed all the time, and that epileptic of yours who falls during inspection? Maybe you'll remember some detail, some face, some particular incident, something funny or something that hurt you. Scars will remain, that's for sure, they'll stay with you for the rest of your life, but all that won't be connected any longer with here and now, they'll just be dry, dead crumbs without any meaning. In a few years' time you won't remember anything alive, real; only the present gives things life. That's why the damned in Dante's *Inferno* don't know what's happening in the present, because they're no longer alive. They only know the past and the future."

"Then I'll have to invent them," I said, "make up new memories from my imagination, instead of the ones that have disappeared, create a new past for myself."

"An artificial limb," said Arik, letting out his breath and giving vent to his creaking, bitter laugh, after which he raised his head and fixed me with the lenses of his glasses, as if trying to ascertain whether I had been speaking seriously and, if so, where such nonsense had sprung from.

We entered the lines of his platoon. He looked at his watch, couldn't make out the figures, ran over to the lamp shining on the roof of one of the buildings, came back and said: "I've got another half an hour."

We went on walking until we reached a little hill overlooking the path leading to the staff quarters. We sat on top of it.

Arik said: "There's only one alternative — to have a family. Get married, have children. That's the only relationship that's worth investing in. The only thing that really stays with you. All the rest is childish nonsense, romantic dreams. Today I understand this better than ever. Precisely now, when my parents are getting a divorce."

I was embarrassed and didn't know what to say. Arik enjoyed such moments, when he succeeded in shocking his listeners. He looked at me, relishing my embarrassment, and smiled triumphantly.

"They've gone mad," he said, "at their age! How long have they got left altogether? The truth is that they were never happy together, and it was only because of me that they never separated years ago. By now they just can't stand each other. They don't even hate each other. They're like two strangers, with just one son, me, joining them together. No memories, you understand, no sentiments, only this great common project — me. Imagine the sense of responsibility, the sacrifice, the endurance they must have needed. What a sense of mission! And all for the sake of bringing up this wonderful, unique Arik!

"He wants to leave the country and go and live in Germany. Germany of all places! Him of all people, who escaped from there at the last minute, and saved himself from the camps and the war and all that. Go understand what happens in the hearts of people whose families were all wiped out over there, mother, father, brothers — everyone. I never understood, even though I grew up with them. They never talked about it. Never. Maybe in order not to poison my childhood, not to complicate my life, so I wouldn't feel different, not to spoil my Israeliness. Nice of them, actually. In any case he intends to go to Germany, he'll get a lot of money there, and he'll die in the only place in the world where he feels at home. So they sat down and talked to me. I'm a soldier now, a big boy, I can take it. On the face of it, they're leaving it up to me to choose what I want to do after the army, join him and live in Europe, with all the possibilities and advantages that implies, or stay in Israel with her. But the truth is, he's leaving me with a sick old woman whom I'll have to carry on my shoulders and take care of alone. I won't leave her here on her own, I'm already trapped in the net of their responsibility. Besides, I don't want to leave Israel. I might go abroad to study for a few years, enjoy myself, see the world, but I can't see myself living there. There are too many things tying me to this lousy place. I only wish I could get rid of them, but I can't. And I don't want to be a refugee, like my parents.

"Anyway, when they were sitting and talking to me, afraid to look me in the eye, ashamed of their failure, as if they were guilty of something, I felt real love for them for the first time in my life. I actually wanted to get up and embrace them — seriously! Suddenly I sensed how much they'd sacrificed, how serious the whole business of marriage and family is, how complicated, what a terrible responsibility. It really is a life's work. All kinds of things that up till then had seemed to me small, insignificant, self-evident, now seemed to me, looking back, like a kind of quiet, humble heroism. I know I want that kind of depth for myself.

"And that's why, when people talk about loyalty to friends and pacts of friendship and all those phrases, it sounds ridiculous, infantile. All those childish ties are superficial, it's all one big bluff. You can't build anything serious on them, they don't involve any real responsibility. Those relationships don't give any real depth to your life. They're as fruitful and stable as shifting sand. In short, a dubious business. And please note: I'm not talking about love now — I'm talking about starting a family. Like my parents. I'm certain there was never any love between them. Not one single day of love. At any rate, not since I've known them. It was a kind of contract. Maybe the result of necessity or of circumstances I know nothing about. I don't know. And in my eyes it's beautiful. Look, I've got to go now, it's time for my guard."

He let out a curse on the privilege of guarding the Motherland.

I said: "Do you remember that moron who crapped on the teacher's desk on the last day of school when we were in grade school?"

"Of course! Benny-trousers."

"You know what," I said, "he's an instructor in our platoon."

"What do you say! I hope he's changed his trousers since then."

"He's changed everything!" I said. "I hardly recognized him. He reminded me who he was."

"What's he like?"

"Terrible. A real sadistic animal. And he's learned to talk, you should hear him. What cynicism, what hatred. Not to mention the new methods of harassment and humiliation he brought with him from the paratroops. It's no joke, I'm telling you."

"And I suppose you get special treatment from him. They're the worst. The losers, the underdogs. So it seems that what he did then on the teacher's desk wasn't his swan song. His career's only beginning now. I don't envy you."

"He's completely different," I said. "You wouldn't recognize him."

"You know," said Arik, resuming the tone in which he'd once delighted in reporting on the scientific discoveries he read about in foreign journals, "this is their chance to rise in the world, the nonentities, the neurotics, the ugly, the stupid, the ones who were always left out of everything and didn't dare open their mouths, the ones everybody laughed at, who were never promoted at the end of the year. Listen, there's justice in the world, here's where they get their compensation, where they can realize their dreams."

"I thought about what you said last time, that evil is power. I think you're right. But what's it's opposite? Is good weakness?"

"No," said Arik. "I don't know." He quickened his pace so as not to be late for his guard, and it was evident that his heart was no longer in this conversation.

After we parted I returned to the hill where we had been sitting before then descended to the road leading to the staff quarters. Maybe I would find my way back to the platoon from there. The darkness, which always upset my weak sense of orientation, was denser and more definite than on other evenings. For a long time I walked along the broad road searching for the path branching out from it, leading to the mess or the canteen, from which I would know how to get back to my platoon. I tried one of the paths that was illuminated by a garish light. I stood not far from a building unknown to me, a long, narrow edifice, windowless and roofed with galvanized tin, surrounded by a barbed-wire fence, the bulb burning on its facade lighting up the two recruits on guard next to it. Before they noticed me and made me give the password and made a fool of me or worse, I quickly retraced my steps and found myself standing again on the road leading to the staff quarters, trying to remember how I had returned to my quarters after my previous conversation with Arik, about two weeks before. But it wasn't the same place. The darkness had changed it beyond recognition, obliterating all the ways out, shuffling like a pack of cards all the landmarks I had succeeded in rescuing from oblivion. I tried to get back to the little hill where Arik and I had been sitting not long before, but it had disappeared. A strange feeling, the likes of which I had never known before, began to clutch at the back of my neck: This must be what a fugitive felt like! Something standing in his way, inimical to him, making him go around in circles, closing off all his exits. But instead of the circle closing in on him, it expands like ink spreading on blotting paper, like a slow fire in dry grass. Time too begins to betray him, conspiring with the hostile forces on the ground.

After my eyes had become accustomed to the inner circle I had drawn to prevent myself from becoming utterly lost, after traversing it a number of times and familiarizing myself with the objects I encountered again and again from different directions, as I approached from far and near, I was confronted with an essential question, a question of principle: How to proceed from here? Should I try to break out of the circle, set out on the long road and advance in a straight line that led in an unknown direction and might even take me farther from my goal, expose me to danger, and waste my time? Or would it be better to remain within the inner circle, within the few dozen square yards I had marked off and already knew from every side — and gradually, cautiously, methodically expand it. This question, for all that it was cold and matter-of-fact, subject to the calculations of practical logic and in need of a quick reply, sent a fierce pain running through me, as if I had been hurtled through a kind of shortcut to the moment of blindness, to the point of disorientation, to the sensation of the first step dragging my feet in the opposite direction and drawing me to a place that did not exist in reality but only, apparently, inside me, in the nocturnal topography of my fear. The pain was accompanied by a sick feeling of nausea at the loathsomeness of this Sisyphean running around myself, around the uniqueness of myself, like a vortex ceaselessly accelerating under the spell cast by the first moment of disorientation, the moment that repeated itself over and over inside me, like the beats of a machine. Perhaps the silence that had fallen over the camp and the platoon in the afternoon was yet another mirage intended to put my fears to sleep, to draw my feet toward the trap. Perhaps at this very moment one of the instructors was entering the barracks to carry out a sudden inspection, to see if anyone was missing. How would it happen? What would be the punishment for disobeying this explicit order? More hard labor, more humiliation, more harassment, more senseless suffering, to the last drop of air in my lungs, to the threshold of oblivion, to the breaking point? There was no limit to their ingenuity, so intimate was their acquaintance with the power of fear, their skill at putting it into effect. How would it happen? I tried to imagine it without success.

I turned off the road, walked a few dozen paces down the hillside to a meager clump of eucalyptus trees, sat down at their feet, closed my eyes, rested my hands against my cheeks, and waited for something to happen to the decision I had to make, but a kind of sleepiness dimmed my ability to think, turned my limbs to stone, choked up my throat. At the same time it became clear to me that the moment of disorientation was the moment of awakening. If I fell asleep, perhaps I would return to the moment, to the place, to the error, and begin everything over again. Incredible how far the platoon building was from here, how distant those friends, their names, nicknames, faces, voices, as if years had already gone by, as if it were already necessary to bring the imaginary memories to bear, to add the artificial limbs. Perhaps the barracks were visible from a turning in some path that I had overlooked. However I tried to frighten myself with something that might be happening now in the platoon, I knew that this fear was nothing compared to the other fear in my heart, the nameless fear that on this evening had turned this place into a dark

forest in which to go astray. The fear calling to me to surrender, to
abandon myself, to accept the situation with love, not to make any decisions, not to exert myself in any direction, to observe it like a stranger, to
rest without expecting anything, to lean against the tree trunk, to close
my eyes, to dive into the fear, to let myself be borne away on it to other
places, empty of people, empty of myself.

The light breeze shaking the leaves of the eucalyptus trees, making
them look like a quorum of thin old Jews swaying in silent prayer on
Yom Kippur, died down. There was not a rustle to be heard. I didn't
know if I had dropped off for a moment or if my mind had been distracted by some thought that had suddenly been forgotten. But the voices
of the evening began to filter through the silence surrounding me, as if
tiny holes had been pricked here and there in the delicate, transparent
veil that had enveloped me up to now, separating me from the outer
circle, like the sky above me, which up to this moment had been covered
with an impermeable layer of clouds without a star to be seen, until the
cover had begun to disintegrate and the radiance of the night had become
brighter.

They've gone mad, at their age! How long have they got left altogether?
This was how Arik always spoke of his parents, with a certain coldness
and dismissiveness, objectively, sometimes even sneeringly. His father
was a dentist who had not succeeded in learning Hebrew in all his years
in the country. They had a big new house in one of the better streets of
the town. Arik avoided inviting his friends home. Now they were getting
divorced and his father was going to settle in Germany. "There's only one
alternative." Was he in love with Naomi? Perhaps it was her he meant,
Naomi who was in love with Eli Shapiro, who used to be and perhaps
still was his best friend, and who wasn't in love with Naomi but felt only
friendship for her, and ignored all the rest. *Look: I'm not talking about love
now.* Why not, in fact? Why did he thrust this aside as something irrelevant? Did he consider love too as a dubious business, as fruitful and stable
as shifting sand? I had never succeeded in getting to the bottom of what
he thought, which may have been the reason why I was always going
back to him, breaking all my resolutions never to fall into that trap again.
Did he still love Naomi? Maybe he hoped that one day she would realize
she didn't have a chance with Eli Shapiro, that she should forget him, and
that the years of close, intimate friendship between her and Arik would
miraculously bestow the grace of complete, true, mutual love. Was this
what he believed? Was this the reason he extolled marriage as a contract,
as the result of circumstances, seeking the lowest possible point of depar-

ture, holding less disappointment and more possibilities of hope? And maybe he expected to meet the love of his life as a manifestation of destiny waiting for him somewhere along the road, like Avner's story about meeting the love of his life at Hanan's party in Jerusalem. There was no knowing. I knew so little about Arik, after all those talks, after all these years. It was impossible to think of Arik as married to someone who wasn't Naomi, who loved somebody else more than she loved him, a chaste love, full of silent, despairing protest.

Between the clouds an almost full moon was suddenly revealed, illuminating the trees and the broad patches of shade and the dirt road with a pure, watery radiance such as I could remember only in the bedroom window on the most remote nights of my childhood. The landscape around me spread out and stretched into empty expanses on the sides of the road, next to the buildings, between the trees, taking the place of what had a moment before been a dark, dense forest.

The sound of voices and footsteps approached along the road. I stood up immediately and hid behind a slender tree trunk. The voices were those of two girls. Soon I would be able to distinguish between the two voices and hear what they were saying. Soon I would see them passing me. The inner circle grew narrower and narrower, the outer circle washing over it from every side. Soon it would turn into a tiny island, be flooded and disappear. The louder and closer the voices became, the more conspicuous I felt, vulnerable and exposed to the moonlit landscape that had opened up around me. The two girls burst out laughing. And after the laughter there was a silence, and then a voice again, a low, soft, clear voice, monotonously reciting words it was still hard to decipher, but whose cadence held a promise of delight, of secrecy and security.

"Pansies, thoughts that stay hidden in the heart. Peony, I blushed with shame. Honeysuckle, friendship, generosity, and devotion. Jasmine, charm, sweetness, amiability. Quince, temptation and danger. Anenome, illness. Cyclamen, modesty. Harebell, I can always be relied upon. Bay leaf, I change but in death . . ."

The two girls passed me and I succeeded in seeing them only from behind. I felt an urge to follow them, to break the spell of the disorientation, and I had hardly taken a step out of my hiding place when the monotonous recitation stopped. One of the girls turned around and stood looking about her as if she had heard a suspicious noise. I stood rooted to the spot. It seemed to me that I recognized the face bathed in the moonlight, the short haircut, the inclination of the neck, the alert, confident, untamed stance, like that of a noble beast raising its head, sniffing signs of danger, thrilling the heart as a reflection of the night no less than she had thrilled it then, when she was first revealed in the dusk of the day with her two dogs. Now she was wearing the skirt of her uniform with a striped civilian blouse, whose color I could not make out.

Her friend asked: "What's up?"

Ofra did not reply but lifted her chin and went on sniffing, to discover the direction from which danger was liable to come, after which she turned to face her friend and looked at her for a moment, as if trying to remember the point at which she had stopped her recitation. They went on walking, and she said: "Bluebell, my constancy is boundless. Asphodel, my regret follows you to the grave. Rosemary, I'll never forget."

"I've never even heard of most of them," said the voice of the other girl. "I've never heard their names."

"Because they're real, they're from nature," said Ofra. "You don't know anything about nature."

"And the rose, what about the rose?" asked the girl anxiously, almost in distress. "The rose is my favorite flower."

"The rose is three things at once," said Ofra. "The three attributes of love — beauty, desire, and pain. Its color is beauty, its smell is desire, and its thorns are the pain of love."

"Oh, how sweet! I have to write them all down so I won't forget," said the girl.

"You can always ask me," said Ofra. "I'll remember for both of us." She added something else, which I couldn't hear, but I heard them both laugh as a result. Their voices faded into the distance. I waited another minute or two, stepped out of my hiding place, and walked silently after the two shadows, not taking my eyes off them for a second, in case they vanished down one of the side paths and I lost the chance getting back to my platoon again. There was something disturbing and spellbinding in the atmosphere of the night surrounding the two girls whose shadows I followed from a distance, in what little of their conversation I had managed to overhear when they were close to my hiding place, and in all I could hear of it now, the rising intonation of their voices, the ringing laughter, and the silences, silences full of beauty that my heart did not dare to fill with pictures of its own creation.

The two girls turned onto one of the paths on the right of the road. I quickened my steps in order to keep them in view. When I turned into the path I saw that they had stopped not far from the corner to look back over their shoulders. About ten paces separated us. They turned on their heels and stood looking at me. This moment could have gone on forever.

Ofra's face was very calm, the light of the lamp cast soft shadows on her cheeks and under her eyes and on her cleft chin, and there was only a hint of astonishment in her light, wide, inward-gazing eyes. Her friend, who was slightly shorter than she was, with short curly black hair and a cheerful face, and who bore a surprising, hard-to-define resemblance to the girl glimpsed for a moment, like a fleeting shadow, leaving the company office with Benny on the night of that ill-fated guard. She smiled and glanced from me to Ofra and back again, curious to see what was going to happen. My eyes fell suddenly on the end of the path and the group of buildings there: the staff barracks. In my straying I had been sure that they were at the other end of the main road. Fear shook my heart, a concrete, defined fear, with a cause and an object and a host of possibilities each worse than the next. I realized that I now knew the way back to the platoon, but I couldn't move from where I was standing.

Ofra roused herself from her reverie. An impatient expression appeared on her face. She made a gesture of weariness and disgust with her hand and turned her face away, her friend followed suit, and they both turned around and walked slowly toward the staff quarters. I stood and watched them walking until I heard them burst out laughing. I assumed that they were laughing at me. I was seized with shame. I would have given a lot to know what they were saying to each other that made them laugh so much.

The familiar buildings were all standing in their expected places. My feet already knew the way. I approached my platoon lines. Were my ears deceiving me? They were still singing in 3 Platoon. The lights weren't out yet. How long had I been lost? Far less time than I thought. I stood next to their building to listen to their singing: "The wheat sways in a golden sea, Merrily the herd bells peal, These are the fields of my country, This is the valley of Jezreel. May my country blessed be, From Beth Alfa to Nahalal . . ."

Not far from the platoon, on the path leading to the armory, I saw a silhouette; someone was bending over in front of a tree, as if in prayer or supplication. Strange, hoarse grunts, choking and gasping, rose from the bowed figure. I turned off from the path and came closer to see who it was. Hedgehog was vomiting up his supper.

CHAPTER 21

There was a shout of "Attention!" Raffy Nagar entered the room with Benny, Muallem, and five MPs. The platoon stood rigidly to attention, every man in front of his bed, and the faces of the instructors were stern and solemn, important with gravity of the occasion. The MPs immediately surrounded Sammy's bed. One of them ordered him to open his knapsack, overturned it, spilled its contents on the floor, and began examining the items one by one. A second MP overturned Sammy's mattress, spread the blankets out and shook them, and searched the pouches of his webbing. A third opened the locker next to his bed, emptied its contents onto the floor, and began to search through it. Raffy Nagar stood a few paces away, watching the proceedings with a stern, thoughtful expression on his face. Benny and Muallem paced up and down the aisle in the middle of the room, making sure that no one stepped out of line. One of the MPs, holding a large flashlight, knelt down next to Sammy's bed and shone the flashlight underneath it, after which he moved the bed from its place and turned it upside down. His colleague began searching Sammy's clothes. When he found nothing, he ordered him to get undressed and take off his shoes. Sammy took off his clothes and stood barefoot, in his underpants, his small blue eyes staring indifferently, colder than ever, at the MP searching the clothes that lay in a heap on the floor, a thin, rather forced smile on his lips, the ugly scar on his cheek twitching in a gloating sneer. Everything was done in silence; even their questions and commands were addressed to Sammy in an undertone, a dry, efficient, unemotional staccato. And it was this that made it so sudden and shocking: the scream that pierced the silence, like the shriek of screeching brakes, when the MPs quickly surrounded Sammy in the corner between his upturned bed and the wall and hid him from view: one brief cry of terrible, bestial pain — "No!" — and when they withdrew, Sammy was writhing on the floor, his body doubled up and his hands waving up and down like those of a drowning man signaling for help.

Raffy Nagar hurried to the corner: "In the balls?" he asked, in concern or perhaps surprise.

"It's nothing," said one of the MPs, "He's just putting on an act. We know his type."

"Get dressed!" Raffy commanded Sammy.

Sammy went on writhing on the floor, his face twisted in pain.

"Get up! Stop malingering!" Raffy Nagar yelled at the top of his lungs. "Get up immediately if you don't want another dose!"

Sammy rose laboriously to his feet. He couldn't straighten up. His face was very red. Whenever he tried to move he closed his eyes and held his and optimism, an ostentatious, exaggerated demonstration, as if to cover up some guilt: Has he seen? Nahum's face is flushed with suppressed excitement; he smiles his distant, astonished smile. Miller is sunk in some private reverie, showing no interest in what is happening around him. Ben-Hamo's face and posture display concentration and curiosity instead of their usual stupid complacency. A rare flash of intelligence and cunning as well as a hint of malice illuminate his features and his dark, narrowed eyes, which glitter as they dart quickly from Avner to the MPs and Raffy Nagar and back to Avner, encountering mine and avoiding them guiltily, and then returning to the MPs and to Avner. Does he know something? Will he talk? There's no telling how he will act. Peretz-Mental-Case stands rigidly at attention, as grave and solemn as if he's on the CO's inspection. Only his jaw and cheek muscles tighten and relax without stopping, regular as clockwork. Zackie's face is overshadowed by a dull, listless gloom. His eyes, with their thick, brushlike lashes, are downcast, his shoulders slumped, as if all the energy has drained out of his body. The laughter, the childish games, the jokes, the obscenities are over: Is this the moment of truth? He seems to know something. He won't talk. Raffy Nagar announces that the minute is up.

One MP joins each of the two instructors, who divide the rows of recruits between them. The third MP walks up and down the aisle with a slow, deliberate, menacing tread, to make sure that nobody moves or does anything suspicious. They work quietly and thoroughly; they have plenty of time. Only the barked commands disturb the busy silence every couple of minutes as they pass from bed to bed, from suspect to suspect.

"Did he give you anything?"

"No, sir."

"Did anybody else give you anything?"

"No, sir."

"Did you see him give anything to anybody else?"

"No, sir."

"Get undressed!"

Suspect after suspect strips down to his underpants and bare feet. They shake his clothes, search his pockets, shake out his socks, shine a flashlight into his shoes. They search the bed and its surroundings.

"Empty your knapsack here!"

Suspect after suspect empties the contents of his knapsack onto the floor in front of his bed. They pick up every article of clothing, every object, and pass it from hand to hand; they delve to the bottom of the knapsack in case anything has been left behind. They order lockers to be emptied, they shine their flashlights into the corners. They examine web-bing, pouches, straps, belts, canteens, they strip blankets from beds, shake them, overturn mattresses, examine the ticking and feel the stuffing, they shine their lights under the beds, and when they find nothing they give the suspect a long, searching stare and pass on to the next one. And the whole performance begins again.

Out of the corner of my eye I can see Avner's feet on my left standing at ease, every now and then shifting his weight from one foot to the other. There is no telling what he's thinking, no knowing if his face reflects his thoughts. Is the slowness of the proceeding agony for him? How alien to me he is at these moments. People like him never learn their lesson. How I loathe that element in his personality that attracts trouble like a magnet, how I detest his dubious friendships, his strange loyalties to principles, to people, that endanger him, that are liable to involve others too, whose only crime was to have been accidental eyewitnesses to his guilt. How dared he! Apparently people couldn't change. How lonely he is at moments like these, alone confronting his fate. His character is his fate. So let his fate be fulfilled, let him be caught, let him be punished!

Alon is already packing his things, slowly and carefully, with a calm, contented air, as if he has returned from a successful mission and is get-ting everything ready for the next one. They pass on to Micky, and soon will reach Avner.

"Don't be smart! Don't forget what you are!" the MP suddenly yells at Micky.

I turn my eyes in the direction of Micky's bed and can't stop myself from getting in a quick look at Avner as I do so. My eyes meet his, which say *What have I got to do with you?* and immediately part, like a brief encounter between enemies. Avner's face betrays nothing. His thick brows, slightly raised, wrinkle his forehead in an expression of indiffer-ence and disdain; his shoulders slump as if he is tired of standing and waiting for nothing.

Sammy's cry of No! — the cry of a wounded animal, sharp and menacing — is still echoing in my ears, and beneath the deceptive silence, the dry voices, the brief commands, the footsteps of the MP pacing up and down the aisle, beneath the sounds of activity, some terrible violence lies slum-bering, biding its time.

What did Micky say to bring down the wrath of the MP on him? There is no knowing. Whatever it was, the inspection drags out, perhaps to punish him for his impertinence. And just as on that dawn when Avner was caught asleep at his post and robbed of his gun, now too I feel that I have it in my power, the power of fear, the power of treachery, to prevail against the weight of time, to influence the action, to summon it into reality. My eyes fall on the dark window in the opposite wall. The feeling takes hold of me that someone is standing outside in the darkness, watching us. I stare at the window until I seem to see a kind of black, rectangular eye gazing into our souls, omniscient, understanding, forgiving.

They move from Micky's bed to Avner's. I say to myself: *I can't see anything, I'm listening to a play on the radio.* Did he give you anything? No, sir. Did anyone else give you anything? No, sir. Did you see him give anyone else anything? No, sir. Get undressed and take off your shoes and socks. The rustle of clothing. Breathing. Footsteps approaching. Raffy Nagar's voice: He was in jail. What for? Falling asleep on guard. Abandoning his weapon. Faster! Yes, sir. Shoes falling. Turn your socks inside out. The rustle of clothing. Your field dressing's torn. I didn't know, sir. I didn't see that it was torn. You tore it. No, sir, perhaps it tore by itself. Why did you tear it? I didn't tear it, sir, I don't know how it happened. Look inside the dressing, maybe he hid it there. Silence. Give me the dressing. Empty your knapsack here. The noise of things falling on the floor. What's this? Silence. Breathing. Pass it over here.

In the opposite row they're searching Zero-Zero. Benny and the MP bend over the heap on the floor. Benny suddenly straightens up: "Disgusting! Disgusting!" The MP suggests: "Let him pick up whatever we tell him himself." Benny cries: "It stinks like a carcass here! What did you put into it?" Zero-Zero mumbles: "Nothing, sir." "What's this, a towel?" asks Benny. "You piece of filth, it's like a cesspool in there, it's rotten with dirt. You'll pay for this. What's this here, this black bit, blood?" Zero-Zero says: "Yes, sir, it's from shaving."

A roar of laughter erupts from those who have already been searched and who are now busy putting their belongings in order, and those who are still awaiting their turn: It begins in a kind of hum, timid and hesitant, and immediately turns into loud laughter, as if in defiance of the solemnity of the hour. Raffy Nagar turns red and yells: "Stop it!" A silence falls, in which it is still possible to sense the liberating tremor secretly flowing from man to man, like friendship, uniting them in the bonds of a new love, as if the necessary violence has already been done, as if the sacrifice has already been made, as if their hearts have already been cleansed and purified.

On my left the talking has almost stopped, except for the questions of the MP asking "What's this?" without pausing for a reply. Something is waiting in the wings there, delaying its emergence into reality. They're turning over the mattress, pushing the bed around, shaking the blankets; there comes a rattle of mess tins, the creak of nailed boots on the floor. Open it. Take everything out. Is this yours? Yes, sir. Hand it over.

"Stand at attention when your instructor's talking to you!"

At first I don't understand what's happening. Muallem and the MP are standing in front of me and I don't know who they are. I am supposed to do something, but for a second my memory goes blank, I don't know what I'm doing in this terrible place and who the people around me are. Like the moment when I began to regain consciousness after I fainted during the silencing-a-sentry exercise. Muallem shouts something. His shout triggers something inside me, reactivating the automaton that came to a standstill and introducing a certain order into events. No, sir, no, sir, I reply to his questions without paying any attention to their content. "Did you see him give anyone else anything?" No, sir. "Get undressed and take off your shoes and socks."

My body, still slow to wake, moves clumsily, fettered, heavy, and weary. My fingers are unable to undo the laces of my gaiters. My hands are shaking and I don't know why.

"Faster!"

After taking off my shoes and socks and turning the latter inside out, I bend down to remove my trousers, and my eyes fall on Avner on my left getting dressed. The knowledge strikes me like a flash of lightning, with overpowering clarity: He has not been caught. And immediately afterward, like a thunderbolt: They'll find it on me!

My body breaks out in perspiration and seems to me to be weeping. I stand in front of them in my underpants, my body's tears flowing down my neck and chest, watching them searching my clothes, as curious as they to know where it's hidden, as eager to discover it. If only I knew, I would help them gladly, to shorten the process, to realize the fear. *I don't have any idea how it got there,* I repeat to myself, *I don't know, I don't know!* There isn't a chance of convincing anyone. Nobody will believe me. Even in my own ears the words sound false, ingenuous, hollow. This time I'm the scapegoat, it's my turn now. Something is coming to an end. Sammy's scream echoes deafeningly inside my head: *No!* Something's coming to an end and something new is beginning. Maybe this is the way one identity is concluded and another one begins, detail added to detail, story after story, like falling down a steep slope from rock to rock, a new memory, a new will, a new dream. My clothes and possessions lying on the floor are passed from hand to hand and my heart denies them, glad of their humiliation. *I'm being destroyed,* I say to myself, *without fear or hope, I'm being gradually destroyed.*

At the end of the search, after they had passed on to the bed at my right, my clothes and possessions stared at me like a heap of corpses after the battle, after the defeat. The sigh of relief was slow in rising to my chest. Something of the nausea I had felt on the evening I lost my way after the meeting with Arik troubled me now too. Avner had already made his bed and folded his blankets and was standing at ease in front of the bed. I got dressed, and as I bent down to tie my laces I sensed Avner looking at me, as if he wanted to say something. I looked at him out of the corner of my eye but his face was expressionless, apart from sadness and a great weariness. I bent down over my boots again and a surge of gratitude toward this strange fellow suddenly flooded my heart, and I didn't know why. Perhaps it was the sigh of relief that had taken so long to come.

Raffy Nagar surveyed the platoon, his eyes hard. "He'll talk under interrogation," he said. "In the CID they know how to make people talk. He'll tell us who he gave it to. This is the last chance for whoever's got it to think again if he wants to be incriminated and go to jail, if he wants to be tarred by the brush of the underworld for the rest of his life. Whoever's got it has got until lights-out to make up his mind. I'll be in the company office, he can come to me and make a clean breast of it and forget about it. Every one of you has to make his own reckoning. Who do you want to defend, who do you want to cover up for? Ask yourselves what you want to turn this country into. There are some good lads here, lads that your instructors and I have come to know and think well of. There are high school graduates among you with enough education to understand what I'm saying, and decent chaps with open minds and honesty and goodwill who're trying to keep their noses clean and overcoming their difficulties, and they can be good soldiers and be useful to the country and also develop and learn all kinds of things that will help them in civilian life. I know every man in this platoon and I know that most of you are men no commander need feel ashamed of. I can't see any reason why they should suffer because of a few criminal types who landed up in the army by mistake and will be vomited out by the IDF in any case, like the healthy body vomits up poison and filth. I'm talking to now not just as an instructor and commander, but also as a friend. Believe me, I feel sorry to see you come to such a pass. I'm giving you the chance to repair the damage, to return to what you're capable of being, if you want to. I believe in you, and I'm sure you won't disappoint me. You've got time to think it over, until lights-out. I'll be waiting to hear from you."

Raffy and the instructors and MPs left the room. For the first few minutes after the platoon was left on its own there was an uncomfortable silence. Until it was broken by a moan from Zero-Zero who let out a Romanian curse and groaned: "Oy, that's all I needed now!" He had been ordered to appear on parade the next day with his knapsack and his personal effects clean and laundered and not smelling like a rotting carcass, and he didn't know how he was going to manage it. His complaint gave rise to general merriment. The laughter encouraged him, and he called: "Ben-Hamo, go and give it to them. How long do we have to suffer because of you? Where did you hide it? In your backside? Hurry up, take it out and go to the platoon commander and get it over!"

"Fellows, it's no joke," said Alon. "It's a dirty business. I hope that nobody here is mixed up in it. Not that I'm in favor of informing and all that, but if the underworld has already infiltrated the army, then the situation's serious."

Hedgehog came up to me: "You remember, Melabbes, when we were on kitchen duty and he had a fight with that cook, and the cook yelled at him: *Either you bring me the money or I'm going to tell on you.* I suspected right away that they were talking about drugs."

"Why jump to conclusions?" said Micky. "Maybe it was stolen property, maybe smuggled goods, how do you know? Did you hear anyone mention drugs? Have you got any proof?"

"Trust my instincts," said Hedgehog. "Those people are bringing all the Arab shit into the country. Soon they'll begin drinking opium here and God knows what."

Avner sat on his bed avidly smoking a cigarette. Slowly he looked around him with suppressed anxiety. I gave him an encouraging smile. "These idiots," he whispered, "what are they shooting their mouths off for? The MPs are probably hiding behind the windows and listening to every word."

I opened my mouth to say something, and Avner silenced me immediately. He hissed without moving his lips: "Don't say anything now. I know you saw. We'll talk about it later."

I looked behind me and saw that there was nobody listening. And then I whispered rapidly, trying not to move my lips like him: "You're a remarkable person. That was fantastic. Good for you."

Avner gave me a blank look, as if he hadn't heard a word I said, as if something more urgent has distracted his attention. But suddenly I saw his features twisting, his brows frowning, and the corners of his mouth beginning to tremble, and I was horrified, because I had only wanted to make him happy, to express friendship. His voice choked: "You don't know me, you can't imagine what I'm capable of."

"For good or bad?"

He averted his face from me, either to make sure that nothing suspicious was happening behind him or because he sensed what was happening to his face. In the end he turned back to me and said: "Both. Don't you understand that the one depends on the other?"

And he hid his face behind a screen of cigarette smoke, which got into his eyes and made them blink.

An unexpected, inexplicable happiness descended on the platoon. People grew animated, their tongues loosened, as if we had undergone some purifying ordeal that had returned some lost meaning to us, provided us with a new code from which to take our bearings. Hanan and Hedgehog came up to Avner, smiling conspiratorially.

"What was it?" asked Hanan. "Was it really drugs?"

"Why are you asking me, how should I know?" said Avner. "What's it got to do with me?"

"Do me a favor, Avner," said Hedgehog confidentially, as if they were partners in some daring adventure. "We saw him running up to you to give you something before they arrived."

"He came to ask me for a cigarette. And I gave him one. That's all. He didn't give me anything. Melabbes saw him — did he give me anything?"

"No," I said, "he came running up, grabbed hold of your hand, and asked you for a cigarette. He looked frightened. He must have known they were behind him."

Hanan said: "I wondered how you could have hidden it so that they didn't find it."

"And if he had given it to you," said Hedgehog slyly, "would you have told on him?"

"Look," said Avner, "I don't even want to think about it. That's all I need: to get mixed up in that kind of stuff. He could just as easily have given it to you. Why me of all people?"

"How should I know? You're quite friendly aren't you?"

"Where did you get that idea?"

"Birds of a feather flock together," said Hanan in English, no doubt quoting something he had picked up from Peter Cheney again.

Zackie came up to Hedgehog with a scowl on his face. "One day," he said, "a few of the guys are going to catch you and roll you in a blanket and give you such a hiding that you'll never open your dirty mouth again. Does my father drink opium? Does my mother drink opium? What's going on here? First we're not Jews at all, and now we're already drinking opium. What next? What else are you going to say about us?"

"What's the matter with you?" said Hedgehog indignantly. "Why do you have to take everything personally, as if it's about you and your family? I'm talking generally. Why pretend you don't know how all those drugs get into the country and where they come from? Don't you know who brings them in and who uses them? You know as well as I do who the Jaffa underworld consists of. But I didn't say they were all like that, I didn't say everyone who comes from Iraq, Morocco, and all those places does it, as if they were gangsters. Did I ever say anything bad about you? I think you're great, I love you! Really!" And in order to demonstrate this, Hedgehog put his arm around Zackie's shoulder.

Zackie shook off this dubious gesture of friendship with revulsion. "Don't do me any favors and don't love me. I don't need it. But have some respect, respect for me, for my family, respect for our people."

Hedgehog sighed. "Your problem is that you all suffer from an inferiority complex. Of course I've got respect for you and your family and whoever else you like. But if there's something wrong, I'll say so. If it's about Ashkenazis or Sephardis. This country's a democracy, and everyone can say what they think. You'll have to get used to it."

"You're not a human being, Hedgehog," said Zackie, with an expression of insult and hatred on his face. "You're not a man, you don't have a heart."

Hedgehog looked around him in embarrassment. "What does he want of my life?" he asked. "Why's he insulted? I wasn't even talking about the Sephardis. I was talking about the Arabs."

"Don't talk about the Arabs either!" called Peretz-Mental-Case. "You don't know nothing about the Arabs. You've got a lot to learn from the Arabs too. No Arab would talk the way you do, they don't have such big dirty mouths."

"Now they're sticking up for the Arabs!" declared Hedgehog. "I'm talking to Zackie, not you."

"I don't want to talk to you," said Zackie.

Hedgehog's face darkened, but the fighting spirit didn't leave him. "Let's see you roll me in a blanket, let's see you! It'll be the end of you!"

"That's enough," said Zackie dryly and impatiently. "That's enough! Nobody's going to do anything to you, nobody's going to touch you, I didn't mean it. Just don't talk to me again. I don't want to have anything to do with you."

Zackie returned to his bed, sat down on the edge, and looked at the floor. Hedgehog went up to him, embarrassed and hesitant. "I didn't mean it, believe me," he pleaded. "You didn't understand what I said. If you were insulted, I'm not to blame. Shake hands, Zackie, I'm sorry. Shake hands and let's forget it and be friends."

"I don't want to," said Zackie. "You're not a human being. The only thing you know how to do is insult people. To make fun of people. Why d'you have to imitate the way we speak Hebrew all the time? Copy every word we say. You think it's funny? If you came to a different country, would you know how to talk exactly like the people who were born there? Why d'you have to laugh at us all the time? Leave us alone, talk to your own friends."

"Okay, okay," said Hedgehog. "I'm sorry. Let's shake hands and be friends."

"I don't want to," said Zackie.

Cries went up all around: "What's the matter with you? He said he was sorry. Shake hands! Why are you making such fuss? Be a human being yourself, Zackie! Shake hands, be a man!"

Zackie offered his hand limply, turning his face aside as if about to receive an injection. "Okay, I'm shaking hands because I'm sick and tired of you, and I don't want to hear any more, just leave me in peace."

Hedgehog said: "I promise you I won't talk that way anymore, I promise! Okay?"

"No," said Zackie. "I want you not to think it in your head either."

Lights-out was approaching. Like shadows lengthening in the afternoon the threats implicit in Raffy Nagar's ostensibly friendly words reached out to touch us. But nobody seemed seriously disturbed by them. There is an intoxicating pleasure in sensational events that dims our sense of reality and dulls our anxieties, just as the news of a familiar person's death makes the possibility that this will be our lot too recede from our hearts, and we mourn his loss without identifying with his fate, looking down on this vale of tears with sorrow, perhaps with guilt, as if we were immortal.

Muallem arrived for lights-out, alone, silent, solemn, and mysterious as befitted the gravity of the occasion, and after he left it was possible to sense how the last vestiges of this intoxication were slowly fading away, how sleep was procrastinating, it was almost possible to see the dozens of pairs of eyes wide open in the darkness, as if in expectation. Avner was smoking in bed. I knew that he was waiting for everyone to fall asleep so that he could go out and get rid of whatever it was that he hidden so well. Micky and Alon went out to guard the armory. And eventually the air was filled once more with the hoarse, rhythmic breathing, the sudden mutters, with all those sounds of sleep that had long since seemed to me like the spirits of sickness leaving the bodies of the sleepers to wander in the night. Avner sat up in bed and pulled his boots onto his bare feet. After that he pulled out from somewhere or other a bundle of the tissue papers used to wrap oranges that he had brought with him from home. From the depths of my childhood I recognized their faint rustle and unique smell, sharp as a strange medicine. I would have known them from a distance, with my eyes closed. Avner stood up and looked around him. He was going to the latrines to get rid of what Sammy had given him. If he was caught on the way, he would have his excuse ready. He walked softy to the door, stuck his head outside and looked from side to side, descended the three steps, and his footsteps receded and faded away in the darkness. There was a tense, hostile silence outside, but no voices challenged him in the darkness. Maybe they were waiting for him in the latrines, and they would discover what he was hiding there? Would he get out of it this time too, as he had during the search, thanks to his thief's ingenuity? And precisely now, after I had resolved to wait for Avner's safe return, I felt myself giving way to the relaxation preceding sleep. The windows were dark. The night was cloudy. There was something heavy and oppressive in the air, ready to burst.

The sound of approaching footsteps told me that I had fallen asleep. I roused myself and opened my eyes. Avner's silhouette was moving slowly toward his bed. When he stood in the space between our beds, he leaned over to see if my eyes were open. I raised my hand as if in greeting, to let him know that I was awake. Avner made a gesture that said: *It's all over, everything's okay.* I managed to make out his features in the darkness as he bent down to take off his shoes: His eyes were shining in a smile of satisfaction and pride.

And after an unclear interval of time, suddenly, as if from the bowels of the earth, a kind of strange rumbling arose, where from exactly I could not tell. I heard a column of MP jeeps pulling up and stopping at various points around the barracks, their engines running softly in neutral, waiting for something. But then a cry of joy rose in my heart: I must have fallen asleep. I raised my head to hear more clearly, to banish the remnants of the dream. Was it really the common, monotonous, domestic sound that was always capable of touching my heart with delight, like an unexpected meeting with faraway places? I listened to this sound, wanting to be certain that I wasn't mistaken and that I wasn't sleeping.

"Can you hear?" I whispered in the direction of Avner's bed.

Avner couldn't hear. He was sound asleep. Everyone was sleeping. I got out of bed, went over to the door, and stood looking at the first rain.

CHAPTER 22

After the death of summer it comes to life, it breathes. Can't you feel the warmth of its breath, its marvelous smell. See how sweet it is, like the breath of the girl you love. The smell of the dust and the dry soil beginning to wake up. Sometimes it seems to me that if only it was quiet, perfectly quiet, you'd be able to hear that breathing. You'd be able to hear the earth breathing. Can you just imagine it?"

Micky mumbled: "It's always like that after the first rain."

They were standing huddled under the little roof over the entrance to the armory, out of the heavy downpour. The air was full of a sharp, delicate new chill, bearing the odors that had been washed clean of the summer dust. The smell of rifle oil, which until then had been standing almost still in the air, now mingled with the scent of the wet eucalyptus leaves, the smell of the wooden walls of the barracks and the tin of their roofs, the smell of the steam rising from the concrete, the smell of the red loam, whose smell was different from that of any other soil. Alon took off his helmet in order to concentrate more fully on the rain. He stared in silence, abandoning himself to the sounds, listening intently to the whispers of the breathing and awakening that he sensed around him. Now, said Micky to himself, he looks like a religious man. The more I know him the less I know him. The obsessed, lonely expression on Alon's face reminded him of the hostility the kibbutznik had aroused in him during the first weeks of their friendship, when he had taken advantage of every opportunity to provoke ridiculous quarrels and arguments over matters that he had never, in fact, felt very strongly about. Did he already understand that it was a kind of battle to establish the conditions of their friendship, its limits, its depth?

"I suppose you think it's silly," said Alon.

"No," said Micky.

"Don't think it's just sentimentality."

"On the contrary, said Micky, "I envy anyone who can allow himself to be sentimental, to say what he really feels straight out, without complexes, without worrying about the impression he's making or if he'll regret it later. It's not weakness, it's strength. I've never been capable of it."

Alon said: "It doesn't detract from anything else. My girlfriend says it leads me to take the wrong decisions. But that's not true. The question is if a person wants to be what he truly is. Or if he's prepared to deny his truth. In order to conform to some idea in other people's heads. Or to prove something to society."

"I've never known a kibbutznik before," said Micky. "You're a special race to me."

"Don't learn about kibbutzniks from me. I'm not typical. Don't think they don't have problems with me. I'm not like them."

Was he boasting of it? Micky wondered. No, this was apparently his way of telling the truth. Of being a real person, of being what you really were. What a task! *Because it was he, because it was myself* — he heard his father's voice reading Montaigne's essay aloud to him. *How beautiful it is!* The voice of his old father, older than he had ever been, trembled when he uttered this admiring exclamation, spitting it out like a declaration of hatred against the rest of the world, in a voice full of rage and protest against the simple, ordinary, natural things, the little lies.

"My father," said Micky, "hates the kibbutzim. When he came to the country he was on a kibbutz for a while. And ever since then he's hated the whole idea of the kibbutz, and as far as he's concerned Ben-Gurion is the symbol of everything he can't stand here."

"Seriously?" said Alon a little apprehensively. "Why?"

"He thinks the state of Israel won't last long. He thinks it's a question of no more than ten, twenty years. In his opinion the destruction of the state is inevitable anyway, but Ben-Gurion and the kibbutzim will hasten the process."

"He hates Israel," said Alon.

"My father's sometimes hard to understand," said Micky. "Don't think I'm not fond of him, or that I don't respect him. He's a special, unusual person, with ideas of his own and a world of his own. I'll never know what he knows, what he's read, what he understands. But I'm critical of him too. When he says that the state won't survive, maybe it's what he hopes; maybe it gives him a kind of satisfaction to think so, to blame everything that happened to him, all the sadness, the mistakes, the failure, on the state, on Ben-Gurion, on the kibbutzim, and God knows who else."

"How could you have asked me to come home with you for Rosh Hashana?"

Micky snickered in embarrassment and did not reply. Eventually the rain stopped, and in the silence they could hear the water gurgling. From the armory roof and from the tops of the trees heavy drops of water fell in a steady rhythm to the ground.

Alon said: "Come and see something."

He opened his shirt pocket, took out the wallet with his papers, and beckoned Micky to follow him to the lamp on the corner of the roof. Carefully he removed a small snapshot from the wallet and laid it in Micky's hand. Micky saw a young man, tall and thin, in short khaki pants, a submachine gun dangling from his shoulder, his mop of thick black hair blown sideways in what must have been a strong wind when the photograph was taken. His face was thin and sharp, small in comparison to the size of the black mop; his smile was broad, proud, demonstrative, as if to cover up shyness or anxiety. His hands were on his hips and his attitude impatient, as if he were in a hurry to get somewhere.

"This is the last picture we've got of him. Two weeks after it was taken he fell. When I look at it I sometimes get the feeling that I have an appointment to meet him one day — when I reach his age. That'll be in twelve years' time. You remember how we argued about Uri Illan? All the time I was thinking about my father. It could have been him. If he'd been that age, at that period. That's how he would have behaved. His letters to my mother are in *Scrolls of Fire*. Once I knew them almost by heart. I read them so often. I liked reading them in that book more than the actual letters themselves, I don't know why. Over there they seemed more real, more relevant, more serious. You should have seen the way he wrote, the language, the ideas. Afterward I started reading all the other things in *Scrolls of Fire,* by all the other fallen. Whenever I had a minute to spare, I would sit and read it. Instead of social activities in the group. They took it away from me. They locked it up somewhere. Because I really went too far, it began having a bad effect on me. It cut me off from reality. It's unhealthy to let yourself sink too deeply into those things. Socially as well as psychologically. The truth is that I'm still suffering from the ill effects to this day. I didn't understand it then."

Micky gave the snapshot back to Alon, who examined it for a moment before putting it carefully into his wallet and returning it to his pocket. It began to rain again. They took shelter under the armory roof and listened silently to the noise of the water for a moment. Alon, clasping his helmet to his chest, narrowed his eyes, concentrating on the sounds. His yellow hair and jutting cheekbones gave him the air of a scalded man, burned in some ordeal by fire. His tense lips, which always looked wounded, were slightly parted, as if uncertain whether to speak.

In the end he said: "After they took the *Scrolls of Fire* away from me and locked it up, I started reading and rereading 'Friends Talk About Jimmy,' the letters in *Native Son,* and all those books about the Hagana and the Palmach and the War of Independence — they were all in the kibbutz library and they couldn't lock them all away from me. You can imagine how all that stuff turned into one big muddle in my mind. All the fallen took on one face — his face, that I could barely remember. Until I saw that snapshot for the first time — the one I just showed you.

It was only a few years ago. I never saw it before then. It's his last picture. It was taken a few hours before the last battle. I don't know why they hid it from me. Maybe they left it lying somewhere and forgot about it. I don't know. In general they tried not to talk to me about it too much. They thought it gave me problems. But when I came across that picture accidentally in my mother's room and I looked at it, I realized that I'd gone too far. All the stories and the books about the fallen, and their letters and their diaries suddenly didn't fit in with this particular person in the picture. He looks so arrogant here. He became one, private, not mine or anyone else's, not even my mother's. Only his own. I would look at that picture for hours on end. Trying to understand what he was trying to tell me. I never succeeded in hearing anything. I came to the conclusion that he wasn't trying to tell me anything. He didn't know me, just as I didn't know him. So much time had passed since then. I was a child of ten and he was a young man, a soldier. Time had blurred everything, cut off all the connections. I was sure that if there was one thing he wasn't thinking about, when he was standing there on that hill before going into action for the last time, it was me. Maybe he was thinking about my mother, but definitely not about me. What he must have been thinking about was his comrades-in-arms, the men who were going into battle with him, who would come back and who wouldn't. About his responsibility as their commander, about this land, the dream of this land and the ancient covenant with its soil, which was the beginning of everything. And once, at the Passover Seder, they read excerpts from Alterman's *Poems of the Plagues of Egypt.* I think they read it every year, but I never paid any attention. But that night I suddenly heard a passage that rang in my ears like bells. I felt that my father's picture was speaking to me through those lines. I found the book and I read them over and over again. I'll remember them as long as I live. They go like this: 'My son, my first-born son, the darkness will not divide us, for bonds of darkness and rage, of blind, hot tears, bind father to son, bonds which were not woven here nor here will be undone. My father, into a great light as into a palace we will come. My son, a marvelous light will shine tomorrow on Amon. Amon is watching, Father, her eyes pierce like the light. Tomorrow is your night, my son, make ready for tomorrow night.'

"Do you understand?" asked Alon.

Micky said nothing. The words touched on areas that always gave rise in him to resistance and revulsion, which he covered up with mockery. But the polemical spirit had left him. Just as his father's words had ceased to anger him and give rise to contempt for his weakness, so he could no longer react with denial and scorn to Alon, not even secretly in his heart. There was something here with which it was impossible to contend. And so all he found to say was: "Times have changed since then."

"What's that got to do with it?" said Alon.

"People change with time, society changes."

"The war's going on all the time," said Alon, "but people are less and less willing to fight. The countries haven't changed, the dream hasn't changed. The only difference is that today people prefer to make careers for themselves, to live comfortably and make money. To let others do the dirty work for them, shed their blood. And afterward they'll call them murderers for hire, mercenaries, like you yourself said about the fighters in Arik Sharon's commando. You remember, when I told you about them that first time. To this day I can't forget how you said it. It was so insulting. You can't possibly have really thought so! They're continuing the tradition of the Palmach, of the War of Independence. They're the chosen few, the elite, who voluntarily sacrifice themselves for all the rest. What, do they do it for money? Do they get anything out of it for them-selves? You didn't mean it, admit it, go on admit it! Like you didn't mean what you said about Uri Illan, without having the faintest idea about what really went on there. To look at those things from here, from Training Base Four, in this platoon, with men unfit for combat who spend all their time whining and thinking up ways of shirking and don't want to learn anything. With drugs and God knows what else and CID investigations. To look at that from here — it's like thinking of people from another world, a world of legend, perhaps. But they're real people, I know them. I've seen them. I've heard them talking about their mis-sions. I've seen them relaxing and having fun. Most of the things are secret and I can't talk about them. But even from the little I have told you, you can see what kind of fighters they are. When they broke them up and attached them to the paratroopers, in my opinion it was a mistake. Like the mistake they made when they dismantled the Palmach and attached them to the IDF. But still, despite everything, it's still going on in the new framework. It'll always go on. There'll always be some people who're prepared to give everything, give their lives, for this land, for other people they don't even know, who won't even appreciate it."

Micky said: "You didn't understand what I meant when I spoke about mercenaries. There was no reason to get insulted. I didn't say they were hired murderers, that they did it for money or anything like that. I only said you couldn't be sure that they risked their lives purely out of Zionism and patriotism and all that. It's possible that they need that stuff for psychological reasons — that it's necessary to them for themselves. It's possible that if they didn't have the opportunity to live that kind of life in a respectable military framework, and to be considered heroes of Israel, they would find other ways of expressing their instincts. It's possible that they have to prove something to themselves: that they're not afraid of death, that they're superior to other people, that they're permitted what's forbidden to others. I don't know. But it's possible, just possible that some of them might have turned into murderers to find an outlet for their instincts. That's what I meant. But don't think that I don't respect them. Don't think I don't know what it means to the country and the army to have people like that who raise the standard, who give an example of courage and sacrifice and devotion. I don't take it lightly at all."

"Do you find that kind of devotion in a gang of murderers? You don't know the kind of comradeship that exists among them. I never told you about how Jibli was captured. It's a lesson in friendship, in loyalty, in love. There's nothing farther from selfishness in the world. So someone who was capable of that isn't capable of loving his country? I know that today we're ashamed of admitting it. Not only you. Even with my friends on the kibbutz, it sounds ridiculous when you talk about it. And the truth is that that's how they treat me there. As if I were weird or something. But I don't care. I'm not ashamed to admit it, and I don't care what people say. I love this country. I really love it. A thousand times over I'm prepared to give everything for it — my blood, my life. So what? Don't you believe me? You think I've got selfish reasons for it?"

"No, I didn't say so."

"When we climbed the Arbel a few years ago I had to turn away to hide the tear of emotion, of love, that came into my eyes when I looked down at that landscape. They call that love of country. Today it's ridiculous. Okay. The Palmachniks didn't like talking like that either. But they felt it. I know they did. You can read it in their letters to their families or their girls, you can read it in their diaries and the poems they wrote. Have a look at *Scrolls of Fire* one day. You should. Wherever you open it, you'll find it. But on the outside they were like you, a bit cynical, tough, anti-sentimental. As if they didn't care about anything, only having a good time. But in their hearts they cried too when they stood on top of Masada and looked down on the desert, and when they read Eleazar Ben-Yair's speech in Josephus. Believe me — they had to turn away too in case anyone was watching, in case anyone saw the tears in their eyes and made fun of them."

"Don't think I don't love the country," said Micky. "Don't think I don't understand. But I know that a person can't only experience his country. That's one experience. But there's the world outside your country too, and there's the world inside yourself, your most private world, that accompanies you wherever you go, whatever you experience. The world that distinguishes you from other people."

"What," scoffed Alon, "is our soul divided into compartments then, one for private affairs, one for social affairs, one for national affairs, and so on? All these things constitute our private lives. There's no difference. The difference is only in the individual's willingness to renounce his personal convenience, to do things for others, to suffer for them — that's the difference between those who only like taking and those who like giving, those who only think of the present moment and those who think of the past and future too, about what existed before them and what will exist after them. Anyone who lives only in the moment lives a miserable life. Anyone who doesn't know how to give, give the maximum, doesn't know what the real value of life is. Anyone who thinks of himself exclusively as a private individual and not as part of something bigger — a nation, a landscape, nature, history, an idea, all that — is a poor person. His life is empty, it lacks meaning. There are some people who suffer from attacks of depression. One of the women on our kibbutz suffers from it. It's an illness, a real illness. When it happens to her, she doesn't even want to move. Because she hasn't got any reason to. There's nothing to make it worth her while. All her strength leaves her. Nothing interests her at these times, sometimes it goes on for days and even weeks. It's worse than death. Because life's going on all around her, and everyone wants her to behave like a living human being too. And she can't. She hasn't even got the strength to pretend, because that's not worth her while either. Everything bores her, tires her, it's terrible. You see, her interest narrows down to such an extent that all she's interested in is the one little point of her pain. Does it hurt less or more if she does this or that? How can she blur the pain, suffer less? How can she forget? That woman happens to be my mother. I know that problem intimately.

"And sometimes entire societies, entire nations are sick with this illness. It's their way of disappearing from history. Because they've lost their interest in themselves, in their past, in their future. In the recognition that there's something that's worthwhile for them. That there's something that makes it worthwhile for a society to exist, for a nation to live. In other words, something it's worth dying for. Because anything not worth dying for isn't worth living for either. And if there's nothing worth living for, what's life worth? So all that's left is a kind of quiet, slow, gradual death. And that's why I don't distinguish between private life and social and national life. It's all interdependent."

Alon put his helmet on again. The sound of the dripping was growing quieter. Silence fell. The sky was rapidly clearing, spreading over them newly washed and crystal clear. For many nights the sky and all its hosts had not seemed so vivid and so false, like a stage set. Alon gave Micky a brief, sidelong glance, to ascertain his reaction to his long speech, wondering perhaps if he had gone too far. But Micky saw the look and took it as a reprimand. You're still unspoiled, he said to Alon in his heart, life hasn't spoiled you yet, perhaps because you're a bit weird. With me something was spoiled at the beginning. How different we are; everything about us is the opposite, even our fathers.

"Did your mother remarry?" he asked.

"Yes," said Alon, "she's got a husband. They've got a daughter. I've got a little sister. She's really sweet. Maybe you'll see her when you come to visit me on the kibbutz. But my mother's sick. Nothing can help her anymore. It doesn't influence my life too much; we don't spend a lot of time with our parents, you know. My peer group, for example, is much closer to me, and there are other members on the kibbutz whom I have strong attachments to; they're like family for me. But the person I'm closest to is my girlfriend, Dafna, of course. We became friends when we were little kids. From the beginning we knew that we would always be together. And ever since then we can't stand being apart. I miss her terribly here. There are things I can only talk about to her. And she's the only one who can understand me. Although sometimes even she doesn't understand. Or doesn't want to. Because there are other people who influence her about me. But our love is very strong."

Micky said: "Maybe you won't believe this, but I've never gone to bed with a girl."

"Why not?" said Alon with a worried expression.

"I'm unlucky in love." Micky giggled in embarrassment.

"What's it got to do with luck? It's not a question of luck."

"I don't know. Fact. I'm a virgin. Girls aren't attracted to me. Maybe I'm not good looking enough."

"Are you crazy, Micky? You think girls are interested in looks? It's personality that interests them. They're attracted to character, masculinity, intelligence, strength. And you're a star! You're famous, you've got fans!"

"Fact," said Micky. "It's a fact. When it comes to sex, they don't want me."

"I can't understand it," said Alon.

Micky was silent. His face fell, exhausted by the effort it cost him to open his heart. Like someone who had made up his mind to jump into cold water, with his eyes closed, come what may, wondering if the moment would ever arrive when the heat of his body and the coldness of the water would balance each other out and recovery would set in. This isn't self-flagellation, he repeated to himself, it's liberation, I have to talk about it to someone, and I've never had a friend like this before.

"When it comes to love," said Micky, "it's a man facing a woman, the way God made them, and being a soccer star doesn't help."

"Why do you think you're not good-looking? Where on earth do you get that idea from?" asked Alon, with a strange resentment in his voice.

"You can't understand," said Micky. "You have to see it in a girl's eyes. You can read it like a book. There's a girl I like, and I want her. But as soon as I begin to try, she won't let me. She's a wonderful girl. I'll never make it with her, I know. And there were others. There was one girl in my class in high school, and another one I met at a friend's place. And it was exactly the same. Sometimes I think I'll just have to get used to the idea that no woman will ever love me, that that's how it's going to be all my life. It's a terrible thought, you know that?"

"Micky, you're crazy. You've got a complex, I'm telling you. At our age most guys haven't been to bed with a girl yet. What do you think? Look at our platoon, how many of them do you think have had anything serious to do with a girl already?"

"Don't try to comfort me," said Micky. "I told you because I wanted to share something personal, something that hurts me, with you. Like you told me all kinds of things. Maybe in the future something will change and everything will work out. But for the time being, it's hell. It's so insulting to be rejected. You can't imagine. Nothing can make up for it. Not fame or soccer or anything else. When we went out that time to the transit camp on Saturday night and they talked about that girl Gita, and the guys said we should go there once, I felt my stomach turning over inside me. On the one hand, I was terrifically attracted, and on the other I don't want to go to a prostitute or someone who opens her legs for everybody. At least the first time I want, I need for it to be the real thing, for it to be someone I love, and for her to love me. Not just some girl who goes to bed with everyone, or some poor, sick, ugly nymphomaniac. I'd rather jerk off."

"Everyone finds the girl he loves and who loves him in the end. What do you think, that you're cursed or something?"

"Yes, sometimes I'm sure of it."

"That's the last thing I would have believed of you, Micky. You're not thinking logically. I'm sorry for you, really sorry."

"Everything else seems silly and pointless to me. All that soccer, I spent my life on it, and now I'm sick and tired of it. And tomorrow I have to go and train. The whole thing's a bore. I don't know why I agreed to it."

"No, it'll be good for you. Good for your state of mind. You'll feel that you're worth more than other people again, that you're a star. You're suffering from an inferiority complex and forgotten who you really are."

"To go away for a whole week and come back here before the outdoor training series, and then go back again. For something that doesn't interest me anymore."

"Don't do anything you don't believe in," said Alon.

"Of course I don't believe in it. What's there to believe in? I'm not a baby."

"It'll be boring here without you," said Alon. "I don't connect with anyone else in the platoon."

"Once my pride wouldn't have permitted me to talk about such things to anyone. Now that I've spoken to you about it, it seems easier, simpler. Have you got a picture of your girlfriend?"

"No," said Alon, "she didn't want me to take a picture of her with me. I don't know why."

"What was that story about the paratrooper who was captured, if it's not too secret for me?" asked Micky.

Alon did not catch the irony, or ignored it. "Everything's secret. What do you think? All those things are top secret. But I trust you not to talk about it to anyone. I myself only know about it because there are paratroopers who served in the commando on our kibbutz. Once Meir Har-Zion himself came to spend the weekend with us. And other guys from the unit came too, and they all sat and talked and joked and laughed. And me, I was just a little kid, I sat in the corner and tried to make myself invisible. Listening to every word that came out of their mouths. Looking at them as if they were gods come down to earth. You can't imagine the kind of men they are. I'd already heard of their operations and their hikes and trips to all kinds of places across the border. Anyway, the incident with Jibli happened last year, when they were all already in the paratroopers. I heard about it about a month before my conscription, from someone on the kibbutz, an officer in the paratroops who knows all the fighters from the commando and who's really friends with them.

"Last summer they went out one night on an operation in Azun, not far from Kalkiliyeh. They attacked a Jordanian camp and Jibli was badly wounded in the leg. They began to withdraw and Jibli was wounded

again, this time in the neck. The bullet entered at the back and came out
in front. The Jordanians opened fire on them from all sides, very heavy
fire. Har-Zion took Jibli and began to carry him on his back. Jibli's blood
poured over him, it covered all his clothes, and he went on carrying him,
panting like a bull and hearing Jibli's groans and his cries of pain the
whole time. Until they arrived at an olive grove, outside the range of the
enemy fire. They began to take care of Jibli. It was two o'clock in the
morning. They had another eight miles to walk to the border, over difficult mountain terrain full of enemy ambushes. And Jibli began to plead
with them to leave him behind and go back without him. Wounded as he
was in the leg and with a hole in his neck, bleeding, he thought about
them and he didn't want them to fall into enemy hands because of him.
And they didn't want to listen to him. Either they all got back or they all
stayed behind. They didn't leave wounded comrades behind in enemy
territory. And Jibli, in the state he was in, almost unconscious from pain
and loss of blood, began to kick them and shout at them to go! Go! Leave
him alone! He realized that he was a burden to them, that as long as they
had to carry him they wouldn't be able to get through the ambushes and
cross the border in safety. Davidi, the commander of the operation, and
Har-Zion conferred between them and in the end they decided to do
what Jibli asked. For them it was a terrible decision to take. Nothing like
it had ever happened in that unit before — to leave a wounded comrade
in the field, in enemy territory. Jibli asked them to leave him with a canteen and a grenade. And so they left him there and got back safely to
Israel. But their sufferings were only beginning. They wouldn't rest until
they had brought Jibli back. And for that they had to take prisoners from
the Legion, to exchange for Jibli.

"That same night Jibli lay in the olive grove, wounded, suffering terrible pains, barely conscious. Until day broke and a Legion platoon arrived
with their English officer. That was his luck. Thanks to the Englishman
Jibli stayed alive and wasn't killed on the spot. They took him prisoner
and began to torture him, to make him give them information about the
army and the unit. He didn't open his mouth. Whatever they asked him
he repeated his name, rank, and serial number. And if he added anything,
it was only his blood type and shoe size. It drove them wild. They tortured him without stopping and he didn't say anything. He didn't betray
us. Like Uri Illan behaved in the Syrian prison a little while later. None
of us knows what it means to be tortured. We can't imagine it. What happens to a man when he's subjected to such pain, when his body's broken.
What happens to his will then? To his mind? To his life force, which is

so strong, so dominant in us? What kind of strength do you need to remember who and what you are when they break your body, when the most terrible pains cloud your mind, so that you begin to forget who you are at all?

"Har-Zion and all his other friends suffered terribly. They identified with what was happening to Jibli all the time, they understood exactly what he was going through there. Every single one of them felt as if it were happening to him personally, that Jibli was suffering for them. They kept exerting pressure to go out on raids and capture Legionnaires, to exchange them for Jibli. And they went out and took four Jordanian prisoners. The Jordanians returned Jibli and got their men back. Dayan gave him a commendation for his behavior in captivity, for his silence under torture. And not long afterward he was already going out on all their operations with them again. He told his friends all about what he'd gone through. He told them about that night lying wounded in the olive grove, losing blood all the time, without knowing if he would survive the night, if he would be discovered and taken prisoner. He knew that if he fell asleep in the state he was in he would never get up again. So he did his best not to fall asleep, he concentrated all his remaining strength on singing to keep awake. He lay there wounded, losing blood, alone, in the dark, in enemy country, and sang 'The Cannons' Roar' over and over again. Do you know it?"

Alon closed his eyes. In the shadow of his helmet Micky could see his face twisting in pain and intense emotion. He was lying alone in the dark, bleeding in enemy country, fighting for his life, for his clarity of mind, waiting for day to break and his captors to arrive:

> Silenced is the cannons' roar,
> The field of slaughter is forsaken.
> A solitary soldier wanders there,
> Singing with the clouds and wind.
> From the hills a vulture rises,
> Then it falls upon the corpses.

In the stillness of the camp, in front of the armory door, opposite the clear sky, shining with a new brightness after the rain, his hoarse, parched voice rose softly in the darkness, anxious not to break, struggling with the tune of the song in grim, stubborn solitude, like a man clinging to consciousness with the last remnants of his strength, as if his only hope of salvation lay in staying awake.

When he came to the end of the song he took a few steps forward, averted his face, and was silent.

CHAPTER 23

His heart told him what was about to happen and gloom descended on him in the midst of the hullabaloo in the showers after a day of training on the obstacle course. They were all trying to outshout their neighbor, to gain attention for their stories, how they had held back at the last minute, how their bodies had refused to jump, how they were sure they were going to fall right onto the barbed wire, how they'd closed their eyes and jumped, come what may, through fire and water. Amid the noisy elation, the arguments and singing and jokes, gloom descended on him. His expression showed that he felt lonely, rejected, and cheated.

On the way from the showers to the barracks he abandoned his companions and walked alone, wringing his towel in his fists, threatening to tear it to shreds.

Before setting out for the showers, when everyone was pouncing on the mail, perhaps he had intercepted a glance, overheard a remark. Perhaps he had understood. In any case when Yossie Ressler said, "You've got regards from Ziva," Avner's face was sealed, as if he were hearing his sentence passed, a sentence he had awaited without hope. We were walking from the showers to the barracks, and the Jerusalemites, who were in particularly high spirits, approached him, and Yossie gave him the news. Hanan added: "You see, you made an impression on her. She's sending you regards already." He didn't reply.

We got dressed for supper. Every now and then Avner sent a suspicious, hostile look at the Jerusalemites, his eyes narrowed, and in the end he said: "To hell with them!"

"What's wrong?" I asked.

"She's playing a cruel game with me, don't you understand? Sending me regards in a letter to Ressler. I know those games girls play, but this time it's a game whose rules I don't understand. What does she want? It would have been less insulting if she'd ignored my letters completely and done nothing. But sending me regards in a letter to Ressler? What for? I don't understand it."

"Why don't you accept it simply for what it is without trying to find hidden meanings and interpretations? She sent you her regards, and that's all there is to it."

"Nothing here is simple, man. I can't stop thinking about her, I miss her all the time, I talk to her in my imagination. There's nothing simple about it. Everything's complicated already. You don't understand. Even after everything I've told you about her and our meeting and our feelings, you can't imagine what a special, delicate, beautiful thing came into being between her and me. It was the beginning of something big, of the love of our lives. Something that happens very slowly, deep, basic, and she said to me when we parted, *If you write to me, I'll write to you too.* You should have seen the letter I wrote her. It's not the kind of letter you show to a third person, it would be like desecrating something holy, but if you had seen it, you would have understood why I feel like this now. What, is she trying to give me the brush-off? Now? After all this time?"

"You said yourself that you didn't have a chance, that she had a boyfriend, that she wouldn't give him up, that she was only interested in friendship and all that."

"You didn't understand a thing!" protested Avner. "It's true that that's more or less what she said, but the way she behaved was different. The body sends its own signals, the way someone behaves says something. What happened between us was falling in love, on both sides. I've had plenty of time to think about it, to go back and remember all the signs and examine them in the light of my experience with women. At a distance of time and space you begin to understand things that you couldn't go into when they took place, because at that time you were inside the experience itself. Maybe Ressler wrote to her about me, who knows what he wrote her, that gossip. He's not a man at all, he gossips like an old woman. What could he have told her? What did he invent about me? I'd like to beat him up, even though I know I don't hate him. I really don't hate him. On the contrary, I actually feel quite benevolent toward him, I'd do anything to protect him or help him if he were in trouble. But at the same time I feel like hitting him, like humiliating him. Why should I blame him? I get myself into a mess and he deserves a beating? But did you see the way he sneered, the way he gloated when he told me that she's sent me regards? Pretending to be indifferent, but he couldn't hide his happiness."

"I didn't notice anything. It sounded perfectly natural to me, without any special hidden meanings. She wrote and asked him to give you her regards, and he did."

"Whatever I say now, you'll say the opposite, I know that trick." He looked at me through narrowed eyes, as if trying to read my thoughts, to expose my hidden intentions, my conspiracy with Ressler and the Jerusalemites against him.

I recoiled and said nothing. My revulsion must have been apparent in my expression or physical reaction, for Avner noticed it with a certain satisfaction. Anger and hatred are not only a threat of violence, they themselves are a violent imposition of intimacy. Later, I knew, it would be the turn of apologies and sentiment, which was even harder to bear, and for the same reason.

Avner said: "Now you can go to the little darlings and talk about me behind my back and make fun of me with them to your heart's content."

"Don't talk nonsense," I said. "I won't interfere in your affairs if you don't want me to. It's really none of my business. I've never poked my nose into in anyone else's private affairs in my life. But you tell me things, you involve me, and so I react. I haven't the least intention of making fun of you or talking about you behind your back. I haven't done it yet and I don't intend doing it in the future."

"Okay, okay, that's enough," said Avner, "I don't want them to hear what we're talking about. She mustn't know that I was hurt by it, that I give a damn. If there's any chance of making her come to me, on her knees, without any conditions, it's only if she thinks that I don't give a damn, that I've forgotten her, that she has to make an effort to seduce me, and not the other way around."

"Okay."

"What's the matter with you? Why are you so sour all of a sudden? Can't a person talk to you frankly and sincerely anymore, like a friend, even if the subject's disagreeable? What's wrong with you?"

I didn't reply. The situation began to remind me of the evening when he brought the falafel from Ramle. The imposed intimacy doubled the sense of alienation and of absurdity, which gave rise to a wish to burst out laughing. But the laughter refused to come. Instead I felt the nauseating futility of the absurd rising up in me.

Avner was unable to stand by his decision. He was overtaken by panic, his face expressing confidence and hopelessness by turn. His eyes darted around as if seeking the right path, as if he were standing at a busy inter-section and didn't know which way to turn. After we came back from supper, in the few minutes left before we went out on night training, he asked Hanan to step outside with him for a talk.

Hanan didn't understand what he was talking about. "Are you excused from training?" he asked. "Aren't you going? The inspection is in a minute."

"There's time, don't worry," Avner reassured him.

"Are you crazy, Avner? What's the matter with you?"

"Go to hell!" said Avner.

Everyone was busy dipping their fingers in the black paint and smearing it on their faces. Avner stared at them like a stranger who had unwittingly arrived at a fancy-dress party. Suddenly he made a panic-stricken dash for his bed — perhaps some light had switched on inside him for a second and brought him back to reality. He put on his webbing and his helmet, gripped his gun, and concentrated on his thoughts, trying to remember if he had forgotten anything. At the same time he muttered in my direction: "Did you see? Did you see? What have I done to them for them to hate me so much? How is such hatred possible at all?"

"Go and black your face," I said to him.

"I want to smear shit on my face," replied Avner.

All around us rose a silly, childish, noisy merriment, for no evident reason, except perhaps that the blackened faces, and the weariness of our bodies after an exhausting day that was not yet over, made it easier to forget. But Avner was untouched by the hullabaloo.

I went to paint my face. Ressler, who was standing next to me, asked: "What's the matter with him?"

I shrugged and kept my mouth shut. Avner was looking suspiciously in our direction, certain that we were gossiping about him. Yossie glanced at Avner for a moment, turned back to me, and smiled a strange smile. "Has he got problems?"

"Don't worry," I said. "He'll be all right."

"Do you think something's upset him?"

Avner came up to black his face. I said to him in my heart: *I don't feel sorry for you. You're the strong one here. In this huge sausage machine that grinds up everything, memories, dreams desires, plans, ambitions, longings, you hang on to your Hollywood movie plots, you go on living your romances, not surrendering, not ground down. It may be ridiculous, irritating, and unfair to others too, but it's amazing and no less admirable than the way you behaved during the search, the night they arrested Sammy. If you want to go crazy, go crazy — you can afford to. You've got something to suffer for. Your spark hasn't died.*

"Everyone'll be black now," said Avner, and his would-be ironic smile looked more like a grimace of nausea. "All the cats will be black tonight. It's nice of you, Yossie, to worry about me and want to help. Don't worry, it'll be all right, everything will be all right, from every point of view. When you reply to her letter, give her my regards too. Why not? Regards from black Avner — so she'll know who you're referring to. She must have forgotten me by now — she needs to be reminded of my distinguishing characteristics. But friendly regards, mind, only friendly, no more than that. There's nothing between us but friendship. And hardly that. What do you want? I scarcely know her. You meet some girl at a party, you see her home, and that's it. What can come of it? Not even a kiss. Nothing."

"Okay, okay," said Yossie.

We went outside to fall in for inspection outside the building. The instructors, they too with blackened faces, conducted the inspection in whispers, as if the silence of night discipline had already come into force. Every man was ordered to jump up and down. Every clinking buckle, rattling canteen, and thudding piece of equipment elicited a curt, dry whisper, announcing punishments, special parades, extra guards, a delay in beginning the exercise, the loss of hours of sleep. Everything was carried out with an air of tight-lipped gravity, it was all so real that this time too, as on the other night-training exercises, the strange suspicion stole into my heart that this time it was serious, like in the combat units, and I longed to enter into it wholeheartedly, with total identification. Avner jumped up and down. At the sound of the noise he made Benny kicked him and pushed him out of the line, undid the half-full canteen from his webbing, spilled its contents on the ground, whispered his punishment to him, and sent him to join the group standing outside the ranks, to correct whatever was in need of correction.

When I myself reached this group I saw Avner bending over to tighten the straps of his webbing and smiling. "Did you see?" he whispered. "He kicked me again. Everything's happening according to plan. Every kick like that adds years to my life, believe me! It does me good, believe me!"

In a long line we set out from the base, walking in single file, passing on the commands coming from the head of the line in a whisper from ear to ear, stopping and setting out again, hugging the side of the road, hiding from an invisible enemy. We went on walking for a long time in the silence, leaving the area of the big camp too, above us a clear sky and a full, cold moon shedding its deceitful light over us. The chill of the autumn night was sharp and surprising, even intoxicating. The head of the column stopped in front of a dark mass, which looked like a citrus grove, at the end of the road. The platoon split up into squads, each squad, with its commander, setting off silently in a different direction. Among the shadows walking in front of me I made out the silhouette of Alon, turning his head from side to side, scanning the moonlight-dappled expanses, sniffing the air like a wild animal tracking its prey.

The news about the agreement between Czechoslovakia and Egypt, the Czechs undertaking to supply the Egyptian army with weapons on a massive scale, had made a profound impression on Alon. He couldn't find anyone with whom to share his anxiety and concern. Micky was away training for the soccer match. There wasn't even anyone he could have a serious argument with. "You don't understand," Alon expostulated, "there's going to be a war. It's the second round! They're getting jet

planes and tanks and Russian arms. In huge quantities. Russia's behind it
all. And Nasser isn't Farouk; the Arabs today aren't the Arabs of the War
of Independence. This country's in danger." And Hanan said: "There are
people at GSHQ who get paid to worry about it. I can't help." Alon was
withdrawn, solitary, morose, hurt. He hardly spoke to anyone anymore.
He relieved his loneliness by endeavoring to excel at all the tasks and
duties imposed on the platoon. He was ridiculous. He looked like a child
raptly playing at soldiers and war. Behind his back and even within his
hearing sarcastic remarks were made about his devotion and zeal and his
sycophantic efforts to suck up to the instructors. He was behaving as if he
had nothing to lose: the mocking, even hostile, atmosphere only rein-
forced him in his position. Sometimes it seemed that he was deliberately
demonstrating his independence from us and what we thought of him,
and that he was even taking a peculiar satisfaction in annoying us, in
arousing our hostility and scorn.

The squad advanced along the edge of the orange grove, far from the
other squads, which had disappeared from view and whose footsteps too
could no longer be heard. Not far from a long, half-ruined building the
whispered order was given to lie down and take cover. Muallem tapped
Alon on the shoulder and beckoned him to follow. After circling the
building, they approached the entrance, went inside, and were swallowed
up in the darkness. Soon afterward they came out again, and Muallem
beckoned the rest of us to gather around him in a circle. When the movement ceased, he was silent for a moment, pricking up his ears to the
sounds of the night. In the end he was satisfied. He began to whisper in
a monotone, pausing deliberately between one sentence and the next for
emphasis, fixing his eyes on the men crouching around him with a look
that bespoke confidence, seriousness, responsibility, and danger.

"This is no longer an exercise," he said. "From now on this is for real.
This is a true combat operation. Everything that happens here is top
secret. No one will speak about it to anyone. Intelligence has received
information that gangs of fedayeen are prowling round here at night.
They may be over there, opposite us, they may be hiding in the orange
grove. They may arrive soon to take shelter in this ruin." He stopped and
looked at us in the dark, trying to gage our reactions, the extent to which
we believed him. "Now you're IDF soldiers, not Training Base Four
recruits. Now you'll have to put everything you've learned in your night
training into practice. This squad is responsible for the sector from this
grove to that hill over there, after the road. I'm going to divide you now
into ambush details and recce details, and you'll carry out orders according

to my commands and according to the drill you've learned. Arms at safety. Nobody releases the safety catch without an order from me personally or from the head of the detail. The heads of the details will receive their orders from me in a minute . . ."

He went on whispering, explaining the tasks of each detail and appointing the leaders. He pointed out various features of the terrain and gave them names. The password was whispered from mouth to ear.

"Any questions?"

Silence. The men look into each other's faces, seeking an answer to their unasked questions there. What power tempts them to believe that it is all God's truth? Who could possibly imagine that they would send recruits from Training Base 4 to catch infiltrators in the vicinity of Sarafand? The whole story is too childish and ridiculous for words. So why is there something so palpably sincere and serious in the air? What is it that gives the silence of the night and the danger it breathes, the whispered commands and the thrilled attention to which they give rise, the blackened faces and the cruel, atavistic memories they awaken — what is it that gives all these the unmistakable stamp of truth, a different, parallel, inner truth? Less than an hour's walk from the base, the place where they sit is gradually transformed into a foreign land, hostile and remote — enemy territory, full of treachery and violence.

One detail, with Alon at its head, sets out to reconnoiter the orange grove. A second, led by Albert the Bulgarian, goes to scout the open land. Two ambush details are positioned at either corner of the side of the grove facing the entrance of the ruin where the infiltrators are expected to appear. The sound of the breathing of the people crouching next to me in the ambush is tense and rhythmic, full of suspense. I can see the gleam of their eyes staring into the night, wandering between the silent shadows, waiting for those other shadows, which will never appear. Perhaps they too feel that this time the game — however silly — has to be played seriously, wholeheartedly, in the suspension of disbelief and with a sense of danger.

Opposite us lies the ruin with the dark shadow of its entrance, and beyond it — a valley full of shadows and contours tinted blue in the moonlight, a few anonymous trees and the road stretching out like a pale, curving ribbon, like a long, emaciated, sickly arm reaching out to embrace the shoulder of the hill. Who knows what this place looks like in daylight. I have no night vision. Even the few landmarks I have singled out in the nocturnal landscape opposite me are worthless. Soon they will begin to shift, to disappear, to change, to reappear, to come closer, to recede into the distance. Lying there without moving is still pleasant, bestowing a certain feeling of security, a hope of merging with the inanimate objects on the ground. It's getting colder and colder. The orange grove behind us is full of stirrings that are neither sound nor silence. The fear is not of encountering infiltrators; that story is simply a framework, a pretext for being carried away by another fear, whose source is not in living people but in the shadow theater that will soon take place before my eyes. A strange sound rises on my right, a mechanical, metallic noise, as if an alarm clock has begun to ring under the pillow laid on top of it to dull the noise so it will not wake all the members of the household from their sleep. Hedgehog's shoulders are shivering with cold where he lies on my right. His teeth are chattering and he can't stop them. When he sees me looking at him he gives me a strained, miserable, apologetic smile — and the chattering continues. Zackie and Nahum on my left have apparently not noticed anything. They're slowly sweeping their eyes over the sector. The cold is growing worse. The steel of my helmet breathes a chill over my face, exposing it to the eyes of the night, naked and guilty, as if its whiteness is showing through the black camouflage. The night grows gradually brighter and the shape of the objects steadies and clears, as if they're getting ready to move. Suddenly a dog barks. Fierce, savage barks, stunning the silence, coming from an unknown distance behind us, apparently from the depths of the orange grove. Perhaps Alon's detail has bumped into a dog. Better to be walking through the grove with Alon now than lying in an ambush, silent and motionless, easy prey to the visions of the night. The barking goes on for a long time, shaking the theater opposite like cries of despair, freezing the shadows, stopping the flow, exposing the faces. Then it ceases abruptly and there is silence again, leaving the nakedness of the faces revealed to the night with nothing to cover itself.

Until the movement begins. From the shoulder of the hill to the valley of the shadows, which look like a lake that has dried up but whose bed still preserves the memory of the waves in its wrinkles, its shifting patterns of darkness and moonlight, a very slow movement begins, imperceptible as that of the hands of a clock. Huge, clumsy animals, millions of years old, stately and grotesque, proceed slowly down the hill, moving as if in obedience to another force of gravity, refined and harmonious, gliding down to bathe in the dried-up lake.

Night after night a cry for help would rise from one of the houses. When I woke at the sound of those cries, I would always see my father or my mother standing at the window next to my bed, looking at the garden and the empty field behind it, watching over me as I slept. In the heat of the summer nights they couldn't close the windows and bolt the shutters with the big screws bought especially for this purpose. All night they stood guard at my bed with a whistle in their hands. Gangs of robbers from the surrounding Arab villages were roaming our little town with no one to stop them, especially in its eastern part, near their borders, knocking on doors, shouting: "Open up!" breaking in by force, shooting, killing, looting, and going on their way. The police did not interfere. The twilight zone between one reign and another, between the departure of the British and the organization of the new regime, was like a time in which packs of wolves will invade a town struck by disaster, somehow knowing that the borders have been destroyed, that everything is permissible, that the age-old war is beginning again. In the daytime everything vanished like a bad dream. The neighbors met and decided to buy whistles, hold shifts, and rush to the help of the household under attack when the whistle was blown. The robbers were armed with guns and pistols. How could they be deterred? At night the air was full of wailing whistles and cries for help. Sometimes we heard people running too, with rapid, heavy steps, and there was no knowing if they were the people running to help their neighbors, or the robbers themselves. The walls of the house seemed to become transparent, letting the uncertainty, the ambiguity of things filter in.

"Where did that come from?"

"The women's training farm, I think," said my father. He stood at my bedside, smiling at me in the darkness of the room, making light of the whole thing, as if it had nothing to do with us. "There are people there who'll deal with everything."

"So it's already over for tonight?" I ventured.

"Yes, go to sleep now, there's nothing to worry about, it's all over."

My mother came into the room. My father left and she stood next to the window, less practiced in putting a calm, reassuring face on things, more impatient with my questions. For a moment it seemed to me that she was swaying on her feet, as if she had suddenly lost her balance.

"It's all over," I said to her. "They're at the training farm. There are people there who'll catch them at last. Why don't you go to bed?"

In the moonlight coming from the window I saw the tears gleaming on her cheeks, until she quickly averted her face. And because I didn't really understand the situation, and also perhaps because of my natural reluctance to accept any responsibility, I said to myself that she was crying again for her younger brother who had been killed in Hebron many years before. Whenever she talked about him she cried, refusing to be consoled, refusing to forget. He was a boy with beautiful dark eyes in a large cloth cap shading his slender face, the face of child who had learned to appreciate his own worth, a face expressing concern and determination, as if he guessed in advance what the future held in store. This was how I knew him from the oil painting hanging in my maternal uncle's house and the yellowing photographs I had come across here and there. I knew that however good I was, I would never succeed in consoling her for her murdered brother, or making her forget him. I would never gain the right of entry into this closed compartment inside her, closed to me, closed perhaps even to my father, a shrine of tears dedicated entirely to this youth who never lived long enough to be my uncle, who would look forever like the illustration to Bialik's poem about the yeshiva scholar in our literature reader. In one of the closets there was a bundle of old letters and photographs sealed up in a box, forbidden, exerting a capricious, mysterious fascination and arousing destructive desires. His letters, written in another Hebrew, from the yeshiva in Hebron to his father and family at home, and letters from his teachers at the yeshiva to his father, praising his diligence and intellectual gifts in flowery rabbinical phrases, and calling him a genius, and afterward, letters eulogizing him from one rabbi and a handful of his fellow students who had survived the massacre. The smell of death hovered over these letters and over the photographs tied up with them in the box, the smell of tears and the smell of the years that had passed since then without healing the wound. One day I heard my mother telling one of her friends in a whisper that some of the people in Hebron had saved their lives by lying on the pile of corpses and pretending to be dead, so that the murderers passed over them.

There were whistles coming from outside again, and my mother raised her head in order to see what was happening. I decided to pretend to be dead in order to save my life. I pulled the sheet up over my head and lay still. And before I fell asleep, while I was still fully conscious, I saw the big, ancient beasts for the first time, sliding slowly from the shoulder of the hill into the valley of shadows, to bathe in the dried-up lake. In one of my schoolbooks, or in the encyclopedia, I had seen their skeletons and the reconstruction of what they had probably looked like, and the landscape surrounding them. The world had become a place for small, agile, cunning creatures. Not only did everything become harder, obtaining food and having to fight and defend themselves in a treacherous environment, but their will to live diminished too; the new order didn't make any sense to them. There was no point in making an effort to understand it either. It was the wrong size. Alien to their former habits, indifferent to their status. They were proud and pathetic, they did not want, they were not able to adjust to the new conditions. There was no reason to do anything. This too was a kind of decision, perhaps of heroism. The choice was not between extinction and survival, but between two ways of extinction: in surrender and adjustment or in resistance and protest and total refusal to cooperate. They refused to acknowledge the change. They bore the clumsy heaviness of their bodies like an ancient heritage that nobody wanted anymore. The remnants of a forgotten dynasty, gradually, discreetly, fading away in the land of their former kingdom, which had turned into the land of their banishment. Amid the teeming eagerness of the busy, ambitious new creatures growing ever more at home in the changing world, they were betrayed and persecuted, going unwitting and unquestioning to their doom. Tremor by tremor they sank into the eternal darkness, taking the secrets of creation with them. Without sorrow they parted from the world, insensible to the travail and the promise of the new life coming into being. The last of them stood on the top of a bare hill, overlooking a broad valley full of moon shadows, buzzing with new voices never heard before, voices to which they could never grow accustomed. My heart pounding with glee, I waited for the moment when they would descend into the valley, which in their ancient, demented memory was still inscribed as a lake, and when they came at night to drink and bathe their bodies — only at night, when they could still imagine that they were alone in the world — they would crash into the parched earth in terrible thirst, in utter incomprehension, as they sailed away into their last dream. More than the triumph of their enemies, I was glad of their defeat, their stupidity, their punishment for refusing to understand. I was glad of their possible pain, just before they died, when at long last the realization might perhaps dawn on them that the world neither needed nor wanted them, that they were superfluous, ugly, in the way, that they were the last of their kind, that their hour had come and that it was impossible to undo what had already been done. And at the same time, under the sheet covering my head, hiding my body and my face that were pretending to be dead, I became reconciled to fear. I took no further interest in what was happening outside, I did not want to see my father or mother standing by the window, and thus I was gathered into sleep, alone, waiting for the beadle from the Yemenite quarter to start crying into the night, calling the people to prayer, and his call would sound like a cry for help and it would bring with it the knowledge that morning would soon be there. Ever since then I can't fall asleep without covering my head with my sheet, and even a breath of air from

outside penetrating the sheet and brushing my face is enough to give rise
to the feeling that something has been left unfinished — something that
should have been done has not been — and to trouble my mind with endless questions in the attempt to remember what I have forgotten to do,
and why it bothers me so much.

What were those shadows opposite us? A group of trees on the
shoulder of the hill, a ruined building, clouds gathering on the horizon?
Too late to go back and try to discover their material source. More and
more their shape resembled the shape of those other shadows, arched as
domes and pointed at their tips, the point of the head and the point of the
tail. There were two or three of them there; sometimes one of them disappeared behind the others, and sometimes it returned to take its place
between them. Slowly they slid down the slope, so slowly that they
seemed to be floating down to the valley. And this time I wanted passion-
ately to stop them before they reached the bottom, so that the movement
would go on and never stop, so lovely, so exalting, was it, the splendor of
the majesty that betrayed them, such a clumsy, ridiculous majesty, so
pathetic and grotesque, amid the shrieking commotion of the oppor-
tunistic apes, in the logical, dizzying world of the predators, rushing to
and fro like a wild wind, establishing a new regime. I knew that the best
moment of all was the moment of the first astonishment, which I was
never privileged to see eye-to-eye but only imagined in my heart, because
sleep always intervened and brought the curtain down on the pictures.
The moment had to be postponed for as long as possible, the revelation
had to be delayed. Why was I so certain that this was the last time I would
see them? My eyes open, my face exposed to the night air, guilty, responsible. The ground was cool and dry, and in the surrounding silence
Hedgehog's teeth went on chattering like an unstoppable machine.

There was a sound of footsteps in the grove behind us. As one man we
raised our heads, listening to the dark, looking at each other. Zackie, the
leader of the detail, rose slowly to his knees, trying not to make a noise,
and crawled toward the orange grove, in the direction from which the
footsteps had come. Was it Alon's detail returning from their reconnais-
sance? Was it one of the instructors? As in a flash the night landscape
cleared before my eyes, the objects took on their final form, the event on
the shoulder of the hill froze and vanished. I knew I hadn't fallen asleep;
it was only the sense of my body coming back to me, prickly and sudden
as waking. Nahum who was lying next to me took a deep breath, held it,
and let it out forcefully, as if he were giving vent to a sigh of pain or relief,
who knew, and turned to look at Zackie, who had advanced to the first

trees, where he stopped and listened. The footsteps receded farther into the grove. After a moment they were heard no more. Zackie crawled back to where the rest of us were lying.

Suddenly Hedgehog stood up and whispered compulsively: "Where are they? What's going on here? Why isn't there . . ." and Zackie jumped up and covered his mouth with his hand. Hedgehog resisted and tried to push his hand away. Zackie maintained his grip. They began to wrestle, fighting soundlessly, without anger or enthusiasm, and only the sounds of their breathing and their bodies thudding on the ground were heard in the silence, like the groaning of some nocturnal beast encountering an unexpected obstacle on its path, an obstacle it could neither surmount nor circumvent. There was a strange contrast between the surrounding silence — a silence that seemed to be trying to convey the feeling that time had stopped, that nothing was happening — and the fight that proceeded as if in response to some hidden signal, like the continuation of an invisible event that never stopped for a second, under the cover of the darkness, of the silence. Nahum and I watched them indifferently, waiting for it to end, looking from the fight to the ruin and back again as if there were some connection between them. It didn't take more than a minute before Hedgehog was lying on the ground with Zackie's one hand holding him down while the other gagged his mouth. Little by little Zackie removed his hand from Hedgehog's mouth, testing to see if he would try to talk. Hedgehog was silent, puffing and panting, accepting defeat. His teeth were no longer chattering. He sat up and stretched his limbs, as if he had just woken up. Zackie crouched opposite him as if waiting for the next piece of foolishness.

Suddenly a shot shook the air, and in the silence that fell afterward the reverberations of the report could still be heard, spreading out from the center in expanding circles until they disappeared into the distance. Zackie and Hedgehog immediately returned to their places, grabbing their guns, which had fallen to the ground in the fight. In the ruin opposite nothing stirred. Nor was there any sign of the second detail, which was also watching the ruin from its ambush on the other corner of the orange grove. The shot was so close that it was impossible to tell where it had come from, so violent and all-embracing that any one of us could have imagined it came from his own gun. But at the end of the moment of paralysis, when our muscles relaxed and we got our breath back, a gleeful inner cheer ran wordlessly through our ranks like an electrical current, knocking again and again at hearts that refused to believe the news: Someone's gun had gone off! The orange grove and the hill and the

ruin came home from their long and dangerous sojourn in enemy territory; they were no longer cloaked in the strange, mysterious beauty of
treachery. Hedgehog buried his face in his hands and burst into silent
laughter, covering his mouth so as not to let a sound escape. Who was the
poor devil who had fired the shot? It wasn't difficult to imagine how he
must feel, or what was in store for him. Nahum whispered: "Dear God!"
Zackie didn't even bother to react; he no longer cared about enforcing the
rules of the game, as if his appointment as leader of the detail had now
been canceled too. In the end Hedgehog's laughter and Nahum's exclamation infected me and Zackie too. Nahum looked at the three of us
writhing in laughter beside him with a baffled expression on his face.
The game was over. The deception exposed. Someone else would pay the
price of this awakening.

Night discipline continued in force until we reentered the base, like a
ritual whose reasons had been forgotten. In one of the corners of the big
parade ground, next to a lamppost, the platoon formed up in squads
facing their instructors. There was a long minute of silence. The instructors glared at the men in front of them. Benny counted the number of
threes, to ascertain that everyone had returned to base.

"Who fired that shot?"

Alon took a step forward. His head was lowered, and even in the dim
light of the lamp it was possible to see how pale his face was, all twisted
with pain, as if he were about to burst into tears. The instructors looked at
him incredulously: Perhaps he was volunteering to cover up for someone
else?

"You?" cried Benny in amazement.

"Yes, sir."

Raffy Nagar arrived. He had not put in an appearance during the exercise itself — presumably one of the instructors had been sent to tell him
what had happened. He looked at us expressionlessly and nodded to
Benny to carry on.

"Why did you do it?" asked Benny. He sounded aggrieved, as though
he had been let down personally.

Alon was silent.

"Why?" This time the question sounded almost imploring. "Why?"

"Sir, I saw a suspicious armed figure advancing toward us."

A tremor of silent laughter ran through us, shaking our shoulders, a
burst of suspect glee, a promise of freedom and strength.

"A suspicious figure?" said Benny. "Maybe it was the citrus grove
guard? Maybe it was one of the instructors? Maybe it was a shadow? And

maybe you were hallucinating? Did you hit anyone? What happened to the suspicious figure after you fired at it?"

"There was nothing there, sir."

Raffy Nagar intervened: "Are you the one who wants to apply for a transfer to the paratroops?"

"Yes, sir."

"You're nuts! You shouldn't be allowed to carry a gun."

"I know I made a mess of things, sir," said Alon, "but I'm ready to take whatever I've got coming to me."

"You're ready?" inquired Raffy Nagar with a sneer. "Who gives a damn if you're ready or not ready? What do you think this is, a request program? Have you forgotten where you are?"

There was no reply to this question. Raffy Nagar again nodded to Benny to continue.

Benny called out: "The whole detail, step forward!"

Avner, Peretz, and Hanan stepped forward.

Benny asked: "Did you see anyone approaching you with a weapon?"

"No, sir," said Hanan.

"You!"

"No, sir," said Peretz.

"You!"

"I saw something," said Avner, "but I wasn't sure if it was a person or not."

"Stop trying to be smart!" Benny spat out. "If you want to get into hot water together with him, just say one more word. Don't you ever stop looking for trouble?"

In the few minutes that were left until lights-out, while the rest of us quickly got undressed and lay down on our beds, Alon stood there, looking more lost and beaten than I had ever seen him, as if he didn't know what to do first in order to prepare himself for going to bed. Did he sense the looks of scorn and hatred sent in his direction, the satisfaction at his downfall? He was so absorbed in himself, so preoccupied in hiding the pain and shame from showing on his face, fumbling for the blankets on his bed, turning around in circles, as if searching for something. Perhaps he wasn't even aware of the looks and hints directed at him; perhaps he was waiting desperately for the lights to go out, for the darkness to come and separate him from us. And he would return to the place where there was a real meaning to every act, every danger, every enthusiasm. Because here everything is based on a lie, on a game of *let's-pretend,* on bluff and delusion. None of them realizes the terrific power possessed by his hands holding the gun, a gun with live bullets in it. How much strength you need, from one minute to the next, to keep your mind clear and concentrated, to control your thoughts. To remember that the game is a game and reality is reality. Not to allow yourself to be carried away by the real call of the dream, when the whole game is based on a lie. That's the biggest disgrace — to fall into the trap of the lie. Not what they would say about you or what they would think of you or how they would punish you. All those things could be overcome with will power and endurance.

There are some situations in which only the individual himself, all alone with himself, can find the way back to the starting point, reconcile himself to what he has done, acknowledge it. Like a scout returning alone from enemy territory, but along precisely the same route he used before, on his way in. He sees his footprints — fresh, solitary footprints that breathe as if they are alive. This is where I stopped to look at the map. Here I lay down behind a bush until the jeep disappeared into the distance. Here I stopped to have a drink of water. Here I stopped to piss. Here I heard a rustle, like a snake crawling in the grass. Here I heard people talking and I clung to the ground. So he retraces his steps. Recognizing in every footprint, every sign, something of himself, something he had left behind him, as it were, on his way. He can almost sense his smell in them, his heat, his thoughts, the moments of fear, the navigational instinct that guided his feet. And suddenly it seems to him that he is like a tracker sent to discover his own tracks. To pursue himself, to catch himself. And he knows that if he flees from himself, he will become detached and lose his way. Only when he reaches the border and crosses back to our side will he be able to feel how all those little moments, all the thoughts of fear and danger, all the footprints that remained there on the path and reattached themselves to him on his way back — are him. And what joins them together until they compose a particular person, and what attaches that particular person to him — isn't just memory, but belief. That he had not done what he did like a machine. That he understood the significance of his actions, and identified with this significance with the full force of his love. And thus, like a solitary scout returning after a mission, you have to travel that road alone, from point to point, from sign to sign, until you reach your borders. Without answering questions that you don't know how to answer, whose answers you are not obliged to know, because they're not your questions, but somebody else's. There was no suspicious figure in the citrus grove. There's no point in deceiving yourself. Not even now, when it would be convenient to begin believing it. No figure.

You invented it. Something impelled you to try. Something tempted you to go to the limit, to cross it, to feel what it was like, to get inside the part, to live it. As if it were all true. To play *let's-pretend* like a baby. That's your weakness and you should know it. True strength means knowing where your weakness is and how to bypass it; knowing where your strength is and how to activate it. How fine the line is between strength and weakness. How blurred it is. How dangerous that no-man's-land is. When everything takes place within the game of *let's-pretend,* the truth comes to resemble a lie and the lie to resemble the truth. How can you navigate there at all?

Now you need a good sleep. And sleep shuns you like a leper. Your body thirsts for action, not sleep. For love, not solitude. A wrong, unhealthy kind of alertness sharpens your senses, tenses your soul, for nothing, for nothing. Your mind is clear and sees things with a cruel, terrible clarity. You're losing your belief in yourself. Like a body losing blood. Now it's only a question of time. They'll cancel the application to the medical board. You can forget about your dream of a transfer to the paratroops. In any case you didn't have a chance. Nothing is working out the way it should. Something inside you is working against you, like a fifth column. Tripping you up, deceiving you, flattering you. The belief is draining out of you.

> Sleep will provide you with the clearest proof of what I say. In sleep souls left to themselves and free from bodily distractions enjoy the most blissful repose and, consorting with God whose kin they are, they go wherever they will and foretell many of the things to come. Why, pray, should we fear death if we love to repose in sleep? And is it not absurd to run after the freedom of this life and grudge ourselves the freedom of eternity? It might be expected that we, so carefully taught at home, would be an example to others of readiness to die.*

Did he really mean it? Did he believe it himself, or was he just trying to rid them of the natural, physical, paralyzing fear of the deed? Of the hatred of death? Funny you never thought of it before. It's the way a politician talks. Choosing the easy, short, efficient way of persuading them to do what he thinks best. How cheap their sacrifice becomes. It stops even being a sacrifice. It's a good deal, worth their while. Selfish,

---

* From the speech of Eleazar, leader of the defenders of Masada, urging suicide upon his followers. Josephus, *The Jewish War,* The Penguin Classics, Penguin Books, Great Britain, 1959, p. 362.

even, repose instead of suffering. Eternity instead of transience. How terrible and beautiful the sacrifice was when it was performed in pain, in the
love of life, in the relinquishing of it for the sake of a great cause, for the
sake of others. Of a people. Of friends. Without any reward. Without any
consolation. Flying in the face of self-interest. Under an olive tree, with
the summer sky above you clear and deep, full of stars like windows into
infinity, on enemy territory full of the smells of an ancient, rural Canaan,
you feel the blood of belief ceaselessly flowing out of you and soaking into
the earth, returning to it after its wanderings, homeward bound.

> For life is the calamity for man, not death. Death gives freedom to our
> souls and lets them depart to their own pure home where they will
> know nothing of any calamity; but while they are confined within a
> mortal body and share its miseries, in strict truth they are dead. For
> association of the divine with the mortal is most improper. Certainly
> the soul can do a great deal even when imprisoned in the body: it
> makes the body its own organ of sense, moving it invisibly and
> impelling it in its actions further than mortal nature can reach. But
> when, freed from the weight that drags it down to earth and is hung
> about it, the soul returns to its own place, then in truth it partakes of
> a blessed power and an utterly unfettered strength, remaining as
> invisible to human eyes as God Himself.*

To lie on the ground at night and wait for morning to break and not to
fall asleep, not to give in to the temptation, not to relinquish the suffering,
not to make the sacrifice too easy, worth your while. There was no figure.
Peretz-Mental-Case was the only one who believed it. The only one to see
what you wanted them to see. You walked with them through that
damned grove, cloaked in a mysterious silence, enjoying your status as
head of the detail. One of the few in whom Muallem had confided the
truth. You have to give them the feeling that it's all for real. Now you're
the commander, even if it's only temporary, you're like one of the instructors. Again and again you have to silence Hanan and Avner, who keep up
a constant chattering, as if the whole thing has nothing to do with them.
About girls and parties and so on. They react with mockery. Make fun of
you. Their cynicism angers you more than their personal attitude toward
you, toward your role. Because you know the truth. You know they're
right. It even angers you that in your opinion they're tramping too

---

* *Ibid.,* p. 362.

heavily on the grass, trampling contemptuously, defying the rules of silence and secrecy. Only poor Peretz-Mental-Case, who's terrified, behaves properly. The trouble is that it's a dangerous game: When you try too hard to excel, you're liable to overstep the boundaries of logic and to destroy everything. As if it's such a big deal to be the outstanding student in a platoon like this. But the need to shine is a struggle against despair, against futility. It wasn't pettiness. They thought you wanted to make an impression on them. That you were playing leader on their backs. If there was some truth in this, it happened later. At first it was just the desire to excel, to perform the mission properly, perfectly. It wasn't petty. At any rate, until they encountered the dog.

Even in the dark you could see that it was a poor hungry mutt and not a real watchdog. When it approached you, it stopped a few steps away and went on barking furiously. Now they started to get really scared. The two Jerusalemites were apparently not used to dogs, and perhaps not to any kind of animals at all, and Peretz-Mental-Case looked as if a devil disguised as a dog had suddenly loomed up in front of him. This was the moment when cool nerves and resourcefulness were called for. You indicated to them to stay where they were without moving, and you approached the dog. There was something phony about its fury. You can always tell with dogs. There was something terribly pathetic about that fury. So the main thing was to show it that you weren't afraid of it. You held both your hands out to it. It retreated and went on barking, thrusting its head forward threateningly with every bark. Judging by the signs it was possible to see in the dark, the dog didn't have rabies. At least there was nothing to worry about as far as that was concerned. Again you approached it and held out your hands, trying to touch it. The other three stood there next to the tree silent and tense. You could feel their fear, their admiration. It gave you strength and concentrated your mind. The dog began a new trick: It retreated, sprang at you, barked, and retreated again. All you could do was keep advancing and force it to keep retreating. If only you could give it something to eat. But there wasn't anything. You had to make contact. There was no other way of shutting it up. And so you gradually receded from your detail. The dog retreated and you advanced, it sprang forward and barked, you held out your hands and stayed where you were, until it backed away with you behind it. It stopped barking for a minute, looked at you, then looked sideways. Contact was almost established. And then it turned around and trotted off into the darkness. You returned to the other three. Signaled them to stay put and keep still. You knew the dog would be back. It wasn't over.

You seemed to know its habits. They obeyed you. You'd proved something. You could sense their gratitude. They knew they were in good
hands. Here something began pulling you strongly toward the edge. The
feeling that you were capable of far greater things. That you wanted to
give your all. That in the circumstances you had to forget a few things
and concentrate on the moment and its possibilities. A minute or two
later the dog silently reappeared. It stopped not far off, and stood there
without barking, looking at you. A sigh of impatience escaped the three
men. Slowly you advanced toward it. It advanced toward you. You held
out your hands and touched its body with both of them. It moved a little
to the side, careful and suspicious, as if shyly. But it remained standing
where it was. Waiting for you. Again you stepped forward and touched
it. At first with a light, fluttering stroke, barely touching, and then more
firmly. A shudder ran through it at your touch. A shudder of strangeness
and resistance. But it let you do your will and it didn't move from its
place, it didn't make a sound. You passed your hand over its body, you felt
its damp, alien warmth, its sharp ribs under the taut skin, arching like
waves — the rough coat spotted with bald patches, lumps, scabs. You
stroked its neck and addressed it soundlessly: If I had no alternative, I
would choke you to death. At that moment, rising straight out of its
stomach, a choked whimper broke out of the dog's closed mouth, beginning in a kind of gurgling growl and ending in a imploring whine.
Begging for its life. As if in response to your thoughts. You straightened
up and returned to the other three. It trailed after you. As if expecting
something. Again you set off, all four of you, with the dog at your side,
still expecting something. From that moment on it was as if you had
entered a patch of cloud. The dog's whine burst into your ears, filled your
head. Like a dialogue that had been interrupted a long time ago and
unexpectedly renewed. It changed the route. There was pain in it.
Perhaps the pain of love, the longing for the unattainable. And a feeling
of strength ran through you, a fierce, intoxicating physical sensation.
When you looked behind you at the men following you in single file, you
couldn't help despising them. They kept looking sideways at the miserable cur trailing along next to them instead of doing what they were supposed to be doing, watching out for suspicious movements or figures
hiding among the trees. How alien they were to your dream and how
necessary to it. The more the sense of power grew in you, the more you
were aware of your dependence on them, of the silent war taking place in
the dark between you and them. The dog suddenly detached itself from
you, ran about ten yards ahead of you, stopped, and began barking into

the darkness opposite. To anyone watching from the side the scene would probably have looked like a betrayal, an inducement into a trap and a summons to the enemy to emerge from his ambush. But you, so good at understanding the true feelings of animals, you knew that the dog was on your side, warning you of some hostile presence over there, in the shadows.

Here the footsteps end. Somehow all the signs have been wiped out and it is impossible to continue on the way back. The darkness refuses to give back the picture that flickered then for a second, clear, certain, stronger than any truth. Perhaps it was all worthwhile for the sake of that moment — whatever happens to you now because of what you did, whatever price you have to pay. You stop and you don't know how to get back to your borders. A section of the road is lost — from here to the sound of the shot: the faces of the three men staring anxiously at you, standing a little way off, afraid to come any closer to you. It's impossible to discover the footprints in the lost section of the road and get back to that moment, the moment of the flickering in the dark. Keep the memory of that moment alive in your heart. Perhaps it will strengthen you in the evil days to come. The minute the shot was fired, the dog ran away and was swallowed up in the darkness. Returned to the place from which it had come. Its mission accomplished.

CHAPTER 24

Whatʼs all this compared to the torture of Uri Illan in the Syrian jail, or the suffering of Jibli in the Jordanian jail? Here itʼs only a game of humiliation. Here the forces are more or less equal. Despite everything, the game is fair. He gets up and stands at attention again; the tremor in his knees is a little better, he can control it now, thanks apparently to the jolting of the kick and the fall. "Pick up the weapon, nut! Pick up your weapon!" The shout echoes in his ears. He is standing not far from the company offices, an old broomstick in his left hand. For the third day. Occasionally one of the instructors with time on his hands volunteers to put him through arms drill, accompanied by yells, curses, and abuse. He doesnʼt know which is worse, standing stiffly at ease for hours without moving, until his limbs begin to tremble and his legs to give way under him — or running dementedly to and fro with the broomstick and the deafening yells, which no longer insult him, which have destroyed the barriers and are now acting directly on his nerves, like violent, ugly noises. It all depends on him — if he breaks or not. This is his chance to prove to himself and to them how strong he is, to show that he is made of different stuff. At mealtimes they order him to cover the ground to the platoon at a battle dash, under the eyes of all the recruits on the way, join the parade and go with the others to the mess. And they never stop telling him how lucky he is and how lightly heʼs getting off.

The short, red-faced Romanian CSM emerged from the office and Alon sprang to attention. The CSM looked at him. For a split second Alon dropped his eyes and saw the CSMʼs tiny blue eyes under his frowning eyebrows — which were narrow and arched as a womanʼs, and the rhythmic twitching of his cheekbones. "Youʼre moving, nut, youʼre moving!" Alon mobilized the remnants of his strength to stop the trembling of his knees. But the harder he tried the more they trembled, and a feeling of giddiness threatened to pull the ground from under his feet. "Stop moving when youʼre standing at attention, moron! Nut!" The kick on his calf instantly upset his balance and made him fall to the ground. "The weapon!" he heard the CSM yelling, "pick up the weapon, nut!"

He has never felt so acutely how much harder it is to stand still in one position than even the most backbreaking physical activity. Heʼs losing his sense of time. Any connection between his suffering and anything he has done or not done is growing fainter all the time. The suffering demands all of him for itself, tempting him to believe that he has willingly taken it all upon himself, that he is paying the price for all of them, because he is the best of them all. How wretched they appear in his eyes, precisely now, when he is ostensibly the lowest of the low. The CSM goes on shouting and Alon looks at the ground at his feet. His eyes fall on the reddish brown streakings of the loam soil, a strange mixture of colors that have not merged properly together. An act of creation performed in haste and not completed. Here and there the reddish soil is spotted with drops of whitewash that dribbled from the brush when they were painting the eucalyptus trunks and the stones bordering the paths, adding to the peculiar hodgepodge. The CSM goes away, and he is alone again. He stands at ease, standing the broomstick next to him on the ground. The colors of the soil give everything a feeling of transience. Something here is awaiting its correction, its completion, something barren, twisted. And a voice inside him, the remnant of robustness, like a souvenir of other days, says to him: Don't fall in love with your own suffering. A shadow falls suddenly on the ground. The light is growing gray. A fine drizzle falls on him. It increases in strength and turns into a shower. It hasn't rained since the night he was on guard with Micky. Soon the reddish soil has turned into a rust-colored paste. The rain falls on him and refreshes his breath. For a moment he closes his eyes, searching for the smell he loves, without finding it.

After Meir Har-Zion heard that he was going to be transferred to the commando unit, he began walking round the Nahal base in short trousers and sandals. The instructors were flabbergasted. He took no notice of them, disobeyed orders, treated all the rules of discipline with contempt. He knew that he was going there, that he didn't have anything to do with them anymore. The last days were days of license. Complaints and reports were made against him — and he knew that none of them mattered. He was going where he belonged. Someone over there was thinking about him, summoning him. Arik would come and take him away, dismiss all the charges against him, laugh at all the complaints. A new life would open up. And indeed, not long afterward, a command car appears at the base with Arik Sharon inside it. All the officers on the base begin to shake in their boots, they go mad with excitement, sucking up to Arik. Arik hardly bothers to answer their questions. He takes Har-Zion, and the command car charges off at terrific speed, leaving a cloud of dust and a legend behind it. Is everything on a question of belief and self-confidence?

Benny leads him to the platoon and the mess for lunch. Enemy to the left! Enemy to the right! Up! Down! Up! Down! The shouts sound to him as if they're coming from behind a thick screen. Only something in his nerves responds to them and activates his body. The mud in this place smells like rust. His face is stuck in it, his body suddenly refuses to rise. Benny kicks his thigh: "Up! You miserable nut! Get up!" No one's coming to rescue him. No one's waiting for him anywhere. There's no other place for him. "What's the matter with you? Where's all your terrific fitness?" Benny says laconically, without any hatred. "The fighter who's going to the paratroops, who's too good for Training Base Four. Get up!" Benny's boot pushes his face into the mud, his eyes are closed, and like a sigh of relief the temptation wells up in him not to open them, to go on burying his face in this soft, damp lap whose taste is the taste of rust, and to fall asleep. Benny's voice calls again: "Up! Up!" but the pressure on his head doesn't let up. In other words, he has to fight, they won't let him surrender. Benny bends over him, the pressure on the back of his neck ceases. "That's enough, get up!" The tone of the voice is different. He stands up. Benny looks him up and down with a puzzled smile. I haven't broken yet, Alon says to himself, I've still got a long way to go from here to the breaking point, from the moment of the shot to now. So long that it's not me anymore. It wasn't me who fired a shot in the dark in the orange grove, it was someone else, someone I'm paying for now. How good it is to pay for others. I never knew what a great feeling it is! This is my war — and in it I feel strong, and just. Benny marches him to the platoon barracks. He orders him to go into the showers and wash the mud off his face. "Dismissed!" he shouts in his ear, and the shout echoes in the dim, empty room like a call to rebellion. Benny stands silently next to Alon as he washes his face and hair. Lacking a towel, the water drips down his face and neck. Alon tosses his head again and again to shake off the water, and in the meantime drops keep falling like big raindrops and he wipes them away with the back of his hand, stealing a glance at Benny, who looks at him in a blank, enigmatic silence. Alon feels the need to confirm his presence by his side, and he smiles at him unwillingly, a smile of complicity. Before he leaves, Benny stands in front of him and bars his way; he obviously has something he wants to say to him, and hasn't made up his mind how to formulate his words. A triumphant happiness surges up in Alon's heart, a pride he cannot contain. Perhaps the ordeal he has endured is somehow bringing him closer to the place to which he will be called?

In the end Benny said: "This is the second time I've managed to persuade the CO not to court-martial you. The first time was on the firing range. You owe me something for it. You owe me an explanation. I want to understand. I have to understand."

"Sir —" said Alon.

Benny interrupted him: "I'm not talking to you now as your instructor, but as a private individual. I'm only asking one thing of you: Explain to me. Explain why you did it. It interests me, it's important to me to know in order to understand a lot of other things. Why did you do it? Why you, of all people?"

"I don't know either, sir," said Alon. "I myself don't understand. But I did see something, at least believe that. And I was sure that it was the right thing to do. It was only afterward that I realized that it was madness. Sir, I don't belong here. But I know that I don't have a chance of getting transferred anywhere else now. I had big dreams about what I was going to do in the army. Maybe when you want something too much — you lose it. I don't know."

"You could have been the outstanding student of the platoon, it was in the bag. You don't understand what it means to be in the army. Do you suffer from psychological problems?"

Alon was silent.

"I'm not saying it to hurt your feelings. It's not a disgrace. You needn't be afraid to tell me. I'm interested in things like that. I'm trying to help you. Do you understand?"

Alon said: "I don't have any more problems than anyone else."

"If you don't want to be a jobnik, there are lots of things you can do in the army. You can go to a Squad Commanders Course, even an Officers Course. Despite your medical category. You can be an officer, an instructor, even right here on Training Base Four."

"Sir, I wanted to be a fighter."

"You wanted! You wanted! So what if you wanted? I wanted all kinds of things too. Everyone wants. Live in reality. Take what reality can offer you, why not? If it's good enough for me, why isn't it good enough for you? Are you worth more than me? Why? Because you're a kibbutznik? That makes no difference at all. I'm talking to you like a friend. Before we go back to being instructor and recruit again, in the military framework, with everything that implies. Being mentally healthy means adjusting to the situation, living in reality. Otherwise you'll go crazy, you'll run amok, you'll come to a bad end. If you pull yourself together, you can go far, I'm telling you. You know what it means to be an instructor here on this base? You know how much power it gives you? I showed you that before, when you were lying in the mud. I didn't do it out of sadism. Why should I? I did it to make you feel the difference between us, the power they give an instructor here. If you still needed to learn it. An instructor on a training base has more power than an officer in a lot of other units. You control people, you can play with their lives however you like, you can decide their fate. You have to be just, of course, but they're dependent on you. Do you understand that?"

"Yes, sir."

Benny looks at him with a frown that is contemptuous and suspicious at once. His eyes move restlessly behind his glasses; perhaps he's regretting his frankness? Why is he so interested in him? Why is he talking to him in such a friendly way all of a sudden? To give him an idea of the capricious and irresistible charms inherent in the prestige and power of an instructor? More and more Alon realizes how much he hates this place, this hour above all other hours, his benefactor standing in front of the door, his drawling, ingratiating voice, trying to establish an intimacy between them. And for the first time in his life he hates himself. Not contempt, not pity, hate, like the hatred felt for an enemy. As if the voice speaking to him is a part of himself, a voice forgotten in the chorus of voices, a voice breaking out of the depths, emerging from within him and taking up its position against him, like a fifth column.

"Sir, why do you care about me so much?"

"Because you're not like all the rest of the bastards in the platoon. You're the only one who might amount to something afterward. All the others will be parasites, lousy jobniks, human garbage. If you really are such an idealist, this is your opportunity. I have to explain it to you."

Alon says nothing. Something breaks inside him. In the middle of the day, on the training base that is always pulsing with the feverish, rhythmic clattering of nailed boots, the instructors' yells, the terrified chorus of the recruits, the hoarse, broken, stammering, breathless voices raised in song, roaring in joy or despair, all the sounds he stopped noticing long ago, all the sounds that he never imagined acted as a wall protecting him from waking up, from himself — all of them have ceased. An unendurable silence falls in the gloom of the shower room where the smell of carbolic acid lies heavy in the air, dragging him down, down, to the most broken-down, purest, most sterile elements. He is seized by a weariness that even the energy of the hatred coursing through him cannot overcome. What trap is he trying to make him fall into, why is he trying so hard to impress him, to make him believe that he has it in his power to influence and decide his fate? Alon can hate him as much as he likes, but he can't uproot from his heart the things he has heard, the hope of the other possibilities, the temptations of power.

"And one last thing, before I go back to being your instructor and you go back to being what you are — a miserable recruit: You're going in a dangerous direction. You're losing your way. I've seen it before, believe me. The strongest break first. Use your head, think, you're not a child. Now go to the platoon. On Sunday you'll be told what happens next."

There is no sigh of relief. No victorious happiness. Only the sense of time returning to normal. What does he mean he'll be told on Sunday? On Monday morning the outdoor training series is due to begin. Can they actually be cruel enough to leave him behind on the base when the rest of the platoon goes on the series? The pain of this possibility jolts him from his passive stance in the dimness of the shower room, goads him to join the platoon at once. Frantic to save whatever can still be saved.

The platoon has already left for the mess hall. He takes his mess tin, evading the eyes of the men on duty guarding the barracks, and goes to join the queue in front of the mess hall door. They're all standing there and his eyes fall immediately on Micky, still wearing turnout dress; he must have only just arrived. Micky, whom he forgot while he was serving his punishment, during the time-not-time when he was standing in front of the company office with the broomstick in his hand. He struggles with his face, his hands, with all the movements of his tired body, not to betray the joy welling up in him and brimming over. Micky hasn't seen him yet. Something in the way Micky is standing speaks of sadness, loneliness; his profile is frozen in a kind of miserable half smile. Muallem is standing next to them maintaining silence and order. He orders Alon to join the last three. Micky, standing in one of the first threes, turns his head and sends Alon a brief smile of encouragement, almost like a wink, and immediately resumes his former gloomy expression.

Will he despise me now? wonders Alon. Lucky he's not one of those types who can't wait to start preaching at you.

"Let's go outside for a minute," he said when they returned to the building.

"Okay," said Micky. "In a minute. Don't think I didn't have any problems there. I quarreled with the coach. I know that character from way back. In the army every shit thinks he's somebody. It almost ended in a report. That whole business was one big mistake."

In the meantime Alon glanced through the newspapers Micky had brought for him.

"Is it a holiday eve today? What holiday?"

"Simchat Torah," said Micky. "This year all the holidays come on Saturday, to save us days off."

Alon showed no interest in what Micky had to tell about his soccer-training period. What did Micky know about the egoism of the suffering? Alon said to himself: Why does he try to console me with his troubles? Why is he so patronizing? But nevertheless he's glad, he's very glad, that Micky has come back and that he's here. In the mere fact of his presence there's something that assuages his loneliness. If only it were possible to renew the tradition of arguments, to reach a new confrontation, they would have been able to complete another stage in their acceptance of each other. But that was a part of road they had already traveled, and they could not go back to it. Why, despite all his self-confidence, despite the strength and authority he tries to convey, do his intimate relationships, whether in love or friendship, always follow the same, unvarying pattern: Why do people protect him, treat him like an invalid, give in to him, save him from himself? He hates it — maybe it's a form of hating himself?

They left the building and Micky suddenly called: "Alonchik! How's tricks?" as if they had only just met and everything up to then had only been for form's sake. Micky smiled, without hiding a certain emotion: "What going on with you?"

"Listen," said Alon, "I think they're not going to let me go on the series, because of what happened. I suppose you've heard what happened."

"Yes," said Micky, "not that I understand exactly why you did it. But it's not my business. Benny spoke to me about it. He wants me to influence you. I didn't understand too well what he was getting at."

"Maybe I'm just frightening myself," said Alon. "Don't ask what I went through. He came to talk to me too. Like a friend, so called, not an instructor. To warn me, to promise me, that if I'm okay, I'll be able to get on in the army."

"Maybe he really wants to help you?"

"I don't want his help. I can't stand him. You don't understand, he's the opposite, the absolute opposite, of everything I believe in and everything I want to be in my life." He fell silent and glanced at Micky, whose face had clouded over with a worry that Alon was certain was for him.

"I saw something," said Alon. "It's important to me for you to know that, for you to believe me. Only you. In the dark, in the orange grove, there was a moment of brief illumination, like lightning, something like that. And there was someone standing there, a man with his face covered with a keffiyeh, and only his eyes showing. You know I'm not crazy. You know me. He was there and he was pointing a gun at us. You don't believe me."

"It doesn't make any difference," said Micky.

"Yes it does!"

"What matters is that they don't believe you, and the guys are making a joke out of it too. There's no point in trying to prove it and convince them."

"I didn't try. I'm just trying to explain to you."

"Alonchik, before long you'll forget all about it. Before long we won't be here. Basic training doesn't go on forever. And when we leave here we'll take our real problems with us, our real aspirations. Forget it, stop torturing yourself."

"You'll say anything, except that you believe me that I saw him, that he was standing there opposite us, which is the truth."

"How can I convince you that I believe it's the truth?"

"There's no way," admitted Alon. Then he was silent for a moment, examining Micky's eyes anyway to see if he believed him. "Benny said that on Sunday they would let me know what's going to happen to me."

"He told me," said Micky, "that thanks to him you're getting off lightly, without charges and all the rest. He's apparently in with the CO. He really likes you, you know."

"I don't want him to like me and I don't want his help. I don't mind getting what I deserve. As long as they don't think I'm crazy. I saw something they didn't see, do you understand? Before, in the rain, he made me do battle jumps and he forced me to stick my face in the mud. He pressed his boot down on my neck."

"Maybe that's what they do in the paratroops?"

"Maybe. Listen, something really weird happened. At the height of my tiredness, the climax of despair and humiliation and pain, with my face in the mud, I suddenly felt sexually aroused."

Micky sniggered: "What do you mean?"

"Don't laugh. Seriously. I don't understand why, but suddenly, when my head was deep down in the mud, I could hardly breathe, it happened, without any connection to a particular girl or desire, just like that, of its own accord, for no reason. Maybe it's something physical, connected to muscle tension, or blood pressure. I don't know. Like it happens in the morning, without any dream, without any stimulating thought, purely a physical reaction. But in this case I did feel that it had some connection to what was happening to me, as if it were some kind of rebellion of the natural life force against the pressure, against the repression. When he yelled at me to get up, I didn't want to. As if he were interrupting me in the middle of making love to the most beautiful girl in the world."

"I gave up trying to understand the body long ago."

"I keep talking about myself and I haven't even asked you what it was like there."

"Nonsense," said Micky. His face dropped its lighthearted, smiling expression and clouded over despondently again. He was silent.

"What happened?" asked Alon.

"Something terrible happened."

"What is it, Micky?"

"A guy from my hometown died. A while back his jeep drove over a mine when he was on his way to Nahal Oz, to visit his girlfriend. He lay wounded in the hospital, unconscious, and a few days ago he died. We almost grew up together. He's the brother of a girl in my class. He was a really good guy. On my way back to the base I dropped in to see my folks, and they told me that he died. It's the first time someone I know died."

"The ones who fall are always the best," said Alon. "Don't you think?"

"I don't know," said Micky, reflectively and not argumentatively, "but I knew him. I can't stop thinking about it. I just can't. I want to write a letter to his sister, I keep thinking about what to say to her and I can't find the right words."

Alon said: "I got a letter from my girlfriend." He opened his trouser pocket and took out an envelope, which he turned over in his hand to show that it was still sealed. "I haven't opened it yet."

"Read it now," said Micky. "I'm going to change."

Micky turned away and walked toward the building. Suddenly he stopped, looked back at Alon, smiled very sadly, spread out his hands in a gesture of helplessness, and turned back toward the barracks — a slow, stooped, hopeless figure.

The religious boys were setting out for the synagogue to celebrate the holiday. The sound of community singing rose from the platoon in the opposite building. Avner lay on his bed in the position in which he always slept, rigid as if he were standing at attention, his face looking straight at the ceiling, but now his eyes were open and narrowed in concentration beneath his thick, frowning brows.

"What's the time?" he asked.

"Half past seven," I said.

"My watch has stopped," he said, and after a moment's silence he added: "If I ever commit suicide, it'll be on a Saturday or a holiday. I hate them, even though they're days of rest. They fill my heart with a terrible boredom, a kind of emptiness, a feeling of oppression. There are moments when I feel so sad I think I'm going crazy." Again he fell silent, his hands on his face, his body still. After a while he removed his hands from his face and got up, stood for a minute as if wondering where to go, sat down on the edge of his bed, leaned over toward me, and said softly: "Man, I had a wonderful girlfriend, whom I loved, who loved me, who risked everything for me, who suffered terribly for me. And I threw her over for some glamorous snob who makes fun of me with her friends. For a hope that hasn't got a chance. For a dream. It happens so often — we deliberately chose the wrong alternative in order to destroy what we have, rather than to gain what we lack."

I said nothing. I had decided not to react to stories about Avner's personal life anymore. He looked at me in surprise: "You're afraid to say anything already, in case you get it in the neck. Don't be an idiot. Our friendship is too strong to be broken because of some outburst or moment of anger. What can I do? It's my nature. But I've got good sides too. Believe me."

"I don't have any complaints, you don't have to apologize."

"You remember what you said then, after the search, when they arrested Sammy? It was nice of you, it was generous."

"I never said anything special," I said innocently.

"You shit. You're regretting it already. You think it was a moment of weakness, of sentimentality. You don't understand that those are a man's finest moments, those moments of generosity. But you can't take it back, you know, the words remain. They don't get lost. They hover in the air all the time around the people who said them, around the people who heard them, accompanying them even when they try to forget them, even if they do forget them. They're there in the air. And these are the words that you said then: *You're a remarkable person. That was fantastic. Good for you.*"

"I don't regret it," I said. "That's what I felt. I've never seen anything like it."

"So that means something, no?" said Avner. "If it's true what you said, then you should forgive the other, ugly, bad things."

"Yes, you're right."

"I told you then that you can't imagine what I'm capable of, for good or evil, because the one depends on the other. Anyone who's incapable of great evil isn't capable of great good either."

"In other words, it's a question of power."

"Of course it's a question of power. Without power there is no good or evil. There's only living as if you were asleep, letting yourself be swept along with the current, without movement, without resistance. Doing good or evil means swimming against the tide, resisting it. For that you need strength. And I know that I'm strong, I've proved it to myself often enough. It's the strength to stand like a rock, alone, to declare your independence. I know what that means."

How could he talk about himself like that so shamelessly? Where did he get all those phrases from? From the movies he'd been brainwashing himself with for years? It sounded like a part he'd learned by heart.

"I think I understand what you mean," I said, "I've felt it myself, at least once that I remember very well."

On the evening of my treachery during our guard, I had indeed had a feeling of power, and it had indeed been connected to the knowledge that the act was evil. My attitude toward that act took on different guises on different days and in different moods. But one thing I hadn't felt up to now was true penitence, the wish to undo what had been done and behave differently. It was becoming clearer and clearer to me that my act, inasmuch as it stemmed from a conscious decision, was necessary. Only hindsight could have revealed this.

In the corner of the room where the Jerusalemites' beds stood, a crowd suddenly gathered. Everyone hurried over there; there were cries of astonishment, and also loud laughter.

I stood up and went over to see what was happening. Avner remained on his bed, lay down and turned over on his side, and immersed himself in his Hebrew grammar book. Through the circle that had gathered round Yossie Ressler's bed I saw the musician sitting, his face gray with pallor, frozen into a mask of horror. On his knees lay his guitar, which he had just removed from its case, and it was all smashed, its belly crushed and its strings torn and wound around the neck, which had been snapped off its base, like Medusa's hair. The onlookers went on laughing at this sight, and even Hedgehog, his friend who was standing next to him, could not suppress his laughter, although he muttered as he laughed: "Bastards, bastards."

Albert the Bulgarian said: "Never mind, Yossie, a good carpenter can fix it for you in a jiffy. I know a carpenter in Jaffa —"

This advice, which came from a heart full of goodwill, infuriated Yossie to such an extent that it aroused his fighting spirit: His eyes flashed with a fire I had never seen in them before.

"Idiot!" he yelled at Albert. "Idiot! There's no way it can be fixed. It's ruined, you understand? It's completely ruined. Whoever did it will pay for what he did! Barbarians! Human garbage! Scum of the earth! Filth! Filth!"

"Maybe someone did it by accident, when they were cleaning the barracks. Maybe it fell on the floor," Zackie offered.

"Don't talk rubbish!" Yossie yelled at him. "That didn't happen from falling on the floor. Can't you see?"

He lifted the poor corpse of the musical instrument a little, and the scene looked almost like a painting of the Virgin Mary mourning her crucified son, whose dead body lay on her lap.

"Perhaps someone who can't stand a certain kind of music did it?" said Hedgehog, with heavy emphasis.

"Hedgehog, are you starting again?" asked Zackie threateningly.

"No!" said Hedgehog. "I wasn't referring to anyone in particular. Keep your hair on."

Zackie said nothing. He had no wish to show disrespect for Ressler's sorrow by dwelling on his own grievances.

Yossie said: "I won't keep quiet about this! I'll put in a complaint about the whole platoon, everyone without a single exception. Let them send the CID to investigate, I don't care. They're not going to get away with it. I won't stop until they find whoever did it and throw him in jail."

Hanan said: "Calm down, there's nothing you can do about it. What's done is done. Take like a man."

"What bastards," said Yossie in a choked voice. "What bastards. I got this guitar as a present from my parents on my fourteenth birthday. My mother told me I shouldn't take it to the army. She knew what kind of garbage I'd be living with here. But I thought I'd be able to contribute something to other people, I thought they'd appreciate it. What an idiot I am, what an idiot . . ."

I think it was only at that moment, when he said *What an idiot I am, what an idiot,* that I realized the full force of his catastrophe, and how inadequate his words were to express the depth of his heartbreak. He closed his eyes and bit his lip. From 3 Platoon's barracks the sounds of melodious community singing, in two voices, continued to reach us, old songs, youth movement songs, soulful and effusive, as if the singers had been bound to one another for many years by ties of heartfelt affection and comradeship. Ressler's Jerusalem friends stood around him, sat next to him on his bed, silent, chastised, guilty. Alon and Micky, who had also witnessed the sorry sight, returned to their beds. Alon whispered something to Micky, and they went outside.

When they were outside, Alon said: "Listen, I think I know who did it."

"Who?"

"It's only a suspicion, but it seems quite logical to me. When you went on leave and I stayed behind with Ben-Hamo, he told me about how he was at boarding school on a kibbutz and how they chucked him out. On the day he left, he broke a guitar that belonged to one of the girls from the boarding school who hated him. He even described to me how he smashed it, and it's exactly the same as what they did to Yossie's guitar."

"What do you say!" said Micky. "He really is the scum of the earth. It would be just like him to do something like that."

"But why should he?"

"Don't you understand? It's the revenge of the weak against the strong. To destroy in secret. Ressler's playing humiliates him, it humiliates what he considers beautiful, what he loves. His pathetic belly dancing, the disgusting songs they sing. Yossie Ressler's culture proves how ugly all those things are."

"Now you're talking like Hedgehog," said Alon in surprise.

"It's much more complicated than Hedgehog thinks," said Micky, without going on.

"Don't tell anyone else. I only told you about it because the idea suddenly popped into my mind. It's only a suspicion," said Alon, "there's no proof. No good can come of it."

"What are you talking about!" exclaimed Micky angrily. "You're quite wrong. We have to go into it. We have to talk to Ben-Hamo and see how he reacts. Listen, we'll all suffer because of this business. Ressler's a neurotic baby. You saw how he reacted. He's capable of getting the whole platoon into trouble. He might really put in a complaint and there'll be an investigation, and that's all we need now. It's doesn't make sense for the whole platoon to suffer again because of some Ben-Hamo. I'll talk to him. He's afraid of me. I'll get the truth out of him."

"Don't do it," requested Alon. "Just leave it alone. I'm sorry I told you."

Micky was infuriated by the thought of Ben-Hamo's suspected crime. He said to Alon: "Haven't you got enough troubles of your own? Just leave this to me."

Alon said nothing. Micky's face, which was gloomy and crestfallen, apparently because of the death of his friend, took on a belligerent expression. A distraction from his pain, perhaps?

Yossie put his shattered guitar into its case. When he saw me looking at him, he said in his normal, colorless voice, "There won't be any more two-part singing with accompaniment," and gave me a beaten look, almost as if I were an equal partner in his loss.

"You know how much a guitar like that costs?" said Hedgehog. "You know how much it costs?" He addressed this stern question to me, almost as if I were an equal partner in the vandalism too.

Micky came into the room and headed straight for Ben-Hamo.

"Do you know who did it?" Micky asked Rahamim.

"How'm I supposed to know?"

"Because you did something similar once before," said Micky.

"No I never! I never did anything like that in my life!" protested Rahamim, raising his voice, while his eyes darted around in search of rescue. He was confused by the serious, businesslike note in Micky's voice, the same Micky who had once forbidden Rahamim to speak to him. Suddenly Rahamim's eyes fell on Alon as he entered the room, and a look of illumination dawned on his face, as if all was now clear to him. Alon stopped and stood not far from him, hanging his head in embarrassment and helplessness. Rahamim took a step toward Alon, and Micky stretched his hand out to his shoulder and shoved him back.

Rahamim cried: "What are you doing? Don't touch me, it's not allowed."

Those who had not been following the exchange between Rahamim and Micky up until now stood at the sound of Rahamim's shout and gathered around. Rahamim went up to Alon: "Did you tell him what I told you, about how I left that kibbutz school?"

"Yes," said Alon in a faint voice.

Rahamim gave him a contemptuous look, and nodded his head as if to say: *Yes, I understand, I understand.*

"I didn't mean to tell tales," said Alon. "I'm sorry it came out like this."

"I thought you had a good heart," said Rahamim. "I just told you all kinds of things. And now you think it was me that did the same thing to Yossie's guitar as I did that time on the kibbutz."

"No, I never said that," said Alon.

"So what does he want?" asked Rahamim, pointing at Micky.

"I want to know why you're lying," said Micky. "You said you'd never done such a thing in your life."

"I was a little kid then," said Rahamim. "I didn't have a clue."

Hedgehog stationed himself next to Micky: "What do you know about him? Have you found something out? He's the one who broke the guitar, right?"

Micky said: "He told Alon, when they stayed behind on the base, how once, when he was on a kibbutz, he did the same thing to some girl's guitar there."

"What's this," said Rahamim, "are you putting me on trial here?"

"Yes," said Micky, "we've got the right. We're not going to suffer because of you again. Understand? We're going to settle this between us."

Rahamim's friends, with Peretz-Mental-Case at their head, arrived to hear the charges and observe the proceedings from close up. Peretz said:

"Ben-Hamo, tell the truth now, you hear? If you lie, I'll kill you! Did you do it?"

"No," said Rahamim, "on my mother's life I didn't do it."

Peretz looked Micky in the face and spread his hands out in front of him, as if to say: *There you are, there's nothing to be done, the case is closed.*

Zero-Zero said: "He can swear on his mother a thousand times, I don't care. You can see on his face that he's lying."

"Don't talk so silly!" Peretz flared up. "What proof have you people got? What do you want of him? What do you know?"

Micky ignored these questions. He asked Rahamim: "What did you do to that girl on the kibbutz's guitar? How did you break it?"

Rahamim was silent. His eyes examined the people standing opposite him frantically. He tried to smile, as a demonstration of indifference indicating his innocence, or an expression of contempt for the hostility confronting him like a wall, the contempt of those who have nothing left to lose.

Peretz cried out to him: "Why don't you talk? Tell him what he's asking you."

Rahamim said to Micky: "You won't put me on trial. You're not a judge."

Hedgehog cried: "We'll all put you on trial! The whole platoon will put in a complaint against you. If you won't talk you must have something to hide. Either we'll settle it here between us, or we'll let the CID deal with it."

"Good," said Rahamim. "Let the CID do it. I'd rather have the CID than you."

"Nobody's asking you what you want. All you want is to get us into trouble and make everybody suffer because of you," said Hedgehog.

Micky said: "Answer my question: How did you break the guitar that belonged to that girl on the kibbutz? Show us how you did it."

Rahamim was silent. Micky leapt over the space between them and punched him in the stomach. Rahamim let out a shriek and fell to the floor, writhing in pain, real or pretend.

Alon grabbed Micky's arm. "Stop it!" he cried. "You're going too far!"

"Leave this to me," said Micky.

"What's gotten into you," whispered Alon.

Micky did not reply. The nature of the account he was settling here was not clear. It was hard to believe that he was so upset by the fate of Ressler's guitar, or so afraid of the musician's threats, to put in a complaint and demand an investigation. The fire of justice and righteousness that was now burning in his bones was foreign to Micky's nature, to his habitual irony and reserve, the distance he kept between himself and most of the platoon: For a long time he had hardly exchanged a word with anyone, except for Alon and one or two others he considered worthy of his notice.

Almost furiously he shook off Alon's restraining hand and moved closer to Rahamin, who was still lying on the floor and writhing in pain.

Suddenly Miller was standing there, a clown from a different comedy. He stationed himself between Micky and Rahamim and cried: "Madmen! What gives here? Madmen! Why to hit Rahamim all the day?"

His appearance released loud peals of laughter. He himself joined in gladly, as he often did at his ridiculous performances. As if he understood that there was, indeed, good reason to laugh at him. Everyone laughed except for Micky, who did not move from his place and demanded once more of Rahamim that he answer his question about how he had broken that other guitar, on the kibbutz. Rahamim writhed in pain on the floor.

Zackie cried to Rahamim: "Why don't you just tell him what he wants? If you didn't do it here, what have you got to be afraid of?"

Rahamim rose to his feet. He thought for a moment, raised one of his feet and stamped it twice on the floor, very hard, making no attempt to hide a smile of dreamy satisfaction as he did so, as if consoling himself with memories of bygone days of glory.

Hedgehog said: "That's exactly how he smashed Ressler's guitar too."

"Fellows," intervened Alon, looking very miserable, "you don't have any proof. Don't talk loosely. It could have bad consequences."

Hanan said: "It's clear now. He did it. That's exactly what he did to Yossie's guitar."

"We should break his arms and legs," said Hedgehog.

"What do I care?" whispered Yossie Ressler. "What difference does it make to me what you do to him? I want my guitar, that's all. And if I have to set the whole of the military police by the ears and go all they way up to the advocate general I'll do it, I won't give up." Again he bit his lips as if he were afraid he might say things that were better left unsaid.

Miller went up to Yossie. "Rahamim do nothing," he said. "I know, I know."

"What are you interfering for?" demanded Hedgehog. "What do you know about it? Get out of my sight!"

Hanan said to Yossie: "I don't know what you want. Nobody can bring your guitar back, as if nothing happened to it. Tell us what you want to happen."

Hedgehog answered for Ressler: "Revenge, that's what, to teach him a lesson, to make him pay for what he did. Don't sneer at revenge."

"What do I care about revenge?" Yossie burst out. "Why don't you just go to hell, all of you, just go to hell!"

Rahamim approached Ressler. "Believe me, believe me I didn't do it," he said. "Why should I break your guitar? What for? What am I? I'm nothing, Yossie."

"Go to hell," said Yossie, and bit his lip again.

Rahamim turned to Alon: "Do you think I did it?"

"No," said Alon, "I believe you that you didn't do it. All this is my fault. I didn't mean it. It just happened, because I spoke without thinking. I'm sure that you didn't do it."

"What if I once did something like that, do I have to go on doing it again all my life? I was a little kid, I didn't have a clue. Why should I go and do a thing like that? Why does everybody always blame me?"

"I believe you," said Alon. "I know it wasn't you."

"Why did he hit me for nothing?" asked Rahamim, pointing at Micky, who was standing to one side, his eyes full of suppressed rage.

"I don't know," said Alon.

"You haven't gotten what you deserve yet," said Hedgehog, "and you're going to pay through the teeth for it, believe me."

Lights-out was approaching. The religious men came back from the synagogue, flushed with happiness and dancing. Everything remained up in the air, awaiting a resolution. The Jerusalemites clustered in the corner where their beds stood, holding secret consultations, making plans, who knows. Rahamim kept glancing anxiously in their direction — he knew that they were talking about him, and that they meant to do him no good, perhaps that very night.

I went back to my bed. Avner lowered the book of Hebrew grammar that had been hiding his face all this time, his eyes met mine, and my heart sank in astonishment and fear. It was one of those rare, unbelievable moments when a crack suddenly opens in the blank wall enclosing the mysterious alien presence we call the other, and we can never understand why it should be happening now, at this moment rather than another: And from the crack things that have not yet become words look out, like places you once visited long ago, with all their secrets still alive in your memory, ready and waiting for you to meet them again. His face was still hidden by the book; only his eyes appeared above it, looking at me beneath frowning brows, and twinkling in them, reserved, inquiring, and suspicious, a smile, part question and part confession, a smile that said it all, with a certainty beyond doubt, plainer than words: *Have you guessed? That's right, I did it.*

My lips must have parted to say something. My hands went out as if to stop myself from falling. Slowly he lowered the book from his face and put it down beside him, and before I could say anything he hissed between his teeth, without moving his lips: "Shut up." His face was beaming with pride and triumph.

My eyes asked: *Why? Why?*

And he hissed between his teeth again: "Shut up."

His ironic look studied my reactions. I was horrified. I had become his accomplice, trapped in his secret, his motives, his responsibility, in the consequences yet to come, perhaps even in his remorse, if it ever materialized. For a long time after lights-out I couldn't fall asleep. A rhythmic snoring rose from Avner's bed. He was sleeping the sleep of the just.

What's the matter with you? What are you so afraid of? It's the fear of living in a world where everything's permissible. And the fear of knowing that as always, I'll do nothing, I'll let things take their course, without any intervention from me, according to the wishes of others. No one's going to blame you for it. And the knowledge itself — that doesn't make me guilty? Would you prefer not to know? Now that I do know, that question's meaningless. But why did you have to tell me? What annoys you more? That I did what I did, or that I told you about it? I'll tell you: Your problem is that you always want to keep clean. Get a bit dirty! Living in the world means getting its mud on you. But you want to stay a sissy. Are you still trying to educate me? I don't give a damn about your education. I did what I wanted to and I'm not sorry. There are things you can't understand. For example, why I did it and why I wanted you to know. What am I supposed to do now? Are you asking me? That's your problem. Decide for yourself. If you think you should tell everybody who really did it — go and tell them. Like you once told on Benny, that it was him who crapped in the classroom. You accused me of doing him an injustice. But now it's you who're doing the injustice. Everyone's sure that Ben-Hamo did it, and you don't care that he'll have to suffer because of you for something he didn't do. If you care so much about Ben-Hamo, why don't you go and tell that it was me, and save him? I can't do it. Why not? I don't know. I don't want to get involved. You can't be on the side of justice and at the same time stay on the sidelines and keep your hands clean. If I felt the way you did, if I cared more about Ben-Hamo than about Avner, I would go and tell what I knew. In other words, as far as you're concerned the whole thing is a question of personal relations and not of justice and injustice. What a question! Justice is blind, as they say. What a dubious compliment! Personal relations, the relation to one specific person, is an open-eyed, true, complex relation. That's something worth fighting for. How can you live in such a world? What, do I have to worry about the world, to reform it? It's enough for me if I save myself, it's enough for me if I can help the people I love.

I opened my eyes and woke up at once. Something had stopped the clamor of words, the torrent of words that sank at once into a subdued, rapidly disintegrating murmur. The part of me that had remained awake while I slept, observing, had signaled my sleeping part to open my eyes. I saw the shadows rising and leaving the Jerusalemites' corner. Slowly and silently, as if they were floating on their bare feet, they advanced on Rahamim's bed, and as if at a secret signal they fell on him as one man. Rahamim succeeded in uttering a brief wail, which was immediately choked — someone must have gagged his mouth — and he was rolled up in his blanket, held immobile in their hands, and they were beating him. Everything took place in complete silence, even the blows sounded like muffled thuds coming from far away. No one's sleep was disturbed — only Zero-Zero, who slept very lightly, and perhaps had not even fallen asleep yet, sat up in bed and watched them in silence. After a minute he hurried over to them.

"That's enough, boys. Stop it. Don't kill him."

The shadows stopped at once, perhaps dismayed at their discovery, and slipped back to their beds. Ben-Hamo began moving on his bed, carefully unrolling the blanket in which he was wrapped, and even in the dark I could see him trying to straighten his body and stretch his limbs.

Afterward he began to cry. Soundlessly; only his broken breathing was audible, and his sniffing, as if his nose had begun to run. And Zero-Zero was still sitting up in bed and looking at him in silence.

I wasn't sure that these things were actually happening. The silent weeping went on for a long time, and then it stopped. Zero-Zero moved about on his bed, lay down, sat up again, and stared at Ben-Hamo's bed. In the end he got up and went over to Ben-Hamo's bed, bent down slightly, and looked at him. Apparently he was reassured. He went back to bed, lay down, turned over onto his side, pulled the blanket over him, turned onto his other side, shifted about as if to find the right position, despaired, lay on his back, pushed the blanket down to his waist, sighed profoundly, and whispered an interminable Romanian curse.

CHAPTER 25

We have to get to the wall!" The words resound in my head, empty, solemn, lacking any real meaning — a password given to the wrong side by mistake. These words do not belong to me, nor to those standing beside me. We are crowded in the middle of the floor, in the dark, thrust forward and backward and sideways, falling on each other, without balance, without a grip for our feet. The smell of the sweat souring in the sealed coach surrounds us like a poisonous miasma. The intense, sweltering heat and the stifling, ever-thickening air are beginning to numb our senses. Soon, when the last barrier of resistance falls, everything will seem like a game of shadows in the dark, without shame, pain, or pity.

At first there was darkness. The doors creaked rapidly in their grooves and closed on us with a decisive slam and a click as final as a judgment. Darkness descended immediately. An artificial, blank, uniform darkness, like a black curtain, came down on our eyes so that we couldn't see each other's faces, even though we were standing packed together, without moving. Until the train moved off, there was silence, like a moment of recovery. The noise of the locomotive sounded threatening in the darkness of the day, a savage accompaniment to the sounds of our breathing, like a pump gradually emptying us out until we were weightless.

"Melabbes, is that you?" Avner's voice whispered at my left.

"I'm not sure."

"Don't be smart. We have to get to the wall. When we start moving, everyone's going to fall on top of everyone else. It'll be total chaos. Can you see me?"

"No."

His hand came down hard on my shoulder. "Stick to me, you hear? Push as hard as you can. Don't think about anything. Just push. We have to get to the wall."

Gradually I began to recognize shapes again. The figure next to me tried to turn. Someone near us shouted: "What are you doing? You're crushing me!" Others cried: "Stop shoving! It's impossible to breathe!"

Hedgehog's voice called from somewhere: "Hey guys, stop making waves!"

No one laughed. The figure that a moment before had been Avner was swallowed up in the dark confusion. Only the shouts that greeted his efforts to advance made it possible to guess the direction in which he was moving. How did he know where the wall was? What sense guided him? What memory from the world of bodies outside, which had not yet been extinguished in him, directed his progress toward the invisible support he sought? The helmet in the hands of the figure in front of me was pressing the pouches of my equipment webbing into my chest with intolerable force. The barrel of my gun pressed against my collarbone, sending a sharp, crushing pain through me; any attempt to move increased the pressure of the steel on the bone. My eyes were beginning to distinguish the bodies pressing up against me and I recognized their faces. And as I did so I was flooded with hatred for them, for the visible and the invisible, for those standing in the middle and those leaning safely against the wall, who were going to bring catastrophe on us all. The figure opposite me was holding his helmet in front of his chest like a shield and its dome was pressing against my pouches, which were pressing against the barrel of my gun.

"Nahum, I want to let my gun down. It's pressing on my bone, move a bit."

Nahum's face didn't react.

"Come on! Move a bit!"

He didn't reply.

"Nahum!"

His eyes stared. From close up it now became possible to see them, wide open, expressionless. His face was stony as the face of a dead man who has given up the ghost standing up, in sudden terror. I flattened my hands against the dome of his helmet, trying to push it back with all the strength of the cold hatred that flared up inside me, that I fed and fanned with the smell of his shaving cream stinking up the showers every morning, with the wall of silence behind which he hid in order to guard his soul, with the ludicrous way he looked when he set out for the synagogue, full of a sense of vocation, silent and solemn, as if purified of our constant presence, self-regarding, set apart. Room to breathe and relief from the pressure of my gun on my collarbone became the pretext for a war for the right to hate, to punish, to hurt, to change others. Accordingly, when I failed to thrust him back, because the resistance of the object facing me was stronger than the force of my hands, I went on pressing on the dome of his helmet, in order to at least force him to break his silence, animate his expression, bring him back to reality, until he understood his guilt, until he suffered for it.

Micha, who was pressed up against my side with a silly, tortured smile on his face, heard my request and tried to move. But at that moment the train started moving and everybody fell backward with a loud clatter of nailed boots, clashing of helmets, thudding of rifle butts on the metal floor, like the sound of a terrified flight. The pain of the steel crushing my collarbone stunned my mind, which immediately numbed and blurred, as my body's sense of identity vanished underneath the weight of the bodies falling on top of it. Gradually the bundle came apart. The deceptive balance defied attempts to stand up. Everyone swayed drunkenly and fell on their neighbors, seeking a support. My eyes were already accustomed to the darkness. Now it seemed to me that there was less of a crush, as if the sudden jolt had been able to introduce a certain order into the way we stood, to spread us out a little, so that we would have enough room to fall. Zero-Zero had fallen onto Micky, who was standing next to the wall and hanging on to it. Micky kicked him and he fell on his face, and at the same moment the train went around a bend that, although not particularly sharp, was enough to throw the people standing in the middle onto the opposite wall, and back again, to where there was no support. *The division is right,* I said to myself, *a power outside us is imposing order here. Everyone has received his proper place in one of the circles of this hell.* The clever ones had unloaded the mountain of rucksacks and blankets and tents and tent pegs and spades as soon as they were pushed into the train, and laid them at their feet. The simpletons had gone on carrying their loads on their backs, like huge humps, weighing heavily on their shoulders and upsetting their steadiness on their feet. Like strange, clumsy animals whose bodies had swelled to monstrous proportions while their legs withered. Whenever they tried to turn, they hit someone behind them with their mountain of equipment. It was impossible to move. Only to be pushed by some external force. It was impossible to reach the wall. The places had been determined in advance.

Zero-Zero did not get up. He sat where he had fallen after Micky's kick and mumbled to himself: "It's better to sit, you have to sit." A few people who overheard his mumbling and understood that he was right, followed his example. Nahum, whose neighbors sat down too, depriving him of support, collapsed and fell like a lifeless body. Slowly the fear crept into my heart: Was there a dead man in our midst? There was no way of summoning help. The instructors were in a different coach. No one would hear our shouts from the sealed coach. How far did we still have to go? Why was it so important to inform someone outside that there was a dead man among us? Why was it much more important and urgent even than the chance of saving him?

Hedgehog's voice announced in a sudden cry, almost a wail, so upset was he by the force of the revelation that had struck him: "Hey, guys! They're transporting us in a cattle train!"

I didn't know why, but at the sound of this cry, all my limbs were seized by a strange trembling that in other circumstances would have been accompanied by wild, anarchic laughter. But now, because of the drowsiness that had overcome my body, and because I was positive that I was breathing in the hot, close air exhaled by the others in hoarse, rhythmic pants, as after a long, long run, the laughter died before it was born. Only the familiar inner tremor, nervous but full of the promise of freedom, went on shaking me, bearing with it tidings of glee, at their expense and mine. And a voice, my own voice, like a visitor from far away, said inside me: *Don't resist what happens, only try to understand, to decipher it, to read it like fate, to hear what it says to you. There's no point in reaching the wall; there's no point in being sorry that you couldn't reach it. Cattle have no problems with balance. Better to be a beast now than a man.*

The train went around a bend again and again bodies fell from side to side. As I fell I managed to say to myself: *Now I'll have a place to sit.* Among the melee of the falling bodies my feet sought a space to sit. Slowly I collapsed to the floor, and after a few of the fallen had steadied themselves I found myself next to Nahum, who began shifting about as if he wanted to move to another place. But he had nowhere to move to. He stretched his arms out stiffly in front of him and held up his hands opposite me, as if to mark a boundary line: *This far and no farther;* like someone defending himself against people who wanted to kill him.

I succeed in sitting up. Nahum's next to me again. His sheltering hands hide his face. *They're transporting us in a cattle train.* Whenever I think of this sentence I vibrate with soundless inner laughter. My body and my uniform are wet with sweat. The relative repose of my new, seated position makes me acutely conscious of the presence of my body and the weight of its singularity. I look at Nahum sitting, his profile facing me, holding up his hands to protect himself from me. My eyes already see well in the dark. Between the men leaning against the wall narrow slits of light coming from outside are visible. Nobody speaks to his neighbor. We're running out of air to breathe. The heat is making my face burn, my eyes sting. Only the floor of the coach touches my fingertips with a faint, damp reminder of the coolness of metal. I turn back to face Nahum and again he holds up his hands against me.

"What's the matter with you?"

Nahum doesn't reply. After a moment he drops his hands and puts one of them on his head to check if his skullcap's in place. Then he places both hands on his knees, which are up against his chest, shrinking into himself as much as he can, like a picture of a fetus in its mother's womb, lowers his head onto his knees, hiding his face behind his forearms, his shoulders and neck twitching convulsively. Is he experiencing difficulty in breathing? Is he saying one of his prayers? Is he taking advantage of the cover of darkness to weep silently into his lap?

The train stopped. There was a suspicious silence. The silence lasted longer and longer, until the prisoners in the dark cattle car began to regain confidence in their sense of balance, to approach each other and to talk. Suddenly the doors opened with a creaking sound and a click, just as they had closed before an unknown period of time, and a harsh, burning white light dazzled our eyes. A chill breath of air from outside touched our sweat-soaked clothes and flushed faces. Fresh, rich air, making us feel slightly dizzy and nauseated.

Until the barked command came from outside we didn't dare look out into the blinding light. At the sound of the command we plunged out instantly, the mountains of gear on our shoulders, our feet still seeking a hold on the ground. On a hill facing us stood our instructors, bright and fresh, with the rest of the company commanders. They had traveled in a passenger coach. All around the other platoons were gathering and forming up in front of their instructors. Nobody shouted, nobody hurried or ran. Benny and Muallem descended the hill and approached us, suspiciously quiet and patient. And while we were still stumbling about with our eyes on the ground, unable to bear the harshness of the light, we heard Benny's slow, sleepy, drawling voice saying to Muallem: "Look, look."

Then he sprang forward and charged into our stumbling ranks at a light, bounding run. "Halt!" he cried, and we stood still and watched him go up to Nahum, snatch the canteen out of his hand, hold it aloft, and say quietly, with pretended astonishment: "Drinking without orders?"

And holding the canteen high in the air, he spilled the water in a long stream onto the sand. Nahum looked at him uncomprehendingly, without showing any sign of fear, as if the whole affair had nothing to do with him. He saw the instructor waving the canteen about in order to shake out the last drops of water and then throwing it at him for him to catch in mid-flight, like catching a weapon after inspection. But Nahum let the canteen fall onto the sand at his feet. Benny looked him up and down with an expression of loathing on his face, and when Nahum did not bend down immediately to pick up the canteen, he said with menacing, mocking gentleness: "Are you waiting for me to pick it up for you?"

Nahum bent down and picked it up, closed the lid and replaced it on his belt. Benny returned to his position on the hill. Until we formed up for inspection, we all looked into each other's eyes, as if seeking an answer to a question that had not been asked. We were experiencing a moment of recovery from the journey in the cattle car. The feeling of togetherness came back to us, breathing new strength into our bodies.

We stood formed up in threes in a desolate landscape, sparsely dotted with strange bushes. At one end of the horizon there were a few little houses, without trees or any sign of cultivated fields. And at the other end, strips of shifting sand. We set out, relaxed and refreshed, marching in single file with our instructors at the head of the column. We reached the places where the shifting sands invaded the brown soil, clinging to the mounds of the bushes, filling the hollows in the earth. We marched for a long time until the command came to halt for a rest break. Suddenly Muallem appeared in our midst. He made straight for Nahum.

"Be grateful for getting off without a report," he said to him.

Suddenly Nahum's voice rose louder and clearer than I had ever heard it before, with no sign of effort visible on his face, as if he were inspired, as if someone else were speaking from his mouth, lying to save his soul from disaster: "Sir, I never drank, I swear, I never touched the water, I only opened the —"

"Without orders?"

This question silenced him. He began to stammer. As if he had seen something that suffocated him with fear, and returned him to himself. His shoulders beneath the mountain of equipment made a shrinking movement, as his hands had done in the train, when he held them up out-spread to protect him from the darkness, as from an enemy seeking his soul. I said to myself that in a world of masters and slaves, beaters and beaten, persecutors and persecuted, these were the moments when the spark of rebellion might be ignited, not out of protest and the wish to destroy, but out the justification of fate, out of the wish to identify and the hope of reconciliation and the desire for punishment, as a final, desperate gesture of love for the oppressor.

Muallem asked: "Don't you know yet that you don't drink without an order? Or even open your canteen?"

"Yes, sir," mumbled Nahum.

Muallem looked at him in amazement, as if he had never come across anyone like him before.

"When the command to drink is given, your friends will let you have some of their water."

And Muallem looked at us, as if seeking confirmation for this com-radely idea. There was something grotesque in his concern, in his wish to ingratiate himself with us, to establish clandestine ties of friendship with us. In a world of masters and slaves, beaters and beaten, persecutors and persecuted, Muallem didn't have a chance. His deep-set little eyes were like the eyes of a fish out of water. His whole person gave off an air of failure and futility.

When the command to drink was given, Muallem came back to make sure that Nahum got a drink from one of the other men. But Nahum refused to touch any of the canteens offered him.

"Don't you know what an order is in the army?"

"Yes, sir," said Nahum.

"Drink! That's an order."

"I'm not thirsty, sir," said Nahum. "I didn't drink before either —"

Muallem said: "If you don't drink, you're refusing to obey an order."

"Yes, sir," mumbled Nahum.

"What d'you mean — *yes, sir*?" said Muallem angrily. "Is he an idiot or something?" he asked the people sitting next to Nahum.

"Yes, sir!" a few voices responded gleefully.

Muallem removed the canteen from his belt, opened the lid, and held it out to Nahum. "Drink, that's an order!"

Nahum took a small sip of water, swallowed it with a visible effort, and gave the canteen back to Muallem.

"Drink more!" commanded Muallem.

Nahum tipped a little more water into his mouth.

"What's the matter with him?" asked Muallem. "Does it make him sick to drink from mouth to mouth?"

He turned back to Nahum and explained: "In the army everybody's like brothers, don't you understand? Everyone can eat from everyone else's plate, everyone gives his life, his eyes for his comrade. What's wrong, aren't we Jews?"

"Yes, sir."

"Okay, that's enough!" said Muallem.

"Yes, sir," repeated Nahum.

Muallem said: "Take off your helmet!"

Nahum took off his helmet and remained in his little skullcap, which was stuck to his head with a girl's hair clip. Muallem emptied his canteen onto Nahum's head, the water pouring onto the little skullcap and trickling down his face and body.

"Wake up!" cried Muallem. "Wake up!"

"Yes, sir," said the wet and startled Nahum, as if waking from a trance. He put the helmet back on his head and avoided the eyes of the men sitting next to him.

Muallem hooked the empty canteen onto his belt. A smile of satisfaction appeared on his fleshy lips, the upper one of which otherwise drooped over the lower in an expression of perpetual displeasure.

Hedgehog took advantage of this moment of grace: "Sir," he said, "why did they put us on a cattle train?"

"What did you expect?" said Muallem. "A Cadillac?" He looked at us, waiting for a reaction to his humorous remark, and when the reaction failed to manifest itself, he added: "You know what a series is? You don't have a clue! You think this is going to be a vacation camp? You don't know what's waiting for you. Soon you'll wish you were back in that train."

And so saying he turned his back on us, angry and disappointed, and went over to where the instructors were sitting. Not far from us we could see the people from 3 Platoon, whose barracks were opposite ours, laughing at a joke that one of them had presumably told.

Hedgehog said to Hanan: "You see that guy over there, the fat one sitting and lacing his gaiters? He's a medium. He claims that he can get in touch with the spirits of the dead."

"How do you know?" asked Hanan and burst out laughing.

"We were together on kitchen duty," said Hedgehog, "and him and his mate were talking about it. Melabbes!" he called me, "You remember that character?"

The medium suddenly turned around to face us — either because he had overheard Hedgehog's raised voice in the normal course of events or because his supernatural senses enabled him to hear farther than ordinary mortals — let his gaze rest on us for a moment, and returned to his gaiters.

Hedgehog said: "I think he's already carrying out experiments in his platoon. His pals say that he learned all kinds of spells from some Yemenite rabbi in Rehovot, as well as how to get in touch with the spirits of the dead."

"Disgusting," said Micky. "How morbid can you get? How can they take freaks like that in the army?"

"Some people believe in it. Not me," stressed Hedgehog.

"On his light-footed steed in a night black as pitch, King Saul came to Endor to seek out the witch, In a house by the roadside they saw a dull glow, You'll find her in there said the youth speaking low . . . ," recited Micha the Fool, rattling the words off like some unstoppable machine.

"If you only knew who went to the spiritualists," said Alon to Micky. "*They* do."

"You're kidding!"

"When one of them falls, they can't forget him. It's as if he were taken prisoner and they have to keep in touch with him, not to forget him. They leave no stone unturned in the attempt to make contact with him. As if a limb has been cut off their body. They won't let him leave them. He has to come back. Don't you understand? What do you know about comradeship between fighters like them? They used to go to a woman in Tel Aviv to teach them how to get in touch with that other world. What do we know about it? Nothing. The important thing is, not to give up. To keep up the struggle to go on being together. It's a form of longing, like love."

"And you believe in the spirit world?" asked Micky.

Alon reflected for a minute, not knowing how to reply. "No. I don't know. But that's not important. What's important is the willingness. The devotion. Keeping faith with the memory. That's a kind of danger too, a different danger, that they're prepared to undergo for the sake of a comrade-in-arms."

"They simply break down," said Micky. "Like the bereaved families, they break down, they go mad with grief."

"No," Alon protested, "you can't call that breaking down. They know a lot more about death than you and me. They encounter it almost every night, they face it, touch it. They know what they're doing."

There was a strange expression on Micky's face, an expression of revulsion and fear. He looked at the squat recruit from 3 Platoon, whose face was so heavy and mature for his years, as if he were his enemy, a threat to his personal safety, to the thing that was most precious to him of all.

We knew that the sea was not far off, but there was no sign of its presence. The parched expanse of shifting sands we had entered looked more like a desert. Was this the wilderness that had to be crossed in order to experience the transformation, to forget the journey, to lose our way in it in order to reach the real destination? The wilderness that remained in the end only as an image, a theater waiting for the drama to be enacted in it when the time came? A low, dull, colorless sky stretched out over our heads like a veil, hiding the real, deep sky from us, sifting pure, merciless light onto the dunes, which reflected the glare and diffused it into the surrounding air. And again our feet stumbled on treacherous ground, after touching solid land again, on the way from the railroad tracks to here.

After a few minutes the long single file snaking through the dunes disintegrated into groups, which thinned and fanned out and scattered over the sand. The instructors marching at the head of the column, without the knapsacks and blankets and tents and the rest of the equipment heaped up on our shoulders, fresh and light, disappeared behind a sand hill, and we were left to our own devices, to trudge through the sand without getting ahead, to find our way by ourselves. Before long I found myself in a small group of stragglers, wandering amid the dunes, not looking at each other, like the survivors of a shipwreck each trying to save his own life. Suddenly I was relieved of my silly, childish dread of the army's vengeance: the certainty that that I would not arrive at the meeting point on time, that I would never catch up, that I would be punished, paled into insignificance. Another, far more terrible dread yawned inside me, the terror of the trap of nature. We were scattered over an area of about ten square yards, each of us struggling alone with his fate, but it seemed that vast distances separated us, and that if any of us called out, his voice would not reach the others. The place looked as if no one had ever passed through it before, as if it was not intended for human passage at all. My boots sank into the sand. I could not advance. The load on my back dragged me down, the sand slipped beneath my feet. I sank into it, and when I tried to pull one foot out, the other sank deeper. Fewer and fewer of the stragglers remained in sight. The horizon was deserted. The place was getting emptier all the time. I mobilized whatever strength I imagined I still had left and tried to run, to shorten the time my feet would have to stay on that accursed ground. The mountain of equipment swayed on my back, repeatedly hitting my neck, my shoulders, my waist, to force me to the ground, to fix me here forever, hitting with an unbearable weight. I had to keep trying to run, it was my one impulse, to run blindly, in desperation, in terror of the trap — and without any hope of extricating myself from it, without calculating my chances. Every hop took my breath away and made my heart beat as if I had the weight of the world on my shoulders, and my legs began to tremble. At first I didn't understand what it was. As if the ground were trembling beneath my feet, something alive was flowing, moving between the soles of my shoes and my feet, something was striving against them. I stood still and looked at my feet, at my boots buried in the sand. A demented kind of laughter began bubbling up inside me, convulsing my body. The heat was like a furnace, I was bathed in sweat, my face was blazing, stinging, it was trembling too. Everything told me: *You've had it.* I knew there were tears in my eyes. Maybe it was only the weight of the equipment on my shoulders, pressing me down, down, and the trembling of my collapsing legs that caused me to find myself suddenly, unintentionally, bowing down and kneeling in the sand, weeping with a dumbstruck heart, imagining that I had been left there all alone, forsaken in an accursed universe, facing an unknown God.

When I raised my eyes I saw Zero-Zero standing a few steps away from me, his face gray, his eyes staring, his back bowed, and I heard him mumbling: "What happened? Where did they go? Where's everybody? Where are we going?" Hedgehog and Ressler, who were trudging a few yards in front of him, disappeared behind a sand dune. Ben-Hamo dragged his feet, indifferent to his fate, as if he had time to spare. As if he had nothing to worry about. Not far from him Miller swayed on his feet, his eyes on the ground, his breath coming in rhythmic, groaning pants, as if he wanted to shout but had lost his voice. Zero-Zero mumbled in a squeaky voice: "Damn them! Damn them! Where are they?" Another four or five were trying to make their way to our left. I didn't know them; they were apparently from another platoon and had lost their way and attached themselves to us. The strange, lost faces gave me back my sense of context and time. The need to hurry up and get to the bivouac struck me like a blow, together with the fear of what awaited me there because of my failure to keep up and because of the whole chain of foul-ups and failures that were bound to come in its wake. I knew that I was saved.

From behind one of the sand dunes to the right Alon suddenly appeared, his face flushed as red as blood, puffing and panting like a bellows. He looked terrible, red and grunting like a bloodthirsty animal. He plowed through the sand, his neck outstretched like the neck of some bird of prey, dragging the rest of his body behind it. For a moment he stood and looked around him, as if his rage had subsided, the webbing pouches on his chest rising and falling with his breath, examined the faces of the men scattered here and there, then his face resumed its ferocious expression, his neck stretched out in front of him, and his feet trampled the dunes, spraying sand around him. He reached the place where Ben-Hamo was trudging desultorily, carelessly, pensively, as if trying to make the most of this lull that had unexpectedly come his way, perhaps even happy to be alone at last. Alon seized his arm to drag him along behind him. Ben-Hamo slipped out of his grasp.

Alon panted: "I'll help you. The first ones are already there."

"Leave me alone," said Rahamim. "Don't do me any favors."

"I'm trying to help you, you fool!"

"Don't even talk to me. Don't worry about me. I'll get there."

"What's your case?" Alon burst out angrily. "I'm not asking you! Let's see who's stronger!"

He pulled Rahamin's arm hard, but the latter resisted him and succeeded in staying where he was. Alon went around behind him, took hold of his equipment, and gave him a shove. Rahamim fell on his stomach. Alon bit his lips. The redness of his face was strange and intense, as if it were about to burst. He pulled Rahamim to his feet, took hold of the equipment on his back again, and tightened his grip, as if about to lift him from the ground. And he pushed. Rahamin stopped resisting but tried to make his body as heavy as possible. He let himself go limp and closed his eyes in protest and insult. Alon went on pushing him. Suddenly he stopped, took a deep breath, wiped the sweat pouring down his face with the back of his hand, squatted, grabbed hold of Rahamim's hand, pulled his arm over the equipment on his back, slowly straightened up, and Ben-Hamo's feet left the ground. Alon took a few small steps over the sand, bowed down under his burden but steady on his feet. At first his steps were small and deliberate, as if testing his ability to bear this load, then he broadened them, but without changing the tempo of his slow, measured pace, taking a step and transferring the weight from foot to foot, steadying himself and then taking another step. And the ungainly, domed, double figure, like the primeval beasts I once saw under my sheet on the nights of the marauders in the village, going down to the desolate valley of shadows to quench their thirst, patiently and stubbornly bearing its load, plowed ahead with heartbreaking strength. I unhooked the canteen from my webbing and drank. The warm water, with its bitter, metallic taste and bad, stale smell, sent a frisson of life, in all its exciting, stimulating vanity, racing through me. I drank more and more, without thirst, as if out of a sense of obligation.

The sands grew shallow. On the horizon hilltops appeared rising out of the sand, and pale brown spots of solid ground emerged here and there like islands. From time to time I felt the chill of a breeze brushing my sweat-soaked clothes. Perhaps it was coming from the sea, the sea that was not far from here, although it could not be seen and was so difficult to imagine. As the sand grew shallower and the spots of solid earth multiplied, I imagined that we were straying from the path and getting farther away from the sea, but the truth was that we had entered an enclave between two sand dunes. I didn't look down at my feet but let them carry me forward, while my eyes followed the spot swaying in the blazing glare of the light, moving slowly ahead, resolute and bowed, Alon carrying Ben-Hamo on his back.

When he stood still and unloaded his burden, the place was already in view. Even from a distance it was possible to sense its aura of quiet, confident happiness. No one was waiting for us. No one reprimanded us for coming late. The whole atmosphere was friendly and relaxed. Alon sat down not far from Micky, spread out his arms, and slumped forward, bowed over and panting for breath.

The place where we had assembled was higher than the surrounding area, a patchwork of sand hills and stretches of soil, as if the war between desert and inhabited land were still being waged there. The wind grew stronger and blew up columns of dust around us, whipped sand into our faces, covered the piles of equipment, and the yellowish dust penetrated every corner of our bodies, made our teeth gritty, flew into our eyes, invaded our nostrils. The heaviness of our bodies when we had been trudging through the deep sands left us, and something wanted to blow us away with the wind.

While we were putting up the big tents for common use, and the wind swelled the canvas, blowing us from our places, the sounds of laughter rose into the air again. And even the instructors, who had begun to shed some of their sternness, took part in the work and the laughter, as if we were no longer tainted and untouchable, almost like equals among equals. Soon it was possible to imagine how the place we were going to live in now would look, and all that remained was to put up the pup tents that would serve as our living and sleeping quarters during the series. Each of us was carrying half the canvas, tent pegs, and other requisite gear. The command was given to pair off in order to pitch the little tents in the rows marked out for them. Immediately everyone stood ready with his partner; there was no hesitation, no embarrassment about choosing, as if it had all been planned in advance. The instructors showed us how to put up the tents. Immediately we grasped our spades and got ready to dig the pit above which the tents would be erected. Benny saw Ben-Hamo working alone and his face lit up. "Haven't you got anyone to share a tent with?" he called out. "Can't you find anyone?" We put down our spades and watched the grotesque spectacle. Ben-Hamo stopped digging and looked straight at Benny without saying a word. His face was still locked into the same expression of protest and insult it had worn when Alon had forced his help on him. Benny glanced around, looked at us, a happy, amused expression on his face, and said: "Doesn't anyone want to be in the same tent as Ben-Hamo?"

Miller suddenly popped up at the end of the row. He too was without a partner. "Sir," he said, "I go with Ben-Hamo together."

Terror appeared on Ban-Hamo's face: "No! No!" he cried. "Sir, I don't want to, I can't!"

But Miller took no notice. He came up to Ben-Hamo and said: "Don't be afraid, we together in the tent. If I fall, it is nothing to be afraid for. It is nothing. I help to you, you help to me. Everything okay."

Like an electrical current the special, familiar laughter ran through us. Beginning in a dangerous tremor, dark and pleasurable, and continuing in a liberating outburst, purifying and unifying, as if an evil spirit were being exorcised. Rahamim's face began to quiver, breaking up the expression of protest and insult that had afforded him a kind of self-respect and erected a barrier between him and the rest of us. Now the laughter bubbled inside him too, tearing the proud, reserved mask off his face and exposing the expression of habitual stupidity beneath it. He began to prance about, as if to shake off the closeness of his would-be benefactor, while Miller's shriveled parchment face lit up strangely, like a comic who had finally found the longed-for role, the right partner, the fruitful situation, and the audience to be conquered. He spread out his hands as if to express his helplessness, so frustrated in his endeavors to remove a troublesome misunderstanding, so eager to reach agreement and fellow feeling. If only he could explain, set the record straight, all the difficulties could be resolved, but the task was impossible.

He approached Rahamim, and Rahamim ran away from him, shrieking in a convulsion of laughter, "Go away! Go away! What do you want of me? Leave me alone, I want to be alone, alone!" I couldn't help saying to myself that the two of them were putting on a comic act for us, that like us they too only half believed in their roles, but they enjoyed miming for us, as in a distorting mirror, the story of how we run hither and thither in the vicious circle of our need for one another, and the fear, humiliation, and absurdity to which this dependence gives rise. The spectacle could have gone on forever, endlessly repeating itself in its fixed circle, but Benny halted it when it stopped being amusing. Rahamim suddenly realized that he was really going to have to sleep in the same pup tent as Miller, and it was no joke. He was more frightened of Miller and his illness than the rest of the men, who had already stopped paying attention to it. His face began to tremble. He muttered: "Why does it have to be me? Why?"

But Miller took no notice of his protest. He gripped the spade and began digging a pit in the place marked out for their tent.

CHAPTER 26

W hat's that? Show me! What are you throwing away there?" Alon asked in alarm.

We were afraid that the incident of the grenade on the firing range was repeating itself. Alon hurried over to the place and began digging in the sand.

"It got broken inside my pouches," said Zero-Zero. "I found it over there, next to the high place, when I went to piss. Pity it broke. It was like a toy."

Alon found the two potsherds in the sand and gazed at them in excitement: "It's a lamp," he said and joined the two pieces together until the little pottery vessel was restored to its original shape, round and closed, with rings encircling its mouth and a flat, elongated spout. We gathered around to look at it. Zero-Zero, seeing how precious the object was to Alon, repeated his tale of how it had been broken in the jolting of his equipment.

"Is it old?" asked Hedgehog.

"Yes," said Alon. "Look" — he turned to Zero-Zero — "you don't need it, right? You threw it away."

"You can keep it," replied Zero-Zero generously. "It's a pity I didn't give it to you before, when it was still whole. You would have looked after it. I don't know what it is. I thought it was an Arab cup that they drink coffee out of."

"It's a lamp," said Alon, examining the two pieces joined together in his hand. "They filled it up with oil, and over here there was a wick." He pointed to the jutting spout of the artifact.

"There are Hanukkah lamps like that," said Hedgehog. And he added immediately: "Maybe they used them for idol worship?" His eyes gleamed with sinful glee.

"No," said Alon. "They used them for light."

"How old is it?" asked Hanan. "Is it from biblical times?"

"This area, round Ashkelon," said Avner, "was Philistine territory. Maybe it's Philistine?"

"No," said Alon. "I think it's from the Arab period. But I'm not sure. I have to show it to someone on the kibbutz, who knows much more about it than I do. Look how beautiful it is, what wonderful workmanship. I'll stick it together again."

"How much can you get for something like that today?" asked Hedgehog. And he answered himself: "Thousands, I bet. Antiques are worth a fortune."

"Really?" asked Zero-Zero. "Is it valuable?" His protruding eyes rolled around in alarm at the thought of having given away a fortune, and in the end he consoled himself: "But now it's broken. I always break everything. Maybe there's more stuff like that over there. I didn't look."

"Maybe you're right," said Alon. "It's an ancient mound. I don't know which one. But this whole area is full of ancient mounds. We should go over there and have a look."

"Listen guys," said Hedgehog, "we'll go there as soon as we get a chance and dig everything up, sell it and divide the money among us." He looked around, counting the number of people standing next to Alon, potential partners in this secret enterprise; perhaps he even calculated how much each of them was likely to get out of it. "And don't tell anyone!"

Alon pulled a strip of flannel from his pocket, wrapped the two pieces of pottery carefully in it, and put them away in one of his pouches.

"If it's from the Arab period like you say," said Hedgehog somewhat doubtfully, "then it's not so old, is it?"

"Do you know when the period of Arab rule dates from? Do you know how many hundreds of years they've been here? You don't know the first thing about the history of Eretz Israel," said Alon. "All you know about, if anything, is the persecution of the Jews."

The rest break came to an end. We were trekking far into the dunes, making for the point at which we would each have to find our own way back to the camp. We had to fix the prominent landmarks and contours of the terrain in our minds and remember the direction. We walked in a column through an area we had not yet trained in with Muallem in the lead, making the route as difficult to remember as possible. Avner walked next to me, silent and thoughtful. He had been like that ever since we set out from the bivouac. Suddenly he said: "You shouldn't change people, it's not moral, you know?"

"I never had any ambition to do so," I said. "I've despaired even of changing myself."

"Understand," he said, "I can't live by time. I'm simply incapable of it. Even after all this time in basic training, I try and I don't succeed. It's not that I don't want to, I simply can't."

That morning our tent wasn't ready for inspection. Avner moved with demonstrative slowness, as if to show his contempt for the wretched slaves to time, afraid of punishment, like me. Then he disappeared. It was almost time for the inspection, most of the platoon were already standing outside their tidy tents, and I was running up and down looking for him, because it was impossible to shake the sand off the blankets, tighten the ropes, collect his scattered gear, and get everything ready in time for the inspection alone. When he reappeared at last he was in good mood, while I was boiling with rage and resentment. I bit my lip to stop myself from sounding sanctimonious, from telling him what I thought of his behavior, informing him of my unwillingness to suffer on his account and complaining of my misfortune at having him as my tent mate. I answered his questions dryly and briefly. I wished for the blow to come and fall on our heads, hoping that it would rouse him from his apathy. When the instructors struck our tent, to the accompaniment of threats and yells and the imposition of punishments, I felt a measure of relief, while Avner frowned and looked at them with a resigned expression on his face. When we were left alone with our collapsed tent, with a few minutes to put it up again and get ready for the extra inspection, Avner began to laugh softly. In response to my astonished, reproachful look, he said: "Man, if you only knew what you looked like, you'd laugh too."

I kept quiet.

He went on: "Hysteria — that's your trouble."

As we worked, hurriedly putting up the tent again, shaking the blankets and folding them, raking the sand in front of the tent and cleaning our weapons, Avner didn't stop talking for a minute. He talked like one possessed, as if the spate of words had it in their power to stop time, perhaps even to conjure it go backward to the point of the fall from grace and its pardon. He told a strange story about one of his sisters, a seamstress by trade, who was sitting one day at her place of work and suddenly took it into her head to imagine what would happen to her if she swallowed the needle in her hand. The idea took hold of her imagination to such an extent that she began to feel the effects of this reckless, imagined act in her body — she writhed in pain, she vomited bile, her face turned blue, she lost her breath and fainted. They took her to the hospital. "She nearly died," said Avner, "and it was only after she regained consciousness and the doctors began to question her about what had happened that she began going backward in her memory and remembered that she hadn't actually swallowed a needle at all, that the whole thing had taken place in her mind. When she came home my father gave her such a beating that the whole neighborhood heard her screams."

When our squad finally set out, after the extra inspections and punishments, and we were marching along under the soft light of the cloudy sky, with a cool, pleasant breeze in our faces, and one way or another my anger and resentment had subsided. I too began to see the morning's mishaps as petty and ridiculous. Once Avner had broken his silence and begun to apologize and explain about his inability to cope with time, I said: "Do me a favor and try, at least try to avoid situations like that. Because apart from all the suffering and punishments and hassle, I feel ridiculous as well, terribly ridiculous. I can't stand it. Do you see?"

"Of course, it isn't fair. I know. But admit, admit one thing: You can't say that I'm an egoist, that I don't help out when necessary. It's just that I'm not organized —"

"Okay, okay," I said quickly, before he got carried away by the monologue with which I was already familiar ad nauseam, along the lines of: *On the one hand I'm this, and on the other hand I'm that,* and so on and so forth, wallowing in the narcissistic stream that so frequently flooded him. "Okay," I said, "that's quite true. So for God's sake, just try to be there when I need your help and there's no time."

"Don't worry. I'll get organized. It's only a question of getting properly organized. We have to cut the things to do in the morning to a minimum, save time, prepare in advance. You'll see, it'll be all right. When I pull myself together, there's nothing to worry about."

The squad came to a halt at Muallem's command. We gathered around and listened to his explanations about procedures for the exercise. He gave us a short rest break. We were standing at the foot of a sand hill, and at the command "Dismissed," everyone began looking for a place to sit down. We circled the sand hill, and when we were behind it, a very strange sight, which at first sight seemed like a mirage, was revealed: On the plain, a few dozen yards from where we stood, we saw a small group of trees rising out of the desert of sand. We approached the spot. We were standing on the edge of a wide, shallow pit, about a yard deep, with a few sabras and acacia bushes that had almost completely dried up around it, the remains of a hedge with only a few bits of green to testify to the remnants of life still surviving in it. And in the middle, crowded closely together as if for protection, five or six trees, figs and pomegranates and a single plum tree. Thin trees, whose few slender branches stretched up like arms crying out to heaven. And their fruits were still hanging on them, some shriveled up for want of anyone to pluck them, some still good to eat: The pomegranates looked dry and shriveled, but the figs looked juicy and sweet, honey bursting out of their skins with over-ripeness.

A few of the men tried to go down into the pit and reach the fruit, when Muallem suddenly appeared out of nowhere and shouted: "Stop! Stop! Anyone who goes into that area gets put on report! Idiots! What are you, children? Get away from there! It's dangerous!"

We retreated from the edge of the pit and stood looking at the strange trees. There was something terribly poignant about them, in the pathos of the way they stood there in the pit, as if determined to maintain a facade of normal life in the heart of the wasteland closing in to suffocate them. The sand had already covered the bottom of the pit, but apparently not in a very thick layer, and it was still possible to imagine the existence of a different kind of soil underneath it, where orchards had once been planted. Although the hedge surrounding the trees was already almost entirely covered by sand, it still served them as a wall against the drifting sand, which accounted for the difference in height between the hedge itself and the bottom of the pit. I didn't understand what the nature of the danger referred to by Muallem was, and to this day I still don't know what he meant. Was he afraid of mines left over from the war? This seemed illogical to me. Why there of all places? But the sense of danger was there. Above all the sight of those trees gave me a feeling of death: I remembered once reading somewhere that dead people's hair and nails went on growing due to some automatic impulse that did not know they were dead. This was to me the real danger: Those trees seemed to me to be poisoned, and anyone who tasted their fruit would be poisoned too.

"How do trees come to be in a place like this?" wondered Hanan. "How can they grow here?"

"Before the war this whole area was full of Arab villages and orchards," said Alon, "and after they fled, the sands spread and covered everything. Seven years is a long time for shifting sand, when there's nothing to stop it. In another year or two this place will be covered too, and these trees will die. In the meantime their roots draw nourishment and water from the soil that can still breathe. But in the end they will be suffocated when the sand covers them like it's covered everything around."

"It's better that way," said Hedgehog. "To begin everything from the beginning."

Micky said: "People lived here, for generations. At least in other places new immigrants came and moved into their houses, and life somehow goes on there. Here everything's been buried, not a trace will remain."

"Don't worry," said Hedgehog, "there are still too many Arabs in the country anyway. It's a pity they didn't get rid of them all in one go."

Alon ignored this remark. He said to Micky: "Look, this is the Majdal-Bet Guvrin line, where the Egyptian forces cut the Negev off from the rest of the country. They intended holding that line and expanding it more and more. And Bernadotte already had a plan for a state of Israel without the Negev. The Negev and Yiftah Brigades fought here in the Yoav campaign. A lot of fighters spilled their blood so that the Negev would be ours. At the very last minute, after the truce had already begun, after trying and failing again and again and so many casualties. We wouldn't give up. Until the Egyptians broke and fled to the Gaza Strip. And the inhabitants fled with them. And anyone who didn't flee was expelled. Because there wasn't any choice. There was no room for them here. Today they're over there in refugee camps in Gaza. And you can feel sorry for them, Micky. There's certainly good reason to feel sorry for them. But you should know that most of them are still hoping, dreaming, they haven't given up hope of returning to their homes one day. And now that the Egyptians are getting all those weapons from the Russians, and preparing for the second round, those hopes aren't so fantastic. So you can save a few tears for us. Because we have to be awfully strong. Only the strong will last here. Only those who believe in what they're doing here, those who're prepared to sacrifice everything for it — only they have a chance of prevailing and surviving here."

At the end of this speech, which he made with downcast eyes, lowering his voice and addressing himself exclusively to Micky, Alon raised his eyes and saw us standing and listening to him. And for the first time since we had been thrown together, he read on our faces our agreement with what he had been saying, our identification with his views and our admiration for his eloquence. The silence that fell when he finished speaking was pregnant with the seriousness of the moment, the kind of moment at which a man might become a leader.

The silence was broken by Micky, who said: "You're preaching to the converted."

And Micha the Fool, since the silence had been broken, cried like a beggar rattling his tin: "Give to the Defense Fund! Give to the Defense Fund!"

The thin, dreaming trees, standing up to their knees in sand, sucking up the last of its dwindling vitality from the depths of the suffocated earth, and their infected fruit transmitting its deadly allure were like some disturbing, unsolved enigma. The rest break was nearly over. As if in obedience to some secret, inner command we rose as one man, approached the edge of the pit, unbuttoned our flies, and urinated into it. Most of us aimed at the solitary plum tree growing close to the dry hedge, some of whose fruits were hanging on the branches at our feet; others aimed a little farther and tried to reach the pomegranates. When we were finished, we felt as if we had settled our accounts with the place, and we returned to the other side of the hill to form up in front of Muallem.

While the men were being sent out one by one, at intervals calculated to ensure that they would not be able to help one another find their way, we sat down at the foot of the sand hill to await our turn.

Avner said: "In biblical days there were plenty of fine, cultivated orchards here, in the land of the Philistines. And in the valley of Sorek, which must be not far off, Delilah sat in such an orchard, eating a big, juicy fig, or some other fruit, like Hedy Lamarr in the movies. Oh, how she eats it! Taking slow bites, as if she's kissing it all over, licking it, enjoying every touch, and suddenly all the juice squirts into her face, and she swallows it at the last minute, and goes on sliding her lips over the fruit and nibbling, swallowing the juice, and there's a kind of smile on her face, half bored, half mysterious, as if to say: *It's not what you think, it's much more.* I've never seen anything so sexy in my life. Hedy Lamarr, the first love of my life. I dreamed about her every night. She drove me out of my mind. I couldn't stop thinking about her for a minute. I went to see every single film of hers, I went every day, every night, to meet my beloved. In the movie *Ecstasy* where she appeared naked, absolutely naked, I went bananas. I went to see that movie about ten times. I would sit and wait for the moment when she emerges naked from the water, with my heart beating like crazy, and I never managed to see anything. It was the same every time. Perhaps out of excitement, I don't know, or maybe they did it like that on purpose, so it would be all blurred and over in a flash. What a woman! God! Give me Hedy Lamarr and take my life. Hedy Lamarr . . ." He repeated her name in a whisper, in the passionate voice he presumably kept for the boldest of his seductions.

All this time I had been suppressing the fear that I would lose my way in the dunes during the navigation exercise and would not succeed in getting back to the bivouac. Now the fear returned and began to weigh heavily on me. Muallem sent everyone out in a different direction, and only after traversing a certain distance, which the instructor indicated according to features of the landscape, was the person supposed to start making his way back. I imagined encountering on my way ancient mounds strewn with potsherds and the remains of orchards buried in the sand, like evil omens, traps set for us by time. These shifting sands, which within the space of a few days had become our natural environment, neither hostile nor welcoming but a material like any other filling the space around us, these sands upon which my feet had learned to tread, now seemed to me like a kind of camouflage spread over the real ground, over the ancient mounds, over the ancient life that went on stirring underneath it. In this place-not-place, in the sands of Barnea, which we knew lay somewhere between Nitzanim and Afridar, I suddenly felt that I

didn't know what I was stepping on, and that the life that might be stirring beneath the camouflage of the shifting sands was hostile to me, hostile to what I represented.

The group of those remaining grew smaller, and I said softly to Avner,
while Muallem was standing a few paces away from us with the next in
line, pointing out the beginning of his route to him: "Listen, I've got a
feeling that I'm going to wander around and around in the sand without
finding my way back to the bivouac. I can't orient myself. I've got no
sense of direction. Like you've got a problem with time, I've got one with
space. In places I don't know I'm like a blind man."

"You've got nothing to worry about," said Avner. "This isn't the Sahara
Desert. You'll always land up at a place where people are living, or a road.
After a few days you'll recognize the terrain that you've already crossed
a few times, and you'll know how to find your way. You'll meet people
too, that you can ask. At night you'll see a campfire burning in the distance, and you'll know it's us. And don't forget the stars" — he raised his
eyes to the sky — "no, its cloudy. The stars won't help you. I think it's
going to rain. In short — everything will be all right."

Muallem returned and put an end to the conversation. Avner's irony
reminded me of the story he had told me in the morning about his sister
who had been overcome by hysteria because she imagined she had swallowed a needle. Fear was a dangerous game, an act that was liable to turn
into reality. Was this what he meant by the heavy irony of his words? I
was waiting for him to offer me help, to show a bit of his famous
resourcefulness. I knew that he would have no difficulty in finding his
way. That was how the world was divided.

By now only four or five of were left. Avner was sent on his way.
Muallem accompanied him for a few dozen yards.

I asked Yossie Ressler: "Do you know the way?"

"No," he said, "I don't have the faintest idea. And I don't care. As far
as I'm concerned, they can come and look for me in the dunes. They can
force me to do their tests, but they can't force me to pass them. And I
haven't the least ambition to do so. I'm not planning on a career as a scout
or a tracker. It simply doesn't interest me."

"I've got signs," said Hedgehog. "On the way here I made myself all
kinds of signs that are easy to remember. I'll get there without any problems, you'll see."

Ressler snorted and laughed. There were lines of bitterness and
loathing etched at the corners of his lips. Ever since the smashing of his
guitar he had sunk into a gloomy silence, hardly speaking even to

Hedgehog and the rest of the Jerusalem crowd. Now I saw him laughing for the first time since it had happened.

Muallem accompanied me to the starting point he had chosen for me, and slapped me on the shoulder to send me on my way. I said to him: "Sir, I don't know where to go, I don't have the first idea. I'll get lost here."

"Don't talk like that!" He retorted as furiously as if I were somehow accusing him and his fellow instructors of failing at their task. "What are you, a baby? Stop whining. Did you pay attention to the way we got here?"

"Yes, sir," I lied.

"So stick to that and remember everything you've learned in training."

"Yes, sir."

I started walking and didn't dare look behind me. When I had covered some distance and reached the place where the sands grew deeper, I turned my head, and there was no one there. I stood still for a moment, trying to decide which way to go. It was afternoon and the sun was moving to the west, toward the sea. I knew that I had to get away from the sea, and I turned in the opposite direction. All around me the sand dunes stretched from horizon to horizon, except for a strip of ground with brown spots on the horizon to my left. Perhaps that was the direction I should take.

The sand at my feet was smooth and free of footprints, pure sand, sieved and heaped by the wind into a temporary order until fresh winds came and blew it in different directions, other shapes. Only now I realized how beautiful this place was, how much gentleness and reconciliation there was in its barren monotony. A wonderful feeling of freedom took hold of me, an inner cheer of exultation, a delightful physical sensation of weightlessness and faith in my ability to soar, and boundless gratitude that I was alive, that my childhood was already behind me, that I was young, that I was an Israeli, that I didn't care what happened or where I landed. I heard myself whistling, as I always did when walking alone, unconsciously, without hearing what I was whistling. I went where my feet carried me, I discovered new shapes in the sand, new folds in the earth and vantage points from which to gaze at the horizon. Above me was a gray, cloudy sky, perhaps it really was going to rain, and all around me there wasn't a living soul, or a sound, apart from the sound of my whistling, only the wind blowing very softly, like the murmur of a seashell, occasionally gaining strength, throwing handfuls of sand and scattering them about, like an infant playing. It was so long, so very long, since I had been alone.

I wanted it to last longer and longer — until I met others lost in these sands. I wanted my head to be empty of thoughts, and to abandon myself utterly to the delight of walking, to the softness of the desert sand beneath my feet, to the sensation of weightlessness that had taken hold of me, to respond to the cry of freedom rising within me. *They can't force me to pass their tests* — I echoed Ressler's words. My failure to pass their test would be my success in passing another test, a test I would set myself. What this test was — I did not know. But I remembered the firing range, which was also in a desolate area, like this one, but in a different place. After firing at the targets we'd sat down to rest and wait for our turn to throw the grenades. The ceaseless sound of the detonations and the smell of the shots scorching the air, a nauseatingly bittersweet smell, had given that place a feeling of fateful strangeness, as if we had been brought there to do battle against a force we would never be able to overcome. My right shoulder sent waves of pain shooting through me from the blows it had received in the recoil of the rifle butt. *Nature's revenge,* I said to myself, *a punishment for every shot, a blow for every violation of the silence, the primordial silence we've been tamed into forgetting.* And Avner sitting beside me had suddenly said: "I wouldn't have come back. I would have run away. I know it. If only something had happened between us that night. I wouldn't have come back. Afterward I would have paid a heavy price for it. I know. And still it would have been worth it. There are some moments that are worth paying for with eternity!" He pulled his helmet down over his forehead to shade his eyes, smoked a cigarette, and spoke softly, as if he didn't want to add to the noise of the grenades exploding and the shots, which were upsetting the spirits of the place in any case. But the truth was that he didn't want the Jerusalemites to hear: Whenever he talked about the girl he had met at Hanan's party, he looked around to make sure that nobody could overhear.

"What are you looking at me like that for?" he had asked.

"It's your way of going on from where you left off. As if nothing ever stops with you, despite all the time that's passed, despite everything that's happened in between. As if you've never left your closed, inner world. What percentage of you takes part in what's going on around you? Ten percent? Five?"

"You'd better believe it! What do you think? I sold them my body, not my soul, not my feelings. Should I stop living in the meantime, should I stop dreaming?"

"I envy you. You need strength for that."

"What a tactful way you have of telling someone that he's crazy. You think I don't understand? Okay, I know I'm crazy — I'm not blind to myself."

"I don't think you're crazy. I really do envy you. I feel that I've already sold them my soul too. Maybe because my body's not such a big deal."

"You don't have anything to protect you, you don't have a dream."

"A while ago I realized something. I said to myself: They're always trying to humiliate us, break us, telling us how unsuitable we are for the army, what rubbish we are, how we're shit and garbage and how we'll never be soldiers. Suddenly I asked myself: Does it ever occur to them that maybe they're not exactly my aim in life either? That this isn't my cup of tea? That if it was up to me to choose how to spend these years, the army might come last on the list? What makes them so sure that it's the greatest honor in the world for me? They keep refusing to give me a gift that I'm not in the least bit interested in."

"But still, what they say insults you like hell."

"Right. And I don't understand why. I keep adjusting myself to their point of view, accepting their opinions about me, looking at myself through their eyes. As if that's the only way to keep going. And it seems to me that by doing that I'm selling them my soul. So that's why I think it takes strength to make the division. To give them the minimum and keep the maximum inside and protect it. I don't have the strength to see the real situation. You need courage to face this raving lunacy without giving in to the brainwashing that seduces you into believing that this is the normal world, that it's okay, that this is real life, that these are your dreams."

"What got into you all of sudden? You've been part of the game for a long time now, and you're always complaining to me that I don't respect its rules."

"I discovered the extent to which they've succeeded in brainwashing me," I said. "During the target practice I never succeeded in hitting anything. Whenever I fired a shot I felt as if the blow from the butt came before I pressed the trigger. And it moved the barrel off target and the bullet flew off to one side. It was the fear of the recoil, obviously. Of course I'm no good at it. I've never had any illusions on that score. I've never had any ambitions to excel at it. So why did it humiliate me so much? Why did missing hurt me so much? Because I already see myself through their eyes. It was only afterward, with an effort, that I began to think: Those targets, they're even cut out in the shape of people — head, shoulders, heart. I don't want to kill anyone, no one at all, not Arabs or Jews or Christians or anyone. I don't want it at all. I doesn't interest me. It doesn't belong to my real life! And still it hurt me that I missed, I despised myself so much, I hated myself. And that's how I began to understand that I'd already sold them my soul."

Avner had stuck his cigarette butt in the sand, held it by the end, and stared at it, as if waiting for the second when it went out. I knew he wasn't interested in what I had to say — he was busy saving his own soul. But the need to say what I had to say was stronger than I was, like the overwhelming need to admit failure; I had to hear myself say these things to somebody.

He'd said at last: "What do you know about your real life? Man, you haven't even begun to live it yet."

And now, in the heart of this wilderness, rescuing an hour of freedom and solitude from the satanic circle into which I had been cast, I agreed with Avner in my heart: It was true, I didn't yet know what I wanted. But I felt quite happy about this state of affairs, there was no need for me to make any decisions, I was content to walk in the shifting sands to wherever my feet carried me, and as far as possible to empty my head of all thoughts and memories, until things ripened of their own accord.

"Hey! Do you know what you're whistling?"

Avner appeared behind me. I still hadn't relished the hour of solitude and grace that had fallen to my lot to the full, but I was glad to see him anyway, because it was somehow connected to the thoughts that were occupying my mind, which refused to empty itself.

"No," I said, "I don't remember."

"You shit," he said, "you don't want to admit it."

"I promise you I don't remember."

"It's that dance from Prokofiev's Classic Symphony! Doesn't it remind you of something?"

I remembered but I pretended innocence: "No."

"On the first day on the base, when we were sitting and waiting, I was whistling it, and you kept staring at me as if it were getting on your nerves."

"The opposite!" I said. "Now I remember. Actually, I was admiring the accuracy of your whistling, because it's hard to whistle it right, with those semitones and transitions."

"And you thought: *What on earth is that black monkey whistling Prokofiev for? Who does he think he is?* Admit it, go on, admit that's what you were thinking."

"No it wasn't."

"Then let me tell you, that's exactly why I was whistling. And I chose that passage on purpose. The little darlings were sitting there and jabbering. They hardly knew me. As usual, they were trying to make a big impression on everyone, showing off how clever they are, how brilliant and witty. How inferior everybody else is to them, because they come from the upper crust, they're cultured and well educated."

"Do you know where we're going?"

"Sure," he replied. "It's over there." He pointed. And indeed, a minute or two later we saw other figures, coming from different directions, dotted over the dunes. "We didn't know what was going to happen to us," said Avner, "everything was new, strange, frightening. And Hedgehog and Micky began having that idiotic argument of theirs, about the strong and the weak and all that rubbish."

As he spoke a gleam of longing flickered in his eyes. I too felt a tremor at the memory, like the pain of loss for some beauty that had passed from the world. If we remembered that first day with such nostalgia, spoke of it with the longing with which one always speaks of distant new beginnings, as of an hour steeped in the innocence of the past and the promise of a pure future — it could only mean that time had passed, that we had indeed come a long way, and that we were close to the end. I hadn't forgotten the dread and the strangeness of that hour, the humiliation and helplessness in the face of the expected and unexpected revelations of evil, the violence, the agony of the body and the sinking of the soul. But the stamp of longing was stronger than all these, it was impossible to dismiss it as a distorted perception, as bribery and corruption.

"Strange that I was whistling that of all things," I said. "I wasn't paying attention to what I was whistling."

"I thought it was a signal to tell me where you were, that you were sending for me, calling me to come and help you find your way. After Muallem left, I walked for a bit and then I stood and waited for you to begin wandering around. You said you were sure to lose your way."

"I knew that that was what would happen, but I forgot that I should accept it willingly, even with love. Not to try and change the rules. That's how the world's divided. Some people are born to find their way and reach their goal without an effort, by instinct. It's part of their system. And others will never find their way, they'll always get lost, always take the wrong road. Like there are some people who'll always reach the wall of the coach to find support, and others who'll stay in the middle, with nothing to get a grip on, and fall on top of each other."

"What nonsense. You can't really believe it."

"I don't doubt it for a moment."

"A typical attitude for pampered people. The real division is different: Some people are led by the hand all their lives, given what they need, and have everything done for them. And others have to take care of themselves from the word *go,* and of their families too. Because if they get lost, there'll be nobody to save them. Nothing was built in ahead of time. Life taught them to cope. The beatings they received taught them to go out and get what others take for granted without having to lift a finger. Get it? I came to basic training after I'd already done part of the training by myself, because I didn't have a choice."

The fire began to burn in the hollow dug in the sand. It was already pitch dark, the wind that had been blowing early in the evening had dropped, and there was a stillness in the air. Our bodies begged for sleep after the backbreaking efforts of the day, the night exercises and the sudden emergency inspections that constantly disturbed our sleep. But the campfire too was an order. A few people tried to start singing, but their voices soon died away. Nobody felt like singing. We sat wearily staring at the fire, taking hold of the twigs we had gathered from here and there — they too, perhaps, the remains of orchards from the villages that had once stood here and been buried in the sand.

"Where's his fiddle?" asked Muallem. "Why didn't he bring it with him?"

"Someone smashed it up on the base," said Zackie.

"Smashed it?" asked Muallem in astonishment. "Who smashed it?"

A chorus of cries and laughter went up, and Ben-Hamo said sulkily: "It isn't true, sir, it isn't true."

"Ben-Hamo," said Muallem, "why did you smash up his fiddle?"

"I didn't do it, sir," said Ben-Hamo. "I don't know what they want of my life. Anything that happens, it's always: Ben-Hamo, Ben-Hamo!"

"Poor thing," said Muallem. "You're a saint."

"Sir." Miller, who seldom took part in general conversations, piped up. "Sir, Ben-Hamo good boy, he do nothing wrong."

The burst of laughter that broke out in response to this remark went some way toward relieving the dullness, the fatigue, and the need to withdraw into ourselves that had descended on us as we sat around the campfire. Even Muallem, however hard he tried to maintain the seriousness of his expression, the reserve proper to an officer in his position — his thick upper lip began to twitch, his face twisted as if he were about to burst into tears, and he could no longer restrain his laughter.

"Are you a good boy, Ben-Hamo?" asked Muallem. In the middle of the sentence his voice broke, and he gave way to a bellow of irrepressible laughter.

Benny returned from the kitchen tent with a number of recruits bringing cans of battle-ration mincemeat to roast on the fire.

"Why aren't the lazy buggers singing?" inquired Benny, amazed at the sounds of laughter, especially Muallem's, which was not frequently heard.

And Muallem, who had already surrendered completely to his laughter and was no longer trying to disguise it, said: "Somebody broke his fiddle" — he pointed to Yossie Ressler — "they say it was Ben-Hamo, but he says he's a good boy." His voice broke again.

"It's a guitar," said Benny, "a guitar, not a fiddle."

"Now it's nothing," said Muallem.

The fire showed signs of going out and Benny ordered kerosene to be thrown on it. Then he looked at the flames that leapt up as a result and were reflected in the lenses of his spectacles. Without moving his lips, as if talking in his sleep, he asked: "How did they break it?"

Zackie volunteered: "It was flat as a pancake. He must have stamped on it."

Benny smiled, as if imagining the sight to himself and relishing it to the full. Then he said: "In grade school I was once in the same class as Melabbes. On Fridays, when we had programs in honor of the Sabbath, he would bring his violin to play for us. He would scrape away and produce the most ghastly sounds. You've never heard anything like it in your lives. The teacher would close her eyes in ecstasy, and we would split our sides laughing. You should have seen him, standing there like a sissy, teacher's little pet, who ran to tell her tales about everybody to suck up to her, standing in front of the music stand and scraping on his violin. What a joke! He deserved to have the same thing done to his violin, I'm telling you. But nobody there would have had the guts to do it."

The laughter and cries of appreciation followed at once, either in true enjoyment of Benny's story, or in the desire to please the instructor. And he, as soon as he had finished talking, approached the fire, in order to supervise the grilling of the meat. He bent down over it, his lips parted, exposing the broken incisor, and his face bathed in the reddish glow of the flames and full of flickering shadows lost its sharpness, suddenly shed its mask of maturity, cynicism, confidence, and for a split second became the face of Benny-trousers, clenched in an expression of childish obstinacy, like a declaration of opposition, of noncollaboration, of the readiness to resist and take the consequences. This was the first time since we had met again that I fully recognized the face of that child in him. I felt as if I had succeeded in breaking a code that I had labored long to decipher and failed. And the happiness of this meeting between the ends of time, for a split second in the glow of the fire and the play of the shadows, moved me and sweetened the pain and insult and pointless lie of his peculiar story.

Benny straightened up, and as he returned to his place in the circle he turned his face to me and asked: "Remember?"

Like someone reminiscing with a friend about some shared experience in the distant past. From the way in which he put the question it was clear that there was no need for a reply. I knew that he was aiming more at the people sitting around than at me. My eyes suddenly met Yossie Ressler's, which were fixed on me, calling to me. I heard what they were saying very well. In his own unique way, in silence, his eyes were calling to me in a cry of brotherhood; presumably the brotherhood of artists persecuted by a society that did not understand them, was incapable of understanding them; the brotherhood of artists wounded by mockery, the crucified Messiahs of a narrow-minded society, who transmuted their agony, the essence of their heart's blood, into the gold of creation. I knew his views and my whole being revolted against them; I wanted no part of this brotherhood, it had no place in my heart. I was repelled by his identification with me in this silly situation. Ressler's wrath aroused in me a courage inconceivable in other circumstances, and I dared to reply to Benny.

"No, sir, you're confusing me with somebody else. I never played the violin to the class. Never."

"And he was always a liar!" said Benny with the same nostalgic, reminiscent air. "Like all cowards, he was a liar. Like he's lying now. People don't change." And he turned toward Muallem and continued in the same tone: "What's the matter with the lazy little bastards, why don't they sing? We lay on a campfire for them, and they think they're doing us a favor by sitting around it and taking whatever we hand out to them. Maybe they want us to entertain them too?"

"Come on, Ben-Hamo," called Muallem, "come and dance for us, give your friends a bit of fun!"

"I can't, sir," said Rahamim, "I don't feel well."

"He got his period today," explained Zero-Zero, "too bad."

Zackie and his friends broke into an Oriental song, again they produced a tin can to drum on from somewhere or other, and they called to Rahamim to come and dance to their singing. But he stubbornly refused.

"Then sing!" cried Muallem. "I'm telling you to sing!"

Rahamim shifted restlessly in his place, trying to protest, to explain, to plead. But nothing helped. He saw that he couldn't get out of it, and he surrendered. Everyone hushed the singers, who were already being swept away on a wave of enthusiasm, and waited for Ben-Hamo to get up and stand in the middle of the circle and perform. But he remained seated where he was, and his voice suddenly rose, soft and quavering, choked, singing the French national anthem.

The surprise in itself was enough to give rise to delighted laughter, but the way he sang too, his manner of pronouncing and emphasizing the French words, the pathos swelling his voice, the swaying of his head in to the tune — all these were grotesque beyond measure. Undeterred by the laughter and critical comments he continued, as if carrying out an order, verse after verse. The tense silence that had fallen over the sand dunes surrounding us in the evening hours, when the wind dropped, disintegrated, and it began to rain. Ben-Hamo did not stop singing until he had concluded the last verse. But many of us left the circle, running to take shelter from the rain. The rain came down harder; the fire went out. The half-cooked hamburgers were transferred to the kitchen tent, and we gathered under the canvas to receive our share.

The rain did not stop even after we had crawled into our pup tents and lay down to sleep. Avner got into his sleeping bag and said: "I'm not even taking off my boots. When they wake us up, I won't have to waste time putting them on."

"It's against orders," I reminded him. "It's forbidden to sleep in your boots."

"They won't know," he said.

"It's unhealthy too," I remarked.

"Rubbish," he said, "I have to get organized to give myself enough time for everything in the morning."

The rain beat down on the tent without stopping. Big drops leaked through the gaps in the corners, but we were protected. A chill pervaded the air, and the sleeping bag was pleasantly warm and cozy. From the adjacent tent I heard Micky saying: "What a waste of all this rain, lost in the sand." And Alon's voice answering him: "A lot of the rain seeps into the soil and reaches the groundwater. There are huge lakes of water in the depths of the earth. If they drill, they'll reach them."

CHAPTER 27

An irresistible impulse told me to move into the other coach. The coach I was in was densely packed with darkness, which was not, however, the black darkness of night, but a white darkness, as if I were standing in full light with my eyes closed. But my eyes were open, and I couldn't see a thing. It felt good there. I was lapped in a damp, pleasant, primordial warmth. I didn't want to move, but another will, an alien will that had attached itself to my own, overcame me and drove me out. Thus I found myself standing next to the passage into the other coach, which was a kind of big tunnel, folded up like an accordion, its opening no wider than my body. I was obliged to insinuate myself into it. I inserted my head and my body followed easily, as if it were being sucked inside. In the middle of the tunnel I got stuck and couldn't advance or retreat. I felt that the force sucking from the other coach was unable to pull me any farther. A sense of suffocation overwhelmed me. In a flash I knew: Come what may, I had to get back. There it was good. Here it was bad. I exerted all my strength but I couldn't move an inch. A groan escaped me from the effort.

"Melabbes, have you seen what's happening here?"

The voice sounded like a disembodied echo coming from far away. After having identified it as Avner's, I realized it was announcing disaster: The fact that he had woken spontaneously from his stonelike sleep was sufficient in itself to sound an alarm. The rain, which had been coming down steadily for several days now, lashed mercilessly against the canvas, pelting down with a deafening, menacing roar.

"The pit's full of water."

Now the voice sounded close, not in the least disembodied, and accusing.

We were lying in a pool of water that had collected in the pit under the tent. Our blankets were soaked and full of mud, our sleeping bags, clothes, equipment, weapons. I heard a commotion in the adjacent tents, cries, laughter, groans of despair; I didn't want to move. The lukewarm wetness in which I was lying was like a shield against the outside. I had no idea what we were supposed to do.

"What's the time?" I asked, as if it could make any difference, further any practical plan.

He put his hand into his pocket, took out a box of matches, and tried to light one, to see his watch. "The matches are wet," he groaned, and added a curse.

"Lucky we're not on guard tonight," I said. "Imagine being outside in this rain, lying on the ground for hours."

"Man! Are you awake? We're lying in water!"

Why did he insist on giving me the bad news, on ruining the illusion of home I had finally managed to create under this canvas?

"I feel like a baby who's peed in his diapers," I said.

He shifted about, looking around him for something, at his head, in the pockets of his clothes. In the end he found his cigarettes and again he cursed: "The cigarettes are wet too."

"Listen," I said, "we'll do what everybody else does. We've got one more night to be here, we'll get through that too."

"Maybe you're right. But I want to smoke. I have to smoke. I'll go mad if I don't smoke a cigarette now."

He began moving around again, got on his knees, lifted the flap and looked outside at the rain, and in the end he made up his mind and crawled out. A little while later he came back, dripping with water, with a lighted cigarette shielded in a cupped hand. "It's the same everywhere," he said, "don't ask; what a balls-up."

"What did you think, that it was only us?"

"Do I know? My luck's always unique."

He crept into his wet blankets and smoked silently. The damp warmth encompassing me began to fade and cold seeped into my body. I shivered.

Avner said: "We'll all come out of this sick. Lucky I stayed in my shoes. But they're soaking wet too."

I gathered my knees to my chest, shrank into myself, and curled into a ball, to reduce the area of contact with the wet, to contain the warmth of my body, but the cold increased, and with it my shivering. The rain stopped. In the silence that suddenly fell we could hear voices talking outside. Somebody called: "Guys! Come outside!"

I emerged from the tent. There was a group standing between the two rows of tents. One by one more refugees from the storm joined it, wet and excited. There was a smell of rebellion in the air. From somewhere or other Muallem appeared, spick-and-span as usual. "Get back into your tents immediately! You've got five seconds to return to your tents!" he shouted. "What do you think this is? The central bus station? Anyone who doesn't go back gets put on report. Have you forgotten what night discipline means? Have you forgotten where you are? Five seconds!"

Nobody moved. Muallem looked around him with an air of concern rather than anger. Suddenly his voice grew conciliatory. "What's the matter with you?" he asked.

Nobody answered. Nobody wanted to be the spokesman for the mutiny. Muallem surveyed the figures standing opposite him in the darkness and his eye fell on Hanan. "What's the matter with you? Why aren't you in your tent?" he asked him.

Hanan said: "Sir, it's full of water in there, everything's wet. It's like lying in a cold bath."

"So what's the big deal?" said Muallem. "Don't you think your instructor knows what's good for you better than you do?"

"Yes, sir," said Hanan.

"So your instructor is telling you now to go back to your tent. That's an order. Move it! Everyone back to their tents. You've got four seconds. Get cracking!"

Nobody moved.

Muallem didn't lose his temper. There wasn't a drop of anger, not even a hint of hatred or cruelty in him. He acted in accordance with the rules as he knew them. Presumably he felt that in these moments, as after some act of recognition in a relationship full of vicissitudes, we were meeting him at a new crossroads, and the new love for him stirring within us was about to be tested.

"Night training for the whole platoon!" called Muallem. "Orderly-student!"

The orderly-student presented himself and stood to attention.

"In five minutes exactly the whole platoon will be ready for night training. Combat webbing equipment dry, weapons clean, blackface on, canteens full, like soldiers on a night exercise!"

"Yes, sir!"

At the command "Move!" all the shadows rushed to their tents. The mad race against the missing minutes and seconds began, the frantic chasing back and forth to the fall-in place for the inspection, to the tents, and back again, with Muallem allocating and reallocating the minutes and seconds, inspecting the tightness of the webbing, the dulling of the polish, the blackface. Opposite the slowly brightening sky he held up the rifles and gazed through the bore at the starlight, which was apparently sufficient for the purposes of his inspection. We set out in single file. We passed the ring of guards lying in their posts at regular intervals around the bivouac, a gunner with two riflemen at his sides, wrapped in blankets against the rain, which did not appear to be doing them much good. From the dismay and desperation on their faces it was evident that they were wet to the marrow of their bones. We trudged through the sands a good way until we arrived at a broad road, one of the new roads laid in this desolate area in anticipation of the construction of Barnea, the Israeli movie town soon to go up here. Once we were on the road, the command was given to halt and form up in threes. From there on we ran.

The din of the nailed boots on the asphalt shattered the silence of the shifting sands, which we had been told harbored bands of fedayeen, especially at night. I didn't know where he was leading us, to what punishment. This running was like a deliberate defiance of the danger, the real fear. As it warmed our bodies it restored their strength, banished fearful thoughts from our hearts, overcame our sleeplessness, and gave rise once more to a feeling of happy camaraderie. After running for a long time we were given the command to go over to walking, to stretch our limbs and get our breath back. We left the road and returned to the sand hills. After a while we stopped. Muallem sent guards to take up positions at a few observation points on the terrain, to secure the platoon. In obedience to his instructions we sat around him in a close circle at the foot of one of the hills. He stood in the center and surveyed us in silence.

After a while he said: "What's the matter with you? What have you got to cry about? You're already at the end of your basic training, and you still don't know anything. You don't have a clue. When are you going to be men?"

Nobody answered. No answer was required. There was no anger on his face, only sorrow and concern, which looked, in the pale nocturnal light, like personal disappointment.

"You know what you did there? In the army that's called mutiny. You know what mutiny means? I should have called the CO, and everyone who was standing there and refusing to return to his tent would have been court-martialed. They would have been thrown into jail. What are you, spoiled children? What do you think, that you're better than anyone else? You deserve more than them? Water got into your tents? So what? You know what's going on in the country now? Floods everywhere. In the transit camps. In my own family they're probably being evacuated from their shack now, because everything's full of water, everything they possess is ruined. Old people, sick people, women with babies, they've got nowhere to stay now, until someplace is found for them. I should have been there now, with my family, to help them. But I can't, because in the army you do what you have to, and I have to be with you. To listen to you whining and complaining all the time. What makes you any better than my family? Than my sick, old father and mother? Go on, tell me. You're so good at talking, you're so well educated. Why don't any of you talk now? Talk! I'm speaking to you now like a friend, not a commander. Go on, don't be afraid, I want to know. Say what's in your hearts, I want to hear. I want to understand what you want."

Nobody said anything. There was an oppressive silence. Muallem continued: "It's not only me. There are quite a lot of guys in this platoon who live in camps, whose families' houses may have been destroyed by the rain. What makes you any better than them? You think you deserve something special? What do you want, for me start feeling sorry for you? For me to dry your tents, so that you can sleep well? Haven't you got any sense?"

He surveyed us with his small, deep-set eyes. His protruding upper lip, which always made him look on the verge of tears, was now pursed, full of determination to get to the bottom of things. He fell silent and waited for someone to say something.

Zackie spoke. "It's not only now," he said, "it's been like that from the start. There are some people here who think that if they're sabras, the whole world belongs to them. If they're sabras, it's only so they can laugh at other people, make fun of the way they talk, tell jokes about them behind their back. As if they're not people, as if they're dogs, to show them your boot. It's not nice. Why? What harm have we done them?"

Muallem said: "It's disgusting!"

"It was only like that at the beginning," said Alon, "when we didn't know each other. It hasn't been like that for ages. I don't remember anything like that recently."

"Bullshit!" said Zackie. "I hear everything. I notice all that stuff. It hasn't stopped. Don't you understand that it hurts? What kind of army will it be, what kind of state, if people treat each other like that?"

"Come on, Zackie," said Hedgehog, "you look for it, you want to find it. What's the good of talking about it? There are things that come and go of their own accord. That's life. But you have to drag it up on purpose. When people live together they sometimes fight. And then they make up and forget it. But you don't want to forget. However much people apologize and promise you that from now on everything'll be okay, that it was all in friendship, no harm meant, just for a laugh — you jump on it, as if you needed it. What did you have to drag it up for? The instructor was talking about something else, a specific situation. And you push it in a different direction. Why do we have to talk about it?"

Alon said: "I think we should talk about it. People have to get it off their chests. If there's anyone in the group who feels that way, then the rest of us should know about it. It should be talked about openly."

Behind me I heard Avner snoring faintly. He took no interest in discussions of this kind. In his view the night was made for love or sleep. A few others also fell asleep in the crowded circle, which was composed of a number of circles surrounding each other, leaning on the backs of the people in front of them, or squatting in peculiar positions on the sand. Muallem was silent. He let the conversation take its course, even though it strayed from the point for the sake of which he had made us run all the way here, seated us at his feet, and preached us a sermon. If he had intervened, perhaps it might have dispelled the atmosphere to which his silent presence among us gave rise in that strange hour, neither day nor night, when hearts open without shame and barriers fall.

The night grew paler and paler. The shifting sands around us glowed with asoft grayish light that gradually grew clearer and began to fill in the lines of the landscape, to dissolve the pools of shade, to smooth out the domes and slopes and plains. And to our right, on the horizon, we saw a strip of blue-gray sea emerging in the radiance of the dawn breaking behind us, shimmering, elusive, distant as a dream, casting off the curtain of the night. The blackened faces, makeup left over from another play, seemed transfixed to this place and this hour, refusing to yield to the clarity of the dawn.

Muallem's eyes fell suddenly fell on something suspicious at the edges of the circle. He hurried to the place where Miller lay without moving. He bent over him and shook him, held his head in both hands and raised it a little from the sand, examined it and let it drop to the ground, face-down in the sand. Then he squatted down and held Miller's wrist in his hand, feeling for the pulse. In the end he stood up, his face very grave, radiating strength and suppressing terror. He called Alon and Micky to him and told them to run to the bivouac and bring the medical orderly back with a jeep. "Do you remember the way?" he asked Alon. Alon nodded and the two of them ran off immediately and disappeared from view. We heard the pounding of their boots on the road, and soon that pounding too was silent. We sat in silence, looking at Muallem as if seeking an answer to our questions, but he returned to the place were Miller was lying, knelt down next to him and gazed at him as if hoping to discover some sign of life.

"Sir," Nahum suddenly asked in a quiet, almost throttled voice: "Is he dead?"

Muallem said: "He may be."

And Nahum leapt up as if he had been bitten by a snake and began to run into the dunes. Muallem called to him to come back. We thought he was hysterical with fear. He went on running for a few dozen yards, looked back, stopped, and sat down.

Muallem looked at us and then at Nahum and weariness settled on his face, as if he had decided to cast off some of his responsibility and not get involved any further. "What's the matter with him?" he asked.

Hedgehog said: "He must be a Cohen, and it's forbidden for him to sit next to a dead person; it contaminates him."

In other circumstances Hedgehog would no doubt have gone on to express his opinion of religion and superstitions, their danger to the state and the need to fight them and those who believed in them, but the circumstances were not conducive to speech. Muallem distanced himself a little from the circle and stood staring at some point on the horizon, perhaps in anticipation of the noise of the jeep approaching from that direction, perhaps in the need of a few moments of solitude, of detachment from our eyes fixed on him, demanding satisfactory answers, immediate solutions, refusing to accept the possibility that at a moment like this, face-to-face with the inconceivable, he was in the same boat as the rest of us. When all was said and done, he was slightly older than we were, and more experienced in army life. That was all. We sat still and silent, as if fearing to disturb the dead man lying in our midst, looking at Muallem and waiting for him to say something at last, sensing the treachery slowly taking shape in our hearts.

All at once morning came down on us with the full heat of the sun, with a pure blue sky, without the hint of a cloud, with the fierce glare refracted from the shifting sands. Now it was possible to see clearly the lumpy skin in which the rain had clothed the dunes, like a kind of crumbly armor that disintegrated at the touch of a finger, the traces of the water that had passed through here on their way home — to the abyss.

Muallem returned from his vantage point at the edges of the circle and approached Miller's body lying on the sand again. He stood at his head and contemplated him. Did he expect the body to start moving at the sight of the rising sun, showing signs of life and putting an end to the bad dream at last? A look of sadness and dread appeared on his face. *He's scared! He's pissing in his pants!* said the looks that passed between us, swift as an electrical current, plainer than words, uniting us in a bond of brotherhood and a sense of strength: He would pay dearly. The love of the night melted in the light of day.

About fifty yards away from us we saw Nahum stand up and face the east, purifying himself according to his lights from the contamination of the death among us.

All this can't be accidental. Some lost voice is trying to get in touch with me, asking me a riddle with very transparent clues. My fears about my

father's health, during the holiday. Amos Drori, and now this. Seeing it
for the first time like this from close up. Frightening how simple it is,
how banal. Nothing special. The big fear. And what now? What circle
will be closed? The most morbid thoughts are the thoughts about death.
This running's more like a flight than a mission. We're running for nothing.
There's no reason to hurry. But we have to run in order to deaden the
fear. To blur the morbid thoughts. At moments like these you discover
new strengths. You can overcome the little fox gnawing at your stomach,
be open to new trials. Grow more mature from day to day, as if it will
never end. Be less proud. Less hypocritical. More authentic in all this
degradation. I don't belong to myself anymore. I don't know how to
answer. Except by screaming. But I don't even know how to scream.
Who's there to scream at? Who'll take care of it? Soon the road'll end,
we'll have to go down to the dunes and turn left. We're both running in
step. It's ridiculous. Why? Why shouldn't the thudding of our boots
sound out of step? There's no instructor dictating the cadence. But there's
something in it. Together. With a friend. Running to get help that is no
longer needed. I don't know her, but I'm sure I'll fall in love with her on
the spot. He must have told her about me. Maybe she even heard about
me before. I'm no Clark Gable, that's for sure. But neither is Alon. When
I go to visit him on the kibbutz, I'll see her, and it'll happen in a flash. I
know it will. I don't have the faintest idea what she looks like. In my
imagination she changes all the time. And I'm already in love with her.
I'm not realistic. Now we're on the sand we're not keeping step with each
other. And we're not really running either. I'll stop when he does. Sooner
or later we'll have to stop and rest a bit. Maybe he's waiting for me to stop.
What is this, a race? What are we in such a hurry for? What's he thinking
about? Maybe he's imagining that he's one of those ancient runners who
ran alone for miles and miles in order to announce victory. Or defeat. The
runner from Marathon who ran twenty-six miles and dropped dead the
minute he'd finished announcing the victory. It wasn't a victory for him,
that's for sure. He can't live without comparing himself to something
great, special, ancient. He can't be satisfied with his own, true, private
limits. Who's going to stop first and let us rest a bit? There are moments
when reality suddenly stops seeming real. How much I want to live. How
much I want love at long last. I'll have it, I'm sure I will. So why do I suddenly feel frightened? He's looking at me. Say something, idiot. Why
don't we stop running for a bit? What's the hurry? My strength is beginning to leave me. After a sleepless night it's not so easy. He's got strength.
Physical strength and terrific strength of will. A picture: him carrying

Ben-Hamo on his back like a bag of flour on the trek to the bivouac, in the deep sand. Will I ever understand that picture?

As one man, as in response to a command, they stop to get their breath back and relax their limbs. Then they go on bounding over the dunes, in an imitation of running. And Alon says, panting: "Maybe I'll apply to go on a Squad Commanders Course. To come back here and keep coming back with a new intake of recruits on the series."

"You like this place."

"Yes. A lot."

"That makes sense."

"You come too. They're sure to let you, all you have to do is apply."

"Can you see me instructing recruits?"

"Why not?"

"Do I know?"

"We'll be together."

"Maybe I will. You know what, it's a possibility."

"What do you say about Muallem? It looks bad for him, don't you think? He could be in big trouble. But he's okay, he really kept his cool."

"I think that with Benny it could never have happened. He would have noticed right away that there was something wrong with him. You have to be on your toes all the time. It's a question of responsibility. With Muallem there's something resigned, fatalistic. A commander, an instructor, has to be alert all the times, he has to be on the ball, to sense everything that's going on, and not to want to be liked so much."

"And what about the firing range? When Zero-Zero threw the grenade backward? Where was Benny then?"

"Right. It can happen to anyone. He's not perfect either."

"But when he slapped me in the face, I have to admit he knew what he was doing. I think it was really the right reaction on his part."

"Are you crazy?"

"Look, I think I did the right thing. But so did he. Because if everyone started running to catch every grenade that fell it would be a proper mess-up. He understands the meaning of discipline. Of responsibility. He sees things from a different point of view."

"That's why I'm not so keen on being an instructor or an officer. I want to finish as a private. I don't want to be responsible for anyone. Only myself."

"The only thing that can give content to your life is taking responsibility for others."

"Okay. So you've reached the right conclusion for yourself. And I'm

glad that you have. And you'll finally stop suffering from the disappointment over what you wanted at the beginning. You'll go far, Alon, you've
got a lot of strength."

"I don't know. It depends on my mood. It changes all the time. I can't
control it. But this place attracts me. I feel happy here."

The bivouac appears on the horizon. As in response to a secret inner
command, as one man, they break into a proper run. Micky wonders:
What does he feel about the death that happened over there? An
anonymous, modest, unheroic death. Without any big ideas. Without
self-sacrifice. In solitude and strangeness and silent submission. Like a
cat. It touches me more than all the ideas in the world. That way seems
more human to me. What difference does it make what the instructor
did? That's how it happens. Why do I feel such shame that it happened
to him? Why is it so humiliating? It should make me feel respect. It
happened and nobody can change it.

Benny walked between the tents, looking at us as we spread the wet
blankets out to dry in the sun, next to the rest of the gear that got wet in
the night. He scolded in his dry voice, goading the stragglers. Midday
approached. The morning's training program had been disrupted. The
afternoon would be our last here. The sleepless nights had left their
mark. Our movements were slow; a strange intoxication blunting the
edge of reality for us, closing our hearts to fear, emotion, expectation.
Benny sensed this. It was obvious that he was being careful not to destroy
the peculiar immunity protecting us. He spoke briefly, suppressing his
hatred and cynicism. Observed us from a distance, like some unavoidable
nuisance. At times it seemed as if we were all ill — something had
infected us in the night.

"What's the matter with you? Why are you limping like that?" he
asked Avner.

"It's nothing, sir."

"Then stop it!"

Benny turned his back to us and went to stand by one of the tents.
Avner contemplated him with a frown, as if trying to make him out, as if
he had just met him for the first time. "I can't step on my feet," he whispered to me. "I don't know what happened to them."

"I told you, it's unhealthy to keep your boots on all the time. What are
you going to do?"

"Suffer."

When we marched to the training area it seemed to me that he was
overcoming the pain in his feet. Maybe the movement did them good.

But he was in a bad mood and hardly spoke. We trudged through the sand for a long time, to a place where we had never been before. We reached a hill higher than any we had encountered before. This was the objective we were supposed to take by individual stalk. Benny gave the command to begin, and immediately sprinted off and disappeared behind the hill. We began to crawl through depressions in the ground and dead zones, as we had been trained to do. There was no instructor with us, but we knew that invisible eyes were watching us as we stole toward the top of the hill. The sun was in our eyes and we advanced carefully, slowly, crawling and stopping, trying to comb the objective, to discover the enemy hiding out there. Changing direction, trying to disappear into the face of the earth, to merge with it. This performance was familiar to us in every detail. There was a suppressed, suspect silence surrounding us. I could hear the breathing of the people crawling not far from me, scrupulously observing all the rules.

And suddenly there was the sound of a shot, and then another one. Bullets began whistling over our heads and flying past us. I hugged the ground with my body and buried my face in my hands, without daring to look in the direction from which the bullets were coming. After some time had passed, I looked around me at the others, who had also stopped crawling, and in the shade of their helmets their faces were terrified. "They're shooting at us," I heard Yossie Ressler's colorless voice saying. "Now they're already shooting at us."

Impossible. Something must have gone wrong in coordinating among the different platoons. We had probably stumbled into someone's field of fire by mistake. How long would it take them to sort it out so that we could carry on without danger? Were any of us hurt? The main thing was not to move. The report of the shots and the whistling of the bullets went on tearing incessantly through the air.

Zero-Zero shouted behind me: "Madmen! They want to kill us! What's wrong with them? Madmen! Madmen!" I looked behind me and saw him suddenly getting up, standing erect, and running for his life down the side of the hill. All the shots were now aimed at him. I saw the bullets falling next to him. He ran erratically, turning from one direction to another, as if trying to pass through a heavy shower without getting wet. He ran around in circles and yelled: "Stop it! Stop it! Madmen! I don't want to! Leave me alone!" Suddenly he stopped, stood still, looked around him, swayed, and fell to the ground.

The thought flashed through my mind: *None of this can possibly be real.* And as at similar moments, when a feeling of helplessness or utter incomprehension overcomes me, words reverberated inside me, words strung together as if of their own accord, accompanied by their own tune, like a recitation for other circumstances: *Your days as a soldier did not last long.* This sentence, which had popped into my head when I woke up in the morning, had come back and given me a moment's secret amusement when we were sitting and waiting with Muallem for the jeep. It occurred to me then that it would make fitting epitaph to carve on Miller's tombstone. And now I heard it inside me again: *Your days as a soldier did not last long.* What was it about these words, what was it in the way they sounded, that held me spellbound in the midst of the stunned fear and astonishment, on the slopes of the hill with the bullets raining down?

Everything happened with a curious slowness, as in a dream. Zackie suddenly appeared, crawling toward Zero-Zero. The shots were aimed at him. He ignored them. He crawled straight ahead, without zigzagging as he was supposed to. He reached Zero-Zero, who was lying as still as a corpse on the ground, and began to shake him. Zero-Zero woke up and yelled: "What do you want of me?" Zackie burst out laughing. "Don't be afraid," he said, "it's just a noise, it's nothing," and he kept on shaking Zero-Zero, urging him to move. Hedgehog shouted at him: "Zackie, are you crazy? What are you doing? You want to commit suicide for him?" But Zackie went on laughing. He knew something we didn't know.

All at once the shooting stopped. Silence fell. From the top of the hill we heard the voice of the company commander, Raffy Nagar, rolling thunderously over the dunes — he was apparently speaking through a megaphone.

"The company will continue with the exercise immediately! Advance according to instructions! Who told you to stop, you little bastards? Chickenhearted babies! Anyone in too much of a funk to advance will begin again from the beginning. Advance! Advance!"

I saw Alon advancing at a dash higher up the hill, springing forward and dropping to the ground, changing direction, combing the area around him for cover. This was his hour. This was the dance he liked. Now there was nothing ridiculous about his seriousness in his game of soldiers. The firing began again. It was aimed at Alon. He was the only thing moving on the hill. He was undergoing his baptism of fire with thrilled excitement, defying danger, realizing a fraction of his dreams.

A few more bold spirits joined him. I saw Avner too making a flanking dash for the hilltop, oblivious to the pain in his feet, carried away by the enthusiasm that only the danger of death can arouse. I tried to move from my place, and immediately heard the report of a shot and the whistling of a bullet over my head. I was overcome by a kind of stupor, perhaps because of fatigue and lack of sleep, an unwillingness to understand what was happening around me, and a detachment from it. If I pretended to be dead, the bullets would pass over me. And then the cry went up from mouth to mouth, the strange, incredible news, pathetic as the consolation of fools: The bullets weren't real. They were firing blanks at us, bullets that couldn't hurt us. It was only to frighten us. The bullets were harmless!

By the time I took in the significance of this news, I had emerged from my stupor and begun to feel the effects of the fear I had previously suppressed. My body was bathed in sweat, my heartbeat could not adjust itself to the new rhythm. *Your days as a soldier did not last long . . .* the morning's chant started up again, tempting me to get up and run for my life down the hill. I didn't believe the story about the blanks. At moments like these anything was possible. They, hiding up there on top of the hill, were capable of anything. Death too had become a matter of no importance. The mysterious goal justified this means too. This was the last illusion, really the last. Yossie Ressler began to advance, not far from me. Laboriously I managed to begin crawling again. I drew closer to him. The firing continued, the bullets whistled overhead. More live and piercing than ever. There was a smell of gunpowder in the air. Was that simulated too? I knew that sickening smell. Both of us buried our faces in the sand, until there was a break in the firing. And he began to crawl again.

"Aren't you afraid?" I asked him.

"I am afraid."

"They say they're only blanks."

"So what? You want to get a blank in your bum?"

Hedgehog approached us, his little face swallowed up in the shadow of his helmet, only his eyes gleaming, mean and furious. He said: "They're having fun up there, the bastards. Enjoying every minute of the performance. Laughing themselves sick to see how scared we are. Playing with us as if they were God."

The first men reached the top of the hill. The firing died down and stopped. Now we could clearly see Raffy Nagar standing up there with Benny at his side, looking at us through binoculars. Raffy lifted the megaphone to his lips and his voice thundered.

"You there!" He pointed at us. "You'll go down to the bottom of the hill and begin again from the beginning. This is an individual stalk, not a bunch of old women gossiping on a park bench! Get back down!" We ignored the instruction and began advancing up the hill, but Benny took the megaphone from the commander and repeated the instruction, this time calling our names.

At a rapid dash, we charged down the hill. We heard the megaphone calling other names and ordering them to go down and repeat the exercise.

The feeling of security at the bottom of the hill, far from the eyes of the officers hiding up above like cruel gods, filled us with the joy of survivors: From now on it was only a game again. The battle wasn't a battle. The shots weren't shots. The fear wasn't fear. If we stuck to the rules of this game, if we let them enjoy themselves and frighten us by shooting blanks, if we forgot about our honor, which had been destroyed long ago, we would emerge the victors. Someone suggested going around the hill and taking them by surprise from the rear, in a full flanking movement. We were possessed by the excitement of the game, and the memory of the man found dead among us, together with our speculations concerning the whereabouts of Muallem, our anxiety about what was going to happen to him and our obscure, murky feelings of guilt toward him, as if he bore our sins — all these were postponed to the fast-approaching end of this game. Micha the Fool flung out his arm in a salute and cried: *"Ave Caesar, morituri te salutant!"* and again we set out crawling and dashing from cover to cover to conquer the top of the hill.

"I told you," whispered Hedgehog, "look how happy they are! Miserable sods! That's what turns them on. Frightening recruits. Shooting at them and watching them panic, running, hiding, trying to save themselves. I'd like to see them in the same situation."

When we reached the top of the hill we took cover and waited for the others to arrive, and Hedgehog, who had not yet learned to forgo his honor, stared at the officers malevolently. He did not share in the feelings of relief and satisfaction that we had reached the end of the game and what came now would be different. "They're taking it out on us," he explained. "For not being in combat units, real fighters, for being chocolate soldiers, lousy jobniks like us. Instead of fighting the Arabs they shoot bullets made of wood or rubber or something at us. There's no difference between them and us, they can't fool me."

Ressler said: "What do you care about them? Soon it'll all be over. We'll go away and never see them again in our lives. We'll forget them. We'll forget this whole pile of shit."

"Hedgehog wishes he could fight them," said Avner.

"You bet I do!" said Hedgehog, smiling dreamily. "Boy, would I love to fight them! No — what I'd really like to do would be to sit up there and shoot at them. See them panicking, running like animals for cover."

After supper the sky grew overcast and the farewell campfire was endangered. We gathered round in a circle, not far from the edge of the bivouac, in a broad depression in the dunes, the instructors came and sat among us, and when Muallem, whom we had not seen the whole day, appeared, a deafening chorus of welcome broke out. "For he's a jolly good fellow! And so say all of us! And so say all of us!" we roared in growing enthusiasm, to the accompaniment of rhythmic clapping. Muallem's expression was stern and glum, and his small, deep-set eyes glittered in the light of the campfire, darting here and there as if to make sure that we were all present and correct. He sat down next to Raffy Nagar and they spoke to each other in an undertone. After a while Muallem got up and went away. When he came back he was carrying an accordion. God knows where he found it, whom he'd gotten it from.

He held up his hand to silence the singing of "For he's a jolly good fellow," which had continued uninterrupted, and asked Yossie Ressler: "Do you know how to play this too?"

Ressler's face darkened. Perhaps he had taken a vow never to play for us again after the smashing of his guitar. Muallem held the accordion out to him, and Ressler said: "Sir, I can't —"

"Do you know or don't you?"

"I do, but —"

"Then play. I'm telling you to," Muallem insisted.

"Is that an order?" asked Ressler.

"No," said Muallem. "There are no such orders in the army. Do it for us, for all your friends, to make us happy, to make us feel good at the end of the series."

Raffy Nagar and the other instructors did not interfere in this dialogue between Muallem and Ressler. They looked on with something between amusement and curiosity, as if Muallem were being tested. People called out to Yossie to go on and play, but he stood his ground.

Muallem asked: "Do you really know how to play it?"

"Yes, sir."

"Come on, play. Muallem's asking you."

At these moments there was something beautiful about Muallem, something I had never seen in him before, something spare, dry, very vulnerable, as if he had already unconsciously begun to serve his term of punishment.

Ressler took the accordion in his arms, clasped it to his chest, and began running his fingers over the keys to accustom them to the instrument.

"Why don't you accompany Ben-Hamo? Let him sing the French

national anthem again," suggested Benny. "That was really something," he explained to one of the other instructors who had not been present at the previous campfire.

"No," said Muallem, "our own songs, Israeli songs."

Yossie began to play a medley of old tunes, and the singing broke out, spirited and disciplined, rising and swelling as we passed on to humorous, bawdy songs, when the thunderous clapping nearly drowned out the sound of the accordion. Benny stood next to the fire and fed it with twigs. Then he put a big pot from the kitchen on it to boil up the coffee. When it was ready, the singing died down and each of us, mug in hand, went up to Benny to get his share. We all sat in a circle, sipping our coffee, and Raffy Nagar began to speak, summing up the series. He spoke in his natural voice, not threatening or barking, occasionally hesitant, distant and matter-of-fact, like a man speaking to men. Had the hour of reconciliation with them really come at last? When Raffy finished speaking, Muallem called out in honor of the company commander: "Hip! Hip!" and our voices roared: "Hurrah!" The cry was repeated three times, and the third time we cheered: "Hurrah! Hurrah! Hurrah!" It seemed that in these cries, which had been transmitted to us by the youth movements from some ancient, anonymous tribal tradition, whose language had been forgotten and whose words were unintelligible to us, we were giving expression to some heartfelt emotion we did not even know we possessed, and would not have been able to express in our own language. And when the echoes died down Alon stood up and cried in honor of Muallem: "Hip! Hip!" and our voices roared in response: "Hurrah!" and the third time: "Hurrah! Hurrah! Hurrah!" And when we fell silent, we could hear Muallem mumbling, perhaps to us, perhaps to himself: "Enough, boys, enough."

Yossie struck up a new song on the accordion, and before we had time to join in we saw Rahamim rise to his feet, his eyes closed, his face furrowed by lights and shadows from the fire, quiet and concentrated as that of a sleepwalker, advance with little steps, raising and dropping his shoulders, and stop next to the fire. An expectant silence fell. For a moment he stood still, as if in search of a starting point, and Benny said to the instructor sitting next to him: "Now the artistic program will begin." But Rahamim no longer heard. He was already sailing away to the distant realms of his strange dances, as on that other night, at the beginning of basic training, when our weekend leave had been canceled and he had first danced before us. Suddenly he flung up his arms, as if requesting silence and attention, or calling for help against the alien forces overpowering him once more, or perhaps he was actually invoking them to come and take possession of him. His body began to tremble, at first with a faint, barely perceptible tremor, and then with quick, jerky movements, as if he were hitting out at the shadows of the flames flickering next to him. He did not move from his place; his feet were planted on the ground while his body tried unsuccessfully to free itself of this hold. And like then, now too a brief, choked scream escaped his lips, a cry of pain or pleasure, perhaps a shout of triumph. His friends slapped their thighs, as if beating drums, with strong, rhythmic slaps, without singing or shouts of encouragement. He moved to and fro, his body writhing, bending and straightening, his head swaying with the movements of his body as if it had no strength of its own.

With little skips he began to encircle the campfire, and as he did so he held out his arms to it, in supplication, in longing, in love. As if the fire imprisoned in his bones were calling out to the fire of the campfire: *Mother, Mother.* No one joined the thigh slapping by clapping or calling out. Everything took place in silence, as if for fear of disturbing the mysterious force making him dance, as if he were hanging from a very frail, slender thread, and the passage back to the starting point was full of danger. Muallem watched the dancer with a suspicious frown, occasionally casting his eyes over the spectators with an expression of disapproval and curiosity, to see the effect the dance was having on them and guess what they thought of the spectacle.

I tried to translate the gestures and expressions of the dance into a story, but was unable to find any thread connecting them into a meaningful whole. Was he saying something, speaking for all of us as our representative? Like then, now too I heard Avner's sentence about his fellow prisoner repeating itself in my mind: *Maybe he's seen things we'll never see.* I didn't know what these things might be. Avner himself was no longer watching the dance. His head had slumped onto his chest, his hands were lying on his drawn-up knees, with his gun between them, sticking up over his shoulder and slanting like the mast of a sinking ship. We could hear Ben-Hamo's rhythmic breathing. Now he was running in a circle round the fire, his face toward his audience, stretching his arms out and gathering them in, moving his shoulders backward and forward, up and down, his face bathed in sweat and twisted in pain. Suddenly he stopped, as if waking from a dream. He bowed his head and panting heavily went slowly back to his place, sat down, and placed his hands on the nape of his neck, as if he were having trouble getting his breath back.

Zackie broke into the tremulous notes of an Arab song, perhaps hoping to fan the fire that had died down in Rahamim's bones, but Rahamim did not react. He covered his face with his hands, as if ashamed of having exposed himself to us again. And Muallem said: "Play, Yossie, play our own songs. We don't want Arab songs."

Zackie fell silent. Yossie played, and this time the community singing was not successful. The fire, no longer fed with twigs, died down. We gathered around and unbuttoned our flies to put it out in the traditional way, and when it started to rain we made for our tents.

The blankets had not dried completely during the day. A strange, sourish smell emanated from them. The rain came down on the tent in a thin, monotonous drizzle, without any wind. Avner groaned. He tried to take off his boots and failed. For a long time he tossed and turned. I was on the point of succumbing to the exhaustion of nights without sleep. Already I could feel myself beginning to drift away when suddenly the tent was filled with an appalling stench, the stench of a rotting carcass, a fierce, brutal smell that descended on me like a blow. I opened my eyes and saw him looking at me, to see if I was already sleeping or if I had noticed anything. The smell was unbearable, like a suffocating cloud of poison gas.

"It's terrible, isn't it?" he said in a whisper, as if he couldn't believe what had happened to him.

I held my breath, I couldn't breathe. It was the smell of death, the smell of the death of the flesh, stunning in its ugliness, its intensity, its sticky, suffocating intrusiveness, seeping and penetrating everywhere. He lit a match and examined his feet, and when the first match burned down he lit another. "Look what happened," he said.

I sat up in my sleeping bag and looked at his feet. They were red, and I didn't know how much of this redness was from the flame and how much from his feet. They were as red as raw, peeling flesh, very swollen, and covered with strange, damp spots and blotches. As he looked at his feet an expression of terror came onto his face. He blew out the match again and lit a new one.

"I don't know what to do. Forgive me, I'm sorry you have to be next to me now."

"You shouldn't have kept your boots on all the time," I said, "especially after that night when everything got wet."

"Better not to look." He sighed and put out the match, then lay down again. There was a moment's silence, and I heard him groaning softly.

"What's up? Does it hurt?" I asked.

"No. It stinks. And it's humiliating. That somebody else has to smell it too."

"Forget about me. It doesn't matter."

"You're only saying that to be nice. But it's awful. I know it is."

He took the blanket lying next to him and covered his feet with it. I wasn't sure that this was the right thing to do, after his feet had not been exposed to the air for several days already. At the same time I hoped that it would afford some relief from the miasma of poisonous rottenness filling the tent and pounding inside my head like a sledgehammer. And again he groaned softly and sniffed.

In the end he said: "I'll put on my boots again. At least it'll put a stop to the smell." He sat up, threw off the blanket, took up a sock, and tried to pull it onto his foot. "My socks have gone rotten," he said, "they're all slimy." Nevertheless he put on both socks and tried to put on one of his boots. But his swollen foot would not fit into the boot. He pulled with all his strength and groaned with pain: "It's impossible. It won't go in. If I were a decent human being I'd go outside and sit in the rain all night long. I wouldn't make someone else suffer."

But he fell onto his sleeping bag and went on groaning and sniffing instead.

I pulled the blanket over my head, covered my face, and buried myself inside it. But the terrible smell came from all directions, sinking into everything, adhering to the blankets, me, and the damp ground beneath me. It was inescapable. Like a wild animal the stench of the dead flesh raged, penetrating, attacking, paralyzing. He stirred. I lowered the blanket from my face and saw him moving again and again, and the movements, which looked at first like an attempt to change his position or relax, turned into a constant writhing and repeated beating of his body on the ground, as if he were struggling with some demon that had taken possession of him. I averted my face in order not to look as if I were spying on his privacy. Behind my back I heard the thudding of his body beating against the ground and his groans. After a while there was silence. I turned my head discreetly in his direction. He had raised the tent flaps and stuck his feet outside. Rainy air from outside entered the tent, mingling with the dense, heavy, sinking smell. Soon the remnants of the stench were left only in our blankets, clothes, and gear and in the ground, and more than lingering as a smell they were like the remains of some sticky, sickening sweetness, which was absorbed by the sour moldiness of the damp blankets and disappeared into it entirely. In the darkness I could see Avner's eyes gleaming as he lay with his legs sticking out of the open tent flaps. The rain fell on his sore feet and washed them as if it possessed healing properties.

I said to him: "There's something I have to tell you."

"What?" His voice was anxious, like that of a person haunted by guilt.

"On that guard, when they caught you sleeping and sent you to jail . . ."

"You saw them coming and you went away on purpose without warning me."

"You knew?"

"Sure I did."

"How?"

"I saw everything."

"You weren't sleeping?"

"And how I was sleeping."

"So how did you see?"

"There are some things you can see with your eyes closed," he said without elaborating. He sank into a mysterious silence.

"Why didn't you ever say anything to me about it?"

"I was waiting for you to tell me."

"I don't know why I did it. It was some force I couldn't resist."

"It's called hatred."

"Maybe."

"And it annoyed you too that I didn't give a damn for their rules and regulations, that I wouldn't be their slave, that I wasn't afraid."

"You may be right."

"I hoped that one day you would feel that you had to tell me. Say, you're turning into a human being!"

"So how did you keep it in all this time and go on being friendly, as if nothing had happened?"

"You don't know me. On the one hand, I . . ."

I was happy to see him on top of his form again, but the revelation that he had known about my treachery all along was too astonishing for me to satisfy my curiosity with this all-too-familiar verbiage.

"When you were sitting in jail and suffering," I said, "didn't you want to revenge yourself, didn't you curse me?"

"I don't judge anyone. I don't know why people do the things they do. I hardly know why I do what I do. Understand? And I believe in the power of forgiveness, there's nothing like the power of forgiveness, and the more terrible the deed, the greater the forgiveness. So I'm glad you asked my forgiveness, but there are certain conclusions to be drawn. I remember for instance that I decided then that certain things I wanted to tell you about myself, about experiences I once went through, and I even said once that I would tell you — I decided not to tell you. Not as a punishment, but because I realized that it wasn't fitting, it wasn't right, after everything that had happened. And I won't tell you."

"Why did you get jail? They don't dish out such long sentences for a thing like that."

"The company commander said I was impertinent to him. He transferred the case to the commander of the base. And he sentenced me for impertinence too. They decided to throw the book at me."

"What was the impertinence?"

"I wasn't impertinent at all. The CO began yelling at me that the gun was my woman, and all that rubbish. He wanted me to say it too. I wouldn't give in and I refused to say what he wanted me to say."

"Why did you refuse?"

"Why? What kind of a question is that? There are some things you can't give in on, they're sacred. If a woman is a gun, there's no point to my life. My life's not worth a fart! If I have any hope, any endurance — it's because a woman is a woman and not a gun."

He fell silent for a moment and then asked suspiciously: "Tell me, why did you chose now of all times to tell me about that time on guard? Because I'm so stinking and degraded?"

"No. I felt that I had to say it sometime, and there's not much time left."

"My father knows all kinds of legends and stories. He used to tell them to us when we were small and he was still in shape. One of the stories is about a gypsy and a bear. Once there was a gypsy and he had a bear, and he would appear with it at circuses and fairs. Once the gypsy lay down to sleep on the roadside, or maybe it was in the forest, and suddenly some murderers fell on him, or maybe they were wild animals, I don't remember. And anyway it was always changing. In any case the bear jumped on them and killed them. And the gypsy was saved. The gypsy was moved and grateful to his bear for saving his life, he hugged him and kissed him, but the bear turned his head away and said: *Your mouth stinks.* The gypsy said to him: *It's a pity you saved my life.*"

"I don't understand the moral."

"There is no moral. It's just a story. You can read anything you like into it."

· PART FOUR ·

THE CANNONS' ROAR

CHAPTER 28

Where's Alon?"

"He'll come soon. Don't worry. Come with me, I'll show you your room and you can put your rucksack down in the meantime."

Why did she say don't worry? What's there to worry about? And actually there is a note of suppressed worry and embarrassment in her voice, disguised by inner poise and a frank, friendly smile. Is there something about his presence that embarrasses her? The tension of strangeness? Maybe she's busy and he's disturbing her? When he got off the bus and saw that Alon wasn't there, as arranged, he realized immediately that the girl in boots, in blue pants and a checked shirt, raising her chin and narrowing her eyes to see the people getting off the bus, was the girl he had thought about so often without knowing how to give her a face and a body. But she is less beautiful, more ordinary than he had imagined. Does he interest her at all? Maybe she has something more important on her mind. Where's Alon?

They walk down one of the kibbutz paths. Men and women passing them nod and smile at her, stealing curious, sidelong glances at him. This is the first time he has ever set foot in a kibbutz. His friends had all had a taste of kibbutz life in the youth movements, on work camps. He thought then that he had better things to do in the long summer vacations. Today he's sorry that he missed the experience, the fun and camaraderie, the proximity of the girls, the mystery of the nights in those places, the new feeling of freedom. The memory of the stories his friends told when they returned still pierces his heart with the painful consciousness of having missed something. Walking along these paths now, he feels a certain tension, as if he has entered the domain of a sect whose rules and prohibitions are unknown to him, and he is afraid that he might do or say something without thinking that will arouse their anger, or even worse: their ridicule. If Alon came to meet him, as he said he would, he would feel more comfortable. But Alon isn't there, and he feels a stab of resentment against him. There is a smell of mystery in the air, and he hates mysteries.

Dafna leads him into a room in a long, narrow building. There are a number of beds in the room, one of which will be his for the night.

"Maybe you're not used to conditions like these, but this is how we live here."

"Has anything happened to Alon?"

"Nothing's happened to him. I told you not to worry."

"When people tell me not to worry I start worrying right away. Has he gone to work or something?"

"He should be back at any minute. He went somewhere."

"Went somewhere? Where?"

"I don't know."

"Maybe there's no reason for me to stay?"

"There's every reason for you to stay. You must stay. Put your things down and come outside. I'll show you around."

Items of clothing lie scattered over the other beds. Their owners have apparently gone out and will be back soon. Have they heard of him, will they recognize him? An uneasy feeling of strangeness takes hold of him. He's intruding in a place where he doesn't belong. He finds himself — after so many years — agreeing with the things he's heard his father constantly repeating about the kibbutzim, about the "inhuman" method they had invented to repress the spirit of the individual. Now he has to take somebody else's bed. And what if the owner unexpectedly returns in the middle of the night and wakes him up and demands his bed back? How humiliating. His anger at Alon increases. How dared he? Why? How could he have taken off after inviting Micky to come and visit him? There 's something fishy going on. He should pick up his knapsack and go straight to the main road, to get a bus or hitch a ride home.

They walk for a while in silence. He senses her preparing herself to explain what has happened to Alon. She isn't beautiful like he thought she'd be. But neither is she as plain as she seemed at first, when he got off the bus. She has a kind of serenity about her, a powerful self-control. The boots, the long blue pants, the thick, loose checked shirt blur the lines of her figure. She is rather tall, her nose is tilted, her eyes are small, light brown, very clear, and they have a lively, shrewd, skeptical gleam, which seems to hold a knowing smile: She's the kind of girl you'll never catch losing her head, the bossy kind that manage your life for you.

"He told me what good friends you are," said Dafna. "He thinks you're great, he's really proud to be your friend. It's lucky he found someone like you there. Because he doesn't usually get on so well with other people. You must have noticed how he's sometimes strange, how he does things that nobody can understand. Well, he did something like that today. He dressed up as a lieutenant in the paratroops and went out to see what it felt like."

"What do you mean?" he asked, even though he understood it all, immediately, despite the way she made light of this grotesque, off-putting story. "'To see what it felt like'?"

"Someone saw him slipping out to the main road by a side path this morning, dressed in a paratroop officer's uniform, with the insignia, the beret, the boots, the Uzi — everything. Later it turned out that the uniform belongs to my brother, he's home for the weekend. It disappeared from his room. Alon took it. I suppose he went to town to show off in it, see what kind of impression he was making. You know how disappointed he was at not being taken into a combat unit. In the towns perhaps people don't care so much, everyone lives his own life separately, but over here, when you're the only one of your group who's going to be a jobnik in the IDF, it hurts. He'll probably walk around the streets for a bit until he calms down, and then he'll come home. He knew you were coming. He was looking forward to it. I'm sure he'll be back soon. It's just a question of the luck he has hitching rides."

Micky's heart sinks. What has this story got to do with me? he wonders. She's looking at him to see the effect of her words. Her eyes hiding that suspicious smile give rise in him to something he can't define. What kind of a relationship is there between her and Alon? The way she talks about him, as if he's sick. Is she his girlfriend or his nurse? There's something wrong here.

They left the center of the kibbutz and reached the edge of the fields, where they sat down on a couple of wooden crates. On the horizon Mount Gilboa lay like a splendid slumbering animal. Dafna lowered her head, her hand groped at her side for a hold on the crate, then she tightened her grip and turned her whole body sideways, with all her weight on her hand and arm. Through her thick shirt, now pulled tightly around her, he could see the curve of full high breasts and the soft, mysterious line slanting down from her armpit via the swelling of her bosom to her slender waist. Micky was pierced by the pain of desire, after he had already made up his mind that there was nothing special or captivating about her. There was something so intimate in the way the material was stretched over her body, in the contours of the body thrusting against the pressure, as in a lover's struggle — stubborn, yielding, with a marvelous mutuality. A moment as daring and revealing as nudity.

"But lately," said Micky, "he's come to terms with it. He said he wanted to go to a Squad Commanders Course. I thought everything was okay."

"Of course he'll come to terms with it in the end. But suddenly he got this silly idea into his head. The trouble is that he might be caught. If some MP wants to see his papers, or something like that, he could be in serious trouble. But he probably looks very convincing in that uniform. No one'll suspect him. As long as he doesn't do anything silly to draw attention to himself and then it'll all come out. There, now you know everything."

She sat up straight on the crate and the thick checked shirt fell loosely around her again and hid the lines of her body, but her face had emerged from its neutrality. It was slightly flushed from the exertion, and behind that flush was a burgeoning femininity, modest and healthy. She smiled and Micky felt a dryness in his throat; he could hardly swallow his saliva.

"Please, don't hurt him."

"Why on earth should I?" asked Micky.

"I know that all you want now is to go home quickly and run away from all this unpleasantness."

"I don't really know what to do."

"Stay and wait for him. Please."

He gave her a look of agreement but was unable to pronounce the words to confirm it.

"I have to go back now. I can't stay with you any longer. Will you manage on your own?"

They got down from the crates and walked back to the center of the kibbutz. He knew that the right thing to do would be to leave right away, but he also knew that he wouldn't dare to do it. In the strangeness and the embarrassment, the surprise at what Alon had done, the confounding of all his expectations, he felt that a circle had been opened. And he wanted to pass this test. Not to listen to the old voice tempting him not to get involved, not to make himself ridiculous, to return to himself.

"I'll wait for him on the main road and see him as soon as he comes."

If he comes at all, he added silently to himself, with not a little malice, which took him by surprise, and reminded him of the first days on the base.

"I know," she said. "You feel uncomfortable staying here by yourself. I'm really sorry that I have to go back now. I've taken a lot of time off already and they'll be angry with me. I don't have a choice. That's the way things are."

"No problem. I'll wait on the road. Don't worry."

She gave him a long, scrutinizing look, and her skeptical eyes seemed to plumb the depths of his soul. Perhaps she doubted his sincerity. And again she asked him: "Please, don't hurt him. You know him — he's got a pure heart, really pure. He doesn't know how to be mean, or petty. There's no limit to what he's capable of doing for others."

Was her voice really on the point of breaking? Why was she telling him all this?

"Why on earth should I hurt him?"

"I don't know. I feel something hard in you, something evasive. And he expects you to be at his side when he falls, to help him up."

Not far from the bus stop, at the side of the road, he sits down on a big stone. His rucksack's still in the room, blocking the temptation to flee. And as he sits there, opposite the road leading to the gate of the kibbutz, suspended between coming and going, it seems to him that he is beginning to come to terms with the sorrow of parting, with the certainty that he will never see the Alon he has come to know and love, with all his strangeness and contradictions, again. A line has been drawn between the past and the present moment. And in his longing for the figure who has departed, never to return, he feels a kind of hatred for the usurper of this identity, the other Alon, shamelessly mad, setting out alone on a hopeless journey, a ridiculous adventure, to act out his sick fantasies, like some lousy Don Quixote, like a parody of Don Quixote, like a parody of a parody. I won't be his Sancho! — the angry, defiant cry rises from his heart — I'll never be his Sancho! What's the time? Twenty to three.

He'll never get used to it. Not to the shrinking of fear, not to the choked cry of pain, not to the groan of relief and the inner melting, always unexpected, rising from his depths and spreading through all his limbs, swelling in his chest like a new breath, harsh as a sob, broad and even as sleep, blurring his memory, bursting the bounds of his body, sharpening the sense of the moment like a point of light, the newborn moment, the astonishing moment, the fading moment, the past moment, an incessant flickering of moments, strengthening their grip, relaxing their grip, in a rapid, giddy tempo, with the heartbeats of pursuit and flight echoing from the earth and drumming in his temples: There's a long way still to go, there's a long way still to go, there's a long way still to go. His uncle pulls the blanket more tightly around his shoulders, as if he feels a sudden chill. In his eyes the embers of the chastising fire are still smoldering, but his lips are beginning to tremble. Rahamim approaches him, sits at the foot of the bed, on the floor, his head downcast, his eyes red but dry, his face frozen, supposing that the hiding is over. When the hand swoops swiftly and hits him in the face, he falls flat on the ground with his hands protecting his cheeks, in a strange gesture of amazement. The old man stoops slightly to see how he is. The uncle's thin, pale face is covered with gray and white stubble. His skinny body is lost in his pajamas, which are too big for him. Once more he tightens the blanket around his shoulders and his clear, surprisingly youthful voice asks Rahamim if he will keep to the straight and narrow. Rahamim takes his hands off his face, sits up, and nods. The old man demands to hear him say it. Rahamim says he'll keep to the straight and narrow. The old man demands a promise that he will be a good soldier and obey his commanding officers. Rahamim promises. The old man sighs bitterly, a sigh that contains both skepticism and a lament for his miserable fate. He rises slowly from his bed, as if afraid any untoward movement might break his fragile bones, and stares at Rahamim expectantly. Rahamin knows what's expected of him. He remains seated on the ground and turns in a semicircle with his face to the door of the hut and his back to the uncle. The old man secludes himself in the corner with his pile of belongings, turning his head again and again to see if Rahamim is fulfilling the duty of discretion, removes from its hiding place a little knotted bag, totters back to his bed, and calls Rahamim. Rahamim gets up and goes to him. The old man slowly unties the knots, takes out a bill, folds it, and gives it to Rahamim. Rahamim says it isn't enough for his needs and he doesn't know when he'll be coming on leave again. Again the old man's strong, youthful voice rings out, demanding a detailed account of his expenditures. Rahamim is silent. The rules of the game are fixed. He is sick and tired of them already. The uncle folds another, smaller, bill, places it in Rahamim's palm, and gives him a hefty push on the shoulder. Rahamim recoils a few steps backward, returns, takes the uncle's hand and kisses it.

After going out and shutting the door, he stands still for a moment, trying to hear what's happening inside the hut, deliberates, raises his hand to the wooden board as if to push it open and go back in, drops his hand in resignation, and turns away, heading slowly for the wadi. He sits down on a broken suitcase lying there, all cracked and swollen out of shape by the rain, looking at the mud in the creek and the rubbish sticking out of it. During the previous winter's floods water had streamed here like a river, sweeping up everything in its path, and the wind had uprooted everything not planted firmly in the ground. This winter was calmer. The water collected in the creek, still and slowly sinking. He hears the voices of people walking behind him. He does not turn his head to see who they are. Something has hardened inside him like a scab, like armor. When the idea first came to him, he was afraid. He thought that his body would betray him when he came to do the deed, that his hands would shake, his feet would refuse to move, his head would spin, his eyes cloud over. But now his heart is full of quietness and confidence. He feels that he will have no difficulty carrying out his resolution and that he will not falter or regret the deed when it is done.

A truck stops at the side of road. When it sets off again, he sees Alon standing there in the paratrooper's uniform, the Uzi hanging from his shoulder. Alon is standing with his back to him, looking quickly around him and at the path leading to the kibbutz gate to make sure no enemy forces are concealed there. Micky freezes where he sits, hoping that Alon won't look in his direction. It would be better if Alon goes into the kibbutz first, to straighten things out and change his clothes, before meeting Micky. Better for him not to know that he has seen him in his disgrace. Micky averts his face, hunches his shoulders, and lowers his head, trying to merge with the stone he's sitting on, to be as hard and still as it is. Suddenly he hears a rhythmic pounding on the ground. He looks carefully out of the corner of his eyes and sees Alon breaking into a run at the side of the road. He watches him until he turns right and disappears into a clump of trees growing on the verge on the road. Perhaps this was the way he stole out in the morning, to avoid meeting anyone from the kibbutz.

Micky stands up and stretches, as if waking from a disturbing dream. It is clear to him now that all this time he has been hoping that Alon wouldn't come home. He was almost sure of it. His heart told him that something would happen to Alon, that his imposture would be discovered, that he would be locked up, court-martialed, jailed, punished. Maybe a hard blow would bring him back to his senses, to reality. And not for that reason only, but because he hates him. He has never hated Alon before, not even at the beginning when he sneered at his opinions and expressions, when it all seemed a pose to him; nor during the period of the never-ending arguments, with the will to win and humiliate involved in them. He never hated him. What is the meaning of this hatred? Where does it come from? It's a far cry from the friendship whose description his father read to him from the essay by Montaigne. There is no such friendship. It's impossible. Only in love, perhaps, is such mutuality, such unity, such wholeness possible if you're lucky. And most people apparently aren't so lucky. There is a lot of misery in relations between people. There is far more chance of disappointment and hatred in human relationships than of purity and perfection. Why did she say: Don't hurt him? How did she guess? What did she see in me? Something hard and evasive. Once more her image blurs in his memory, growing as neutral as it was when he first set eyes on her, just a girl like any other, and not one of the prettiest either. I wish I were hard and evasive. I wouldn't have been sitting here if I was, I would have gone home a long time ago instead of hanging around in a strange place to pry into other people's private lives, to be a part of his sickness, I don't want anything to do with it. I don't want anything to do with it! How can she be his girlfriend? Micky clenches his fists in the rage that suddenly grabs hold of him, trying to throttle it and push it down as deep as he can. He surveys the wide-open spaces around him. The traffic has almost stopped. A silence, more like indifference than tranquility, hangs over everything. Clouds like white sheep float in the pale sky as the sun turns to the west. A transparent, solemn melancholy descends on the fields and plantations and on Mount Gilboa. How have the mighty fallen!

And here comes Alon again, emerging from the kibbutz gates, running down the dirt track to the main road. Now he's wearing civvies, disguised as a kibbutznik.

"You said you'd be here after four," he apologizes, puffing and panting, touching Micky's shoulder, smiling in embarrassment. "I didn't see you when I came back. Where were you?"

"Here, next to the bus stop."

"Did you see me?"

"Yes."

"Look, I don't know what to say."

"What got into you?"

"Nothing. It was just a joke." He turns his face toward Micky, who is walking next to him. "What's up? Are you mad at me? Look, as far as I knew, you were coming after four — that's what we arranged, no?"

"I saw you when you came back, I looked at you and your fancy dress. I was ashamed for you."

"Come off it, Micky, don't make such a fuss."

"I brought you all kinds of newspapers you probably don't get here."

"Great! It's terrific you came. Dafna's awfully pleased too. It's a pity she had to go back to work and couldn't stay with you."

"You've got a wonderful girlfriend."

"She has to suffer for my nonsense too. What did you think when you saw me on the road? How did I look?"

"It suits you. You looked just like one of those guys, you really did."

"But you were ashamed for me, nevertheless."

"Yes."

"Micky, I'm ashamed now too, believe me. But the shame comes in the end. When you're actually doing it you forget everything, you only think about what it feels like. If only it was real . . . If only that was my real uniform!"

"What do you need it for? What are you — a clown?"

"What's the big deal? We're still young enough to play the fool sometimes. Listen, I hitched a ride to Haifa, I hung around outside the Palace for a bit, to feel the glances, the admiration, the gratitude in the eyes of the people looking at you. You begin to believe that you really are what they think you are. It's a fantastic feeling. I suppose it sounds completely ridiculous to you."

"Yes, it does. And they could have caught you too. You know what you can get for posing as an officer?"

"I wanted that too, those moments of danger. Like playing with fire. And anyway, they didn't catch me."

"I thought you'd gotten over all that stuff, that you'd given up that dream, that you were going on a Squad Commanders Course, that it was all fixed. And so I put in an application to go on the course too. But now I don't know if you're still going to do it."

"Definitely! No problem. It was just a joke, I'm telling you. You can trust me."

"Tell me, don't you care what people think about you here? What your friends think about you?"

"I don't have any friends here. And in any case they never had a good opinion of me. I know what they say about me behind my back. And not only behind my back either. So they'll have another reason to make fun of me. It doesn't make any difference anymore. Apart from Dafna and my mother, there's no one here I feel a strong bond with. And my mother's not in good shape, by the way. Maybe you'll see her later, so I'd better tell you now. Once I thought that if I got into the paratroopers, the army would be my framework, my new home. From the social point of view too. And now everything's pushing me back here. The kibbutz isn't the ideal place for someone who's not accepted by the group. But the way of life here has a lot of other advantages. I don't think I could live anywhere else. Certainly not now."

On the face of things it's the old Alon again, his good friend, solid and familiar. But who knows what he's hiding. What else he's planning. What's brewing in his mind. When his childish fantasies will suddenly take hold of him again. Who knows what more he's capable of. A strangeness falls between them, and however hard Micky tries to cover it up, however much he talks and acts as if nothing has happened, there is no escaping the certainty that something has been destroyed, something precious and irretrievable.

"Where are we going?"

"You'll see in a minute. There's a place I like going to in these twilight hours. It's beautiful there now."

"What's Dafna doing now?"

"She's gone to rest. She got up awfully early in the morning, and this afternoon she worked hard."

"You're lucky to have such a wonderful girlfriend, who loves you so much."

"I know," says Alon, and he looks into Micky's face for a moment with a sad smile in his eyes. "You'll have a girlfriend who'll love you too. You'll meet her, just like everyone meets their girl."

Micky feels uncomfortable talking about it now. There isn't the same intimacy between them now as there was on that night guarding next to the armory, when the first rain fell, when he told him that he had not yet known love. So he says, in a noncommittal tone: "Yes, I suppose so."

They walk past an orchard hedged in with a row of cypresses. At the foot of one of the cypresses they sit down, leaning against the trunk. In front of them is a plain surrounded by hills, steeped in a golden, dusky light, part of it sown, part plowed, part stubble, a patchwork of dark brown and light brown, yellowish squares. And opposite, on the mountain range on the border, the omnipresent Gilboa again. The twilight casts long shadows over the fields. Alon is silent, he sits and listens to the stillness, waiting for something. He glances at his watch and his eyes scan the broad fields in front of them. They sit in silence for a long time, and Micky thinks to himself that it's for the best, there's really nothing they can say to each other now. On the base, they sometimes didn't have enough time to tell each other everything that was in their hearts.

In the end a strange, ugly, startled screeching goes up: *Chook! Chook! Chook!* Alon taps Micky softly on the arm to show him the flock of partridges that has appeared in the field, not far off. A dozen or so rusty gray birds are hopping over the furrows, pecking and shaking their heads with peculiar movements. Alon's eyes are fixed on them. After a while he inserts two fingers in his mouth and lets out a short, sharp, piercing whistle. The partridges rise a yard or two into the air, fly heavily through the air, drop to the ground, and fly again, repeating this performance until they recede into the distance and disappear from view.

"Why did you frighten them away?"

"I like to watch them fly. That's the maximum they're capable of. They can't fly any higher. It kills me when they fly like that. They're more hens than birds, but they think they're birds and they think that they're flying!"

"Why? Because they're so stupid?" asks Micky, astonished by the malice in his own voice.

"They're not in the least stupid! They have tremendous natural intelligence, real cunning. Look, they nest over there, in the rocks and bushes under those hills. And when their chicks hatch and they go out to look for food, if they encounter an enemy, man or beast, they begin their flight in the opposite direction of their nests. To draw their pursuers after them and distance them from their chicks. A kind of deflection operation. You call that stupid? They draw the enemy fire in order to protect their homes. Don't you think that shows intelligence — and self-sacrifice too, if you don't mind?"

"Do you really think that there's such a thing in nature as self-sacrifice? There's no such thing as the protection of the weak in nature. They're a lost cause. They don't have a chance. What you're talking about is a purely egotistical drive to defend their offspring, to preserve their culture. You know that better than I do."

"You'd tell them to stop flying, if they can't do it. But I think there's something beautiful about it, even if it looks grotesque. As if they remember that once, at a different stage of their development, millions of years ago, they could fly like birds, and they still preserve that — to the best of their ability."

I've never thought about my clothes. It never entered my head to waste money on them. I was always so sure of myself, there was no room for any change or improvement in my appearance. In front of the mirror, shaving, one sad, dark smile, promising the world — and I knew I had what it took. I had it all. So why on earth is it beginning to bother me now? As if I'm beginning to grow old already. Afraid of looking ridiculous in these clothes, looking at them with their eyes, those mean, pitiless eyes. These are a child's clothes, not a man's. And they're too small, they're simply too small for me. My arms and legs are too long, they stick out, and the darn in my sweater, on the elbow, my mother's darn. I can't afford to be ridiculous. Not now. You can't be expected to like it. Pity, yes. Maybe hang on to it as a keepsake, for the days when she's no longer here — to kiss it, to weep into it. Yes. Like a letter from her. She didn't know how to write, so that's how she wrote to me. And I've got all the rest of my life to try and decipher her handwriting. She sat with her weak eyes, her tired hands, her heart heavy with memories, with presentiments of disaster and bad luck. And with him pestering her all the time, complaining and flying into rages. Blaming her for everything. I remember that night. The light too dim to see properly. Her eyes narrowed with the effort, her whole face wrinkled up. Her eyes almost completely closed. You can't even see the slits she's left, to concentrate all the light in them. How long it takes her. She finishes, looks at it, holds it farther, closer, and displays it. Making an effort to convince herself, or me: You can't see a

thing, just like new. That belief in the power of words to change reality.
I inherited it from her. Like hell you can't see! You must be joking. A
hole would be better! But I didn't really care. I didn't pay any attention
to my clothes. It was only stubbornness and the wish to tease her. And she
insisted: No one will notice. You'll see, they won't notice. It merges into
the pattern and the colors. A tremendous glee in my bones: No! You can
see it! You can! Only to annoy her, because I don't give a damn about that
stupid sweater, and whether it's got a darn in it or not. But her efforts to
lie, to pretend innocence, to demolish every problem with words, with
pretense. What a laugh. Everything turned into a game. Where did it
come from, that gleefulness? Maybe the appalling discrepancy between
the plain facts and her pretense. And maybe the glee broke out whenever
I discovered that it was something I had in common with her. How well
I know those reactions in myself, those deceptions. Avishai said, "As soon
as he began to wear it, he made a hole in it. I wore it all the time, and
there was nothing wrong. Nothing's good enough for him."

"What are you interfering for?" She shuts him up. She holds back her
laughter with an effort. She too is swept up in the hilarity of this game.
You can see it, you can't. As if it mattered. I never gave my clothes a
thought. Ignoring such things, perhaps even poverty itself, seemed more
manly to me. What's happening to me? It's not cold now. We'll take it off.
Like this — over the shoulders, with the arms knotted around the neck.
That's it. It's the fashion. That's how she wore her sweater too, on that
night. The fashion today is against uniforms. My lousy luck. The minute
you get home you take off your uniform. Why? Uniforms are actually
attractive, they're manly. But no. That's the fashion today. As if it's a disgrace to serve in the army at all. My shirt looks okay like this. I'm losing
my self-confidence. What's happening to me? There's no answer from
anywhere. How many hours am I going to go on standing here?

A chilly wind blows through the pine trees in Lincoln Street. There are
lights on in the windows. His heart tells him that she's at home and that
in the end he'll see her coming out. If only he knew her family name, he
would go in and look for it on one of the doors, ring the bell and ask for
Ziva. He feels that he would have the confidence to do it. But he can't go
from door to door and ask if there's some Ziva living there. And what if
she doesn't come out of her house all night long? And what if she isn't at
home at all and only returns late at night? Should he listen to his heart,
which tells him she's at home and in the end she'll come out and see him?
Every now and then he crosses the road and walks along the pavement,
trying to see something through the windows. Maybe her face will catch

the light and he'll be able to locate the apartment. But most of the windows are curtained and shuttered, and there's nothing to see. He gathers up his courage and goes into the stairwell. He'll listen outside the doors. Maybe he'll hear voices, maybe he'll hear her voice. He pauses outside every door, reads the names on them, tests to see how they sound in combination with Ziva's name. He strains his ears. There's someone coming down the stairs. The fear of being caught like a thief galvanizes him: A religious woman descends to the landing where he's standing. He addresses her and she ignores him. Is it out of modesty? He persists and addresses her again, more in fear of his presence there seeming suspicious than in the hope of getting an answer out of her: "Excuse me, madam, maybe you know where Ziva lives?" She ignores his question, takes no notice of his presence, and continues descending the stairs. Maybe she doesn't understand Hebrew, perhaps something about him frightens her? Maybe it's his old clothes?

He waits for her to leave the stairwell and continues making his way from door to door, listening for voices. And how does he know that he'll recognize her voice, even if he does hear it? So much time has passed since he spoke to her, so many voices have clamored in his ears since then. He only met her once. And her voice was sometimes choked, so subdued it was almost inaudible. The whole affair begins to seem exceedingly strange to him. On the second day of hanging about outside her house, with the patience of a saint, the stubbornness of an animal, the question suddenly strikes him like a thunderbolt: What does he want of her? What's he to her? Instantaneous sobriety, a sinking heart, shame. He rushes out of the building. Lest she see him in his disgrace. He must look like a madman. She'll begin to be afraid of him. Again he stands in the street, opposite the house, wanting to go away and unable to do so. Something still tells him that this is a rare opportunity, that if he misses it — all will be lost. Perhaps it's the inner voice of life, which is wiser than common sense? Why should indifference and toughness be the sign of manliness? Maybe it would be more manly to lie opposite the home of the beloved all night long and howl like a mad cat, to pierce her with the pain of his terrible longing, of his inability to live without her, without metaphors or clever words from the movies — just a huge howl, straight from the guts, which would surmount all the barriers and obstacles and demand the fulfillment of the promises made to each other by their bodies, when they were so close, when they thirsted for contact and were prematurely parted.

He's already told himself a hundred times as he paces the pavement outside the building that she might be with her boyfriend, in his room. He's trying to hurt himself, suppress his hopes, get out of the trap. In the circle of light cast by the lamp in the student's room he imagines them necking, laughing, talking about philosophy, sufficient unto themselves, full of themselves, steeped in unexampled beauty; the special beauty she casts on everything connected with her. He has no place at her side, no place at all. The student tells her about his travels to dangerous places beyond the border, about the red rock of Petra that marks a man for life. An admiring blush suffuses her face, whose complexion is so fair and soft, sensitive to every shift of feeling, almost transparent, and her stooping shoulders and outstretched neck sway in devotion and gratitude.

The street is already completely dark. Every now and then the light goes on in the stairwell, someone coming out, someone going in. The desire to see her is as painful as a disease. Something in his chest begins to quiver in rage, in supplication, in despair — is this the howl seeking to break out? Didn't I sit there on the wall opposite Terra Sancta and embrace her? Didn't I stand here in front of her house as she walked away and didn't she turn around, before going inside, so that I could see her face again? Didn't she tell me all those things? She wouldn't make a fool of me. We're twin souls. I won't give in now. I won't. There's no choice. I'll have to humiliate myself and exploit the little darlings. He succeeds in tearing himself away and heads for Rehavia.

He could see part of the illuminated room through the flimsy curtain, but the musicians were invisible. Perhaps they were in the other part of the room, or in some other room not facing the street. Although the windows were closed he could hear the music clearly. He knew that they played chamber music on Friday nights, but not so early. He'd never heard this particular piece before. But if he listened carefully, he would hear something very familiar: the sense of danger and the intense excitement the danger arouses in him. Like the thrill of walking on the edge of an abyss. The moment when you can win everything or lose everything. For a long time he listened and calculated his chances according to the music, waiting for them to finish playing. His agitation subsided somewhat, perhaps because at the last moment he found a strategy, and was no longer running around in a void.

Ressler's mother opened the door. When she heard his request she said, "Come in," but she called Yossie to come out into the hall. Avner remained standing there until Yossie arrived, his face frozen with astonishment at seeing him.

"What's up?" he mumbled.

"I have to talk to you," said Avner. "Could you come outside for a few minutes?"

"We're just about to have dinner," said Yossie. "What's wrong?"

"Ten minutes."

"Wait a second."

Yossie returned to the room and held a whispered conversation with his parents. His little sister suddenly peeped into the hallway, her eyes met Avner's, he smiled at her, and she immediately withdrew and laughed. Yossie came back and they went outside into the street.

"Listen," said Avner, "I feel that I have to tell you something, and I can't put it off. All I ask is for you to promise me that it won't go any farther, and you won't tell anyone."

"All right," said Yossie, somewhat impatiently. "What is it?"

"I broke your guitar."

Yossie didn't say a word; he only looked at Avner in the darkness with an expression of disbelief on his face, wondering what was coming next.

"You don't believe me," said Avner.

Yossie was silent.

"We stayed behind at lunchtime, on duty, Albert and I, Albert went out to take a leak, and I was left alone in the barracks and I broke it. I know you won't forgive me, but I can't keep it to myself any longer."

Yossie took a few steps and sat down on the bench next to the bus stop. He mumbled: "It's impossible."

"Melabbes knows about it," said Avner.

"Was he in on it too?"

"No. But he guessed afterward, when it was discovered."

"Why? Why?"

Now Avner was silent.

"How dare you? You and your big act. As if you love music. You're just scum. You know what it means to break a musical instrument? It's like killing life. It's murder!" At last his rage flared up, reconnecting him to that moment when he sat on his bed, mourning the shattered guitar lying on his knees, like the body of her son on the virgin's lap. "You were always a criminal and you've remained a criminal. You'll pay for this!"

"In any case I intend paying you however much it costs. After basic training, when I'm in some unit, I'll use all my free time, all my leave, to work. I'll scrape the money together and pay you the price of the guitar. I promise you."

"I don't want your favors! I don't want to have anything to do with you anymore. You hear? Nothing at all! What harm have I ever done you? Why did you do it? What do you want of me?"

"I came to confess to you, to ask you to forgive me."

"I don't need your confessions. I want my guitar. That guitar. It was given to me as a present. I was already beginning to forget about it. All the pain. And now you come and stir it all up again. Who asked you to come and talk about it? What do you think, that if you come and confess and ask forgiveness, then I'll forgive you? I'll never forgive you as long as I live! It doesn't wipe out what you did. It doesn't bring back my guitar. You murdered it. You're a murderer!"

Yossie fell silent for a moment, then he frowned and fixed his eyes on Avner: "And what about Ben-Hamo? We blamed him for nothing, we beat him up for nothing."

"Yes," said Avner, "he had nothing to do with it. He didn't do anything. So you see, you and your pals aren't saints either."

"Damn you, Avner, damn you! You're to blame for that too. It was all your fault, you should go and beg him to forgive you. You saw him being beaten up, you saw him being blamed for what you did — and you sat there watching and you didn't say a word."

"Why did you pick on him for nothing, without any proof? Why did you make him into your victim? You're big heroes when it comes to a poor bastard like Ben-Hamo, who hasn't got any friends to come to his help."

"How dare you preach to me? Can you hear what you're saying? When you're the one to blame! You did it!"

"My guilt toward Ben-Hamo is my business. It's between the two of us. I'll tell him everything and ask him to forgive me. Don't worry. However primitive and stupid he is, I'm sure he's capable of more understanding and forgiveness than you are."

Yossie looked at his watch. "I have to go home now." He stood up. Avner put a hand on his shoulder, pressed down hard, and made him sit down again.

"You'll stay a little longer. I haven't finished what I want to say to you yet."

"They're waiting for me to come and eat. What do you want of me? I don't want to talk to you!"

"I'm opening my wounds to you, and you tell me that they're waiting for you to come and eat? What are you, a little boy?"

"Tell me, do you think that this is some lousy Hollywood movie? What do you want of me?"

"Your friendship."

"What?"

"Your friendship. I did what I did because you're mean to me. You're all mean to me, you and your friends. You think you're superior to everybody else. That you can trample on other people. And now I'm appealing to your better nature. I need you to help me. Show that for once you can be generous, that you can behave like a man instead of a spoiled child. Don't waste this opportunity. Man, I'm appealing to your better nature."

He waited for Ressler's response, but it didn't come. He saw his face in the darkness, his lips were trembling, as if he were whispering something furiously and soundlessly to himself. Now he knew that the way was open before him.

Avner said: "Where is she?"

Yossie looked at him inquiringly.

"Where is she?"

"Who?"

"Ziva. You know. Stop pretending."

"I don't know. What do you think I am, her keeper?"

"What's her family name?"

"Shorr."

"I never saw that name on any of the doors in her house in Lincoln Street."

"She doesn't live in Lincoln Street. She lives in Gaza Street."

"Not in Lincoln?"

"No."

"That's strange." Avner reflected for a moment, giving Yossie a suspicious, penetrating look. "Tell me, does her boyfriend, that student, live in Lincoln Street?"

"I think he's got a room in the German Colony."

"I have to see Miri," Avner announced.

"Go ahead, who's stopping you?"

"Help me, for God's sake, behave like a human being. Where does she live? What's her family name? Where can I find her?"

"She lives in that big apartment block on King George Street, next to the Knesset. Entrance Three. Their name's Guttman. Am I free to go?"

"Wait a minute. Don't tell anyone about this conversation. I'm asking you. Be a friend for once in your life!"

"I never want to talk to you again."

Her fallen face is lifeless as a mask. The sight of this face makes it possible to understand a lot of wasted words. Its features sag, as if they've lost their grip. A terrible weariness makes them slump, a weariness of life, a total surrender. The eyes have black hollows under them, dull eyes, hardly moving in their sockets, half closed behind the cigarette smoke. They rise laboriously to greet him, and the two lines running down the cheeks are the only features in this face that are not limp but fierce, cruel, vehement, deep. As if that's where the crack took place, where the collapse began. She tries to smile and her hand tremulously crushes the cigarette in the ashtray.

"Micky's a famous soccer star," says Alon.

Her hand shakes as she gropes for the pack of cigarettes lying on the table next to her, and as she lights the cigarette. With the first puffs she straightens her head, which was drooping and tilted slightly to one side, and the hand holding the cigarette goes on shaking. Her eyes widen slightly as they examine Micky's face. Her husband fills in the silence with a few polite questions about where Micky lives and his family and plans. And again her head falls forward and sideways, and she breaks into harsh coughing and lays her hand on her heart. As opposed to the ruin of her face, her light chestnut hair is untouched by gray. In the remnants of the ruins it is still possible to discern a certain resemblance to the lines of Alon's face. Her voice is thick and very hoarse.

"Everything's all right," she said, "everything will be all right."

Her husband asked about Micky's sporting achievements and those of his team. Then he went to make them tea.

She said to Micky: "You know, Alon has a talent for drawing. Has he ever shown you his drawings?" Her thick, hoarse voice choked again on a fit of coughing. She put out the cigarette she just lit in the ashtray, shaking her head as if to say: No, no. Her voice tried to break through the coughing, to say something, but without success. Her face reddened with the effort and her eyes filled with tears. All this added a little vitality to her appearance.

Alon said: "You smoke too much."

The husband shook his finger at him quickly from the doorway, telling him silently to drop the subject.

When her coughing subsided, she drew her lips into an apologetic smile: "I'm not feeling too well," she croaked, "I'm a little ill. But everything's all right. Everything will be all right."

Perhaps her words conveyed a prearranged signal between them. In any case Alon did not wait for tea to be served. He rose and left the room, with Micky following him. Alon did not seem particularly upset; perhaps he was used to it. Micky didn't know what to say. When they were outside, Alon showed him a little cardboard box in his hand, opened it, and said: "Look." He displayed the little pottery lamp that they had found broken in the sands of Barnea, and which was now mended and whole again. He held it out to Micky, who took it, examined it, and said: "Fantastic, you can hardly see the join. You did a great job."

"Look at these rings going around it, how precise and delicate they are," said Alon, "and the shape, with the neck rising like a jar. They really did make lamps like this one on a wheel, like jars, and not in molds, like the other candles. It's a pity the handle's missing." He showed Micky two flaws on the back of the vessel — the places where the rounded handle had been attached to it. "Remember I said it was from the Arab period? I was right. I asked someone who knows the subject. This type of lamp is called a shoe-lamp, because of its shape, which is supposed to resemble a shoe. Look at the lip — you can still see the soot. Imagine, this lamp you're now holding in your hand was in somebody's hand in Eretz Israel a thousand years ago, maybe even more. Before the Crusader conquest! Maybe he was a Jew. There was a Jewish community in Ashkelon during that period; maybe they were also in the place where we found it. Fantastic, isn't it?"

"Yes," said Micky. He held the lamp out to Alon.

"You take it," said Alon. "A present from me. A souvenir of the series."

"Are you crazy?" Micky protested. "I can't take it from you. I remember how excited and happy you were when you discovered it, how precious it was to you."

"If it wasn't worth something to me," said Alon, "I wouldn't give it to you."

"Really," said Micky, "it makes me feel uncomfortable. I don't deserve it. I'm an ignoramus about those things. I don't have a clue about the history of Eretz Israel, I don't know a thing about archaeology. For you that lamp is full of meaning and importance."

A pain pierced Micky's heart, and he didn't know where it came from. Was it the beginning of guilt? He didn't want to accept the lamp, he absolutely didn't want to. For some reason it gave rise in him to a feeling of strangeness and reluctance, as if he were touching some mystery that carried a curse. Alon returned the little pottery vessel to its cardboard box and put it into Micky's hand. He said: "The history of Eretz Israel is the history of us all, including you, even if you don't know anything about it. It belongs to you as much as it belongs to me."

"You never told me that you drew," said Micky.

"Nonsense," said Alon. "I stopped long ago. My mother makes a fuss about it."

"Show me something."

"Nonsense, leave it alone."

"What do you care, show me something."

"You really want me to?"

"Yes, absolutely."

Alon looked at his watch. They had some time before going to fetch Dafna for supper in the dining room. They went into a room in one of the buildings and Alon smiled in demonstrative relief to find it empty.

"I'll show you something no one else has seen. No one knows I did it. Except for Dafna, of course."

Alon pulled a cardboard file from the bottom of one of the cupboard drawers. They sat down on his bed. He removed a large sketching pad from the file, closed the file, and placed the pad on top of it. When Alon opened the pad and leafed through it, Micky caught his breath: The pages were full of pencil and charcoal sketches of a nude girl whose identity was unmistakable. Alon turned the pages slowly, looking for a few drawings that seemed to him most successful and worthy of display. As he did so, the nude pictures passed before Micky's eyes, in various poses of standing, sitting, and lying down. Micky's heart pounded in amazement and excitement. Alon did not seem in the least embarrassed to be showing him his girlfriend's nakedness. He stopped turning the pages upon reaching a pencil drawing in which she appeared sitting on the edge of the bed, one knee raised, hiding her pudenda, one hand behind her nape, lifting one breast higher than the other, her neck stretched, slightly tilted, her head thrown back, her eyes closed and her lips slightly parted, exposing the tips of two flawless, shining front teeth. There was something especially moving in the oblique line stretching from her exposed armpit, with the hair etched in delicate detail, to the erect breast and the dropped breast, with their flowery nipples, and the smoothly narrowing waist. A marvelous combination of innocence and pride. Micky sensed Alon's eyes on his face, trying to gauge his reaction. He turned his eyes away from the drawing and looked down. His heart pounded; he was shaken to the core. The picture seemed glorious to him, heartbreakingly beautiful. Alon went on turning the pages, and once more there passed before Micky's eyes the various shapes of her nudity, the shadows of her pudenda, the curves of her breasts, her amazingly narrow waist, her belly. He wanted to say something but his throat was dry.

Alon paused again at a portrait of her face and the upper half of her body. She was looking directly at the viewer with the same secret, quizzical smile in her small, clear eyes. The line of her neck and the slope of her shoulder were drawn caressingly, with a sure, gentle hand, full of love.

In the end Micky exclaimed: "Listen, you're an artist! You're a real artist! I didn't know! I didn't know that you were capable of anything like this!"

Alon smiled a shy, gratified smile, his eyes thanking Micky for the compliment. "I gave it up long ago," he said, "I lost interest in it."

"You don't realize what a tremendous gift you've got!"

"Today I'm interested in other things."

"How would the people on the kibbutz react if they saw them?" asked Micky.

"They wouldn't like it," Alon admitted.

"I thought that on kibbutzim people were more liberal about such things."

"Where from! Not on your life! You're probably thinking about free love and all those stories. All that belongs to past history. If they found out about these pictures, I'd never hear the end of it. You can't imagine how much gossip there is on the kibbutz, how much hypocrisy. In any case they already think I'm not all there. This is all they need to decide I'm a sex maniac too, and to throw mud at both of us. But don't worry, they'll never see them."

"Where did you draw them?"

"In my mother's room, when she was in the hospital and her husband went to see her there. We had plenty of time. I see that you really like them."

"They're wonderful!" said Micky. "I can't get over it. I never knew you were so talented. You draw marvelously. And she's really beautiful."

Alon smiled again, restraining his happiness, and examined Micky's eyes to see how sincere his admiration was.

Micky went on: "You're simply an artist. That's all. You're an artist, and that can explain a lot."

"You think artists are weird. Is that what you mean?"

"Sometimes there's something strange about you, hard to understand. Something about the way you behave. The courage not to give a damn about all kinds of things, not to care what people will think of you, what they'll say. To believe in yourself."

"I don't see myself as an artist," said Alon. "I've lost interest in it. Like you've lost interest in soccer. Maybe I'll go back to it one day as a hobby. But it can't fill my life."

"I wouldn't like Dafna to know that I've seen these drawings," said Micky.

"Why?"

"Maybe she'll be embarrassed at the idea of me seeing her naked."

"I don't have any secrets from her. I never lie to her. I'd be incapable of it."

"But you don't have to tell her everything."

"You didn't see her naked. Of course you didn't. You saw my drawings, the nudity that I invented for her. It's not her. It's not a photograph of her. It's how I see a nude woman. And I'm not ashamed in front of you. I don't have any secrets from you either. Does that embarrass you?"

"A bit, at first," Micky admitted.

There was a sound of footsteps approaching the door. Alon closed the pad, put it back in the file, and tied the laces carefully, as if they were a complicated lock, impossible to open. Someone came into the room. Alon exchanged a brief "Hi" with him, returned the file to its place in the cupboard, and went outside with Micky. What made him so sure that none of his roommates would pry into his file and discover the secret drawings? Micky wondered. And maybe they already had and Alon in his innocence didn't know it? Better not to ask and undermine his confidence. Because he himself would never dream of prying into other people's belongings, he was sure that everybody behaved the same way. Micky could not get rid of the uneasy feeling that he had taken advantage of his friend's innocence and desecrated his most beautiful secrets.

What's eating him, why is he so restless? his mother asks him. His eyes look strange, she says to him. Why should she say that? It seems to him that he is quite calm. Has she guessed something? There's nothing to be afraid of. Everything will be over soon. Why didn't he eat anything at supper? she asks him. Something in her voice accuses him of hiding something from her. Why doesn't she go to visit their neighbor already, as she usually does at this hour of the evening? In an hour's time his sisters will come. From them he has nothing to fear, they leave him alone, they hardly speak to him. His hour is the time between her going to visit the neighbor and his sisters' arrival. The kerosene lamp casts strange shadows over the walls of the hut, you could see entire stories in them, like movies. There were old women who might know how to guess the future by these shadows, but for him who had made up his mind to do the deed there was no future. To renounce everything and cling to the moment. To detach the act from its immediate or far-reaching consequences, to concentrate and listen only to the silence of the action. As if it had all been done long ago and now you were only going through the motions, repeating the steps, the beats. Like a dance. Without hope. In supreme necessity. In free will. The body knows the plan. This is the secret of serenity. For the body is free and only the soul is bound in chains. A smile rises to Rahamim's lips. His mother gives him an angry smile, full of reproach. He begins to hum.

The narcissus has bewitched me, the flowers of the stock fall like rain. I turned hither and thither, my sadness subsided. The nectar of the rose bursts forth, healing all pain. To breathe its scent restores one's soul. Oh, friends, he is of the dawn . . .

His mother mutters something. What's he up to, humming to himself, staring at the shadows on the wall? What's eating him, why is he so restless?

They stand next to a carob tree, on the pavement of King George Street, opposite the Yeshurun Synagogue, after having walked a little way from her house. She has a dark-gray cardigan slung over her shoulders, and she pulls the two halves tighter to her chest, because it's cold outside.

"Don't be shy, Avner," she says, "tell Auntie Miri all about it. If you've shown up on my doorstep, you must need something. So don't be shy to use Auntie Miri. That's what she's here for, after all, to be useful."

He listens and smiles what he regards as his darkest, most mysterious, most captivating smile — will she be able to make it out in the dark? How well he knows that bitter, knowing style of talking, that ironic, provocative self-abasement, with its ostentatious display of disillusion and lack of expectations. She gives him a look calculated to show that she can see right through him, that his motives are crystal clear to her, and that she has no intention of falling into his trap again. He knows that to get her cooperation he must be sincere, speak with the humility that bears the stamp of the truth. But the need to go beyond the truth, to test the other possibilities, is stronger than he is: Sometimes the pleasure of playing the game is worth even more than the joy of winning it.

"What do you want? Let's have it. I don't have all night."

He remains silent and subjects her to his special smile.

"It's cold standing here. What are you waiting for?"

"I've got a place."

"A place?"

"I've got the keys to my brother-in-law's shop. There's a little store-room there, it's quiet, no one will disturb us there."

"What are you talking about? Have you gone mad?'

"Come, be with me, I'm terribly lonely."

"It seems to me that you're trying to put on a repeat performance of something you already did once before."

"No. I really want you. I need you badly. Be good to me, please. Not like I was with you then. Give me a chance to show you that I'm not what you think I am."

"Look, if you're trying to persuade me to let you go to bed with me, you can forget it. I don't want to. I simply don't want to. Do you understand? Don't make any mistake about it!"

"Okay. Then give me an hour and be with me like a friend. I need to talk, I have to pour my heart out, and there's no one to listen to me."

"I'm not the welfare bureau."

If she were as sure as she sounded, she would have gone home and left him standing there.

"But you're kind," he says, "and I need your kindness, your under-standing. Give me that chance."

"You don't know anything about me. You've seen me twice. What kind of demands are you making of me?"

"I know that you're kindhearted and that you'll help me."

"Look, don't think I'm stupid. You came to ask me where Ziva is. Why don't you come straight to the point?'

"No," he says, "I don't have a chance with Ziva. That was just a dream. I've woken up. I know she's making a fool of me. If you like, we can talk about that too. There are things I want to understand, and you're the only one who can help me. Once I thought I knew all there was to know about girls. Now I've come to realize that I don't understand the first thing about them."

"Why do you think that she's making a fool of you?"

"That night, after the party at Hanan's, when we were alone together, I saw her home, to the building she said was where she lived, in Lincoln Street. And now I know that she doesn't live there at all. She was trying to get rid of me. She took me there to get rid of me, so that I wouldn't know where she really lives. So I wouldn't be able to get in touch with her again. After I left, I suppose she must have slipped out and gone home."

He tries to read her face for signs of confirmation or refutation of this supposition, but her face is blank.

"And now that you don't have any other choice, you're prepared to make do with a substitute — me?"

"You're not a substitute! How can you say such a thing? I reached you after other stations on the way, like reaching the end of a journey at last."

"I'm not a station on some line that you're traveling on, get that clear.

In any case I might as well tell you right away that she's not in Jerusalem at the moment. She's gone to Tel Aviv and she'll only be back on Sunday. Now you've got all the information you wanted. So you can stop playing absurd games with me. Don't make a fool of yourself. You're no good at it, Avner, take it from me."

"You don't understand me," he says, "I've woken up from that dream. I don't interest her. I've never been to Petra, I don't know anything about philosophy, so why not make a fool of me. Tell her she needn't worry. I won't go looking for her."

"What, she told you her boyfriend's been to Petra?" Miri snorts ironically.

"Isn't that true either?"

"I don't want to talk about it. I don't know anything about it." Her smile is malicious.

He nods. Gradually the lies and the empty words are becoming true: He desires this ironic girl, not as a means of reaching Ziva, not as a substitute to fill the loneliness of the evening ahead of him, he desires her in truth, for what she is.

"Won't you stay with me? Just for an hour. We'll talk. I won't do anything you don't want me to. I promise. I love you. I really love you."

"And you're sure that you're going to get what you want."

"Yes," he admits.

"What makes you so sure?"

"I've got this special power that brings out the best in people, the kindness, the generosity, the forgiveness. These qualities exist in everybody, but they don't always come out. I know how to bring them out, to make them bud and blossom like flowers."

"You're just a demagogue, Avner."

He suppresses the joy that breaks out in his heart at the sound of these words. The international words, her words and Ziva's words, that sound like strange, mysterious, Hottentotish melodies! Miri's long silhouette under the shade of the carob tree draws in her shoulders, gathers up the cardigan under her neck, as if she's afraid of the cold, or in some impulse of needless modesty. How much beauty and femininity there is in her gesture! The light from the street lamp falls on her obliquely, caresses her slightly bowed back, her dark, sleek, abundant hair. More and more he is convinced that his heart is far from tricks and wiles. Something reserved in her early-burgeoning femininity, something in the armor of bitter irony with which she clothes herself, to protect her from harm, from disappointment, from exaggerated hopes, something in her smile, skeptical, resigned, despairing, makes it very clear to him who is the lady here and who the ruffian. All this floods him with desire and impatience to charge and conquer, with a stubborn readiness to risk everything for the faint chance of touching the real thing, of miraculously transforming himself and her.

He draws nearer to her, and puts his hand on her waist, urging her to move, to come with him. She walks silently at his side, very slowly, he smells the smell of her hair — the fresh scent of some expensive imported soap, he imagines. He whispers in her ear: "You'll see, I'll be good to you, better than I've ever been in my life. You know how to hear, don't you? You can hear the things that aren't said. Can you hear that I'm telling you the truth?"

She doesn't reply. She walks with him and her face is sad, as if she is being led away to serve her term of punishment. He knows that she is saying to herself: I'm doing something I'll regret again. I'm acting against reason again, against experience, even against feeling. I don't want this. Why am I going with him?

> The whole valley was illuminated by the fire. Evening had already fallen and the sky was red with the light of the flames, while the dense, heavy clouds of smoke spread over the entire area. The fire broke out at six in the evening in the yard of the regional plant. At about seven o'clock we reached the spot and a terrible scene greeted our eyes. A large part of the cotton bales were on fire. There were about fifty tons of processed cotton in bales of a quarter of a ton in the yard. More than half went up in flames. The warehouse too and many of the platforms were burned. The fire engines from Afula were already there and dozens of trucks with people from all the kibbutzim in the area arrived. Afterward fire engines arrived from Ramat David and Haifa too. Luckily, the plant itself was undamaged. Together with the people from the surrounding kibbutzim and policemen and soldiers who came to help, we put together big bales for removal from the danger zone. We were all very depressed. How much labor and sweat, anxiety and hope we had invested in growing and picking the cotton; now it was all being ruthlessly consumed by the fire. The older members probably remember what it feels like from the days of the troubles in our country, when the Arabs burned the fields. But this time there was no enemy. Only blind chance, or carelessness. We spent a gloomy New Year grieving for the fruits of our labors that had gone down the drain, but we did not despair. This year we'll sow double the amount of cotton, and

once more contribute our share to the crop of the future, which will lead our country to economic independence. Gideon M.

Micky goes on leafing through the stenciled pages that Alon handed him after he had finished reading them himself. Before supper one of the members gave Alon a few of the kibbutz news sheets from recent weeks, which have apparently been kept especially for him, to inform him of what has been happening on the home front when he comes on leave from the army. After the meal they pushed the tables and chairs into a corner, struck up folk-dance tunes on an accordion and an Arab clay drum, and the young people and a few of the older ones began dancing, in couples and in a circle. Alon and Dafna sat next to him on a bench against the wall. After he explained to them that he didn't know how to dance, that he didn't have the first idea of how to set about it at all, they remained at his side, instead of joining their friends. The noise of the music and singing made it impossible to talk. Micky glances through the newspapers handed to him by Alon, reading a paragraph here and there. He finds nothing to excite his interest, nothing that deserves thought, nothing capable of explaining the things he has difficulty in understanding. It is impossible to explain a person's behavior by the place where he was brought up. He finds it difficult, too, to comprehend the nature of Alon's relationship with his peer group. A few of them come up to them, are introduced to Micky, express their surprise and pleasure at discovering the famous soccer player in their midst. Others walk past them and exchange hidden smiles and quick, mocking winks: The story of the stolen uniform has apparently taken wing, gone to join a whole stock of anecdotes about Alon and previous exploits of his, which Micky knows nothing about. There are no secrets in this family.

Dafna is wearing a white blouse embroidered around the neck and shoulders in different colors, in line with the prevailing fashion among the girls. Her hair is still damp from the shower. She is sparkling with freshness. Something about her says that she has a secret. He thinks he knows what the secret is. This secret has been thrilling his heart ever since he saw her nakedness in Alon's drawings. Sometimes he is afraid to look in her direction, in case she discovers her desecrated secret in his eyes. Her small, brown eyes, which are so clear and penetrating, smile secretly to themselves as they ceaselessly scan her surroundings. Her snub nose, with its pointed tip, underlines something childish and arrogant in the calm face, whose expression is one of inner harmony and poise. She protects him, Micky says to himself; she shields him from the smiles and winks, from the mockery and sneers of the group. Micky feels an urge to demonstrate his reservations to the people around him, to make it clear to them that he has nothing to do with Alon's affairs. And immediately afterward his heart contracts in a pang of shame and guilt: What do I care about all these people, what are they to me compared with him?

"Why don't you dance?" he asks them. "I don't want you to sit out on my account. On the contrary, I'd like to see how you dance."

Dafna looks inquiringly at Alon, as if to ask whether to take Micky's words at face value. Alon smiles sadly. Apparently he doesn't want to dance. Dafna looks at the dancers, who have begun to dance "For Love Delights," and joins softly in their singing, swaying her shoulders and her head in time to the music. Alon gets up and they join in the dance. Micky watches them curiously. Strange to see Alon dancing. It seems so incompatible with his general air of clumsiness. But so does his artistry in drawing. He's full of contradictions that Micky can't resolve. They merge with the other dancers, executing the steps to the delicate tune neatly and precisely. A surprising beauty bathes them in its glow, an intimacy in the way they hold hands, as they bend and straighten, singing with the others. And her full breasts in the embroidered blouse are outlined against the material, press up against it and separate from it, revealing once more the glorious body he saw in the drawings. How stupid of him to think she wasn't beautiful, when he saw her as he got off the bus. Her face is full of a quiet, confident beauty; the loveliness of her body illuminates everything about her, including Alon. How beautiful they are as they execute the complicated, artificial steps, together with all the other dancers, a part, despite everything, of this big family, this special world, which is so remote from his. Beauty should lift your spirits, make you happy — why then does the beauty suffusing Dafna and Alon as they dance "For Love Delights" give Micky a feeling of dull pain, shame, and bitter resentment against himself: Why did I come here? What did I need all this for? *Come let us dance, for my heart desires it, for love delights in the dance.* He feels his chest tighten with suppressed tears and insult, like someone knocking again and again at a door that does not open.

He waits a moment longer until he is sure that his mother is settled in at the neighbor's. He leaves the shack, arrives at the hiding place where he has secreted the parcel wrapped up in newspaper. He conceals it under

his shirt. It's quiet outside. The old man must be back from the synagogue already, he's probably gone to bed. He approaches the little hut.
There's nobody in sight. He puts his ear to the door, and it seems to him
that he can hear him snoring. He takes the newspaper parcel out of his
shirt, unwraps it, and grasps the bottle by the neck. He opens it and
begins walking around the shack, pouring the contents of the bottle onto
the bottom of the walls. It isn't enough to go right around, but the corner
where the bed is situated is well drenched. He takes the box of matches
out of his pocket, lights a match, holds it to the wet patch at the bottom
of the wall, and waits for the flame to grow and spread.

Everything is accomplished slowly and silently and in complete tranquility. To such an extent that he deviates from his original plan. Instead
of running straight to the wadi, throwing the bottle and the matches into
the water, and hurrying home before the flames leap up and the commotion breaks out — he stands and waits, watching the beginning of the
fire, with no desire to run. There are moments of stillness in the night
when the air fills with the spirits of the dead who come to see us, to touch
the miracle of our bodies. Something in the silence of this moment and
the height of his longings resembles those moments. It's impossible to
take a step, to look around, to move a muscle. His whole being is spellbound by passivity, as in a dream. The cloak of stillness enveloping him,
for all its impermeability, is thin and stretched to the breaking point. And
it keeps stretching all the time.

All at once his ears, his head, his chest are invaded by the sounds of the
shouts and the commotion. The flames leap up and illuminate the faces
of the people around him, carrying pails of water, beating blankets,
pouncing on him. And his mother's face huge and terrible, screaming
into his face, and he can't understand a word she says. As if the words
are being spoken in a foreign language. They drag him away and he lets
them do as they will with him. The terrible voices fall pitilessly on his
ears, they deafen him, and the leaping flames blind his eyes. They seize
him by the arms, they drag him, they pull him with great force. In a
moment they'll tear him to pieces. He offers no resistance. He pants for
breath, as if he has come running from a long way away. His body trembles. His body is afraid, his body weeps. His body dreams of its wholeness, of its freedom. *The narcissus has bewitched me, the flowers of the stock
fall like rain. I turned hither and thither, my sadness subsided. The nectar of
the rose bursts forth, healing all pain. To breathe its scent restores one's soul.
Oh, friends, he is of the dawn . . . The night star fades and day breaks like a
smile, trusting in whatever the Master of Destiny decrees. Oh, my friends, he*

is of the dawn . . . Suddenly morning will reveal itself in its nakedness, restoring life to the sleepers, calling them to set forth again. Oh, friends, he is of the dawn . . .

"Come on, dance with us, why don't you," Alon urges him.

"I told you, I don't know how to dance."

"But it's a Horah — you must know that!"

"No, I'm telling you, leave off."

She stands to the side, without interfering. If only she asked, he would join the circle and dance with them.

"I understand, you're still mad at me because of what I did this morning."

"No, of course not. That's finished and done with."

You can't stand the expression of sorrow and insult and victimization on his face. Why does it matter so much to him for you to dance with them? Does he see it as some kind of ceremony of reconciliation? After he gave you the antique lamp as a present, after he showed you the secret nude drawings, what else can he do to appease you? You steal a glance at Dafna, surprise her eyes examining you, curious, skeptical, suspicious. Will you pass the test? Don't hurt him. He doesn't know how to be mean. I can sense something hard and evasive in you. And he expects you to be at his side when he falls and help him up. Again you feel ashamed of your earlier reserve, when you tried to set yourself apart from Alon and the crazy things he did.

You dance with them. You haven't danced a Horah for years, but your feet still remember those skips and stamps. In the circle with them, with their friends, between the two of them. Your hand touches her, feels the warmth of her body, remembers the secrets of her nakedness. You can no longer separate her physical presence from the pictures haunting your imagination, thrilling you, and torturing you. You're haven't fully emerged into the adult world yet. You're still sleeping. Cradled in the cocoon of your dreams. When will you break out at last? You feel her eyes examining you. Maybe she can feel it? Maybe she knows? Something has happened between you, after all, something very intimate that no one must know about. As long as she doesn't realize what she's doing to you. As long as Alon doesn't tell her that he showed you the drawings. You hear Alon's voice croaking the words of the song next to you. His face is flushed with enthusiasm. In this too he invests himself wholeheartedly, honest and loyal as always. Somehow the reconciliation is accomplished. It's good to be with them. How full of love and beauty their world is. They're stronger than you are. Something deep still separates you from them. These moments, moments of premature longings, burn feverishly with the intoxication of illusion. You can't detach yourself from them, you can't resist them. Blindly, you can only soar with them and fall slowly to the ground, as in a dream — alone.

CHAPTER 29

Once more, as in the beginning, they isolated themselves, huddled together, consulted each other, defending themselves from the looming hostility, as if the barriers that had already fallen between us were unconsciously springing up again. As the hour of judgment, the hour of parting, approached, their hearts were no longer in the illusory friendship that had somehow, despite everything, come into being between us. The hour of awakening was at hand, when the old, established order, which was stronger than everything else, would reinstate itself again. Sitting at the end of the long line in front of the company offices, they sent dark, suspicious, helpless looks at the open door, as if it held the answer to the question in their hearts. Behind the table blocking the doorway sat the interviewer, the lieutenant who would decide their fates. They lowered their voices, spoke in whispers, like conspirators.

Peretz-Mental-Case suddenly raised his voice, breaking their self-imposed secrecy, defiantly challenging danger: "This is all eyewash! They wrote it all down long ago! At the beginning, at the intake center! This is just to make it legal. So they can say they talked to everyone, to find out where they want to go. As if they care what you want! Like hell they care! They wrote it all down long ago where we all are going to be."

They shut him up angrily, and he smiled under the narrow line of his mustache, the forgiving, superior smile of one who has learned the bitter lessons of experience. Peretz's interpretations of military law had long ceased to have any currency with his friends; nobody valued his knowledge in this field anymore. And he wagged his head at them as if to say: *Just wait, you'll soon see who was right.*

Zackie, whose family had lived in a mansion with servants to wait on them in the old country, the shrewd, good-humored Zackie, was down at the mouth too; he could not contain his pain. "What difference does it make?" he whispered. "They wrote it then, they wrote it now — if you're one of them, they'll put you in an office, you'll have a nice, clean job, maybe you'll get to be an officer. If you're black, you'll be an RP, they'll stick you in the kitchen, they'll make you clean shit. That's what it's like in Israel."

Ressler returned from his interview. In reply to the questioning eyes of his friends waiting their turn, he said: "He didn't tell me anything. But I think it'll be the IDF orchestra. I told him I wanted to be in an entertainment troupe too, but he asked me about playing all kinds of instruments, about my musical education. I don't mind which of the two it is."

Avner smiled sarcastically, as if to say: *There you are.* As if Ressler's words only went to confirm Zackie's complaint.

I asked: "What's wrong? Don't you think it makes sense for Yossie to be in the IDF orchestra or one of the entertainment troupes? Why shouldn't they take advantage of his talents?"

"Man!" said Avner. "You know that Zackie's terrific at math. Micha said so himself. They had a competition. So what do you think? You think it'll do him any good? He won't go where Micha's going, or where you are either."

"You don't know that."

"Trust me."

"And what about you?"

"I don't know. On the form they gave us at the intake center I said I wanted to be an MP. Maybe they'll think I'm good enough for that."

"Why did you ask for that of all things?"

"I didn't know then that it was something shameful. I had no idea about army folklore. I thought the uniform would suit me, that I'd look attractive and handsome in it. That hat and all those shining badges, and the white belts. Walking down the street like that — I thought it would impress the girls. Childish, I know. But that's what jumped into my head then. In any case I don't regret it, even now. Maybe because of it I won't be sent to something a lot worse."

"You know the kind of discipline they demand there, the order and punctuality? You and your problems with time."

"I'll have problems wherever I go, so what difference does it make?"

A pleasant breeze rustled the leaves of the eucalyptus tree not far behind us. Clouds sailed lazily through the sky, and a mild, warm winter light caressed our backs. Time slumbered like a cat in the sun, basking in the warmth of the day. And they sat apart from us, consulting each other in undertones, smoking glumly, as if the laughter was over, the squabbles and storms were over, the hour of reckoning had come, and the intimacy that had come into being, the camaraderie of daily life together, would not be counted to their credit.

"Actually, the most important thing as far as I'm concerned," Avner went on, "is being close to home. Maybe even in Jerusalem, in the Schneller barracks. It's really important to me to be able to work and earn a bit of money during my army service. They promised me at work that it would be okay as far as they're concerned. For you people it probably doesn't come up at all."

Benny stood next to the door. He had lost interest in us. His little eyes behind his glasses gazed into the distance. He was hardly aware of our presence. Each interview lasted two or three minutes. The queue advanced rapidly. Micky, who would be going off the next day on a training program that would end in a game against the Nahal team, counted the number of days left on the base after this, and the sense of the approaching end loomed up with astonishing clarity, filling him with an inexplicable joy. He saw the back of Alon, who was sitting on the chair in front of the table blocking the entrance to the office. The officer stood up and went into the room, coming back a moment later and resuming his seat. Micky was standing at the foot of the bottom step, a few yards from Alon's back. He was the next in line. It seemed to him that Alon's shoulders suddenly slumped, as if he had been hit. Alon stood up and saluted the officer, and when he passed Micky on the stairs, his face was flushed and his eyes evaded Micky's.

Alon sat down at the end of the line, under the eucalyptus. He was obviously very upset.

When Micky's interview was over, he went up to him immediately: "What happened?"

"Military police."

"He said so?"

"No, I saw it written on the form: Course for Military Policemen."

"Are you positive?"

"Yes. You know I've got good eyesight."

Micky was speechless with astonishment.

Alon said: "You know what this means to me? Listen, I don't know what's going to happen. I can't. I just can't. I'd rather not serve in the army at all."

"Maybe it's the CID. That could be interesting."

"Are you crazy? Can you see me in an MP's uniform? Can you see me coming home to the kibbutz like that? It's all over for me. I won't be an MP. Never."

"Why don't you talk to Benny? When we talked to him at the series about the Squad Commanders Course he said it would be okay."

"Benny? He did it to me. On purpose."

"Did you say in the interview that you asked to go on a Squad Commanders Course?"

"Yes. But he didn't even answer. He nodded and closed the file and the interview was over. What about you?"

"I don't care. If we're not together on the Squad Commanders Course, then it makes no difference to me where I go."

"Can you see me coming to the kibbutz with a Brasso uniform? Can you just imagine it?" Alon repeated the nightmare vision.

Again Micky feels anger building up inside him. Uniforms again. Why are uniforms so important to him? Alon is going off the rails again, turning into a Don Quixote, blocking off every possibility of communication, of help. And Micky feels a sense of relief at the thought that tomorrow he'll be leaving the base for a week, far away from all this misery.

Muallem came and took over from Benny guarding the office entrance. Benny descended the stairs and walked past the people sitting in line, waiting for their turn. When he passed Micky and Alon, Alon stood up. "Sir!" he said, "about the Squad Commanders Course, will it be okay?"

"What did the interviewer say?" asked Benny.

"He didn't say anything," said Alon.

Benny spread out his arms in a gesture of helplessness, as if to say: *If he didn't say anything, what can I say?*

Alon's voice shook: "But sir, I asked you, right?"

Benny stared at him with a kind of puzzled smile, he looked at him for a long time without saying anything.

Alon continued: "Sir, you said it would be all right."

"When did you ask?" Benny inquired.

"On the series, sir."

"Maybe it was too late. I don't know. But when I talked to you then, after you fired that shot on the night exercise, and I promised you that I'd try to help you, you weren't overenthusiastic, if I remember rightly; you had other ideas then, apparently. Look, you're not a child. Take responsibility for your decisions. You remember what I said to you then, about being strong? So be strong now."

"Sir, I'm asking you to help me get to a Squad Commanders Course. It's awfully important to me. I've learned something in the meantime, I understand more."

Benny said nothing. He smiled faintly, looked Alon up and down, as if he had never come across anything so peculiar in his life, and continued on his way.

I wasn't here then either, Micky remembers. I was training with the team, and he did something crazy. What's he going to do now? Perhaps I should stick by him now, to guard him from himself. So he doesn't do something crazy. Try to encourage him. But I have no choice. That's the way things worked out. And there's nothing I can do to change them. I have no choice in the matter. And for some reason I'm glad. Why should I deceive myself? I'm glad to have no choice in the matter, to have the decision taken out of my hands. He would have done everything he could to help me, to save me from myself. He would have behaved differently, no doubt about it. He would have found a way to get out of the training, to change the no-choice situation. He would have taken a risk for me. There's no doubt about it. But I don't know how to do it. I want to run away. I have to be tough, think about myself, get back to the main thing. And that's exactly what she said about me: something hard and evasive. She knows me. Better than I know myself.

They looked at Benny walking away. Alon narrowed his eyes, as if straining to concentrate on some saving thought.

"What did he say to you then about the strong?" asked Micky.

"He said they always broke first."

"Rubbish," said Micky. "You'll be fine. You hear? Don't do anything silly. I'm asking you. As a friend, I'm asking you. Control yourself, even if it's awfully strong, even if takes hold of your imagination. Promise me you won't do anything silly, that you won't break."

"Calm down," said Alon. "What are you afraid I'll do? Do you really think I'm crazy? Don't worry. I won't break. It'll be all right."

The thudding of heavy, dragging feet, and the rhythmic, threatening shouts accompanying it, rises at the bottom of the road, coming closer. Until the greenish animals appear, bowed down under their loads, frightened, running in a body of threes, knapsacks and other gear on their shoulders. New recruits from the intake center are standing on the hill, lowering their gear to the ground in front of them, sitting down, and standing up in time to the shouts. Even from far away we can see the too-tight berets squashed down on their heads, their staring faces, stiff with dread and strangeness, their lost eyes. As in the mirror of time we see the picture reflected in all its repulsive ugliness, riveting and provocative. None of us is roused to cry: *Raw meat! Raw meat!* Only one or two spit out a venomous curse, to banish the dull, heavy sadness it awakens in their hearts. And we can't take our eyes off it. They're sitting on exactly the same hill, their instructor has gone off and left them there, sitting and waiting for the unknown. At first they're afraid to move, as if some hidden eye is watching them. Then they grow bolder, turn their heads, and settle into more comfortable positions. They don't seem to be talking to each other. Probably they don't know each other yet. Or perhaps they're afraid that talking is forbidden. It's difficult to distinguish typical faces among them. Perhaps they too have their Miller, who is reading a book in a foreign language and who will die one night on the sands of Barnea, and their Ben-Hamo who is collecting somebody's cigarette butts, and who will not return from his leave because he has been arrested for setting fire to a shack in the transit camp, and others who will fall by the roadside, who will pay on behalf of them all the price of the transformation and the removal of the taint and the sense of rebirth, the price of the immunity and the sinking of the soul, the price of the transient friendships between strangers, the price of the promises of intimacy and camaraderie, which had been fulfilled, which had failed. They look like lumps of raw material over there on the hill, formless, undifferentiated, like clay in the hands of the potter. This, at least, is what it looks like from a distance. And this, in any case, is what I want to believe, for it is inconceivable that it was all for nothing.

"You're not listening to me!" cries Muallem, as if trying to wake us from our sleep. "What are you looking over there for all the time? Haven't you ever seen new recruits before?"

We sit in front of him, competing to dismantle and reassemble the machine gun in the shortest possible time. And Muallem, seeing the expression on our faces as we look at the hill, smiles the smile that makes him look as if he's crying.

"What's the matter with you? You were just the same when you arrived here from the intake center. Before we began to make men of you."

The bonds of time are growing looser, the extent of interest in us is lessening, sometimes it seems that there's nothing left to do with us. In the intervals between training, we know hiding places on the base, where we can sit among the eucalyptus trees when they're looking for people to do all kinds of made-up jobs to fill in the hours of idleness. And during the training itself the breaks are becoming longer and longer. More and more everything is being done perfunctorily, without enthusiasm, without anger, without desire. Less and less are the instructors to be seen prowling the company paths, seeking victims. Presumably they have more important things demanding their attention.

There was a stir on the hill opposite us. The instructor returned with two supply men, laden down with fatigues, which they threw onto the ground. In response to a command the new recruits rose to their feet and fell on the pile of clothes, like ants swarming over a crumb. Their commander stood to one side and watched them. Some of them found what they wanted immediately and held the shirts and trousers up against their bodies to measure them, while others went on rummaging in the pile, which now consisted of old, shabby garments in unusual sizes. The quicker off the mark were already taking off their uniforms and changing into the fatigues, and amid the stir and bustle it was already possible to distinguish different faces, characteristic types and modes of behavior. One of them, unusually tall, was wearing a U.S. Army fatigue shirt with a sergeant's stripes on it. He strutted about like a peacock, showing off his stripes to his friends, congratulating himself on his good fortune. Their instructor went on standing to the side, letting them amuse themselves, glancing occasionally at his watch, calculating the moment of surprise and fear.

Alon had finished dismantling the machine gun, the various parts were set out side by side in exquisite order on the blanket, he knelt down in front of them, an expression of intense concentration on his face, and before he began to reassemble the gun he spread both hands out in front of him, his narrowed eyes scanning the parts on the blanket, like a pianist waiting for the right beat to place his fingers on the keys and strike them. And immediately he began to assemble them, unhesitatingly choosing the parts in the correct order, and in a minute the machine gun was assembled, resting on its stand, without a part or particle left lying on the blanket. Muallem pressed his stopwatch again, and at the sight of the work of his hands Alon's somber, distant face broke into a triumphant smile. It was easy to see from his appearance that the triumph he felt was not over his friends, but over himself. After Micky's departure for his training in anticipation of the match against the Nahal Command team, Alon had hardly spoken to us, withdrawing into himself as in the early days in the platoon, as in the days when his pride was wounded or when reality rose up against him and tripped him up. He looked depressed but his functioning seemed unaffected.

Muallem announced Alon's winning time and said: "You could have been the outstanding student of the whole platoon, if only . . ." and the rest of the sentence was left hanging unfinished in the air, but we knew that Muallem was referring to the incident during the night training, when Alon fired a shot in the orange grove.

Alon dropped his eyes. It no longer mattered to him whether he was chosen as the outstanding student or not. In the evening he lay on his bed and stared at the ceiling. He had even stopped reading his newspapers. We had never seen him staring so apathetically at the ceiling before. Hanan went up to him and invited him to play a game of chess. Alon shook his head. Hanan sat down on the edge of his bed: "Why are you in such a bad mood?" he asked. "Is it all because of what Muallem said about being the outstanding student?"

"Don't make me laugh," said Alon, and his voice sounded different. "It doesn't interest me in the least. My future isn't here. They're waiting for me somewhere. In a certain secret unit. I'll be taken out of here even before the end of basic training. It's a matter of a few days. Outstanding student! That's child's play. In the place where I'm going the issues are a bit more serious, more dangerous."

Hanan looked at him in astonishment. Alon had spoken in a casual, confident tone. But this was not sufficient to overcome Hanan's natural skepticism, his tendency to take everything with a grain of salt. He left Alon alone and returned to the corner where the Jerusalemites' beds were situated. The whispers and sniggers that ensued must have been audible to Alon, but there was no telling from his face if he actually heard them. Externally he looked absorbed in his own thoughts, proud, strong, not broken, very remote from us.

The next morning, when we returned from the morning run and the showers, Alon refused to fall in for inspection. He lay on his bed in his gym shorts and contemplated us scornfully as we got ready, cleaned our weapons, made our beds, spruced ourselves up.

Avner went up to him: "What's the matter with you? Aren't you going to get ready for inspection?"

"No," said Alon.

"What's up?"

"It simply doesn't interest me. This isn't my place. I belong somewhere else."

"Alon, for God's sake, why make trouble for yourself now, when basic training's already over?"

"Leave me alone."

Avner tried to drag him off his bed and make him stand up. Alon resisted and wrestled with him. We gathered around Alon's bed to see what was happening there. Zackie and Albert the Bulgarian joined Avner in his attempts to rouse Alon and bring him back to his senses. Alon pleaded in a sad, quiet voice: "Fellows, please, leave me alone. It's nice of you to worry about me. But you don't understand what's going on. You don't understand that I'm leaving here for another place, and all these games don't interest me anymore."

"The only thing that's waiting for you is a court-martial and prison. I can tell you all about the pleasures in store for you," said Avner. "Get up and get ready for inspection. There isn't much time left."

"Believe me, I know what I'm doing," said Alon.

Albert pulled him roughly off the bed and stood him on his feet. Alon gave in, standing there limp and uncertain. Zackie took his gun and began to clean it, Avner made his bed, and Albert handed him his uniform. Alon refused to put it on, and Albert forced him, strapped on his webbing, and sat him down on the bed to put on his boots.

"What's the matter with you?" asked Albert. "Are you sick? So ask to go on sick call. But now you have to get ready quick and go outside."

"I'm not sick," protested Alon. "I'm perfectly healthy. I'm tired of being here."

"Put on your boots," Albert urged him. "For God's sake, do it for us, we love you and we don't want you to get into trouble."

Alon bent down and pulled his boots onto his feet. He began to lace them up, and in the middle he stopped and hung his head. Avner sat down in front of him. "Look at me!" he called loudly. "Look at me, Alon!"

Alon responded to his call, raised his head and looked at him. Avner swept his hand backward and slapped him hard in the face. Alon was shocked and for a few seconds he was stunned. Then he covered his face with his hands, and when he took them away there was a red mark on the slapped cheek and he looked around him with a slightly bemused expression. The remote, contemptuous look in his eyes was gone. He bent down again, laced up his boots and gaiters, glanced sideways at his made bed, took his cleaned weapon from Zackie and said: "Thanks, fellows, thanks a lot for helping me."

Avner said: "Forgive me, Alon, there was no other way. I understand these things."

"Okay, okay," Alon mumbled impatiently, wanting to get the whole thing over as quickly as possible. If he could have, there is no doubt that he would have dissolved before our eyes and vanished into thin air, but as things were he addressed himself to getting ready for inspection.

I looked at him and I wasn't sure if he had really woken from his dream and returned to reality, to the rhythm of real time and its obligations. He looked to me as if he were still sleeping and only pretending to be awake, in order to be left alone to go on dreaming, giving in order not to give up.

These days were suffused in the light of the approaching end, like a light of weariness and forgiveness. I no longer feared the sarcastic remarks of the instructors. I stood with Yossie in the showers; we flooded the floor with vast amounts of water and swept it up with the rubber bars at the end of the sticks in our hands. We worked at a leisurely pace. We knew that if we finished too quickly, we would be detailed to perform some other duty. And Yossie, after maintaining a prolonged silence, as if in concentration on his work, suddenly stopped, gave me an accusing look, and said, "You knew that it was Avner who smashed my guitar."

His long, thin, ascetic face was flushed with anger now too, long after the incident in question. He scrutinized my face, hoping to discover the truth as a consequence of taking me by surprise. I was too startled to reply. I frowned in pretended perplexity.

"You knew and you said nothing," said Yossie.

"How do you know?"

"I know," he said, and added mysteriously: "I have ways of knowing."

"I didn't see him doing it. It was only later, when it was discovered, that I guessed it was him. He never said anything to me. He sensed that I'd guessed and all he said was: *Shut up.*"

"And you shut up."

"Why did he do it?"

"Are you asking me? I thought you might know. What have I got to do with him? I hardly know him."

"I thought it might have something to do with some girl in your crowd that he fell in love with."

"Who's stopping him from falling in love with her?"

"Did he tell you that I knew about it?" I asked although I had no doubt that this was the case.

"He's a dirty swine," said Yossie, "listen to what I'm telling you. Really dirty. And I'm not talking now about what he did to my guitar. He'll pay for that, I'll see to it. But he saw what they were doing to Ben-Hamo, he saw how he was getting the beating he should have got himself, and he kept quiet. What does he care if someone else gets beaten up because of him?"

"And do you really care now about Ben-Hamo being beaten up?"

"Of course I care! It really hurts me. I feel guilty too." He clenched his lips in a peculiar way, as if he wanted to bite something. "And you, don't you care?"

"No one would have dared to hit Avner. That's why there's always some Ben-Hamo to get beaten up instead," I said.

"I can't share your cynicism. I don't want to. But don't worry, Avner'll get what's coming to him, I promise you."

"In your opinion, should I have told on Avner?"

"You're talking like a kid in grade school, who doesn't want to tell on someone who copied from him in a test. What kind of nonsense is that? All those codes of friendship and loyalty are phony. They were invented for the sake of convenience, so we wouldn't have to struggle too much with our conscience. So that in the name of friendship and loyalty we can do the most terrible things in the world — and feel righteous. To see somebody behaving like an animal and trampling on others, and to keep quiet, because it's not nice to tell tales, it's not the right thing to do. But keeping quiet means consenting. It means collaborating. You can't be loyal to friendship and to your conscience at the same time, if some friend of yours does something that you think is a dirty thing to do, if your friend steals or murders; you have to decide what's more important to you, friendship or your opposition to those acts. You can't hold the rope at both ends. And if you choose loyalty, then at least be loyal to someone who won't sell you for a ha'penny the minute it's worth his while. Because loyalty at least should be mutual.

"He needed me, to find out where that girl was, so he came with the excuse of saying he was sorry, as if he had such a bad conscience that he couldn't stand it anymore. And right off he told me that you knew about it too. Because at the beginning I couldn't believe that he'd really done it. Why, for God's sake? What harm had I ever done him? With that dirty bastard everything's a bribe, payment for prostitution — words, feelings, friends, the lot. Altogether, he's got the mentality of a pimp."

"I don't mind him telling you that I knew. I don't have anything to hide."

"Don't imagine that I think I'm such a saint," said Yossie. "On the contrary, when they beat up Ben-Hamo, I was pleased as punch. I thought he'd done it. I was only sorry they couldn't actually kill him. I didn't know they were planning it. The only reason they suspected him was because of that story of Alon's that Ben-Hamo once told him. But when they hit him, I was glad. Now I feel that they dirtied me. And I still haven't had the guts to tell them that I know it wasn't Ben-Hamo, that they picked on him for nothing, and that instead of helping me they did me a terrible injustice."

We heard footsteps approaching the door and went back energetically to work. The corporal from the CSM's office looked at us wordlessly for a moment, in a silence full of meaning. The smell of carbolic acid rose ominously from the open tin in his hand.

He said: "You'll clean the latrines over there too." He stopped talking to see the effect of his words on us, and continued: "And don't fool around either, or I'll find something else for you to do, something special!"

He left the tin on the floor, glared at us malevolently, and walked away without waiting for our reaction. We finished sweeping out the water and began sprinkling the carbolic acid on the floor. The shower room was flooded with the harsh smell, wiping out everything that had been there before it: the stink of sweaty feet, the miasma of tired bodies, and the stench of the religious men's depilatory shaving cream.

I said to Yossie: "We're gradually getting thick skins."

"Sure," he said, "wherever a wound heals, wherever you received a blow, your skin thickens. That's what I don't want. I don't want a hide like an elephant. I prefer to feel the pain. Not to lose the ability to be hurt. For every blow to be as painful as the first. That's what it means to be an artist. To keep your string tight all the time, so that everything that happens to you makes it vibrate and play your tune. When we saw those new recruits I suddenly felt jealous of them. I swear. Not that I'd like to go through the whole business again from the beginning, but because they don't have thick skins yet. The blows'll do it eventually. In the end we stopped even being afraid. We got used to it and became a part of it.

"Have you noticed that ever since Miller died at the end of the series, no one has even mentioned his name? As if he was never here with us. As if some cat died next to us. And that's someone who wrote an article on Rilke in a literary magazine. What did we know about him? Nothing. Who knows what he was writing in those black notebooks of his all the time? Perhaps there's wonderful, artistic stuff in there? Perhaps one day someone will find those notebooks and discover a new Kafka? Imagine, it could happen. But our skins have grown so thick. Nobody cares. Nobody remembers. Why does it only hurt me?"

After lunch, in the time left before we fell in for inspection and went back to training, we sat in front of the barracks and she came before us again, wearing long pants and an army sweater with her corporal's stripes sewn onto it, holding her whistle on its cord in her hand and twirling it in front of her in the air as she walked. For a moment we were dumb with astonishment. She sauntered past, her hair and face fair and summery in the winter clothes, humiliatingly beautiful, utterly absorbed in twirling the whistle at the end of the cord. And after the dumb astonishment, glances were exchanged and whispered remarks, until Micha the Fool suddenly called out loudly: "Can I take you out one day? When are you free?"

A roar of laughter immediately broke out. Ofra stopped, turned around very slowly, stood there for a minute looking at us, and began walking back toward us. The laughter stopped abruptly. We looked at her from close up, and she must have sensed our caressing, pleading, anxious looks. But her face remained clear and calm, with the hint of a smile in the corners of her mouth and the two dimples that appeared in her cheeks. Her square, cleft chin lifted in contempt. She rested her weight on one leg, with the other one limp at its side, half her foot in the air, swiveling to and fro on its heel, as if seeking a comfortable hold on the ground, making her whole leg move. Her eyes expressed all the infinite distance between us.

Suddenly her voice rose: "Who said that?"

There was a silence. Her face showed patience, determination, and an awareness of her own power. Her voice jarred nervously, a coarse voice, at odds with her appearance.

"Is there an orderly-student here?" she went on.

Zackie said in an unrecognizable voice: "Yes, miss."

"Call me Corporal!"

"Yes, Corporal!"

"Who said that?"

"I don't know, Corporal, I didn't notice."

"Your details!"

"Corporal —"

"Give me your details. You'll pay for this. You'll all pay through the nose." Her voice became shriller and more jarring, as if she had no control over it. She sounded like an old fishwife.

Micha stepped forward. "I said it."

"Repeat what you said!" commanded Ofra.

"I — I can't," mumbled Micha.

"I can't — what?" shrieked the fishwife hidden inside her.

"Corporal!"

"Give me his details too!"

Zackie told her what she wanted to know and she took a notebook and pencil out of her pocket and wrote down the details. Then she turned to Micha and looked him up and down with an expression of loathing and astonishment on her face.

"Good God," she muttered, "God almighty! How ugly you are. What ugliness! There isn't a girl in the world who would want to go out with such a disgusting, ugly, repulsive creature!"

Avner took it upon himself to say something, to try to appease her. He displayed one of his most wheedling, captivating smiles: "May I say something, Corporal?"

"No! Give me your details!"

"What did I do, Corporal?" said Avner plaintively.

"Shut up! Give me your details! Speak when you're spoken to!"

Avner gave her his details.

When she turned and walked away she flicked the whistle at the end of its cord again, twirling the cord rapidly around, until the whistle spun like it had before. And she sauntered slowly off, confident in the awed silence accompanying her, until she vanished into the distance and turned into a dream again.

The silence continued for a while, even after she disappeared from sight. In the end a few curses rose into the air and Hanan shouted furiously at Micha: "Why can't you keep your mouth shut, you idiot? Why?"

Micha didn't know what to say.

"Do you know what's going to happen to you now?"

"What did I say?" he asked: "I've forgotten what I said to her." His lips went on mumbling soundlessly, incomprehensible words that his brilliant, stupid, mathematical brain went on endlessly emitting, like a machine that had broken down and nobody knew how to stop.

"How evil she is," said Avner, "the bitch. Strange how that evil makes her even more beautiful. What an evil beauty. Why didn't she stay on Training Base Twelve? Why did she come here to drive us crazy? She's not real, I'm telling you, she's not real at all. She's a randy dream!"

"Nothing will happen," said Albert the Bulgarian. "All she wants is to show off. What does she come sashaying around here for? Just to provoke us. She likes it. So what's she going to do to him? She wants people to talk to her like that, to want to take her to bed." He turned to Micha: "Don't worry, she won't make trouble for you."

"I don't remember what I said," Micha mumbled again.

Now we were all overcome with laughter at the sight of his grotesque confusion, his desperate attempts to undo what he had done, to repair the damage.

Hedgehog too tried to cheer him up. "Remember what you told us then, at the party, about the king of Persia's horse? Now it was you who smelled the female and began to run. You're a man, Micha, for confessing so that we wouldn't all have to suffer for your sake."

"What does she want of me?" said Zackie. "The whore! The whore! What's she doing here in a camp full of men, without a single woman, trying to make fools of us! What does she think we are — a bunch of kids? One day a few guys should grab hold of her and show her what a woman knows how to give a man. They'd take her down a peg or two. Just because she's pretty she thinks she's got everyone where she wants them. The whore!"

Nothing was comparable to her first appearance, in the beginning, in that cruel, enchanted hour of grace, when she appeared before us with her two dogs, and the twilight gleamed like gold on the smoothness of her skin. Only the memory of this vision was capable of effacing the coarseness of her voice, the shrill, fishwife tone, which had suddenly transformed her into the ridiculous caricature of an army officer — and returning her to the image of mystery and longing in our hearts.

"I can't get her out of my head," said Avner, "she's driving me crazy. Her evil, her hatred, they're so provocative. No less than her body, her face, the color of her skin."

He lay on his bed, fell silent and sunk into a trance. I was harboring a grievance against him, because he had told Ressler that I knew what he'd done, instead of keeping quiet like he had demanded of me. He had betrayed my trust. I wanted to reproach him for it. I planned how I would question him, in all innocence, how I would catch him out in a lie. I was sure he would lie. But I knew that this wasn't the time to talk about it.

Exclamations of surprise rose from the people near the entrance to the barracks. We saw Sammy, in civilian clothes, coming in and striding rapidly toward Avner's bed, and the latter, astounded, sitting up. Sammy grimaced in a kind of brief, purposeful smile.

"Hello!" said Avner.

"Give me what I gave you then," said Sammy in his gruff voice. His baby face had grown up a little, grown gray. His narrow eyes, light as the glint of a knife, stared at Avner. "I have to get out of here fast," he said.

Avner spread out his hands uncomprehendingly, looked around to make sure that everyone was listening to their conversation, and shook his head: "I don't have anything."

"Like hell you don't have anything! I gave it to you!" Sammy's cheeks, one of which was traversed by the ugly scar, twitched. His temples pulsed nervously.

Avner said: "Let's go outside for a minute, we can talk there."

Sammy said: "I'm in a hurry. I have to get away from here."

"I threw it away," whispered Avner, hardly moving his lips. "They searched us. I was lucky they didn't find it. Later I threw it away."

"Where?"

"In the latrines."

"Are you out of your mind?" said Sammy furiously. "You know what you did?"

"They would have caught me with it otherwise."

"Come outside," said Sammy.

Avner pushed his feet into his boots without lacing them and followed Sammy, who was waiting for him at the door with a scowl on his face.

After they went out, the rest of us followed them cautiously. We peeped around the corner of the building and saw them standing next to the wall with the light from the window falling on them as they argued in undertones. Suddenly Sammy gave Avner a violent push on the shoulder and punched him in the stomach. Avner hit him back and they began to wrestle. We approached and stood around in a semicircle to watch them. Much to our surprise we saw Sammy getting the better of Avner, and forcing him to the ground. We would never have guessed that Sammy was so strong. Albert and Zackie went up to separate them. And when they bent down to seize hold of them and drag them apart, Sammy sprang up, abandoning his prey lying on the ground, and pulled out a knife whose blade flicked and flickered in the dark. He moved the knife to and fro in front of him. Zackie and Albert retreated. And Avner, who tried to get up and slip away, was trapped between Sammy and the wall. Avner thrust both hands out in front of him and began circling Sammy, who moved in a circle too, his knife in his hand.

Alon, who had only now emerged from the barracks, pushed his way through us as we anxiously watched the spectacle, and when he was standing not far from them, he called out to Sammy in a commanding voice: "Drop the knife at once!"

Sammy glanced rapidly in his direction, snorted contemptuously, and went on circling with Avner, brandishing his knife in front of him.

Alon pounced on him, seized the wrist of his hand holding the knife, and squeezed until the knife fell to the ground. Avner picked it up, gazed at it wonderingly for a moment, and then looked back at Alon, who was pummeling Sammy like a man possessed. Alon threw Sammy down, sat on his back, pinned his shoulders to the ground, and gasped for breath.

"Let go of me, I'm getting the hell out of here," said Sammy in a choked voice.

"Yes," said Alon, "get the hell out of our lives. Get out of the life of this country. What have people like you done to our country? What have you brought here? We don't want it. Do you understand? We don't want it! We don't want it!"

"Why don't you let me go?"

Alon got off his back. Sammy stood up, shook the dust off his clothes, looked around him, and said to Alon: "I want the knife back. I won't do nothing with it. I'm getting out of here."

"You're not going to get it," said Alon, and to reinforce his words, he went up to Avner and took the knife from him.

Sammy looked at him. There was something about the way Alon was standing and the expression on his face that persuaded him not to wrestle with him again. He started walking slowly, demonstratively, to show that he wasn't running away, that he wasn't afraid of anyone. And when he walked past Avner, he spat and said: "I'll get you. There's a couple of other guys out to get you too. Thief. We'll find you wherever you are. You sold it, I know you did. You'll pay for it. All of it. Thief. Sonofabitch," and he spat out a curse and walked away and was swallowed up in the darkness of the paths between the buildings.

Alon was agitated. When we returned to the barracks he didn't stop talking, and Avner, depressed and humiliated, shut his ears with his hands and whispered: "Why doesn't he shut up already, I can't listen to it. Why doesn't he shut his mouth."

"Everything's being ruined here," said Alon, "everything that once existed in this country. What a wonderful nation there once was here. What great things they did here. Now it's all going to the dogs. Soon none of it will be left. Even the Hebrew language won't be what it once was. In a few years' time the children won't understand the Hebrew of the Bible. People won't be able to read Alterman's poems and Yizhar's stories. They'll talk a new, ugly language. And the Arabs are already preparing for the second round against us. They're getting vast quantities of weapons. Who's going to stand up to them here? The underworld? Everything that was built here, all the blood that was shed, all the suffering and disease and hunger, for the sake of building a new nation, a new country, is it all going to be for nothing? Are the foreignness, the madness, the egoism, the underworld going to destroy it all? What are the Arabs amassing all those weapons for? All they have to do is wait, their work's being done for them right here . . ."

It wasn't clear who he was talking to. He sat on his bed staring into the distance. Perhaps he was talking to us all, perhaps to himself, perhaps to history. Suddenly he got up and went over to Avner.

"Listen, we'll have to report it. They have to know what happened here with that character. What did he want of you? Did he really give you something? What was it? You have to report it."

Avner said: "All right." It was clear from his expression that he had no intention of doing anything of the kind.

"I'm keeping his knife as evidence," added Alon. "I'll give it one of the officers. The whole affair has to be gone into."

"No," said Avner. "Throw the knife away. Get rid of it. You'll only get into trouble. Give it to me, I'll keep it."

Alon didn't even hear him. He said: "Why is this happening to us, fellows? Why? We wanted to create a new culture here, a new, better society. Where do these worms come from, crawling into the fruit and rotting it? We should never have brought people like that here. They'll destroy us, they'll destroy everything that was built here."

The Jerusalemites could no longer restrain their laughter. But Hedgehog rebuked them: "He's right. What are you laughing about, you idiots? It's true. Everything he says, he's absolutely right!"

Avner said to Alon: "Enough, Alon. Stop it. It's over. He's gone and he won't be coming back, not after what you did to him. We won't see him again. Just leave it alone."

"But he'll be somewhere else!" said Alon. "Carrying on with the same dirty business. You know what his business is? Drugs!"

"No!" Avner pretended to be shocked.

"Yes! Drugs. The whole of Arab society has been destroyed by those drugs. It's a well-known fact. I read about it. And now they're bringing it here. And the country is full of new people, weak, desperate, who can't adjust to our way of life, a life of hard work and war. That's all we need now. If it finds its way here, it'll spread and destroy us too. Don't you understand? It's entered the army now! What's going to become of us? Everything will be destroyed. Everything that's been built here!"

Avner could bear this speech no longer. He didn't know which annoyed him more — Alon's Zionist slogans or the laughter his words aroused among the Jerusalemites. He said to Alon: "Stop talking. Can't you see that you're making a fool of yourself? Can't you hear the way they're laughing over there? What are you, some senile old pioneer? What are you babbling about?"

"Let them laugh, I don't care," said Alon, "I say what I believe, what frightens me, what's important to me. You have to uproot the witchgrass wherever it appears, as soon as you see the first stalk coming up. Otherwise it'll suffocate everything growing around it. Our fighters are spilling their blood in action while those people are still feeding the sicknesses they brought with them from the diaspora, trying to create a new diaspora over here. We mustn't let them do it! Don't you understand?"

Hedgehog asked Avner: "Why did you lie then? You said he didn't give you anything. And now he comes to get it back from you. Where did you hide it then? They turned everything upside down and they never found anything. You see how your lies catch up with you?"

"Are you interrogating me? Do I have to answer you?" said Avner.

"Yes," said Hedgehog, "and not only me. The whole platoon. It affects us all. We're all in the same boat here, we're responsible to each other. I didn't laugh at what Alon said. I agreed with every word he said. It isn't funny — this is our country and we're responsible for it. Maybe that sounds like Zionist propaganda, but I'm not ashamed to say it!"

Avner listened patiently and answered loudly, so that everyone would hear, and this time, trapped between the frying pan and the fire, he apparently decided to risk everything and play the game of truth.

"You've still got a lot to learn in life," said Avner. "As far as I'm concerned, when someone in trouble comes to me and asks for help, I don't cross-examine him. I don't care what he did. First of all, I try to help. Understand? I'm not a judge or a policeman and justice isn't my business. I decide according to my own conscience. And my conscience tells me that you have to offer help quickly to anyone who asks for help. That's why I did it. That's why I kept his secret. I'm not an informer. If anyone wants to inform, let him go and inform on me. And I'll pay the price for what I did. But I'll know that I was true to myself. I hope there won't be anyone in this platoon who'll want to get me into trouble, just because I'm prepared to help anyone who needs help with no questions asked. I don't know what was in the package he gave me and it didn't interest me. He wanted to get rid of it, and I was prepared to help him. With no questions asked. I took the risk of being found with it, of being thrown into prison. I don't care. Even now, after he hit me, and threatened me with revenge, despite everything I did for him, even now I'm not sorry I did it. Even though he's a shit and he doesn't deserve to be helped. Even though there's a danger that him or his friends will get me. They might even kill me. I know they're capable of it. And still, I'm glad I did it. Because if I'd have told the CID the truth and betrayed his trust, I would never have forgiven myself as long as I lived. I would have been ashamed to look at myself in the mirror. I would have looked to myself like a leper. Can you understand that? Is that something you're capable of understanding at all, Hedgehog? It's a question of honor. Do you know that word? There are rules that are as important to a man as religion is to someone who believes in God. What's wrong is wrong. And no arguments about it."

My eyes met Yossie Ressler's, searching for me from the far end of the room. They looked straight at me with a meaningful look, as if in continuation of our conversation in the showers. There was something off-putting and irritating in his arrogant, righteous, gloating expression; even though I was convinced that he was right.

All Hedgehog could find to say was: "When it comes to talking you always turn out to be a saint! You do what suits your own book, and then you find all kinds of interpretations that make you out to be some kind of hero and martyr!"

Avner said: "Man, my life's in danger! The day might not be long off when I'll be lying dead in an alley with a knife in my belly!" He glanced around him, to see the effect of these words on his audience. "Types like Sammy and his friends are capable of anything. Killing is a small thing to them. I'm telling you that even now I don't regret helping him, not informing on him. What did I get out of it? You saw how he thanked me, the way he threatened me, despite what I did for him."

Alon intervened from his position seated on his bed: "Those are the codes of honor of the underworld. If everyone behaved like that, the whole country would turn into the Jaffa underworld."

Zero-Zero went up to Alon. "What you said's right," he said. "It's the truth. I'm afraid too. What's going to become of our state? What's going to happen here, with things like that going on, with crooks like that Sammy roaming around? Everything'll go to hell! It's not funny! They'll mess up our state. It'll be an Arab country, not a Jewish state. In other countries they chuck all of them in the calaboose. So why're they walking around free here? Is everything going to pieces? What's going to happen? I want to live here, I want to have kids here, for them to grow up somewhere good. You're a decent person, you understand what's going on. Those others don't have a clue. They're like babies. They don't understand but I do. I'm afraid for our state!"

Alon looked at him glassily, as if he didn't recognize him. Again he stared silently into the distance. Zero-Zero went back to his bed and began to prepare himself for sleep. Suddenly he turned his head and looked at Alon again, in the row of beds opposite him, a worried, unhappy look. Alon roused himself from his apathy, got up, and also began making his bed. You're leaving yourself behind again, said a familiar voice, one of his many voices. You're going away again, and afterward you'll have to travel the same road back, retracing your footsteps, avoiding ambushes, overcoming fear, until you return to your borders. Why are you going away? The enemy is hiding inside you. The longings for the meeting are terrible, they are impossible to overcome. On the ground, in the shade of the olive tree, on a bed of earth that nothing can surpass, as dawn begins to break, and the cries of the hunters are not yet heard, life runs out, it runs out, the blood returns to its source, like the payment of a debt of love. Hard, hard, are the fathers to die, as the oak to be torn asunder.

Avner, as was his habit, lit a cigarette before lights-out. "My rotten luck is still pursuing me," he sighed. "I'm in trouble," he whispered, perhaps to himself, perhaps to me, as I made my bed to go to sleep, "so soon before the end, when you can already see it in the offing. How typical of me, of my luck. Have you noticed how that sports instructress brings me bad luck? The last time we saw her, they caught me sleeping on guard afterward and threw me into prison. Strange, isn't it? I'm not usually superstitious. But now I'm beginning to believe that every time I see her I get into trouble."

"Why are you so surprised?" I said to tease him. "Sometimes time returns. A circle closes, a circle opens, the past begins to repeat itself. All kinds of insignificant little details begin connecting with each other, taking on meaning, hinting at something, some story, like the solution to a mystery beginning to emerge. You're returning this evening to that night on guard. Now you have to go back to those minutes, to fall asleep, in order for them to catch you, to seize the gun from your hands, to put you on trial and send you to prison. All that's missing is the traitor, to stand to one side, to see them coming and not to wake you, not to warn you of the danger — so that everything can happen all over again —"

"Melabbes!" exclaimed Avner, "You wouldn't do it to me again!"

We laughed. Avner grew gloomy again. He said: "Lucky I'm not on guard tonight." Then he added: "I would never have believed that shit had so much strength in him. Even though he looks like a child. I couldn't get the better of him, I swear! He's terrifically strong! He's got tremendous power in his hands. Why, why did he do it to me? I risked my neck to save him. I wanted to be friendly to him. You remember what you said to me then about the way I behaved when they conducted that search? It wasn't easy, believe me. I thought he would also realize what I went through for his sake. Now he's turned into my enemy. As if I lacked enemies. Did you see how happy the little darlings were to see what was happening me? Do me a favor, ask them one day why they hate me so much. What harm have I ever done them? Why? Why?"

"Is that what you concluded from the argument?" I asked. "That's it's simply a question of hatred? Not a conflict between points of view?"

"I understand," he said. "You're sorry for what you said then. You've changed your mind. One day you'll understand that ideas aren't a house you can live in; that the real issues are decided between you and yourself, or between one man and another, when history goes to sleep, when ideas and points of view disappear from sight, and all that's left is love, friendship, hatred, loyalty, treachery, jealousy, ambition, anxiety . . ."

He finished his cigarette, sighed deeply, set his head straight facing the ceiling, stretched his body, his arms and his legs, closed his eyes, and prepared himself for the plunge.

The sound of a brief, dreadful scream woke Alon instantly from his sleep. He caught his breath. He opened his eyes and looked around him.

In the dark room the silence of the sleepers smothered the echo of the scream. He remembered that he had just fallen asleep, and not completely either. The echo of the scream was still reverberating in his heart. Who had screamed? Perhaps someone outside the barracks. Perhaps someone had screamed in his sleep. And perhaps the scream had come from within him. Perhaps it had only been heard inside him. He could hear its sound — like a cry of horror and warning against an enemy unexpectedly discovered, somewhat reminiscent of the yells he had tried to produce during bayonet practice, a short scream, full of terror and cruelty. For a long time he tried to go back to sleep, but his heart was still pounding in his chest, making his body shake. He got quietly out of bed, turned here and there, as if he didn't know where to go. Then he bent down over his knapsack, opened it, thrust his hand deep inside it, and groped among his belongings. Until his hand felt the chill of the switchblade. He pulled the knife out of the bag, laid it on his bed, pulled on his trousers, pushed his bare feet into his boots, put the knife into his trouser pocket, and walked slowly out of the barracks.

Outside the two guards stand huddled in their overcoats. At the sight of him they stop talking and stare at him in silence as he walks past. He feels cold in his shirt. The still, dry, sharp air of the November night makes his shoulders shiver, continuing the inner trembling that had broken out in him before, at the sound of the scream. He goes to the latrines, and before entering the building, he turns from side to side to see if anyone is there. He goes inside, throws the knife into the hole, unbuttons his trousers, and pees.

When he emerges he can feel a curious clarity gradually spreading through him. The oppression has lifted, the remnants of the anxiety have disappeared, something has been purified inside him. He feels like a man who has made his reckoning and whose reconciliation with himself is approaching. As he felt during the period of the series, the happiest time he knew in basic training. The night is so clear that if he raises his eyes to the pure sky he will be able to see all its myriad stars, each star and what lies behind it in those pellucid depths. An unexpected beauty lies over the base; everything is steeped in an unfamiliar stillness. From time to time the gentle purring of a car impinges on this silence, recedes, and dies away. A dog barks suddenly from the direction of the orange groves, angry and threatening, and another dog answers it from another direction, and silence descends again. There is no movement in the air, no stir of a breeze, no rustle in the eucalyptus leaves. Everything is striving toward some supreme stillness, the heart's desire that can never be attained. As he turns onto the path, the barracks stand on either side like protected reservoirs of human warmth, the warmth of the sleepers' breath, the warmth of the bodies being charged with new strength. The warmth of being together. Love awakens in his heart, a new love before which everyone is equal, as if he is standing at a great distance from here, remote in space, remote in time.

When he gets into bed intense longings for her attack him, longings for the smoothness of her body, for the warmth of her touch, for the smell of her breath, for the restrained, confident joy trembling inside her as he gathers her to him. The pain of this lack echoes inside him like a song, calling him home from his exile.

Like a sandstorm the command car bursts into the base, without stopping at the gate, racing wildly over the paths and the whitewashed stones, trampling fences, overturning barrels, sending everyone flying in panic-stricken flight. Abruptly it comes to a halt next to a clump of trees, surrounded by a pillar of dust. Through the haze its occupants are gradually revealed, goggles on their eyes, their hair gray with dust, their faces floury. They sit and look at him, lying motionless on the ground. Although he has never seen the man before, he knows who it is sitting next to the driver, packing a pistol, without any insignia of rank, without any airs of command, calm, brisk, and businesslike. His driver looks at him questioningly, but his face does not betray his intentions. He goes on looking at the figure lying on the ground, and a hint of disapproval and disappointment appears on his tough, emotionless face. And behind him, on the side seat, under the sand goggles and desert dust, Micky too looks at him, waiting with them for him to stand up and get onto the command car, and on his face is an expression of amazement, like when he said: *Listen, you're an artist, a real artist!* Micky, all of whose stories about soccer training were nothing but a cover-up for his treacherous secret. He's already one of them. As if rent by a knife, his body is split by a bitter cry: "You were like a brother to me, a brother!" For a little longer the dusty figures go on looking at him from the command car as he lies on the ground unable to move a muscle. A little way off a crowd has collected, the company instructors, the CO, the red-faced CSM and even the RSM, recruits from the platoon and from other platoons, gazing at the command car and its occupants, afraid to come closer, respectfully silent, waiting to see what will happen next. Only the engine hums quietly in neutral, monotonously counting the beats of the time running out second after second, hope after hope, toward the supreme silence. In the end the man sitting next to the driver instructed him with a faint, economical nod to set out again. In the midst of the neutral humming you could clearly hear the gnashing of the metal as the gear locked into first with a light but powerful touch, and the steering wheel twisted farther and farther to the right until it jammed, and the wheels creaked slowly over the ground as the tires crushed the dry eucalyptus fruits, grinding them into powder, until the car turned around in a semicircle and broke into a sudden charge that sent the spectators flying in all directions. Clouds of dust rose from the ground and wound upward, surrounding the car and its occupants like a pillar of smoke and whirling around it like a sandstorm as it raced past the company lines toward the gate of the base. And on the path where the wheels had passed, a train of burning dust went on swirling, as in the wake of a fire.

"Come outside for a minute, I want to talk to you," said Avner.

He put his hand on Alon's shoulder and led him out of the barracks. Ever since he'd awoken in the morning Alon had been smiling, a quiet, cunning, dismissive smile. He'd gotten ready for inspection, and Avner had hesitated for a long time whether to talk to him or not — for there was no knowing how Alon would react, and perhaps he would do more harm than good. In the end he braced himself and approached him.

When they were outside he said to him: "Don't make trouble for me, for God's sake. I've got enough problems as it is. Don't make a fuss about what happened here last night."

"It's all right," said Alon and looked at him with his quiet eyes, his dull, ironic, weary smile. "What did you think, that I was going to inform on you?"

"I don't know. Last night you said all sorts of things. You said we have to report it, hold an investigation. I'm just a victim here, a scapegoat. All I wanted to do was help someone in trouble. That's all. I didn't ask any questions. That's my only guilt."

"I was in that kind of mood last night," said Alon, "but it's over. I'm not going to save the state and army anymore."

"What about the knife?"

"I threw it away last night."

"Where?"

"The same place you threw what he gave you."

Avner looked at him suspiciously: What schemes were being hatched behind the tired, mischievous smile on Alon's face?

"You're a nice guy, Alon. I know you are. But sometimes you see things from too high up, from the point of view of history. But down here there are little people with little problems that are ruining their little lives. And from all the blows that have come down on their heads they can't lift them high enough to see the things that you see."

"It's all right," said Alon, "there's nothing to worry about. I'm already down there too."

He looked at his watch. It was nearly time for inspection and he wasn't ready yet. They returned to the barracks. Alon went straight to his bed and began folding up his blankets and straightening them on the bed. Avner watched him with a worried, mistrustful look. He whispered to me: "These righteous characters are the ones who frighten me most. They're the ones who make all the trouble."

On morning inspection Micha, Zackie, and Avner were charged with impertinence to the sports instructress Ofra. Micha was sentenced to four days in prison, while Zackie and Avner, whose crime was less grave, got off with nothing more than a reprimand and general guard duty.

"You see," said Avner, "it really is repeating itself. That bitch! I'll still fuck her. She's no less of a female than any other girl. I'll fuck her one day. She won't get away from me. And on this guard I won't smoke, I won't fall asleep, I won't make any mistakes. I'll do everything by the book. I'll break this vicious circle if it takes every bit of strength I've got. I won't give in. There won't be any balls-ups. I won't give her the satisfaction, the bitch. When I really want something, nothing can stand in my way. You'll see!"

When the guard went up to the parade ground to lower the flag, we saw Alon running toward them. Puffing and panting he reached the men forming up in threes, jumped to attention, saluted the commander of the guard, and took his place among the guards. On their return to the guardroom, to reserve their beds, Zackie asked him what had happened. "There was a guard missing," said Alon calmly, with a faint, dismissive smile. "Benny came to look for a victim. I volunteered."

"Why?" they asked in astonishment.

"What do I care?" said Alon. "They'll cancel my guard tomorrow."

When the guards were detailed and the sentry posts allocated, Avner was glad that he and Alon had been given the same shift, at points not far from each other next to the fence of the base. There would be eye contact between them. If his spirits fell during the long hours of standing alone at his post, and he was in danger of giving way to the temptation of smoking, dropping off for a minute, or ignoring one of the rules, he would look over at Alon — perhaps he would see his shadow in the darkness, performing his duty with all his usual loyalty, seriousness, and responsibility — and he would serve as an example to him to overcome his weakness. His desire to get through the night without any trouble was intense, if only in order to prove to himself that the fatefulness of the recurring cycles would not prevail this time, and the bitch-instructress would not come out on top. This thought cheered him.

Nevertheless, he refused to wake up when they tried to rouse him for his shift. For a moment he sat up in cursed silently, and then he lay down again, stretched out, and fell asleep. Alon, who was already dressed and ready to set out, went up to him and slapped him hard on the cheek. Avner started up, stared at him in alarm, and put up his fists like a boxer ready to engage his opponent, until he recovered his senses and said to Alon: "Okay. Now we're even."

Alon said: "Sorry, Avner. I had no choice. I understand these things."

And again the new smile flickers in his eyes, the faint, mischievous smile that accompanied him since morning, giving rise to the suspicion that his generous candor has left him and he is beginning to plot some evil.

Avner looks at Alon's silhouette not far from the bend in the fence. Sometimes Alon stands erect and motionless, drawing himself up as if about to salute, and sometimes he marches a few paces to and fro along the fence. The bend is illuminated by a ray of light from an unseen lamp, and the reflection of the light falls on the edge of a building in the next base. The cold penetrates his bones. Avner knows this cold from the winter nights in Jerusalem, the clear nights, with their sharp, dry chill. Not even the overcoat and sweater are a match for this cold, which sends shivers down his spine. The chill of the metal helmet falls on his face, bringing tears of cold to his eyes. He is dying for a cigarette, but his resolution to get through the night without any trouble and not to give in to his weaknesses is still firm. If only he were guarding with somebody else, at least he would be able to pass the time by talking. But these guards are performed alone, in solitude. The cold stings him like an insult. Self-pity and resentment at the injustice of it all overwhelm him. There's something about me that attracts girls to me, but also insults them, annoys them. And I have to pay for it. Why do they always want to revenge themselves on me in the end? What do I do to them?

His talent for lying and pretending and finding excuses for everything, so useful in times of trouble, betrays him precisely at moments like these, when no trap has caught him and no pressing need assails him, but for the need to sweeten the sorrow he has caused another, to blur the traces of the injustice. At moments like these he is sentenced to the muteness of truth. He becomes transparent; only the evil inside him is visible, without the good: the good that hurts him when he sees it so wounded, so humiliated.

There's no point in trying to talk to her. She can read him now like an open book, whatever he says will sound like a lie. All because he couldn't smile back at her lovingly at the critical moment. Her hands held his head, his face was so close to hers that he could see the minute pockmarks on her cheeks and the places where she plucked her eyebrows to make them narrow and arched. Her brown eyes, set rather deeply in their sockets, seek his shifty, evasive eyes, wanting to say something to him, calling him, pleading — in vain. But he can't. He's simply incapable of lying to her. As if he's been turned to stone — he cannot give her a look of affection, of intimacy, of gratitude. Who knows what strangeness looked out at her from his eyes, what denial, perhaps even contempt and hostility. In any case, she dropped his head immediately, drew away from him, stood up and began hurriedly getting dressed, her back to him, her movements nervous, her heart embittered against him. What can he do if these moments of deflation, the moments when everything is over, are so hard for him. Harder, perhaps, than for other people. I wasn't playing with you, he would have liked to say to her, everything I said to you was sincere and honest. I wasn't using you to make Ziva jealous. I really desired you. I loved you. I needed you terribly. But now my loneliness is eating me up. I know, I'm losing you now forever.

Instead he hears his voice saying: "What's wrong, wasn't it good for you with me?" A hoarse, hollow, coarse voice. It's hard for him to recognize his own voice.

He doesn't even dream of saying to her: Wait a minute, I'll come with you.

The long, dark road in front of her, from here to her house, will give her plenty of time to think whatever she likes about him, to feed her hatred, to cultivate thoughts of revenge.

She really did make me happy, and on that night I lost her forever. I know. But even that happiness was lacking something. The thing that I'll never stop looking for as long as I live. I won't rest until I reach it. If anyone ever does reach it. Better to be consumed in this thirst than give up the aspiration to quench it.

"Halt! Password!"

The voice was Alon's, echoing in the darkness. Avner could see his silhouette at the edge of the ray of light shed by the lamp behind the bend in the fence, moving to and fro in the attempt to identify the person coming toward him.

When no answer was forthcoming, Alon called again: "Halt! Password!"

The figure did not halt. Alon cocked his gun and aimed it at the shape looming out of the darkness.

"Stop it, nut! Stop showing off!" Benny's voice rose out of the darkness. "What are you aiming your weapon at me for, are you mad?"

Alon held his ground: "Password!"

Benny gave the password.

Alon saluted. Benny did not return the salute. Instead he said: "Give me your weapon."

"Why, sir?"

"Give it to me! That's an order. I want to discharge the bullet you loaded into the barrel chamber. I don't trust you."

Alon hesitantly gave him the gun. Benny opened it and dropped the bullet into the palm of his hand, put it back into the magazine, closed the gun, aimed it at the sky, and pressed the trigger. After the empty click was heard, he returned the gun to Alon.

"What did you aim the gun at me for, you imbecile?"

"Sir, I was obeying orders. You didn't give the password."

"Didn't you recognize me?"

"It's impossible to be sure, sir."

"Maybe you thought you were seeing some infiltrator, like you saw then on the night training, in the orange grove?"

"No, sir."

"Why did you volunteer for guard duty tonight?" asked Benny.

"No reason, sir. I don't mind."

"You don't mind standing outside for hours at night, in the cold, like a dog, instead of sleeping?"

"No, sir."

"Sometimes I'm not sure if you really are crazy, like everyone thinks, or if you're making fools of us all."

Alon said nothing. Benny looked at him as if he wanted to examine his face, to discover signs of ridicule on it. In the shade of the helmet, Alon's face was sealed, clenched, and only a hint of irony glittered in the slits of his eyes, indistinguishable in the darkness.

"I suppose you think you're better than everyone else," said Benny.

"No, sir," said Alon. "I'm no better than anyone else."

"When I was an instructor in the paratroopers, I had a lot of kibbutzniks there. I never understood why they were so full of themselves. True, they've got some good fighters among them, a lot of them are physically fit. But no more than among the kids from the towns and the moshavim. Besides, you've got quite a lot of screwballs too. What's wrong there, in the way you live, that produces so many nuts? You were supposed to produce the finest, the elite! The ideal Israeli. What happened? What went wrong?"

"I don't know, sir."

"I can't stand the way you're all so pleased with yourselves. As if the whole world was created for you. As if everyone has to admire you, worship you. Wait for some amazing thing you're going to do."

"I don't think about myself like that, sir."

"I know. You haven't recovered yet from the fact that you're on Training Base Four. For you that's the worst humiliation. It may be okay for all your mates in the platoon from the towns, for the new immigrants, but not for a kibbutznik like you, right?"

"Sir, when we were on the series, I asked you to help me get into a Squad Commanders Course so I could be an instructor on Training Base Four. I wanted to be here."

"It was too late. By the time you came to your senses, you'd already been posted somewhere else. I know where you've been posted. You want to know?"

Alon was silent.

"You're going to the military police. Are you satisfied?"

"Sir," said Alon, barely able to suppress the trembling in his voice, "I'm not going to be in the military police."

"I tell you that I know you've been posted there. You're going from here to a course for MPs. So you're telling me that you're not going there?"

"Sir, I know that I'm not going to be in the military police," insisted Alon.

"Explain yourself," said Benny.

"There's no explanation, sir."

"Are you trying to make a fool of me?" asked Benny.

"No, sir. I mean every word I say: I'm not going to be in the military police."

"So where are you going to be, in your opinion?"

Alon was silent.

Benny shrugged and looked at Alon with a mixture of amusement, astonishment, and anger.

Avner saw him standing and talking to Alon. From where he was standing he couldn't hear what they were saying. The conversation went on for a long time. In the end he saw Benny leaving Alon, walking off and disappearing behind the bend in the fence. Now he waited for him to reappear when he least expected him, from the most unexpected direction. Like a dog he sniffed the air, staring into the darkness for the flicker of a stir, straining his ears for the hint of a sound. Wondering where Benny was going to appear. But all around him lay a tense, suspect, treacherous silence, hiding what was to come. The sense of danger choked him. He clasped the gun to his body. No one was going to get it away from it. This time they wouldn't take him by surprise. This time he would get through the night without any trouble. His whole being was alert to danger.

And then came the sound of the shot.

A brief, terrified scream escaped Avner's lips and he sprang from his place in alarm. Something in him had expected it, and it was this that gave rise to his terror. He was sure that it was him they were firing at, him they had hit. The echoes of the shot went on reverberating in the air, and when they subsided the treacherous silence descended again, and Avner knew he had not been hurt. And as if it were only a problem of memory, to determine what came first, and as if it were a question of music, to distinguish the note particular to every shot, to every catastrophe — the certainty flashed through his heart, cutting like a knife: I know that shot. I've heard it before.

CHAPTER 30

S traight away I looked in Alon's direction. I couldn't see him anymore. But I was certain he was lying on the ground, wounded. I didn't have any doubts about it. I wanted to fly there straight away, to see what had happened to him. But I was afraid that that shit Benny was just waiting for me to move from my post so he could come and stick me on a charge. I stood there for a minute, torn between the wish to run to Alon and the fear of getting into trouble again. In the end I took my courage in both hands and ran over there. And he really was lying on the ground."

"Was he conscious?" asked Micky.

"I'm sure he was. He knew me, he saw me. I called him: *Alon! Alon!* But he didn't want to answer. As if he had something more important to do and I was disturbing him. But I'm positive he was conscious and he knew who I was. I decided to look and see where he was wounded and then I heard someone running. I knew it was Benny. He heard the shot and came straight back there, he hadn't gone far. He came rushing back as if he were expecting it to happen. He began yelling at me: *What are you doing here? What did you leave your post for? You'll pay for this!* He was in a panic. I had the feeling he saw me as a danger. Maybe I was a witness to something he didn't want known. And that made me feel sure he wouldn't do anything to me. He examined Alon and bandaged him with his field dressing. Then he told me to stay there. And he ran off somewhere. When I was left alone with Alon again, I suddenly heard him trying to sing. I heard a few words. About the vulture coming to eat the corpses. I think he was trying to scare me. I don't know. Anyhow that's what he sang, you could hardly hear him, in a kind of whisper. How could he have the heart to sing?"

"There really is a song like that," said Micky, "I know there is."

"'The Cannons' Roar,'" said Hanan. "It's a Russian song.'

"Ah!" said Avner, as if this answered all his questions. "It was terrible to hear him singing like that. I began to shiver. By then I didn't know if it was from cold or fear. I didn't know what to do. In the end Benny came back with another two guys, medics, I think. He yelled at me to go back to my post. When I got there, I couldn't see them anymore. They'd taken him away."

Micky had returned to the base after the soccer match. We sat around him in the barracks, in the evening, and talked about Alon. We didn't know what his condition was, if he was dead or alive, if his wound was fatal or if he had a chance of recovering.

Micky said: "I don't understand, I don't understand how you can do it with a Czech, the barrel's so long, how can you reach the trigger and shoot yourself?"

"Like this," said Zackie, and he took his gun, sat down on the floor, set the butt of the gun on the floor, reached for the trigger with his right hand, and aimed the barrel at his chest with his left. Everyone began yelling at him: "Stop it! Cut it out!" and Hedgehog leapt behind his back and tugged at the butt until the gun dropped to the ground.

Zackie raised his eyes, looked around with a sly smile, and said with pretended astonishment: "What's the matter with you? You don't have to be so worried about me. Why are you so worried about Zackie? What does it matter if some black Iraqui dies? We have to die someday, no?"

Micky said: "The question is, if it's only the shoulder that was hit or the chest too. If it's the chest too . . ."

Zero-Zero approached Micky, who was sitting on his bed, next to Alon's empty bed, with his perpetually razor-scratched face and his perpetually inflamed eyes popping out of his head, full of dread and anguished doubt: "You think he won't live?" he asked, "What, you think he might he die of it?"

Micky shrugged and did not reply.

Zero-Zero said: "How can anyone do such a thing to his own body? Why? Why? Look at me, a sick man, with a useless body — I want to live so much. To live like a dog, like shit, but to live. And him — a sabra, strong, healthy, handsome, with such a good heart, who loves our state so much, why should he do something like that to his body? What happened to him? He was angry. I saw it all the time. But what made him angry, I don't know. Maybe it was because of Sammy coming back like that? He talked about him, he talked about our state, how crooks like him were going to destroy it till nothing was left. What he said was right, he's better than all the rest of us. He saved my life on the firing range. Except for him I would've died on the spot. There wouldn't even have been anything to bury. The pieces would've flown all over the place, there wouldn't have been anything left. He saved my life!"

Peretz-Mental-Case intervened with a comment from the legal field: "If he gets out of it alive, he'll be put on trial."

"Why?" asked Zackie. "What'll he be accused of?"

"Damaging army property," said Peretz solemnly.

"What kind of a joke is that?" said Zackie. "Is this a time for making jokes?"

"What do you understand about it?" said Peretz.

There's a hungry little fox clawing at his stomach. Micky still doesn't understand the real meaning of this pain. What does it matter if Alon lives or dies? Everything's over in any case. The remnants of the anger and the hatred, which filled his heart when he stood opposite the kibbutz that Friday waiting for him to return, well up in him again: Lousy Don Quixote. I won't be your Sancho. A huge desire to be rid of it all, to get back to himself, not to feel guilty. What could I do? I wasn't here. He was waiting for it. He had it all planned. There are limits to friendship, the borderlines between the self and the other. So what's the meaning of the pain? Perhaps it's only fear, the terrible fear of the powers within us over which we have no control, the fear of what I'm capable of doing to myself, against my will, against my reason. No, it really doesn't make any difference if he lives or dies. That friend is finished for me, finished forever. Dead or alive, he's gone far away, too far for me to see him anymore. And that's not all. Those drawings, and especially one in particular, where the naked girl's depicted in sure, delicate lines, with incredible tenderness, raising her arm. The secrets of his love. It's all there in the images of my memory, like the traces of a crime you can't rub out. He should never have shown me those drawings. There are some things you should never show a stranger, and a friend's a stranger too. I don't want to think about her, and I can't stop seeing her as she was on that evening, dancing "For Love Delights" with him, with his drawings showing like dark hints through her embroidered blouse, inciting to betrayal, conquest, love. If I sat down to write a few words to her, maybe that would distract me from the fear digging its claws into my belly, gnawing without cease. To understand the pain of this fear, I'd have to know it better, live with it, make a friend of it. The picture of those two breasts, innocent, challenging the laws of friendship and loyalty, her two breasts, one bigger than the other when one of her arms is raised, different in shape, in firmness, in softness, in relation to the rest of her body, spoiling its striving for symmetry, like a call of freedom, full of poetry and vitality. What is she doing now? Perhaps she's at his side in the hospital? Perhaps he's already dead. Dead or alive — he's already dead to me. Strange, that apart from the dull, oppressive fear of the constant threat inside you, there's no sorrow for the dead man himself, no pity, no anguish at parting, no sense of loss. Perhaps just a hint of anger at the insult of the body, the insult of this ridiculous, contemptible death.

"What did Benny talk to him about before it happened?" asked Micky.

"I couldn't hear," said Avner. "They were too far away. You think there's a connection?"

"I don't know. Maybe. He had his eye on him from the beginning, he was waiting for his chance. Who knows what he said to him. He knows how to hurt people, how to humiliate them, make them despair, that bastard. His evil is on the lookout for a victim all the time."

"If this was a platoon of men," said Zero-Zero, "we'd have put him in a blanket already and given him a hiding he'd never forget as long as he lived. Some guys have done that to their instructors at the end of basic training, to teach them a lesson. But in this platoon, who'd do it? Everybody only thinks about himself, everybody's only frightened for himself. Who'd do it for Alon? My heart hurts for him all the time, I think about him all the time."

"He's right!" cried Hedgehog. "He deserves it, the bastard! What d'you say, guys? On the last night, after the party, we follow him and catch up with him in the dark and put him in a blanket and give him the biggest beating he's ever had in his life."

Benny was nowhere to be seen during the following days. We didn't know if he had gone on leave or if his absence from the base was connected to what had happened. Most of our training hours were devoted to the mustering-out inspection. For hours on end we had arms drill with the CSM. First on our own and then with the other platoons, in preparation for the company display. The mechanical repetition of the complicated, superfluous movements on the parade ground already seemed completely ridiculous, not to mention the yelling of the CSM and his curses and threats. But Micky felt that he had to take it seriously. Something in the automatic movements and wheelings of the body in obedience to the barked commands, something in the rhythmic stamping of the feet and the uniform mass movement of those drilling with him relieved the oppression in his heart. Every ounce of energy and concentration he devoted to the precise execution of these stupid exercises seemed to him to detract from the weight of the fear in the depths of his being.

One evening Muallem came into the barracks for a heart-to-heart talk, as he did from time to time, and we learned from him that Alon had been operated on and that his life was still in danger. Muallem examined our faces as if he were trying to grasp something that was not yet clear to him. In the end he came right out with it and asked: "Why did he do it? Don't you know?"

When nobody answered, he asked: "Has he got personal problems?"

To this too he received no answer. He appealed to Micky: "You're his friend, you were always together. Don't you know?"

"No, sir," said Micky. "I wasn't here."

It seemed to Muallem that he was coming up against a wall of deliberate, hostile silence. And he made haste to explain: "I'm asking for myself. It hurts me. Because I actually liked him. He's intelligent. He's okay.

Someone like him doesn't do things like that. It's disgusting for a person to shoot himself! I suppose he's got personal problems. And so he makes problems for the army, for the state, for everyone."

"Maybe the instructor Benny knows," said Hedgehog, "He saw him just before, at his post."

Muallem said: "Alon volunteered for that guard, he asked for it especially. He had it all planned. You don't do something like that at the last minute. Maybe he's sick in his head. He's got problems. You could see it then, on the night exercise, you remember, when he began shooting in the orange grove and said he saw fedayeen. Maybe there's somebody else here who wants to do something like that? Boys, don't lose heart. The basic training's almost over. If anyone's got problems, he can always come and talk to Corporal Muallem. I'm not only your instructor. I'm like a father to you, like a big brother, you can come and pour out your heart to me. I'll always help someone who's got problems, just don't let anything like this happen again. What are you, crazy? A man should kill himself? The Arabs aren't enough for us?"

The party committee had already begun preparing the program for the festive event, in which parents and families had been invited to participate as well. After Muallem left the room the argument between the committee members broke out again: What if Alon died? Were we going to ignore it and carry on as usual? And now, after having heard what his condition was from Muallem, the question became real and pressing. And once more, it was decided to wait and see what happened, and in the meantime, as long as he was alive, to carry on with the preparations. Once more Yossie Ressler was presented with the accordion he had played at the bonfire during the series, and once more the sounds of music and singing were heard in the barracks, cautious, inhibited, and growing increasingly freer. Hanan undertook to compose the humorous songs and Micha the Fool, who had been cast into total confusion, frightened silence, and loss of wits by his days in prison, gradually recovered his senses and agreed to imitate a couple of the instructors, after he had been assured that on the last night everything was allowed and no harm would come to him, and that they would even get special permission from Raffy Nagar, the company commander.

Yossie was practicing on the accordion, improvising different adaptations and variations on tunes and songs. The party committee was still looking for something serious, some recitation that would be appropriate to the occasion and the circumstances.

"He plays well, the shit," whispered Avner.

"He's terrifically gifted, even though he can sometimes get on your nerves," I said, "but you can't hate anyone who plays like that."

"I don't hate him," said Avner, "not really hate him. But he really gets on your nerves. There's something repulsive about him, something disgusting."

"Did you break his guitar because of that girl in their crowd that you fell in love with?" I asked.

"Ziva," he said pensively, the hint of a dismissive smile on his lips, without answering my question directly. "Her name's Ziva. No, she's not for me. Actually, I knew it from the minute I set eyes on her at the party. I was just going through the motions, out of boredom. Maybe to prove something to myself. Nonsense. She's not for me. She's a spoiled, deceitful snob. She doesn't know what she wants. I can't stand the games she plays. But during the last leave something serious started, with her best friend. She's something else entirely. And I'm making it hard for her. She'll have to adapt herself to me if she wants me. And she'll come running, I promise you. On her knees. I'm educating her. Man, I've got no patience for spoiled, screwed-up little girls. I want a normal woman, a real woman. Her name's Miri. And I love her. It's true love, I know. She suits me. I want her to be my wife. The trouble is that she also belongs to their crowd" — he pointed his chin in the direction of the Jerusalemites — "but I'll get her away from them. It's them or me. There's something poisonous about those people, something absolutely barren. They don't want to grow up. They keep an eye on each other all the time. Bombard each other with irony all the time, afraid of failing, of looking ridiculous, because all the others are watching them all the time, gossiping about one another, pretending to be God knows what."

He fell silent for a moment and then added: "But he knows how to play, the shit. He's terrifically talented. He'll be famous one day, I'm sure. And I still owe him a guitar. I have to settle my accounts with him. As soon as I make any money, it goes to buying him a guitar. I have to get him out of my memory, out of my conscience. I don't have any room for types like him."

Micky, who was lying on his bed with an open book in front of his eyes, suddenly got up and went over to Yossie: "How does that Russian song, 'The Cannons' Roar,' go?" he asked. "Do you mind playing it for a minute?"

Yossie began to play the song.

Micky asked: "Do me a favor, sing it with the words. I want to hear it."

Yossie asked Hanan to sing with him. And although Hanan was sick and tired of Hebrew songs altogether, never mind the Russian songs from his youth movement days, and he was only interested in the modern songs with the English words constantly broadcast by Radio Ramallah, he magnanimously agreed for Micky's sake to join Yossi in singing "The Cannons' Roar" to the accompaniment of the accordion. Their pale voices rose quietly, softly singing in thirds, and the strains of the accordion too were hushed, with Yossi occasionally making the notes tremble gently, like the sound of choked breathing. They sang slowly, without emotion, as if performing a duty that could not be shirked, pausing longer than the beat required between the lines, then gathering their dying voices, renewing their strength, and the quiet, measured, monotonous singing pierced the heart with its strange, surprising beauty, as if the wind had carried it here from far away:

> Silenced is the cannons' roar,
> The field of slaughter is forsaken.
> A solitary soldier wanders there
> Singing with the clouds and wind.
> From the hills a vulture rises,
> Then it falls upon the corpses . . .

Micky sat next to them on Yossi's bed, listening expressionlessly, as if trying to decipher the secret buried in the song. His eyes were narrowed in the effort to take in every word and note. And suddenly he seemed to shudder, his neck muscles jerked, and his shoulders slumped. He stood up and ran quickly down the aisle between the beds and rushed out of the room.

Immediately the music and the singing stopped. There was an oppressive silence. We looked at each other, smiling in embarrassment, as if we were guilty of something. Avner said: "He's broken. We have to do something for him."

He turned to Zackie and Albert and a few other experts and they held a consultation and decided that the first time we had a free evening, they would go out to have a good time in the neighboring transit camp and take Micky with them to visit the famous Gita.

Shortly before lights-out Micky returned to the barracks, puffing and panting, flushed and perspiring. His eyes evaded ours, his face was proud and denying. We saw that he was feeling better. He stood and made his bed, slowly and reflectively. Avner went up to him, put his arm around his shoulder, and said: "How's it?"

Micky smiled: "I went for a run. I ran right around the base. Now I feel great. No problems."

He sees a man walking in the dead zone between the folds in the earth. The man is seen from the back, from the waist up, there is no knowing if his legs are sunk in sand, wallowing in a swamp or wading through water. Only his back is visible and his shoulders bearing their load, and his arms swinging at his sides, to ease his progress, to speed his pace. Judging by the way his head thrusts forward and his back alternately slumps and straightens, you can guess how heavy the load weighing on his shoulders must be, how bad and treacherous the terrain beneath his feet. Sometimes he stops and his arms fall to his sides and his head drops to his chest and his breath feels about to burst. But the baby sitting on his shoulders will not let him be. His little legs beat impatiently on his chest, his hands push his shoulders. For there is no time to waste. The man tries to turn his head to the baby, to see his face, perhaps to ask him not to be such a burden. But the little hands grip his head with great force, turning it back toward the road ahead, and the little legs kick his chest again. The opposite bank seems so near, why then is the way there without end? For a moment, it is impossible to understand what stops the weight of the burden from making his legs collapse, what stifles the groan of the final effort to prevail and take yet one more step, until it appears that the two forces are equally matched and there will be no more movement in any direction, time will come to a stop and the hour of the ultimate contest will arrive. Gradually the vantage point grows higher and the dead space is revealed. Now the man can be seen standing sunk to his waist in the strip of water. The two halves of his body are struggling against two opposing laws of gravity. There is no grip for his feet, the water jostles them to and fro, while the weight on his shoulders strives to push him down. The babe on his shoulders weeps. The weight is not the weight of his body. It is a weight that is not of this world. And how terrible it is. All the weight of the world is in it, all the weight of its suffering.

As soon as we were given permission to leave the base in the afternoon, Avner went up to Micky, took him aside, and invited him to join the little group that was going to look for a good time in the transit camp. Avner expected a proud refusal and was prepared to coax and urge him, but Micky smiled in embarrassment and blurted out: "Why not?"

Hedgehog sensed that something was cooking without his knowledge. He approached the conspirators, who fell silent and avoided his questions. He saw them counting their money, making calculations, whispering,

giggling, He must have guessed what it was about. He began pacing restlessly between his bed and them, his face flushed with affront or indeci-
sion. In the end he gathered up his courage and voiced his complaint: "It's
not nice of you, guys. It's not right. What's the matter? Aren't I good
enough to come with you?"

Avner said: "This is a matter for men, not for babies."

And Albert added: "Don't worry, Hedgehog. Wait till you begin to
shave. Afterward the rest will come too."

Zackie, who apparently felt some kind of obligation toward Hedgehog,
after all the quarrels and arguments and reconciliations, pleaded his case.
They looked at Micky, as if waiting for his agreement. At that moment
Micky evidently realized that the whole plan had been conceived on his
behalf. His face suddenly darkened. He muttered something unintelligible and gave them a hostile look. But then his face immediately cleared
and he said: "Why not? Let Hedgehog come too."

The room emptied and only the party committee remained to work.
Ressler settled down to his improvisations on the accordion, Hanan
opened the notebook in which he had written down suggestions and
ideas, and we began discussing them again. The main difficulty lay in the
"serious part," which was supposed to open the program. All the suggestions were rejected due to the opposition of one or another member of the
committee, either on the grounds that they were boring or ridiculous, or
because they would take too much time at the expense of the entertaining
part. The only thing we were agreed on was that Yossie would begin the
program by playing a military march by Mozart or Schubert on the
piano. Yossie made this conditional on the piano in the hall where the
party was to be held being tuned for the occasion; he had tried it and
announced that he wouldn't degrade himself by playing on a piano that
was so out of tune. We promised him and we knew that he would play
even if the piano wasn't tuned. In any case it was clear that the question
was one of his honor as an artist, which demanded satisfaction in words
at least. Micha the Fool gave us a few imitations of the RP in the jail and
various prisoners with their different accents, stories, and complaints. For
a long time we couldn't stop laughing. It was decided that his performance was worthy of being included in the program, and Hanan wrote it
down in his notebook. "Now don't let us down, you hear?" he said to
Micha. "Don't dry up and stand there like a dummy moving your lips."

Micha took no notice of this warning, carried away by his imitations,
his head full of the characters from the jail, he didn't stop for a minute,
and we fell about, shaking with laughter.

Suddenly we saw two people from 3 Platoon coming into the barracks. I knew them from the kitchen duty with Hedgehog: Ginger with his skull ring and dream of becoming a window dresser in Tel Aviv, and his short friend with the strong, square face who had operated the Voice of Youth radio station in Rehovot.

"What's new, guys?" asked Ginger. "Getting ready for the party?"

Micha responded with an imitation of a lisping Moroccan prisoner complaining about having the "sits" (shits).

Ginger laughed and said: "I can see your party's going to be a riot."

"In our platoon," said the square-faced shortie, "they're organizing a whole choir with three voices, all kinds of patriotic songs, 'Arise Ye Wanderers in the Wilderness,' and something by Bach too." He put a pious, sentimental expression on his face, so mature for his years, rolled up his eyes, and sang tremulously: "Oh that my head were waters, and mine eyes a fountain of tears, that I might weep day and night for the slain of the daughter of my people . . ."

"Have you heard anything about your suicidal kibbutznik?" asked Ginger. His eyes betrayed the fact that he knew something we didn't. In response to our suspicious silence, he added: "He's gone."

"How do you know? Who told you?" we asked. The shortie replied instead: "I know."

"Where from?"

He maintained a proud silence and his redheaded friend said: "You can rely on Ze'evik. He's got connections with the next world. He's already proved it. He gets reports from there."

Hanan said, in English: "My dear, that's no laughing matter."

And Ze'evik himself rebuked him: "What are you babbling about? There are ways, there are ways of knowing." He did not elaborate.

After they had gone off, Yossie Ressler said: "They're revolting, those people, they're scum. But maybe they know something?"

And all our ideas for the party program seemed dubious, inappropriate, silly. And once more we had to rethink everything from the beginning, just in case.

Micky went into the room. Avner and Zackie remained sitting in the hole of a kitchen with the old woman. There wasn't enough room in the kitchen, and Gita insisted that no more than two people remain with her mother — perhaps she was afraid that she would be harmed if everyone came in together. The old woman talked without stopping in Yiddish, in a tearful voice, wringing her hands, laying her right hand on her breast as if she were swearing an oath. She was evidently telling them her troubles. Avner and Zackie nodded their heads solemnly in agreement, biting their lips in order not to burst out laughing, winking at their friends waiting outside, next to the open door.

From behind the closed door in the room that Micky had just entered, Gita's voice suddenly cried angrily: "What's the matter with you? Why don't you take off your underpants?"

The old woman burst out laughing. There was no knowing if she had understood what her daughter had said in Hebrew, but in any case she was amused and appeared to expect her two companions to join in her laughter. But Avner's face darkened, he drew his thick brows together as if trying to understand something, and Zackie whispered: "What's going on? Isn't he a man?"

And again Gita's voice rose from behind the door: "No, I don't want it like that. If you won't take them off, you can go and take your money back. I won't do it."

Again there was a silence, and again they heard Gita's voice: "Don't bullshit me. You're talking nonsense. I can see that everything's all right down there. What are you afraid of taking them off for? What's wrong, are you afraid of getting me pregnant?"

And again the old woman burst out laughing, as if enjoying her daughter's wit and the stupidity of the soldier there in the room with her. The men standing outside the door too heard and laughed.

For a long time there was no sound from the room. And when Micky came out, there was an embarrassed smile on his lips, his face was flushed, but his eyes expressed a certain satisfaction. He mumbled: "What a lot of fuss she makes."

Zackie went into the room. Avner accompanied Micky outside. The people standing at the door greeted Micky with glad cries: "Why didn't you want to take off your underpants? Were you shy or what? What did you go to her for then? What did you want to do to her?"

Micky smiled without replying. He and Avner went into a huddle a little way off, and Micky said: "I was afraid of getting some disease. I don't know why she made such a fuss about it. And besides, after all the others who've been with her before, it's a bit like going to bed with them too. It puts you off, no?"

Avner said: "She's got her professional pride too."

"Yes," said Micky, "I suppose I hurt her feelings. Actually, she's quite nice. I thought she'd be something ugly, twisted, rotten. But she's pretty, you know what, she's really pretty. I let her take my underpants off, I decided to give in. Look, maybe that's part of her professional pride too, but she was awfully nice to me, she behaved as if she really liked me, as if she even loved me. I know it's not true, but that's the way she made me feel. I thought I would come out of it with a feeling of disgust. Not a bit of it. No disgust at all."

"Did you enjoy it? Did you come?"

"Yes." He smiled in embarrassment, trying to hide his surprise at the question. For a moment he examined Avner's face, blurred in the twilight, and in the end he braced himself, put his hand on his shoulder, and said: "There are things you feel without knowing how to say them, or that are awkward to talk about, in my case at least. I don't know how to say this to you. But I'm sure you know how I feel. Avner, you're the best. You're a great guy."

"All for one and one for all," said Avner.

"And now we'll have to wait and see if I catch some venereal disease."

"You don't need to be so frightened. Today there are cures for all those diseases. And if God forbid it happens and you don't discover it yourself, they'll discover it for you in the VD inspection in your unit. And you'll get whatever treatment you need. The main thing is not to be ashamed of it, if it happens, you hear? Don't be ashamed. It's nothing to be ashamed of. Like there's nothing shameful about being wounded in battle."

Micky snorted in laughter at the comparison. "Nevertheless," he said, "I hope I escape without damage. All I need now is a venereal disease. Not that I know exactly what it means, but it sounds quite scary. All I really want now is to get back to the base and take a shower."

"The whole thing seems like a dirty business to you, right?"

"Look, she's a whore isn't she? And after all the men she's been with."

"Sure," said Avner. "Tell me, it's your first time, right?"

"Yes," said Micky. He was silent for a moment and then he went on: "I always hoped that the first time would be different. With someone I loved, someone who loved me. But it all turned out differently. I don't have any luck with girls."

"Nonsense!" Avner protested. "What do you mean?" He put his arm around Micky's shoulders: "Someone like you? Any girl would be attracted to you. Any girl would want you. Listen to me, I'm experienced, I understand these things, I know that tribe of women only too well. Someone like you is exactly what they're looking for."

"Fact, up to now I haven't had any success. Nothing ever happened. I don't know. Maybe if I was better looking —"

"Are you crazy? You know how much trouble I get into because I'm good looking? Sorry, because they think I'm good looking. And why do you think you're not good looking? You're a man! You're a famous athlete, you're strong, masculine. What kind of nonsense are you talking?"

"Yes, someone else already told me the same thing. In exactly the same words!"

"Alon?"

"Yes."

"It's true. Look, even the whore wanted all of you, without anything on. If you didn't attract her as a man, she wouldn't have insisted, despite her professional pride."

"Yes," said Micky, "she really did give me that feeling. She was so nice to me."

Hedgehog, who was standing with the others waiting outside, deliberated with himself. He went into the kitchen and began bargaining with the old woman again. She was already sick and tired of the argument, which they had already been through before, and she began to curse him in Yiddish. He answered her in fluent Yiddish, and it was impossible to tell if it was his stinginess that was prodding him into this new round of bargaining, or his insatiable thirst for argument, or whether perhaps he had been overcome by doubts about the deed itself and looking for a way of getting out of it without disgracing himself. In any case, all his protests were useless. He cursed her; she grabbed him by the shirt and pushed him violently outside. He fell onto his friends standing by the door, muttering as he did so: "Old witch, what a filthy mouth! If you could have heard what she said!"

Micky and Avner joined them. Hedgehog announced that he was ready to "forgo the pleasure and the honor" and return to the base. Avner laughed and looked him up and down with an amused expression on his face: "What's wrong, Hedgehog? Haven't you got enough money? Come on, I'll lend you some."

"Don't do me any favors," replied Hedgehog sullenly. "The last thing I want is to be in your debt."

"Are you afraid of losing your virginity, poor baby?" asked Avner. "Are you regretting it at the last minute? What's the matter? Are you afraid it won't work?"

"Don't worry about me. It works very well thank you. Nobody has to learn how to do it at the university. Even cats and dogs know how to do it just as well as you. You behave as if you invented it and the rest of humanity should come and thank you for it. Don't you worry about my sex life."

Hedgehog turned around and walked away, to the sound of ironic cries and laughter. At the same moment Zackie emerged from the room and joined the group waiting outside, and when he saw Hedgehog beating a retreat he called after him: "Donkey, you don't know what you're missing!"

Hedgehog stopped and turned to face them. For a moment he appeared to vacillate. But for the darkness that had fallen and covered everything, they may have seen his crestfallen face, his anxious, defeated eyes pleading for his life, just as when he had been caught cheating during the silencing-the-sentry exercise and apologized to the instructor, at the beginning of basic training. In the end the gravity of the decision proved too much for him and he turned on his heel and continued on his way back to the base.

When he entered the barracks he found the members of the committee there together with several others who had returned before him. The way back from the transit camp to the base had proved sufficient for him to recover and return to the old, familiar Hedgehog.

"Listen guys!" he cried. "Don't ask what a laugh we had there! Micky went in to the whore and he didn't want to take off his underpants. She started yelling at him. We heard it all from outside. And he was so frightened of her he took them off. What went on there! Don't ask!"

And they did ask, and he elaborated on his story and went on telling it to the people returning to the barracks, who repeated the amusing anecdote to those who came after them, adding various embellishments as they did so. And when the other members of the expedition returned and Avner discovered that the story had become public knowledge he seethed with fury. He sat down on his bed and clenched his fists, and I saw that his hands were shaking. I knew from experience that at moments like these he was capable of anything and wondered whether this time he would control his anger. At the end of the room, in the Jerusalemites' corner, I saw Hedgehog. It was evident that he too had noticed Avner's mood; he kept sending apprehensive, guilty looks in his direction. He apparently realized that he crossed some boundary and entered the danger zone. He whispered to his friends, and they too looked in Avner's direction, as if they were planning their strategy. There was war in the air. The only question was which would come first — lights-out or the explosion of Avner's rage.

Avner whispered: "The last time I hit him we were still kids. And he still had his side locks, hidden behind his ears, and the skullcap he hid in his pocket. I beat him up on the railings in Zion Square. Afterward I was sorry. Even then he had a big mouth and strength of a sparrow. And I beat him black and blue. But it wasn't enough. Tonight I'm going finish the job. I won't let him get away with it. I've got no pity for him."

He stood up and walked slowly over to Hedgehog, narrowly watching his reactions and the reactions of his friends. He stood next to them and looked at them. Suddenly he grabbed Hedgehog by the collar and lifted him off the ground. Then he lowered him slowly to the floor and hit him hard in the face. Hedgehog dropped onto his bed, stunned. He didn't even try to resist or defend himself, and allowed Avner to do what he liked to him.

"Tell me!" shouted Avner. "Are you a man at all? What are you? What sex do you belong to? You miserable bastard! You're nothing but an old maid full of spiteful gossip, *tee-tee-tee-tee-tee!* Where do you get off telling tales on other people? And you? What did you do there? You didn't even have the guts to go inside! You ran away at the last minute, when it was your turn to go in. You were afraid she would see what you've got in your underpants and start laughing. Because what you've got there is a joke. You need a magnifying glass to see it. Any girl would die laughing at the sight of it. You miserable, rotten bastard! What gives you the right to open your mouth? How dare you talk about Micky? Look at him and look at you! You're not worth his little finger!"

"Leave me alone," said Hedgehog. "Just leave me alone. I don't want anything to do with you."

"And you begged us to take you with us. You wanted to peep! That's what you wanted! People who can't do it themselves want to peep at others. You know what you are? You're a Peeping Tom!"

Micky, who felt that the storm had broken out on his account, and who may have been sorrier for Avner's rage than for Hedgehog's distress, interposed himself between them. He said to Avner, with the same embarrassed smile on his face: "Do me a favor, leave him alone. I really don't mind. I've got nothing against him. I'm not trying to hide anything. I'm not ashamed of anything. What difference does it make? Nobody here's got any secrets or privacy, when you live the way we live here. It doesn't bother me anymore, I swear! I don't care if the whole platoon knows what I did and what I didn't do in her room. What difference does it make to me? In any case it'll all be over soon, and we'll all get out of each other's lives, and whatever's left isn't important, it really isn't important."

"You don't understand," said Avner. "I've got a score to settle with him. With them. With all these little darlings. And if I don't settle it here, I'll settle it in Jerusalem, after we leave —"

"After you give me back my guitar you smashed!" cried Yossie Ressler.

"What? Was it him who smashed the guitar?" Cries of astonishment rose from all directions. "Not Ben-Hamo?"

"He did it! He admitted it himself! And Melabbes knew too," said Yossie.

Hedgehog gave Yossie an offended, sullen look: "You didn't tell me. Why didn't you tell me?"

"I've told you now," said Yossie.

Zackie asked Avner: "What, is it true that Ben-Hamo didn't do it? That it was you who did it?"

"Yes," said Avner. "It's true."

"Remember the hiding they gave him then, poor bugger," grinned Zackie. "The poor bugger. Why did you let them beat him up?"

"Suddenly everybody's sorry for Ben-Hamo!" said Avner. "When he was here, nobody was so sorry for him. Nobody went to his defense, to stand up for justice. Now you're all full of righteousness. I didn't hit him. Let the ones who hit him be sorry now, if they want to."

Zero-Zero said: "I also thought he did it at first, that it was the kind of thing he'd do, but after they beat him up in the dark and I heard him crying quietly like that, I knew for sure it wasn't him. However much I hate him and know what he deserves for all kinds of things, I swear it hurt me to hear him crying like that in the dark."

"He got a punch in the belly from me," said Micky, and he asked Avner: "Why didn't you say then that it wasn't him? You didn't even have to say that it was you. All you had to do was say you knew he wasn't guilty. I came and said I knew it was him, because of that story he told Alon, about what he did on the kibbutz."

Avner burst out shouting: "What's the matter with you? What do you want of me? That's what happens when people take it on themselves to be judge and jury. You decided it was Ben-Hamo and you took it on yourselves to punish him. And now you come and blame me? Don't be judges! Nobody appointed you to be judges. If you don't set yourselves up as judges you won't make mistakes and nobody will suffer for nothing. And now you want to judge me? I'm not Ben-Hamo! It won't work with me!"

Breathing heavily, he went back to his bed and began getting it ready for sleep, since the hour for lights-out was approaching. Micky came up to him and said: "Listen, the only person I blame is myself, I wasn't accusing you. I went and repeated the story I heard from Alon. I was to blame for the whole thing. It was all because of me. I don't blame you. Please don't get me wrong."

"No problem," said Avner with a smile. "Between us there's no problem." And the smile cost him a great effort.

When Micky went back to his bed, I heard Avner muttering softly, to himself or me: "Once there was a gypsy and he had a bear. One day in the forest robbers fell on him, or perhaps they weren't robbers but wild animals . . ."

A cry of "Attention!" made us all jump to the foot of our beds. Muallem took roll call, and when he was satisfied that no one was missing, we got into bed. Before he went to put out the lights, Muallem looked at us, his face that always seemed about to burst into tears passing slowly from bed to bed with a reproachful expression. In the end he said: "I have to tell you something not good that happened. Your friend Alon died today in the hospital." He was silent for a moment, looking at us with his deep-set eyes, his upper lip protruding over the lower one, and then said abruptly: "Good night."

CHAPTER 31

Silence comes down on you. It surrounds you like a transparent, impermeable sheath. All the lights have already gone out inside you. You know what you are supposed to feel at a moment like this — and you feel nothing. When it wasn't clear if he would live or die, the hungry fox cub gnawed at your stomach, frantic, ceaselessly reminding you of the terrible fear of unknown forces, of the things for which there is no explanation. And now — silence. Everything inside you has stopped, come to a standstill. How should you greet this silence? Should you welcome it? There's a certain relief, a peace of mind, as if in confirmation of what you have kept repeating to yourself, that dead or alive — to you he's dead. When they sang his song you couldn't hold back your tears, something that hadn't happened to you for a very long time. You rushed outside and went for a run so as not to cry. And now — silence. What does this silence say? What does it hold in store for you?

A man stands on the edge of the water. His face scans what lies before him, as if measuring the distance to the opposite bank. He is seen from the back, his body is sturdy and tall, broad-shouldered, drawing himself up to his full height in front of the water, his burden on his shoulders, the burden that is incomparably heavy, with a weight that is not of this world. He strains his legs, bows his shoulders, spreads out his arms to maintain his balance, and takes a small step forward, with the result that his hands are already skimming the water. He moves slowly, his feet seeking a grip on the slippery riverbed. His outspread arms flutter like the wings of a bird unable to fly. The knees of the baby sitting on his shoulders grip his neck tightly, choking him. Every step he takes churns up the water, creating waves that buffet his body, dislodging his feet. He is already up to his waist in water. His feet are jostled by the currents, they no longer seek a hold on the riverbed but row through the water. And he arches his back as high as he can, to save his burden. He feels the baby's hands pinching his arms at the place where they are joined to his shoulders. A sharp pain saws through his body, running through him like a scream, trying to break out and remaining stuck in his throat. But behind his ears he hears the baby weeping unendurably.

At reveille it is still completely dark outside. In the barracks the electric light is switched on. Waking up to the cold of the night is hard. The guards on the last shift shake the sluggards, swearing loudly. Groans and whimpers rise from under the blankets, and the murderers of sleep are roundly cursed. The waking faces are crumpled, long, agonized. A few early birds, who have already put on their running shorts and their boots, ready for the morning run, jump up and down to ward off the cold.

Micky bends down to lace his boots, and the news from last night, which he has somehow forgotten, erupts in his memory. And the silence inside him shatters.

When we emerged from the base onto the road, the darkness began to pale and the sky over our heads was low and gray. The thudding of the boots of the runners kept the beat of their singing, which increased in volume, dispelling the befuddled dregs of sleep. Other platoons could be seen running a short distance ahead of us on the road, and suddenly a platoon of girls from Training Base 12 came into view, running toward us. We could hear the sound of the whistle keeping time, and we could hear their singing too: "He'll be wearing no pajamas when he comes!" And despite the provocative words of their song, calling for some rude retort, there was something innocent and charming about their singing. A feeling of happiness and excitement filled one's heart at this encounter, at the sound of this strange singing, as if this were the first time we had ever met a girls' platoon on our morning run. When the platoons approached each other, we saw their instructress running at their side, advancing toward the forefront, and it was Ofra the sports instructress. Avner looked at her sullenly. I knew what he was thinking: What trouble was he going to get into today? I knew that he believed that she brought him bad luck and gotten him into trouble, and that every meeting with her ended in disaster.

As they ran past us Ofra called out to them: "Why are you running like corpses? Pick up your fat backsides and run in step. Haven't you ever seen boys before? Show them how you can run, put them in their place, the show-offs!"

Indeed, they were not keeping step, and altogether they looked like inexperienced new recruits. We often met platoons of girls on our morning run, but for some reason this bunch looked prettier than them all. Their cheeks rosy with effort, their plump, white legs quivering in their brief running shorts, even a certain ungainliness and lack of unison in their running — all these added to their charm, arousing a feeling of warmth and affection toward them rather than any desire to call out rude and provocative remarks. There were a few of them who looked older than their companions, more developed, but most of them looked very childish, far younger than we were, however illogical it sounded, for of course we too had only been drafted a few months before. As soon as they had passed us, the instructor running at our head ordered us to turn around, so that we went on running not far behind them. When Ofra turned her head and saw us following them, she smiled a surprised, mis-

chievous smile. We could not tell if her smile was directed at us or at our
instructor, but in any event it was free of malice or revulsion. Her cleft
chin rose proudly in the air, her tender, stalklike neck taut, and her smile
illuminated her face, restoring its exquisitely beautiful lines. She was
dressed exactly as she had been on the day when she first appeared to us:
The twilight had then gilded her legs and arms and face, bathing her in
a strange, primordial light, and her pair of twin dogs were like attendants
escorting her to the realms of mystery from which she came and to which
she would return. All her appearances since then had been different from
each other, capricious, elusive, challenging memory and expectations.
Was this to be her last appearance, closing the circle in a final vision of
conciliation? Not in Avner's opinion, to judge by the angry look and
frowning brow he directed at the figure running in front of us, with light,
economical movements, as if every touch of her feet on the ground
charged them with the power to glide through the air. He had vowed that
he had a long score to settle with her and that he would not rest until he
had gone to bed with her. Did he still believe this?

"Why have you stopped singing?" shouted our instructor.

We hadn't even noticed. We ran in silence, our eyes fixed on her,
waiting to see her face again.

She widened her stride, overtook the first three of girls, and disappeared from view, and immediately afterward the whole platoon turned
on their heels and ran past us. Our instructor immediately gave the command to turn back again and run behind them. Once again Ofra turned
her head toward us, and when she saw us running after them, she burst
into loud laughter. She gave a command and suddenly we saw them all
waving their right hands behind their backs as they ran, as if they were
waving us good-bye.

It began to rain, at first in tiny drops that mingled with the beads of
sweat on our bare backs, and then in a heavy shower that soaked us
through. Again the instructor gave the command to turn around, this
time in the direction of the base. There was still a long way to go, and the
rain pelting down on us did nothing to dampen the joy and enthusiasm
that seized hold of us, but only made it seem as if nature itself were participating in the happiness of parting from this place and the sorrow of
longing for it, a foretaste of which we were now experiencing in advance.

In the showers we burst into song again, something quite at odds with
the atmosphere of the place in the early-morning hours as we had known
it up to now. And Zero-Zero, bleeding profusely from his shave, contemplated his face in his broken mirror and began to snigger: "In the end I

won't have any blood left in me and I'll die of it. Why doesn't it dry? What kind of lousy blood have I got?"

"It's all nerves," explained Peretz-Mental-Case, with all the weight of his experience in this field, in which he was no less of an expert than in that of military law.

"What kind of bullshit is that?" said Zero-Zero indignantly. "You know what kind of sicknesses I've got? At first I couldn't even run ten yards. My heart beat like bombs going off inside me: Boom! Boom! Boom! I thought I was going to fall down dead any minute, that my whole body was being cut to pieces. And now! Look how I run with everybody else, all the way! I'm telling you, I'll never understand it! A person never knows what can happen to him. That I can run like that! But shaving — no, that's something else. Every bit of my blood it's costing me. And anyhow I don't have enough blood to live."

"There's nothing wrong with you," said Peretz. "If you don't think about it, you won't be sick. It's only nerves that make you sick. Just don't think about it."

"So what should I think about? Your sister?" inquired Zero-Zero. But suddenly his face grew grave, and he said softly, as if to himself: "It's not funny. I have to be healthy now. I have to be strong." He fell silent and gazed thoughtfully into his broken mirror. He stopped trying to stanch the flow of blood with the styptic stick he kept especially for this purpose, or the bits of cotton he stuck on his cuts. He let the blood flow down his cheeks and chin and drip onto his throat like big, red teardrops. And his bulging, bloodshot eyes glazed over with a film of maturity and seriousness. "Now I have to be strong," he muttered to himself.

The rain went on falling all morning long, disrupting the arms drill in anticipation of the mustering-out inspection. Many of us were given various duties, but there weren't enough jobs to go round. After lunch most of us were in the barracks, left to our own devices. Micky closed his book, unable to concentrate. He saw Hedgehog standing at the door, looking at the rain. He got up and went to stand next to him. Between the branches of the eucalyptus trees and the roofs of the buildings bits of dark gray sky were visible, charged with enough rain to last for days. Would it go on like this until the end? Suddenly it seemed a shame to spoil the passing-out inspection after all the tedious, complicated drills and exercises. There should be some brief hour of military splendor to mark the end, never mind how fatuous its pomp and ceremony. From the opposite barracks, 3 Platoon's barracks, we heard the choir practicing for their graduation party, repeating a difficult passage over and over again.

Micky placed his hand on Hedgehog's shoulder. "Tell me," he said, "do you remember before we started marching to the bivouac on the series, when we were sitting there after the train, you showed us someone from Three Platoon and you called him a medium?"

"Yes, sure," said Hedgehog, "I met him on kitchen duty. Why do you ask?"

"I'm curious. Will you go over there with me and show him to me?"

"What, in connection with all that business?"

"Yes."

Hedgehog examined him suspiciously, trying to see how serious he was: "What, really?"

"Are you afraid of things like that?"

"Do me a favor! It's all a cheat. There's no such thing. Spirits and devils and ghosts. Not even my grandmother believes in them anymore."

"And what about God?" asked Micky and looked at him in amusement.

"Are you crazy? What do you take me for? You think I believe in all that? I finished with it ages ago!"

"So what's the problem? What do you care? I'm simply curious. Come on, let's go over there."

Hedgehog said: "No problem. You can trust me, Micky. I'll keep my big mouth shut. No one will know. I won't talk. Believe me."

"What difference does it make to me? I'm not trying to hide it from anyone. It's not a secret."

"I suppose you think I'm a big gossip. Don't listen to what Avner says about me. If I wanted to talk about him, you'd know what kind of a character he is. But I don't want to gossip. About last night . . . I don't know what got into me, I swear. I was wrong. I behaved like an idiot . . ."

"Never mind all that. Those things don't interest me. I don't care about your telling everybody what happened there. I'm not ashamed. I wouldn't mind being transparent, and letting everyone see what's inside me, the good and the bad. Believe me."

"You don't give a damn what they think."

"No. I, how can I put it? I'm here with everyone else. No better and no worse. After everything that's happened, what difference does it make what people know and what they don't know."

"Listen," said Hedgehog, "when we were in the transit camp, that guy, the medium, and his crazy friend, came to our barracks and said that Alon was dead. They already knew then."

"You're kidding!"

"When I came back, they told me. I didn't believe it then. How could they possibly know? Those two are liars, and they're not normal either. They stick their noses in everywhere. Maybe they heard it from someone who knew. I don't believe they got their information from the spirit world. There's no such thing."

"You see. They do know something. Come on, let's go over there."

They ran quickly in the pouring rain to the door of the barracks opposite. And when they went inside they saw about ten recruits standing in a semicircle at the end of the room and singing, conducted by a tall, bespectacled boy who was waving his arms about just like a real conductor. "And he said unto me, Son of Man, can these bones live . . . ," sang the choir in a strange, unnatural, modern harmony. Hedgehog scanned the room and its occupants until he discovered the redhead with the skull ring sitting on the floor, in the space between two beds, building something with matchsticks, a kind of tower narrowing to a pointed roof, red with the sulfur of the heads of the matchsticks. They went up to him and stood in front of him, but he did not raise his eyes to them or even seem aware of their presence, so absorbed was he in what he was doing. The tower was about twelve or fifteen inches high, and on the floor next to it many apparently empty matchboxes lay scattered. On the third finger of his left hand was the ring with the skull engraved on it, which had so excited the staff sergeant in the kitchen. He finished putting a match in place, lying on its side, its red head joining the heads of the other matchsticks at the point of the tower, and carefully removed his hand without dislodging the match. Only then did he lift his head, rise slowly to his feet, holding himself as still as possible so as not to cause a breath of air and bring down his tower, roll over the bed behind him so as not to step over it, and land on his feet on the other side.

Hedgehog asked: "Where's your friend, the one who knows how to get in touch with the spirit world?"

"Oh! It's you! What's up?"

"Where is he?"

"Ze'evik? They sent him to grease guns in the armory."

"When's he coming back?"

"How should I know? Maybe before supper. What do you want him for?"

"My friend here," said Hedgehog importantly, "wants to talk to him."

Ginger looked into Micky's face: "Is it about the kibbutznik who killed himself? You were good friends, weren't you?"

"Yes," said Micky, to the evident displeasure of Hedgehog, who did not like the crude way in which he had spoken of Alon, or Micky's frank, overly familiar, reply. And Micky went on: "Do you mind telling him I was looking for him? My name's Micky. And if he can, ask him to come over to our platoon, because I want to ask him something."

"His powers are limited too, you know," said Ginger. "But I'll tell him. It's up to him. I'm not his impresario." He somersaulted over the bed again and landed next to his matchstick tower. "How are you getting on without your instructor, Benny?" he asked.

"We don't miss him," said Hedgehog. "What's he up to?"

"Don't you know? He's gone on an Officers Course!"

Ginger bent down slowly, trying not to move the air, took a matchbox out of his pocket, removed a match from it, lit it, and set the flame carefully to the red top of the tower. The matchstick heads exploded into fire, broke apart, igniting the wooden sticks, and in a moment the whole tower was aflame, layer after layer, match after match catching fire in its turn, while Ginger squatted next to his handiwork as it went up in flames and collapsed, gazing at it with narrowed eyes, like an expert severely inspecting his masterpiece.

"How do you know everything that happens on the base?" asked Hedgehog somewhat resentfully. "How do you know that Benny's gone to an Officers Course?"

"They call you Hedgehog, right?" asked Ginger. "They should call you Mole."

When they were outside, and the rain stopped, Micky said: "What a weird character."

"Being weird's in fashion nowadays. Didn't you know? Anyone who behaves normally, like everybody else, doesn't count. You can crush him underfoot. Today you have to be original, special, incomprehensible, poetic. That's the latest fashion, straight from Tel Aviv. Everyone wants to stand out, to attract attention. You know what the ambition of that Ginger's life is? To be a window dresser in Tel Aviv. Go and make an army out of people like that. Go and build a state with them. It all comes from Tel Aviv, all the corruption in the country comes from there."

"Do you know Tel Aviv?" asked Micky.

Hedgehog smiled in embarrassment. "You won't believe it. I've never been there in my life. I only passed through the central bus station once or twice. But I know what goes on there. All they care about is having a good time and to hell with the rest of us. Like during the siege. When we didn't have anything to eat, and there was no water or kerosene, and the shells were flying over our heads — they went on living in luxury. They didn't care what was happening in Jerusalem. I call that corrupt. Not that I'm a socialist, God forbid, on the contrary. I'm in favor of free enterprise and people making money and benefiting the country as a whole from it. But they have to be honest. In Tel Aviv everything's run by the Labor Party bosses. That's where all the people with connections are, all the parasites. And what's the result? Degenerates like that Ginger, who try so hard to be different and special that in the end they couldn't be normal if they wanted to."

The day was rapidly growing dark. They lingered outside, taking advantage of the pause in the rain. There was a sharp smell of eucalyptus leaves in the air. The choir was still practicing in the 3 Platoon barracks, repeating the same passage over and over again: Their conductor was evidently striving for perfection. A squat figure approached them in the gathering dusk, coming down the path between the two buildings. Hedgehog said to Micky: "It's him."

They waited for him to reach them. When he was about to turn toward his platoon's barracks, Hedgehog called: "Ze'evik!"

The squat figure turned his square, clumsy head toward them.

Hedgehog said: "Remember me? We were on kitchen duty together. My friend wants to ask you something. But keep it to yourself and don't go gossiping all over the base about it afterward. It's a personal matter."

Ze'evik looked at Micky, demonstratively ignoring Hedgehog's mediation. He asked: "What is it?"

"I heard that you know how to get in touch with . . . with people who've died," mumbled Micky, trying to choose his words so as to avoid giving offense to his interlocutor and his beliefs.

"Are you asking in connection with that kibbutznik of yours who killed himself?"

"Yes."

"Do you want to get in touch with him?"

"Yes."

"It isn't possible yet. He only died yesterday."

"So what?"

"It's too early. Some time has to pass first. A few months at least. Then I can try to do it."

Micky said nothing, disappointed. Hedgehog, like a true businessman, tried to persuade him: "Can't you do something special for him?"

"But he isn't there yet," said Ze'evik, "he hasn't arrived yet."

"What does that mean?" asked Micky.

"It takes time."

"Do you have to do basic training there too?" said Micky bitterly.

"Something like that." Ze'evik grinned.

"So where is he now?" asked Micky.

"Neither here nor there. It's complicated to explain. If you like, we can meet sometime and I'll explain it to you."

"Yes, I'd like to meet you. How'll I find you? Do you know where you're going to be?"

"I'm staying here in Sarafand. I'm going to a Signalers Course."

"Great! I'm staying here too. First a Squad Commanders Course and after that I'll be an instructor here on Training Base Four. There won't be any problem about meeting."

"You were good friends," said Ze'evik.

"Yes," said Micky.

"Let's bet you won't meet me. You'll forget."

"How do you know?"

"Let's bet on it."

"Are you a prophet too?" Hedgehog could not resist the urge to interfere in the conversation.

"Do people forget?" asked Micky.

"Most do," said Ze'evik. "They get over it and they forget."

"Should they forget?" asked Micky.

Ze'evik said: "I don't know. It depends on the individual. What I do know is that they don't forget. They miss us."

"I bet you that I won't forget," said Micky. "I'll come looking for you."

They shook hands to confirm the bet.

Ze'evik turned away and went to his platoon. Hedgehog gave Micky a long look, to see if he was serious: "Tell me, do you really believe in that stuff?"

"I don't believe and I don't not believe. I don't know anything about it. But I'm curious. I'll go and see him one of these days."

"You remember how you said yourself, on the march to the series, that it was disgusting, that it was sick to take freaks like him in the army."

"I thought then that I knew everything."

"Perhaps it's a passing weakness," said Hedgehog. "Don't do anything you'll be sorry for later."

"You know that the toughest paratroopers went to séances? After their mates were killed. I'm strong enough not to be afraid of it."

"I don't believe in all that nonsense. It's only despair that makes people go. But if — if something like that actually happens, and you somehow or other talk to him, ask him what Benny said to him that night when he was on guard, before he shot himself. I'm sure there's a connection. And now that bastard's gone to an Officers Course and he'll be a commander in the IDF. Who knows how far he'll go and how many guys'll still have to suffer because of him. Ask Alon that."

Muallem came into the room with a strange smile on his face, a kind of laugh that he was trying to suppress. He went straight to Zero-Zero.

"Hurry up and put on turnout dress and go home till twelve o'clock tomorrow. Congratulations! Your wife's given birth to a son. You're a father!"

At the sight of Zero-Zero's face on hearing this news, Muallem could no longer restrain himself and he burst into loud guffaws of laughter, his face twisted into something resembling a tragic mask, his thick upper lip quivering and his deep-set eyes almost closed. Zero-Zero stood stunned, his eyes wide open, bulging more than usual, and his face gray. Muallem controlled his laughter. "Here's your pass," he said, "get a move on! Get dressed! Don't you want to see your wife and child?"

And when Zero-Zero still did not move, Muallem said: "What, didn't you know there was a baby on the way? Did your wife make it all by herself? Or is it somebody else's?"

We all burst out laughing.

Zero-Zero mumbled: "Sir, I thought it would come next week. It's a bit early. And yesterday I was at home and nothing'd started yet."

After Muallem left the room, Zero-Zero sat on his bed, limp and sagging, with only the fingers of his right hand playing nervously with the pass. Everyone gathered around to congratulate him, slap him on the shoulder, make joking remarks at his expense, and ask him questions about various intimate particulars. The whole business seemed absurd and grotesque, like some wildly obscene joke, like a freak of nature.

He was overcome by weakness and unable to get off the bed. He placed his hand on his heart, to feel the heartbeats, which were presumably echoing inside him like exploding bombs. Boom! Boom! Boom! Suddenly he raised his head and looked at us standing around him, and a smile came to his lips, a wondering kind of smile, as he had smiled that morning at his ability to run the full course with everyone else: full of amazement at the mysterious ways of fate. "I've got a sabra son," he said, "a sabra like them," and he pointed to a few of our number. "He'll be like the kids who grow up here from the beginning. He'll talk Hebrew like them. He won't know no foreign language, only Hebrew, and he'll sing their songs. Here it's a good place for kids to grow up. They turn out better looking, healthier, strong. I won't call my kid any of those lousy names from over there, Lupu, Shmupu, Berko, Shmerko. I'll give him a sabra name, one of them new names, not losers' names. What a crazy world, I'm telling you, that I've got a sabra kid! I'll bring him up like one of them strong, nice-looking kids, so he'll fit into this country. So he won't be shit like me."

Something flickered in his eyes, their focus blurred, and two enormous tears, like transparent marbles, hung from his red eyelids and dropped onto his cheeks. Little streams of tears on his thin, frightened face.

"What are crying for, you donkey? What are you scared of?" cried his friends.

"I'm happy," explained Zero-Zero in a trembling voice, sniffing again and again, "I'm happy. For something good to come out of me at least."

"How will you manage, a family with a child?" asked Hedgehog. "On the money we get from the army?"

"My wife works. She'll leave the child with her mother when she goes to work. But I don't know. Maybe the army pays more?" He looked at us as if seeking our advice. "Never mind, he won't lack for nothing. I'll give my soul, my lousy life, to see he grows up right, like a sabra, not like a loser."

He rallied and stood up to change his clothes, wiping away his tears, and it was no longer possible to see that he had been crying, since his eyes were always red anyway. When he was ready to leave, he smiled shyly, spread out his hands in a gesture of apology, turned toward the door of the room, and looked anxiously at the rain, which had started to fall again. In the end he hunched his shoulders and ran outside. He ran in short, zigzag dashes, in the way we had been trained to advance under fire, trying to avoid being hit by the increasing downpour. We clustered outside the barracks, accompanying him with our eyes, until he disappeared into the darkness and the tumultuous din of the rain. And from the opposite barracks the 3 Platoon choir could still be heard rehearsing the same passage over and over again, striving to improve the combination of voices, in a difficult harmony, discordant to the unaccustomed ear, harsh in its strange, unpleasant intervals: "Son of Man, will these bones live . . ."